ANGUS DUNN has worked in the circus; was a maths teacher in a Buddhist monastery in Nepal; worked for King Hussein of Jordan, furnishing his new palace; planted trees; been a lumberjack and a fishing ghillie; ran a bakery in Kathmandu, been a radiographer, animator, graphic artist, fruit picker, beggar, set builder, storyteller, gardener, vegetarian chef, tattie picker, hypnotist, railway lineman, a transvestite cabaret singer and a winkle picker... only one of these is untrue, and he's not saying which!

Winner of the 2002 Neil Gunn Competition and the Robert Louis Stevenson Award in 1995 and author of numerous works of poetry and short fiction, his work has featured in *Shorts* – The Macallan/*Scotland on Sunday* Collection and been broadcast on BBC Radio 4 and BBC Radio Scotland. He has also served as the Writer in Residence for Aberdeenshire and the Scottish Sculpture Workshop. An enthusiastic supporter of writing events, Angus helped to set up and run the first Cromarty Book Festival and has acted as a reader/tutor at many events supported by Scottish Book Trust.

Writing in the Sand

ANGUS DUNN

Luath Press Limited

EDINBURGH

www.luath.co.uk

First published 2006
Reprinted 2006

The paper used in this book is recyclable.
It is made from low-chlorine pulps produced in a low-energy,
low-emission manner from renewable forests.

The author's right to be identified as author of this book
under the Copyright, Designs and Patents Act 1988 has been asserted.

The publisher acknowledges subsidy from
Scottish
Arts Council
towards publication of this volume.

Printed and bound in Great Britain by
Biddles Ltd, King's Lynn, Norfolk

Typeset chiefly in 10.5 point Sabon

Thanks to John for his gall bladder, Steve for his name, Colin for getting me started and Alex for showing me, long ago, what a few pungent words could do. Thanks also to Eiko for translating the Japanese and to those who commented on early versions of the text, including (but not limited to) Fran and Cynthia.

For Alastair

PART I

THERE WAS LOW cloud over the Firth, lying as mist on the sea. A man stood by the sea wall, staring into the whiteness. Dampness condensed out of the air onto his head and neck. He ignored it.

Invisible in the mist, the marker buoy sounded its siren, then fell silent again. The sound of a boat became audible, moving from west to east, past the town. Then the low sound of its engine changed to a slow idle, out near the salmon cages. The man reached up his hand and wiped the moisture from his bald head.

After a few minutes, the engine throttled up again, then its sound faded away as it rounded the headland. The siren moaned again, then was silent. Only the waves on the shore moved.

The man adjusted his overalls, straightened the flower in his buttonhole, turned and walked up the Muckle Vennel towards The Fisherman's Arms. Ancient low fisher cottages crowded the dim lane, their small dark windows looking blindly across at each other. He peered this way and that in the gloom, studying the roofs and windows, checking the doorways and the small gaps between houses. As he approached, a cat appeared out of the shadow at the foot of a wall. It moved swiftly across the lane and into a dark corner, where something small shrieked and died.

The man did not hurry, but neither did he linger.

As he reached the main street at the end of the Vennel, his eyes strayed towards the bright windows of The Fisherman's Arms. The door opened and the barman hauled out a set of sandwich boards and set them on the pavement. 'Dominos Tonight!' they declared, as if this was a big event. The barman looked up at him.

'Coming in for a dram, Jimmy?'

Jimmy pulled a child's windmill from one of his overalls pockets and waved it to and fro thoughtfully.

'Later,' he decided. 'First there is work to do.' He turned the other way, heading for the west end of town, the harbour and his house.

On the Castleton slipway stood George MacLear, looking across to the Dark Isle. He had a small rucksack over one shoulder and a frown on his face. He could see the ferry pushing through the sparkling waves, he could see green fields dotted with grazing sheep, he could see brown hillsides speckled with golden patches of gorse. And he could see a hint of dark clouds, far away in the east, at the very tip of the Dark Isle where the village of Cromness lay.

The ferry was nearly in, its ramp lowering slowly as it edged its way in to the jetty. The waiting crowd pushed forward. George stayed where he was.

Passengers walked off, cars drove off, then people and cars moved up the ramp onto the ferry. Only at the last moment did George sigh and walk down the jetty, stepping onto the ferry as it began to pull away.

He went to stand at the bows. Salt spray blew in the breeze. Gulls floated overhead. The Dark Isle grew closer, the hills seemed higher, the gorse more golden. It was beautiful and peaceful and George could hardly remember why he thought there was danger there.

On Cromness beach, two small groups of salmon fishers were grunting in unison as they heaved a dripping net from the sea. Out in the water, a long semicircular ripple showed as the net moved slowly shorewards. Big Irwin pulled at one end, his thick muscles barely straining, though it was heavy. By his side was old Sammy Poach, making a show of pulling along with him. Sammy was too old to be much help, but the landowner, Mr Mor, employed him anyway, hoping that if he was being paid to fish during the day, he wouldn't go out poaching salmon at night. At the other end of the net, three men hauled, barely keeping up with Irwin.

As the loop of net grew smaller, they could see a disturbance in the water.

'We've got one at least, boys,' called Irwin.

The last of the net was pulled up onto the stones, a few big silver fish thrashing amongst the wet brown cords. The men dispatched the fish with their clubs and began to carry them up the beach to the Land Rover.

'What's this?' Sammy Poach was holding a salmon. It was a fine fish, a female of about fifteen pounds. It was silver-bright and plump, but its tail was ragged.

Irwin glanced at it. 'A dolphin's bitten its tail. Or maybe a seal.'

Sammy shook his head impatiently. 'Aye, aye. But what's this?' He grasped the fish behind its tail and held it up. They all moved closer to look.

Around the damaged tail was a loop of black rubber.

Alice sat in the big armchair in her front room and thought. She weighed over eighteen stones, and judging by her face, her thought was as weighty as she was.

'Doreen.'

The young woman watching the television did not move.

'Doreen!'

Doreen turned. 'There's no need to shout. I'm not a mile away.'

Alice gestured impatiently at the screen. 'Turn that thing off.'

'You could ask politely. I'm not a bloody teenager.' She turned the TV off. 'What is it?'

Alice frowned. 'We have business to deal with.'

'Oh.'

'There's something wrong,' said Alice. 'Something... Something is disturbing the atmosphere.' She looked sharply at Doreen to make sure that she understood. Doreen nodded reluctantly.

'Someone is watching us. Watching too closely. Do you know what I mean?'

'No, I...' began Doreen, then paused. 'What does it feel like?'

'Thick. Dense.'

'You mean that heavy feeling, as if the sky is pressing down?'

'Exactly.'

'I thought it was the weather.' Doreen looked uneasy. 'You're sure it's not the weather?'

'Yes, I'm sure. You know what we have to do.'

Doreen looked away, then turned back, though she could not manage to meet Alice's eyes. Her face was pale. 'No,' she said. 'We *don't* have to do that. We could ignore it. We could get the others together and call up a mist to hide us. Or, Alice, why can't we find someone who can speak to Lugh – or the Dagda. There must be someone.'

'The Dagda, indeed! Do you think he's senior to Herself? No, this is our responsibility.'

Doreen looked miserable. She nodded slowly, without conviction.

'You carry the tradition. You were born to it.'

'I suppose so,' said Doreen in a small voice.

'And you can have a new set of silk underwear.'

Doreen sighed. 'All right. If I have to.'

At the west end of Cromness, within view of the old red sandstone harbour, Jimmy Bervie's house stood, so close to the sea that his garden petered out into the sand of the beach. Jimmy was standing there, a rake in one hand, staring seawards. The mist had lifted and he could see across to the mainland. Far off, mountains glowed in the low sunlight. He reached up with his free hand and adjusted the flower in the buttonhole of his overalls.

Jimmy stood perfectly still for a few minutes, then reached out with his rake, dropped its head onto the sand and pulled. He stepped sideways, reached out and pulled, stepped sideways again, then again. The tines of the rake hissed as they pulled through the sand, rang as they knocked on small stones. He pulled the rake one last time and stepped back, looking at the lightly furrowed surface. He nodded with satisfaction. It looked just right. A regular pattern of tiny furrows – a picture of perfect harmony.

Except for one place. He frowned and bent down to study the sand more closely. It was not a large irregularity – but it was odd. Some of the little ridges did not lie quite straight – in fact, they appeared to be twisted. Jimmy's hand reached out, not touching the sand but gently moving in the air above it.

At last he shrugged. 'So it's not perfect,' he said, as he stood up. His frown cleared. 'Almost perfect is good enough.'

He looked down the long beach to the sea. The tide was still going out, but it would be turning soon after sunset. By midnight it would have washed away the marks that he had made, and there would be a blank smooth expanse of sand once more. Good.

He walked slowly up the garden path, studying the growth of the dockans, the nettles, the dandelions. Yes, they were doing well enough, for this time of year. He propped the rake against the house wall and went inside to change his clothes. Off came the overalls and on went the kilt and sporran, the dress shirt, the coarse Harris tweed jacket. He picked up his shoes. They were clean and shining. He put them on. A few essentials in the sporran, and he was ready for a stroll around the town.

Almost ready.

He opened the door to study the weather, then turned to the hatstand by the door. He reached up and selected a wig. It was a long blonde wig, with ringlets. Before he put it on, he glanced out at the shore, where the raked sand was just visible.

'Nothing to worry about. Nothing at all,' he said.

Then he looked at the wig, shook his head and hung it up again. He reached down another wig and carefully set it straight on his shiny bald head. It was his favourite, an old-fashioned mop-head. He shut the door and strode down the path. His kilt swung as he opened the garden gate and stepped out into the street. His red face gleamed between the bangs of white string.

From *Exploring Rossland*
published by the Highlands Tourist Association

Cromness, near the eastern tip of the Dark Isle, looks out into the North Sea past the headlands known as the Suitors – the North Suitor on the mainland, the South Suitor on the Dark Isle itself. There, the hillside that rises from the edge of Cromness turns into the cliffs of sandstone that edge the Island. Along the south coast of the Isle there is a series of sandstone cliffs, headlands and bays with Redrock Gorge and other smaller creeks breaking through.

The town of Rossmarty lies a few miles west of Cromness, nestled on the beach at the foot of one of the small glens. Further along the coast are a succession of smaller villages. Finally, twenty miles to the west at Castleton, a car ferry links the Dark Isle to the rest of the Highlands of Scotland. The ferry runs during the hours of daylight every day of the year, excepting Christmas, New Year and the day of the Dark Isle Show.

Despite himself, George was beginning to feel as if he was really home. He walked out of Rossmarty and into Glen Grian, where the road ran among ancient trees. The sun was low now, but still warm, and the burn down in the Glen was audible even up on the road. Soon he gave up the chance of a lift and dropped down from the road to walk along beside the water.

Other people were enjoying the Glen – a few family groups, a jogger and an old man walking his dog. In the green depths George ambled slowly along the paths, remembering other times. A red dog came down the path, sniffing at the bushes and wagging its tail. George was far away, remembering expeditions to pick hazel nuts in autumn, to poach salmon in the burn, to just run wild up the little side valleys.

The memories were clear but not complete. He couldn't remember exactly what it was that he did in the side valleys, or who it was that he gathered nuts with. He barely noticed the dog as it came close and sniffed around him. George absently patted its head.

'Good boy,' he said.

The dog licked his hand and simultaneously snapped at a passing fly.

'Yes, yes. Good boy.'

He watched as the animal ran off into the woods and disappeared. He walked on up the Glen, past the waterfalls and eventually out onto the road again. Where the track met the road there was a statue of a dog with two heads. George stopped and studied its worn features, the eyes mere dimples now in the misshapen heads. The statue was one of the local mysteries. Some claimed that it was from ancient Greece, brought to the North by Lord Elgin. Others claimed it had been made by the local mason Hugh Chandler, who met the beast one night down in the Glen. It was said that it lived there still, or its offspring. There were tales of other eldritch beasts: a Kelpie, so it was said, lived in the small loch near the village. George looked back down into the Glen. The low sunlight was on the leaves, and everything below the canopy was mysterious.

He lifted his head and looked across the Glen. Over there he could just see the roof of the farmhouse at Rossfarm. That was where Veronica lived. Her father was the farmer. She had gone to a private school, so George hadn't met her until he'd left the Dark Isle and gone to college.

He shivered. He always did when he thought of Veronica. His head swam too, and he lost all capacity for rational thought.

Veronica said that talk of Kelpies and two-headed dogs was superstitious nonsense. She lived right next to the Glen, so she should know. Such stories were the inventions of feeble minds, fabrications created by people who could not accept the truth, which was much stranger and more wonderful.

There were Elves in the Glen. That's what she told him, and she was serious about it. They were the physical expression of a spiritual reality, so she said, and George had found himself unable to confront such a glorious young woman and tell her that she was dottled. He was hoping to see her sometime during the summer, and he had hopes for something better than an argument about the nature of reality.

So apart from the Elves, the beasts of the Glen were all mythical. A diplomatic belief that didn't distress his sense of integrity too much.

He patted the statue's heads for luck, and turned along the road to Cromness.

From *Architecture of the Dark Isle* by Dougal Willis

Several miles to the west of Cromness, on the edge of the Redrock Gorge, stands Redrock House. This splendid edifice was constructed in late Victorian times by the eccentric laird, Sir Thomas Farquhar, and was built of Old Red Sandstone quarried from the gorge. This is generally considered to be a delicate compliment to the famous geologist Hugh Chandler, a native of Cromness.

In the early nineteenth century, Chandler had discovered fossil fish in the Old Red Sandstone of Redrock Gorge. After a great deal of thought and painful soul-searching, Chandler, a devout Christian, realised that the fossils proved that the process of creation must have taken several million years, rather than the Biblical period of seven days.

Sir Thomas Farquhar at first fiercely attacked Hugh Chandler and his findings, accusing him of fabricating evidence. Even after being shown the actual fossils – embedded in the 500-foot cliffs of the gorge – he still refused to give way to Chandler, though he could not deny the evidence.

In a letter to the *Inverness Crier*, he wrote: 'While we cannot deny the evidence given us by the Bible, namely that the Lord created the world in seven days, it is necessary for us, as rational men, to understand that days were very much longer then.'

The fossils nevertheless fascinated him, and on discerning a certain resemblance to his grandfather in one of the fish, he accepted Chandler's viewpoint and turned wholeheartedly to the study of palaeontology, investing most of his fortune in the attempt to trace his pedigree back to the primeval fish.

This he failed to do, but he built Redrock House from the Old Red Sandstone, favouring those stones which contained fossil fish most closely resembling him and his ancestors. As a receding chin was a family feature, such stones were in plentiful supply.

The construction of the house used up the remains of his fortune, and he was compelled to sell off most of his other property. His family declined with his fortunes and when he and his heirs were eventually laid to rest in Saint Regulix churchyard, both the Estate and Redrock House passed into other hands. Inevitably, tales are told of strange happenings around the family vault, and even in Redrock House itself.

The meeting should have been coming to an end. The drawing room of Redrock House was filled with smoke from Mr Mor's cigar: they had been talking for over an hour and Mr Mor was growing impatient with the evasions and half-spoken objections from the rest of the committee. It was time to present them with a bald choice.

He stood up from his seat at the head of the mahogany table. 'There are two options,' he said. 'We either have a local team or we have a winning team. I am happy to put up the money for the transfers we have discussed, but this is a committee. We must have agreement.' He looked at his watch. 'And soon,' he added.

The other men avoided his eyes, each waiting for someone else to explain.

The Nailer stood up, smoothing down the front of his boiler suit with his rough hands. 'We are all grateful for your offer, Mr Mor, and it is indeed a most generous one.' He looked around at the other men, encouraging them to agree with him. They nodded and murmured without actually using any words. 'It's just that until recently there was no more than a few hundred pounds in the kitty.'

'In the bank account,' put in Mr Siller.

'Yes, in the bank account.'

'Two hundred and twelve pounds and some odd pence,' said Mr Siller, consulting the sheet of paper in front of him, 'at the last accounting.'

'Yes. Thank you, Mr Siller. Two hundred and twelve pounds. And some odd pence,' he added, seeing that the treasurer was about to interrupt again. 'As you can see, your kind of money is quite out of our league – if you will pardon the little joke.'

Several men smiled. Mr Mor did not smile. The Nailer coughed and continued.

'We are uneasy – I think I can speak for us all here – we are uneasy about getting in beyond our depth. I know that most football teams nowadays are fully professional – it's a business as much as a sport. But the Dark Isle League has always been a friendly one, and basically, as you point out, a local one, and there seems to be something a little... eh, not so much underhanded, but perhaps unfair about buying players of that calibre to play for us.' He sat down with some relief amid general murmurings.

Mr Mor stood up. 'Thank you for your comments,' he said, in a tone that did not suggest gratefulness. 'I now understand you better. However, you do not yet understand me. Since I took over the estate four years ago, I have been studying Cromness and the Dark Isle. Studying it most carefully.

'This town has been steadily going downhill since the seventeenth century. It used to be a major trading port but it is now so far from prosperity that it would be flattering to call it poverty stricken. The town is on the edge of one of the best natural harbours in Europe, but who uses it? A dwindling fishing fleet and a few rowing boats. Cruise ships dock at Invergordon – why not here? Where are the yachts, the pleasure boats? In the marina at Inverness. Why not here? There's money in that. Cromness could be prosperous again! But the jetty is crumbling away – and that's no surprise. The harbour dues are a pittance, barely enough to keep the navigation lights lit!'

He paused and took a pull on his cigar, looking round the room at the bank clerk, the joiner, the undertaker, the minister, the fisherman: the committee that had run the town football team for the last fifty years – or if not them, then other local worthies so similar as to be indistinguishable.

'When I arrived, the Redrock Estate was nothing more than a run-down collection of farms, woodland and heath, none of which...'

The Nailer looked at his watch now. There was a domino match this evening in the Arms. He glanced at Aristide Coupar across the table. Aristide nodded gloomily. He had plans for the evening also.

Mr Mor continued. 'There was no local employment worth talking of...'

The door of The Fisherman's Arms creaked open and a thin-faced man in a tweed overcoat entered. The mist floated in with him and chilled the room. In the far corner, two old men huddled over their drinks. The barman put down his copy of the *Fishing Times* and stood up.

'What can I get you, Major?'

'A wee dram, if you please,' said the Major, 'and a dash of Crabbe's ginger wine in it.'

'A cold, is it?'

'No. I'm in perfect health.'

The barman looked at him. 'No-one ever asks for that stuff unless they've got a cold.' He poured the green liquid into the golden whisky and clonked the glass onto the bar in front of him. 'No-one.'

'I do.'

The Major counted out coins onto the bar and took his drink over to the corner by the fire. From his inner pocket he took out a copy of the *Racing Final* and laid it on the table. Then he sat there staring at the picture on the wall. It was a portrait of Jimmy Bervie in Highland dress. Every now and then he lifted his drink to his lips and sipped.

The barman glanced round at the empty tables. Ashtrays, beer mats. Boxes of dominoes on the bar. Everything was ready. He pushed a cassette into the deck. The strains of 'The Dark Island' filled the room with its syrupy melancholy.

Outside the light was failing. A car moved along the street, its headlamps lighting up the windows for a moment as it passed. The clock ticked.

The door banged open and Big Irwin came in. He still had his fisherman's jumper on and his waders were rolled down to the shins.

'Evening, Major,' he called out. 'Cold tonight.'

'No, no. I assure you, I'm in perfect health.'

Irwin was at the bar ordering before he could work out what the Major meant. By then, the rest of the salmon fishers had come in and the room was full of bustle.

The Major sipped his drink and sat, watching but saying nothing. More people came in, taking boxes of dominoes to the tables with their drinks. The chink and clatter of dominoes being mixed could be heard over the murmur of voices. The room filled up and the barman rapped on the bar.

'Ladies and gentlemen, I want to see a fair fight, no low punches, no gouging, biting or spitting...'

'Hold on a minute,' shouted Irwin. 'The Nailer's not here.'

Sammy Poach muttered to the room at large, 'Can't start without Nailer. We haven't got a chance without the Domino Dominie!'

'Where is the bugger?' roared Irwin. 'It's not like him to miss the dominoes.'

'Ladies and gentlemen, please,' shouted the barman. 'It's time to begin.'

Irwin turned to the corner by the fire. 'Major... the Nailer hasn't turned up. Will you take his place?'

'I'm not that fond of flatfish. I thought you fellows caught salmon?'

'No, dominoes. Will you play dominoes? We're short.'

The Major wondered if he should point out that they were all well above average height, but that was perhaps a bit too clever. He didn't want anyone to take an interest in him. Dominoes was a good chance to get into conversation, though.

He wet his lips with the whisky and Crabbe's and went over to sit opposite Sammy Poach. Sammy was concentrating on rolling a cigarette and didn't notice the man's sharp gaze.

'Very satisfactory,' thought the Major. Perhaps it might be as well to win a hand or two. Might be asked to join in again.

'Catching many salmon?' he asked.

At Redrock House, Mr Mor was still trying to convince the Cromness Football Club Committee. He was more used to simply ordering people about. His face was red and he had begun to pound the table with the flat of his hand.

'We cannot succeed in this kind of atmosphere, the atmosphere of defeat...'

The Reverend Dumfry coughed and raised his hand. Though he himself was renowned for the length of his sermons, he was unused to having to endure a speech of such length from anyone else. It was almost an affront to his calling. He glanced at his watch. It really was time to wind things up. There would barely be time for a blessing of reasonable length at the end if he was to reach his next appointment.

In his busy schedule he had managed to make a little space for personal instruction, and this evening he had arranged to visit the young woman Doreen, who stayed with her aunt at Wayland Crescent. There was, he was sure, something unhealthy about Doreen's relationship with *that* woman. He shuddered, then a small involuntary smile touched the corners of his mouth. Yes, Doreen must be led in the ways of righteousness. He began to search his mind for suitable Biblical texts with which to instruct her.

Mr Mor ignored the uplifted hand and continued.

'It is not just industry we need, not just full employment. What is needed first, the seed to begin the process of economic recovery, is a boost to morale.' He paused and looked around the table.

In the sudden silence, they all turned from doodling on their notepads or looking at their watches. The minister took down his arm. Everyone looked at Mr Mor expectantly.

'For the regeneration of this town we need a symbol,' he said. 'A powerful symbol,' he said, 'A positive symbol.' He slammed his hand down on the table. 'A football team that wins.'

There was silence, while Mr Mor stood alone at the head of the table, looking down the two lines of faces, waiting for a response. They all looked uncomfortable. Aristide Coupar spoke up.

'But the team is already doing well. We're top of the league.'

Several voices agreed. 'That's because of Irwin!'

'Aye, as long as Irwin is on our side, we've nothing to worry about!'

Mor shook his head. 'But Irwin MacKerril is not immortal! He's not going to play football for ever!'

'I suppose not, but he'll see us through this season. Hell, he's better this year than ever before!'

'To continue to win,' Mor said, 'we need good players. The best available. The talent simply does not exist in Cromness. All right, all right. Apart from Irwin. Who will not last for ever. We must buy players in – from outside the Island. I am prepared to put up the money, but we all, as a committee, must agree to this forward-looking step.'

He sat down and waited.

Eventually, because no-one else was going to do it, the Nailer stood up. 'Yes, Mr Mor. Very well put, sir. Indeed your sentiments are very uplifting, eh... exciting. Fine stuff indeed. Rousing. Ambitious.' He coughed. 'But...'

'Well? But what?'

'Alice wouldn't like it.'

From *Walks of the Dark Isle*
published by Cromness Chamber of Commerce
Route 7: *East Cromness to the head of the Suitor*

At the east of Cromness, follow the shoreline, where there is a rough path. In season, the visitor may see many wildflowers by the pathside: Sea Campion, Splurge and Old Man's Breeches among them. (A full list may be found in the companion leaflet *Plants and Flowers of the Pathside*.)

Thornapple, Deadly Nightshade and Witches Eye may also be seen beside the path. These were reputedly used in times past by the wise women of the locality, who claimed that they could develop second sight and mystical abilities by the use of these plants – but experiments are not recommended!

The visitor wishing a shorter walk may make a detour where the path turns uphill towards the famous Hog Graveyard. Here the 15th Baronet Farquhar interred the most illustrious boars from his experimental pig farm. The statues which remain are considered by some to be among the finest examples of late 17th century farmstock sculpture.

Continuing, pass to the seaward side of the Clach Mor (Big Rock) to avoid the Bog of Morrigan, where a battle was fought in 1254 over possession of the Red Pig of Newton. The monument – erected by Sir Thomas Farquhar in 1883 – has unfortunately suffered catastrophic subsidence, but the upper part of the monument is still visible when the bog subsides in periods of dry weather.

Alice handed the glossy catalogue to Doreen, who sat like a queen in the big armchair.

'Here's the catalogue, Doreen. The silk underwear is near the back. Go on, now, pick yourself a nice set. And would you like me to get you a cup of tea?'

'And a biscuit, please,' said Doreen. It was only at times like this that Alice made an effort to be nice. Doreen had few chances to play the prima donna in the house, and she might as well make the most of it. 'Two biscuits.'

'Of course, dear.'

Alice lumbered towards the kitchen while Doreen turned the pages of the catalogue. She shook her head in amazement at the full-colour pictures of accessories and gadgets that she could not imagine anyone needing. Spiked shoes for aerating lawns. Underblankets with built-in fire alarms. Underarm depilators. Dental bridge grinders. Beach balls with radio transmitters.

When Alice came back with the tea, Doreen was still leafing through and imagining, with a half-pleasurable shudder, the sort of people who would buy these things.

'They're at the back, dear. Next to the medical supports.'

'I know, Alice. I'm just looking to see if there's anything else we need.'

Alice began a caustic retort, then swallowed it. She smiled brightly as she put the tea down on the chair-arm.

'Did you bring the biscuits?'

Alice put the two biscuits down beside the teacup, saying nothing.

'Thank you.'

'Silk underwear, Doreen,' Alice said impatiently. 'At the back.'

Doreen looked up, saw Alice's face, and meekly turned to the section at the back.

Alice sat down heavily on the sofa. 'I'll send in the order tomorrow and it should come by Wednesday,' she said. Doreen looked down at the catalogue.

'Do you understand?'

Doreen looked up. Her face was set and white. She opened her mouth to argue, but shut it again and nodded.

'Good. If we start your purification on Wednesday we can do the Seeing on Friday night.' Doreen looked at her blankly, not seeing her. 'Agreed?'

Doreen spoke quietly. 'Yes. Of course.'

Alice leant forward, trying to make her face look understanding. 'You know I'd do it myself, dear, but I'm just too big now.' She held her arms out to demonstrate her bulk.

Doreen wondered spitefully whether she had grown fat just for that very reason, but she said nothing.

'Now. The underwear.' Alice pointed to the catalogue. Doreen looked down again.

There it was. Just the thing to help with a Seeing. Thermal silk underwear. As worn by intrepid explorers at the South Pole. As supplied to the Icelandic expedition to Everest.

She looked at the models, a smiling man and woman, dressed only in the long silk underwear. The fine material hugged the shapes of their bodies. She trembled in excitement, thinking of how the silk would feel on her naked body.

Alice was watching her from the sofa.

'Doreen,' she warned. 'This is business.'

Doreen blushed and studied the selection available. Small, medium and large. Blue, white or peach.

From *Walks of the Dark Isle*
published by Cromness Chamber of Commerce
Route 5: The Town – Glimmerings of the Past. The Vennels

Local legend has it that the Muckle Vennel used to be the main thoroughfare to an even older part of Cromness, now lost beneath the waves. The Wee Vennel is a smaller alley, lying parallel, which creates the second boundary for this area, commonly known as The Vennels. This is the oldest surviving part of Cromness, and consists mainly of fisherfolk's houses, now in a poor state of repair. Although the architecture is vernacular rather than monumental, it is worth a visit to see how the old town must have looked.

Many of the ghost stories of Cromness originate in the Vennels or nearby, and it was here that the 18th century mystic Wandering John disappeared, while addressing a meeting of fisherfolk. (See the companion leaflet: *Hermits and Holy Men – an Ecclesiastical Study of the Dark Isle*.)

The fifteenth Baronet Farquhar attempted for over a decade to have the Vennels area cleared to build a town-house, but met with fierce opposition. The struggle seems to have diminished his prodigious energies, for when he finally abandoned the fight, he turned to smaller-scale buildings, which occupied him for the rest of his life. His famous

Hog Graveyard dates from this period.

(The Vennels have no lighting, as a local by-law prohibits public lighting on streets of less than twelve feet width. Consequently visitors are advised not to use these streets after dark.)

George walked in over the moors, towards Cromness, until he reached Redrock. The fences and walls around the Redrock Estate had been repaired recently and the old shortcut was closed. He looked up at the wall. It was seven feet high. There was even a strand of barbed wire along the top. He shook his head. Perhaps the new owner was starting a safari park. He turned and walked along by the wall until he could join the road. Here there were big steel gates with a sign – PRIVATE. NO ENTRY. In the dusk, lights were blazing in the big house and he could see that the drive had been levelled and tarred. The old gate house was occupied too. The new laird had money.

The sun had gone and light was draining from the sky. He arrived on the hill above Cromness to find the moon sailing over the sea between the two Suitors. Silver light gleamed on the rock of the two headlands, a mile away. As he turned down the old cobbled street from the graveyard, he paused to watch the scene. There were a few wisps of mist, white streaks lying on the black water. The black massifs of the Suitors framed the view out into the sea that stretched all the way to Norway. The buoy marking the channel blinked its light three times, paused for a count of fifteen, then blinked again.

He stood there a long time, telling himself that it was time to go down into the town, but unable to move. The sea and the sky and the headlands. He'd been carrying their image around with him for the last three years, unnoticed but certainly there. He began to shiver from the cold, and at last looked down to the rooftops and lights below him.

The town looked small, so small. All the houses were laid out below him like a child's toy, the streets barely wide enough to allow cars to pass each other. He could see the sign for The Fisherman's Arms: its windows were bright and cheery, and singing could be heard faintly – he could even make out the tune – 'Tatties and Herring'. He felt he could reach over and lift its roof to see what was happening – a darts match, or dominoes. He wanted to go and see what was happening, he wanted to join in, but at the same time he was nervous of meeting people he knew. He felt like a spy in his own town, looking down to the streets and brightly-lit house windows. His grandfather was still living here, in a cottage at the end of the Vennels, but with his grandmother dead and his mother gone away, George felt like a stranger here.

To one side, wind rustled in the bushes along the path to the Foxes'

Dens. It was dark along there, only a patch or two of moonlight among the trees. He nervously turned from it and edged down the steep cobbled street.

He slipped along a couple of streets until he reached The Fisherman's Arms and stepped up to the door. He did not open it. He should go to see his grandfather first. He wasn't looking forward to the prospect. Searching for an excuse to put off the meeting, nostalgia suddenly grabbed him, the desire to see something of his childhood. He'd been gone only three years, but it seemed like a lifetime. He remembered the maze of small streets around the Vennels and long days spent playing in there with... with whom? He could not recall.

So much of his childhood was a blank. It hadn't been a problem until he noticed it, but now it was constantly nagging at him, the worry that there was something wrong with his mind.

Just to his right was the entrance to the Muckle Vennel. He stepped quickly over and disappeared into its darkness.

Jimmy Bervie walked through the streets, his brown brogues clapping smartly on the pavement, the white string of his mop-head wig swinging in time with his kilt. He watched the trees as they swayed in the breeze, he checked the angle of flight of the seagulls that wheeled over the harbour, he savoured the salt smell from the beach.

All seemed to be well. Up Harbour Road he could see a few people chatting around Ali's late-opening shop. He could see a handful of children running on the pavement, chasing a ball, he could see a hen perched on the wall of a garden. He nodded to himself. Not bad, not bad at all. The scene was harmonious, but he could sense something missing.

His pace slowed and his face creased in concentration, waiting for the moment, looking for the crack in the world where he could intervene. He didn't know what he was looking for, but he felt the need to adjust reality. His inner sense was speaking to him, leaving him with an uneasiness that would not disappear until he had harmonised the world.

A man was just leaving the Coastguard Station at the corner of Lighthouse Road. Jimmy stepped forward confidently, seeing his moment.

'Hello, hello,' he called heartily. 'Ian Coast, is it? Just the man.'

'Hi, Jimmy.'

Jimmy looked him in the eye. 'Now then, you're a man that uses a boat.'

'Yes, indeed Jimmy, I've been known to use a boat.' Ian smiled uncertainly. You couldn't tell with Jimmy. He was old and he was strange and sometimes you thought he'd lost his marbles. Then you found that he'd stolen a march on you while you were humouring him.

'Well, would you be interested in a new boat?'

'I'm always interested in boats,' Ian said warily.

'For it just so happens that I have one here in my sporran.'

Ian laughed. 'Is that so, Jimmy? And I've got a rescue helicopter in my pocket!'

'No, no, no. I have a boat in my sporran. Would you like to see it?' He opened the sporran and pulled out a small paper boat, made of a greenish paper. He tugged it into shape and sat it on his open palm. 'There you are. A bonny boat?'

'Aye, Jimmy, a bonny boat. Now I'd better be getting along.'

'Just a minute though. What would you say if I offered you this boat for only a pound. Would you buy this boat for a pound, now?'

Ian Coast laughed. 'You're not on, Jimmy! A pound, for a paper boat! I could make one just the same for the cost of a sheet of paper.'

Jimmy looked gloomy. 'You're sure now? It's not often you get the chance of a boat for a pound.'

'Sorry Jimmy,' Ian said awkwardly. It wasn't like Jimmy to go around begging money – for that was what it was, really. He almost felt like buying the boat just to be rid of him. 'No. Now I've got to go.'

'Before you go...'

Jimmy took the boat in his two big hands, carefully undid the folds and laid the paper flat. It was a five-pound note. He smiled at Ian, a big beaming smile. Ian smiled back and shook his head.

That was it, the wee adjustment that the world needed. You could feel the right thing to do, even though you couldn't tell what it did to the world. Jimmy walked off up the street. He nodded at the people outside Ali's shop and called to the children, who looked away shyly or called him names according to their disposition. The streetlights had come on, bright in the twilight. All was well in this street.

Perhaps now was the time to try the Vennels again. He nervously rubbed his hands together, then reached into his sporran and took out a child's windmill. He looked at the strange writing on the vanes. Some of it was in Tibetan script, but even the words in Roman letters were meaningless to him. OM AH HUM VAJRA GURU PADMA SIDDHI HUM. He'd thought of asking the Dalai Lama for a translation when he'd sent the thank you letter, but so long as it worked, it didn't really matter. As he walked along, he held it up so that it spun in the breeze. Calmness fell upon him. After a few seconds he put it away in the sporran. No sense in wearing it out.

He walked along Beach Road towards the Vennels.

From *Cromness: The Harbour of the North* by Dr Angus
MacDonald, published by Rossland Press, 1985 (now out of print)

Of all the harbours of the Dark Isle and the surrounding mainland,
Cromness was the most cosmopolitan, being a merchant port as well as
a fishing port. In the other important fishing towns, such as Rosshaugh
and Castleton, there were a few main family names: MacKenzie,
Patience, MacKerril, Dory, Kedge. In Cromness, in addition to these,
there were names of Danish origin, English, Flemish, Norwegian,
even Spanish. These were the descendants of emigrants willing and
unwilling, shipwrecked mariners or sailors who jumped ship – or were
thrown off.

In the 17th century Cromness was a rich and bustling port, and
the town itself was of unsurpassed importance in the North. It must
have seemed a desirable haven for crewmen tired of their berth. The
hospitality of the townsfolk was and is well known, and there were
many places to hide among the haphazard collection of shanties on the
Links – a grassy area of common land next to the shore.

Though most of the hovels were the respectable homes of fishermen,
there were, in the darker alleys amongst the timber bothies, a number
of establishments where men with a little money might find female
company. This, in the short term at least, was a great attraction to sailors
newly off ship.

But friendly as its folk may be, the climate can be unwelcoming.
When the east wind moans in off the North Sea and dry snow blows
through the chinks in the walls, a man longs for some human warmth.
When the desolate sounds of winter fill the hovel, a man hungers for
those comfortable pleasures which we enjoy as much as the beasts of
the field.

And so some of these gangrels of who-knows-what pedigree would
take to themselves a wife, either with a ceremony or without it, in the
old tradition of Handfasting. Though the men were of strange foreign
parts, the women were of the land and lineage of the Dark Isle. And
so therefore, were the children, who took sometimes the mother's
name, sometimes the father's – when he had been scrupulous enough to
register the marriage.

In the 17th century the Links would have been a theatre of great
activity, with nets and ropes being repaired, boats out of the water being
overhauled, hawkers selling goods and children and dogs fighting.

Nowadays, the grassy area of the Links is unused, save for recreation
– though small boats are stored there through the winter, when they are
laid upturned on baulks of timber, making a most picturesque scene.

Even in the summer a number of boats remain there, either awaiting repair or too old to be used safely.

After Doreen had selected her silk underwear from the catalogue, Alice filled in the form.

Doreen was feeling restless. Her moment had passed, and she now felt uneasy sitting in the big comfy chair. Alice said nothing from her place on the sofa, but it was a weighty silence.

'Tea, Alice?' she asked.

Alice grunted assent and Doreen went through to the kitchen, an elegant and diplomatic way of allowing Alice to get back into her throne. Another time she might have stayed in the chair for a few minutes more, just to make a point. But not tonight. Technically, Doreen was a free agent in the house – she was, after all, nearly twenty-five – but in fact, Alice's word was law, and there was no pulling the wool over her eyes. She might be too big now to do the Seeing, but she was sharp enough to see a needle under a rock.

When she came back with the tea, Alice was sitting in her easy chair once more. The envelope with the order form in it was on the arm of the chair.

'Here you are, Alice. I brought you a piece of cake too.'

'Cake, is it? Trying to butter me up are you?'

'No, Alice. I just thought you'd like a piece of cake. I made it this afternoon.'

'Hmph.' Alice took a bite of the cake then picked up the cup and sipped. 'Nice enough,' she acknowledged.

Doreen looked at the envelope, and thought about the silk underwear. She also thought about the purification which was to start soon. She'd have to stay in for three days. No alcohol, no sex and a special diet. That was the rule. She glanced at the clock. It was getting late. Almost eight o'clock.

Alice sipped her tea.

'I suppose I could slip out and post the order?'

Alice smiled to herself. 'No, no, Doreen. Don't you bother yourself about it. It can go in the morning post.'

'I'd like to see it in the post tonight,' said Doreen. She stood up and reached for the envelope. 'I want to be sure it gets there in time.'

Alice put her hand over the envelope. 'Oh, it'll get there in plenty of time. Or maybe I'll take it myself later.'

Doreen lost her temper. 'You? Get out of that chair to post a letter? Fat chance! Give it to me you great besom!'

Alice roared with laughter. 'That's a terrible fuss to be making over a wee letter. You wouldn't have anything else in mind would you? Some other reason for leaving the house at this time of night?' She handed the letter over to Doreen, who took it and slammed out of the room.

Doreen was fuming with anger all the way to the post-box, giving only a curt greeting to the few people on the street. Then she saw the moon laying its silver hand on the grass and the black shapes of upturned boats lying along the Old Links. Her anger gave way to excitement and she laughed to think of herself and Alice snapping and sniping at each other like two hens in a cage. Out here was the real life, where anything might happen. She could walk into the dark and disappear, or a stranger might walk by and change her life. Across the Firth she could see mountains with snow still on their peaks. From the beach beyond the Links she could smell the sea and hear the waves breaking along the shore.

She walked down to the grass and took off her shoes to walk barefoot in the moonlight. She was happy. She untied her hair and shook her head so that her hair blew in the breeze.

A dark figure could be seen walking along the Links from the other end. She couldn't recognise him in the dim light and at this distance, but she could see that he was looking around himself nervously. Probably a new one. Good. She veered towards where the boats lay, swinging her shoes in her hand and humming to herself.

The folk singer was giving it laldy in The Fisherman's Arms, thrashing at the chords on her guitar. Dominoes chattered irregularly on the tables round the room. Big Irwin was singing along to 'Tatties and Herring', his deep tones audible over her voice and the hum of conversation:
'...*the lads that was brought up*
on tatties and he-e-e-rring.'
At the next table Sammy Poach was still speaking furiously to the Major, shouting over the music.

'Salmon is it, indeed! There's barely a man now catching salmon in the whole of the Dark Isle. And why? Is it the monofilament nets? Is it the poor poacher catching a fish for his starving weans? Is it the Norwegians over-fishing the breeding grounds?' He slapped down his domino and sat back in his chair. 'No. It's that great gollochan Mor that sits on his fat arse up at Redrock House!'

Sammy downed his whisky and caught the barman's eye, who filled a glass and leant over to hand it to Sammy.

'On the slate?'

Sammy nodded and the barman made a mark in his notebook.

Sammy clicked down a domino. The Major looked at his hand, thinking what his next move should be.

'And how is it Mr Mor's fault?' he asked. 'Does he not own the

Cromness fishings? You're fishing, and does he not pay you?'

Sammy spluttered as the Major laid a domino on the table.

'Yes, he pays us! But if we're still working it's entirely at his whim. He has the Rossmarty fishing rights and the Redrock fishing rights and God knows what else: he owns all the fishing rights on the South side, from here to Castleton – and not a man-jack is working those fishings. No! It's worse! His own men are taking the fish – and they're putting them back into the sea! What kind of nonsense is that? Scientific research, so he claims, but it's a plain damned nonsense! He's just another bloody capitalist playing a game of Monopoly with peoples' livelihoods.'

He paused and sipped his whisky, then sat upright and pointed a finger at the Major. 'And he's got the river fishings too! If there's a rod or two still working the Redrock Burn, then that's just his pals, the ones that arrive at night in big black cars – Mafia, as like as not. You mark my words, he's playing some deep game, and it's not us that will benefit from it.'

The song finished. Big Irwin leant over from the next table as he applauded heartily.

'That's the song we should have for the football team,' he said. "Tatties and Herring". That's the food that made the Highlanders great, and it's a fine song.'

The Major raised an eyebrow ironically. 'But man does not live by tatties and herring alone.'

Irwin looked at him. 'I do.'

'Surely not. Not *just* tatties and herring.'

'Well, that and porridge. That's what my granny made for me when I was a bairn. She said it would make me grow up big and strong. And it worked.' He held out his big arms to demonstrate. 'So I've never ate anything else.'

'You must buy them wholesale,' said the Major.

'That's just about right. I get a freezer full of herring whenever the fishing boats are in.'

'And a truckload of tatties from the farm?'

Irwin shook his head. 'I used to – but my mam has arthritis and she can't peel them, so I get sacks of Instant Tattie. Mr Mor gets them for me – he knows the wholesaler. Gets me sacks of oatmeal too.'

'That's very good of him.'

Sammy broke in. 'It's just another tactic for keeping the peons under his thumb. He has ulterior motives, you mark my words. He's a man without loyalty or principle.' He turned to Big Irwin. 'You mind he wanted you out of the football team when he was made chairman.'

Irwin wriggled uncomfortably. 'Aye. But that's behind us now. He reckoned I wasn't playing well – and I wasn't. But then he got that coach to come in and look the team over. It's made a big difference to my game. It helped all of us. I don't think he's a bad loon. Just didn't understand the way we play football here.'

'Damn right he doesn't. Committee meetings in Redrock House, by God! What's wrong with the football pavilion? We had meetings in there for years before he came.'

'I suppose it's more comfortable,' said Irwin. 'Ach, come on, Sammy, the man's not half as bad as he was when he first came here.'

'You mark my words – nothing good will come of it.'

He looked at his dominoes and shook his head. He picked one from the table and swore. 'Chapping!'

The biggest of the boats upturned on the Old Links was a fishing coble, sixteen feet long. It was raised from the ground on baulks of timber, waiting to be repaired. It had waited now for some five years, looking every year more ancient and more picturesque. It was a favourite among the tourists, who took photos of each other standing in front of it.

It was also Doreen's favourite.

Under the old coble it was dim, though a band of twilight showed all around, where the boat was raised up on the timbers. There was a pleasant smell of tar and earth, as well as a more complex musky scent. Doreen lay on an old tarpaulin shivering occasionally, but not from the cold.

Her eyes adapted to the dimness as she waited and she let her gaze linger on the lines of the planking. She looked back at the flat stern of the boat, then let her eyes follow the planks forwards, above her and on to the bow. Left side, right side, the lines swept forwards and inwards to the prow, where all the lines met.

Sometimes she lay here for hours, always in the evening, often in complete darkness, but the sweeping lines of the boards had graven themselves on the back of her eyes. The arched roof in the South Church had a similar pattern, and on Sundays she sometimes fell into a reverie, drifting away from the church during Reverend Dumfry's sermon.

There was the sound of footsteps on the grass and she saw a pair of shoes under the edge of the boat. Brown shoes with black lace-holes. John Ritchie.

She moved over a little as he scrambled under the boat.

'John,' she said. 'I hoped you'd come tonight.'

He reached for her without a word and in a moment his hands were under her clothes.

'John,' she rebuked him, 'Slow down.'

'Boat sails in half an hour,' he said.

She sighed, and gave herself up to his hasty lovemaking.

From the *Rossland Advertiser Sporting Supplement*

...but it's goals that count and in the end the best team won.

The man of the match once again was surely big Irwin MacKerril, the kingpin of the Cromness team in the old-fashioned position of centre half. Irwin has literally carried the Cromness team on his broad shoulders for over eighteen years, by sheer physical presence. His record speaks for itself, which is just as well as he is not a man of many words! His detractors have been known to claim that he is solid from the neck up, but his opponents on the field of play are all too well aware that he is solid everywhere!

No-one has ever accused Big Irwin of being a tactician, but speaking after the match today, he was persuaded to reveal his own opinion as to the continued success of Cromness FC. He said that he was of the opinion that tatties and herring was the source of their success. Asked if that was all, he replied, 'And porridge.'

Irwin (35) is at an age when it would be sensible to look for a replacement, but he just goes on and on and on. Though he seemed to lose form last season, his performance this year has been, if anything, better than ever. Never a great runner, his strength has always lain in his solidity and his sense of physical presence. To that must now be added his surprising turn of speed, which the Cromness coach has discovered and nurtured.

A source in the Cromness Committee informs me that last season the Chairman, Mr Mor, had planned to retire Irwin – but fortunately good sense won the day. In addition to his skills on the field, Irwin's presence guarantees a good gate – the Cromness side always attracts a large crowd, many of them women, anywhere from 15 to 50 years old, fascinated less by the ball-play and more by the way that Irwin's muscles fit into the Cromness strip!

Irwin has never married, and his bachelor status makes him even more of an attraction to the female members of the fan club. We will not, of course, assume that his athleticism continues off the pitch!

Is he thinking of retiring? Well, let us leave the last word to Irwin. I asked him that very question after the match, and he said, 'No.' Nuff said.

Play on Irwin!

The door of The Fisherman's Arms opened and the Nailer came in. He looked around the smoky room, searching for his team among the tables full of domino players. Irwin called him over. 'Nailer! Come and get a drink. What kept you so long?'

'Och, it was the football meeting,' said Nailer, as he walked over. The chatter of dominoes hushed as people nearby stopped to listen. 'Mr Mor had his heart set on buying players for the team, and talked at us for long enough.'

'Well?'

Nailer shrugged. 'I told him Alice wouldn't like it – and he wanted to know what she had to do with it.'

'What did you say?'

'I said she was a well-respected woman in the community and we had to consider her feelings in the matter.'

Irwin nodded. 'That's true. So what happened then?'

'It came to a vote, and he lost. Only the minister sided with him, and that's just because he doesn't like Alice.'

'What did he say about that?'

'So Irwin's got to carry the team a bit longer. That's all. He didn't like it, but there was nothing he could do.'

People began to play dominoes again.

Sammy was looking disgusted. 'Buying players!' He looked around at the roomful of people and raised his voice. 'Isn't that the telling phrase, eh? Buying players! Dampt capitalist! Isn't content with the wage-slave lackeys he has running around his estate – he has to go buying football players too.'

The Major laid down a domino and leaned forwards. His smooth soft voice betrayed little of his satisfaction at being given such an opening.

'A capitalist, eh? Now that's an old-fashioned word nowadays.'

Sammy's face grew redder and he began to splutter.

'Old-fashioned is it, old-fashioned? Well let me tell you, *Major,* that the exploitation of the masses does not go in and out of fashion. Whether it's wage-slaves in the factory or peasants in the fields, it's oppression pure and simple!'

Irwin laughed and patted his shoulder. 'Keep it down Sammy. We've all heard it before.'

'Not this so-called Major.' In a sudden fit of spite, Sammy leant over the table so that his wind-beaten face was close to that of the Major. 'Major, is it, indeed! Your bloody pretensions to status don't cut ice with me! I reckon you're just another lackey of the financial imperialists, the bloated capitalists that run this country!'

He was shouting now, and the Major turned white and looked away.

'All my life I've said it, and I'll not stop now. There is war in the land! Class war! And there will be no peace until the last capitalist is dead and the means of production are in the hands of the workers!'

Irwin spoke as he pulled a chair over for the Nailer. 'Losh, Sammy, our means of production is modest enough. A piece of net is all you need, and from what I hear you're well supplied with that.'

There was a general laugh and Sammy Poach subsided, muttering to himself. He turned back to his table and picked up a domino. 'Damn! Chapping.'

Reverend Dumfry was walking slowly up Wayland Crescent, nerving himself to approach the door of the house where Doreen lived. He recited some inspirational phrases under his breath and commended himself to God's care. Then he opened the garden gate, walked up the path and knocked on the door.

He could hear Alice lumbering down the corridor and his nervousness increased. He clasped his hands in front of his stomach and uttered a short prayer.

'Dumfry,' Alice said, unceremoniously, as the door opened. There was a hint of surprise in her voice, but not enough to give him any advantage. Then she just stood there, uncompromising, waiting for him to speak.

He coughed, then spoke. 'I have an appointment, Mrs... eh, Mrs...' He realised that he didn't know her surname. 'With Doreen.'

'Oh. Aye. I warned her you'd be getting the hooks into her if she kept going to church – but I think she likes the singing.'

'Doreen is a fine young woman with a proper respect for the Church and our Saviour. She has requested personal instruction, and I think she would benefit from it.' His hands were nervously rubbing against each other. He laced his fingers and clasped his hands tightly.

Alice leered at him. 'Aye, well, one of you would benefit, that's for sure.'

Rev Dumfry grew suddenly impatient. 'May I come in?'

'Och, there's no point in that. She's not in. Unless you'd like to wait? She may be some time.' She beamed and stepped to one side.

'Thank you, no.'

'I thought not.' Her big smile grew wider. It was not a friendly smile.

Rev Dumfry felt defeated. After all his effort, that it should come to this. In momentary petulance, he said 'We had an appointment, you know. Where did she go?'

Alice had already begun to close the door. 'She went to post a letter half an hour ago. Most likely she went for a walk.'

The door closed and the minister walked away. His stomach was churning. That woman had no respect! No notion of how to behave. She was a heathen.

Despite his anger, he kept a calm face, greeting the few people on the streets. Jimmy Bervie passed on the other side of the street.

'Ah, the good doctor,' he said, and politely raised his mop-head wig as he bowed. The minister found himself bowing back, then waved a hand at him, feeling foolish.

Old Miss Semple was just leaving the ship's chandlers. She raised a hand as he approached. He nodded politely and went to pass by, but she took hold of his arm and he was forced to stand and listen while she told him a preposterous story about Satanists in the old graveyard.

After he had nodded sympathetically and assured her that he would look into it, he managed to escape, shaking his head. She just wanted a bit of attention, poor old bat. But then, what if it was true... who would be involved? Alice. Yes, Alice! She could easily be one of these Satanists, dancing around in the old graveyard, naked men and women under the moon, among the old trees, concealed by the mist. Dark secrets underneath the quiet surface of the town, babies sacrificed... who knew what they might get up to! He thought about Alice, naked and dancing in the graveyard. He shuddered. No. Perhaps she was mistress of ceremonies.

He counselled himself against his dark thoughts as he walked on to the post-box at the end of the street. Doreen was not there, of course. He looked around. In the twilight he could see the old boats laid out on the Links and one or two young people strolling nearby. He frowned. That had been Miss Semple's last bit of nonsense. Goings-on under the boats on the Old Links. He shook his head and smiled. She was just a garrulous old spinster. But then, he'd mentioned the matter to the Nailer, and he'd shrugged and muttered something about young folk having their fling. Perhaps, after all, there was some truth in the rumour. The streetlights flickered on. The Old Links seemed darker by comparison.

He thought about going home, to the manse, to the empty kitchen, the empty sitting room, the empty library. He should prepare a sermon. He should write some letters, long overdue. He decided that the moral guidance of the community was more important, and stepped down the hill to the Links. If there was something going on, he'd soon put a stop to it.

The *Suitor's Lass* ploughed into the waves, spray breaking over the deck where the passengers clung onto the guardrail. As the boat rounded the cliffs of the North Suitor, the waves began to come in at an angle. In the cabin Barry Ellis whistled tunelessly, trying to keep the boat head-on to the swell. He glanced backwards. In the fading light, the passengers looked sickly, but most of them were weathering it well.

Maria slid the door open and edged into the wheelhouse.

'Gosh, it's not awfully warm out there, Barry,' she said. 'And the passengers are getting dreadfully wet.'

Barry smiled to himself at her accent. It was odd to hear a voice like that on an old converted fishing boat in the north of Scotland. Still, she had talents that more than made up for the refined English accent – though some of the passengers were surprised at it, expecting to find nothing but Scots this far north.

'For goodness sake, Barry. I'll take the helm.' She reached out and grasped the wooden spokes.

'Aye, aye sir,' Barry grinned, moving aside.

As Maria's small hands toyed with the wheel, the boat settled easily into the swell of the sea. The bow sliced neatly into the waves and the spray ceased to drench the passengers. Her face was wholly absorbed as she cast her gaze around, watching for the Whistler Buoy to the south and the rocks of the Suitor to the north. 'Time to do your thing,' she said.

Barry turned on the mast-head light, unhooked the crutch from the wall and hung it on its string round his neck. He slid the door shut as he hopped out.

'Now, ladies and gentlemen, boys and girls, we'll soon be coming in to Cromness Harbour. We've had to go a long way today, but I think you'll agree it was worth it. After all, you weren't looking for a pleasant cruise on a luxury yacht, were you – though we've been lucky to have such a fine day for your trip!'

The boat bucked and Barry took a firm hold on the mast. The breeze whipped a fine spray across the boat. He took a handkerchief from the breast pocket of his blazer then reached up and dabbed the salt spray from his left eye. His right eye was covered by a black eye-patch. He wiped the patch dry.

'No, it was the sea-beasts you came to see, our sea brothers, the dolphins of the Cromness Firth. The most northerly school of bottlenose dolphins in the world. They live here, they feed here, they breed here; and we live here with them.'

He looked at the row of pale faces along each gunwale, staring back at him. A mixed bunch. An American grandmother with bright sharp eyes, a German family with cameras, an intense young man and his pale girlfriend. There were one or two familiar faces among them, people who'd been out before. There was the couple that were staying at the hotel, Mr and Mrs Deace. He always looked dour, but she was bright and lively. A pretty woman too. Anyway, they'd have heard the talk before. Maybe try another one today. The Old Mariner come home? Yes, that should do.

He nodded to Mr and Mrs Deace and looked around the others as he stuffed the handkerchief back into his blazer pocket and stood up straight.

There was a heavily-built man, bald from the ears up. Barry took out his pipe and tapped out the old ashes while he tried to place the man. He couldn't recall him being on the boat before but he looked familiar. He filled the pipe, bent over to create shelter against the breeze and struck a match. The bald man wasn't a local – perhaps he'd just moved here. He sucked at his pipe until it was going, then he tamped it with a horny thumb and turned it upside down so that the spray wouldn't get in.

The passengers were watching him, looking as if they were prepared to be distracted from their dampness and discomfort. He turned so that he could see the harbour lights, bright in the twilight. Now they were in past the twin headlands of the Suitors, the waves were quieter and the boat was making better headway. Fifteen minutes, maybe twenty. The Old Mariner it was, followed by a few words about the base of the food chain.

'As well as the dolphins, we've seen porpoises, seals and that savage marauder, the fiddle-nosed grunion – not to mention innumerable seabirds.'

A boy held up his hand. 'Please, Mr Ellis, I didn't see the fiddle-nosed...'

'No, they're terribly shy beasts. I just caught a glimpse of them myself as they came up to breathe.'

'But you said they were savage marauders.'

'Indeed they are. But shy too.'

The boy's parents smiled and nodded and shushed him.

'But what this trip was all about is the dolphins, and there's no-one knows these dolphins better than I. Twenty years ago I left Cromness to travel the world, and I've seen the dolphins of the China Seas, I've seen dolphins off South America, I've seen the fresh-water dolphins of the Ganges. In the Pacific, they would come up at night and lie around the ship, so that the air was filled with the sound of their breathing, like cows in a byre. This wooden leg here,' he slapped his right leg and lifted it with one hand so that it stuck straight out in front of him, its wooden tip clearly visible, 'is testimony to the bond between the beast of the billows and me. It was dolphins that saved me from the sharks of the China sea.'

He let go the leg and it swung down to the deck with a dull clonk. 'But it was also the end of my career as a sailor, and I came home to settle down. But the sea wouldn't let me be. I remembered the wonders of the world's oceans and wanted to share them with others. Twas then that I bought the *Suitor's Lass* and started taking visitors out to see the sea, so to speak.' He sucked on his pipe and gazed for a moment into the sky then blew out a gust of smoke and turned back to his audience.

'But we're not here to talk about me, but about the sea and our cousins that live in it.'

Maria had opened the door so that she could hear him talking. Watching through the window she could see Barry pointing to the waves breaking white on the jagged rocks below the cliffs of the Suitors. Now that he had their attention, she could hear him telling the passengers about the absorption of oxygen and the life-cycle of tiny sea creatures. The light from the mast-head lit up his flamboyant figure: the loose white trousers, the frilled blazer, the eyepatch, his black hair pulled back in a tarred pigtail. He took the pipe from his mouth and pointed with the stem. The passengers were hanging on his every word. They wouldn't forget this trip.

She swung the boat towards the harbour mouth as Barry settled the crutch under his armpit and hobbled round the boat handing out leaflets, his wooden leg clicking on the boards.

Davy MacLeod kissed her one last time and scrambled out from under the boat. Doreen took a bonbon from the small white bag beside her and sucked it as she straightened her clothes. The sun had set long since, but enough light came in under the sides of the boat that she could still see the lines of planking above her.

A line of shadow fell across the bar of dim light on one side. Someone else was out there, someone walking quietly. She took the half-sucked bonbon from her mouth and pressed it against the wood of the hull above her. The sticky toffee stuck there.

She watched as the shadow moved, then stopped.

'Here I am,' she called sweetly.

'Oh. Hello. Is there someone there?' The voice was strained and false. Doreen smiled and put on her hostess voice.

'Yes. Do come in. It's really quite nice under here.'

There was a hasty scramble and then a young man was crouching beside Doreen. His head was against the planking of the hull and in the enclosed space under the boat she could hear his breathing, fast and uneven. She tried to make out his face in the gloom. One of the MacLean boys – or the MacFarquhars? Small farmers, some fishermen in the family. His mother, now. That was important. How did she bring him up, what stories did she tell him, what would reach him? She reached for his hand, trying to sense the ancient connections that ran from mother to grandmother and back into the bogland of pre-history.

She pulled gently until he lay down beside her, his body rigid.

'You're nervous,' she said.

'Oh no!' His voice was shrill. He coughed and tried again. 'Oh no.'

She stroked his face then let her hand run down his body, leaning over further and further until at last she bent and kissed him on the lips. His body relaxed and he lifted his hand to touch her breast, more of a pat than a stroke. She broke the kiss and watching his face in the dim light, she undid her blouse, took his hand and pressed it against her bare skin.

'Is this your first time?' she asked.

'No! Of course not,' he said. Then, 'Yes.'

She began to unfasten his belt.

'Then your life is about to change.' She took hold of his jaw and looked straight into his eyes. He looked back, more than a little afraid of her and her dark deep eyes.

He swallowed and his mouth opened, trying to find something to say, searching through a mind gone completely blank. 'Is it that nice?'

She laughed.

'Nice?' she said. 'Believe me, my young friend, there is nothing – absolutely nothing – one half so much worth doing as messing around in boats.'

He looked puzzled. The words were familiar, from long ago, but where did they come from? Doreen's eyes held his and would not let go.

'?' he said, but it was too late for talk. Doreen took hold of the moment. The sound of a zipper filled the silence as her mouth covered his.

One hundred yards away, Rev Dumfry strolled along the Links. He nodded and gave a good evening to a young man walking the other way, whistling to himself. One of the MacLeod boys. Nice lads. He veered towards the line of old boats. There was nobody there of course. He sat on an upturned dinghy and watched the fading glow in the sky to the West. Obviously just another of old Miss Semple's daft notions.

When the boat had tied up, Barry and Maria stood at the gangway, shaking hands with the passengers as they left.

The American grandmother held on to his hand and looked Barry in the eye.

'And just how exactly did you lose your leg, Mr Ellis?'

'Och, that's a long story.' He looked uncomfortable. 'And I'm not keen to talk about it, if you understand me.'

She let go his hand. 'Oh my. Of course, I quite understand.'

Mrs Deace stepped up.

'May we buy you a drink in the bar, Barry?'

'Thank you, Mrs Deace, but it'll take me an hour or so to see that the boat is shipshape.'

'That's all right,' she said, 'I'd like to change first anyway.' She put a hand on his arm and leant forward so that her perfume wrapped round him. 'Do call me Ann. And this is Bill.' Mr Deace nodded. 'We'll be down in the Harbour Bar in about an hour.'

Barry nodded. 'Fine. I'll see you later then.'

The bald man was making his way along the deck. His suit was of fine linen, well-cut, hanging perfectly except for a bulge over the inside jacket pocket. Barry was framing the obvious jocular comment about the gun in his pocket, but he brushed past with a quick, 'Howzitgoan, pal,' that obviously expected no answer. Barry looked after him as he walked off down the quay while Maria smiled and shook the next hand.

'Barry.'

'Sorry.' He turned to the next passenger. 'I was just studying the cloud formations. Fine day tomorrow, but a bit of a breeze I think.'

Maria winked at him. She'd heard the radio forecast too.

As the last passenger left Barry caught a glimpse of a Land Rover pulling to a stop beside the bald man. He climbed in and the vehicle turned under a streetlight and drove away. As the light caught it, Barry glimpsed the livery on the door: a fish crossed with a rampant boar gules. That was the Arms of Redrock Estate. Baldy worked for Mr Mor.

He and Maria tidied the ropes and checked the engine then walked up the quay. Barry winced as he walked.

'Never mind,' Maria said. 'We'll go straight up to the room.'

'But I've got to see the Deaces in the bar.'

'We've got twenty minutes.'

Barry sighed. 'I suppose it's better than nothing.'

Maria frowned as she held open the door of the Harbour Hotel. 'You could have said no. It was a long trip today.'

He shrugged. 'Customer relations.' He waved to the receptionist as they walked past the desk.

'Of course,' said Maria. 'On the other hand Mrs Deace, or rather Call-Me-Ann, has a rather shapely bosom, hasn't she?'

'Is that so? I didn't notice.' Barry fumbled the key into the lock and opened the door. The room had no bed. Instead, there was a masseur's table covered in black leather. Several eye patches hung on the wall, and beside it a rack holding an assortment of wooden legs.

'Maybe you should take your patch off. You might see better. She practically thrust it at you.'

'Them.' He grinned as he pulled the lever to lower the table. He sat down on it and undid his trouser belt.

'Don't be crude, or I'll withhold the benefit of my talents.'

'Don't do that!' He laid down and began to wriggle his trousers off. 'Hey, maybe she wants my body.'

She pulled his trousers off and looked at him critically. 'Doubt it. But she wants something.'

Miss Semple's suggestions of nefarious goings-on were evidently unfounded. Evening on the Old Links of Cromness was a quiet though dim scene. As is the wont of men of the cloth, Rev Dumfry's mind turned to matters beyond this world as light faded from the sky in a metaphor of the end of all Earthly life. He settled himself on the hull of the upturned boat, watched a late stroller coming down the track from the harbour, and gave himself up to that melancholy occupation, a meditation on the nature and meaning of Death. His thoughts grew long and slow, like waves coming in over the ocean of consciousness, which a storm far off has stirred into motion.

He had dismissed heathenish notions of rebirth and the Papist ideas of Limbo and Purgatory and was well started on a strong current of thought heading towards entry to paradise based on justification by faith alone, when he was distracted from this gratifying but doctrinally prickly area by an anomaly.

The late stroller had ceased his late strolling. His motion no longer had the slight implication of direction suggested by the word stroll, and he had begun to pace, indicating, by the restless to and fro movements, the existence either of disturbance in the soul or of impatience. What was more, his pacing activity was taking place right beside one of the boats lying upturned on the grass. A sixteen or eighteen foot coble. The minister's suspicions, lulled by the sense of immanence in the beautiful evening, returned with full force. He slid to the ground and began an approach to the coble.

The stroller, noticing his approach, made as if to hail him, then as he grew close enough to make out the white dog-collar, turned and exercised his strolling skills in the opposite direction.

Doreen was half seeing and half imagining the lines of the planking above her. She could see the majestic sweep of the timbers as they approached the prow, all ending at one line, all the curves reaching their end simultaneously. There was a stately court music that went with the imagining and she felt herself to be transported into realms beyond the merely physical. In order to enhance this feeling, she was pulling the boy Fergus MacFarquhar into a deeper and more intimate embrace when there was a sudden knocking on the boat hull. Fergus cried out, but Doreen held him tight.

'It's all right,' she murmured, 'Don't stop what you're doing.'

She pulled Fergus's face to her and breathed in his ear. He began to thrust again, with an urgency that would have indicated to an anthropologist or other keen observer that some conclusion was nearly at hand. There came another loud knocking. Fergus jerked his head up in distress, striking it hard on the planking of the boat above him.

'Argh!'

Doreen tried to calm him, but while she was reaching for him there came a third fierce knocking on the wood.

Outside, Rev Dumfry hammered on the boat hull. He knew there was someone there. He'd heard the cry. He would not be ignored. He stopped knocking and in the sudden silence he heard an exasperated but somehow familiar voice cry out from under the boat.

'Jesus Christ, man, can you not wait your turn?'

Rev Dumfry gasped in astonishment and outrage. 'How dare you! Come out of there this moment, the two of you.'

'Oh God, it's the minister,' whispered Fergus as he rolled off in panic and tried to pull his trousers up. 'What'll I do?'

'Run for it,' she said simply.

He rolled out on the opposite side to the minister and ran off with his jacket wrapped round his head. He ran straight into another boat and fell over with a cry of pain. In a moment he was up again and running.

Dumfry ignored him and addressed the boat.

'Doreen? That is you, isn't it? Come out at once.'

'No. I'm quite happy here.'

'Doreen, I want to speak to you.'

'Well? You're speaking aren't you?'

The minister almost swore. He looked up to the sky, begging heaven for strength. Under the first streetlight at the end of the Old Links the figure of the boy was visible, heading up the street, still running.

The minister's ire was high, but neither the authority of the Church nor respect for her minister was sufficient to coax Doreen out of her nest. Instinctively he appealed to her good manners.

'We had an appointment this evening,' he said. 'I called, but you weren't in.'

Doreen's voice sounded uncertain. 'Oh yes. So we did. Sorry minister. I forgot.'

'So, will you come out and talk to me face to face?'

'No,' said Doreen. Then her voice brightened. 'But you can come under here.'

Dumfry drew breath in astonishment and affront. The very idea! A minister of God's Church to go crawling under boats, of all things. Creeping into dark places with a young woman of dubious morals. No, not dubious, not dubious at all. It was pretty clear what her morals were. And all the more reason not to go in there. What would people think?

If they knew.

Almost furtively, he looked up and down the Links. The grassy stretch was still visible in the gloaming, and it was plainly deserted.

For a man in the public eye this was a crucial moment. Was it worthy of him as a public pillar of rectitude to go sneaking under boats? Or was it more contemptible not to do it just because of what other people might think?

He sought within himself for guidance. Christ had been happy to spend time with publicans and sinners. And fallen women. And this was a fishing boat – after all, He had spent a lot of time with fishermen.

Perhaps, he admitted to himself, it was his duty to go under this fisherman's boat with Doreen, a sinner, and instruct her in the ways of righteousness. But was he strong enough? He knew not what he might have to confront.

A surge of confidence rushed into him. Yes, of course he had the strength to confront immorality, and to confront it without quaking! His heart leapt. What need he fear from the prurient interest of the townsfolk? He spoke out loud to the gathering dark around him.

'Lo, I have the strength of ten, because my cause is just!'

Doreen spoke out. 'That's grand, minister. Are you coming in, then?'

He quelled the impulse to look around. He cared not if he was observed. He was on a mission of righteousness.

'Doreen,' he said, 'only because I am your minister and you are in need, sorely in need of instruction, I am coming in there.'

Doreen quickly put her bag of sweets away, swept aside a few crumpled tissues and, having done what housekeeping she could manage, she lay back to see what would happen.

Dumfry knelt down on the grass then crawled in under the boat.

Jimmy Bervie walked the seafront muttering to himself. As he approached the Vennels, he took out the Dalai Lama's windmill again and let it turn in the breeze. His muttering quietened and he walked more slowly. He raised the mop-head from his bald head for a few seconds to let the breeze cool his scalp. Soon he was completely calm again.

Out in the Firth he could hear the engine of a small boat making its way past the salmon cages and back towards the harbour. He wondered briefly who it was and what they were doing out so late, then turned his mind firmly back to its task. Investigating the Vennels.

There were many places in the Dark Isle that might be worth

investigation, but the Vennels was certainly high on the list. There was something not canny about the area. Most people, if they were aware that it existed, thought of it as a run-down pair of streets overdue for renovation. Those who lived nearby found it an odd and uneasy place, and most of them avoided it. But with Jimmy it was more than just uneasiness. His sense of reality was affronted by it. Even after a lifetime in Cromness, he had no idea who lived in the dilapidated houses. He even found it difficult to remember how many houses there were. The Muckle Vennel was no more than a hundred yards long and the Wee Vennel about sixty, but there seemed to be a monstrous number of houses crammed in there.

'Damn!' In his ruminations he had walked right past both Vennels and was at the foot of the Suitor road. He turned and walked carefully back, past the Wee Vennel, past the Muckle Vennel, past Kirk Way and School Brae and kept on going until he reached the old Jail, where he stopped and wondered what he was doing there.

He turned and faced along Shore Road and set his eye on the streetlight at the end of the Muckle Vennel and began walking, determined to let nothing distract him.

A small group of tourists were looking in the window of the Fisherplace Art Gallery. As Jimmy drew near them, three pigs came trotting out of School Brae, a big mamma pig with long rough bristles and a sharply ridged back, and two young ones, still pink and smooth.

A woman spoke. 'Good God! Pigs!'

The tourists watched and exclaimed in amazement as the big sow led the way to the sea-wall where she grunted and snuffled in the tussocks of grass, finding broken crisps and crusts of bread dropped by visitors.

The woman turned to Jimmy as he approached. At first she only saw the burly figure dressed splendidly in full Highland dress. 'I say, do you always have pigs in the streets of Cromness?' Then she noticed the white string wig and the little windmill whirling in his hand. She stepped back among her friends.

Jimmy, though he was trying to concentrate on his task, was loth to let the moment pass.

'Not always. They've just wandered down from the moors.' They all stood and watched the piglets roaming around while the big pig contentedly rubbed herself against the wall. 'Wild boar, you see,' he continued. 'They live up on the moors. But now and then they come down into the village, looking for scraps – or maybe just for the change of view.' He laughed jocularly. 'Or maybe they came for a change of company. They're bright animals you know, and I doubt they find much conversation up there.'

They smiled nervously at him so he offered to sell them a paper boat, as a distraction. There were no takers. They edged away from him and the pigs, watching both ways. As he waved goodbye with his windmill, there was a furious barking. A dog came out of Kirk Way, pulling a man on a leash. The man stopped by Jimmy and managed to haul the dog to a stop too. It barked and lunged, trying to attack the pigs. The big sow grunted and watched the dog while she rooted in the grass.

'Jesus, Jimmy! Where did those pigs come from?'

'Ah, it's yourself, Duncan.' Jimmy turned and waved to the tourists who were now out of earshot, then turned back to Duncan. 'They just came down School Brae. But between you and me, I've never seen their like before.'

The Dark Isle Show
From *A Visitor's Guide to Rossland*,
published by the Rossland Tourist Board

One of the oldest and most popular of the Agricultural Shows, the show is always held at or near the time of the quarter moon. This year it is on the last Thursday of August.

In addition to the Farmstock Competitions and the usual Agricultural events, such as the Ploughing Contest, Turnip Hurling and Tractor Tug o' War, this show is unusual in that there are various Fishing categories also, including Netted Salmon, Line-caught Salmon, Basket of Prawns and the Nerval Memorial Lobster Pair.

Beginning early in the week, while competitors are still arriving, there will be a wealth of activities, including live bands in the Grand Marquee as well as continuous jazz from the Rossland Rhythm Rulers in the food tent. We can also expect the most elaborate fair north of Perth. As well as the rides and hoopla stalls there are traders selling everything from revolutionary oven cleaners to waffle irons – a must for those of you who have crumpled waffles!

If you are still undecided, then consider that this is a once-yearly opportunity to walk dryshod to the Dark Isle. The fishing boats of Cromness, Rossmarty and Castleton unite to form a barrage across Castleton Sound, and a timber road is laid across them. For this reason, the Show is arranged to coincide with the moon's first quarter, so that the tides may not disrupt the crossing. Motor vehicles are prohibited from the causeway and most stock are brought across in the old style, led by drovers.

Visitors should note that the normal ferry service is suspended for the duration of the Show.

Duncan and Jimmy watched the pigs ambling along the seafront until they disappeared behind the Old Jail. Jimmy knew he should be doing something else, but Duncan was telling him about an event called a rave that they were having soon, over at Rossmarty, in the big barn on Rossfarm.

Duncan expressed his opinions of the young folk wasting their youth on dancing and drugs and wild parties.

Jimmy listened and nodded. 'Aye, Duncan,' he said, 'it sounds like a grand ceilidh. I'll have to visit one of these rave things and see what they're like.'

And then Duncan had to tell Jimmy about preparations for the Dark Isle Show and who was going to win the Heavy Horse section this year, and who would be in the running for the Nervous Lobster Pair. Jimmy nodded absently and wondered if he should go home and watch the tide sweeping away the patterns he had raked on the sand. There was a sublime content in watching the waves smoothing out the long straight lines – and there would be extra pleasure in seeing that odd irregularity washed away.

And that reminded him of his business. The Vennels. Everything seemed to be conspiring to distract him. Something underhand was happening in the Vennels, and it was his job to find out what it was.

He nodded vaguely to Duncan and walked away in the middle of a sentence.

Barry flung open the door to the Harbour Bar and stood there for a moment with his head turned slightly, just long enough for everyone to notice him. His black eyepatch gleamed in the bright lights, his tarry pigtail stood out in relief against the white door. He had his white dress trousers on. From the left trouser leg his best teak wooden leg stuck out. It had been dressed with linseed oil and it shone warmly. Round his neck on its string hung his crutch, over the nautical blazer which completed his outrageous outfit.

Dan MacFarquhar was standing at the bar with his cronies. 'Well, well, if it isn't One-eyed Jack, the pirate chief!' They all laughed at Dan's wit, while Barry turned his right eye upon them.

'Not at all,' put in one of the hangers-on. 'It's Hopalong Cassidy!'

'Oho, judging from the standard of repartee I see that it's the meeting of the Cromness intellectual elite. Very amusing, mateys.' Barry gestured to the barmaid. 'Drinks for these gentlemen, Pauline. The only time they're quiet is when they're drinking.'

Pauline began pulling pints as Barry headed for the table where Mr and especially Mrs Deace were sitting. She had changed into something much more comfortable that encouraged the flow of air over her tanned skin. He was wearing the same clothes that he had worn on the boat. She was smiling charmingly, while he merely glanced up from a pamphlet entitled *Walks of the Dark Isle*.

Mrs Deace stood up and reached for Barry's hand. 'Do sit down. What may I get you?'

'A nip of Glengrianan please Mrs Deace.' She kept hold of his hand as she sat, guiding him into the chair next to hers, close enough that he was enveloped in the subtle cloud of her perfume.

'Pauline?' she called, 'A large Glengrianan, a gin and tonic and a lager.' She turned to Barry again and smiled prettily. 'And do call me Ann. And this is Bill.'

'Of course, Ann.' He nodded to her husband. 'Bill.'

Bill grunted a greeting and returned to his pamphlet. He had a number of them on the table in front of him, all published by the Cromness Chamber of Commerce. He evidently wasn't going to be taking much part in conversation.

'But where's your delightful assistant? Maria, isn't it?'

'She's finishing the bookwork. She may be in later.'

Pauline brought the drinks and set them on the table.

'I do hope you're not driving, Barry.' Again, the bright smile.

'No, Maria will drive me home later.'

'You don't stay in Cromness?'

'No, I live over at Castleton. Maria has a flat there too.' Barry sipped his whisky and relaxed into his chair. It seemed as if Maria was right. Mrs Deace did seem to be prying, gently. And her husband, though he had picked up another pamphlet, called *Celtic and Pictish Rituals in the Oral Tradition*, was evidently listening too.

'Isn't that a little awkward? I suppose you have to stay in Cromness when you have two trips on the same day?'

'I keep a room at the hotel here – just a place to relax between trips.' He rubbed the thigh above his wooden leg. 'I get a little tired.'

'Of course. How did you lose your leg, Barry?'

'It's rather a painful memory Mrs Deace – Ann, I mean.' He smiled at her and she smiled beautifully back at him. She really had a lovely smile. 'I'd rather not talk about it, if you don't mind. And where do you come from?'

'We stay near Bearsden. Do you know the area?'

'Not at all.'

'Well it's very nice, but not so... atmospheric as Cromness. That really is a lovely harbour.' Bill kept his attention on survivals of the cult of Lugh in North-East Scotland.

'Yes. We're hoping to extend it with European funding.'

Barry noticed a flicker of interest on her face.

'It's a busy harbour then? Do have another drink. Same again?'

'Yes, thanks.'

'Pauline? Same again please. Sorry, the harbour is a busy one, you were saying.'

Well, well. She wants to talk about shipping movements, does she? Barry finished his whisky and smiled broadly at Mrs Deace. What exactly did she want, and why did she want it?

In the darkness under the boat, Reverend Dumfry grew aware of the sound of his breathing, harsh and loud. He deliberately calmed himself with suitable portions of the Psalms, recited silently.

His breath grew quiet and he could hear another breath, Doreen's, low and regular. For the sake of inner peace and fortitude, he recited his favourite lines aloud: 'Those that seek my soul to destroy it, shall fall by the sword, they shall be a portion for foxes.'

As always, the words brought a complex shiver. There was a horrible desolation in the idea of being 'a portion for foxes,' and the shiver of horror was compounded with relief that it was not he who was that portion. Then, having strengthened the inner man, he turned to the business at hand. Doreen.

She was so close that he could feel her body-warmth at his side. The thought of her so close disturbed him and he suddenly wanted to leave again. But he called on his Guide and Comfort for strength, growing calm again and finding, with a surge of confidence, that he had the strength to remain.

Doreen's voice murmured in the dark. 'I never thought I'd be seeing you here, minister.'

'How can you see anything? It's pitch black under here.'

'Your eyes grow accustomed to it. After a while.'

He snorted. 'I don't expect to be here long enough.'

Her hand grabbed his arm. 'Oh don't go.'

Mixed with the tar of the boat and a disturbingly familiar musky smell, he could smell her perfume. He'd noticed it before – she wore it to church. It was a sweet scent and rather lovely, but he thought it was not really suitable for times of worship – though he'd never told her so.

'Please,' he said, 'don't touch me. This is already a rather compromising situation, and I will have to leave if you make it any more difficult for me.'

'No, don't go,' she cried, pressing herself against him. 'Don't leave me alone in the dark!'

He almost laughed. That her wiles should be so transparent! He could almost feel her eyelashes fluttering theatrically in the dark.

'My dear,' he said, patting her arm, 'I rather think you are more used to the dark than I.'

'Of course. I'm sorry.'

'Now, no more of this nonsense between us.' He noticed that she still had her body pressed against his, but to his surprise found after all that he had the strength to let her lie close beside him. 'You must be forthright and honest with me.'

'Yes, of course,' she said meekly.

'Now, it seems to me that, not to beat about the bush, you have been coming here for some time, to meet people of the other sex. And to...'

Doreen said nothing. In the silence Dumfry thought about what it was that he thought Doreen might be doing with young men under the boat, and how he was to express himself on the matter. The silence grew long and Doreen's body was warm against him.

'Is this the case?' he asked in desperation.

'Yes, I'm afraid so,' she murmured. Her voice came from a place in the dark very close to his ear. He could feel her warm breath on his neck and he felt the sudden danger of her closeness. He shifted uneasily and Doreen drew back a little, then, as he lay there unmoving, moved closer again. Guide and Comfort notwithstanding, he wasn't sure if he had the strength to let her warm breath caress his neck. Not for very long, anyway.

He coughed to clear his throat. 'So Miss Semple was right.'

'Miss Semple? So that's the besom that's been spreading gossip!' Her voice sounded resentful. 'The wee fat spider – she's not been in Cromness a year yet and she's poking her nose into everyone's business. She's a malicious wee busybody. Don't you believe a word she says!'

Dumfry frowned. 'Now, now. There's no need to go name-calling. And after all, she was right about you wasn't she?'

Then he stopped breathing for an instant. If Miss Semple was right about this, perhaps she was right about the Satanists too, in the churchyard. He tried to dismiss the thought, but it grew large in the dark around him.

'I suppose so,' said Doreen, sulkily.

'What?' Dumfry had forgotten what they were talking about. He had had another thought. He was already suspicious of Alice: perhaps she had recruited Doreen. Was Doreen one of those who performed dark rites to the Evil One in the graveyard? He turned to look at her in the dark. He could see her face now, as a paler shape in the darkness, but it was almost obscured by the disturbing image of Doreen dancing naked around the gravestones, performing unspeakable acts with other...

'Doreen.' His voice was harsh.

'Yes?' Her face floated in the dimness. Were there signs of evil there? He tried to discern her features. He could just make out her eyes, looking back at him.

'I want the truth now. You don't dance in the graveyard do you?'

She sounded surprised. 'Of course not.'

Her voice was without guile. He believed her. 'Thank God,' he said, and reached to put his hand gently on her head. 'Thank God.'

Doreen laughed. 'You're a queer sort,' she said, and pulled him close.

Her scent and her warmth enveloped him and he found that he had the strength to give in to them. His body relaxed and he stroked her long hair. Her face was pressed into his neck, just below his chin, in the most endearing way. He was powerfully aware that there was no-one else within a hundred yards, and that no-one knew he was here. Something warned him that he might find the strength to do something he might later regret.

Sadly he said, 'I think we should sing a psalm.'

His deep voice took on the unctuous tones of a preacher and he began to sing.

Doreen sighed and reached up to the place on the boards where she had stuck the toffee. She fumbled in the dimness, unable to find it. It was gone. She rustled another one out of the paper bag which she kept on the boat seat and popped it into her mouth.

The sound of the music from The Fisherman's Arms faded behind him as George made his way down the Muckle Vennel. Memories were stirring. There was a smell of old mortar and damp, of seaweed and salt, mixed with other less identifiable smells. The crazy edge of the ancient cottages showed in outline against the grey sky, a jagged silhouette that seemed to have little to do with the actual buildings of the street, a mix of architectural styles and periods: crow-stepped gables, Dutch gables, roofs of slate, pantiles, corrugated iron, even a few with heather thatch.

The houses fronting on the cobbled pathway seemed to be empty, but beyond them smoke drifted up from a few of the chimneys. The chimneys were also a mongrel bunch: here an Emperor chimney pot stood beside a plain nine inch can, and beyond that a square chimney head with no pot. There were even a few with no chimney at all, only a hole in the roof where smoke escaped.

George walked down the cobbles slowly and thoughtfully. He could see the light of the streetlamp at the other end, though the Vennel itself was unlit, and a figure stood there, a burly figure wearing a kilt.

Suddenly a cat dashed from a dark doorway into deep shadow in a corner. In the shadow, there was a small scream followed by a crunching sound and a satisfied purr. George jerked back in fright, leaning against the wall behind him. It was the corner of a house. He slipped round it and into the narrow lane beyond. The smell of sea grew stronger as he stumbled forwards then tripped over a fishing net left lying by a doorway.

Something was wrong, he could feel it. He knew that there was no lane in the Vennels, only a double row of houses back to back, fronting the Muckle Vennel and the Wee Vennel. Yet this place was as familiar as his clothes. It fitted him and he belonged in here. Before him in the dimness were shacks built of tarred wood, sheds of timber and clay, slumped houses of rounded stones with sand and lime mortar. Candlelight was flickering in one or two tiny windows.

Years of growing up in the small-town atmosphere of Cromness faded away. Years spent trying to belong, to be like the other people in the town. His three years spent struggling with meaningless subjects at college were less than a dream now, and the memories were fading. This was where he'd spent his real childhood, in here with... with whom? He still couldn't remember, but that didn't matter now. He was back, he was home, and soon he'd be seeing Them again.

Jimmy stood and looked up the narrow alley of the Muckle Vennel and tried to see it clearly. Somehow it was difficult to get a perfectly accurate idea of the whole street. The first house was obviously a red sandstone fisher cottage, the next was harled in dingy white. The next had yellow sandstones at the corners... and after that it was the tarred shed – or was it corrugated iron?

A figure appeared at the far end of the Vennel, a dark shape against the lights of Kirk Road. A young man. He looked familiar, but Jimmy couldn't quite make out who it was at this distance and in this light. He idly watched him walking down the Vennel. Something dashed across the cobbled alley – a cat – and the young man stepped to one side, disappearing into the shadows.

He did not reappear. After a minute or two, Jimmy began walking up the Vennel. The cat was still there, he could hear it eating something in a dark corner, but he couldn't see it, no matter how he peered. He took out the windmill again, for comfort. There was no breeze to make it turn, so he waved it absently to and fro as he walked on, checking each doorway, looking for a corner where a young man might be hidden. There was nothing, there was nobody.

Fergus MacFarquhar walked through the streets, choosing the darker alleys by preference. Anyone seeing him would have thought – *there's someone with something to hide.* He was almost sure that the minister had not seen his face when he rolled out from the other side of the boat and ran for it with his jacket over his head. He groaned and bent to rub his shins where he'd run into the other boat. The trouser legs were torn.

But what if he had been recognised? Oh God, what would his mother say?

He walked down to the East End of Cromness, instinctively staying away from his own part of town. He walked up and down the alleys, trying to think his way out of the mess.

As he came along Kirk Street, he could hear a folk singer in The Fisherman's Arms and a crowd singing along. They were having such a good time that he felt even more miserable. He could probably have bought a drink in the crowd, but his mother would smell it on his breath. As he walked past, Jimmy Bervie came out of the Muckle Vennel, holding a child's windmill and looking worried.

'Can I sell you a ticket to Mars?' Jimmy asked, reaching into his sporran. But his heart didn't seem to be in it.

Fergus muttered a greeting and walked past, admitting to himself that a ticket to Mars was just what he needed.

Jimmy wandered slowly along the pavement, wondering to himself where on earth that young fellow in the Vennel might have disappeared to. He waved the windmill vaguely, half hoping that the Dalai Lama's inscription would bring him understanding. It didn't work.

He opened the door of the Arms and walked into a wall of noise. Shouting over the music and the general hubbub, Sammy Poach was giving a speech to the crowd. His theme tonight, as usual, was the downfall of the capitalists and the inevitability of the workers' uprising. His words seemed to be especially directed towards that strange cratur they called the Major, who was flinching in his seat. The Nailer and big Irwin were both trying to quiet Sammy down.

Jimmy stepped into the tumult, his kilt swinging as he pushed among the tables. 'Good evening madam,' he said, doffing his mop-head wig. 'And good evening to you Mr Barman. A glass of your amber spirit if you will.'

He leant on the bar and watched Sammy Poach work himself into a frenzy. Not well-balanced, that family – and the female side was worse. Like calling to like.

Then he realised who it had been in the Vennel. It was Sammy's grandson, George, the daft chiel that had gone off to college. Jimmy worked his way through the crowd towards Sammy Poach, who had finally been quelled and was slumped over his drink muttering dire warnings to any landowners within his reach and to Mr Mor in particular.

'Samuel!' bellowed Jimmy.

Sammy looked up at the glowing red face beside him. Jimmy's mop-wig was now perched on his shoulder and the windmill was in the breast pocket of his jacket. 'Aye, it's yourself, Jimmy.'

'What would you say, Samuel, if I told you that I'd just seen your grandson disappear?'

Sammy shook his head. 'I'd say very good, Jimmy, but I'm not in the mood just now.'

'Not in the mood for disappearing grandchildren? Indeed the world is a terrible place nowadays. Not always was it so.' He beamed down at Sammy.

'Och, don't take it hard, Jimmy. I'm just worked up about what that gollachan Mor is up to. Sit down and I'll tell you about it. I'm about finished with dominoes anyway.' He leant forward and whispered loudly, 'I've got that nitwit, the so-called Major, for a partner. A lackey of our imperialists rulers.' He noticed the Major squirm uncomfortably at this, and smiled to himself. The local branch of the Revolutionary Workers Party would be striking a blow for freedom soon, and if that blow didn't include a stone through the Major's window, then Sammy would be very surprised.

Fergus eventually admitted to himself that he would have to go home sooner or later. He walked through Cromness and found himself going down past Wayland Crescent. That was where Doreen stayed. He stopped in the middle of the road, remembering what he and Doreen had been doing when the minister arrived. The horror of that moment would never leave him. Perhaps he was scarred for life. He put his hands to his face, trying to blot out the memory.

A car hooted and he opened his eyes. A vehicle had stopped in front of him, its driver gesturing at him to get out of the way. He stepped aside and watched it pass, a grey Landrover with a pig and a fish painted on the door.

Afraid of being seen near Doreen's house, he hurried on, past his own road-end and down past the Harbour Hotel.

The Harbour Bar, thought Fergus. That's where Dad would be, most likely. Dad wouldn't mind what Fergus got up to. But he wouldn't stand up for him either. It was hopeless.

Fergus kept his head down as he walked past the Bar and out to the waterfront. He leant on the railing of the pier. The tide was in and nearby streetlights dimly lit the waves surging queasily against the sandstone wall. He looked out to the end of the pier and thought about throwing himself in. That seemed melodramatic, even in his present state. After all, his mother couldn't know anything yet. How could she? He shrugged miserably. Somehow, mothers knew. It was an occult gift that they had.

'Now then, now then!'

Fergus turned. Across the road came Constable MacFearn.

'What you doing hanging round the Harbour Bar at this time of night?' He looked closely into Fergus's face. 'Angus, isn't it? Angus MacFadyen.'

Fergus nodded. MacFearn beamed. 'Never forget a face. Now get on home before I tell your mother what you were up to.' He chuckled to himself at Fergus's guilty start. Underage drinking no doubt – they were all the same, these young lads. 'Not so easy to pull the wool over my eyes, eh? Off home with you now.'

Fergus made his way back to his own street and walked past his house, checking which lights were on. Just the living room light. His mum would be watching TV. His dad would still be drinking in the Harbour Bar.

He crept up the grass beside the gravelled path and opened the front door without a sound.

'Fergus? Is that you? Where on earth have you been?'

'Just a minute, Mum.' He dashed into the bathroom and locked the door. He ran water into the basin and washed his face and hands. He tucked his shirt carefully into his trousers and splashed some aftershave under his chin to hide Doreen's sweet scent. Then he stood there wondering what to do next. He couldn't stay in here all night. Eventually he had to leave the room.

'Fergus! Fergus! Come here this minute!'

'Coming.'

He walked into the living room. His mother turned down the volume on the TV with the remote control and stood up to face him.

'Now, my boy, where have you been until this hour?'

'Just walking, Mum. It was a lovely evening.'

'Lovely evening my foot. You were up to mischief, I'll be bound. You weren't hanging round with these MacPhee boys were you?'

'No, Mum.'

'Humph. I hope not. I've told that Mary MacPhee times enough if she doesn't take her boys in hand then the police will.'

'Can I go now? It's time I was in bed.'

'No. Come here. Have you been drinking?' She sniffed. 'What's this?' She stepped forward and took him by the shoulders and sniffed again. 'Is that your father's aftershave?'

He swallowed. 'Yes. I had to shave.'

'What? At this time of night?'

He looked at her defiantly. 'Yes.'

She looked back at him grimly. 'I suppose you'd best be off to bed then.'

He turned with a sigh of relief.

'Oh by the way...'

'What?'

'Just where did you go on this evening walk of yours?'

He'd thought about this. It had to be somewhere that no-one would have seen him.

'Up the Suitor and back by the Foxes Dens.'

'So that would explain the tear in your trousers.'

He nodded smugly. 'It was getting dark and I stumbled on a log.'

'Who was with you?'

'No-one.'

'No-one?'

'No. I didn't see anyone else at all.'

'And you were just walking, all by yourself, for over two hours.'

'Yes.'

She reached over and tugged at his hair.

'Then why is there a toffee stuck to your head?'

The folk singer had caught Big Irwin before last orders and she seemed unlikely to let go of him. As they climbed the stairs to the guest room of the Arms, she had her arm through his, and as she smiled and breathed words into his ear she squeezed this immense limb, reassuring herself of the physical reality of him. If she expected that the girth of his biceps might be indicative of his nether dimensions, she was lady enough to display no disappointment later, when they played at the merry hams in the big bed. After all, though his physique was impressive, her affections had really been captured by his heartfelt rendering of 'Tatties and Herring'. A man who could sing with such commitment must have soul.

Actually what Irwin had was simple gusto, a heartiness of spirit which extended into all his activities, and had fortunately not yet been affected by his problem – which he was too shy as yet to discuss with his doctor.

The crowd in the Arms slowly moved out into the street as the barman began to turn out the lights. Jimmy waved goodnight to Sammy Poach, who had ceased his tirade against the capitalists of the world in general and of the Dark Isle in particular, and had developed a drunken crafty look. The Major, uneasy at Sammy's hostility, had slipped away almost unnoticed as soon as time was called.

The Nailer had been well plied with drink and was trying to get home, but Ellen MacRee had caught him just outside the door of the Arms. She had one of his coat buttons in her strong fingers so that he could not escape without violence and she was interrogating him about Redrock House. About the furnishings, the number of servants about the place, the fish tanks in the old stable block, the heavy-duty wire mesh fences behind the house, and about Mr Mor's taste in brandy.

As the Nailer dredged up what details he was able to remember, Ellen's mind was working on this raw material, elaborating it into gossip fit to pass on to her neighbour, Miss Semple, who was developing nicely as a confidante. Though she'd only been in Cromness a year, Miss Semple had already shown great talent in creating good solid rumours out of hints and hearsay.

From the Nailer's mention of a small mirror on the sideboard, Ellen had already deduced that Mr Mor was a cocaine addict. In a film, she had seen a mirror used in the ritual of sniffing cocaine, and she now regarded a looking glass with the suspicion more generally reserved for a copy of the *Necronomicon*. When the Nailer said that the chauffeur had a low forehead, Ellen converted this into blatant evidence of criminality, and created for Mr Mor a complete gang of out-and-out thugs. The brandy she took for evidence of an extravagant lifestyle appropriate only for a drug-smuggler or arms dealer. The fish-tanks though, had her stumped. The salmon that his henchmen caught were, according to the Nailer, kept there. In Ellen's experience, fish were caught to be sold and eaten, and Mr Mor's procedure was too outré for her to develop a suitable thread of calumny. The wire fences also had her at a disadvantage. They were too commonplace and agricultural for her. She would just have to wait and see what Miss Semple could make of them.

Mr Mor used his mirror for no such purpose, of course. It was merely there so that he could adjust his tie at a suitable moment and watch how people behaved when they thought he wasn't watching. Just now, there were only two of his men in the room, the driver and the man with the bald head, and he did not need to watch them.

He pulled a little vial from under his shirt, where it dangled on a gold chain. He unscrewed the top and dug into it with a small silver spoon. He held the white powder up to his left nostril and sniffed heartily. The powder disappeared.

'Good,' he said. 'A good batch.' Then he repeated the procedure, this time with the other nostril. 'Balance,' he said, as he shut the vial and popped it into his shirt front. 'Balance in all things.'

'Night traffic? Not a lot. You see, after sundown, it tends to get...' Barry waved a hand vaguely as he searched for a suitable word. 'Dark. That's it, dark. And you'll have seen our harbour lights – just two old street lights mounted on the pier. Of course I've seen commercial ports without even that. I remember when I was in Penang...'

'Gosh, Barry, you've been all over, haven't you. But the harbour isn't completely abandoned after dark?'

'Oh no. Sometimes boats come in. Sometimes they leave.'

Maria came into the bar. As she ordered a drink, she glanced at Barry, one eyebrow raised. He winked at her and turned his attention back to Ann Deace's blue eyes and golden skin.

'Maybe a lobsterman, late back. Aristide, for instance. Now there's a man with a boat. Converted it from a fishery research vessel. Thirty-five feet at the water line and steady as a rock even in a gale.' Barry's eye was watching Ann Deace, but he could see Bill's hands, holding the pamphlets. There was a momentary tension in the fingers at the mention of Aristide's boat.

'Or maybe Mr Mor's salmon boat. That's a good boat – out there at all hours, in all weather.' Bill's hand grew still and tight.

Deep sea boats then. That's what they were looking for. Barry shrugged and spread his hands. 'Though who knows what moves out there that no-one sees.' He reached up to his left eye and tapped the eyepatch. 'I have a certain handicap in the seeing department.'

'Last orders, ladies and gentlemen. Last orders please.' Pauline flicked the lights on and off.

'She doesn't mean us Barry, we are residents.' Ann took Barry's arm. 'Do let me get you another drink.'

'No, no, Ann. Delightful as your company is,' he paused to focus on her a gaze approximating delight, 'I have a boat to take out tomorrow and I still have to drive home.'

Maria walked over from the bar. 'I'll drive, Barry,' she said.

Barry swung round to face her, rather too vigorously, so that whisky slopped on to the table top. 'No, by God you won't. I can drive better than you sober when I'm drunk, which I am not.'

'And we ought to go now.'

'We will not! Ann was asking me about my eye, wasn't she, Ann?'

'I don't think I was...'

'But that's because you're the shoal of discretion and a deeply sensitive woman. Isn't that so, Bill? You're a lucky man.'

'Barry, I really think...'

Barry ignored Maria and focused on Ann.

'Not always was the skipper as you see him now, o best beloved.' He turned to Bill. 'No offence. Squotation from Kipling. But perhaps you've never Kippled?'

49

Bill's mouth tightened. 'I haven't a clue what you mean. Perhaps you had better go.'

Ann reached out and put a hand on Barry's shoulder. 'No, Bill. He needs to talk about it.'

Maria sighed and sat in an empty chair. 'This may take some time.'

Barry continued. 'Not always was I a seafaring man. In fact, occasionally, between ships, there were periods of time when I had to find honest work to keep body and soul together. One time I was stranded in Liverpool, waiting for my next berth, and I had to take a job as a door-to-door salesman. Selling door-to-doors. No. Ha ha. Just joking. I was selling vacuum cleaners.

'Now, if there is one class of person that annoys me more than any other, it is the vacuum cleaner salesman. Don't they know that everyone has got one already?

'But what we were selling was no ordinary vacuum cleaner. It was a Kirby. A complete home cleaning system with the power of a Jumbo jet and the delicacy of touch of a hundred pound whore, begging your pardon, Ann. We nauticals develop a homely but expressive language.

'This Home Cleaning System could clean everything from a deep shag carpet, begging your pardon, to... well, it could polish a wedding ring or clean up the house after the invasion of the Visigoths. We spent a week training first. We had to be convinced of its unique qualities before they'd even let us try to sell one. It had a pressure cut-off sensitive to one tenth of a gram per square centimetre, it had a hydraulic filter release and a special buffer to polish itself clean. They'd even developed a special attachment that would inflate bagpipes, for pipers who had had to have a tracheotomy.'

Barry looked gloomy and he gulped the rest of his whisky, wiping a tear from his good eye. 'Unfortunately, I was a better mariner than vacuum cleaning operative. On my first day I went into a flat where there was a woman with eighteen children, all under five. I suppose she was child-minding. She was a large woman as I recall, and she couldn't get the wedding ring off her finger, so rather than risk her finger, I demonstrated on a curtain ring which I had brought with me. I showed her the easy-fit hydraulic filter release. I poured a pint of water on the floor and sucked it up then polished her linoleum. All was going well, and I anticipated my first sale.

'Next, it was time to demonstrate its facility with a deep shag carpet. The only one was in her bedroom, so I engaged the drive and led it through from the room where the children were playing and began the demonstration. Almost at once, the machine died on me. I improvised. "If this should ever occur, the pressure relief valve needs adjusting," I said.

I turned it up to the highest level and tried again. The motor wouldn't start. Panicked in case I lost my sale, I looked down the tube in case there was a blockage, just as a child in the other room turned the switch back on at the socket.'

Ann looked horrified, and even Bill looked perturbed. Barry sipped from his glass, which had been refilled while he was talking.

'You hear all these stories these days,' he continued, 'about surgeons sewing back anything from a leg to a fingernail, so I drove to the hospital at speed, with the Kirby Home Cleaning Machine in the car.' He shook his head and sighed. 'They couldn't do anything with it, of course. But the surgeon said it was the cleanest eyeball he'd ever seen.'

Maria said 'Time to go.' Barry stood up and stumbled across the room to the door with Maria hovering beside him. He turned and his crutch swung on its string, banging against the wall. He waved to Mr and Mrs Deace. 'Goodnight.'

They waved back. Bill shook his head as Barry stumbled out of the door. 'Look at him,' he said. 'How many whiskies did he put away? He's practically...'

'Don't say it,' said Ann.

'...legless,' said Bill.

Ann smiled sourly. 'Now that you've got that out of your system, let's go upstairs and talk this over.'

Pauline sighed with relief and wiped the bar as they waved goodnight.

Jimmy walked home by way of School Brae and the Old Jail, without seeing any sign of the wandering pigs. Once past the Jail, he strolled out into the darkness of the Links. Ambling across its grassy surface was always a favourite part of his journey home. In the darkness and the silence, he could let ideas well up from the depths and commingle with each other. The connection between peppermint rock and the fourth dimension had occurred to him while walking here, as had his plan for mapping the reality quotient of the Dark Isle in semi-random accretions of silica granules.

His steps slowed as he walked on the grass. The clouds to the west had cleared and he could see the stars gleaming on the inverted black pudding-bowl of the sky. His mind opened. He could hear the waves running in to the shore, he could hear a dog barking across the Sound of Cromness, he could hear the sounds of the stars singing to one another, so clear that he could almost make out the words. In fact, he *could* hear the words. It was a psalm, in a recognisable though rather hoarse voice.

'I to the hills will lift my voice, from whence doth come my aid...'

It was coming from under one of the boats. Doreen's boat.

'Good evening minister,' cried Jimmy. He put a hand on the boat and leaned down, waiting for an answer. He felt that perhaps the minister needed prompting. 'And a fine night it is to praise the Celestial Boat Maker, under the keel of heaven and the twinkling copper nail-heads of the stars.'

'Indeed,' replied Rev Dumfry's voice, but the voice was strained and somewhat tired, without its usual deep resonance. There was a long pause, then the minister spoke up again. 'I haven't seen you in church recently, Jimmy.'

Jimmy nodded solemnly. 'Aye, well, minister, you know how it is yourself. If there's nothing to see you'll not see it.'

The truth of this was so evident that Dumfry gave no reply.

'Goodnight, then.' Jimmy thumped the planks by way of a farewell and walked on. Behind him, he thought he heard two people scrambling out from under the boat, but he was tactful enough to make no further comment. He was particularly thoughtful as he strolled along within earshot of the beach, hearing but scarcely noticing the hissing of the sea on the sand.

Jimmy was without a philosophy. If, in the normal way of things, he needed one, he borrowed it from others and patched it up so that it would not leak. When he was finished with it, he left it on the beach for anyone else who needed it.

Nevertheless, he was convinced that there was a deep underlying connection between events. In 1425, the herring changed their habits and no longer visited the Baltic Sea. The Baltic fleets, had, until then, supplied large amounts of dried fish to Britain. They were bankrupted, and along the East Coast of Britain, local herring fleets developed to cope with the demand. Boats from Cromness and other East Coast ports now traded herring to the Baltic states, along with hemp rope, whisky, nails and other goods. Business was good. Cromness developed into a major trading port.

At the same time, as it happened, the Emperor of China developed a passion for painting cats and dogs. This same emperor valued music so much that he kept 3,800 musicians. He was, after all, the emperor. He could have had 3,800 artists painting cats and dogs, but he did not. He did it himself.

Not only that, but Tsong K'a-pa had died in Tibet just shortly before – Tsong K'a-pa, that great bodhisattva who had reformed Tibetan Buddhism.

The web of connections was almost meaningful. All along the Links he wrestled with the ideas. He remembered that Henry the Navigator was trying to find Prester John's empire about the same time – a venture destined to fail, since Prester John was a complete invention. At the edge of his garden, Jimmy stopped and removed the wig from his bald head, hoping the cool air would calm his brain. The Dalai Lama would have to be told about this. It was too much for just one man to cope with.

Or maybe it was just the whisky thinking.

'The boat wis up the coast near Balmahomack when we saw the dolphins. If they wid stay up there, they'd be nae trouble.' Baldy shrugged. 'But the captain said they'll be back by Rossmarty and Redrock in the morn.'

Mr Mor strode about the room, now glancing at the map of Cromness on the table, now drumming his fingers on the brazen boar's head standing on a plinth. 'They're intelligent,' he said. 'Maybe they can be trained.'

The driver spoke from his chair near the door. 'You can't train all of them.'

Baldy stood straight and looked tough. 'Ah'd just shoot the lot.' He brushed a piece of lint off his cuff. 'Nae mair problems.'

Mr Mor stopped pacing and turned to face Baldy. 'Listen to me, bonehead. We do not shoot them, we do not harm them. We do not even think about harming them. Understand?'

'But...'

'Understand?'

Baldy bowed his head, looking sulky. 'Yes, boss.'

'What's the point of the pigs, the farming, the estate, the football team and the rest of it, why be here in the first place if we go shitting in our own nest?'

Baldy looked sideways at the driver, who avoided his eyes.

'Sorry, boss.'

'Listen, Baldy, you leave the strategy to me, okay? If you want to go and shoot something, you can go out on the moors and kill a grouse. With a shotgun. Anything else is out, prohibited, *verboten, nicht hinauslehnen, e pericoloso sporgersi. Comprende?*'

'What?'

Mr Mor sighed. 'No shooting. No aggro. No double parking, even. Stay clean.'

Baldy subsided into a chair beside the driver, looking sullen. Mr Mor leant over the map of Cromness. He had red lines marked out for the marina, the shopping centre, the theme park, the football stadium. The new road was marked in black, a dual carriageway to replace the single track road with passing places. He had blue lines showing which parts of Cromness he already owned, green lines showing the parts he still had to obtain. He frowned at the green-lined areas. Too many of them, especially round the Vennels. It wasn't a money problem. There was plenty of money, but it wasn't always easy finding out who owned what. He wondered if he should broach the subject with Siller, the treasurer of Cromness Football Club. He was the local bank manager, so he might be able to help, though he would have to be kept in the dark about most of the plan.

Patience, he chided himself. The place would be a mint, and the money would all be clean. More than that, it would be his.

Suddenly it was not enough, just looking at the map.

'Hold the fort. I'm going up the tower,' he said. 'Stay here.'

He went through the small door in the corner of the room. There was a spiral staircase there. Two hundred sandstone steps. He began to climb, fast.

The tower room was of bare red sandstone, with indirect lights playing up against the wooden beams of the conical roof. There was a curved desk against the wall, a rack of CDs and a player on the desk.

Mr Mor was breathing hard when he arrived. He fumbled under his shirt and brought out the vial, waiting for his breathing to slow down before he dipped the little spoon into it. Then he turned on the CD player and put on Beethoven's Fifth Symphony, changed his mind and put on *Also Sprach Zarathustra*.

He opened the window and stepped out onto the balcony. From there he could see the town lights, far off and far down. He could make out where the streets must be, and he could imagine where his stadium was going to be, the marina, the park...

The timpani sounded from the speakers in the room behind him. The night air exhilarated him, turned to fire in his blood.

It was like being God, looking down on the town. It was almost in his hand.

Jimmy Bervie arrived at his garden, where the soil petered away and blended into the beach sand. The tide had done its job. The raked lines had been swept away. The sand was smooth and almost dry, a blank slate waiting for the touch of a breeze or a bird's foot, or a rake.

It was time to try again. Twice in one day was unusual, but things were changing fast.

He took the rake from its place against the house wall and stood looking down at the sand, gathering himself. He took off his jacket and laid it on the ground, carefully folded, with his mop-head wig placed on it. The windmill he laid on the top. This was no time for distractions.

The moon was looking out from the clouds to the east and the sand was silvered by its light. Out beyond the Suitors he could see tiny lights moving on the water. Luminescent sea-creatures from the icy depths of the North Sea drawn up by the moonlight to perform their mysterious mating dance. Or fishing boats at work.

He put all speculation from his mind, lifted the rake, then lowered it and drew it through the sand. With his fingertips he could feel the deep grain of the old wooden handle, he could sense the movement of the tines through the sand, the slight dragging effect of the dampness, the occasional jar as a tine knocked on a stone then rode past it. The space around him was vast and empty, bigger than the North Sea, bigger than Scotland, bigger than the world. Cromness inhabited that space momentarily, like a fleck of foam on a wavetop. The entire world lived in that space like a mayfly in a river.

Jimmy Bervie stood in his brogues on the damp beach, his hands reading the lay of the sand through the rake handle, his bald head cool in the night air, the smell of the sea in his nostrils, the sound of the sea in his ears. He reached and drew, reached and drew, repetitive and irresistible as the tides.

When he was done, he turned from the beach and walked up the path to set the rake back in its place against the house wall. He returned to the beach, put his jacket on again, and only then looked back at what he had made.

The lines of his raking were as close to perfect as anything he'd done. The slight repetitive wave in the lines spoke to him about harmony in the underlying nature of the universe while the jagged edge to the tiny furrows talked to him about the weeds that grew on the top of the police station wall, the sound of a child crying in a garden, Mr Siller's bony hands counting pennies slowly in the bank, Alice chasing a cat out of her garden with a broom.

These irregularities were to be expected. It was like the rough texture of his tweed jacket, a necessary part of the world. But right in the middle of the raked pattern was a strange twisted shape that didn't belong there. It wasn't normal, it wasn't necessary. If the texture of the world was like the weave of a tweed jacket, this anomaly was like a third sleeve.

'Maybe I need a new rake,' he muttered, but he didn't convince himself.

Doreen slipped back into the house quietly. Alice was sleeping, but woke briefly to register the sound of the door closing and fell asleep again as Doreen climbed the stairs to bed.

Rev Dumfry sat in his kitchen drinking cocoa with his Bible in front of him. He carefully stood it on its spine and let it fall open at random. The words of the Song of Solomon lay before him. So much for bibliomancy he thought, and went off to bed without washing up his mug.

Irwin and the folk singer, upstairs in The Fisherman's Arms, were in each other's arms and fast asleep, though they would wake before dawn to deepen their acquaintance.

Sammy Poach was in the stupor of a drunk, his rich whisky breath filling the room, which had little else in it beyond the bed and an old wardrobe and a worn rug.

Miss Semple was twitching nervously in her sleep, dreaming about odd things happening round dark corners. She knew what they were doing, but she couldn't catch them at it.

In the Harbour Hotel, Ann and Bill Deace slumbered in their twin beds, their notes still spread out on the desk. A map of East Rossland was there too, with a red circle drawn round Cromness. Dotted lines were drawn from the harbour out into the North Sea, with dates and times liberally jotted near them.

Even the pillar of the Law was slumbering. MacFearn snored in his bed, his uniform hung over the back of a chair and his policeman's hat on the bedside table.

In all of Cromness, not a soul was awake, though Mr Mor still stood on his balcony a mile away, looking down at the town.

As for George, he couldn't really be said to be in Cromness at all that night. His grasp on reality was slender at best, and he had slipped out of the town and was far away.

PART 2

GEORGE DID NOT reappear for several days and coincidentally, during that time, the town seemed to be on edge, waiting for something.

There were a number of portents. M Le Placs, the French surgeon who worked in Inverness, predicted the winners of three horse races and won several thousand pounds, which he donated to the Cromness playschool association. Mrs Hitchin's hen laid a double-yolked egg, which Mr Hitchin ate for lunch. M Le Placs had predicted this also, and won ten pounds from Ian Coast with which he bought a round in The Fisherman's Arms. A narwhal was reported on the beach at Rossmarty, though it turned out to be a seal. And there was a naval exercise out to sea, lighting the night sky with brilliant flashes as the ships fired blank rounds at each other.

Jimmy Bervie was perhaps the most deeply affected. He did his utmost to adjust the meters of reality by wearing many strings of beads around his neck. He had plastic children's beads, mirafiori glass beads strung on silk, antique jade, a Hindu mala with a picture of Ganesh the elephant-headed god, blue and fat and full of dimples. There were wooden beads, pottery beads and the seeds of the neem tree threaded on cat-gut. Sometimes he wore a dress-suit, sometimes surfing shorts with rubber boots.

Externally, then, Jimmy seemed unchanged. He beamed at everyone he met, as he tried to melt away his uneasiness in a flood of goodwill.

He raked the sand twice a day, getting no comfort from it. Nothing seemed to help. The people of Cromness were not easy in themselves. Big Irwin nearly confided his worries about his genitals to Sammy Poach. Ellen forgot to tell Miss Semple about the young MacLean girl who'd got herself pregnant. Miss Semple, who kept up a constant chatter inside her own head, began to talk out loud at inappropriate times.

In the bank, Mr Siller showed no unease. He counted out coins with his usual glacial slowness. His customers, however, were less phlegmatic and several closed their bank accounts out of frustration.

Rev Dumfry was afflicted on more than one front, as he had a couple of awkward moral problems to deal with. He began to worry about the church. A large, cold and mainly unadorned space, it had always seemed a little too vast for the congregation, though his voice filled it amply. Now, however, it felt empty. Not just as if there was no-one in it, but genuinely, chillingly empty. He managed to convince himself that he had a cold coming, and took a nip of whisky before entering the church.

He was about to encounter a very serious disturbance in his ideas of the world, and this little self-deception should not be held against him.

Jimmy Bervie stared out of his kitchen window, watching the boats bobbing in the harbour. Morning sunlight shone warmly on the red sandstone pier and glinted on the waves. It all looked so peaceful, but Jimmy was sure that the tranquillity was no more than a veneer covering god knew what disturbances in the deeper layers of reality. It was time to do something.

He turned resolutely and began to search around the room. In the kindling box beside the fireplace he found an old white paper bag. He carefully tore the seams of the bag then smoothed it out flat on the rough wooden top of his ramshackle table. From the mantelpiece he took a stub of pencil. Then he sat down and began to write.

```
Dear Nag-dban bLo-bzan bsTan-'dsin rgya-mts'o,

   All is well with me as I hope it is with you too.
Thank you for the inscribed windmill which is a great
comfort to me. I can not, unfortunately, understand the
inscription - OM AH HUM VAJRA GURU PADMA SIDDHI HUM - and
would be obliged if you would recommend a Tibetan Primer
which I might use to translate it.
Mrs MacKerril was asking after you and hopes you are
well. She hopes to see you back here again soon. Her bed
and breakfast business is doing well and she is pleased
to display your written recommendation on the wall. She
has even had it framed. Perhaps I could translate it for
her if I can find a suitable Tibetan phrasebook.
```

Jimmy paused at this point and chewed the end of his pencil. The Dalai Lama said that he inherited all the memories of his predecessor. And his predecessor had inherited the memories of the Dalai Lama before that. So Nag-dban bLo-bzan bsTan-'dsin 'dsin rgya-mts'o should have all the memories of all the Dalai Lamas back to the first one ever, who luckily lived at just the right time. He continued writing.

```
   I wonder if you could cast your mind back to 1425. You
may not be aware of this, but in that year the herring in
the North Sea changed their normal practice and ceased
to visit the Baltic. This was a crucial moment for this
area. If you recall, Tson K'a-pa had just died, so
the time may well stick in your memory. Was there any
particular event in the worlds to which you have access
that precipitated this? (I note in passing that the
Emperor of China developed a passion for painting round
about this time.)
```

Jimmy was not at all sure just how much the Dalai Lama remembered from one incarnation to the next, and he did not wish to embarrass him if in fact his memories of nearly 600 years ago were fading. After a long pause for thought, accompanied by much pencil-sucking, he continued.

> I know that I keep forgetting where I put the door-key, so I won't be too disappointed if memories from 1425 have slipped from your mind.
>
> By the way, I am having a little trouble with my sand-garden that you were kind enough to praise when you were here last August. An odd pattern keeps appearing that is not a natural disturbance. It is as if something is affecting the fabric of the universe. Studying the pattern of the lines in the sand, it sometimes seems that the tines of the rake have crossed over so that the damaged tine is on the left instead of the right. It almost appears as if the rake is twisting through another dimension. (Thank you again for showing me the practical use of extra dimensions. I remain astonished at your capacity to deal with seventeen of them when the rest of us have trouble enough with just a handful!)
>
> If, as we discussed last summer, a well-raked patch of sand mirrors the state of the surrounding world, then I would guess from this odd pattern that Cromness is about to disappear beneath the waves!
>
> If you have any clues as to what might be happening, do please let me know.
>
> May all beings be happy,
>
>   Your friend,
>
>   James Bervie

> P.S. I have included a packet of Mrs Mackerril's tablet that you enjoyed on your last visit.

Jimmy searched out a battered tartan box for the tablet, wrapped both the sweets and the letter and addressed the parcel to the Dalai Lama in MacLeod Ganj, Northern India, an address that never failed to cause him a shiver of wonder at the interconnectedness of things. A relative of his had been called Hamish MacLeod. Who knows, perhaps he was nicknamed Ganj.

Or perhaps not.

After all, no answer is also an answer, he thought. And perhaps no coincidence is also coincidental.

He selected the pink sunglasses and the matching waistcoat with mirrored pockets and took the parcel to the post office.

From the *Rossland Advertiser Sporting Supplement*
Final Score: Castleton 3, Cromness 5

...astonishingly, Cromness recovered from a three-goal deficit when Big Irwin, delayed by a leak in his boat, turned up at half time. The Castleton side went on the defensive immediately, but to no avail. Irwin ran like a gazelle and within twenty minutes sank a hat-trick deep in the opposing goal.

Five minutes after his arrival, Irwin beat Arnold Jack in a deep run along the starboard side, and jinked round a wrong-footed Castleton defence to plant his first goal in the net. The second resulted from Jim Barraclough's fumble on the twenty-seven yard line which Irwin picked up and ran with from his own manor right into the opponents' eighteen yard box where he drove it home with a right foot like a piston. His third goal came when he picked up a clearance from his own keeper. He left the Castleton side standing with egg on their faces as he jitterbugged round them like Fred Astaire. His blistering speed on the final stretch was like Linford Christie with a rocket up his jumper. Watch Irwin and weep, Jonah Lomu! We have a man here who could run rings round you with his hands tied behind his back!

Sportingly, Irwin left the other two goals to his team-mates. By that time, half of the Castleton team were desperately marking Irwin, leaving gaps in the defence you could have driven a bus through. And they did. There can be no doubt that Irwin is a once-in-a-lifetime event, and we are privileged that it happened in our lifetimes.

This sentiment was echoed by the young ladies in the stand, who were obviously fans of the Big Man, cheering him on and singing his favourite song, 'Tatties and Herring'. The size of the phenomenon that is Irwin can be judged from the fact that there were Castleton girls among them, singing with the rest, at a home match! Irwin, always a gentleman, managed to fend off the ladies without offending any of them.

The only question now must be how long it will be before a first division team comes hunting for him.

Alice had not yet risen when the postman arrived, so Doreen signed for the package and ran upstairs with it. In her bedroom, she tore it open, and there they were, each in its own individual clear plastic wrappers. Silk long-johns and a silk vest. She was filled with mixed emotions. There was a certain excitement in receiving the underclothes, and she fully intended to try them on at once, while Alice was out of the way. On the other hand, their arrival was a physical reminder of the Seeing, inevitably drawing closer.

Doreen had been closeted in the house for three days, avoiding all excitement, drinking only water, eating suitable foods chosen and prepared by Alice. Doreen did not really mind that – after all it was the only time that Alice did her share of the housework – but was the diet of mince, tatties and turnips really suitable fare for a Pythoness about to undergo the ordeal of a Seeing? It seemed more likely that her diet was due to Alice's rusty culinary skills.

She thought sadly about the coble on the links, untenanted for three nights now. But sex was definitely out of the question during her period of purification. This was one thing which Alice absolutely demanded, although she was fairly easygoing at other times. Tonight, Doreen would have to spend the whole night in the darkness of the sanctuary of the Goddess, a place fraught with the shades of long-dead seers, as well as the spirit of the Goddess Herself. Sexual purity was essential. Doreen would not dream of infringing this particular rule.

In any case, Reverend Dumfry would be hanging around the Links, frightening off the less brazen of the young men.

From: Factor's Office, Redrock Estate
To: Dolphin Research Institute, Braehead, Cromness

```
Dear Sir/Madam,

    Mr Mor has been for some time aware of your splendid
work and has studied carefully the various research
papers which the Institute has produced. He feels that
your work is both timely and important and deserves
the support of concerned individuals in addition to
the funding you receive from the Highlands University
Trust.

    In recognition of this, I am empowered to offer you
funding of fifty thousand pounds (£50,000) to be used
to initiate a post for a suitably qualified applicant
to study the subject of dolphin training. Mr Mor owns
the salmon fishing rights to the south side of the Dark
Isle, as well as the salmon farms off Cromness. What he
```

is especially interested in is a non-violent aversion technique to prevent dolphin damage to the farms. As you will know, one of the younger dolphins drowned recently when it was caught in the fish farm nets. We hope such incidents can be avoided in future.

Should you accept this offer, Mr Mor will of course expect to be consulted in setting up the parameters and protocols for the study.

Yours Sincerely,

Peter White (Estate Factor)

From: Dolphin Research Institute, Braehead, Cromness
To: Redrock Estate Office, Redrock

Dear Sir,

We are of course pleased at the interest which Mr Mor shows in our work, but we must regretfully decline the offer of funding for the project you suggest. The Institute is dedicated to the study of Dolphins in a naturalistic setting without human intervention. Dolphinariums, to which we are opposed in principle, train captive Dolphins. Consequently we feel that the training of Dolphins is not an appropriate area for scientific research.

Possibly your employer's money might be better spent on a barrage or a semi-rigid barrier to keep Dolphins and seals away from his fish farms.

Yours sincerely

Joseph Fullwright

(Director, Dolphin Research Institute)

From the barley field on the hillside, Veronica could look down onto the crowns of the trees that filled Glen Grian. This early in the day, the sun was still low and the green leafy canopy was stippled with shadows in mysterious shapes. It was said that there were elemental beings in there – superstitiously called the Good People, or Fairies, or Elves. This summer she was determined to investigate it for herself. Of course she knew the Glen as well as anyone – it had been her playground since she was a toddler. But that wasn't the same as a proper investigation.

Not everyone could see the spirits of the trees and the plants, not everyone was sensitive to the auras of living things. Veronica had begun a regime of tuning exercises, to sensitise herself to these ethereal influences. Breathing exercises, meditation, arcane chants, yoga and a strict vegetarian diet. She took a deep breath and held her arms out to the green Glen, letting its ancient vibrations fill her heart.

She turned for home, along the track by the turnip field and the barn where her father was clearing out the old farm machinery, getting it ready. A company called 2nd Tribal Railroad had hired it for a big dance. It was advertised all over the Dark Isle, posters with wild colours and ambiguous pictures. She thought of the normal barn dance – young men in their best clothes and a half-bottle in the back pocket, young women dressed to kill, flirting with strangers, trying to start a fight. This poster said 'Tribal Encounter – the Meeting of Minds.' Strangest barn dance she'd ever heard of.

She frowned as she walked up to the barn. She hoped that the dance wouldn't disturb the influences from the Glen.

Her father had reached the final stages of clearing the barn. The tractor bucket was full of old junk: fence-posts, a rusty coulter, a turnip chopper, an oil barrel. He stopped the engine and climbed from the cab.

'Hi, Ronny. Had a good walk?'

'Fine, Dad. The Glen is beautiful just now.' She looked at him meaningfully. 'Beautiful and quiet, in fact.'

Mr Ross laughed. 'I hear you, girl. But it'll only be one night.'

Veronica snorted. 'A very long night. From eight until dawn. We'll get no sleep.'

Mr Ross looked at her seriously. 'It's good money and it's paid for. You can like it or lump it. If you're that worried about your beauty sleep, you can stay with your aunt in Cromness.'

'Oh God, no. Not with Aunt Lizbeth.'

'Then why don't you go to the dance yourself?'

'Oh, Dad. I can think of nothing worse than spending the night with drunken sweaty farm labourers pawing me and singing along to the Birdie Song. No thank you.'

He started walking up the track with her. 'Ronny, why don't you? It's just a bit of fun. You're so serious these days, wrapped up in yourself.'

She suspected that this was a criticism. 'It's not just me I'm thinking of,' she said.

'No, no, I'm sure not,' he said turning his head to the side and raising his eyes to heaven.

'It's the Glen. It's a special place. There was a Celtic Christian church there. They've had an archaeologist in to look at the ruins, and there was a Druid college before that – I've been reading about it. People came from all over the world to visit it and study there – even from Egypt. It's a special place,' she repeated.

'Sure it is, Ronny, but the barn dance is here, not down the hill.'

She couldn't explain it to him, she knew she couldn't. But she tried. 'It's a holy place, Dad,' she said, blushing. 'Honest. And its vibrations spread out all around.'

He kicked his boots impatiently against the doorstep to get the mud off.

'Well our barn is a fine place too, though it's a bit short of druids. And a barn dance is a chance for people to get together and enjoy themselves. I'm sure the vibrations of all these happy people will spread out all around too.'

She looked down. 'You don't understand.'

'For God's sake come in and have some breakfast before you fade away. I'll make you a bacon roll, if you promise to eat it.'

She shuddered. 'Not meat, Dad. I'll have some muesli.'

From the *Rossland Advertiser*

It has just been revealed that the Dark Isle Show this year is to be formally opened by one of the most famous of the sons of the Dark Isle. David MacLing, having recently been made Junior Minister with responsibility for Shellfish Harvesting & Pelagic Farms, is not a man with time on his hands, but he is generously taking time from his busy schedule to visit his old home ground.

Now MP for Porthead and Buggan, MacLing was born in the parish of Boblair on the Dark Isle and attended Rossmarty Academy, where he is probably the most highly regarded of former pupils, though the roll of honour includes Army officers, captains of industry and commerce, several research chemists and a ballet dancer.

MacLing, (54) is by no means at the peak of his career. He can surely look forward to advancement before the next General Election. MacLing has been vociferous in his support for the fishermen and looks forward to a future in which the fishing industry is given the support and prestige that it deserves. To suggestions that he is ideally placed to bid for the Cabinet post of Minister for Fisheries and Marine Resources, he merely smiled and said, 'That is in the hands of the Gods.'

During his day at the Show, he is also expected to present some of the prizes, especially those related to his particular field. The Nerval Lobster Pair is the blue riband for inshore fishermen, and it is expected that he will particularly wish to present that. Traditionally, the presentation is accompanied by a few lines from the poetry of Nerval, usually in translation.

Sources in the Highland Police HQ have intimated that there will be extra security in place for MacLing's visit.

Sammy Poach sat on a kitchen chair in his back garden with his net across his knees. He leant back so that he could peer into his window at the clock on the kitchen wall. Nearly mid-day. Just time to finish mending the net.

The garden, though small, had high walls on two sides and the blank gable of a house on the other side. No-one could see what he was doing. He pulled tight a few more knots, then bit off a length of nylon and spat the end into the grass.

The net had not been used for some time but it was ready now. It was a lightweight net that he could wind round his body under his coat. Along the top edge of the net was a semi-buoyant rope that would float just at the surface. The bottom edge had weights to keep it on the sea-bed. The threads of the net were fine clear nylon, invisible in the water. All in all, a grand piece of equipment to be wielding in the war against Capitalist Aggression – personified as Mr Mor.

He took the net inside and carefully folded it away. 'You and me,' he said, 'along the beach, tonight. How's about it doll?' He winked at the net and closed the cupboard door.

Sammy's house was on Shore Road, just past the entrance to the Wee Vennel. In storms, the waves crashed against the sea-wall and threw salt water over his windows, and the wind drove the spray far up the alley. When the windows dried, the salt remained. The windows were now so thick with salt that it was impossible to see through them.

The houses in the Vennel were almost all empty. Sometimes dim lights flickered in the salt-smeared windows after dark or shadowy figures seemed to move behind the glass, but no-one lived on the Wee Vennel except Jenny-Pet. Jenny was ancient and bent. She was from somewhere near Glasgow and she'd arrived in Cromness so long ago that hardly anyone remembered the Wee Vennel without her in it. Her house was tiny and had no plumbing, so she had to get all her water from the stand-pipe in the street. She resisted every attempt to improve her cottage, even when the Social Services offered to do it for free.

'No, pet,' she said, 'I'm as happy with the standpipe.'

It was almost impossible to walk along the Wee Vennel without encountering Jenny-Pet. She seemed to have an organic radar, so that when you went a few paces up the narrow alley, her door opened and she emerged with a bucket.

'Hello, pet,' she would say. 'Just need some water for the washing/tea/cooking/garden.'

Then she would chat away as the trickle from the tap slowly filled the bucket. The result was that people tended to pass along the Wee Vennel at speed, with a brief greeting ready in the mouth, to avoid a long conversation with her.

Visitors of course were ignorant of the proper technique for using the alley, and frequently got caught for twenty minutes as she talked about anything and everything with a blithe disregard for any replies they might make.

Locally, it was felt that tourists were responsible for her short stay in Craig Dunain Mental Hospital, by Inverness.

A couple of tourists went walking up the Wee Vennel and as normal, Jenny-Pet popped out to fill her bucket.

'Hello, pet,' she said.

The tourists ignored her. They were peering into the windows on either side of the Vennel.

'They're all empty,' said the man.

'They wouldn't stay empty long if they were in Dorset,' said the woman.

'Maybe we could buy one – they don't look as if they'd cost much. We could let it out.'

'It's a lovely day, pet. Isn't it a lovely day?'

The man looked at Jenny. She was wearing an old floral dress, dingy with age, and a pair of black work boots. Her grey hair hung around her face.

'I beg your pardon?'

'I said, it's a lovely day, pet. Nice and warm.'

The woman turned from the window she was peering through. 'It's too damn hot, if you want my opinion.'

Jenny nodded. 'It is hot, pet.' She turned off the tap and picked up the bucket. She stepped up onto the doorstep to give herself the advantage of height, then poured the water over the woman.

'There you are, pet, that should cool you down.'

The tourists made a fuss, which could not be ignored. If Jenny had admitted to any malevolence in her act, she would have been all right, but she was quite sure in herself that her behaviour was perfectly sensible.

'She was too hot, you see. I just wanted to cool her down, Pet,' she said. 'So she was taken to the place on the hill for a few weeks.'

Sammy Poach was one of the few people who gave Jenny-Pet any credit for intelligence. It was plain to him that she wanted to keep the outside tap so that she could wage her continual chatter against passers-by. For a while he'd pitied her, thinking it was only loneliness that drove her. But he'd seen the gleam of a bright intelligence in her eyes, and he felt sure that she had deeper motives. She was a pleasing enigma to him and he did not grudge her an occasional half-hour of blether.

She'd been fond of Sammy's grandson George too, who had been happy to babble to her, sitting in the sun in the alley. He'd been lost once, for a couple of days, and half of Cromness had been out looking for him, on the hills, the shore, in abandoned buildings. At last Sammy had told Jenny-Pet.

She said, 'Don't worry, pet, he's as right as rain.' She brought George out of the Muckle Vennel a couple of hours later and took him home. Some suspected that she'd had him in her house all along – but Sammy wouldn't hear of it.

That was about the time when George's mother began to go strange. She seemed to lose interest in George. She neglected both him and the house and started studying psychology books. Since he had no father, George was left more and more in the charge of his grandparents, and Sammy was the closest he had to a father. By the time George left for College, his mother was almost a stranger to him. She went away to Craig Dunain Hospital shortly after and he had never been to see her there.

As it happened, she was happy enough in the hospital, waiting her time and wondering what to say when George turned up to ask about his father. A tricky question.

'Ladies, this afternoon we have Dr Lorraine MacDonald to talk to us on Traditions of Celtic Culture. Dr MacDonald received her Doctorate in Highland Studies and is particularly interested in the North-East of Scotland. As you will recall, she is the author of the excellent book *Cromness: Centre of the North*, in which she presents her thesis that the Dark Isle was a centre of great importance in Pictish times.

'We have here a number of pamphlets which she has also published. We have *Place-Names of the North East, P And Q Celtic in the Literature of the Dark Ages*, as well as *Epona and the Cult of the Horse Goddess*. All of these may be bought after the lecture.'

Dr Lorraine MacDonald looked out on her audience. The Ladies Guild of Cromness was not impressive, though there was a good turn out. The hall itself, the Chandler Memorial Hall, was very Victorian and upright, and it amused her to think of the women in the same way.

Nevertheless, there were one or two oddities. In a niche there stood a carved stone roughly in the shape of a phallus, with a poem engraved beneath it, praising the virtues of the codpiece. This was attributed to the 14th Lord Farquhar. And in the corner on a pedestal was an ancient-looking brass effigy of a boar which interested her extremely.

The audience had its oddities also. There was a very large woman at one side sitting on two chairs. Her bright eyes watched carefully and intelligently. Dr MacDonald turned away from the steady gaze and arranged her notes.

And there was a little bird of a woman, with her knitting out, who looked as if she was here for the tea and biscuits at the interval. She seemed to pay no attention to anything around her, but muttered to herself occasionally, then blushed and knitted furiously for a few minutes.

Would any of these people understand half of what she was trying to say about the Celts and their culture? Still, she was being paid. She felt the eyes of the big woman fasten on to her face as she began to speak.

There was one woman here, she thought uncomfortably, who looked as if she would understand all too well.

As the lecturer spoke, Miss Semple knitted firmly and listened with great suspicion. When she lived in Rossmarty, she had regularly attended meetings of the Townswomen's Guild, where there had been a variety of interesting and educational talks on Wholefoods and their Preparation, Herb Gardens on the Windowsill, and How to Crochet Rugs from Rags. There had also been slide shows on the Holy Land and Vineyards of the Auvergne. These were proper subjects for an Improving Lecture.

She knitted a little faster and dropped a stitch. She breathed a deep breath and started again. She had only come along to support the local Guild – and she'd found herself in the middle of a lecture on heathens of some sort. They were all prehistoric, of course, or nearly so, which was gratifying, and no doubt Educational, but the woman, who seemed to be a doctor of some sort, would insist on speaking about their pagan practices.

'Place-names are particularly revealing,' said Doctor Lorraine MacDonald. 'Cromness is probably named for the Cromm Cruach of the Celts, a golden vessel sacred to the God of Death. Sacrifices were made to the vessel, human sacrifices.'

It was very interesting to know that such practices occurred, a long time ago, but why must she insist on describing the 'binding of the three narrows' and why did she have to describe so precisely the three ways in which the sacrificial victim was killed? Possibly it was because she was a doctor.

But must she suggest that some such practice was carried out in Cromness until quite recently? A horrid thought came to her. Perhaps that was what the Satanists were doing up in the old graveyard. She shuddered and knitted extra fast for a few minutes.

Cromness Town Council: Minutes
Present: Mrs Alma Keivor (Chair), Mr M Siller, Mr Aristide
Coupar, Mr Jonathon Hogg, Ms Epona Rider, Mr Richard
Slater
Apologies: Ms Jan Innes, Mrs Eilidh MacKerril

Item 4: It was agreed that the new lamp-post designs
should pass the conservation officer before erection.
Item 5: After debate, it was decided that both the
planning queries concerning the Vennels area of Cromness
should be dealt with by the full planning committee. Mr
Siller registered his objection to this.

Alma was less than five feet tall, but no-one would dare to ask for the exact statistics. She sat on a thick cushion on her chair and looked down the long table at Mr Siller. He was probably the only person in the room who could sit in that seat and survive.

Alma's personal forcefulness was complicated by a prominent bosom, accentuated by her small stature, and a moustache of fine dark hair. These features caused considerable unease, as it was difficult to avoid the gaze drifting to either one of them rather than confront her little hard eyes. She was well aware of this, and used these characteristics to her advantage in any confrontation. Mr Siller was one of the few people who was immune to Alma's weapons of unease, as he never met anyone's eyes in any case, but looked down at the ground and washed his hands dryly, with a faint hissing sound as the palms slid over one another.

Alma spoke firmly. 'We have two applications here, Mr Siller, and we have to consider both of them. To dismiss one of them at this stage would be inequitable. As I am sure you will appreciate if you reflect for a moment.'

Mr Siller's mouth mumbled for a second as if he was tasting both sides of a penny. 'I believe I made my objections plain, Mrs Keivor, but clearly you do not recall them. I will summarise:

'The proposal from Mr Mor is of an inappropriate size and would oblige the council to invest large amounts of money in improvements to the town's infrastructure. There is, moreover, scant evidence that Mr Mor owns or has any financial interest in any of the property in the Vennels itself, where most of the development is proposed. Only a small portion of the surrounding buildings belong to him and a handful more are under his feu.

'Therefore his application should be dismissed now, as being excessively expensive and in practical terms, unfeasible.

'On the other hand, it seems from the documentation provided that Argent Enterprises already owns or has under negotiation almost half of the buildings around the Vennels and indeed holds the freehold on the land which comprises the Muckle Vennel itself. Their proposal requires minimal improvements to the infrastructure and would involve the council in no financial obligations whatever.

'Therefore this proposal should be seriously considered and passed to the planning committee.'

There was a low muttering from the ranks around the table. Most of them were bent over, studying their notes. Mrs Keivor studied the bent heads.

'Well? Aren't any of you going to say anything?' Richard Slater twitched. 'You there, Headfirst, have you got anything to say?'

Mr Slater muttered something.

'Speak up laddie! We can't hear.'

'I said he's right. We haven't got the money.'

'I thought as much. That's the kind of craven attitude that leaves this town stuck in the seventeenth century. The kind of attitude I would expect from old Siller, but not, I hope, from the rest of you.

'Of course we don't have the money – and we never will have the money if we reject a forward-looking project like this out of hand. By all means pass the Argent company's proposal along as well, but I have to say that it sounds like the sort of proposal that would appeal to a penny-pinching hand-washing anal-retentive accountant rather than a forward-looking dynamic modern town council.'

She looked around the table. Most of the members were sitting up straight again. She caught Mr Siller's eye.

'No offence meant,' she said.

'None taken,' he replied.

The tide was fully in and the water was slack. Rain freckled the surface, dimpling the small waves. Two hundred yards along the shore, water from the Brewery Burn stained the sea brown. It had been raining heavily all night, and peat from the moors had washed into the burn.

The salmon coble puttered along at lowest speed, with two hooded figures in it. One was Sammy Poach, in bright orange rain gear. He tended the net with his gnarled hands, unfolding it into the water behind the boat, making sure that it didn't foul the propeller. The other man had a bright yellow slicker. His face was deep in the hood, and he was sitting obliquely so that he could watch both the unfolding net and the shore. Behind them, the red and white channel buoy showed as a shifting red smear on the grey sea between the two Suitors.

The boat made a long half-circle, coming in towards the shore again. When the net was all out Sammy belayed the rope round a cleat until the boat grounded. Big Irwin waded out and took the ropes while Sammy climbed out to help. As the men on the other end of the net began pulling too, the loop of net grew slowly smaller. The enclosed area diminished and splashing came from the water within the net as the fish panicked. The men hauled together until most of the net had been pulled into wet heaps on the beach and only a thrashing purse of net was left in the sea. By now, Sammy was wading around it, stunning the fish.

'Five,' he said.

'Not bad,' said Irwin. 'This rain has helped.' He nodded towards the brown peat-stain at the burn-mouth. 'They must be able to smell the burn halfway to Norway.'

They pulled the net onto the beach and Sammy took the fish out of the folds. 'Couple of grilse,' he said, lifting out two small salmon, five or six pounds apiece. 'And there's a big one.' He held it up admiringly. 'Must be fifteen pounds. She's probably been back to spawn twice already.' He untangled two big crabs from the net. 'Anyone want a couple of partans?'

'I'll have them. I'll get the wife to make partan bree.' The man took the crabs and carried them up to the Land Rover with the fish.

Sammy and Irwin heaved one pile of net onto the other, turning it over so that the folds lay right. When the rest of the men came back, they lifted the whole wet pile into the coble.

'The other side of the burn?' suggested Irwin.

Sammy nodded. 'I suppose so, there should be fish there heading for the burn. But dammit, if gollachan Mor would let us fish properly, we wouldn't have all this damned heaving about of nets.'

The boatman took the coble out and headed along the beach towards the burn. The others trudged along the stony beach, taking big awkward steps in their waders.

Sammy was still complaining. 'I never saw the like. Fishing with a long net like this, it's all right in a river, but it's ridiculous for sea fishing.'

'He's using the proper nets round the Suitor at Redrock and Rossmarty.'

'Aye, I heard that. But what good is that to man or beast? He catches the fish, but what does he do with them?'

Irwin put a hand on his shoulder. 'Come on, Sammy, what he does with the fish is his business and none of yours. And hell, there's a couple of squads of men now, being paid to do the fishing.'

'Aye, there is! But it's all his own men! Every bloody salmon fisher along the south of the Dark Isle is on the dole now.' Sammy's voice was high with indignation. He made his decision. Tonight was the night that the Workers Revolutionary Party of Cromness would strike the good blow. Mr Mor would rue the day he got his clutching fingers on the fishing rights.

Irwin was uneasy. He didn't understand what Mr Mor was up to and he didn't want to defend him, but he did pay the wages.

'We're still fishing,' he said, 'And he pays us regular.'

'Oh aye, we're fishing, and our fish goes to the fishmongers. But what about the South Side? Nary a fish goes to market. What do they do with them? Why catch the buggers if you're not going to eat them?'

Irwin shrugged. 'Bonnety Bill, the tractor man at up at Nativvy, he was talking to the forester. His wife keeps house for the harbourmaster and he says they take them back out to sea and let them go. Maybe he's tagging them. For research.'

'What bloody for?' Sammy was shouting. 'They'll just come back in again! They can smell the river and they'll keep coming back until they spawn. Any dooley knows that.'

They waded across Brewery Burn. The coble was nosing in to shore a hundred yards along the beach. 'There's your pal now,' said Irwin, pointing up the hill.

One of the Redrock Land Rovers was turning off the Suitor road into the entrance to the Hog Graveyard. Mr Mor was in the passenger seat. Sammy spat on the beach. 'And what's he doing up there? He's got his finger in too many pies for my liking.'

'Och, don't be too hard on the man. Maybe it's a duty visit.'

'What?'

'Maybe he's got ancestors buried there.'

Dr Lorraine MacDonald turned a page of her notes. 'These local details are of course fascinating, but we must try to see it in a more general context: the pattern of growth of the Celtic culture is one particular example of a universal pattern, which we see again and again in different countries, different continents.

'There must be countless similar cases of which we know nothing and can know nothing, but some are fairly well-documented. In India, for instance, there was a succession of invasions, culminating in the invasion of the Aryans. The indigenous peoples were marginalised, reduced in status to servants of the lowest sort, peons, peasants. The heroes of the invaders eventually became the Gods of succeeding generations – Rama, Laksaman, Bhima and so on. The defeated races became the various lower castes which we see even today.

'Similarly with the Celts. The original population were overcome and set to tilling the land and labouring for the victors. Indeed, we only know these natives as the Fir Bolg, the bag people, because they had to carry bags of soil up into the hills to make farmland.'

Some of the women in the audience nodded, either to indicate that they had understood, or perhaps in the hope that nodding the head helped the implantation of knowledge. Miss Semple nodded along with them, while staring at the wall behind Dr Lorraine MacDonald. Alice stared unwaveringly at her. Lorraine began to feel annoyed – both at the unthinking audience and at the gimlet-eyed woman.

'The Celts believed themselves descended from the Great Mother, known as Anu or Dana, and their great heroes became the Gods of later generations: Lugh, Manannan mac Lir, the Dagda, Morrigan and so on. Of these, the Dagda was the great Father, sometimes known as the Good God, sometimes as the Horse-Father.

'The Celts were great horsemen and several of the Gods are known to have horses. There was a Divine Horse who was worshipped wherever there were Celts. And Manannan, for instance, though he was a sea-god, was well-known to have a splendid horse which could ride over the seas.'

There was more general nodding. Lorraine MacDonald felt the sudden childish desire to puncture their equanimity.

'Incidentally, the horse was also of great importance to the Aryans in India. When there was a dire emergency and the help of the gods was required, the greatest sacrifice was of a horse, a white stallion who first had ritual intercourse with one of the king's wives.' She paused, long enough for shock to register on some of the faces. 'A similar rite is known from Ireland, though you will be pleased to hear that no woman was required to submit herself to the embraces of the beast.'

A general murmur of relief spread throughout the room.

'No, in Ireland, the ritual was quite different. The horse was a mare, and the king himself was required to copulate with the horse, in public, before the mare was slaughtered and made into a stew which everyone shared.'

She smiled at the audience. 'Thank you for your attention. If you have any questions, I would be pleased to answer.'

Her glance passed briefly over the big woman. Alice did not look in the least shocked. Her face was pulled into a speculative frown.

A big van drove slowly up the rutted track from Rossmarty and drew up in the courtyard of Rossfarm. A tall man climbed out on the passenger side and walked to the side door of the house.

Only Veronica was in the farmhouse when the doorbell rang. She was in her room and had just finished a set of yoga exercises and was sitting cross-legged on an exercise mat reciting her mantra.

'...*om mani padme hum om mani padme hum om mani...*' Her serene breath carried the repetitive phrases round and round in her head. She was immune to the distractions of everyday life. She wasn't even aware of the doorbell ringing again.

Or rather, she was aware of it, but it didn't impinge on her sense of balance, her delicate poise between the conscious and the super-conscious states. Let the distractions fade away and just follow the mantra '... hum om mani padme hum om mani...'

After all, Ramana Maharshi ignored the ants that bit his thighs when he was meditating – didn't even notice them – or rather, the deep wisdom of his overself gave him the perspective from which such minor events as ant-nibbling were only part of the natural flow. The skin on his thighs was permanently scarred, but did he care? Not a whit.

So a ringing doorbell wouldn't have bothered him in the slightest. He would just have carried on with his mantra as the sound began to drive its way through his skull and why did no-one answer the bloody bell?

'Dad! The door!'

There was no answer.

'Damn! Dad! Da-ad! The bloody door!'

He was probably out in the field shearing the turnips or some such agricultural activity.

The bell-ringing had stopped, but she could hear the mutter of voices and an engine idling in the yard. She closed her eyes and wondered if she could relax again.

The bell rang loud and long. She unlocked her folded legs and waited for the feeling to come back to her left leg. Whoever it was, he was going to get the full benefit of her expanded consciousness right in his ear. She stood up and padded her barefoot way down the stairs along the smooth hardwood floor of the corridor, muttering to herself repetitively, though it was not a mantra that she was repeating. She flung open the door to the kitchen and walked across the cold tiles to the back door. A tall male figure was visible through the glazed door. His back was turned to Veronica and he was talking to the man in the driver's cab of the van. His long blonde pony tail was swinging as he shook his head in negation.

She threw open the door. 'Well? Can I help you? Or are you just leaning on our doorbell for your private amusement?'

The tall man turned to her, a big friendly smile on his broad face. 'Hi. We're the Second Tribal Railroad – bringing the folks home to Eden, ha ha –' He gestured towards the van which was brightly painted with a picture of an antique steam train driving among the stars of the night sky.

'and we're looking for the barn.'

Veronica bristled at the thought of this garish tasteless object parked beside Glen Grian. What that would do to the healing vibrations of the place she hated to think.

'Of course. How silly of me. I hadn't realised that disk-jockeys, having no real need for a brain, have evolved into humanoids with a lump of gristle in their heads.' She smiled sweetly at him. 'A barn is a rather big affair about forty yards long, twenty yards high and, would you believe it, slightly wider than a barn door. If you glance over in that direction,' she waved a hand vaguely towards the Glen, 'you should, even with your attenuated mental faculties and poor eyesight, see something that might fit the bill.'

The man coughed and looked abashed. 'Sorry to bother you, Veronica. I just wasn't sure if it was this barn or your other one up by Glaickbea Hill.'

Veronica looked at him closely. 'Do I know you?'

'Of course. I used to work for your dad at harvest time. Since I was wee.' He looked a little taken aback. 'It's me. Alec.' She frowned and shook her head. 'Wee Eck,' he said.

'Good god! Wee Eck!' She laughed. 'I haven't seen you since...'

'Since you went away to boarding school.'

'That's right. You've grown, haven't you.'

He grinned. 'You too.' His eyes wandered over her body and she became suddenly very aware of the lightweight clothes she wore for exercising. She blushed.

'So, what are you doing with yourself?'

'Nothing much. I'm working with these guys just now. You?'

'Well, I'm at college and... Look, would you like to come in for a coffee?'

'Sure. Great. I'll just tell Tony and the boys.' As he turned, she put a hand on his arm.

'No. Wait.' He looked at her attentively, his eyes blue and steady. 'I meant... I don't want a crowd in.'

'Course, Veronica. I can dig that.' He turned towards the van and waved them on down the hill. 'That's the barn,' he called. 'I'll be down in a few minutes.'

Wee Eck walked in and sat at the table as if it was his own. Veronica put the kettle on and watched him as she put the coffee together. He'd changed a lot, and not just his size.

'I've got decaffeinated if you want?'

'No thanks, I need all the caffeine I can get. Lot of gear to set up.'

He was so confident, that's what it was. He had been a cute kid, a smallish blond boy, but he'd always been a bit shy. He was so sure of himself now, with his ponytail and his sandals and his embroidered denim jacket over a bare chest.

'So you'll be working all afternoon?'

'Not me. We'll have the kit set up in a couple of hours, but then it's all technical stuff. I leave that to them.' He pulled out a tobacco tin. 'Mind if I smoke?'

She quelled the impulse to point to the no-smoking sign which she'd put on the wall and compromised by turning on the extractor fan.

'Go ahead.'

'Thanks.' He opened the tin and began rolling a very large cigarette.

'So, you're not a DJ then?' She set the coffee in front of him and stood leaning against the worktop with her mug in both her hands. She could feel her feet clenching from the cold of the floor tiles. She stood on one foot and rubbed the sole of the other against her leg to encourage the flow of blood.

Wee Eck liberally spooned sugar into his coffee. 'Nah, I don't DJ. I just roadie for them. Setting up and taking down. In between,' he winked, 'they spin the music and I take my ease.'

'You don't do anything?'

'Nah. I take my ease – you know, disco biscuits.' She shook her head. 'Ecstasy.'

'Oh.'

Eck lit his cigarette and blew smoke at the ceiling. It smelt strange, and she suspected that it had more than tobacco in it. She sipped her coffee and watched him. His face was brown from the weather and he had a big gold earring in his left earlobe.

'How come they're doing the event in our barn?'

He laughed. 'I convinced them. That way I can slip away to the Glen if I need to chill out.' He looked at her directly. 'Commune with the spirits of the trees.'

'Really?'

'Yup. They're there if you're open to them.'

Veronica scarcely knew what to say next. Wee Eck used to pick potatoes, and now he worked for a truckload of DJ's. She could hardly believe that he would know about such things.

'Are you joking?'

'Of course not. The animal spirits too. We've all got our totem spirit. Mine's the black panther.'

'How do you know?'

'It came to me. In the night. I turned into a black panther in my dream and hunted deer across the Dark Isle.'

'Just a dream. I dreamt I turned into a cucumber once but that doesn't...'

'I had the same dream loads of times. Once I went for a walk in the woods and found a dead deer just where I dreamt I killed it.'

'Coincidence.'

'That was when I found I could see auras and had healing powers.'

'What? Come on, Eck. You're fantasising.' Veronica was jealous. She'd been meditating for two years and she'd only seen an aura once, when she had a fever.

He puffed on his cigarette and looked confident.

'Argh,' she said, sitting down on a chair and lifting one foot to her lap.

'What's the matter?' Wee Eck was halfway out of his chair.

'Cramp. In my foot. From the cold tiles.'

'Aha. Let me show you my healing powers. Headaches, sore throats and bad trips my speciality.'

In response to Dr Lorraine MacDonald's call for questions, Alice raised one plump hand. No-one else moved. The other women were still shocked and transfixed by the idea of copulation with a horse, even at a distance of a few centuries. Lorraine had to respond to Alice.

'Yes? You have a question?'

Alice shrugged herself into a more upright position. 'Dr MacDonald, I have enjoyed your lecture. A clear overview of the facts.' She looked into Lorraine's face. 'Some of the facts.' Lorraine winced. There was no need for that comment. Alice's attitude was plain in her tone and her set face. 'You have obviously studied your subject well. I wonder if you would be good enough to tell us when you think these practices died out?'

Lorraine shuffled her papers, not looking at her opponent. She was being challenged, for some reason. Best be careful.

'To the best of my knowledge, true Celtic ritual and belief died out more than five hundred years ago, though some practices may have persisted up until the eighteenth or early nineteenth century. There are vestiges of course in the late collections of folk tales and songs. Martin Martin preserved some fascinating relics of an ancient culture, as did Carmichael, just over a hundred years ago. But hints of Celtic ritual in folk songs and charms do not amount to the survival of a culture. They are only its dying echoes.'

Alice grunted, contemptuously. Lorraine became icily angry. She knew her sources. She could quote text and footnotes to this fat boor all night.

'I take it that you believe otherwise.'

Alice smiled unpleasantly. 'You have the facts at your fingertips. I daresay that you have read the books.'

'Where else can we find useful information? All the documents that were there to be found have been found. Oral sources are ambiguous at best. And conclusions based on archaeological evidence are of course necessarily speculative.'

'Have you done any research in the field? Looked at the Celtic rituals that still exist?'

Lorraine smiled back, sweetly. 'You are thinking of the Welsh Eisteddfod, perhaps? Or the so-called Druids who perform their make-believe rituals at Stonehenge?' She turned to the audience at large, sure that she had the big woman nailed. 'These are romantic Victorian confections. The Eisteddfod is a recent invention, an attempt to mimic Celtic culture that owes more to fancy than to scholarship. In the case of the Stonehenge Druids, we have self-deluded mystics with enough money and leisure to indulge an inadequate sense of reality.' She let her gaze rest briefly on Alice again. 'No, what happened to Celtic culture was that it was forced underground and eventually faded out. Its attitudes and beliefs were transformed into forms that were acceptable to the new invaders. If we want to know what happened to the Celts, look around you. Our genes have been mixed with every race in Europe, our culture has been subsumed into today's super-culture that contains ingredients from every imaginable source. Field research into existing Celtic rituals?' She turned her steady gaze on the fat lady. 'I think not.'

Alice smiled broadly back at her. 'No, Miss MacDonald, I did not mean the field in an academic sense. I was making a little joke. I meant the fields that you drove through to get here today.'

Lorraine was flustered. 'I beg your pardon?'

'Did you not see the crows? In the fields?'

'Well, yes, but...'

'Dead crows, crucified in the fields.'

'Yes, of course I saw them.'

And what did you think of them?'

'It's a cruel and stupid custom. As I understand it, the farmers shoot a crow and hang it up as a warning to the others. So that they won't eat the crops.'

Alice nodded and said nothing, while smiling, smiling at the woman behind the lectern.

Lorraine blushed, feeling at a ridiculous disadvantage. 'Well what of it? Perhaps you want to claim it's a kind of sympathetic magic. Superstition. Whatever it is, it's nothing to do with Celtic rituals or beliefs.'

Alice shook her head, tutting loudly. 'Did you never think to ask the farmers? Did you never go up and look at one of these crows?' Lorraine could not answer. Alice let the silence last a few seconds. 'They shoot the crows, Miss MacDonald. Then they break their necks. Then they crucify them.' Lorraine looked back at her bright sharp eyes and waited. 'Does that not sound familiar? You were talking about it yourself earlier, when you were talking about sacrificial victims. The triple killing.'

Mr Ross was seriously worried about his daughter. He'd never been happy about sending her away to boarding school, but his wife had insisted. She had gone there as a child and she had insisted that it would give Veronica untold advantages. He couldn't see it himself. It seemed more as if it had given her untold airs and graces and a contempt for honest toil.

Still, she'd survived the experience, probably without lasting damage, and managed to get to college. Doing some arty farty course that, he was afraid, would only fit her for marriage to some unspecified workshy wally with more money than sense.

And now she was going all theosophical. Healing vibrations, mantas and yogra exercises. Vegetarianism and white loose gowns. She wouldn't look at the boys in Rossmarty because they weren't spiritually refined. She wouldn't even go to a barn dance and enjoy herself.

That was no way to be carrying on.

He turned the tractor for the last furrow and lowered the plough. Great cabs on these new tractors. Protected from the weather and you could hear yourself think.

Perhaps that was why he was thinking so much these days. Mostly about Veronica. He couldn't help thinking that she should be more... more wanton sometimes. She had spirit – God, she was bossy enough – but there was none of the intemperate wildness of youth having its fling.

When he was a student at Agri College, they all had a wild time. Try anything, they would, for a laugh. Even that wacky baccy stuff. That's what being a student was all about. Get that wildness out of you.

But not Veronica. She stayed in of an evening and studied. Her friends were all ever so clever or refined – too damned clever and refined to be brought home to meet Dad. If she even had a good old sexual fling it would be comforting, it would be a sign of normality.

At the top of the field, he turned out of the field gate and headed for the tractor shed. There was nothing to be done. You couldn't encourage her to break out. She had to do that for herself.

He felt helpless. Disappointed. Watching his beautiful daughter turn into a bloodless aesthete. Whatever that might be.

He parked the tractor and walked up to the house. The rave crew had arrived. He'd got a bit of stick from his neighbours about letting them have his barn, but dammit, it was good money and he couldn't turn it down.

He opened the kitchen door and there they were. Veronica was lying on the sheepskin rug and a big young man with a pigtail was kneeling beside her with her legs in his hands. Strangely, he didn't recognise it as lovemaking at first. He thought perhaps the young man was massaging her feet. Then he saw his daughter's absent stare, just before she registered his presence.

She recovered quickly. 'Hi, Dad,' she said brightly. 'This is Wee Eck. Remember him? He was just massaging my feet.'

The young man stood up and shook his hand, while Veronica scrambled to her feet.

'Hi, Mr Ross.'

'Wee Eck? Jings, you've grown. And what brings you up here?'

'I'm with the Second Tribal Railroad.'

'Ah. And this will be yours, I suppose?' He picked up the stub of the cigarette from the table and sniffed at it. 'Smells mighty like wacky baccy to me.'

'I'm sure it isn't, Dad.'

Eck said nothing. Mr Ross winked as he handed it over. 'I'm surprised Ronny let you smoke it in the kitchen.'

'I'd best get down and help them set up.' Eck turned to Veronica. 'See you later?'

'Of course. Bye.'

Mr Ross turned to Veronica. 'What's that about?'

She spoke defiantly. 'I'm going to the dance.'

Mr Ross sat down at the table.

'Make me a sandwich and a cup of tea, will you. I've just come over all weak.'

To his surprise, she did so without a murmur.

The strange thing was that none of the other women at the lecture seemed to have noticed anything. Dr Lorraine MacDonald had been put through the wringer by that woman Then the wife of a local worthy coughed and stood up and proposed a vote of thanks as if nothing untoward had happened.

Because something very untoward had happened. Without the slightest shred of evidence to support her, Lorraine believed every word of what the big woman had said. It was just those eyes looking into hers and telling her the way that it was. And if that woman told her anything at all, she'd believe it.

She gathered her notes together and tried to gather herself together in the process. It didn't work. The thoughts in her head were empty, the words on the paper were empty. Both were based on the academic method and the scholarship that had brought her a Doctorate in Highland Studies. And they were now so much chaff.

She watched the big woman going down the aisle between the seats. At the door she turned and raised a paw to Lorraine and smiled. Then she spoke loudly to the woman next to her.

'I believe I'll just have a Dubonnet and lemon in the Arms. It should be quiet just now. Anyone else coming along?'

She went out of the door with the other women murmuring around her. Lorraine dropped her notes into a waste-paper bin.

She didn't follow immediately. That would have been too obvious, too undignified. She sat on a chair and counted a hundred before she left the hall.

Fom *Totemic Beasts of the Celts: The Pig*
by Dr L MacDonald, published by the Gael Press

...the pig was probably the most important of the Totem animals of the Celts and there are many links between pigs and the Otherworld. As well as being the favourite food for feasts in the Otherworld, hunters may be led into other realms while hunting the beast. The Fianna, for instance, were led through a series of adventures among the Sidhe when chasing a boar with crescent moons on each of its sides. (See the pamphlet '*Fionn and the Red Woman*' pub. by the Gael Press)

The boar is primarily associated with the solar cycle and male mythic figures while the sow is associated with the lunar cycle. The ancient Goddess of the Celts, Scathach, the Shadowy one, for instance, is known to appear in this form.

Remnants of the traditions remained late, especially in rural regions. In the Highlands of Scotland, even as late as the Victorian era, it was considered unlucky to eat the flesh of the pig. (Though a similar taboo exists among the Semitic peoples, they are unlikely to be linked.) The Highland proscription of swine was probably based on a distorted racial memory of Celtic belief, for in Celtic times and in Celtic mythology, the pig was regarded as an important source of nourishment, both physical and spiritual. Manannan mac Lir, the sea-god, possessed seven pigs with which he could feed the whole world, though they would not cook unless a truth was spoken for each part of the pig's body. Several other Celtic Gods possessed pigs, usually magical beasts, and even swineherds were credited with unusual powers.

Several bronze statues of boars have been found, confirming the wild boar as one of the most powerful of the Celtic totemic animals.

Interestingly, the boar hunted by the Fianna (in the legend of the Fionn and the Red Woman, mentioned above) turned out to be the king of the Firbolgs. Little is known of this ancient race, who held Ireland before the Celts and were eventually subjugated by them. Evidently the importance of the pig as a mythic animal predates the Celtic invasions. Other titles in the series: *Totemic Beasts of the Celts: The Salmon; Totemic Beasts of the Celts: The Bull; Totemic Beasts of the Celts: The Uilebheist; Totemic Beasts of the Celts: The Eagle; Totemic Beasts of the Celts: The Dog.*

Rev Dumfry studied the long grass in puzzlement. The grass was crushed and broken, and there was scattered dirt on the green turf – plain marks of a recent interment. Who would have thought that the old hog graveyard was still being used? And why bury a pig here, at an existing grave site? Perhaps, as with humans, the descendants were also buried in the same place? He looked up at the memorial stone.

Fionnladh Mor. Big Finlay. The name, in large letters, was still discernible, but the list of his progenitors was worn down and the date on the white marble tablet was obscured by water stains. There was no clue as to any later interments.

Dumfry stood back and studied the sandstone statue on the top of the memorial, which presumably was of Big Finlay. In the style of the time, his good features had been exaggerated in the sculpture, so that his head and shoulders seemed out of proportion to the narrow flanks. The curly tail was eroded by the weather, only a trace remaining.

Big Finlay was one of the earlier statues. To avoid the tricky problems of carving the thin legs out of sandstone, he had been portrayed couchant.

Dumfry left the statue and wandered along the paths, idly studying the memorials. As the sculptor had gained in skill, he had moved on to more durable stone – imported white marble and porphyry from Boddam. In some of these statues, he had essayed a standing posture. There were even a few bronze statuettes in the antique style and one, in black marble, of Scathach, a particularly productive sow, who was credited with producing 1,396 piglets over a period of twelve years.

For peace, and for the deep solace that absolutes can bring, Dumfry liked to frequent graveyards. There was no doubt about the status of the inhabitants. They were absolutely dead – and at this distance in time most likely they were completely departed also, every vestige of flesh rotted down into the soil. The long green grass growing over the multitude of the dead put him in mind of the Divine balance. Among the gravestones he could wander and meditate and even ponder out loud without fear of being contradicted or misunderstood. Here, in Lord Farquhar's Hog Graveyard he could argue with himself about Doreen and the rectitude or otherwise of her sexuality; and about Alice, her heathen Aunt; about supposed black magic rituals in the graveyard – about the various Big Problems which gnawed at him – all without the slightest chance of anyone visiting to put flowers on the grave of their grandparents.

This privacy was very important to him. He had recently developed certain doubts which he could not share without danger to his livelihood – and even in the empty silence of the manse, where oil paintings of his predecessors hung on the wall, he did not feel entirely secure from observation.

The Elders of the First Reformed and Ancient Presbyterian Church had appointed him and they were always ready to advise him – delighted, indeed, to instruct him where they could – but he nevertheless preferred to leave them in the dark about some of the problems of his calling.

Doreen, of course, was one of these problems. To all outward appearances she was a fairly devout young woman, bright and intelligent, a regular churchgoer. She might be expected to be an example to others of the younger generation – who sorely needed a good example.

How to reconcile this pleasing exterior with her baser side? This was a problem which he could not present to the Elders. They would condemn without understanding. It was a mystery how Doreen herself managed to square her wanton behaviour under the boat with the precepts of the church.

Dumfry adopted the ministerial thinking pose: hands behind his back in the 'reverse fig-leaf' posture, body inclined forward from the waist. He paced up and down a path between rows of memorials.

For there was a personal problem here of moral and spiritual dimensions. How could he, as God's minister, manage to reconcile within himself these two halves of Doreen: Eve and Lilith? Or how, lacking such understanding, could he exercise his Christian charity in his dealings with her?

He was sorely troubled by how to handle this moral porcupine. It was only four days ago that he had become aware of the situation. In the time since then, Doreen had scarcely left his thoughts from his waking at sunrise until, late at night, he fell asleep.

He kicked angrily at a tussock of grass.

And why hadn't she been under her boat for the last two nights?

Jenny-Pet was having a nap. Sammy Poach had brought her a couple of crabs, fine big partans, and she'd cooked them up with a bit of bacon and some turnip. Lovely. When she'd eaten the lot, she'd been so full she'd had to lie down. She would have slept all afternoon, except for the disturbance.

Jenny had lived in the Wee Vennel for more than four decades, and she was delicately tuned to its dimensions, sensitive to any changes. If the humidity increased as the wind backed into the east, her knuckles grew painful. A slight increase in the proportion of positive to negative ions in the air would automatically trigger the erection of hair follicles on her neck. A decrease in the reality quotient of the Wee Vennel would send electrical discharges down the nerves to her feet.

As she lay dozing in the pale sunshine that drifted through her salt-stained window, her feet began to twitch. She swung her legs off the bed and stood up while her eyes were still slowly opening. Her hand was on the handle of the door before she even knew why she was there and she was out in the lane before she realised that she'd left her bucket behind.

She muttered to herself. 'Whatsamatter, pet? Whatsamatter, pet? Whatsamatter, pet?' She caught a strand of hair in her mouth and she chewed and sucked on it as she jittered up and down the lane. Then she saw it happen. Or rather, she didn't. There was a grey-harled cottage across from her own, with a red sandstone shack beside it. As she walked past, she suddenly couldn't see where they joined. She turned to look more closely, and her eyes wouldn't look there, but slid to left or right. It was like a finger trying to trap a blob of quicksilver – you could feel it, but it always slipped away under the pressure. Jenny relaxed and chuckled. Now she knew what was happening.

Without directly looking at the houses, she sidled closer. When she could feel the rough wall with her outstretched fingers, she stopped. She looked down the lane, watching the waves rolling in until they broke on the beach, hidden by the sea wall. Then she focused on the gorse bushes, far-off green and gold lumps on the grassy hillside of the North Suitor. Then she looked even further away, right through the landscape and into the emptiness beyond, looking into the heart of space.

But she was paying no attention to that. With her eyes focused on a non-existent place an infinite distance away, she kept her attention on the walls that she could see hanging vaguely at the edge of her vision, just to her left. Something was coming out of that place. She could feel it coming closer. Something horrible, something awful, she could feel it in her stomach – unless that was the crab.

An enormous pig lunged out of the wall beside her and ran down the lane, running high on its trotters. It was a boar, an immense beast with white markings on its sides. It grunted as it wheeled at the end of the lane and ran out of sight.

So that was it. A pig escaping. A boar, in fact. But why?

Then she cried out, as suddenly He was there, standing before her, straight and strong, His golden hair blowing in the breeze, just as she had seen Him once before, when she first came to Cromness – and then could never leave again, but waited here at the gate, watching.

Then he turned, and she saw that it was not He. Misled by her tired eyes and dazzled by the low rays of the sun, she had mistaken him. The figure seemed to shrink before her and she saw that it was only a young man with fair hair. A young man that she knew, though the name was not ready to her lips.

'The pig, pet. Why did the pig come out?'

'It came with me. It's gone to stay with the big man. He will look after it.'

Then he turned to look at her.

'Jenny,' he said, and she remembered his name.

'So you're back, George.'

'How long was I there, Jenny?'

'You've been away at college for years, George. Years. Did you do well?'

He shook his head. 'No, no. In there.'

'Oh, who knows, pet. How long did it seem?'

'Years.' He tried to move, but stumbled and leant against the wall. She patted his arm.

'I know, pet. I've been in there too, remember?'

'Remember what?'

'I came in to get you, more than once. When you were little, pet, when you were wee.'

George looked at her blankly. 'No, I don't remember.' She saw something fade from his eyes.

'You went in to see your father.' He shook his head. She nodded. 'Yes. You've forgotten, pet, that's all.'

George looked at her and he saw an old woman, daft and dirty. He remembered that she'd played with him when he was small, before she grew so daft, so he was polite to her.

'Well, I'd better be going, Jenny. I just got here, and I haven't even seen my grandad yet. Bye.'

'Bye, pet,' said Jenny. 'Bye.'

She watched him turn along Shore Road, then went inside, shaking her head. He'd forgotten it all, already. Poor boy. What would come of him?

Through the green leaves the rooftops of the Vennels could be seen down below. Patches of the sea were visible amongst the branches. The *Suitor's*

Lass was heading east below the cliffs of the North Suitor, pushing through the white-capped waves. Jimmy Bervie strolled down the Ladies Walk in a state of unease, being extra jolly and occasionally anarchic in an attempt to nudge the world back into its proper state.

On such a fine afternoon, young people were walking together among the greenery of the Foxes Dens. Couples were hiding here and there behind rhododendron bushes or gazing into each other's eyes on the mouldering benches set there by the Town Council many years before. Jimmy raised his water pistol and loudly undid the zip on his windcheater.

He was just about to discharge the water pistol over a bush when suddenly he knew that something important had changed. It was as if someone had silently closed a door in a house. Though you did not hear it, there were tiny clues to let you know that something had changed – changes in the acoustics of the house or the pattern of air currents.

He hesitated for only a moment. There was no external reason, no obvious omen, but he felt the sudden urge to rake the sand. He left the young citizens of Cromness to their country pursuits and hurried back to his house.

Highlands University: Forestry and Conservation Degree Course
From a lecture by Graham Leslie Willis BSc

...and after many hundreds of years of exploitation, less than 1% of the original forests are left in Scotland. Deer and sheep are of course important factors in preventing the regeneration of the Caledonian Forest. But even with fencing to keep them out, the rate of natural regeneration is disappointingly slow.

What many people fail to realise is that an entire layer of the ecology of the Caledonian Forest has been removed. Pigs. Pigs provided a unique and invaluable service to the Forest, but the wild pigs were hunted to extinction centuries ago, and nothing has taken their place.

Consider the pig, searching for food, snuffling in the ground with his strong snout, churning and turning the ground at one end, and fertilising the ground at the other end. The average boar would turn and aerate several hectares in a year, and a whole family of them could reasonably be compared to a heavy-duty rotovator, preparing the ground, turning it into an ideal environment for seeds to germinate and root.

Jimmy drew the rake along the sand one last time and turned, without looking, to set the rake against the wall. Before he turned back to look at the sand, he glanced over the garden.

Convolvulus was boiling out of the corner by the house, strangling the flower bed. Dandelions were in clock already, puffy white balls just above the long grass. Lobster shells from long-past convivial dinners lined a small area of short grass. A stone tablet with some verses in French was propped against the wall, and above it, in white paint, the words 'Nerval Memorial Garden.' Shepherd's Purse seemed to be taking over the lawn area, its tiny white flowers floating on thin stalks above the grass. Jimmy felt satisfied. The world was as it was, and that was fine.

He turned and looked at his sand-garden. The anomaly was gone. Or at least, it had changed. Beautiful lines of sand, not completely straight, but with a slight ripple imparted by the pulse of the harmonic universe. The dropped stitch in the knitted shawl of reality had been taken up. There remained only a vestige of irregularity: the same flaw that had been intriguing him for twenty years. Compared with the gross blemish of the recent major disturbance, however, it was no more than a dimple on the cheek of reality.

He studied the slight wave of the raked lines. What a wonderful sight. Almost perfect. Damn it, it wasn't just almost, it was absolutely perfect.

He thought about the tendency of absolutes to turn into their opposite. A chill passed over him.

'Bugger that,' he muttered to himself. 'What is the opposite of perfect, anyway? Imperfect, I suppose, which is what the world is, mostly.'

Still he felt a certain amount of reassurance in the minor irregularity which still marred the pattern.

It was time to walk the streets, to see what changes might have taken place. In the lobby of his house, he donned a bright orange boiler suit and a fore-and-aft gamekeeper's hat with a child's toy windmill tucked into the hat band. He pinned a large wooden badge on his chest, a model of a flying duck.

Satisfied with his outfit, he strolled out into the street.

Rev Dumfry returned from the Hog Graveyard depressed and no closer to a solution to his problems. He went into the empty church to pray, and found that he had not the heart for it. Perhaps some liquid fortification was in order. Jesus did after all drink wine with his disciples. Almost certainly. He left by the side door and headed for the manse.

His heart sank as he saw one of the Elders approaching him.

'A word, Dumfry, if you please.'

'Certainly, Mr Siller.'

'Dumfry, there is to be one of these 'Raves' in Rossmarty. Iniquitous events. No doubt you have read about them in the papers. Mr Ross is allowing them the use of one of his barns. A very ill-advised decision. I hope we can count on you to deliver a severe sermon on Sunday. We will of course brief you with the names of those who attend this event.'

Mr Siller's sour face was the last straw. Dumfry felt a hot flush of irrational rage.

'Mr Siller! These are our... our constituents. These are the people we hope to attract into the church, the people who will make the church a living place – if we can offer them something more than rigid moral precepts and the threat of damnation. Why do they visit these raves? What is it that they get that they can find neither in their community nor in their church?'

Siller's face twitched slightly, a sign of his great agitation.

'What is it they get, Dumfry? It is drink and drugs, it is lack of responsibility, it is wanton coupling, as the animals do. It is heathen music and pagan behaviour, and you would do well to remember that the church neither condones nor accepts such behaviour, and it would be ungodly to leave it uncriticised.'

'Possibly so, Mr Siller, but I think that we cannot condemn without deeper understanding.' He spoke coldly, but with force. 'Thank you for condescending to advise me, but I have my own plans. I have already resolved to attend this rave to see what it is that we are all so frightened of. I have written of my intention in a circular letter to all the Elders. I presume you have received it?'

'I have not.'

'Then you will, in due course, as soon as the postal service sees fit to deliver it. Good day.'

Inside the manse, he found a sheet of headed notepaper and quickly made up the circular letter which he had described to Mr Siller, dating it for the day before. He wrote out the envelopes, one addressed to each of the Elders, and slipped out to the Library to photocopy the letter.

Within half an hour, he was posting the letters. The delay would be blamed on the Post Office. He walked away, rubbing his hands in satisfaction. He felt little guilt at his equivocation. He knew he had made the right decision.

And he hoped that God would forgive his satisfaction in putting Siller in his place.

Fergus MacFarquhar was walking along the other side of the street. Dumfry hailed him and crossed the road. The poor lad actually flinched as he approached. Dumfry felt ashamed of himself. Lads like this were the next generation, and if they felt nothing but fear for their minister, then there was little future for the Church.

'Fergus,' he said, in his heartiest tones. 'Good to see you. Tell me, will you be attending the rave at Rossmarty?'

Fergus turned white. How had he found out? He'd told his mother he would be staying with his friend Jamie in Castleton. 'Oh, no, sir. Certainly not.'

'Ah.' Dumfry looked at him kindly. 'It's just that I was thinking of going along – to see what all the fuss is about – and I need to know when it's on. And where.'

'I haven't a clue, sir. I'll be at home, studying for my exams.'

'Well, where would I find out?'

Fergus felt as if he had been asked to betray his friends. 'Post Office window,' he muttered, hoping no-one had seen him talking to the minister.

'Of course. Silly of me, I was just there. Goodbye.' He nodded to Fergus and made his way back up the street. He felt somehow that he had failed to put the boy at his ease.

Fergus walked away, feeling seriously as if he must be made of glass. Everyone could see right through him. Now he was going to have to get Jamie to phone up and cancel the arrangements that he'd never made.

Eager to pass on the good tidings, Jimmy Bervie was one of the first through the door of The Fisherman's Arms when it opened at five o' clock. He stood at the bar with his glass of whisky while everyone else found seats. Then he rapped on the counter with his glass.

'A strange thing happened today,' he said.

The barman grunted and studied his *Fishing Times*. The Major sucked Scotch and Crabbe's over his teeth and swallowed it, his little eyes watching everyone in turn. The Nailer continued his discussion of the ructions at the Town Council meeting. The other men at the bar picked draws for their pools coupons or devised methods for obtaining EC grants by setting aside vast acreages of ocean.

'Might I borrow your *Fishing Times*?' Jimmy slipped the newspaper out from under the barman's gaze and held it up. 'Well, well, look at this,' he said. Everyone looked up to see what was so noteworthy in the *Fishing Times*. Jimmy rolled up the newspaper and held it in front of his lips, whipping it to and fro while blowing down into it. This produced a regular fluttering sound. Jimmy stopped and looked around. 'Does that not remind you of the sound of a helicopter? Listen again.'

They all listened as he repeated the action.

'It's a bitty like a helicopter,' admitted the Nailer and one or two others nodded.

'While I have your attention,' said Jimmy, returning the paper to the barman, 'A strange thing happened today.'

'Is that so?'

Jimmy nodded. 'The anomaly which appeared in my sand-garden has nearly disappeared. Just like that.'

'Anomaly? Anomaly? What the hell's that?'

'A kind of sea-bird?'

'A weed?'

'No, no,' said the Nailer. 'It's a conventional piece of wisdom expressed simply.'

Jimmy took the comments as evidence that they were listening.

'In 1425,' he said, 'the herring changed their habits...'

'Come on, Jimmy, tell us something new.'

'...and ceased to visit the Baltic. The patterns of trade were disrupted in ways that permanently affected communities all along this coast.' He held up his glass and gazed into it thoughtfully. 'Yet this hardly had any effect on sand-gardens throughout the north-east of Scotland.'

'God's sake, man, how many sand-gardens were there?'

Jimmy coughed and plucked the windmill from his hat. He waved it to and fro, but failed to distract them.

'Well? How many?'

'Only one that I know of,' he conceded.

'And that would be yours, eh, Jimmy?'

Everyone laughed except Jimmy.

'That may be so. Anyway, that event barely made a ripple in the sand. But just a few days ago I saw the beginnings of a really major disturbance, the like of which we have not seen for centuries. I saw it in the sand.'

'What sort of 'major'? Like, the mackerel changed their habits and started to fly?'

Jimmy looked at the man severely. 'Very major. On the scale of a volcanic eruption or the Great Caledonian Faultline shifting again.'

'Sounds serious, eh?'

'You may well say so. Last time that happened, half of the Highlands disappeared beneath the North Sea.' With a look of utmost gravity he took a lollipop from his pocket and unwrapped it. 'But, as I say, it has subsided, so we may all rest easy in our beds. For the moment.'

The door of The Fisherman's Arms opened and three women came in. The presence of Alice among them prevented any ribald comments from the men, who turned back to their business.

'Dubonnet and lemon for me, Ellen,' said Alice. She scanned the assembled men with a stony gaze and sat at a table near the fire. The barman put aside his paper.

'Dubonnet and lemon, two gins and one bottle of tonic,' said Ellen. She turned to Jimmy. 'What's new, Jimmy?'

'Major disturbance in the sand, Ellen. It seems to have settled down, but I'm keeping a close eye on it.'

'Glad to hear it, Jimmy, we'll all sleep better for knowing that. We've trouble enough without major disturbances complicating matters. You'll have heard about the Vennels?'

'What about them?'

'Everyone's fighting over the place like dogs over a bone. That Mr Mor's got an interest and so has some other fly-by-night operation called Argent Enterprises. They've both got plans to develop the Vennels.'

Jimmy's bluff face creased. 'How can they do that? It's not theirs to develop.'

'Apparently they don't have to own them to get planning permission. And after that, well you know. There's ways and means, if you've got money and the right lawyer.'

The barman put down the drinks. 'You won't need a lawyer for this, Ellen, but I'd appreciate the money.'

Ellen handed over a note and waited while the barman counted out the change.

Jimmy took the opportunity to probe further. 'So, what are they planning?'

Ellen picked up the glasses. 'Mr Mor wants to tart them up, turn them into a visitor attraction and build a marina. The other bunch, Argent, they want to level the Vennels and build blocks of flats.'

'Surely they can't do that if someone else owns the houses.'

Ellen shrugged. 'If no-one turns up to claim them, they can just bulldoze the lot and pay a pittance to the feudal landlord. Whoever that might be.'

Jimmy looked worried. He drummed his fingers on the flying duck pinned to his orange boiler suit. Ellen continued.

'And what about that Mr Le Placs winning the pools? Strange name that. Foreign, I wouldn't doubt. A surgeon, too. What's he doing winning the pools and taking it away from folk that need it more? He gave most of the money to the playgroup, too.' She grimaced. 'he's got more money than sense, if you ask me.'

'Ellen!'

'Just coming, Alice.' She turned and hurried to the table where Alice waited impatiently. Jimmy drank up and left.

Ann and Bill Deace walked up to Ali's shop where a group of women stood talking. They looked the very picture of the holidaying couple: she in a bright loose skirt that blew enchantingly in the breeze, he in light fawn trousers, his short-sleeved shirt open at the neck.

'Could you get me some cigarettes, dear?' she asked as they reached the shop door. 'I'll just pop in and see if the coastguard can give me some idea of when the tide will be in.'

He went in to the shop and bought some bakery goods and cigarettes and a film for their camera.

She went into the Coastguard Station next door and spent some time in conversation with Ian the Coastguard. He was inclined to be condescending. After a while she took something out of her handbag and showed it to him. There was no further argument. She left the Coastguard Station with a set of keys in her bag.

On his way back from The Fisherman's Arms Jimmy Bervie met the Minister, who was reading the posters in the Post Office window.

'Good day to you, minister.'

Rev Dumfry, having rebelled to a certain extent against the Elders of the Church, felt sufficiently buoyant to risk an encounter even with Jimmy, the town buffoon.

'Hello there, Jimmy. How are you?'

'As well as you see me, minister. Can I sell you a ticket to Mars?'

Dumfry laughed. 'No, Jimmy, my work is here on Earth.'

Jimmy glanced at the posters and chose the most preposterous one.

'You'll be checking what time the rave is on, I don't doubt.'

'Well, yes, I was, as a matter of fact.' For the first time ever, Dumfry looked at Jimmy closely. Jimmy's eyes were bright and clear and intelligent. 'How on earth did you guess?'

Jimmy waved his lollipop in vague circles. 'Just came to me.'

'I thought I'd go along and find what the young folk go there for.'

Jimmy folded his arms and looked closely at the minister. The white stick of the lollipop stuck out between his lips. 'And what do the Elders think of this?'

'Hang the Elders,' said Dumfry. 'I'm going.' He had something of the air of a defiant teenager. Jimmy made a decision.

'You'll know about the other ministers that we've had here?'

'I beg your pardon?'

'There's something about Cromness that changes them, you know. Some of them last a year or two, some of them longer, but almost always they change.'

'Change? What do you mean 'Change'? Everyone changes.'

'Begging your pardon, minister, but ministers rarely do change, not once they are installed with their squad of Elders around them. Let me tell you about Harry... No, it's a long story. Do you have time for a cup of coffee?'

Lorraine eventually found The Fisherman's Arms, and pushed through the door. There were a few men standing at the bar. They turned to look at her as she came in. Only one of the tables was taken. The big woman was sitting there with two of the other women from the Ladies Guild.

Lorraine went to the bar and ordered an Islay malt.

'Fine evening,' said the man next to her, moving a few inches up the bar towards her.

She nodded without replying. 'And a Dubonnet and lemon,' she said.

The man glanced at the table where the women were sitting and moved back to his original position. Lorraine sipped her malt, then picked up the other drink and turned towards the table.

Alice looked up, and her eyes brushed Lorraine's face like a flame without heat. 'Why, Miss MacDonald. What a surprise to see you here.'

Lorraine looked back at her and could only speak the truth. 'I thought you invited me.'

Alice's eyes did not flicker, but Lorraine felt something change in them. 'Yes. I see that I did. Sit down. Ellen was about to leave, weren't you?'

Ellen discovered that she had, in fact, been meaning to get home in time for the late news.

The other woman spoke. 'Just a moment Ellen. Let me finish this and I'll see you down the road.' She drank down her gin and stood up.

'Just a minute, before you go,' put in Alice. 'What was that idiot saying at the bar?'

'Jimmy? He's daft as a brush. Saying there was something wrong with his sand, but it's all right now.'

Alice grunted, to let her know that was all.

'See you, Alice.'

'Bye, Alice.'

Alice ignored them and looked at Lorraine, who sipped her whisky and studied the varnish on the tabletop. 'Well, then.'

And Lorraine, who had a Doctorate and security of tenure and a book with her name on it, and who was over thirty years old and should know better, burst into tears.

Alice nodded. 'I see.' She waited until Lorraine had herself under control. 'Did you believe what you were telling us? About the death of the Celtic culture?'

'I suppose I did. All the books say that.'

'I didn't ask about the books. I asked what you believe.'

'I don't know any more.' Lorraine spoke quietly and she wouldn't look up at Alice. 'My mam used to tell me about the old gods. When I was wee she told me the stories. Sometimes she sort of hinted that the gods were real, still in the world, somewhere. Like grown-ups do about fairies.'

Alice's mouth pursed in distaste as she sipped her drink.

'When I went to college, the lecturers talked about it as if it was all gone, all dead. I suppose I was foolish. I sort of hoped they'd be able to tell me where the gods and the heroes all went to. Then I read the books and tried to work it out for myself.' She shrugged. 'Eventually I had to admit that they were right. It was gone. All gone.'

'So what do you want from me?'

Lorraine blew her nose. 'Please,' she said. 'Tell me what's going on.'

'No. I don't think I will. I'll do better. I'll show you. Drink up, then you can come home and make me a cup of tea.'

'Thank you.'

The *Suitor's Lass* made her way down the coast, heading for home. Sea birds swooped around the cliffs, screaming at the boat and at each other. The passengers scanned the waves with binoculars, to catch a last glimpse of the dolphins, while Barry and Maria talked in the wheelhouse.

'For a moment I thought she was going to make a proposition,' he said. 'But if so, she never got round to it.'

Maria laughed. 'With her husband there?'

'Not that kind of proposition. Something to do with the boat.'

'Like illegal immigrants or a drugs run...' She looked at him and shook her head. 'That all comes in by the West Coast – Ullapool and Mallaig.'

Barry shrugged. 'God knows. Maybe they were just making conversation.'

'No. They were after information. They wanted to know what happens in the harbour. Customs and Excise, I bet.'

'Maybe, but we won't know until they make the next move – if they ever do.' Maria reached for the wheel. 'I'll take over in here. It's time for you to entertain the passengers.'

'Aye, aye ma'am. The wheel's yours.'

Barry settled his crutch under his armpit and hobbled out onto the pitching deck. The sea breeze was close to a gale where the cliffs of the North Suitor faced the open sea.

'Ladies and gentlemen,' began Barry. 'What a fine day we have had for our trip today. A grand wee breeze to keep us cool. It reminds me of my time on the China Seas – but there the wind was hot, hot. The dolphins wouldn't even leap clear of the water for fear of drying up.'

He tucked his arm through a rope loop lashed to the mast and began to fill his pipe. Baldy was here again, sullen-faced. He didn't look as if he enjoyed these trips, but this was his third.

'Those were the days, before I lost my leg to cannon-shot.' He slapped his right leg, which gave a solid wooden sound. 'Not real cannon balls of course. The pirates use machine guns these days. Pirates? Oh yes, there are still pirates in those seas. Fierce brigands who would cut your throat rather than look at you. Mostly after the oil they are, these days, but they'll take anything that's going. Slaves to Australia, gold to India, the white slave trade to Arabia.'

The harbour was coming into view around the curve of the headland.

'But enough of the pirates and foreign parts. That's all in the past. Now I'm here to introduce you to our marine cousins. We've seen the dolphins today and the seals, and we've been lucky enough to catch a glimpse of the sway-backed angler fish, a rare denizen of the deep, that feeds on the deep sea worm and comes up to the surface only once or twice a day to breathe.'

As expected, a boy held up a hand.

'Please, sir, I didn't see the sway-backed angler fish and...'

'Well, maybe you'll see it next time...'

'...and if it's a fish, why does it need to breathe?'

Barry chuckled as the boy's parents shushed him. 'The questions these young folks come up with, eh?' He knocked his pipe against his wooden leg to settle the tobacco. 'Dreadfully muddy down there, you know, ' he continued. And when you're fighting a deep sea worm to the death, the mud gets all thrashed up. The sway-backed angler fish is specially adapted to breathe air when the gills are choked with mud.'

He nodded sideways. Maria was watching, and she put the boat into the side of a wave. Spray fountained over the passengers. Always put paid to awkward questions, that did.

'Harry Moncrieff arrived here many years ago,' said Jimmy Bervie, carefully toasting some dandelion roots under the grill. 'He lived in the manse where you stay now.' Rev Dumfry sat on a bench at the table, which was made of three planks placed on fish-boxes. They had the words 'Return to Kinlochbervie' marked on them.

'He used to be round here all the time, he and a few friends. We talked about Philosophy and Palaeontology and Poetry. We discussed Nerval one day, and I mentioned the time he took his lobster for a walk in the Luxembourg gardens.' Dumfry had never heard of Nerval, or indeed anyone else from Luxembourg. He nodded vaguely. 'After that we had regular lobster dinners. Lobster and stout.' He lifted lids from two garishly painted cups sitting on matching saucers and crumbled in the dandelion roots.

'Interesting cups,' said Dumfry.

'Hmm. The Dalai Lama gave them to me.' He poured boiling water over the roots and set the lids on top.

'Indeed?' Out of politeness, Dumfry tried not to look dubious.

'But we were talking about Harry. For a Presbyterian minister, he had an unusual interest in philosophy and other religions, but apart from that, he was by no means unconventional – not at first. He listened to the Elders and preached the party line, so to speak. Then he began to visit other churches, which was unheard of. Not the sort of thing to make you or me raise an eyebrow, though, eh minister?'

Dumfry shook his head without catching Jimmy's eye.

'Then he visited the Pentecostal Church and found he could talk in tongues.'

Dumfry snorted and Jimmy shrugged his shoulders.

'I pointed out to him at that time that it wasn't much use if he couldn't understand what he was saying – but Harry heeded no-one's counsel but his own. I expected the novelty to wear off after a while. But it didn't. He spent more and more of his time with strange folk from strange churches and his conversation grew bizarre and impenetrable. Quite stimulating, in fact. Not, in other words, what one would expect of a minister.'

'Scarcely likely to happen to me,' said Dumfry.

'And that was just the beginning of the change.' Jimmy lifted a lid and sniffed the steam. 'It's ready.' He handed one of the cups to Dumfry and sat down at the table. 'He came across Hugh Chandler's work. You know, the fossil fish in the Redrock Gorge. Harry thought that if God had hidden fishes in the sandstone, then He must surely have hidden proofs of Christianity where men of faith and diligence could find them.'

Dumfry sipped at the mug and put it down again.

'It can be a little bitter,' said Jimmy, spooning some Golden Syrup into Dumfry's mug. 'That should do it. Harry saved up for two years and managed to get some kind of grant from a religious foundation to go to the Middle East.' Jimmy shook his head. 'I had my misgivings, even then. Harry wasn't a young man – though not so old as me. And he'd never been out of Scotland in his life – except during the War when he was an Army Chaplain on Salisbury Plain or some such place.'

'He was in Cromness quite a while ago then?'

'Och yes. Thirty years past, anyway.'

'I don't suppose he found anything much? It seems an eccentric sort of quest.' Dumfry struggled manfully with the coffee and put the mug down again.

'That's just where you're wrong. Harry spent months abroad, and when he got back he had a dozen packing cases with him and he was all lit up from inside with enthusiasm.' Jimmy looked earnestly at the Reverend. 'Another dandelion coffee?'

Dumfry declined.

'He had been away for six months, starting in Turkey, then Lebanon, Jordan and other dangerous places of a Biblical sort. Then it was Egypt, and finally, Israel.

'But Turkey was where he realised that he'd found his life's work – so he said – as a Biblical antiquary. He was taken into the wilds by a guide who led him up high on a mountain and showed him ancient relics which no westerner had ever seen. After a great deal of persuasion the guide sold him one of these, which Harry brought back.

'He told us the story in his front room, after showing us the slides of Holy and Interesting places of the Near and Middle East. The rest of his audience were Pentecosts of one degree or another. They all oohed and aahed, while I suggested that he should have brought a camel home to work the croft.'

Dumfry looked dubiously at the boiler-clad figure of Jimmy, with a flying duck pinned to his chest and a child's windmill tucked behind his ear.

'Were you serious?'

'Of course not!' Jimmy laughed and Dumfry relaxed. 'God's sake, man, where would you get harness to fit a camel?' He dipped his lollipop in his dandelion coffee and sucked it. He used the lollipop to emphasise his story as he continued.

Jimmy's Story

HE WAS QUITE an impressive figure. He had developed a splendid white beard on his travels, and he looked for all the world like Moses himself as he sat there expounding, the lights shining on him. He spread his arms in a most prophetical way as he spoke. I wondered who had arranged the lighting.

'And tonight,' he said 'I will show to you, my chosen friends, the very first relic which I was led to find.'

He lifted a small wooden chest to his lap. We sat there agog as he opened up the chest and reached inside. He held up a shirt.

'Here it is!'

An old shirt, certainly, but not very remarkable. Quite long, made of sheep's wool or something similar.

'That's very nice, Harry, but just what is it?'

Harry nodded sagely. 'Mrs Donneley in the Nairn church has holy water from Lourdes, and a crucifix blessed by the Pope. She even claims to have a fragment of the One True Cross. But this is even holier than that, and certainly more ancient. Preserved by the miracle of high-altitude desiccation, saved down the centuries for our wonder and worship.'

I leaned closer. It just looked like a shirt. 'It's a woollen sark, Harry. It looks fine and warm, but what's so special about it?'

'It's older than Christianity...'

'No! A pagan artefact? That's very broad-minded of you.'

'Pagan? No, indeed! This is an artefact from the true Judaeo-Christian heritage. Older than the Law and the Prophets.' He paused and looked around at us portentously. He held up the shirt for us all to see.

His voice was hushed when he spoke again.

'This is Noah's sark.'

There was a moment of silence. I looked around, surreptitiously. Surely one or two of the better educated were considering explaining some of the basic facts of Bible hagiography to Harry. But no, most of them seemed ready to accept its authenticity.

I began to wonder if this was an inspired piece of anarchy devised by a mind no longer wholly normal. He continued.

'And that is not all. That was only the beginning of a pilgrimage which brought me in touch with the living lands of the Bible, a pilgrimage in which it seemed that my steps were guided to the most precious evidences of the faith, lain unnoticed for hundreds, sometimes for thousands of years.'

A scholar, obviously new to the group, broke in. 'I have some doubts about the authenticity of the... relic. The word 'sark' is Scottish. That such a word was in use in early Biblical times is very improbable.'

'But that's all revealed in the scriptures also. Not only is the Bible a true story of the Jewish peoples, it is also an allegory, a symbolic representation of the history of God's chosen people. The British race.'

I was staggered. 'That's why the Bible is written in English?'

He nodded approvingly. 'Just so. In the King James version, all the major incidents, even the individual words, are coded references to the real nature of the Book. It is a guide and an instrument to lead us.'

'I suppose you all know about numerology,' he continued, 'and how it is used in the Bible?' I mumbled something among the general murmur of assent. 'The wonderful description in Revelations, fulfilling the words of Jesus, when He said, there is not a sparrow that falls from the sky but my father knows of it. He watches over us and numbers our days, and even the beasts of the field. And Saint John tells us in Revelations – 666 is the number of the beast. That's precise. And Biblical.'

The scholar could not be silent in the face of such factual error.

'That's just not right, Mr Moncrieff. I'm sorry, but Henderson

Glaickbea has over two hundred head of cattle himself, and Glaikbea's not a big farm. There must be more than a thousand beasts on the north side of the Dark Isle alone.'

Harry leaned forward to look him in the eye. 'I was just about to say, that it is precise and Biblical – and symbolic.' He nodded his head forcefully and settled back in his seat as if the matter was settled.

Then he sat up again. 'And what about our language? Divinely structured. What language do they speak in North Africa?' He answered himself. 'Arabic. And what language do we speak here? English. Now look at a Spanish phrasebook sometime – you'll be surprised at how many words we share.'

'For instance, mañana,' I said. He nodded to me.

'When the Moors overran Spain, they brought their language with them and it seeped into the local language so that there was a kind of mixture. A language that spans the gulf between the two languages. It spans two cultures. So of course that language is called Span-ish.'

He smiled at us, inviting us to enjoy the inevitability of the name.

I could see that Harry needed no encouragement in his devious schemes. Evidently he was a master in the anarchic style. I stood up to make my excuses.

'Just a minute, Jimmy,' he said. 'There's another holy relic that you really must see before you go.'

'What is it this time? Aaron's rod? Jesse's thorn?'

'Ach, someone's been telling you about my collection, I can see that. But I think we'll save those for another time. No, what I want to show you now is a greater wonder than that. You'll need to come through the house.'

He raised himself from the chair. His white beard seemed even more venerable than before. He shuffled through the room to a doorway, beckoning us to follow.

The room was dim, with niches in the walls. Each one was lit from above, and each had something in it, and a label on the wall below it. There was a model of a head on a shiny plate, a basket full of dusty seeds and so on. As I passed by, I thought I could make out the name Onan on the label below the basket.

Harry beckoned me to the far end of the room. The crowd had followed, and they were quietly marvelling at the room and the relics.

At the end, in a rectangular niche, was an aquarium. There were corals in it, and brownish seaweeds that waved as the bubbles from the aerator drifted past.

'This is one of my greatest finds. In Jordan I managed to get a guide who was deeply versed in Bible history. I persuaded him to take me south, down the sparsely populated shore of the Red Sea, to where the Israelites crossed from Egypt.'

He bowed his head.

'That holy place. I will treasure the memory of that day for the rest of my life.'

Someone murmured 'Hallelujah.' I peered into the tank.

The scholar looked over my shoulder. 'So you brought back some souvenirs then?'

His lips pursed. 'I do not collect souvenirs. I am a serious antiquarian. This collection is in many ways superior to the corresponding section of the British Museum.'

I could feel the hostility of the crowd, at having thus offended the old man. The scholar would not last long in this group. He apologised. 'I'm sorry. The word was not well-chosen.'

I spoke up. 'But what relic did you bring back from Jordan?'

He pointed. 'Look close.'

I leant down and peered into the tank. There was a little sand, some rocks, the weeds. A bit of algae on the glass. Nothing living at all.

'There's nothing there.'

He chuckled. 'None so blind, eh? Look close, now, at that greenish rock there, and tell me what you see.'

It was just a smooth green rock. I was about to say so when it moved. There was a puff of fine sand, and I saw its claws.

'It's a partan. A crab.'

'Aye. What do you say to that?'

'Well, well,' I muttered, being a bitty baffled. The scholar was more forthright.

'It's a crab. A fine crab. But what of it?'

'Losh man, d'ye not know a religious relict when ye see one?'

The scholar had had enough.

'I am as well versed in Archaeology and Church History as the next man, but my studies of invertebrate animals of the Red Sea was sadly neglected. Perhaps you could tell me what that is, as I do not wish to spend the day playing guessing games.'

'Well, well,' he sympathised smugly. 'They didn't teach you everything at that college, did they?'

'Obviously not. Perhaps you could enlighten me.'

'Stand back a wee, then, so that the rest can see.'

We all moved back and stood in a semi-circle around the tank.

Harry pointed at the crab.

'That wee darling,' he said, 'is the partan of the Red Sea.'

There were sighs of awe. As the rest crowded closer for a better look, I slipped quietly through the house. There was a set of keys hanging in the hall. The label told me they were the Keys of the Kingdom. There was a picture of a washerwoman on her knees in a field, scrubbing. It was titled 'Rebecca Cleaning in the Fields.' Was Harry an inspired agent provocateur in the house of God? Or was he just demented?

As I opened the front door, Harry called to me.

'Jimmy, wait. I brought you back something specially.' He pressed a small packet into my hand. I thanked him, but he just smiled and turned to go back to his guests.

As I walked down the road, I stripped off the paper wrapping. There in my hand I held a small tartan box holding a sugary slab of tablet. The Tablet of the Law, of course.

Mr Siller was counting paper pennies in his account books in the flat above the bank. He had sets of title deeds on the table beside him and the safe on the wall was half-open, showing a pile of other papers, some old and battered, some new. The window in front of him looked down the street towards the harbour. People moved up and down the street. He found them interesting, in his own way, and he watched them in his own way. When Jimmy Bervie and the minister went down the street, he barely saw them as people. Jimmy was a sandstone house, old but sound and with undisclosed monetary assets adequate to his lifestyle. The minister was without property, but had a stipend and owned a vague spectrum of shares which he did not tend properly. The stipend was to an extent, under the control of the Elders and Siller found this gratifying, considering Dumfry's attitude last time they'd met.

Sammy Poach came out of Ali's shop. His old coat hung a little low on one side. A bottle of whisky – no, a half-bottle. No assets except for a lease on his cottage near the Vennels. A lease due for renewal soon. Siller's hands automatically reached for each other and began the unpleasant slow hand-washing motion as he balanced interests and calculated courses of action.

He turned back to his account books. His lips were stretched thin in his equivalent of a smile.

George was standing outside his grandfather's door, almost ready to go in. He paused for a few seconds to gather himself. Once again, he had no idea of how he came to be here. He'd been in a dark place with a beast following him, and then he was out in the daylight and Jenny-Pet was talking to him. He was going to have to tell someone about these episodes sooner or later. He wasn't sure if his grandfather was the man to tell, but who else was there?

Disturbing images swam and ran together in his mind. Places darker than night and other, open spaces bright as the sky. Huge figures, gloomy and dangerous, and other tall figures of light, unbearably beautiful, and just as dangerous.

He almost turned and ran. But he had nowhere to run to. He'd just end up here again, sooner or later, hoping for information, looking for sanctuary.

From *Totemic Beasts of the Celts: The Salmon* by Dr L MacDonald, published by the Gael Press

...and along with these other totems ranks the Salmon.

In the legend of Tuan mac Cairill, Tuan recounts the history of Ireland as he has seen it in his different lives. He lived these lives in the form of various different animals: a Stag, a Boar – and in his last life, he was a salmon.

Among the Celts, the salmon symbolised wisdom – as can be seen in the legend of the hazel trees. The Tuatha De Danaan had nine hazel trees, on which grew hazel nuts of inspiration. Five salmon lived in the spring below the trees and ate the nuts as they dropped in the water. The nuts gave their colour to the fish, appearing in red spots on the skin. Any person that ate one of these salmon would 'know all knowledge and all poetry.'

The Celts evidently had an intimate knowledge of the life cycle of the salmon. The Atlantic salmon hatches and grows for a season in a stream or river before venturing into the sea. It swims to the far-distant feeding grounds, where it stays for a number of years before returning to the stream where it hatched. It finds the right stream by swimming along the coastline, tasting the chemical traces in the sea water which are unique to that stream. If it is not caught by humans or other predators it may return many times to spawn in the river where it hatched, and each time it is larger than before.

It is worth noting a parallel to the taboo on pig-meat: (see *Totemic Beasts of the Celts: The Pig*) the name of the salmon is not to be spoken on board fishing vessels. To do so is to court bad luck.
(Other titles are available in this series. Our current list may be obtained from the Gael Press.)

Doreen was sitting up in her room nervously watching the six o' clock news without seeing it. The Seeing was only a few hours away, and she wished it was over. In fact, she wished the whole business of Seeing was over and done with, for good. But Alice was obsessed with keeping the Celtic race alive in the Dark Isle, keeping a connection to the Goddess and the rest of the old Gods.

Doreen sighed. It had been fun when she was young, knowing about the secret meetings, being one of the special ones. Imagining all these wonderful Old Ones still living and walking the world. Doreen had spent weeks at a time imagining herself to be Deirdre of the Sorrows. It had to be Deirdre and not the Lady of Shallot – that was Arthurian, and Alice would skelp her bum if she even mentioned the Arthurian romances. It wasn't old enough. It wasn't from the true source. It was legend instead of mythology.

Now the whole thing was becoming a chore. It was no fun pretending any more. And she had the growing feeling that Alice had more in mind than mythological survival. She had mentioned more than once that the Celtic race had to be kept pure. It was worrying.

And tonight was the Seeing. Doreen scrunched herself into a tight ball on the armchair and chewed at her fingernails. Sooner or later Alice was going to find out that she couldn't See. That she'd been making it up since she was thirteen.

Rev Dumfry stood in his bedroom surveying his wardrobe. What was he to wear? From the bright splashy poster it was obvious that this rave was an informal affair. If he wanted the young folk to remain at ease, his various black suits were out of the question. And that left nothing at all.

Except.

Once before he had gone to an event like this. Well, not very much like this.

At Theological College, there had been a variety of students from many churches. Not all were as foursquare as the First Reformed and Ancient Presbyterian Church, and some were distinctly slack in their practices. There were even some women.

One of these women belonged to an Evangelical Church. She had long brown hair, a heart-shaped face and a guitar. She had invited him along to one of their evening gatherings, where they sang Gospel songs.

'Do come, John,' she had said. 'There's going to be hot chocolate and marshmallows to toast.' She smiled at him guilelessly and her eyes blinked a couple of times as she took a deep breath. 'There's plenty of everything.'

Solely to avoid looking out of place among the members of this more informal Church, he bought himself some clothes that were more fashionable than the suit which, even then, he favoured. When he turned up at the little church hall, excruciatingly self-conscious in his new clothes, the young woman had complimented him. 'You look so much less formal,' she had said, as she gave him a hug. His heart had leapt then, and it did so now, remembering the moment.

But it was only her way. She was a warm affectionate woman with plenty of hugs to go round – and a fiancé who sang to her guitar playing.

With a glance behind him, in case someone had crept into the manse and was watching him, Dumfry climbed on a chair and fetched down a suitcase from the top of the wardrobe. He laid it on the bed and opened it. There were the very clothes. Flared trousers and a turtle-neck sweater.

No point in being outrageous. He'd change in the car when he got to the venue.

He slipped down to the street with the clothes in a carrier bag. No-one noticed him, but the serious black car seemed to accuse him of frivolity as he locked the package in the boot.

Alice lumbered along the street with Lorraine beside her.

'Your explanations are a mongrel mix. Most academic theories are. Half fanciful and half rational. Somebody makes a story up out of facts that they have at their disposal. Then they look for other facts to fit the story. But facts are idle superstitions, where they are not just opinions, and the theories are no more than informed opinions. They have their limits.'

Lorraine turned a bangle to and fro on her wrist. 'But who can we listen to if we can't trust the experts? They've studied the evidence.'

'But not all of it. Informed opinion says that the Loch Ness Monster does not exist – but if the Beast itself crawls across the road in front of your car, that informed opinion is worth nothing. Worth nothing to you, anyway. All the facts that you had on your side now have to be looked at from the other side.

'It's the same with your theories – or rather, your opinions – about the Celtic Gods. They're just one way of putting the facts together. A more or less entertaining exercise. A more or less accurate picture. In this case, very much less.'

Miss Semple nodded brightly to them as she stepped aside to let them pass. They ignored her. She muttered to herself as she pottered off along the pavement.

'If the Goddess once touches you, you can't pretend any longer that she is just an idea that people had long ago, or just a personification of Nature or whatever.'

Lorraine did not feel confident enough to argue. 'Are they alive, then?' she asked.

'That depends on what you mean by alive,' said Alice.

'What?'

'It's not worth asking the question. If you encounter the Gods, the question does not arise. They are as precisely alive as you or I. But if you never encounter them, they may as well be dead, for you. Everything can be explained away. The elasticity of the mind.' She turned her head to look at Lorraine. 'Do you believe me?'

'Yes. Yes I do.'

Alice continued to look at Lorraine as they walked along. Other people on the pavement got out of her way. 'It's not enough. If you just believe what I tell you, you're no better off than when you believed the academic consensus. Faith is not enough.'

They walked on.

'You can stay here tonight,' said Alice, as they entered Wayland Crescent.

Lorraine felt, quite rightly, that it was not just a suggestion.

'George! Georgie, boy, it's you! Come on in!'

George shambled through the door as Sammy Poach held it open wide.

'Hi, Grandad.' George walked uncertainly past the stairs to the kitchen with Sammy chattering behind him.

'Go on through, go on through. Let me see you. God, you're hardly the same boy that went away to Aberdeen. What have you been doing with yourself? Sit down and I'll make you a cup of something. Coffee?'

'Yes please, Grandad.'

George looked around the kitchen as Sammy filled the kettle and plugged it in. He shivered. It was so much smaller and grubbier than he remembered. The bare floorboards were dull with grime and the sink was full of unwashed dishes. The roses had faded on the cheerful flowered wallpaper that his granny had put up. A bare bulb gave a wan illumination, augmented by dim light seeping through the dusty window. A carefully folded fishing net lay on a chair.

The kitchen was not just uncared for, it was empty. Something vital had gone out of it when his granny had died. Sammy had wrapped himself up in a miasma of whisky and communist ideology. That was when George had felt the first cold winds blowing at his back. And then his mother had gone away too, and there was nothing left, no reason to stay here.

Sammy rinsed two mugs under the tap and searched out coffee and sugar while the kettle boiled. He filled the mugs and set them on the table. 'No milk, I'm afraid.' He sat down at the table. 'So, what brings you back here? I thought you'd shown the place a clean pair of heels.'

'Och, I just thought I'd visit and…' George stopped himself and looked across at his grandad. There were broken veins on Sammy's nose and his cheeks and the skin looked grey. When George was young, Sammy had always liked a drink – but now he was a drunk. George remembered him as a fiery communist but now he looked burnt-out. From the grubby jacket and the frayed shirt, it looked as if he couldn't even look after himself properly any more. But he was the only person that George could talk to.

'There's something I have to ask you,' he said. 'When was I here last?'

'Eh? Three years past. Before you went to college. Surely you remember. Why ask me?'

George arranged the words in his head and waited for them to come out. They wouldn't come easily. He had to push them out a phrase at a time.

'Because it seems to me that I was here at the end of next month,' he said, blushing at the preposterous words. You didn't say things like that to your grandfather. Especially when he was a down-to-earth dialectical materialist.

'You mean last month.'

'No. Next month. It was the time of the Dark Isle Show.'

Sammy looked at him uneasily. 'Eh, what… I mean…' He shrugged hopelessly. 'How do you mean that?'

'I can remember it. But it wasn't last year or some other time that I've been to the Show. It was this year.'

'A dream?' Sammy looked disapproving. 'It was a dream. Take no notice of it. Bloody dreams, indeed!'

George gathered himself. 'I don't think it was a dream, Grandad. It was very real. I could smell the mud and I could feel it on my… on my feet.'

'On your feet? You were barefoot, at the Show?'

'Sort of. They didn't feel like feet. They were hard. And there were four of them.'

'For God's sake!'

'They felt like, well, like pig's trotters, really.' Sammy's mouth dropped open. He tried to speak a couple of times. George smiled apologetically and shrugged. 'That's what it felt like.'

Sammy managed to speak. 'Look, you just have to… Listen, just ignore it. It means nothing, it can't possibly mean anything. Dreams, hah!'

'It wasn't a dream!'

'What else could it be? For god's sake, boy, you're not going fey on me are you? One in the family is more than enough!'

'Listen, will you. Just listen. It was at this year's Show. I was in one of the pens – I don't know why. I... I saw myself walk past.' He looked across at his grandfather. 'That's the way it was,' he said defiantly. 'I saw myself walk past among the pens. Later there was a stushie behind the main marquee tent. I pushed under the bars of the pen and ran over – and then I killed someone.'

'What?'

George swallowed and put his hands round his empty mug, looking into it.

'And then I ate him.'

'Jesus Christ, boy!' Sammy stood up and stared at George. He glanced wildly round the room. A half-empty bottle on a shelf caught his eye. He took it down and poured a dollop into his mug, then poured some into George's mug too. He lifted his mug, emptied it at a swallow and poured more whisky in. Then he began to laugh, a strained uncomfortable laugh. He leant over and slapped George on the shoulder.

'You really had me going there,' he said. 'Almost had me believing you for a moment. Quite the joker, eh?'

'Yes. That's right,' said George. He sipped at the whisky in his mug. 'Quite the joker.' But he could not manage a smile.

'...only the most recent of the ridiculous attacks made by their back-benchers. Let me say once again, any links with the various revolutionary socialist organisations, which may have existed in the past, have been severed completely.'

'Thank you. That was Thom Gardiner MP, Labour's Policy and Cohesion Spokesman.'

Sitting on her bed, Doreen watched the TV blankly. Alice should be back soon. It was time to tell her the truth. Time to tell her that she had been fooled for all those years. Time to tell her that she couldn't See at all, but just made it up. If she'd only been brave enough to do it before, she wouldn't have had to put up with so many long dreary hours in the cold and the dark. She stretched herself. Of course, she had a nice set of thermal silk underwear now, but eight years of duplicity was a heavy price to pay for that.

The newsreader's voice changed tone and a picture of the Scott Monument appeared on screen.

'Reports are coming in of an earth tremor, the most recent in a series of earthquakes which have struck Edinburgh in the last month. This one reached 4.9 on the Richter scale and affected the east end of the city. Experts say that further tremors can be expected but it is unlikely that any of these will be dangerous.'

The picture of Edinburgh faded out to show the presenter addressing a serious looking woman across the news desk. A caption read: Martha Nero TRE.

'Martha Nero, of the Terrestrial Research Establishment: you have investigated these earthquakes. Is there any cause for concern?'

'No, of course not. Tremors of this magnitude occur perhaps a dozen times a year in Scotland. It is only because these were in Edinburgh that they have attracted attention. Several much more interesting earth movements have occurred recently along the Highland Faultline, from Fort William up to Inverness, but nothing has appeared in the national press.'

The presenter leaned forward, eyebrows raised quizzically. 'And why is it that these tremors in the Highlands are more interesting?'

'Because the rock movements are occurring at a much deeper level. This indicates unresolved conflicts in the underlying rock on which our geological structures are based...'

Downstairs, the front door opened. Doreen sat up straight and listened. It was Alice, she could tell by the heavy tread, but there was someone with her. She leaned over to the TV. The newsreader was speaking.

'You mean we might see changes in the coastline, for instance?'

'Yes, quite soon.' Martha Nero laughed. 'But of course when I say 'soon,' I am speaking in geological terms. Perhaps 100,000 years.'

'Thank you, Martha Nero.' He turned to the camera as Doreen turned him off. In the sudden silence, she could hear the voices downstairs – Alice lecturing someone. A strange voice replied. A woman. A woman who was frightened of Alice but trying to hold her own.

Curious, Doreen straightened her clothes and left her bedroom.

At Redrock, the big gate was shut and bolted. The boar put its snout against the gates and pushed. They creaked and groaned, but would not open. It squealed and lunged at the gate a few times. The steel buckled, but the bolt would not give way. The gateman came out of his lodge just in time to watch it trot down the road, round the wall and out onto the moors.

He took out his handset. 'Hello? Lodge here. Gate lodge. Who's that? Right. There's a pig at the gate, Baldy. The outside of the gate, trying to get in. A great big bastard. No, of course I don't know its name, it looked like all the others but bigger. Send someone down to catch it.' There was a long reply from the other end. 'So you're loading up the salmon... I don't care if you're copulating with the bloody salmon. Mr Mor isn't going to like it if one of his pigs is loose – and it's a boar. Listen,' he lied,

'I'm recording this conversation, and if there's a pig missing I'm in the clear. But he'll feed you to the boar.'

In the courtyard of Redrock House, a forklift truck was lifting a large grey plastic tank onto the back of a pickup truck. Baldy was standing at the entrance to one of the steadings. He shouted in the doorway.

'If the salmon are nae ready, then get them bloody ready! Last ah heard they wis supposed to be fitted up this efternoon!'

A voice spoke behind him. 'What's going on here?'

Baldy turned. 'Ah. Boss. There a pig at the gate. A boar. Ootside, tryin tae get in.'

Mr Mor frowned. 'Damn! How did that happen? Take a couple of men and go get it.'

'It's no there, boss. It ran aff tae the moors.'

'Then get the ATV and catch it. Take the tranquilliser gun.' Baldy turned to go. 'How are the salmon doing?'

'They're no ready yet. Ah've bin tryin...'

'Deal with the pig.'

Baldy ran off. Mr Mor entered the steading.

Men in overalls were bending over troughs and tanks, looking busy. They all had plastic gloves on and there was occasional splashing as they handled the salmon. A pile of tangled rubber straps lay on a bench among the troughs.

Mr Mor beckoned over a skinny man with a flat cap on. He spoke to him very quietly, but everyone in the shed could hear.

'Docherty. There seems to be a hold-up. Are you responsible for this?'

'It's the harness, Mr Mor. Look.' He held up one of the rubber straps. The rubber had split, showing the orange nylon twine at its core. 'We're having to repair them.'

Mr Mor did not look at the straps but continued to look at Docherty. 'Perhaps I haven't explained myself sufficiently,' he said. 'This is your area of responsibility. All of it. The salmon must have enough time to settle down after they've been handled. Otherwise they hang about in the sea for days. That affects our cash flow – and we can't have that, can we?'

Docherty looked up at Mr Mor, 'No sir, but...'

'So, do I have to find someone else? Someone who can keep things moving smoothly?'

'Oh no, sir. I'm sorry. It won't happen again.' In the background, a couple of the men were smirking.

'I'm sure it won't.' He raised his voice slightly. 'And should you need to... retire anyone in the interests of efficiency, you have my full support. Just let me know and I'll get Baldy to retire them for you.'

The men lost their grins and bent over their work. Docherty managed a small smile. 'Thank you.'

Mr Mor left the steading. Behind him, Docherty's voice spoke with a new sense of authority. 'Now then, you two. From now on, you're in charge of the salmon harnesses. If they're not ready in time, it's your balls in the wringer.'

When they had finished their drinks, Sammy made another mug of coffee for himself and George. He talked about the fishing, about Mr Mor, and his misgivings about him, about the football club and Big Irwin's miraculous skill with the ball. He talked about a suspicious character called the Major, who seemed to be prying into Sammy's background for some reason. He talked about Jimmy Bervie's sand-garden... 'he's dottled, that one, but good for a laugh.'

He talked about anything except George's claim that he had been to the Dark Isle Show a month in the future. The other parts of George's confession were too disturbing even to think about.

'I'm surprised to see you back here,' he said, when he had run out of local small-talk. 'Last time we spoke you'd had enough of the place and were leaving for ever.'

George shifted uneasily and the rickety chair creaked. 'Och, you know. Just couldn't keep away somehow.' He thought about Veronica for a moment, but somehow he couldn't mention her. She was too fey for Sammy. A phrase from a TV programme came to him. 'Just looking for my roots.'

'Hmph. Roots, is it?' Sammy sighed. 'I thought it would come to this sooner or later. I suppose you want to know about your father.'

'My father?' George was puzzled. He knew who his father was. He was... he was a fisherman or something like that. He'd drowned or sailed off around the world. It had never seemed important. He had a mother and two grandparents. The grandparents looked after him. The mother wandered on the shore, her red hair blowing in the sea winds – when she wasn't in her room studying books on mythology and psychology and god knew what. That was the way it was. But he supposed that he should show interest. 'Who was he?'

Sammy shrugged. 'Your mother would never talk about him. He was probably a sailor paid off after a voyage. Took her away for a few months until his money ran out. Then she came back pregnant.' He looked at George. 'Nothing to be ashamed of.'

'No, of course not. Still, it seems a bit careless of her.'

'Careless is the least of it. She took the man's name, but he never gave her a broken groat towards your upkeep.'

'His name? So you do know who he was.'

'Hell, his name's on your birth certificate, though it's most likely a made-up one.'

'Well, what is it? What's his name?'

'Same as yours, of course. MacLear.'

'Yes, but nothing else? What was his Christian name? Where did he come from?'

'God's sake, it's years since I saw the birth certificate. It was something with lots of syllables.'

'Come on, Grandad. That's not much help.'

'That's all I remember!' Sammy said, shortly.

George was taken aback. 'All right, all right. But we must have the birth certificate somewhere.'

Sammy shook his head. 'Hard to lay hands on it just now.'

George said nothing.

Sammy sighed. 'All right. Let me have a look.' He went out of the room and brought back a black tin box. Inside were vaccination forms, a marriage certificate, a few old photographs, a Communist Party membership card and several birth certificates. 'Here they are. That's me, that's your gran, that's your mother.' He pulled out the last one. 'And here's yours, so you can see what the blackguard called himself.' He opened up the certificate and spread it on the table. George pulled it over and read the details while Sammy walked to and fro and fidgeted.

'Here it is! Surname MacLear. Christian name – look! Someone's crossed out the word 'Christian' and written in 'First.' Well then, his first name is Manannan. That's a strange name. It says he's a seaman, and there's an address in the Vennels.'

'That's just made up, I'm sure,' said Sammy.

'What was he like? You must have met him.'

'That's just it. Your mother was going with him for months before she ran away with him. She'd go out in the evenings and we'd see nothing of her until after midnight. I thrashed her until her arse was black and blue.' He looked abashed. 'Things were different then. Nobody thought twice about leathering bairns. That's how they were kept in line.'

George was too impatient to debate changing practices in child-rearing. 'What did she tell you?'

'Bugger all.' He stared into his mug. 'Said it was none of our business. Said he'd shown her another way of life or some such nonsense. I thought it might be some well-heeled prat from the semi-nobility that had turned her head, and I was harder on her because of that. But I think it was a seaman after all. Probably a deck-hand. Who knows.'

'That's all?'

'She was stubborn, I can tell you. Refused to tell me anything. Just before she went away though, she said something strange. Before she went away to Craig Dunain she told me that it wasn't just stubbornness. She said she actually couldn't remember.' He sighed. 'She was pretty odd the last few years.'

'I wish I knew more.'

'Well, you know where to find her. The Mental Hospital up on Craig Dunain.'

As Doreen opened the living room door, Alice's face creased in a smile. 'Doreen. This is Doctor Lorraine MacDonald. She was giving the lecture at the Institute.' Her smile became a little more malignant. 'She'll be staying here with us for a while, won't you, Doctor MacDonald?'

'Oh. Yes, I suppose so.' Lorraine held out her hand to Doreen, who looked at her suspiciously.

Alice spoke again. 'Lorraine is interested in Celtic rituals, aren't you, Lorraine?'

Lorraine blushed and nodded. 'I'm mainly an academic, though. I would be fascinated to see a real ritual.'

'Well, Doreen here is your girl, isn't that so?'

Doreen glared at Alice. 'I don't want a bloody audience, Alice.'

Alice laughed. 'Tradition-bearers don't get much respect from the young.' She turned to Lorraine and whispered loudly. 'She's been purifying herself for the last few days, that's why she's so grumpy.'

'I'm not just bloody grumpy, I'm finished. I've had enough. I'm not going to do it.'

'Doreen, don't be so melodramatic. Go through to the kitchen and make us all a nice cup of tea. Get us a piece of that lovely cake you made.'

Doreen stamped through to the kitchen.

'Don't mind her. Temperamental.'

Lorraine looked uncertainly in the direction of the kitchen. 'She does seem to resent my presence.'

'Nonsense. If it wasn't you it would be the cat, or me. She has to complain about something. It's not easy being a Seer. You don't always See things you'd want to see.'

'I'm amazed that there is a real Seer at all.'

'Yes, of course you are. You've spent too much time reading books. Here in the Dark Isle we didn't bother writing it all down, we preserved the Celtic bloodlines and the racial memory, transmitted from mother to daughter from one mouth to the next down through the centuries. Keeping the Celtic race pure.'

Lorraine looked uneasy. 'I know it's just book learning,' she said, 'but it seems to me that Cromness in particular has been a melting pot of genes from all over Europe. How could you possibly hope to keep track of some prehistoric bloodline?'

'With paternity so open to question, you mean?'

'Yes, I suppose so.'

'Quite simple. It is always completely certain who the mother is. And that has always been the Celtic way. Inheritance follows the female line. Not, perhaps in material goods: but the skills and traditions were passed down secretly. There are dozens of women in Cromness, each with her own part of the Heritage. You'll meet some of them when you're initiated.'

Lorraine finally got up the nerve to ask the question which had been nagging at her.

'Why tell me? If you are the keeper of the tradition – one of the keepers – why did you choose to tell me?'

'Two things. Firstly, there's a tinge of red in your hair. Celtic genes in there somewhere. But mainly it was your lecture.'

'What? You've just been telling me it was all worthless theorising. And I agreed with you.'

'True. But when you asked us where the Celts had gone, you said "we". You said "Our genes have been mixed with every race in Europe, our culture has been subsumed into today's super-culture."'

'Oh. But I was being... I was speaking metaphorically.'

'You were being unacademic. You were being truthful. You can't deny it – you know that you belong with us.' She looked steadily into Lorraine's face. 'There is a connection to the old gods, to the Tuatha de Danaan, to the Goddess, yes and to the Gods too. There is a connection, and we are it.'

Doreen came through with a tray. 'On the other hand,' she said, 'there are those of us who believe that Alice is a cultural fascist. All this talk of bloodlines, does it not remind you of something? Pogroms, concentration camps, so-called ethnic cleansing?' She put the tray down on the low table.

Alice glared at her. 'Doreen! You go too far!'

'Just making a point. It's all racism of a sort, isn't it?' She turned to Lorraine. 'Ask her how many black women have been initiated.'

Alice laughed. 'There are no black women in Cromness!'

Doreen jauntily poured tea into the porcelain cups. 'Typical bigot's answer,' she said.

At Rossmarty the big black BMW turned up the hill to the west of Glen Grian. There were other vehicles on the small road, cars and vans and even buses. The black car slowed to a crawl. Now and then a motorbike shot past, passing the slow line of traffic.

Headlights were on now and in the uncertain light Rev Dumfry nervously tried to make out the occupants of the other cars. They were certainly much younger than he. A blonde girl was watching him out of the back window of a van. She looked no more than fourteen. In the mirror he could see the driver of the car behind. A young man with a shaven head. It was hard to tell how old he was. Twenty? He wondered what they saw when they looked at him.

He sat up straight and pulled in his stomach. They saw a trim young man in his early thirties. Suddenly he remembered how old thirty seemed when you were young.

They saw an old man in a suit, with a dog-collar. They saw The Minister.

He had a sudden impulse to leave, to go home, to bury himself in his work and the stuffy atmosphere of his well-established church. But it was not possible to turn back. The cars were nose-to-tail all the way up to the farm. Dumfry smiled as he realised that his decision was made for him. As for the trembling in his stomach, it wasn't nervousness, it was excitement. He was travelling to a new world, searching for new lives, dedicating this adventure to God.

In the van in front, someone passed a joint to the blonde girl. Dumfry thought she was too young to be smoking, but when she glanced at him he smiled and gave a stiff little wave. She smiled back and spoke to her companions. Several faces came to the window, grinning. He searched his repertoire of responses and found one that he'd seen young people use. He held up two fingers in a peace sign. They grinned wider.

Dumfry relaxed, pleased to be just another one of the crowd.

Doreen sat in one corner of a triangle of chairs. In the other two, Dr Lorraine MacDonald and Alice were discussing farm animals and Celtic social structures.

'It was called the *colpachadh*,' said Lorraine, 'The equalising of cattle.'

'You mean, not all cows are born equal?' put in Doreen, who was feeling left out. Alice ignored her. Lorraine turned a polite smile towards her then continued speaking to Alice.

'We have the rates from several places – possibly the West Highlands is the most extensive.'

Alice grunted, and Lorraine correctly interpreted this as meaning, 'I am interested. Please carry on.'

'Well, one horse was equivalent to eight foals or two two-year old fillies or two cows.' She looked at Alice, who nodded sourly – probably a sign of enthusiasm. 'A cow was equivalent to eight calves or four stirks or two two-year-old quoys. Or eight sheep, sixteen lambs or sixteen geese. These are for live beasts, of course. Eighteen partans or twelve lobsters was equivalent to a dead goose, while a sheep could be had for eight crans of herring.' Her voice had changed to a lecturing tone as she recited the details of the ancient barter system. 'In Argyll, it was different. One cow was equivalent to four calves or five sheep or twenty lambs. This difference probably reflects the difference in life-expectancy for young animals in different parts of the country. If you were bartering a sheep in Stornoway, you wanted lots of lambs, to make sure that at least some survived.'

'Maybe. What was the rate for a pig?'

'Interestingly, there are no lists extant which give a barter equivalent for a pig.'

'So what do you think they did with them?'

'The lists?'

Alice looked at her with an expression of disgust. 'The pigs.'

'Oh.' Lorraine looked nervously at Doreen, who ignored her. 'I don't know. I thought there just weren't many pigs in the Highlands.'

Alice nodded. 'That's right. Why not?'

'Well, I always thought it was because of some tabu, based on the fact that they were totem animals.'

'Or because the Gods wouldn't let ordinary people keep pigs.'

'I've never heard about that.'

'You wouldn't have. It was after the Dagda gave up being Boss God. They all sort of scattered after that – and They always were a thieving and acquisitive bunch. Where did all the wild boar go? The Gods took them for their own.'

Lorraine looked at Doreen again, who shrugged her shoulders. 'But why would the Gods want earthly pigs?'

'Because they were earthly Gods. They weren't immortals, you know, except in the sense that They could live forever. But They could be killed. And They were mean bastards, when it came to livestock. They would slaughter half a herd to provide you with a feast. That was all right, that was hospitality. But wars were fought over just one bull, or a boar. Here, at the Bog of Morrigan, there was a big fight over the red pig of Newton.'

Lorraine looked uneasy. 'But the Goddess and the Dagda... Are you saying they were just, well, just like people?'

'Of course They were! Oh, They've changed a bit over the centuries, but you still have to watch Them carefully.' She looked at the clock and slapped her thighs. 'Time to go,' she said.

Doreen's lower lip stuck out and she folded her arms. 'I'm not going.'

Alice heaved herself upright. 'Of course you are.'

'Am not!'

'God's sake, girl, you've got your thermal underwear, what more do you want?'

'It's cold and it's wet and it's dark and I've had enough!'

Alice lumbered through to the kitchen. 'You've got to do it,' she called through, 'I would do it myself, but I'm not so athletic any more.' She came back through with a plastic box and a thermos flask. 'Here,' she said, handing them to Doreen. 'Sandwiches and coffee.'

Doreen reached out mutely and took them. Stupidly, she was touched by Alice's thoughtfulness. Somehow, her resistance vanished. 'Thank you, Alice,' she said.

'Don't thank me,' said Alice, as she put on her coat. 'It was Lorraine that made them.'

Lorraine smiled shyly at Doreen, who said, 'Thank you,' while swearing to herself. Rebellion surged in her breast, but the moment had passed. She resentfully slid her feet into her welly boots.

They hadn't returned to the subject of George's strange dreams – if dreams they were – but Sammy was painfully aware that George's mother had shown similar signs of mental disturbance. He chatted on about Irwin's increasing success in the football team.

'He's not such a ladies' man any more, though,' he chuckled. 'Time was, he could pleasure any woman he wanted and be up at dawn for the fishing.' He looked at George. He wasn't completely sure that he should be talking like this to his grandson. But hell, the boy was grown up now.

He talked about Doreen and her boat on the links. 'And now Dumfry the minister goes down there of an evening to sing psalms under one boat while she favours the local youth under another. A strange alliance.'

He talked about Alma Keivor and her obsession with the Independence movement. 'But I think she understands that until the Dark Isle is financially independent, we can't afford to leave Scotland.'

He went on to talk about the need for a socialist revolution. 'The concept of nationality would then be obsolete...' but got side-tracked into a diatribe against Mr Mor, 'that wheeler-dealer, that bloated capitalist with his pack of running dogs!'

'He keeps dogs?'

'In the metaphorical sense.'

After a few more drinks, he talked about David MacLing MP, the local boy who'd been to Rossmarty Academy. 'Look at him now, Shadow Secretary for Agriculture and Pelagic Fisheries or somesuch. He's done well for himself.' He took another drink and turned his bleary eyes on George. 'Him and me,' he said, 'him and me were that close.' He held up two gnarled fingers. 'He was the farmer's son and I was the ploughman. We'd sit in the barn and I'd tell him about Marx and Lenin, recommended books to him. He was on fire with it. Then I organised a farm-workers union. That showed them.' He looked down at the floor. 'I was sacked.' He sighed. 'And David went to college and climbed the political ladder. Och, he should have stayed on the croft. By god, if he'd stuck to his principles he wouldn't be a part of that lukewarm revisionist crypto-conservative so-called socialist party that makes him dance like an organ-grinder's monkey!'

By and large, Sammy managed to keep the conversation in fairly neutral channels, but as the evening wore on, he grew restless and began to glance at the net, carefully folded on a kitchen chair.

'Grandad, what are you doing with that net?'

Sammy looked at him aggressively. 'What do you think I'm doing with a net? I'm going poaching.'

'I thought you'd stopped that! You've got a job and no-one to look after but yourself. You don't have to.'

'It's a matter of principle, boy.'

'No it's not! You just want to go out there and break the law!'

Sammy chuckled. 'You'll mind Kropotkin? The anarchist?'

George looked at him dubiously and nodded.

'Well, he was passing through a town and found a bunch of peasants burning down a burgher's house. He joined in with great enthusiasm. A friend asked him why they were burning down the house and he said – and I paraphrase – 'Who cares? It's not the end but the method that counts.'

'Eh?'

'The question isn't whether it's right or wrong to break the law. The question is whether the law should be there in the first place. If everyone went out and caught salmon when they wanted, the law would collapse. That's the basic principle of anarchism.'

'But I thought you were a communist!'

'Aye, of course. Does that mean I can't be an anarchist too? I'm not a vegetarian, but I eat carrots and leeks.'

'Grandad! Let it be. I'll buy you a salmon, if you want.'

'Have you got cloth ears boy? It's a matter of principle. Damn it, I don't want the salmon. Don't I see enough of them? I'll give it to Jenny-Pet.'

He put his hands on the table and managed to lift himself out of his chair.

George tried one more time. 'You're not fit to go out poaching. You can barely stand.'

'Och, the fresh air will soon put me right.'

'I'll come with you, then.'

'No, no. I don't want any fellow-travellers on this. It's an anarcho-socialist crusade, and only the one hundred percent committed are allowed.'

He picked up the end of the net and tucked it under his armpit, then turned slowly, winding the fine net round his body. He tucked in the loose end and put on an old tweed jacket.

'Now you just relax. Go to the Arms. Read a book. Don't wait up. I'll be back before morning with a fish or two.'

He slipped a length of broom handle into his pocket and staggered out of the door.

Down at the harbour, Mr Mor supervised while his men removed the salmon tanks from the truck with a forklift and trundled them onto an old flat-bottomed work-boat. When they were all loaded, the truck driver parked at the pier-end and joined the rest on board.

With the round white moon shining down on the sea, the craft chugged out of the harbour mouth into the smooth swell of the sea. Baldy and Mr Mor climbed into the Range Rover to drive back to Redrock.

Far away in Inverness, a squad of police and dog-handlers were sitting in the canteen, waiting for the word. The ferryman at Castleton had been warned to expect a late crossing.

Alice led the way along Kirk Street, keeping a fast pace, as if to keep Doreen from raising more objections. Doreen lagged behind, looking sulky. Lorraine walked beside Alice, awkwardly trying to get information out of her.

'The Sea God would have been important,' she said, 'in a fishing village like this. I'm told that there was a traditional site of worship in Cromness?'

'Well, there's a surprise. You got that out of a book, I suppose?'

'Yes. Mary Birch mentions it in *Worship and Sacrifice in Scotland*.'

Alice smiled sourly. 'That's academics for you. They talk big, but they know bugger all about it.'

'Oh. She says there was a temple to Manannan the Sea God. In the Vennels.'

Alice frowned. 'She has no right telling people these things.'

'So it's true?'

Alice grunted and waved vaguely towards the jumbled houses at the east end of Cromness. 'Yes, yes. Somewhere in that *bourach* over there.'

'Are there any traces left, any remains?'

'Good god, woman, who's talking about remains? He still hangs about that part of town. If you're interested,' she snorted, 'that whole area is sacred to Him. He claimed it for his own after They all arrived here from Ireland – you'll know that story, I suppose. He was bad enough,' she grumbled, 'but the Dagda tried to hold the entire Dark Isle! He still has to be kept in his place. Every now and then Morrigan whips his backside for him, just to teach him manners.'

'They fight among themselves?'

'Constantly at each other's throats. Territorial squabbles mostly. They're latecomers, usurpers. Everything they have, they stole or fought for, or drove someone else out. Long before they arrived, there were sacred places dedicated to the Goddess and the Old Ones. Groves along Ladies Walk, up at the Foxes Dens, in Glen Grian, and dozens of other places like the White Cave of the Suitors. The corners of the bloody fields were holy!'

'So where is Manannan's...'

'In there, in there!' Alice gestured at the Vennels. 'If you can find a way in. I'll have nothing to do with it, myself. I've better things to do.'

Lorraine looked longingly down the Muckle Vennel as they walked by, imagining the archaeological possibilities in the jumble of mis-matched, decrepit houses.

After they passed, Siller, the banker, emerged from the shadows and stepped out of the Muckle Vennel. He came face to face with Doreen. They engaged in an awkward two-step, trying to pass on the narrow pavement, until Doreen resolved the situation by standing still with her arms folded, glaring at Siller until he had edged past her.

Sound and light fell from the door of The Fisherman's Arms as a man opened the door and held it for Miss Semple's crony. A sly smile was on the man's face as he watched Ellen pass through the door into the bar room. Twangy guitar music flooded out and a woman's voice began to sing a melancholy Country and Western song, then the door swung closed.

Alice and Lorraine were waiting at the end of the street. Doreen deliberately took her time, but they were talking together and barely noticed her reluctant arrival.

When they reached the edge of Cromness, the moon was well above the horizon, laying a silver track across the sea. Two figures ahead of them were walking along the Suitor road, up past the Hog Graveyard.

Doreen noted them as strangers. Holidaymakers – though they were walking at a strangely businesslike pace.

There was a wind hushing in the trees further up the hillside as they turned onto the beach path. Alice was leading the way, with Lorraine trying to keep beside her on the narrow path while talking about Gaelic inheritance customs.

Doreen walked well behind, but the light breeze brought her most of the conversation.

'...of course there was inheritance by the male line as well as the female. It's only that the female line was preferred – and the more easily followed, of course. As you pointed out, there was never any doubt who the mother was.'

'Yes, yes,' said Alice impatiently. 'Everyone knows that. But what about customs that lasted into historical times? Do they have any legal force?'

'Not usually. Though the laws of inheritance are fairly universal. I suppose heritable succession would remain legally unassailable.'

Alice grunted. 'You've got the hang of the legal style, anyway. Could be useful.' She reached out and plucked some pale flowers. 'Witches Eye. Doreen!' She stopped and waited for Doreen to catch up. 'Here you are.'

Doreen reluctantly took the flower heads and popped one into her mouth. 'Alice, I don't know if there's any point.'

'Eh? It works, doesn't it?'

'Well, yes...' she thought about the chaotic images that usually floated through her mind after eating the flowers.

'Well, then!' Alice scowled at her. 'We need a Seeing. For God's sake, girl, there's Christ knows what going on in the town. There's someone watching, I can feel it, someone with little spider legs for a mind, trying to catch us all, someone with bad intent. There may be dozens of them out there watching.' Her voice rose, her eyes rolled in their sockets. 'Then Morrigan may have to come – Goddess as the black crow woman – and pick white their red bones!'

Her voice was loud and shrill, and a shiver ran down Doreen's spine. Lorraine had backed a pace, and they both watched Alice's face as her eyes moved wildly, as if trying to look inside herself.

Alice coughed, blinked a few times, then looked at Doreen. 'And we don't want that to happen, do we?'

Doreen swallowed. 'But Alice, I'm not really sure. What if I can't do it any more. Do people lose the power?'

Alice scowled at her. 'Not you, Doreen. If there's anyone in the Dark Isle can See as well as I could, it's you.' She stripped another handful of flowers from the plant and handed them to Doreen.

And as they walked along the path, Doreen popped flower after flower into her mouth, knowing it wouldn't do any good. She wouldn't See anything at all but swirling plant-shapes and distorted animals. She couldn't give that as an answer. What rigmarole was she going to have to make up this time?

On the path ahead, Alice and Lorraine were discussing academic qualifications. The only merit in them, according to Alice, was that people tended to believe what you said, just because you had the certificate.

Out at sea by the fish farm, a motor could be heard faintly as a boat sailed across the silver track of the moon. Its angular black shape was distinctive. Mr Mor's boat. The Whistler Buoy blinked, blinked again. The boat's masthead light shone, a red spark against the sky. Doreen felt the sound coming to her in waves as the flowers edged their dry way down her throat.

Ahead, the black mass of Clach Mor, the Big Rock, showed against the hillside. The path turned down on to the beach, then disappeared. Alice and Lorraine crunched on across the shingle, Doreen followed.

In The Fisherman's Arms the country singer, accompanied by a drum machine and a man with a steel guitar, bemoaned her fate. It appeared that she was unable to find a man to match her 'dee-zi-urs.' Which inevitably rhymed with 'burning fie-urs.'

At the tables near the small stage, men watched her shapely figure and idly wondered how the conflagration of their sexual inclinations would measure up to the 'burning fires' of her simulated passion, and the more realistic of them accepted that they would never find out.

Big Irwin, looking morose, sat in a corner with the Nailer and Aristide Coupar, playing cards. Aristide and the Nailer were arguing over who was going to win the Nerval trophy for best lobster pair. Irwin studied his cards with little interest and did not join in the banter.

The Major stood at the bar. 'A gin and tonic and a whisky and Crabbe's,' he shouted over the whining of the steel guitar.

'You got a cold?' asked the barman as he pressed a glass to the optic.

'No!'

'It's a funny drink,' continued the barman. 'You'd be surprised how many people drink it.' He tipped in a measure of green ginger wine. 'Thing is, no-one drinks it unless they've got a cold.'

'Is that what you tell them?'

The barman opened a small bottle of tonic water. 'Who?'

'All the other people that drink it.'

'Yes. Yes I do. Never ceases to amaze me.'

Ellen, sitting at a table near the fire, watched the Major as he paid for the drinks and turned from the bar. He was a little old, but quite the gentleman, holding the door for her and courteously asking if he might buy her a drink. He probably had designs on her. Wanted her body, as like as not. Ellen was no longer young as the world measures these things, but she did occasionally indulge in a small affair of the heart. She was, after all, a widow, more or less, and occasional carnal frivolity, as long as it was not too blatant, was not held against her.

This frivolity usually took place on a patch of grass behind the Old Jail, and not just to avoid the unwelcome attention of her neighbours. When the tide was full, the waves broke on the sea-wall nearby, their sound rushing through her like liquid fire as the frivolity reached its consummation – and, incidentally, drowning any involuntary noises. Tonight there was a full moon, which meant the tide would be in around midnight. As long as the Major did not drink too industriously, he should be both amenable and capable by then.

'Your drink, Ellen.' The Major handed the gin to her with a charming smile. Well, it was obviously meant to be charming. She gave him the benefit of the doubt and smiled back. He even poured the tonic into her glass. What an attentive man.

Ellen was pleased to be sharing a table with the Major. Quite apart from his amatory possibilities, she wanted to know more about him. He had been in the town for nearly a year and had not yet featured in any local gossip.

'You know the West Coast, do you not?' she began. 'You must know the MacDonalds, at Gairloch?'

'Possibly,' he replied, sipping his drink. 'But there are so many MacDonalds. MacLeans, too. I remember going through the phone book once, trying to find a Mr MacLean who was a farmer. Hundreds of them. And right at the end of the list I found a most unusual name. MacLing. A farmer near here, I believe.'

'MacLing? The must be David MacLing's father. You know, David is Minister for Shell Fisheries and Fishing and... and other things to do with the sea.'

The Major looked amazed. 'Not that MacLing! Well, well. There's a successful man, and no mistake.'

'I was at school with him,' Ellen said smugly. 'Wee fat nyaff he was, but look at him now.'

'At school? With David MacLing? Surely not. He must be much older than you.'

Ellen blushed. 'He was in sixth year when I was in first year,' she lied.

The Major looked at her dubiously. 'Well, I must take your word, I suppose, but it seems scarcely possible.'

Ellen looked at him shyly and lowered her eyelashes while thrusting her bosom out, a most unlikely set of actions, and almost wholly involuntary.

'Do tell me what he was like at school,' the Major continued. 'Popular, was he?'

'Popular? You must be joking. The strangest cratur you could imagine. No friends, you know, not one. A scrawny wee bugger he was, no good at sports at all – spent all his time with his nose in a book – him and his friends. There was a whole bunch of them, a sort of gang you would say, only they didn't do much together except talk and read. Politics and things like that. The headmaster encouraged them. Gave them books of his own to read – Plato and suchlike. Christ, you would think they had nothing better to do. I told him straight, "David MacLing," I said, "If you don't take your nose out of that books you'll never make anything of yourself." Did he listen? Took not a blind bit of notice.'

The Major sipped his drink frugally. Ellen chattered on about the MacLings, about his schoolmates, about his friends, or lack of them, as the fancy took her. As the evening progressed, the Major refilled her glass as necessary, laughed when it seemed proper and prompted her occasionally with a leading question. He moved closer and inclined his body towards her. Ellen chattered on, smugly aware that she had made a conquest. In the Major's breast pocket, a small tape recorder whirred quietly, the sound inaudible among the incessant chatter from nearby tables and the country singer's whine.

Rev Dumfry sat in his car in a field near the farm. There were hundreds of cars parked in the field, as well as assorted buses and vans. A hundred yards away, the side doorway to the barn was outlined in bright lights. There was a glowing sign above it, with strobe lights bringing it to juddering life: a picture of a train driving across the night sky with the words Second Tribal Railroad along its carriages. Dozens of people were queuing at the door, more were making their way up the road and across the fields. Even at this distance, the beat of the music could be felt as well as heard.

Dumfry gathered his strength as he had learnt to do when under the boat with Doreen. We have the strength if we need it, he reminded himself as he opened the door and walked round to the boot. He removed the carrier bag of clothes and climbed into the back seat of the car, where he had more room. He folded his jacket, awkwardly slipped out of his trousers, took off his shirt and finally, reluctantly, his dog-collar. Then he put on the flared trousers and turtle-neck sweater.

Feeling ready to fade into the crowd, he locked the car and made his way down to the barn.

The music grew louder as he approached. The sweet smell of turnips from a nearby field mingled with the scent of perfumes, incense and sweat as warm moist air boiled out of the doorway. He surreptitiously studied the people in the queue. The young woman in front of him had long golden plaits, but her head was shaved from the nape of her neck to her earlobes. The young man beside her had painted his face entirely blue and his eyes were shockingly mobile in the painted mask. His hands danced and stuttered in time to the music. There was a sweet smell from the couple beyond them, who were smoking. Dumfry suspected they were smoking drugs, but quelled his disapproval by reminding himself that he was here to observe and learn.

The queue moved along and new arrivals joined the line behind him. He felt an elevation of his spirit, as he realised that no-one had noticed anything odd about him. Somewhere deep inside he had feared that he would be recognised as an interloper, with all that that implied. But he was just one of the crowd, another person at this event. He found himself curious to find out what was happening inside, what the flashing lights were, what people were doing. He was curious also to find out what part he himself might take in the event. Curious and very nervous. What might he find himself capable of?

Lord, give me strength to resist temptation, he prayed, then surrendered all his worries.

'Hey, man! Good duds.'

Suddenly he was at the head of the queue and a massively muscled young man with a pigtail and a beaming smile was speaking to him.

'I beg your pardon?'

'Good duds, man.'

'Ah, I see. Thank you. Might I purchase a ticket, please?'

'Ha, ha, ha! You've even got the style to go with it!' He grabbed Dumfry's hand and smacked a rubber pad down on it. There was now a small purple steam train on the back of Dumfry's hand. 'That's twenty quid, please.'

Dumfry paid up while the young man chuckled and his hands did a strange hand-dance.

'Cheers, man.' He clenched a fist in the air between them. 'Yowser! That is one weird get-up. Man, you look like a minister on a night out! Have a good time now!' He leant forward and spoke in a lower voice. 'Eckies?'

'Hm?'

'E's?'

Dumfry looked back at him blankly. 'Pardon?'

'Eckies? Blotting paper? Speed?'

This was a new language. Dumfry was bewildered. Remembering his earlier success, he held up two fingers in a V. 'Peace, man,' he said.

The ticket man grinned. 'Jesus, you're a card all right. Stay cool.' He turned to the next in line and Dumfry escaped into the barn, where he wandered in bewilderment among strange tribal things happening to the accompaniment of driving rhythms and flashing lights.

Thwarted in his desire to attend the rave in Rossmarty, Fergus MacFarquhar moodily wandered along Kirk Street. Cromness was dead at this time of night. Some windows shone with light, but from the empty ones the dark windows seemed to stare out hopelessly. There were quite a few empty ones. Fergus shivered.

The full moon was rising over the crooked roofs of the Vennels. From The Fisherman's Arms came the sound of sad country music. The street was empty.

Fergus swore to himself. 'Heck! Damn the minister!'

In a moment of pique and bravado, he turned up the cobbled street known as the Waye. On the brow of the hill, past the low houses, lay the graveyard. The statue of Hugh Chandler stood on its huge pillar, gleaming in the moonlight. And opposite the graveyard gate was a dark opening amongst the trees and bushes. The Ladies Walk, leading to the Foxes Dens.

He stood on the road for a minute or two, nervously eyeing the dark path through the bushes. There was a full moon and few clouds, but the light only seemed to make the shadows darker.

There were rumours about the Foxes Dens. Dark rumours. In fact, so dark that he'd never had the nerve to go in there after nightfall. But Donnie MacLean had dropped some broad hints. He had suggested the Brotherhood were looking for new acolytes and that if Fergus should turn up one night, he would not be turned away.

Fergus braced himself. After all, it would just be a bunch of guys having a laugh. He stepped into the inky shadow of the path, starting nervously at every stray sound. His breath seemed to rasp loudly, though he tried to suppress it and his heart thudded painfully in his chest. It was almost a relief when several hands took hold of him, threw him to the ground and tied an old sack round his head.

```
Dear Sammy,

       It was good to hear from you after so long. Yes, I am
well, thank you, and I look forward to visiting the North
soon to open the Dark Isle Show. I do not think it would
be advisable for me to visit you at present - the current
```

trend in the Party is against any connection with left-wing politics and, this close to an election, I am afraid the papers would make a meal of it. Your name is still remembered in some quarters! I hope you understand.

My secretary has searched out the information you asked for. Curiously enough, we already had some information about your man. We had no joy with his name, which is most likely a pseudonym, so we had to trace the connections back from Cromness Firth Salmon Farming and Redrock Estate. As you will see, there is an extensive web of connected companies and it was very difficult to trace the actual owner. Perhaps he just wants to avoid the attentions of the taxman, but like you, I suspect he has some dark secrets.

I have appended a list of the societies and charities to which these companies make donations. Some of them are quite surprising. There are no donations to the major political parties, but a sizeable contribution to the Dark Isle Independence Group, chaired by a Mrs Alma Keivor.

I hope this is of some use to you. I am intrigued to know what it is all about, and I hope you can tell me some day.

Best wishes, David MacLing

In The Fisherman's Arms, the country and western singer was singing a sad song. Another sad song. This one was about an orphan.

Almost everyone in the Arms seemed to find the music a stimulating background. They chattered and laughed and drank and played dominoes or cards. But Big Irwin's face was getting longer and longer. He looked over at the singer and sighed.

'I said, it's your deal, Irwin!'

The Nailer was holding out the pack of cards.

'Oh. Aye.' Irwin took them and shuffled slowly.

'God's sake, man,' said Aristide Coupar, 'you've a face on you like a bulldog that's swallowed a wasp. Can you not look a bitty more cheerful?'

Irwin tried a smile as he cut the pack. The other two shook their heads sadly.

'I wouldn't bother, Irwin. Just deal.'

A few tables away, the Major was leaning towards Ellen with interest as she retrieved thirty-year-old gossip from her archives.

'Sammy and David MacLing used to spend hours in the barn, talking. He was always workshy, that Sammy Poach. If he could find a warm place out of sight he'd be happy to sit there with a book all afternoon. Sleeping, as like as not. If he could be preaching revolution to the farmer's son, well, so much the better. He started a farm workers' union, you know, just stirring up trouble. The farmer fired him, of course. Sammy only got what was coming to him, I reckon. Damned communist nonsense.'

'And David...?'

'He ate it all up, hook, line and sinker. He used to talk about it in school. Set up a study group, and they read all sorts of Red propaganda. Marx and Mao Tse Tung and Plato. I told him he'd never amount to anything if he listened to that sort of shite. When he went off to study Law he was half brainwashed already. That Sammy has a lot to answer for! I never did like him. And his daughter... well!' She leaned over towards the Major and spoke quietly. 'She got herself in the Family Way.'

'Not married, I suppose.'

'Of course not!'

'Tut tut. But David MacLing was brainwashed by Sammy, you say.'

Ellen pursed her lips. 'Then he fell in with a bad lot at university. Politics. Demonstrations. That sort of thing. I could have told him that sort of carry-on would get him nowhere.'

'It must have been a surprise when he stood for parliament.'

Ellen bridled. 'Not a bit of it! Always had ideas above himself, the wee fat nyaff.'

'And now he's an MP.'

'But he'll not rise. You mark my words. He's in a dead-end there. No wife, you see. The voters don't like an MP without a wife to stand behind him. I could have told him that.'

The Major nodded. 'Edward Heath, for instance,' he said.

'Just my point!'

'And he never had a girlfriend?'

'I wouldn't say that.' Ellen did something strange with her face and upper body. In another woman, it might have been a simper. 'I think he was sweet on me at one time.' She regained her critical demeanour. 'But I wouldn't have anything to do with him. A woman likes a reliable man...'

She tailed off awkwardly, thinking of her own long-absent husband.

The Major sensed the break in her flow of reminiscence and gossip. 'Let me get you another drink,' he suggested.

At the bar, a dapper man with a little curled moustache held up his hand.

'Mister Barman!' He had a trace of a French accent.

'Ah. Monsieur Le Placs.'

'We had a small wager, did we not? You said that Irwin would score a hat-trick against Boblair United, while I...'

'You said that Cromness would just hold them to a two-goal draw.' The barman looked sourly at the surgeon as he handed a wad of notes to him. 'That's not good crack, you know, winning money betting against your local team.'

M Le Placs nodded. 'That is true.' On the bar there was a collecting box for the Swimming Pool Appeal. He put half of the notes into the box. 'Perhaps that will pacify the gods of luck.'

'What about the rest?'

'The rest I will spend on drink. That will benefit the local business community, will it not? A Black Bog whisky for me – and for you, Jimmy?'

Jimmy Bervie accepted with a broad smile. He leant against the bar, sipping the whisky and watching the crowd. It was almost as good as the sand-garden for studying the state of the universe. There was a depression over the table where Irwin sat, and a thick knot of deviousness at Ellen's table, where the Major was standing and leaning towards her. Ellen was smiling up at him, Jimmy noted. Best avoid the Old Jail on the way home. He continued his survey of the room.

From the country and western singer flowed a miasma of lyrical melancholy, with a core of genuine longing. Her gaze drifted over the audience, lingering now and then on Irwin. Over the rest of the room hung a fog of conviviality punctuated with nervous laughter that suggested that all was not wholly well with the community. The particular edge to the laughter suggested a disturbance of the deep structures of reality, while the pitch of the voices located the disturbance in the mythic realm. Which was annoying, because Irwin's gloom suggested the opposite, an entirely physical disarrangement. Jimmy frowned in perplexity.

Beneath the overlay of voices and music, the tapping of feet on the floor was somewhat hesitant – more of a shuffle than a distinct beat. That normally indicated some major act of criminality. Perhaps one of the local farmers was feeding his bull steroids in preparation for the Dark Isle Show. Or maybe some of the local lads were trying to grow marijuana again. Silly boys. It never came to anything. The weather was too unsettled.

He put his drink to one side and leant over the bar to pick up the mop. As the singer agonised over the question of divorce, separation or just cheating, Jimmy waltzed among the tables with the mop in his arms. His kilt swung, the sequins on his waistcoat glittered, his bald head gleamed in the lights, his wellies squeaked on the floor. The crowd cheered, the nervous overtones gone from their voices. Feet stamped in rhythm.

'It's Fred and Ginger!'

'Go on yersel!'

As everyone else watched Jimmy and the Mop, Irwin stared into the bottom of his glass and found no comfort there.

A bonfire blazed in the clearing and the firelight flickered on the smooth grey trunks of the beech trees. Fergus tried to stand tall as he faced the dark, hooded figure in front of him.

'Do you, Fergus, petition to join the Ancient Brotherhood of Cromm Cruach?'

Fergus recognised the voice coming from inside the dark cowl. It was Bad Bastard, the butcher's apprentice. His bullet head sat on a neck as thick as a bull's. He was muscled like a bull too, and looked as if he should be for sale in the butcher's shop, instead of working there. The other figures under the ring of tall beech trees were in hooded robes too, but he could pretty well guess who most of them were.

'Yes,' he replied. 'I, Fergus, do humbly petition to join the Ancient Brotherhood of Cromm Cruach.' What a daft way to do things. He managed to say the words without giggling, but he couldn't suppress a small smile.

'Is there one among the Brotherhood who will sponsor this supplicant?'

Donnie MacLean's voice spoke. 'I will sponsor him right readily.'

Bad spoke again. 'And do you, Fergus, undertake to pass through the ordeal, that you might be measured in a true measure by the Brotherhood?'

'I do.'

Bad held his arms up. 'Brothers, he is willing!' He stepped forwards and his voice had a hard edge. 'Right, Fergus. Clothes off.'

'What?'

'Brothers, he is not willing!' The dark figures that stood in a circle around him took a pace forwards. 'And he honour not his undertaking,' continued Bad, 'he shall have his privy member cut off and it shall be cast among the embers of the sacred fire!'

'All right, all right!' cried Fergus in panic, remembering rumours of how Bad had got his nickname. The details were unclear, but it was something to do with his butcher's knives.

Quickly he removed his clothes until he stood there wearing only his underpants.

'Brothers!' began Bad. 'He does not...'

'All right! All right!' In a moment, Fergus stood there, blushing and naked, his hands held limply in front of his genitals.

'Shall we accept his petition, Brothers?'

'Yea!' The hooded figures all spoke in unison.

'Shall he be tested?'

'Yea!'

'Shall he therefore be anointed?'

'Yea!'

'Then let the Cup Bearer bring the sacred oil to me!'

A dark figure brought a tin can from beside the fire. It had a paint brush in it. It smelled like warm lard. He handed it to Bad.

'Lie him on the holy ground.'

Four cowled figures took Fergus by the arms and legs, threw him to the ground and held him there, spreadeagled.

Bad stood over him, with the greasy brush held up to the sky.

'Man be-cromness miraftan vaghttike urd didam! Mo'allem-e-ma migoft – Ba inke in asb khub bashad man nemitavanam savar-e-an beshavam –'

He leant down and smeared the warm lard over Fergus's genitals, working it well in.

Fergus struggled and swore, but he was firmly held.

Bad then poured the rest of the semi-liquid lard onto his stomach. The thick greasy stuff ran down his sides, puddling beneath the small of his back. Fergus groaned in disgust.

'Now is the time for the revealing,' said Bad. Even in his present humiliated state, Fergus found the words ridiculous. Bad didn't speak like that. Someone else had written those words for him.

Fergus was pulled up and brought close to the fire. There was a white sheet there, on which he was made to sit.

Bad stood on the opposite side of the fire. He raised both hands to the sky and glared at Fergus. Firelight flickered on the cowl and his little eyes glinted. 'Now it's time for the ordeal.'

Fergus stared at him, aghast. 'You mean, that wasn't the ordeal?'

Bad sneered and smiled at the same time. 'Naw. That was just to get you in the mood.'

Another voice came from nearby. 'Now you must tell us a story.'

'What? I don't believe this. Jesus, why didn't you just ask?'

'Not just any story.' The voice paused. 'It has to be something you've never told anyone before. Something so embarrassing that you don't want anyone to know about it.'

'But...'

'Magar inke beman haghighat ra beguid beshoma komak nemikonan!'

Bad was speaking in someone else's words again. He began to pour various powders into the fire. Scented smoke drifted up.

'Was that Gaelic?' whispered Fergus to the figure to his left.

'Persian.' The whisper came in Donny MacLean's voice.

'Why?'

Donny coughed. 'No-one knows any Gaelic,' he mumbled.

'What does it mean?'

'The first one means, I was going to Cromness when I met a horse. My teacher told me, This is a fine horse but I cannot ride it.' Fergus looked at him in bafflement. 'It's from a phrasebook,' mumbled Donny.

'And the other bit, just now?'

'Oh that's serious. It means, If you don't tell the truth you're in big trouble.'

Fergus glanced at the blocky figure of Bad Bastard strewing incense on the bonfire. 'Look,' he said, 'do I have to do this?'

'Oh yes. Though Bad will be delighted if you don't. Then he gets to say, Brothers, his privy member will be cut off and cast...'

A final handful of powder was thrown on the fire. Bad sat down.

'Now listen and hear and attend,' he called in his ritual voice, 'O best beloved,' he mumbled, 'to the Tale of Fergus.'

Donny stood up. 'And, that no-one might know who is telling this tale, he will be hoodwinked, and made invisible.' He pulled a sack down loosely over Fergus's head.

To his surprise, Fergus felt much safer under the sack. He racked his brains for a story that was embarrassing enough to fit the bill without being completely mortifying. But only one incident would come to mind.

He swallowed. 'There was a girl,' he said, 'Who shall be nameless.'

'Magar inke beman haghighat...' began Bad, in a threatening tone.

'All right! It was Jill.' There was a waiting sort of silence. 'Jill Middleton.'

'Aha!' said Bad. 'The Laird's daughter! Aiming high, were we?'

There was a grumble of complaint at Bad's interruption. Fergus was relieved to see that he was not in complete control of the group.

With much halting, he began his story.

'It was the summer holidays and I wanted to get a job somewhere, so I could get out of Cromness. You know what it's like. But my mum wouldn't hear of it. I think she wants me to die without leaving the Dark Isle. But her sister runs a hotel in the south of England, just a wee one, and she reckoned that Bournemouth was safe enough, so I got sent down to stay for the summer and work on the front desk. My mum said it would give me experience. She wants me to work in the bank with Mr Siller. Yeugh.'

Several people called from around him, their voices muffled through the sackcloth. 'Get on with it!'

'Okay, okay. Well my mum had to make a big deal of it – me going away from home for the first time. We got a special Indian meal from the carry-out before I left and she kept forcing more food on me. She said, "If you're full up, you won't have to buy anything at the service stations." She thinks everyone south of Inverness is a crook. "If you have to buy anything, make sure you count your change." She wouldn't stop giving me stupid advice. As if she knows! In the car, all the way through to Inverness she told me things to watch out for in London. She warned me about drugs, religious cults, strange men, strange women, pickpockets, skinheads, foreigners. By the time we got to Inverness, I was fair sick of it. So was Dad. "And don't come back pregnant," he said when I was climbing into the bus. Mum just glared at him.

'The bus was a fancy one with a big TV screen up front so they can show a video as you drive along. I got a window seat, and I was trying to make out that I couldn't hear my mother shouting more instructions at me through the window when I saw Jill getting on the bus and waving goodbye to her parents. I don't know if you all know Jill? Okay, I suppose you do. Anyway, she's kind of. She's.'

'She's a cracker!'

'Aye. Right. She's real good looking, but, come on, she's sort of in another world. Behaves like it, anyway. Difficult to talk to, you know? I didn't really know her.

'Anyway, you know what she's usually like. But when her parents drove off she looked a bit nervous, you know, and I kind of waved to her. She headed straight up the aisle and asked if she could sit beside me. Just as the bus started moving, Dad knocked on the window and winked at me. I think she saw, but she didn't say anything.

'So she asked me what I was doing and I told her and then I asked her and she said she was going to be staying with relatives in Camberwell, studying, and then going off to college in the autumn.

'Then I ran out of things to say so I asked her what she would be studying and she went into this long ramble about poetry and literature and romance in the modern novel until I was sorry I'd asked. But she kept looking at me as she was talking and I kept nodding. She's got brown eyes. And she was very close. There's not much room in those seats. I was kind of hypnotised, you know?

'But then she brought out a book from her bag. It was called Dark Passion or something like that. I said it looked like it was a romantic novel. I couldn't think of anything else to say. She looked a bit offended and lectured me for a bit about romance and realism and I agreed with her and eventually she opened her book and I said I was going to watch the film. It was already running, and it was a horror movie. She kind of sneered at it, and I suppose it wasn't much good, but it looked better than another hundred miles of modern literature, so I pulled down the little headphones and put them on.

'It really wasn't that bad, once you got into it. Exciting. You could never tell which way it was going next. My stomach was kind of sore, from the Indian food I think, but I ignored it and watched the film. It had a quiet bit in the middle when the hero was romancing the heroine, even though he knows about the terrible beast that is rumoured to haunt her family. There's that kind of music you know, flowery, so that you know that they like each other. And just when it looks as if they're going to do the business, you know, get into bed and that, the Beast turns up. Gave you quite a jolt.

'Then the hero has to fight the Beast, and it's just about there that my stomach acts up again, only worse. Jill is deep in her book so I turn away and rub my stomach and it helps. It hurts less. Except, that wasn't all. Just as the hero defeats the Beast, I feel this wind coming. You know what I mean? A really big fart, and I just can't do anything about it.

'The hero and the heroine are congratulating each other now and falling down onto the bearskin rug in the ancestral hall in front of the ancestral fire and their clothes are coming off to romantic background music and I am in agony at keeping the wind in.

'So they're kissing and things like that on the rug when the music begins to change, and it starts to sound menacing and then the camera shows the pool beneath the bridge and the wounded Beast is crawling from it. Then I knew that I still had a chance. I gritted my teeth and clenched my bum while the Were-Beast came across the lawn. The orchestra was winding itself up all this time, and first you see the wild goings-on on the rug and then you see the wounded Beast, shambling up the road, bent on vengeance.

'Then the Were-Beast comes into the house and the music gets more menacing. The man and the woman are naked now and you can even see a bit of her breast before he moves over her and his shoulder hides it. Now the Beast is in the corridor and the music is getting louder too.

'The man and the woman were getting really into it now, but all the time they were at it, the Beast was stalking up on them, only they were too busy to notice. The Beast got closer and closer and the music got louder and I managed to hang on, though it was difficult by now. Then at last the heroine opened her eyes then opened her mouth wide and screamed as she saw the Beast looming over them, then lunging forward and that was when the music went completely bananas, really, really loud!

'And I relaxed everything and let the wind go. I didn't care about the man and the woman, I just wanted the Beast to keep on battering them until I was finished farting. What a relief. They killed the Beast at last, and the music went quiet again, but I'd finished by then. I sat back in my seat and relaxed. Everything had ended happily.

'Then I looked around at Jill. She was sitting with her back to me, leaning out into the aisle, looking at her book. Her face was bright pink. I remember wondering if it was because the bus was so warm.

'Then the credits started to roll and I reached up to pull off the headphones. Oh Christ, I thought, the headphones. When I took them off I could hear people laughing and there was a choking noise from the seat in front.

'For a moment I thought maybe I got away with it, maybe no-one noticed.

'Then the man in the seat in front turned round. His face was red and he was laughing and he said, "Jings fella, that wis a real bobby dazzler!" And all I could do was sit there in the bus, all the way to London.'

There was a roar of appreciation and the sack was whipped from Fergus's head. Someone whacked him on the shoulder. 'Good one!'

Bad raised his arms for silence. 'What say the Brothers of Cromm Cruach? Shall he be admitted, yea or nay?'

All the voices called out. 'Yea!'

'Right. He is now admitted as a Brother. Let us then leave this sacred grove, but don't forget, next time we're going to have the big Ceremony and I expect everyone to be here, right? No excuses. This is the big one. After the Ceremony, Brother Fergus will receive his name. Until then, he is the Brother without a name.'

Sammy Poach strode along the Shore Road. He liked striding. It was just that he couldn't do it very much any more. He was old, but that was a minor matter. In order to stride properly, you needed a good reason to be moving, you needed a Cause. And tonight he had that, all right. Several nips of whisky helped with the stride too, but it was mainly the Cause.

There was something basically untrustworthy about Mr Mor, and that was what Sammy was reacting to. In many ways the man was no worse than any other bloated unprincipled capitalist. He had, after all, brought employment to the area – which it sorely needed. Sammy glanced at the houses along the sea front. Nearly half of them empty or holiday cottages, which just about came to the same thing. Cromness was almost depopulated for lack of employment.

So Mr Mor had done some good. Not just the salmon farm, but also the potato processing plant at Castleton, the fleet of refrigerated trucks so that herring could be landed at Cromness, the new fabricating works at the Boblair Smithy, and other enterprises too. What made Sammy uneasy was that they were all run by dummy corporations owned by subsidiary companies of other companies owned by that gollachan.

So why was he hiding his ownership? And what about all these causes, some good, some simply daft, that he was anonymously donating to? It didn't fit with the bloated capitalist stereotype. The gollachan Mor was a slippery customer. As slippery as his damned salmon.

And that was another thing that annoyed Sammy. Why did he sell the sea-trout caught in his nets, but not the salmon? It made no sense.

As he stepped off the road onto the Suitor's path, he paused. There was a scent of perfume among the bushes. A woman had passed this way not long ago. The net, wrapped round his body, was well hidden, but still, he didn't want witnesses.

He slipped silently along until the surrounding bushes opened out onto the beach. Under the light of the full moon, he could see all the way out to the headland of the South Suitor. There were three figures on the path, a quarter of a mile ahead. He swore. One was very large and lumbered along distinctively. Alice. One of the others must be Doreen. They'd be doing something arcane out at the cave. He snorted. They thought it was a secret, but he knew what they got up to. More or less.

So he couldn't go that way. No telling how long they'd be. He reached out a small flask from his hip pocket and took a glug as he stood and thought. Up the Suitor, that was the answer, then down the Hundred and One Steps. He hadn't fished there in twenty years.

He walked softly along the path then turned up the hill to the Hog Graveyard. He slinked around the fence, keeping in the shadow of the yew trees and the statuary. Once on the road, he kept to the shady side and began to climb the long steep hill to the Suitor.

As he gained the hilltop, Sammy Poach relaxed. That was the worst of it over. He stopped to catch his breath and swallowed a drop more whisky before taking the road towards the old gun emplacements. From there he could climb the long flights of concrete steps down to the beach. No-one would be up here at this time of night and there wasn't a building for a mile. Except the old Coastguard Station beside the road fifty yards ahead. He could see the white-painted construction clearly in the moonlight. Sammy stepped forwards.

There was a brief flicker of light through the windows.

Sammy stopped. 'Damnation!' he hissed.

Nothing else happened. A flicker of moonlight? No, it was definitely inside. And the Coastguard Station commanded a view of the top of the steps. What was going on? The place hadn't been used for years.

He slipped off the road and crawled through the rustling heather up to the building. He stopped, waiting for his breathing to slow down, and listened. No sound. He slowly raised himself until he could just see into the building.

There was an orange glow – that was a cigarette – and a faint greenish glow. He moved to one side. The dark figure of a man had been hiding the source of the green light. A radar screen. There was a murmur of voices. The man's head turned and Sammy could make out the silhouette of another figure standing by the wide window. A figure with long hair and breasts. The woman was scanning the sea with a large pair of binoculars. She turned to the man and said a few words. He raised a radio handset to his ear and spoke into it.

Sammy eased himself down and rested. His heart was thumping. He watched the skyline nervously, feeling conspicuous against the white boards. What was going on? They certainly weren't coastguards, in there with the lights off. They couldn't be Mr Mor's people could they? Surely not. He crawled back up the slope then turned, looking out to sea. Far out, there were lights moving. Fishing boats, freight carriers, oil tankers. Another light was moving out from the Cromness Firth past the Whistler Buoy.

He took another swig of whisky as he sat and thought. He could go home. No. Dammit, the whisky was keeping him warm, and he was out here on the moors already. Why not poach that gollachan Mor's home waters? The salmon and sea trout caught in the Cromness nets were sold to the fishmonger but no-one saw any of the salmon caught round the other side of the Suitor, on the south side of the Dark Isle. Something special about these salmon, was there? Sammy grinned. In that case, let's take one of the gollachan's special fish.

He set off round the hill towards the Redrock Estate. It was a mile or two, but he could still get there, do the deed and get back before dawn.

There was a chilly breeze off the water. The silk underwear kept her body warm, but Doreen could feel it on her face and hands. The bitter taste of the Witches Eye seemed to be spreading down her throat, like slow green ice. She shivered. The cold didn't seem to affect Alice and Lorraine. They were a few steps ahead of her, their feet crunching on the shingle. She could barely make out what they were saying, though she could tell from the crunching sounds just how many stones lay under each foot. She ran a few steps to catch up.

'We watch the bloodlines carefully,' said Alice. 'You can tell who is going to be Sensitive by the line she comes from.'

'What about the men?'

Alice looked grimly at Lorraine. 'What about them?'

Lorraine was flustered. 'You've been talking about women all this time but aren't there men with talents? Men who are of the Celtic race?'

Alice grunted. 'Of course there are. And if his mother is from hereabouts, we know where we are: this is a man with the genuine Celtic blood in his veins. But if he marries outside of the Dark Isle that's the end of the line. After all, it's not our job to watch over the marriage bed. The children could be the milkman's, for god's sake.'

They detoured down towards the sea to get past an outcrop of rock. Lorraine phrased another question.

'Doesn't that mean that you lose an awful lot of, well, allies? You know, there must be people that are interested...'

'Interested? What the hell has that to do with it? Listen,' Alice stumped along angrily. 'The child of any woman from the Dark Isle belongs here. The child of any other woman is of uncertain lineage.'

The cliffs were encroaching on the shore now, though there was still a wide beach. Moonlight glimmered on the waves that hissed as they broke on the shingle.

'What did I tell you?' Doreen butted in. 'Listen to her! She's a racist. What does it matter who your parents are? If you're brought up in the tradition, you become a part of it, no matter who your parents are.'

Alice turned and looked at Doreen's flushed face, her bright eyes. 'So your mother's not important?'

'I didn't say that! She carries the tradition, passes it on, but she doesn't pass it to you in the womb.' Her head felt as if it were wheeling slowly, like the night sky rotating round the pole star. Slowly but unstoppably.

Alice opened her mouth to reply, but Doreen continued, reflectively.

'On the other hand, she does pass on other things. Hormones and chemicals pass through the placenta. And this flow of hormones is affected by the mother's disposition and her emotions, perhaps even by her thoughts. Hormones affect the thought processes. Perhaps thought processes also affect the hormones?' She nodded. 'Yes, there are influences of some sort.'

Alice leaned towards Lorraine and smiled grimly. 'The Witches Eye,' she said. 'It's talking.'

They had reached an outcrop of rock which ran from the cliff right down to the sea edge. Doreen began to climb without breaking the flow of her discourse. 'And of course hormones affect the way the brain works. A hint of the right chemical at the right time could give the developing brain the nudge it needs, creating a predisposition to Seeing or a tendency to respond to nature in such a way that it becomes an uplifting or transcendent experience. A few molecules of the right chemical could create a predilection to see the world in terms of unifying processes.'

She reached the top of the rocky ridge and stopped. Behind her, Lorraine helped Alice up by an easier route. Doreen stood there with one hand raised, speaking to the empty beach ahead. 'The Mind is a continuum, and when it is calm, we know only the moment we are living. But if we disturb this sea of mind, the waves on the surface of mind can lift the Seeing Eye into another dimension.' She gazed at the white disc of the moon as she spoke. 'From the point of view of the foam on top of the wave, the surface of the sea is visible. Both the future and the past are visible.' She turned to look at Lorraine, who was paying rapt attention to Doreen while trying to lead Alice up by the easiest path. 'The future and the past of the wave, of course, not of the sea.'

Cautiously, so as not to break her mood, Lorraine asked her, 'Is that how you See?'

'No,' said Alice, breathing heavily. 'That's just Doreen talking out of her backside.'

Doreen turned to look at them. 'But I assure you, that is very far from being genetically determined.'

Alice's breath had almost returned to normal. 'Come on,' she wheezed, 'We're nearly there.'

Fifty metres along the rocky beach, near the base of the sandstone cliff was a gleaming white smear of limestone. Water oozed down from the hole above it, a dark oval hole rimmed with more limestone.

Doreen remained silent as they approached the cave.

'What is it?' whispered Lorraine.

'The Drooping Cave,' said Alice. 'A water-carved recess lined with a skin of limestone deposits. The womb of the earth. The Mother's secret place. Take your pick.'

'A horrible cold wet hole in the cliff,' said Doreen. She giggled nervously. It wasn't just a cave. She could feel energy radiating from it.

'Okay. In you go.'

Doreen cautiously began to climb up the slippery wet limestone. Lorraine stayed back, afraid that she might interfere, intrude on holy ground.

'Go on,' said Alice. 'Give her a hand.'

The powerful aura of the cave was thick in the air. 'Should I?'

'God's sake, woman, why did you think I brought you? Last time we came here I slipped on the wet stone. I practically had to crawl home.'

Lorraine stepped carefully onto the slippery limestone, took hold of Doreen's foot and lifted. Doreen stepped up and into the dark entrance.

'Come on,' said Alice. 'Let's get back. You can buy me a drink in the Arms.'

Lorraine was distressed. 'Isn't there any ritual or anything?'

'No, no. Best just leave her to it.'

Doreen watched the figures of Alice and Lorraine disappear along the beach. Lorraine kept looking back towards the cave. Alice did not look back once.

Doreen turned and felt her way into the pitch black of the cave.

George was worried about Sammy, out alone in the night with his salmon net. Which was ridiculous. After all, Sammy was his grandfather. He'd been poaching since he was a child and surely he was old enough to look after himself. But Sammy was a drunk. Was he really capable of looking after himself? George looked uneasily around the dirty and untidy room.

He made himself yet another cup of tea. On a shelf by the cooker there was an inch or so of whisky in a bottle, but he didn't fancy it. Faintly, from The Fisherman's Arms in Kirk Street, he could hear the beat from a drum machine, but he couldn't hear the music that went with it.

There was nothing to do in the empty house, but there was a lot to think about. Should he try to find out more about his father, now that the matter had come to his attention? Should he go to visit his mother? Would she be capable of telling him anything? Was it important? Would Sammy really be all right?

He knew where Sammy used to do most of his poaching – along the beach past Clach Mor. It was safe enough there. The worst that could happen would be if he fell in and got wet. But this new Laird was supposed to be tough. His estate workers looked like gangsters, so what would his bailiff look like?

He left the tea on the table and went out to look for Sammy. He could just stroll along the beach and watch for him coming back. Something of the clandestine nature of his grandfather's activity affected him. He left the house and sneaked up the Wee Vennel rather than be seen walking along Shore Road. The street was dark, with a light showing in only one window. The door opened as he passed.

'Evening! Isn't it a lovely evening? Just popped out for some water for a cuppa.' Jenny-Pet put a bucket under the tap of the standpipe and turned it on. A listless stream of water fell into the bucket. 'How are you then? George, isn't it? How do you feel after coming through the wall? Bit off colour, eh?'

'I'm fine thanks, Jenny.' George slowed, curious despite himself. 'What wall?'

Jenny pointed across the narrow street and winked at him. 'Don't worry. I won't tell a soul.'

'Oh. Fine, fine. Be seeing you.' He waved vaguely and walked away, shaking his head. She was daft as a brush.

As he neared the end of the Wee Vennel he could see The Fisherman's Arms, all its lights on. Now he could hear that the drum machine was accompanied by a steel guitar and a country and western singer. If he found Sammy quick, they could go in for a drink. He turned into Kirk Street and walked to the end, where he could get onto the shore unobserved. Down on the beach, the moon was shining on the sea, the waves were hissing on the shingle, the stones crunched beneath his feet. He passed below the path to the Hog Graveyard. Something nagged at him, something about pigs. Why did Lord Farquhar breed pigs anyway? The aristocracy usually concentrated on horses and suchlike. Clach Mor and the Bog of Morrigan slipped behind him. He reached the first outcrop of rock. The waves were breaking on the lower end. He climbed over and scanned the bay beyond. There was no-one there. Why would anyone be there at this time of night? Unless they were smugglers or...

But where was Sammy? He didn't usually fish this far along the beach. George walked along the shore and clambered over the next rocky outcrop. No-one in the next bay either. The light breeze brought salt spray to his face, from the breaking waves. He hurried along the narrow shore, past the Drooping Cave. The next outcrop was the biggest yet, tricky to climb in the moonlight. From the top, he could see nothing but a receding series of headlands. The beach was empty.

'Damn!' Sammy must have changed his mind, or gone somewhere else. George didn't know all his grandfather's favourite poaching spots and he wasn't going to spend the whole night searching for someone who was probably all right in any case.

He climbed back down. Hell, it was a beautiful night, and a fine place to be. He sat on a flat rock and watched the tide come in quietly, peacefully, inexorably.

He didn't even panic when he found that he'd been cut off by the tide. He laughed at himself, then turned to look at the cliff behind him and quailed. It was probably an easy climb for a rock-climber, but not for George. The moon was full. That meant a big tide. He looked for the tide mark. There was no seaweed on the beach. The tide came right up to the cliff face. There were barnacles on the cliff. The tide went four feet up the cliff.

The waves were breaking close to him now. He could swim round the headland. He put a hand in the water. It was bitterly cold. As a last resort, he could swim.

He looked once more at the cliff then, dubiously, at the wet mouth of the Drooping Cave. It might be better than risking drowning. Just. He'd been in once before. The floor was a series of pools of water with dead pigeons in the corners.

A wave breaking on his foot decided him. He struggled up the wet limestone, clinging to the rock. His clothes were soaked and smeared with white by the time he reached the entrance. He crawled into the darkness, feeling his way blindly, trying to avoid the puddles of water.

Just inside, he remembered, it opened out almost to standing height. He began to stand, reaching above him to feel the roof of the cave.

A strange voice spoke out of nowhere. 'Do you bring a message from the Otherworld?'

He stopped, frozen with terror in the inky darkness.

'Well, have you, or not? Hurry up! Silk underwear is all very well, but it doesn't keep the damp out.'

The country and western singer finished her song with a long drawn out note. The audience recognised it as an ending and began to applaud before she finished.

'Och, Irwin, you're just not yourself,' said the Nailer. 'It's not the football that's getting you down is it? So you only scored once today. Who cares?' Nearly everyone in Cromness, he thought. 'Everyone has an off-day. Christ, we didn't lose.'

Big Irwin shrugged helplessly. It wasn't the football, but he couldn't tell the Nailer. Couldn't tell anyone.

Aristide got up from the table and went up to the stage. He exchanged a few words with the singer. She looked dubious, but he gestured towards Irwin. She looked over at him, then nodded. Aristide went to the bar, smiling.

At a table near the fire, the Major had expended several more drinks on Ellen. He was leaning close to her so that his tape recorder would not miss her words in the din. She thought that he was being especially attentive and had begun to rub her thigh against his.

'Sometimes I would go up to the farm after school, to pull turnips or breach the cereal spalter – it was a special job I had. It needs small sensitive hands. You know what I mean.' She reached under the table and stroked his thigh while looking straight into his eyes.

'Indeed. So you would see David and Sammy...'

'Aye. As often as not, David would be in the barn with Sammy, or in the truckling pens talking to him. You'd always see them together, just the two of them. And sometimes Sammy would have the farmhands in the steading for a meeting. Whipping them up with his communist propaganda.'

'Is this all true?' asked the Major. He leant forwards to catch her reply.

'As God is my witness, not a word of a lie.'

The Major beamed. 'You're a most interesting woman, Ellen. Might I buy you another drink?'

The singer had reached the end of a song about a widow who expected to find her loved one again in the arms of Jesus. After the applause, she shook out her long shiny black hair and held up her arms.

'Ladies and gentlemen, I sing country and western. That's all. But tonight by special request, I am going to sing 'Tatties and Herring' for Irwin, who needs to be cheered up.'

There was loud applause. She adjusted the drum machine and the guitar player valiantly tried to find the tune on his steel guitar. It came out imbued with country and western melancholy. Irwin lifted his head, smiled sadly and looked down into his pint again.

Alice and Lorraine came in the door. In the crowded room, Alice miraculously managed to find an empty table while Lorraine made her way to the bar.

'A Dubonnet and lemon, please, and a Laphroaig.'

Beside her, Jimmy Bervie and Le Placs leaned over their glasses of whisky and discussed methods of prognostication.

'Raking the sand is a favourite of mine, Monsieur Le Placs, but not, strictly speaking as a method of foretelling. The purpose is to mirror the harmony of the universe – and in the failure to do so, in the mistakes, so to speak, we can discover the factors at work in the present.'

'And foretell the future from those factors?'

Jimmy waved a child's windmill languidly. 'Personally, I try to intervene, rather than let matters take their course. But essentially you're right.'

'The Romans, and others, used to study the entrails of chickens and other beasts in order to forecast.'

'Ah. These beasts would have been killed first?'

Le Placs nodded. 'Or simultaneously. But perhaps their death was not a necessary part of the ritual.'

'No? I suppose if you could breed a chicken with a transparent stomach, perhaps you could just lift its feathers and consult it each morning.'

'That would be one solution, certainly, but...'

His reply was drowned in the sound of dozens of voices joining in the chorus of 'Tatties and Herring.' When the singer continued with the verse, Irwin, looking into his pint glass, joined in. Slowly, his head lifted and his voice grew stronger. The singer's voice was clear and sweet, Irwin's was deep and dark. When the next chorus came round, no-one joined in. There was silence for Irwin and the singer, complete, pin-dropping silence. No-one had ever heard Irwin sing like this. His voice was heart-breaking.

When the song finished, the singer came over to his table. There were tears in her big brown eyes. The applause subsided. Every eye was on her and Irwin.

'That was lovely,' she said. 'It was just lovely. I didn't know that 'Tatties and Herring' could be sung like that.' She looked at Irwin.

Irwin looked down. It didn't seem as if the song had cheered him up.

The singer shifted from one foot to another, at a loss. She coughed and smiled shyly. Irwin looked up at her. With a massive effort, he overcame his personal sadness.

'Sit down,' he said. He pulled a chair over from another table. 'Would you like a drink?'

She sat down, hugged his arm and kissed his cheek. He blushed.

The guitarist stood up at the microphone. He glared at the singer, who smiled back at him.

'Now I'll just finish up with a set of instrumentals,' he said. The crowd remembered their manners and ceased to watch the goings-on at Irwin's table.

'Damn it to Hell! What's this?'

Sammy Poach had blundered his way across the rough moorland towards Redrock, only to come up against an eight-foot heavy-duty wire mesh fence with barbed wire along the top. At the bottom it was dug into the soil. In the moonlight he could make out the line of the fence running clear to the cliffs. There was no way through. Half-heartedly he tried to wedge his foot into the mesh, but there was not enough purchase to climb it.

He kicked at the fence. 'You bastard!' he swore at the absent Mr Mor. Everything was against him. First there was Alice and her women on the beach, then that couple of sentries in the Coastguard Station. Now an impenetrable fence. He kicked the fence again.

There was a grunt from behind a knoll. A pig ambled into view and looked at him. A huge sow, red and hairy.

'My God, you're the big beast and no mistake!'

The sow grunted again, then squealed and ran towards him. He stepped back. The sow stopped at the fence, a few yards from Sammy, its snout whiffling in the air. There was a rank smell of stale pig. Behind him came a deeper grunt. He turned round.

There stood an enormous boar, more than four feet tall at the shoulder. Its back was sharply ridged, each of the countless bristles black and distinct in the white moonlight.

'Jesus Christ! It's the Caledonian Boar!' He edged backwards until his back was against the fence. The beast turned its head, so that the moonlight glinted on its tusks. Just how sharp were they? Sammy didn't want to find out. His fingers felt for a grip in the wire, in the forlorn hope that he could climb it if the beast charged. Its little eyes looked at him briefly and Sammy felt a sudden shock of recognition, as if he and the boar knew each other. Then it snorted and trotted away along the line of the fence, to a patch of gorse. A white mark showed on its side as it forced its way into the thorny bush.

Sammy leaned against the fence to gather his wits. It must be one of Mr Mor's pigs. What the hell was he up to? That had to be the biggest and most dangerous boar in Scotland – it looked like some breed from prehistory. Was he trying for a prize at the Dark Isle Show? Somehow that seemed like small potatoes for Mr Mor.

There was a deep grunt from behind him. He turned slowly. There was the boar, inside the fence now, grunting and snuffling at the sow. There must be a way in.

'Time, gentlemen, time, ladies, time, everyone.'

The barman flashed the lights on and off. The lady singer fluttered her eyelashes at Irwin. He hadn't the heart to say goodnight to her. The barman glanced over at him and Irwin nodded.

The Major was in the corridor leading to the toilet, speaking on the phone. 'This is it. Yes, yes, I've confirmed the connection all right. He's in regular contact with the communist leader of the Cromness Socialist Front or something like that. But that's small beer: there's more than that. Listen.' He glanced up and down the empty corridor. 'I may be able to construct a more interesting story. The communist connection will embarrass him, but what about if we could make him out to be a homosexual communist?' He waited for the reply. 'No, of course I can't prove it. But I've got the sworn testimony of a woman who knows them both. She says they used to spend hours in a barn together, when he was a boy. Yes! MacLing and the communist.'

The door opened and a man blundered along the corridor to the toilet. The Major kept silent until the toilet door swung shut. 'Who cares if it's true?' he continued. 'Leak the information to the *Sun* or the *Mail*. They'll print anything. We don't have to prove it. The point is, MacLing can't disprove it. People will say there's no smoke without fire.'

Ellen sat waiting for the Major to return. He was a gentleman, and no mistake. She'd been so absorbed in her conversation with him she hadn't noticed the other goings-on. Like the fact that Irwin had been collared by the skinny country singer, for instance. She had a smug look on her face.

Irwin didn't look too pleased, though. And there was daft Jimmy Bervie talking with that foreign doctor, Monsieur Le Placs – a surgeon, so he claimed. Well, no foreigner was getting his hands in about her innards!

'May I see you home, Ellen?' The Major had returned.

Ellen stood and took his arm.

'Perhaps we could go by way of the Old Jail,' she suggested. 'There's a bench there, and I do so love the sight of the full moon over the water. So romantic.'

'By all means, Ellen. Let's go.'

The bar cleared slowly. The barman locked the door while Irwin and the singer made their way up the stairs to the double bedroom above the lounge. She had him wrapped in her arms before the door was properly closed. Irwin responded with as much enthusiasm as he could muster, not wanting to disappoint her.

Ten minutes later, she cried out. 'My God!' Then she began to laugh.

'Oh be quiet,' said Irwin. Then, 'Shut up!' He didn't normally shout at a lady, but he had been pushed beyond his endurance.

She stopped laughing after a while, then said the most terrible thing imaginable. Quietly and gently she asked, 'Do you want to talk about it?'

In the abandoned Coastguard Station on top of the South Suitor, a faint green light came from the radar screen. There were several blips on the screen. Bill Deace was watching two in particular, one large, one small, about two miles offshore.

'They're closing.'

Ann Deace was scanning the moonlit sea with binoculars. 'I see them,' she replied.

There was silence for a few minutes.

'Contact.'

Ann handed Bill the binoculars. 'See if you can make out any detail.' She lifted a radio close to her face and pressed the buttons.

'Holiday Camp calling. Holiday Camp calling. Do you read me? Over.'

'Blue Bottle receiving you loud and clear. Over.'

'Move in, Blue Bottle. Repeat, move in. Over.'

'Message received. Message received. Move in. Over.'

In Inverness, there were a dozen police officers in the canteen, drinking coffee and smoking. The door opened and Inspector Morrison walked in. Conversation stopped. Everyone sat up straight.

'Okay men, this is it. The freighter has reconnoitred with our target, Mr Mor's boat. The coastguard are waiting nearby but they won't close in until our target gets to Cromness. We've had our eye on this man for some time and tonight we make the pinch. Let's not blow it, okay? I want every man-jack of them. Now go. Check your equipment and make your way to your bus.'

In thirty seconds the canteen was empty. Outside, men were climbing into two minibuses. The engines were already running. A dog handler led his Alsatian into a van and closed the door. The Inspector's car pulled out and the other vehicles followed onto the main road where they headed east through Inverness, at full speed with blue lights flashing.

At Castleton, the captain roused the crew and they hurried to the ferry. The engines roared into life, then settled down to a deep rumble as they waited. The sleepy crew stood in a huddle, smoking.

'Crackdown on drink driving, that's what it is.'

'Don't talk shite. They won't run the ferry at this time of night just for some drunk driving. There's five of us for a start. Four hours minimum call-out at double time. No, it must be a drugs bust.'

'Thought that was all on the West Coast. Ullapool. Kinlochbervie.'

'Maybe Donny MacLean's been growing wacky baccy again.'

'Aye, that'll be right. A squad of coppers will surround Mains Farm Cottage and triumphantly confiscate a few scrawny weeds. No, no. This is the big one.'

'What?'

'Siller has been embezzling the money from the collection plate.'

In the middle of the gorse, Sammy found a tunnel under the fence. It must have been dug by the boar. It was muddy and rank with the smell of pig. Sammy didn't mind. Circumstances were on his side at last.

He crawled through and made for the beach, keeping to the high ground so that he could see the boar if it came for him, though there was nothing he could do if it did.

He had to climb down to the shore, by way of Redrock River, to avoid the cliffs. Just above the beach was the salmon-fishers' bothy. The old shack had been sturdily repaired, and even at a distance the bright new padlock on the door was visible in the moonlight. Sammy edged a hundred yards along the beach before emerging from the bracken. He waited for a few minutes, listening and watching. All clear.

He rolled up his trousers and waded into the sea to set the net. When it was inconspicuously hanging in the water, he found a sheltered spot in the bracken where he could watch the net and finish his whisky.

Reverend Dumfry wandered among the people in the Rossfarm barn. They were lost in a tribal dance, with its own language of moves and rituals. A young man with a shaved head painted green wriggled as if he was trying to get into an invisible jumper, while his hands did a completely separate dance of their own, looking like a sacramental sign language. Sacramental? Yes, that was it. They were leaving their bodies on the dance floor and joining in the group being of the rave, a great animal with a thousand arms and legs, making a dance with its thousand limbs. Only Dumfry's arms and legs did not seem to be part of the great beast.

In one corner there was a screen displaying bizarre images, melting designs, icy patterns. A dancer passed between the screen and the projectors so that her shadow joined the images. Then a coloured aura bloomed from the shadow, leaving a dancing figure when she was gone. A man stepped in, to let his shadow dance with the figure of light. On a podium to one side, a wild man worked at a computer, modulating the light show. The ceaseless beat drove everything. Over it, the repeating trills and gracenotes of the music and strange animal sounds from the DJ.

Dumfry felt a longing to be a part of it, to lose himself in that sacramental dance. He wanted to join in. He walked about the hall, observing, and as he did so, he let his body move with the beat. It jerked stiffly at inappropriate moments.

Someone stood in front of him, blocking his path, shaking both fists in the air. Dumfry flinched, but it was the young man with the pigtail who had been at the door, grinning hugely. He shouted over the music. 'Hey, my man the minister!'

He stepped with the beat towards Dumfry. His hands were dancing and his shoulders were rolling. His shirt was off, but still tucked into his trousers, so that it hung like a skirt behind him. 'Doing that beat!' he cried out.

Dumfry jerked his body so that his arms swung at his sides.

The young man beamed. 'Do that thing! Live that style!'

Dumfry grinned back at him. He twitched again. His arms flung themselves around. The young man did a hand shimmy to match. Dumfry did the twitch again, still grinning. The young man copied his twitch, let his feet glide with it, added an arabesque to the floppy arms. Dumfry followed. His face ached painfully. It had been so long since he'd felt his face muscles doing so much exercise. He didn't care if he got face cramp. It felt good to smile.

'Eck! I've been looking for you.' A young woman with long black hair took the young man's arm.

'Yo, Veronica. Just me and my man doing a little paddy doo here. Hang loose buddy. Time for me and Veronica to chill out.' He waved to Dumfry and turned with Veronica towards the exit.

Dumfry was lost for a moment, then regained his perspective. He was just pretending to be a minister on a night out. That's the key to the kingdom. He knocked on the air with a clenched fist. It looked awkward, inelegant. Just the way a minister would do it.

Great.

Not far from the mouth of the Redrock river, Sammy Poach lay amongst the bracken, sipping the last of the whisky and keeping an eye on his net. Far out at sea a couple of boats slowly pulled away from each other. He could see the lights moving apart, and just below, he could barely make out the dark bulk of the boats. The waves stroked the shingle with a regular hush and there was a faint rustling from the breeze in the bracken fronds. Apart from that, the night was silent. Sammy made himself comfortable: he would hear if anyone came along the shingle beach.

Cosy amongst the bracken, with the whisky warming him from inside, he lay there dozing, his thoughts wandering. He wondered about his grandson, whether he was going the same way as his mother. The boy had been having visions, thought he was going to kill someone – and eat him too, for god's sake! He shook his head sadly. George had been a fine boy, but it was a strange upbringing, after all – brought up by his grandparents while his mother wandered the moors like a madwoman.

On the sea, a movement caught his attention. Tied to his net there was a tiny buoy, no bigger than an angling float, and he could see it dipping and pulling in the waves. He glanced along the beach before leaving the cover of the bracken, then rolled up his trouser legs once more.

'Right Sammy, let's go,' he muttered to himself. He took his head in both hands and shook it to clear away the doziness. 'If there's a moment to strike a blow against the creeping evil of landlordism, then this is it!'

He waded into the sea and took hold of the net. There was a powerful thrashing below the surface. 'Come here you wee beauty!' The silver body wriggled in the moonlight. Sammy brought out his length of broomstick and whacked it soundly on the head. The fish jerked a couple of times, then ceased to struggle. Sammy took hold of the slippery fish and untangled it from the net. 'A fine beast!' He held it up in front of his face. It didn't look quite right, but it wasn't easy to tell, even in the bright moonlight. He grasped it round the end of its body, just before the tail, then tried to pick it up. The tail slipped right through his hand. 'Damn! It's a sea-trout.' He looked at it. 'But it's a fine fish. Jenny can have it.'

He threw the sea-trout to the shore then started to straighten the net. It jerked in his hand. There was another fish in it. He pulled in the net and the silvery shape appeared out of the water, splashing and struggling wildly. A couple of blows to the head and it was dead. He reached below the surface, to grasp it by the tail. This time, the stiff tail did not slip through his hand.

'Ha! A salmon! Ten pounds if it's an ounce.'

But there was something puzzling about the fish, something rubbery tied round the tail. He lifted it clear of the water. There was a harness of some sort tied round the slim part of the body just before the tail. He held the fish by its tail and pulled on the harness. On the other end, there was a length of black plastic tube, with a cap on each end.

There was a crunch on the shingle beach behind him, and he turned. A dark bulky figure with a raised arm stepped into the water. Sammy dropped the fish and tried to fend off the blow, but something struck his head in an explosion of pain and he slipped down into the dark water.

Wee Eck and Veronica walked down the farm track through the fields to Glen Grian. Behind them, the rave lights flashed in the barn doorway. In front, the moon hung placidly in the sky, dimming the stars with its brightness. The leafy canopy of the Glen was dark below them.

Veronica had never been to a rave before, and she wasn't entirely sure whether she should have taken whatever it was that Eck had pressed into her hand. At least, she hadn't been sure at the time. Just now, it didn't seem to matter at all. There was such a pleasant easiness to everything, just letting go, falling into the rhythm of the music, being part of the crowd in the barn. Her father had stuck his head in at one point and she'd actually been pleased to see him. She'd waved and smiled and he'd waved back. They both knew what they meant: they were really communicating.

Wee Eck spoke. 'Wasn't bad, eh?'

Veronica perceived his remark with utter clarity. She was aware that he was expressing an interest in her opinion in order to initiate a verbal exchange that would link them in a shared social network of concepts. (A network that did not exclude the possibility of sexual congress, but did not yet imply it.) She watched the mobilisation within her of massive psychological constructs that reared against each other like the meeting of icebergs at sea. She found herself assessing balances and applying the proper parameters that would mediate her response, while also making allowance for the bandwidth of the communication device being employed – the human voice – and making allowance also for the extent of overlapping experience, shared concepts and verbal patterns. Strangely, this rich pattern of thought seemed to be taking place in her abdomen, and while she was aware that this did not accord with her normal understanding, it seemed right and proper that it should be so.

'Not bad,' she agreed with him. She nodded as she said it, adding this positive reinforcement with her body language to convey the information, which would normally be picked up subliminally, that it was in fact better than 'not bad,' that in fact she was employing an ironic turn of speech (matching his own) and intended to convey a high degree of appreciation by her comment.

Wee Eck grinned and she knew she'd been understood. Still, the narrow bandwidth of communication concerned her. It seemed that a vast universe of experience had to be trimmed down to a tiny thread of meaning in order to be passed from one human being to another.

'We're like funnels,' she said. 'We're talking through the wrong end of a megaphone.'

Eck nodded. This dame was plainly out of it, he could see that. A bit of cooling out in the Glen would definitely be in order. Some calming low-key conversation would help too.

'Yeah,' he said.

Veronica was amazed at just how much could be implied in a communication through the wrong end of a funnel. The moon glinted on the turnip leaves, damp with dew.

'Y'see,' Eck went on, 'We're all creatures of light in human form. And not just humans. Every being is a star. You see?'

Veronica nodded. They'd passed the end of the turnip field now and the barley was standing still and straight and pale to their right, a blanket of awns. That sounded good.

'A blanket of awns,' she said.

'Yeah. And I have opened myself up to that reality,' said Eck. 'My chakras are wide open. Most people just ease them open, and you can do it that way – you can take lifetimes over it if you want – but man, we haven't got the time. This planet's on the way out. Millennium stuff, you know. Plagues and earthquakes and like that. The Brahan Seer knew, and Nostradamus. Though they might have got it wrong with the dating. Like, Jesus wasn't born just on the stroke of midnight at zero AD. There could be a good few years out, like maybe the Millennium will come when we're not expecting it and we haven't got our lamps ready...'

Veronica was listening to the music from the barn. Only the beat was audible at this distance, but she could imagine a melody and words. Her feet were wet from the damp grass in the middle of the track. She could feel the chill coming up her legs and thighs and through her vagina and on up into her stomach where it was exquisitely uncomfortable. She watched in fascination as the chill knotted itself harder then broke. A bubble of inspiration floated into her mind.

'The dance is the heartbeat of the people. People, that is, in the general sense. The tribe.'

Eck nodded wisely and went on with his rap.

'So there's no time for pussyfooting around. Go in there and do it. Blow all your chakras open and let the world come in. Spirit of trees, spirit of the tribes, spirit of the animals. Catch that totem beast and ride together. Ride the wave into the future.' He turned to her. 'Ninety-nine out of a hundred will die,' he said.

'Really?'

He nodded. 'It's like turtles hatching. There are flocks of bad bastards out there waiting for us to make a break for the sea, to pick out the weakest and eat them. But we will survive, for we have seen Eden.'

He beckoned towards the Glen. They were just about to pass into the first dimness below the outlying trees. A path meandered between the tree trunks, until the small moonlit clearings gave way to deeper shadow.

'Come,' he said. 'Let me show you the spirits of the Glen and we can commune with them.'

Veronica was all for communing with the spirits. They passed beneath the trees. Moonlight flickered on them for a minute or two, and then they were gone.

Sammy came back to consciousness as the Land Rover stopped outside Redrock House. The bulky man opened the door and dragged him out. Sammy's head seemed to shatter with the pain. He bent over and vomited on the ground.

'Christ's sake!' The man held Sammy at arms length until he'd finished, then dragged him up the steps into the house.

In the big room Mr Mor was standing at the map table making notes in red ink on the margins of a large scale map of the Easter Dark Isle. Sammy was marched in and stood there. Mr Mor turned.

'Baldy. Do we have a problem?'

'Ah spotted this wan on the beach. Wi nets.'

Mr Mor looked at Sammy. Sammy tried to stand up straight and look him in the eye.

'So why did you bring him here? Take him to the police station.'

'Ah wid, but he caught somethin.'

'A salmon?'

Baldy nodded 'Wan o they specials.'

Mr Mor looked at Sammy. 'You stupid old man. What did you go and do that for?' He looked at Baldy. 'This is one of the salmon fishers from Cromness, isn't it?'

Baldy nodded.

Sammy's face contorted. 'Can't you speak to me yourself, but you have to ask your boneheaded henchman? I've got nothing to hide.'

Mr Mor looked at him in surprise. 'Not only can it talk, it has nothing to hide. Listen old man, you've got a lot to hide. You've been taking my money to work in Cromness and you've been poaching on the side. I wouldn't be surprised if you're the ringleader for the entire poaching ring.'

'Damn it, I went out to take a fish as a matter of principle! I'm not a bloody thief! Isn't it always the way – some fat landlord takes over and the iron glove squeezes on the people of the land. People belong on this land, we're part of it. And the fruits of the land belong to the people who live on the land! Not to some greasy unprincipled capitalist. When I was young a man could walk the moors without let or hindrance and now there's these damned fences everywhere that no-one can cross!'

'Good point,' said Mr Mor. 'How did you get across?'

Sammy was not to be stopped in his flow. 'And not just fences, you've got damned sentries everywhere. That's the sign of the paranoid capitalist outlook, if anything is. God aye, watch your back, Mor, there's a revolution coming!' He spat the last words out and folded his arms defiantly.

Mr Mor wiped his face with a handkerchief. 'Come now, the fences are to keep my pigs in. They're big beasts, and they can be dangerous. And I can't see what's so wrong about keeping a watch on the salmon fishings. They caught you, didn't they?'

Sammy laughed. 'Paranoia, the ravings of paranoia. Och, any laird will watch his fishings, and I should have spotted the man on the beach, but Jesus Christ, you've got fences that a storm trooper would balk at, hoodlums on the beach and a surveillance post on the bloody Suitor!'

Mr Mor spoke sharply. 'What?'

'Why for God's sake keep a post on the Suitor? That's the sign of a paranoid mind – or someone with a very underhand operation. Just what is going on here, Mr Mor?'

Mr Mor looked at Baldy. 'There's no-one on the Suitor, is there?'

'No, boss.'

'Don't come it,' said Sammy, but the certainty had gone from his voice. 'There's a man and a woman up there in the abandoned coastguard station.' Mr Mor shook his head. 'Aye there is. With night glasses and a radar and...' Sammy stopped, realising how ridiculous it sounded. Why would they need a radar to catch poachers?

Mr Mor turned to Baldy. 'Emergency. Cover up plan. Close everything else down. Lock the main gates and get the steadings cleared. Go to it!'

Baldy ran out of the door. Mr Mor stepped over to the wall and pressed a red button. Out in the yard, bells began to ring.

Sammy edged over to the window and pulled back a curtain. Outside in the yard, men were running around carrying pieces of equipment, others were hosing down the yard and the steading floors.

Mr Mor was sitting at the table with a thoughtful look on his face. Men ran into the room with bundles of papers. They lifted a picture off the wall, opened the safe behind it and thrust in the papers. A sheet of paper fluttered to the floor. Another was jammed in the safe door as it was slammed shut. Sammy watched in amazement. The picture was re-hung. It did not hang straight. No-one adjusted it. The men left the room.

He turned round to look at Mr Mor. He laughed. 'I don't know what you're up to, but I would get some better hired help if I were you. God, man, they're a bunch of boy scouts!'

Mr Mor smiled at him. 'I know. You just can't get the staff any more.'

He reached up to his neck and drew a small glass vial up from under his shirt.

'I suspect that we're going to have a squad of police here very shortly. I have some evidence here that must be destroyed. Will you help?' He kept his eye on Sammy as he dipped a small silver spoon into the vial, held it to his nose and sniffed.

'That'll be cocaine, I don't doubt,' said Sammy. 'Why should I help you get rid of it?'

'Well, for a start, it'll fix that headache which I am sure you're suffering from. Also, we have to talk. You have seen more than you should have, and I don't like that. I could just feed you to the pigs, but I'd rather not.'

Sammy gaped. The pigs were big enough to devour him and leave no traces. He had no reason to believe that Mr Mor would not go through with the threat. After all, he was an unprincipled and bloated capitalist.

'I do have a wee bit of a headache,' he said. 'I might just try it, for medicinal purposes.'

'A wise decision,' said Mr Mor, handing over the spoon.

Sammy sniffed deeply. In a remarkably short time, the pain disappeared.

'Now,' said Mr Mor. 'In a way, it's lucky you turned up tonight. Lucky for both of us, I hope. We have a few minutes before the police arrive. Let's see if we can reach an arrangement that suits us both.'

There was a modest uproar in the Hugh Chandler Institute of Cromness. Several snatches of argument could be picked out.

'...set-aside allowances on turnips...'

'...don't think so! Better the St Kilda groat than the Norwegian krone!'

'...new laws! World leaders in growing beremeal and...'

Alma Keivor did not speak particularly loudly, but the rest of the crowd in the Hugh Chandler Institute gradually fell silent.

'...plain that we shall have to adopt a different currency once we are an independent state. We are all, I think, agreed on that. There appear to be two proposals as to how to proceed during the changeover period. One suggestion is that we should appoint a Master of the Treasury, a temporary post, to supervise the conversion of Sterling into Groats. The other suggestion is that we should continue to use Sterling until our application to join the EC is accepted.' She shifted on the cushions which gave her height enough to look over the table. She looked severe and stroked her small dark moustache. As she took breath to continue, Mr Siller stood up.

'I feel bound to point out that the economic base of the Dark Isle, as it stands, is insufficiently developed to maintain itself as a Sovereign State. The Dark Isle is simply too small to succeed in this era of super-nations. Does anyone really take seriously this ill-advised attempt at self-governing status? Only those with a naive vision of global economics.'

'Good points,' said Alma. 'But my esteemed colleague has, as usual, taken a most pusillanimous attitude to what is a pioneering attempt to modify the map of Europe. One wonders what he is doing here, at a meeting specifically called to promote the cause of the Dark Isle Nationalist Party. However, I shall endeavour to answer his questions.'

She raised her shoulders so that her disproportionately large bosom stuck out belligerently. 'First, let me assure you that we shall not lack inward investment. I am in touch with several large concerns that are excited by the prospect of an independent Dark Isle. I can not of course divulge their names at this delicate stage of negotiations. On the other hand, Mr Siller, I could easily make a list for you of independent nations of a comparable size to the Dark Isle. How large is Monaco, for instance, or Hong Kong? Can you tell me, Mr Siller, the size of the Bahamas?' She paused. Mr Siller had no answer, of course, which was fortunate for Alma, since she was as ignorant as he. 'But I have no need of such a list,' she continued. 'We shall succeed on our own terms! As for the legitimacy of our claim for independence – look at the natural boundaries, my friends. We are on an island! Never have we been part of mainland Scotland! It is time to grasp our destiny!'

There was a smattering of applause and conversation broke out. Alma was almost sure she heard someone say, 'What does Alice think?' She set her teeth and smiled grimly.

Through the thick curtains of Redrock House, there was the sound of men busy in the yard. Mr Mor sat on the edge of the huge polished table. He picked a cigar from the box and rolled it absently between his fingers, looking at Sammy, slumped on a chair. The old man's face was grey and there was blood in his white hair.

'I believe you're known hereabouts as Sammy Poach?'

Sammy Poach glared back at him.

'Well, Sammy?'

'Well, Mor?'

Mr Mor chuckled. He laid down the cigar and leant forwards, watching the shabby figure of Sammy. 'So, what did you see, and what did you work out?'

Sammy assessed his chances. He could deny seeing anything, but there was obviously something very criminal going on here, and it was unlikely that Mor would believe him. He shrugged. 'When I pulled the salmon from the net I saw the harness on it. And the container that was hitched to the harness.'

'And what did you think it was for?' Mr Mor watched Sammy carefully.

'The container wasn't very big. It's got to be drugs. A few ounces of cocaine in each canister would soon mount up.' He laughed and shook his head in reluctant admiration. 'So that's why you don't keep the sea-trout. The salmon's tail is stiff enough to take a harness, but the sea-trout's isn't. I'm surprised you didn't try to train the dolphins.'

Mr Mor looked rueful. 'I did try, but I ran into resistance. The Dolphin Research Institute have principles. So I stuck with the salmon. They have the advantage that they don't have to be trained. We just put the cargo in the harness and put the salmon back into the sea. They do the rest, heading straight back to the river mouth.'

'Where you catch them and take them out again for the next shipment. So that's why you have the whole damn area fenced off.'

'Partly. But that's mainly to keep the pigs in.' Sammy looked dubious. 'Really. You should see the size of the pigs.'

Sammy grunted. 'I have.'

'We don't need the fence against poachers. Up to now, no-one but you has managed to catch a fish, though we've stopped a couple of people on their way to the shore. The men are very vigilant.'

Sammy rubbed his head. 'Violent bastards.'

Mr Mor shrugged. 'I have to take precautions – I am a smuggler, after all. A traditional vocation in these parts. As is the poacher, eh?'

'Smuggler? Drug peddler more like! A common criminal.'

Mr Mor's expression was pained. 'No, no. Do you consider yourself a criminal? I think not. Without descending into romanticism, I think we can both be fairly classed as outlaws.'

Sammy's mouth set. 'Same difference.'

'No. I don't think you mean that. Criminals break the law to gain advantage over those who keep it. Outlaws ignore the law on principle.'

The phone rang. Mr Mor picked it up without speaking, then laid it down again.

'They've got the boat down at the harbour. It'll take them some time to be sure that there's nothing illegal on board. Come with me. I'd like to show you something.'

He crossed to the door in the corner. Sammy followed. Together they mounted the spiral stairway.

Echoes of the voice were still ringing as George leapt backwards. His head crashed against the roof of the cave and his feet slipped on the wet stone. He fell to his knees in a puddle of icy water. In the darkness, half-seen terrors seemed to throng the cave. Moonlight seeping in through the entrance made a grey haze over the limestone-encrusted walls. Shapes swirled in the haze, disturbingly familiar shapes: a grey naked woman with skinny breasts hanging past her navel, a terrifying woman with vicious sharp eyes and a nose that looked like a beak, a man with one of his legs twisted and a massive body. George scrabbled backwards until he could move no further, pressed against the cave wall.

'Well? Cat got your tongue?'

There was a brief vision of hillsides and moorland, a forested valley where a huge boar snuffled among the roots, a deer tore at the leaves. A hound with two heads bellowed as it leapt at the deer. The boar lifted its head, then suddenly disappeared. George felt the muscles of his face clench. A huge hand swept away the scenes, and then there was just a man's face, fierce and angular, with red hair and beard. Then it faded into greyness, but not before looking at George for an instant.

George knelt in the water and tried to remember where he'd seen the face before. He heard a cough from the darkness and remembered that someone had been talking about silk underwear.

'Who's there?'

'It is I, Pythoness of Cromness, Seer of the Dark Isle, Favoured One of the Goddess and so on.'

'What?'

'It's me. Doreen.' She spoke more sharply, then returned to her portentous voice. 'Who comes to this holy place in the full of the moon, who dares disturb the Pythoness at her vigil?'

George clambered upright, his breathing more quiet now, but his heart still thudding. The only girl called Doreen that he could remember was a few years above him in school. She had seduced the Physics teacher, who had been quickly transferred to another school. 'I'm George,' he said.

'George?' She was silent for a moment. 'Not Sammy's grandson? That went to college?'

'Yes.'

'Are you sure?'

George thought about what he could answer to such a question, and chose the simplest. 'Yes.'

'What the hell are you doing here?' Then her voice grew deep and resonant again. 'Why come you here from far off? You bring with you the fluttering edges of many worlds. Bring you news of the Otherworld?'

'Not really.' George was feeling more sure of himself now. He was pretty certain that he'd know if he carried a message. He was beginning to make out some details in the darkness. Doreen must be that dark mass against the grey haze of limestone that covered the walls. He stepped forwards, setting his foot in a deep puddle. 'Damn.' He moved to the side and banged his head on the rock again. 'Bugger!'

Doreen's voice came from nearby. 'Do not profane this holy...'

'Oh shut up!' George rubbed his head as he looked around for her. He could just make out the darker shape. He stepped towards it.

'Ouch! That's my foot!'

'Oh, sorry. I thought you were over there.'

'Obviously not,' said Doreen. 'Now, what the hell are you doing here? This is the time of the full moon. Everyone knows we use the cave at the full moon.'

'I didn't. I just got trapped by the tide. What are you doing here?'

'It's a Seeing,' said Doreen uncomfortably. 'There's not supposed to be anyone else here. Especially not a man.'

'Why not?'

'Well, it's a woman thing. Receptive, you know. In the womb of the Mother I receive messages from the Otherworld.'

'Really? That's amazing.'

'Not so amazing. I take some herbs first. Mostly Witches Eye – that liberal shepherds give a grosser name. You can hardly help seeing things. The trick is to remember them tomorrow.' She snorted. 'And make sense of them.'

George stood and thought. 'Look, Doreen...'

'Pythoness.'

'Look, Pythoness...'

'No, that sounds silly. Just call me Doreen.'

'All right, then! Doreen! I'm truly sorry I came in, but now I'm here and I can't go back out without risking drowning. I'm wet and cold I'm getting a crick in my neck from standing here. Is there a dry place where I can sit down?'

'Sit on this rock by me. It's the driest place in the cave.' Doreen's hand took his arm and helped George sit down on a damp rock. He was pressed close to her. She smelt of strange herbal fragrances, not all of them sweet. The effect was disturbing.

She put an arm around his stiff body. 'What's the matter?'

'It's just a rather strange situation,' he said.

'It's a bloody cold place,' she replied. 'Snuggle in close. We can keep each other warm.'

George leaned stiffly against her.

Doreen sighed. 'Look, under normal circumstances I'd be happy to consider this a sexual encounter, and then you might be justified in feeling uneasy. But it's bloody cold, there's an average of two inches of water on the floor of the cave and the roof is too low to stand up straight.'

'Sorry, it's just...'

'Also, you should know that I am the intimate of caterpillars.'

'What?'

'I'm wearing thermal silk underwear next to my skin. Under five layers of woollens.'

George laughed and relaxed. 'So what do you See?'

'Right now?'

'Well, I meant in general.' He shrugged. 'But okay, what do you See right now?'

Doreen closed her eyes. After a few seconds, her voice came out, distant and thin. 'I see, I see... over the Dark Isle, shadows lying, and through the dimness, the Grey Woman, her dugs lying on her belly. I see Morrigan with her beak like a crow, watching the fields, watching the affairs of man, waiting. I see the forest and the wild pig, I see the two-headed dog rending the deer...' Her voice rose. 'The dog's master, Manannan, is hunting for the Great Boar. He is turning towards us, He is looking at us...'

'What?' George let go of Doreen. 'What did you say?'

Doreen's head turned and her blank eyes looked towards him. Her thin voice began again. 'I see the Great Boar... and I see you, George MacLear!'

Her blank gaze was terrifying. George took her by the arms and shook her. 'Oh stop it! What did you say before?'

Doreen shook her head. 'How dare you interrupt!' Her voice was normal again, but angry.

'Tell me what you said before. Please.'

'You shouldn't interrupt! In olden times you could be castrated on the altar for speaking while the Prophetess was Seeing.'

'Sorry.'

'With a blunt stone knife.'

'All right, I'm sorry, but what were you saying?'

Doreen sighed. 'It's just old Celtic stuff. The Gods and the Goddesses and the totem animals. Bits of myths. It's a pain. At first I used to tell Alice all that stuff, but she couldn't make much of it. I reckon it all comes from the collective unconscious.'

'What's that? No, tell me some other time. What were you Seeing?'

'I told you. Just mythic visions. The grey crone and Morrigan, that sort of thing.'

'Doreen! It may just be that sort of thing to you, but I want details.'

'All right,' she said sulkily, 'No need to bully me.'

'Please.'

'There was a forest, the old forest, oak trees and pine and that sort of stuff, with a huge great pig and a deer. One of Manannan's dogs took the deer. That's when I heard your voice and I saw your face in the dimness. The great Boar was there too. In fact, the Boar's face turned into yours. Odd. You're not really that ugly. As far as I can see.'

'Whose dog was it?'

'I told you. Manannan's. Why?'

'I heard the name just a few hours ago. I saw it on my birth certificate. My father's name was Manannan.'

Doreen laughed. 'Don't tell me. His name wasn't mac Lir, was it?'

George looked at her. 'Of course it was. Same as mine.'

Doreen pulled away from him. 'George MacLear,' she whispered.

As they walked down the Kirk Road, Jimmy turned to his companion. 'The question is, do prophecies create the future they predict?'

M Le Placs shrugged. 'Sometimes, yes. The self-fulfilling prophecy is well-evidenced. But if, for instance, I correctly predict the winner of the 2.30 at Aintree, that prediction doesn't make the horse win.'

'No?'

'Of course not! Many other people are predicting also – and they do not predict the right horse.'

Jimmy Bervie lifted his wig to scratch his scalp. 'But the better a prophet you are, the more likely it is that you will get it right.'

'Of course. And as you practise, you must get better.'

'But it is possible that you are getting better at causing events.'

'*Parbleu*! This is ridiculous! Why not choose the most simple explanation?'

'Mine is the most simple explanation. If you are causing it, then it is very easy to tell what is going to happen. In ten seconds, my wig is going to rise in the air and fly over that shop sign. One elephant, two elephant...'

'But no, my friend, this cannot be!'

'...eight elephant, nine elephant, ten elephant.' Jimmy pulled off his wig and tossed it over the shop sign. 'That was easy to predict, because I was doing it.' He caught it and restored it to its usual position.

'*Mon Dieu*! Miraculous! I give way before your superior talents.'

Jimmy bowed. 'Perhaps you might care for some coffee? I can show you the sand-garden.'

'Most certainly, yes. Thank you.'

They turned down School Brae and walked towards the Old Jail. There was a regular hissing from the waves on the beach. Closer to the Old Jail they could hear the repetitive soughing of the aerating machines of the salmon incubators.

'Totem animals, you know,' said Jimmy. 'The salmon.'

'Ah, yes. I am also from a Celtic country. The boar also is a totem, eh? That is why Obelix eats them.'

The sound of the aerators and the waves was joined by a low moaning, regular as the waves, and keeping time with them.

'Ah, yes. Ellen.' Jimmy turned away from the old building. 'A matter of some delicacy,' he explained. 'The grassy bank is occasionally used as a place of assignation.'

They turned along the Links, where the dark shapes of boats were clear on the grass. Doreen had been absent recently, and even the minister was missing tonight.

'But the boar was sacred before the Celts,' said Jimmy. 'It seems to have been special to the Firbolg too.'

'The Firbolg?'

Jimmy nodded. 'The original inhabitants of Ireland. They were defeated by the Celts.'

'There are stories about these people also?'

'Not really. Only a few mentions in the Celtic tales.'

They had reached the end of the Links and the harbour was visible. Mr Mor's boat was just pulling in. Even as the ropes were tied, a squad of men with bright torches rushed from two vans parked on the pier. They leapt on board and grabbed the crew. Sammy and M Le Placs watched as three men bundled the crew up to the vans and thrust them inside. The remaining men set to work on the boat, overturning boxes, rapping on bulkheads, searching cubby-holes, probing small spaces with flexible steel rods.

Jimmy and M Le Placs watched this entertainment as they opened Jimmy's garden door. Down Harbour Road came a running figure. It was Constable MacFearn.

'He-ell-o, hell-o, he-ll-o-o,' he cried as he ran along the pier. 'Wha-at's a-ll thi-is then?'

The men on the boat scarcely glanced at him, but continued to search the boat.

'I am a police officer, and I insist you stop this immediately or I will be forced to arrest you all!'

The nearest of the men turned to him, taking a wallet from his pocket. 'It's MacFearn, isn't it? We were warned you might turn up.' He removed something from the wallet and handed it to MacFearn. 'Do you recognise this?'

MacFearn peered at it in the uncertain light. 'It's a warrant card.'

'It's a warrant card, sir.'

'It's a warrant card, sir.'

'That's better. We are engaged on an investigation here, as you can see, and we do not require your presence.'

'But this is my beat, sir!'

'Unfortunately, it is. Now, is there a hostelry or pub at the other end of town?'

'Yes, sir! The Fisherman's Arms, sir!'

'Good. Go and see if there's any after-hours drinking.'

'I've just done that, sir.'

'Then go and check again!'

'Yes, sir.'

MacFearn turned and marched stiffly back along the pier, his teeth clenched and his face red. Jimmy and M Le Placs stepped into Jimmy's garden and closed the door. Jimmy went into the house to put the kettle on and brought out a plate of oysters and a lime cut into wedges. They sat together at the garden table, from where they could watch proceedings as they ate.

The search was obviously not showing results.

'There's bugger all here!' called one man.

'The boat's clean.'

'Nothing on the crew either.'

'Any news from the Coastguard?'

'They've stopped the freighter and searched it. They say there's nothing there either.'

'Maybe they threw it overboard.'

'Shit! Everyone in the vans. We're going up to Redrock House to talk to the boss man.'

The vans roared away. Jimmy offered the plate of oysters to M Le Placs. 'The night is fine,' he said. 'Do you admire the view?'

At the top of the spiral stairs, Sammy Poach stepped into a circular turret room. It was lit by moonlight flooding in through the windows, which looked out in every direction.

Mr Mor opened a window and gestured towards the cluster of lights down by the shore, a mile away. 'Cromness.'

Sammy walked over to stand beside him.

'An unusual place,' continued Mr Mor. 'A well-preserved seventeenth-century trading port set in a beautiful landscape with access to a wonderful natural harbour. You can hardly walk down the street without wading through history. A jewel for archaeologists, historians and tourists.' He looked at Sammy. 'It tells you that, more or less, in the brochures. But they don't tell you that Cromness can't support itself. The old buildings are growing dilapidated. Some of them are past repair. Every year more young people leave, while few return. It's not just Cromness. The rest of the Dark Isle is little better.'

'Aye,' said Sammy, bitterly. 'It's the victim of creeping landlordism, of the polarisation of economic power. Any new jobs go to the South. Marginalisation of the people of Scotland...'

Mr Mor shrugged. 'It's no-one's fault. It's happening all over. Communities like this are irrelevant to the new politics, irrelevant to the modern world. Urban centres hold the power.' He lifted the small glass vial that hung round his neck and unscrewed the cap.

Sammy looked at him angrily. 'It's easy for you to be philosophical about it. What about the rest of us? Should we all migrate? Head for the urban centres? It's happened before, entire populations vanished away to be ground into dust by the satanic mills.'

'No. That's what I wanted to discuss with you. There is no need to migrate to the centres of power. The solution is to develop the Dark Isle, bring the power here.' He sniffed white powder from the spoon and held the vial up to check the level. He reached out to press a button and the beginning of *Also Sprach Zarathustra* rang out. 'Aah!' The drums boomed.

Sammy laughed. 'You're dottled, man. Crazy. Who'd invest in the Dark Isle? And would we want them here anyway? Dammit, maybe the Island's going downhill, but we don't want a flock of vultures tearing the place to bits and squabbling over the good bits.'

'Look out there,' said Mr Mor. 'Imagine that Cromness was prosperous again. A marina, a few good hotels, the old houses renovated, new ones built on the flat land to the west. A commercial section to the east, with offices and banks. Ferries from Cromness to Tain, to Aberdeen, to Norway, to Denmark.'

Sammy stared at him in astonishment. 'You'd better lay off that white powder. It's giving you delusions. This is a depressed area, even by the standards of the Highlands. There's no damn work! Are we all supposed to dig each other's gardens or what?'

Mr Mor shrugged. 'The shipyard at Boblair should provide employment.'

'What shipyard?'

Mr Mor turned on a wall light, illuminating a map. He pointed. 'That shipyard there.'

'You're daft, man, daft as a brush. Where will you get materials from? Why do you think the shipyards are on the Clyde? Easy access to materials.'

Mr Mor pointed out of the window, where the Dark Isle could be seen clearly, spread out below them in the moonlight. 'A harbour at Oldmills, big enough to take cruise ships and oil tankers.' He turned and pointed west. 'A wind farm along the Ardmeanach ridge will provide domestic electricity, and a tidal barrage at Castleton Bay will give power for industries in the eastern development area. 'He turned again to face south, and pointed. 'Recreational developments at Rossmarty and a village on the shore at the mouth of the Redrock Gorge.'

Sammy laughed. Mr Mor watched him silently. Sammy leaned against the wall, laughing, and managed to gasp out, 'Man, man, do you think it's as easy as that? Even if you had enough money to start such a venture...'

'Me and my backers.'

'Aye, aye, you and your backers, I don't doubt. Even then, do you think they'd let you get away with it? Do you really think it's a mistake that Scotland has lost most of her industrial base over the last decade? We're being whittled down to size. Re-made in the role of twenty-first century serfs.'

'And who is doing this?'

'The government, of course. But not just them. The government is a tool for the people with real power, hiding in the shadows. The bankers and the corporations and the multinationals and the heritably rich, who have grown so used to being in the monied elite that the attitude is bred into them.'

'The government is their tool?'

'Of course it is. What are you, naive?'

'So what if we take that tool away from them?'

'Eh?'

Mr Mor smiled. 'What if we remove ourselves from their jurisdiction?' Sammy looked at him, uncomprehending. 'What if the Dark Isle declares itself independent. Isn't that a whole new football pitch?'

'But,' said Sammy, then stopped.

Mr Mor turned a knob and the music faded. He changed disks. A trumpet rang out. 'Aaron Copeland,' he said. 'Fanfare for the Common Man.'

'You wouldn't know a Mrs Keivor, would you?' asked Sammy.

'Alma and I are on very good terms.'

'Ah.'

The trumpet music was loud and clear, but faintly through the windows could be heard the sound of vehicles coming up the hill from Cromness. Mr Mor glanced out. Headlights were glimmering through the trees.

'So where, if it isn't an indelicate question, will the money be coming from?'

'Suffice it to say that the new state of Dark Isle will have very liberal laws.'

Sammy gestured at the glass vial at Mor's throat. 'Decriminalisation of so-called recreational drugs?'

'Possibly. That would be my personal preference. For obvious reasons. But we have considered a range of laws designed to encourage investment. Banking, recreational facilities, small-scale industry.'

Sammy snorted. 'And the Dark Isle will turn into Hong Kong. Overdeveloped, overcrowded. Housing estates and dormitory towns for Inverness.'

'By no means. I am investing in various other projects, which I will expect to be safeguarded by relevant laws.'

'Of course,' said Sammy sourly. 'You want your cut.'

'I expect a return on my other investments, yes. But I was talking about something else. The Dark Isle National Forest. The ancient Caledonian forest replanted and its natural fauna restored.'

Sammy remembered the huge boar he'd met by the fence. 'Wild pigs!'

Mr Mor nodded. 'Wolves too, and bears, when we can get the area properly fenced.'

Over Mr Mor's shoulder Sammy could see a van leaving the trees and coming out onto the moor, its headlights fanning out across the moorland. A second van followed it.

'But what's this to me? If you've done your homework, you'll know that I'm not of the capitalist persuasion. I'm bound to say that it sounds like you're playing chancy games with the lives of the proletariat, like every other rich bastard that forgot his roots and carved out a place for himself. No offence.'

'Ah. I'm sorry. I thought you might find the political situation to your liking.'

'Eh?'

'We will be a free and independent nation state. If it suits us, we can be an independent member of the EC. We can have a seat at the United Nations.'

'My God!'

'So we'll need a democratically elected government.'

'The Communist Party of Dark Isle!'

Mr Mor nodded encouragingly. 'After all, Marx did point out that a nation has to pass through the stage of industrial capitalism in order to create the proletarian masses who will take over.'

'You're right! Communism failed in Russia – and in China – because they missed out that stage, went straight from feudalism to the dictatorship of the people. Perhaps on the Dark Isle we might be able to create the true Workers' State!'

'Good. I thought the prospect might interest you. Frankly, I doubt if there are enough communists around to take on the committee of the Ladies Guild, but you're welcome to try.'

Down at the main gate, the two police vans had stopped. The gatekeeper was taking his time coming to the door of the lodge.

'They're on their way,' said Mr Mor. 'It's time to decide. You can throw in your lot with the ad hoc committee for the independence of the Dark Isle or I can throw you out of the window. It'll be awkward to explain how you came to fall, but not impossible.'

Sammy looked uncomfortable. 'I don't have much choice, do I? But it doesn't seem right, making deals with a bloodsucking capitalist landowner.'

'An arrangement between equals.'

Sammy glowered at him. 'No, it's *realpolitik*, that's what it is. And I've never liked the taste of that.' His mouth twisted. 'But sometimes it's necessary.'

'And I can trust you to overlook what you saw on the shore?'

Sammy nodded.

'We've still got a little evidence to dispose of.' Mor held out the glass vial and handed him the silver spoon.

'Personally, I'm fed up with the Seeing,' said Doreen. She wriggled her toes, which had gone numb long ago. The silk underwear kept the rest of her warm. 'But it's Alice. She's such a bad-tempered old besom. I'd have given it up long ago but... Well, I didn't like to disappoint her.'

'I'd be terrified to disappoint her,' said George. He couldn't press any closer to Doreen. The dampness from the cave floor was seeping its way up through his clothes.

Doreen thought about Alice, in a bad mood, when she'd been thwarted. A cold fury was the least of it, and it went on for hours, even days. 'Yes. Well. Anyway, I keep doing it, even though I don't really want to. I haven't really got the talent for it.' She turned to look at George. She could see his shape and feel his shoulder, so she knew she was looking in the right direction. 'So I have to make it up.'

'What does Alice think of that?' He felt Doreen shrug her shoulders.

'She just accepts it. It's a funny thing, though. There's lots of stuff here, just now. I can feel it swirling just beyond my eyes. I can See all sorts of things but when the morning comes, it all fades away. I forget almost everything.' She paused to think. 'And then, when I take the Witches Eye, I remember it all again, what happened last time and the time before that.'

George shifted uncomfortably. 'I, eh,' he coughed. 'I know what you're talking about.'

'Really?' Doreen sounded dubious. 'Do you take archaic herbal concoctions too?'

'No, not that. But there's something that keeps happening to me. I go into these places and spend days there and when I come out, I forget.'

'Places? Like bars?'

'No! Sort of in-between places. Like I might slip through the gap between two walls that join each other... or I might go through a doorway and come out somewhere else.'

'Is that so? Have you seen a doctor about this?'

'It's true! It really happens.'

'What sort of places do you go to?'

'Strange places. There are men and women there. They look normal, but they're bigger than usual people, more solid, more real. You know?'

'No, I don't know. Tell me more. Who are they?'

'Just the people that live there. Somehow they seem perfectly normal when I'm there, but when I'm leaving, just as I'm leaving, I think – Is it normal for a man to be nine feet tall with red hair to his waist? Is it normal for such a man to wear gold bracelets as thick as my wrist and is it not a bit odd to have a pack of red and white hounds, some of them with two heads? But somehow I don't feel astonished, you know, not even at the stone he has that always returns to his hand when he throws it.

'And then there's the woman, nearly as tall as him. She has long red braids and a quiver of arrows slung on her back. The strap for the quiver is of doeskin, and it lies between her breasts. When she looks at me with her green eyes, I almost forget who I am.

'Sometimes, when I'm leaving, I stop and wonder to myself, not at all astonished, but just curious about whether this is really the way the world is. Then I step out, and for a moment, the world is like a shadow, a dream. I feel as if I could put my hand right through solid stone. I feel as if I've lost my home,' he finished sadly.

Doreen sat silently in the dark. Outside a cloud had passed across the moon, and the darkness in the cave was velvet black.

'Then in a matter of moments, everything slips away,' George continued. 'I forget it all.'

The moon shone bright again. Doreen could make out George's shape once more. 'George, that's amazing. Does Alice know this?'

'Alice? How would she know?' Doreen thought it unlikely that anything like this would get past Alice, but she said nothing. 'No,' he continued, 'I haven't told anyone but you. I tried to tell my grandad something about it, but he wouldn't listen. Anyway, I couldn't remember much. Just something about a boar, or killing someone. I forget.'

'A boar?' George did not reply. The vertigo of Witches Eye caught Doreen in its grip and she began to mutter to herself. Small clouds were scudding across the moon. The dim light from the cave mouth flickered. Doreen could feel the Witches Eye teasing at her vision. The edges of the cave mouth glowed and distorted. George seemed to be changing shape, his hair growing coarse and spiky, his face elongating. A breeze whistled through the cave bringing the smell of damp leaves, mud and the rank smell of pig. She closed her eyes. She could see sunshine on a patch of woodland that reached down to the shore. An enormous man bearing a spear waded through the waves, watching the forest edge, calling to the dogs baying amongst the trees. A giant boar suddenly sprang out of the woods onto the shingle shore. As the man hurled the spear, it wheeled and dashed back amongst the trees, the spear thudding into a tree by its flank.

The scene disappeared and another patch of sunlight lay on a township by the shore – hovels of sod, shacks of rough timber, one or two small round-houses of stone. Smoke drifted from smoke-holes. Outside, people sat by open fires, talking as they cleaned animal skins, worked a spindle, carved a stick. A young man walked out from among the dwellings. He was tall and his hair was long: his clothes showed the signs of travelling. People turned to call greetings to him. He waved as he passed, obviously pleased to be among friends. He walked down to the shore, and beyond him the distinctive double headlands of the Suitors showed.

'And that's where I used to spend all my time, when I was a boy.'

Doreen opened her eyes. 'What?'

'Down in the Vennels. The old houses with the sod roofs, the people working outside by the fires.'

'Listen, this can't be real. I mean, not really real. I See things, but I don't think they're real.'

'Oh yes, I'm afraid so.' He shivered and scrambled up. 'Damn! Caught my head again.'

'But how does it happen?'

'It just does.' George said. 'I pass near to an interesting looking doorway or a dark corner or something like that. That's when I begin to remember about the place – the memories just flood back. I walk into the doorway, and I'm gone.'

'Just... gone?'

'Yeah. Just like that. Look, see that patch of darkness there, just beside you?'

'Where?'

'Just there. Now, it's just as if I were to step into it,' he stepped over her legs, 'and...'

The moon had disappeared again, behind a particularly thick cloud. For a few seconds, even the cave entrance was lost in the inky black.

'And what?' asked Doreen nervously. 'George? George?'

Moonlight sent its pale light into the cave again, but revealed no trace of George.

From *Meaning in Myth: An Analysis of the Celtic Hunting Story* by Dr Lorraine MacDonald, published by the Rossland Press, 1994

The older version of the story avoids the embellishments of the later re-tellings. Consider this passage:

A hunting party of young men, known as the Fianna, were out hunting, when they passed into a strange mist. They travelled on through the haze, crying to each other and to their dogs, to keep together in the mirk. Passing again into the daylight, they saw a boar as large as a stag, watching them from the edge of a wood. A red woman was standing by its head.

The Fianna cried out in joy at finding such a beast, and set to chasing it. As it turned from them, they saw that it had a shining crescent, like the moon, on each of its sides.

Looking just at these two paragraphs, we can not doubt that we are already well into the realm of the Otherworld. The mist is usually a clue to the passage of the protagonists into Other Realms. The woman is red, the colour of the Otherworld. The great boar itself is plainly supernatural, linked to the Goddess by the symbology of the moon.

The story continues:

The Fianna followed the beast both night and day, seeing ever and anon as they travelled, the red woman, now on the hillside, now among the trees.

At the dawn, the boar plunged into the side of a hill and disappeared. The Fianna were confounded, and milled about the hillside, the dogs baying uselessly, for they could in no wise discern where the beast had gone.

Suddenly the red woman appeared among them and struck the hillside with her staff. The hill broke open and the Fianna entered. Inside was a great hall, lit as by the sun and moon for brightness. A great feast was laid, and at the head of the table, clothed in gold and green, a man who had the look of a king, sitting in a golden chair.

Before they could partake of the feast, the Boar appeared and came close to the king. 'I am going now to my own country,' the Boar said, then turned and ran from the hall.

All day long the Fianna followed the Boar. At the middle part of the day it began to weaken, and as the afternoon went on, it grew weaker, until at nightfall it dropped down dead.

They stood around the fallen beast in astonishment, when once again the red woman appeared among them.

'This too was a king,' she said. 'King of the Fir Bolg.'

In this story we have one of the very few hints that still exist about the nature of the Fir Bolg society. It is fascinating that the great totem of the Celts, the Boar, is associated also with the Fir Bolg, and that the great Goddess is also involved. It is difficult to escape the conclusion that the Fianna are being shown something here about the connection of the Fir Bolg to the country in which they lived, and more specifically, the link, amounting to an unbreakable bond, between the king and the land. There is the exciting hint of a solar hero also in the manner of the Boar's death, and indeed the whole has a premonitory atmosphere, hinting at the themes of the Grail and the Fisher King, to reappear later in the Celtic cycles, particularly, of course, in the Arthurian legends.

'Well that seems to be the entertainment finished,' said Jimmy Bervie, as the sound of the police vans faded away.

M Le Placs looked across to the boat tied against the harbour wall. 'They didn't seem to be at all happy. What do you think they were looking for?'

'Probably the Holy Grail.'

'The Grail?'

'Och, yes. Most likely. Though it might have been the elixir of youth. The blue serge uniform of the British Constabulary covers one of the most venerable branches of an ancient chivalric order. Under the guise of Law Enforcement, they have virtually unlimited licence to search for the arcane secrets of the ages. Through the centuries they have sought for the Philosopher's Stone, the Holy Grail and the alchemical secrets of how to transform base metals into gold.'

'Zut! Is this so?'

'Indeed. They even flaunt their secret quest, expecting no-one to notice – an unwarranted arrogance. The policeman on the beat is known as the copper – and copper is of course one of the base metals. During the alchemical transformation, copper becomes refined to silver.'

'So?'

'At the next stage of initiation, the copper becomes a sergeant.'

'Sorry, my friend, I have become lost.'

'As you will of course know, in certain occult tables of equivalents, the letters s and z represent zero. So if we ignore the letter s in the word sergeant, we are left with Argent – which, in your own language, is silver. This symbolises the beginning of their transforming journey through the levels. Once they attain the major level in this eclectic brotherhood, what are they rewarded with? Gold braid on the uniform.'

'*Mon Dieu*! It is so obvious! You must know, then, why they are also called 'bobbies'. There must be a good reason, no?'

Jimmy winked and conspiratorially tapped the side of his nose. 'A coded reference to their association with occult branches of the Roman Catholic Church. You have heard of Greyfriars Bobby?'

The Frenchman laughed. 'Most ingenious. But also whimsical, hein?'

Jimmy waved his child's windmill. The little wheel twirled merrily, sending out its Tibetan prayer: OM AH HUM VAJRA GURU PADMA SIDDHI HUM.

'Perhaps,' he said. 'The most useful fact about facts is that you can use any one of them to illuminate any other.'

'But no! Not just any facts!'

Jimmy nodded. 'Oh yes. Unexpected correspondences leap out of the twilight of consciousness into the broad light of day.'

'No, no. I think you are joking. This is preposterous.'

'Try it, *mon brave*,' said Jimmy. 'When you find yourself discovering something you could not have learnt by conventional means, you will think again.'

'But this is a... a maltreatment of facts!'

'Och, people give facts altogether too much respect, in my opinion.'

The Frenchman muttered and grumbled as he finished his coffee.

Jimmy smiled. 'There remains a small question as to how you managed to predict the winners in a five-horse accumulator last week? Not to mention a sizeable pools win the week before. There is more there, I think, than meets the eye?'

Le Placs shrugged ruefully. 'It is so.'

'Facts then, are not necessarily paramount... Now, I believe the tide has receded sufficiently. Shall we address ourselves to the discipline of the sand?' Jimmy took the rake from its resting place against the house wall.

Le Placs stood and they walked together to the end of Jimmy's garden. The full moon had swung round, but the sea still shone silver and black, with the headlands of the Suitors standing out jet-black and knife-edged against the sky.

Jimmy knelt down and felt the sand. Le Placs followed his example.

'A little wet, perhaps, but good enough for a little demonstration.' He held the rake poised in both hands. 'The first pull,' he said. Reaching out, he let the tines of the rake dig lightly into the sand then pulled smoothly and easily. 'Look,' he said. A set of clear, straight furrows lay in the sand, the moon's rays giving each furrow a clear dark edge.

Le Placs nodded. 'Looks very good.'

'And again...' Jimmy pulled once more. Harmonious lines appeared as the head of the rake passed over the damp sand.

'It looks easy enough,' said Le Placs.

Jimmy nodded. 'It's not so difficult. A few decades of practice and it comes almost naturally. Would you like to try?' He handed the rake to Le Placs. 'With you being a surgeon, you might well get the feel for it.'

Le Placs took the rake in his delicate hands, reached and pulled. Jimmy watched his technique, nodding his head. 'Yes, good. A good competent pull. Now...' He turned to look at the lines in the sand. Halfway along the draw, the straight parallel lines twisted across each other, producing a confused muddle of lines that was not pleasing to look at.

'*Merde*. Sorry Jimmy. I have done it wrong.'

Jimmy peered at the disharmonious muddle of lines, a puzzled frown on his broad pink forehead. 'No, indeed. Not your mistake, I think.'

He held out his hand absently and Le Placs handed him the rake. Jimmy grasped the pole firmly, reached and pulled. Parallel lines sprang into life behind the head of the rake, but Jimmy was not watching. His gaze was fixed on the single unmoving point, far beyond the sphere of this world. His body reached and pulled again and again, his body seeming that of a Titan, more solid than rock, more real than reality. Le Placs could not take his eyes from the mystical roll and twist of Jimmy's shoulders.

At last Jimmy was finished. He had raked his way across the full width of his garden, where it encroached on the beach. He stood with rake in hand, gazing at the pearly shimmer in the dark sky beyond Dornoch.

Then he looked down.

From end to end, right across the patch of raked sand, was a twisted roiling anomaly, where the lines of raking had been distorted by an underlying disturbance in the nature of the space-time continuum.

'Well, bugger me!' said Jimmy. 'It's happening again.'

Behind the massive fences of Redrock Estate, the largest boar stirred and snuffled at the breeze. The full moon shone on the rolling acres of heather and scrub. A family group of a sow and ten piglets appeared over the edge of Redrock Gorge.

Far to the west, beyond Glen Grian, there was a faint sound of music from the rave at Rossfarm. The boar could hear the sound, but ignored it. To the north, the bright headlights of the police vans were visible, as they raced up the drive from the gate lodge, heading for Redrock House. The boar paid no attention. Out at sea, to the south, coastguards and customs officials had apprehended a freighter and were searching it for the second time, very thoroughly. The lights were plainly visible, and even the dark bulk of the ships could be seen. Strangely, the boar's small brain grasped this also, but he ignored it.

To the east, Doreen was by herself, huddling in a cave below the cliffs. From the east there was silence, and nothing to be seen. The boar was listening and watching.

The sow grunted and headed towards the huge boar. The piglets squealed as they followed her. The boar snorted at her and trotted away.

Not long afterwards, the fence shivered as a huge body forced its way beneath the wire and the beast began to gallop across the moor.

From *The Merry Wanderer: A Touring Guide to the Dark Isle*
published by Dark Isle Tourist Agency, 1958, reprinted 1977

If the visitor to Cromness should decide to return to the Castleton ferry along the south edge of the Dark Isle, he will find, after mounting the slopes that make up the Ardmeanach ridge, that the road descends into the very pretty valley known as Glen Grian (Valley of the Sun). The road winds down among the trees to where the valley debouches into the river-plain, where the village of Rossmarty is to be found.

The plain of Rossmarty is a fertile delta which has been inhabited continuously since Stone Age times. As a centre of some importance to the Dark Isle, it was one of the first Christian centres. The earliest

Christian traces are those of the Culdees, a Celtic branch of Christianity which diminished in importance with the growing influence of the Roman Catholic church.

Before the Christian era, however, the area was already of religious importance. It seems likely that the Culdee centre was based on the remnants of an earlier Druidic college. Traditions suggest that Egyptian priests were sent to Rossmarty for part of their training.

The existing church in the village incorporates several Celtic carved stones in its walls. These may be viewed any weekday afternoon by appointment with Mr Gallagher, Rose Cottage, High Street.

Rossmarty has much to offer to the wayfarer: a fine beach, excellent fishing in both sea and river, a recreation park for children and much quaint and intriguing architecture. Visitors wishing refreshment may profitably make the acquaintance of Mario's Ice Cream Parlour. For those wishing something more sustaining, the Ploughman's Inn serves a selection of fine beers and can also provide meals (within licensing hours).

Wee Eck strode along the narrow path. Moonlight fell in patches through the canopy of trees, so that light flickered across his naked upper body as he moved. He seemed to pass through the woods with the ease of a spirit. Branches and briars encroached on the path, but they seemed to bend aside to let him pass. Veronica hurried to keep up with him, holding one arm up to protect her eyes from the twigs.

'Eck!' she called. 'Eck, slow down!'

Eck stopped and turned, smiling. His pony-tail swung as he turned, and the freckled moonlight danced on the muscles of his broad chest. A branch overhung the path just where he had stopped, and a cluster of leaves hung down just over his brow, so that they looked like a woodland crown.

Veronica was awestruck by the beauty of the moment, even though she could see how the event had come about. Eck was living a fantasy of himself, watching the world as it changed around him, adjusting his perceptions and his personal fantasy to match it. Dancing his way through, listening to the music of the world.

The vanity of Eck was at once amusing and touching. He plainly thought that the moonlight and the woods and the girl had been laid on purely so that he could display himself to best effect. Veronica smiled and shook her head.

'You're at the right place at just the right time,' she said.

Eck stood before her with his arms out, palms held up, as if offering her the trees and moonlight. 'Let us commune with the spirits,' he said.

He beckoned to her and slipped off the path between two birch trees.

It had to be birch trees, she thought. She could almost feel the living presence of the trees, the graceful dryad of the birch turning to watch her as she passed. The leaves gave a delicate shiver in the breeze.

Eck was standing in front of a fine old Scots Pine. The mighty column of its trunk soared up thirty feet in a single clean swoop before the first branches sprang from it. Eck reached out towards its orange bark. Veronica flinched. It seemed almost sacrilegious to touch it.

'Do you see it?' Eck looked back at her. 'Can you see the spirit?'

Veronica squinted at the tree. She could see its shape with unusual clarity, she could almost feel the texture of its bark, just by looking at it. It looked like the very archetype of a Scots Pine, the shape that all other pine trees were trying for, but couldn't quite attain.

'Well,' she said.

'Come here. Stand beside it. Now put your arms around it.'

Veronica trembled at the thought. It seemed such a powerful thing, this tree. She was afraid to be too familiar with it. She reached forward, then paused. And not just that. She was also acutely embarrassed at the thought of embracing it. It was such a... virile tree. That was it. It was far too phallic. She blushed and laughed at the same time. She could hardly believe that any part of her would entertain such ridiculous ideas, still less take them seriously. She shook herself mentally to dispel the idiotic notions. Her mind cleared. Around her, the trees and shrubs seemed to be waiting. Even the grass and the moss was watching. The spirit of the woods was in the very air that she breathed, in the smell of mud and rotting leaves, in the scent of pine resin.

'Do you mind looking away?' she asked Eck.

'Eh?'

She blushed furiously, but managed to look him in the eye. 'Could you look away, please. This is a very private thing.' For the first time, she saw Eck lose his calm certainty – something was going on that he did not know about. She felt more sure of herself. 'Please,' she repeated, firmly.

'Sure, sure,' he muttered and turned his back. She leant forwards slowly and wrapped her arms as far round the trunk as she could. The warm dry bark pressed against her cheek, scraped roughly at her forearms. She shuffled her feet as close to the trunk as they could get, then held tight, closed her eyes and let herself fall into the giddy swimming sensation inside her.

From outside herself, she could see her body in its cotton dress holding tight to the base of a tree. She moved farther and farther away. From a great height she looked down on the valley of Glen Grian and saw the canopy of leaves glowing with life. There was a blue-green vortex of light above the pine tree, and two small figures were sheltered within its aura – a young woman clutching the tree and a young man standing a few yards off, turning his head to look back over his shoulder. There were other creatures in the Glen. Two deer by the mill-pond, countless rabbits further up the hillside and a dog with two heads. For the length of one long breath she hovered over the Glen, then she swooped down towards the young woman in the cotton dress. She felt skin pressing against warm, rough bark and she knew that she was one or the other.

Eck saw her lift her head from the tree's trunk, smiling.

'This is who I am,' she said.

When the police burst in, Sammy Poach and Mr Mor were sitting at the table, each with a glass of brandy. Mr Mor was sipping his. Sammy was drinking his.

'What is the meaning of this?' Mr Mor rose in a theatrical show of anger. 'How dare you burst into my house!'

'Shut your trap!'

'I beg your pardon? This is an outrage!'

'Sorry. Please shut your trap, sir. And read this.' The man pulled a sheet of paper from his pocket and held it up so that Mr Mor could read it. Uniformed police swarmed into the room and began opening cupboards and pulling out drawers. 'As you can see, I am Inspector Morrison, and I am empowered to search these premises.'

'This could be a forgery! Let me see your warrant card!'

Inspector Morrison held out his identification, a thin smile on his face.

'All in order, as you can see.'

Outside in the yard, crashing sounds could be heard as the steadings were searched with extreme prejudice.

'I wish to phone my lawyer!'

'By all means. Bring in all the weasels in Rossland if you want. Our papers are in order and by the time they get here we'll have searched the whole shebang. For the moment, I must ask you to remain in this room.' He looked at Sammy. 'And who have we here? If I'm not mistaken, it's Sammy Poach, the scourge of the salmon and weel-kent local revolutionary. Are you mixed up in this too?'

Sammy opened his mouth to reply. Mr Mor spoke.

'My friend Samuel and I were having a drink when you burst in.'

'Really? I must say this is a most suspicious circumstance.' He turned to Mr Mor. 'You have the salmon fishings, I believe. This man is a well-known poacher. It seems a little odd for him to be here.' He glanced at Sammy. 'Especially as there is blood on his head.'

'Is there, indeed?' The cocaine had dealt with the pain quite efficiently.

Sammy had forgotten about his wound. He patted his head and looked at his hand. 'God, you're right! It had quite slipped my mind.'

The inspector looked at Mor and Sammy suspiciously. 'There hasn't been any trouble here, has there?' He focused on Sammy. 'I would be delighted to charge someone with assault, if you want.'

Sammy held up his hands. 'Trouble? No, by God. No trouble here. Blood on my head? I fell coming down the stairs that's all. Bloody nuisance, stairs, I mean, you'd think some bright spark might invent stairs that went down both ways, to save legwork. Or up both ways, to save falling down. But no. All the bright boys are employed designing the next wave of police uniforms.' A uniformed policeman was checking the drawers in the sideboard. Sammy reached out and flicked one of the silver buttons. 'And damn fine uniforms they are, too. As uniforms go, you know.'

'Sir, we've found this.' A policeman held up a sheet of paper. 'Under the sideboard, there.' He pointed. Inspector Morrison glanced at the sideboard and the picture above it.

'Right,' he said. 'You watch these two and I'll apply a superior intellect to this problem. Pay attention, everyone.' He walked up to the sideboard and held up the sheet of paper.

'That's my private paperwork,' shouted Mr Mor.

'Indeed.' Morrison smiled without humour. 'Constable Spence found this piece of paper on the floor, just about here. Am I right?'

'Yes, sir.'

'Now, your average intellect sees such a thing and says to itself – This may be vital evidence – and forthwith brings it to me, expecting a pat on the head.' Constable Spence blushed. 'So I look at where it was found and what do I see? A bloody great picture on the wall. Just the sort, you might think, behind which to hide a safe. The superior intellect also notices that said picture is squint. Look, gentlemen! The picture is not hanging straight! Does this suggest anything to anyone?'

All the policemen kept quiet, not wanting to attract Inspector Morrison's sarcasm.

'Now that is why I am the Inspector here. You look at a squint picture and say – That picture is not straight. I look at the same picture and say – Someone moved this picture and replaced it in a hurry.' He beckoned to two men. 'You two, take that picture down.'

'Take care! That's an original Landseer!'

The picture was removed, and behind it was the safe.

'Aha! Inspector Morrison leaned forwards and pointed to a corner of white paper showing at the edge of the safe door. 'Further evidence of undue haste, I believe.' He looked at the combination lock. 'Well, Mr

Mor, are you going to save us some trouble and open this safe for us?'

'I'm damned if I'll give you any assistance. That safe stays closed until my lawyer gets here!'

'Oh dear. That won't look well in court. The accused refused to render assistance to the police.' He shrugged. 'Back to work, men. Search everything and everywhere – but I suspect that the answers we need are in that tin box there.' He turned to Mr Mor. 'I could not have more respect for the criminal mind,' he said. 'Take that however you will. You will, of course, forgive me if in this instance I try one or two of the most obvious combinations. Not, of course, that I expect them to work, but just to be thorough.'

He opened his notebook and leafed through it. Then he leant over the sideboard and began to turn the wheels of the combination lock. There was a click and the safe door swung open, revealing untidy piles of papers. The other policemen turned round in astonishment. Inspector Morrison looked first shocked, then smug. He looked across at Mr Mor contemptuously. 'The date of your bloody birthday,' he said. 'So much for the criminal mastermind!'

'These are perfectly legitimate business papers. I insist that you leave them alone!'

'Spence,' Morrison called. 'Bag up this lot.' He leafed through the papers. 'What the hell?' He began to smile. 'Well, well! Looks as if we've got you for fraud as well! If I'm not mistaken, and I rarely am, you've been claiming EC subsidies on salmon that you didn't catch!' He rubbed his hands together heartily, beaming round at the room. 'Oh, we'll bang you away for years!'

Mr Mor looked down at the table and sipped his brandy. Sammy refilled his glass and took a large swallow.

'So, now you've met the spirit of the Pine tree,' said Wee Eck. He spoke heartily, trying to take charge of the night once more.

Veronica nodded. 'A private communion took place,' she said and smiled tolerantly, seeing that he was upset because he didn't know what had happened at the pine tree.

'Okay, let's move on.' He turned away and stumbled over a tree root. He'd lost his grace, now that he had slipped away from the centre of the universe. She watched him treading carefully along the dark path, stepping over the trunk of a fallen tree. His movements were awkward, and the moonlight no longer fell so fortuitously on his muscled body.

'Look!' Eck hissed, pointing at a clearing thirty yards ahead. A deer had stepped onto the path. The moonlight was quite happy to play with its body.

'Wait,' said Eck. 'I can feel it – there's another one.' For a few seconds they all stood still, then another deer stepped out onto the path. Eck turned to look at Veronica. He was smiling again.

He's pleased that he knew about the other deer, she thought, and decided not to mention that she also had known there were two deer.

As Eck turned to look at the deer again, his head automatically ducked to slip past a trailing briar shoot. The deer slipped away into the shadows. 'Come on,' said Eck. 'There's a gorse bush over there. You must meet the spirit of the Gorse.'

The bush was a dense mass of orange flowers, broken only by the wicked green spikes.

'It looks hellish thorny,' said Veronica. 'I hope I don't have to embrace it.'

'No, no. Look.' Eck stood by the bush and held his hands, palms down, over it. He moved his hands in slow circles, a few inches above the blossoms. The dense smell of the blossom drifted over to Veronica. She almost felt she could see the Spirit of the Gorse, stirring sleepily and looking round.

'Let me try,' she said. She stretched her hands out and began to move them, encouraging the golden spirit to rise up from the bush. As the spirit of the Gorse rose beneath her hands, she felt a welling pleasure inside her. This was a creature of the Earth and she was meeting it for the first time. 'Gorse of the thousand swords,' she said.

'Eh?'

'A line from a Gaelic poem,' she said, and knew that she was right. But where had the words come from? For a moment, she seemed to be in a schoolroom, long ago, and she could hear a teacher reciting an endless poem called *The Battle of the Trees*. It was so clear in her mind that she looked around nervously, looking for the teacher – but of course the woods were empty, as far as she could see. There was no-one there except Eck and an enormous boar with gleaming red eyes and white tusks gleaming like sickle moons.

In the moonlight, the boar snorted and took a step forwards. Veronica backed until the gorse thorns were jabbing her thighs. She reached out and took hold of Wee Eck's arm.

'Eck. Eck! Look at that.'

Eck was watching the glow around the gorse bush. 'Yeah. It's really something, isn't it?'

'Not the bloody bush! That!'

Eck swung round and looked where she was pointing. Two birch trees stood with a mass of shadow between them. Moonlight glinted on patches of silvery bark. For a moment it looked almost as if there was a shadowy beast standing there – a stag, or an enormous boar with a white crescent moon on its side. 'Wow! It's like the Spirit of the woods or something!' Then he moved his head and the illusion became no more than patterns of shadow and light.

'It's gone,' she said. 'It just faded away.'

'Yeah,' he agreed. 'Woodland spirits are like that. One minute here, then there's nothing but...' He sniffed.

'Nothing but the smell of pig,' put in Veronica. 'And the mark of trotters in the mud.'

'What?'

'Look there. Just in front of that patch of dark shadow.'

'It can't be!' Eck walked over to the trees. As he bent to look at the muddy ground, someone stepped out of the shadow. Eck jumped backwards, his arms up to defend himself.

'Jesus Christ! Where did you come from?'

'Somewhere else,' said the newcomer. He looked around himself at the trees and underbrush.

'And this looks like Glen Grian.'

'Of course it is!'

Veronica was still standing by the gorse bush, poised to run away if necessary, watching the shadowy figure and wondering if he also was going to fade away into the moonlight. She flinched as he turned to look at her. But his face was familiar. She stepped forwards to see him more clearly. He took a step towards her and smiled uncertainly. 'Hi, Veronica.'

'George!' She laughed with relief and reached out towards him. She took his hand and squeezed. 'I'm glad you're real.'

George, surprised by this turn of events, held on to her hand firmly. 'Yes,' he said. 'I suppose I'm glad, too.'

'What are you doing here? At this time of night?'

'I'm not really sure,' he said. 'Something brought me here. I didn't really have any choice in the matter.'

She stepped back so that she could look into his face. His eyes looked disturbingly deep and dark, but perfectly honest.

'We came down here to chill out,' she said, smiling faintly, 'and to commune with the spirits.'

'You've stepped on the tracks!' Eck was on his knees by the birch trees. 'There's nothing here but your footprints.' He glared up at George. He and Veronica self-consciously disentangled their hands.

George frowned. 'What else would there be?'

'There were tracks here.' He paused for a moment. 'Veronica said there were tracks here.'

'There were. I saw them.'

'Maybe,' said Eck. He stood up. 'It could have been a trick of the light.'

Veronica shrugged. 'Possibly. An enormous boar with white shiny tusks that leaves trotter marks in the mud – nothing but a trick of the light. And of course the smell of pig. A strong smell of pig. Another trick of the light.'

'Decaying leaves,' said Eck.

'Eck,' said Veronica. 'You brought me here to show me the spirits of the trees. And now you're trying to convince me that I'm just imagining things?' She turned away. 'I think I'll get back to the barn.'

'Okay, you're right,' said Eck, hastily.

'About what?'

'Whatever it was you saw. But I didn't see it as clearly as you did. I wasn't sure.' He stepped up beside her. 'Come on, there's a fine willow on the way back.'

Veronica turned to George. 'Are you going to disappear?'

'I don't think so.'

She took his hand and tugged. 'Come on, then. You can commune with the Willow spirit too. Lead on, Eck.'

Eck stumbled on a tree root. 'Damn!'

Veronica let go of George's hand and they walked on through the woods in single file, mostly in silence, but with Eck swearing occasionally.

The police vans left, taking with them some of the staff from Redrock House, all the papers from the safe and a dozen small sacks of white powder found in a locker beside the big fibreglass salmon-tanks. More than half of the police officers remained at Redrock, posted at various points around the house and steadings. Inspector Morrison had called on the radio for reinforcements and was now prowling the house looking for vital evidence that his subordinates had missed.

The remaining staff of Redrock had been gathered into the dining room, and were being guarded by four policemen. Sammy and Mr Mor were sitting at one end of the walnut-topped dining table, talking in low voices. Sammy was drinking twenty year-old malt whisky. Mor was sipping brandy. He did not seem at all worried.

'In this game, you have to be a few steps ahead of everyone else,' he said. 'It's all a matter of psychology.'

'You can call it that if you like,' said Sammy Poach, 'But it doesn't explain a damn thing.'

'They were looking for evidence of criminal doings, and they wouldn't leave until they found some – or wrecked the house in their search. So I let them find the papers in the safe.'

'But what about the cocaine?'

'What cocaine? They took away twelve bags of marine fungicide. If they'd thought to check, they'd have found that it has no stimulant effect at all. And it burns in the nostrils too.'

'But they'll just be back again.'

'I think not. It'll take them a couple of days to test the fungicide. Then I suspect I will be getting a personal apology from Inspector Morrison.'

Sammy looked at him dourly. 'I doubt that. He's obviously a man who values his own good opinion of himself. And what about the papers in the safe? He was on the ball very quick with them, whatever they are.'

Mor chuckled. 'He was indeed, but he was on to the wrong ball. It'll take them a good few days to make sense of those documents. But if the Procurator Fiscal has any sense, he'll not try to prosecute.'

Sammy clenched his teeth. Mor was still a bloodsucking capitalist, and he was damned if he was going to try and draw him out. His underhanded shenanigans were his own business. On the other hand, what was he going to do about the cocaine that was even now swimming towards the beach?

'They'll be watching you closely now.'

'That's all right. I'll be watching for watchers.'

'But what about,' he glanced at the stern-looking policemen at each of the doors of the room. He lowered his voice. 'What about the drugs? The stuff that's coming in just now?'

'What drugs?'

'Damn it, the stuff you picked up tonight.'

'Eh?' Mr Mor looked lazily at Sammy. 'Wherever did you get that idea?'

Sammy swore and looked up at the ceiling. 'God help us! Didn't you tell me earlier this evening that you were a smuggler?'

'Yes, of course. But I didn't say what I smuggle.'

'What? The canisters aren't for drugs?'

'Not at all! Nothing so sordid. Not tonight, anyway.' He paused, and looked thoughtfully at Sammy. 'Let's just say it's connected with stock breeding. Not illegal.' He shrugged. 'Not very illegal.'

'Spirit of the wiry Willow!' Eck stood back from the tree. Veronica could almost be sure she was seeing the spirit of the Willow. She had an impression of sinuosity and toughness. The glow that surrounded the tree seemed to drift free of the wood, then sink into it again.

'Do you see it, George?' she asked.

'I can see something,' he replied, 'But I tend to steer clear of weirdness if I can. I've got far too much of it in my life.'

In the walk up through Glen Grian, Veronica had been watching

George, reading the language of his body. When he had first appeared, he stood straight and sure. Now, the hunched shoulders were defensive, the hesitant steps were nervous and diffident. He seemed almost like a different creature. His whole posture said that he was denying something. She nodded. Eck was a bit crazy, but he didn't deny the reality of the morphological congruencies of the living world. Shit! She thought. Do I think like that all the time? Do I talk like that?

Eck had regained some of his poise by now. 'Some people can see these things, some can't,' he said.

George shrugged. 'Oh, I can see them all right. I just don't want to. It makes me uneasy.'

'That'll be right,' said Eck, dubiously.

'I just don't trust these bloody morphological congruencies.'

Eck scowled. Veronica looked at George curiously. 'You want to explain that?'

'A life form can exist in more than one energy level, but they overlap. In fact, they occupy the same space.'

Veronica nodded. 'Like the tree and whatever it is that Eck calls the spirit of the tree.'

'Something like that. So it makes sense to you?'

'Yes, of course. I just haven't heard it in those words before.'

Eck could make neither head nor tail of this. He butted in before George could reply. 'I hear the jungle beat,' he said. His voice was tense, but he tried to speak lightly. 'The drums are calling.'

Sure enough, there was a faint rhythm of drums from above the Glen.

'It's the heat, Amanda, and the terrible, terrible drums,' said George, quietly.

'What?'

George looked abashed. 'It's a line from a film. About Europeans coming in contact with the savagery of nature – and the nature of the savage.'

Veronica laughed and looked at George with surprise. 'Your brain works oddly, but it gets there.'

Eck scowled. 'Come along!' he called, managing to calm himself. 'The Railroad is rolling!'

They climbed the path up from the Glen and as they topped the valley-side, the thump from the bass speakers rolled over the fields and through them. Eck let his hands dance and twitched his body. Veronica's head moved, her long dark hair waving down her back. George looked across the fields to the barn. A thin layer of mist had formed over the hillside, lying in skeins. Moonlight shone white on the barley in the first field. In the field beyond that, rows of turnips showed their big round heads above the soil, the leaves damp and black. The moon had come round to the west, and it hung above the barn, where light was streaming and flickering from the open doors.

Eck stepped out along the farm track. 'Lo!' he cried, 'The Spirit of the Barley!'

The barley was not yet ripe, and the creeping, swirling light that seemed to coalesce for a moment in the drifting mist before them had the form of a happy youth with just the beginnings of a beard. 'Ho, John Barleycorn!' cried Eck. The other two gave an involuntary bow as the momentary vision faded.

They walked on towards the barn, the music becoming louder and more compelling. Eck stepped and swayed along the track, his pony-tail swinging to the music. They reached the edge of the turnip field. Eck slowed down and eyed it dubiously, then slyly glanced across at Veronica. She looked back at him with her eyebrows raised. He sighed.

'The spirit of the Turnip,' he called, not loudly.

George turned to him. 'What did you say?'

'The spirit of the Turnip!' repeated Eck, more loudly.

Mist rolled slowly down the field. To the eyes of the imagination, it formed into a round, sad face. The air felt suddenly damp and chilly.

Veronica shivered. 'Come on, let's get inside.'

Eck was happy to leave the turnip field behind him. 'You got a ticket?' he asked George.

'Come on, Eck,' said Veronica. 'Who's going to worry about that at this time? It's nearly dawn.'

Eck muttered to himself as they all entered the barn. The dance floor was not so crowded as it had been, but those who remained were still full of energy.

An ungainly figure in flared trousers and a turtle-neck sweater bopped past. He waved to Eck. 'Yo there, my pony-tailed friend!'

'Yeah, yeah. Yo to you too,' said Eck.

Rev Dumfry noted Eck's despondent tones and bopped past again. 'Light up, friend!' he shouted. 'The Railway is running on time!'

George spoke to Veronica. 'I'm going to have to go soon. I have to get home.'

She looked surprised. 'You just got here.'

'I know, I'd like to stay, but it's my grandad.'

She looked at him quizzically.

'I've sort of lost him. It's kind of urgent.'

Veronica nodded. 'There must be someone here going your way.'

'Maybe.'

'Wait here a minute.' She slipped in among the dancers. George watched the strange man talking to Eck. He would utter a word or two, then do a few jerky steps, while Eck tried to find a suitable reply.

Veronica went over to the podium where Chief Stoker was mixing the music. She spoke to him for a few seconds, then the music faded down to let the DJ perform an impromptu rap.

'Calling all trippers on the Eden Express,

'we have a body in the hall needing taken to Cromness.

'Hold up your hand, George, and wave it in the air,

'brothers and sisters, that's George over there!

'Thanks to you all, and lets roll!'

Embarrassed, George waved his hand in the air. The music faded up again.

Veronica reappeared at his side.

'Thanks, Veronica.'

'Nothing to it,' she smiled.

His face was still red with embarrassment. 'You home for long?' he asked.

'A week or two more.'

He coughed and tried to look casual. 'Will you be going to the Dark Isle Show?'

'Of course. Never miss it,' she lied. 'Will you be going?'

'Oh, yes. Do you think...'

The ungainly man in flared trousers was suddenly standing in front of him.

'George?' he asked.

'Yes. I'm George.'

'I'm just about to return to Cromness. You are in need of a lift, I believe?'

'Oh, yes, thanks.' He turned to Veronica. 'The Dark Isle Show. I wonder if...'

'Yes, of course,' she said. She waved to him and danced away. George followed Dumfry from the barn. Dawn was brightening the eastern sky.

When dawn brought pale light into the sky, Doreen stirred from her seat on the cold rock. The visions had stopped some hours before, and the stimulating effect of Witches Eye had also run out. She was deeply chilled, stiff and miserable.

She stumbled through the puddles on the cave floor then clambered down the rock face, the wet limestone leaving white smears on her clothes. She stood on the shingle, stamping her feet and flapping her arms. She stumped down the beach, then back again, until the stiffness grew less and she could walk rather than hobble. She made for the rocky headland at the end of the bay, her feet slipping in the shingle. The sky was now bright with sunrise and when she had scrambled up the rocks she could see two figures at the edge of Cromness, starting along the path.

'Damned if I'm waiting,' she muttered and clumsily climbed down the rocks to the beach.

Letter from Mr Siller to the Elders of the First Reformed and Ancient Church, Cromness

```
Dear Brethren,

    It has come to my attention that our present incumbent,
Reverend Dumfry, has on several occasions behaved in
such a manner that, while it may be (pending further
enquiry) that his motives were innocent, his acts may
have caused the Church and his position within it to be
called into disrepute.
    Furthermore, he has expressed sentiments and beliefs
not wholly consonant with the guidelines set out in our
Articles of Doctrine (1854).
    Wishing to give Reverend Dumfry every support in what
is, perhaps, a temporary lapse of faith, I feel that it
has become necessary to call him before a committee of
Elders, where we may give him necessary Instruction,
that he shall be strengthened in his belief. I hereby
formally request that an audience be called, requiring
that all Elders should be present (excepting for the
purposes of charity and mercy) after the evening service
of the Sunday following this date.

    Sincerely in God's name,
    T. Siller (Elder)
```

The air was cold outside the barn. The sound of the music faded as they hurried to the field where the cars were parked. Rev Dumfry unlocked the shiny black car and they climbed in. The music was cut off as the car doors closed. Dumfry edged the car carefully out of the field and down the farm track. Once the car was purring along the main road, he turned to George.

'My name is Dumfry,' he said. 'I'm the minister in Cromness South Church.'

George stared at him curiously. 'I'm George MacLear,' he said. Then added awkwardly. 'I'm afraid I don't often go to church.'

Dumfry nodded sympathetically. 'I had noticed that we were failing to attract young people to the church. In fact, that was why I was at the event this evening. I felt that I had to know what was going on, why so many young people were turning to the dance and to these raves, while rejecting the church.'

George's sleepless night was overcoming his curiosity. The car was growing warm and he was beginning to doze, but he managed to nod politely.

'Now it seems to me that I understand more,' Dumfry continued. 'I can speak to the young people because... because I understand. They find the dance a sacramental act. They attain a communion. Theologically I have to say that it is a communion of humans, rather than a communion with the Divine – but is there really such a difference? If the Divine in humanity is invoked, then we see the profane becoming the sacred. Don't you think so?'

George roused himself to reply. 'I thought they went to raves to get out of their heads.'

'Yes! A very good way of putting it. Out of their heads and into the transcendent! I must slip that into the sermon tomorrow.' He glanced at the brightening sky and laughed. 'Oh my goodness, the night has passed! Of course I mean today. There are changes in the procedures of worship that I would like to implement also, rather than adhering to the rigid traditional forms.'

George looked at Dumfry's eyes and realised that he was really talking to himself. He yawned. 'What sort of changes?'

'I scarcely know yet. But if the church is to survive we must introduce some of this enthusiasm into the services!'

The car climbed over the top of the Ardmeanach ridge and far off the waters of the Firth suddenly became visible. Beyond the Suitors, the sun was hanging just above the horizon, laying a golden path across the sea. George roused himself to look around at the familiar view, wide and beautiful.

The car rounded a bend and there were the Redrock Estate fences bordering the road, strong enough to restrain a stampede of buffalo. Two miles beyond, across the rolling acres of moorland, the tower of Redrock House stood stark and black against the bright morning sky. George's mouth twisted. He had spent long days of his childhood exploring those moors, getting lost there, discovering lochans and streams, the nests of plover, the skeletons of sheep in bogs. Now no-one could walk there, no-one could wander. What possible use could Mr Mor have for such fences? To protect the grouse? The fences would stop an army, never mind a few poachers.

He sat up straight, remembering his grandfather. Dumfry dawdled down the long slope to Cromness, babbling about the presence of God. He made some stupid joke about Noah's shirt while George gritted his teeth in impatience. Relax, he told himself. Sammy may be old, but he can look after himself.

When Dumfry dropped him off at the top of the Waye, he barely waited to thank him before running down towards the Vennels.

You're being stupid, he thought to himself. The old man is fine. He paused at the door, waiting until his breath had slowed. Then he opened the door of the empty house.

From the Rossland Advertiser
LOCAL LAIRD ARRESTED

Police at Inverness are believed to have uncovered a smuggling ring which has been importing drugs through the Dark Isle, using the tiny port at Cromness, better known as a base for dolphin trips, as the centre for their operations. Last night a special squad of police swooped on the village and arrested the entire crew of a fishing boat before proceeding to Redrock House, where they interviewed the proprietor, Mr Mor.

Mr Mor took over the run-down Redrock Estate just four years ago and has restored it to some of its former grandeur. In addition to the salmon fishings, he is also believed to have a controlling interest in several local companies, such as Boblair Fabricators, Rossmarty Leisure Incorporated and Ardmeanach Windfarms. Aristide Coupar, a member of Cromness Council, confirmed that funding from Redrock Estate was also an important factor in the recent bid for EC assistance to restore Cromness Harbour.

A spokesman for the Redrock Estate said this morning that Mr Mor was voluntarily assisting police with their enquiries. 'Our investigations are proceeding,' said Inspector Morrison in an exclusive interview for the Rossland Advertiser.

'Doreen! You're supposed to wait in the cave until we've done the blessing!'

Doreen didn't even bother getting angry.

'You want to bless that damp pit of misery, you go and do it. I'm wet and chilled to the bone. I'm going home.'

Alice stood grimly blocking the path. Doreen waited, not confronting her, but not giving in either.

Alice spoke through her teeth. 'Someone's got to bless it. It's part of the ritual.'

'You don't need me for that. I'm not waiting.' Doreen stepped down on to the beach and walked round Alice.

'Here, you do it.' Alice handed a plastic carrier bag to Lorraine.

'Me? But will it be all right? I'm not... I mean I've never...'

'I hereby initiate you into the mysteries of the Goddess. Do you swear never to reveal these mysteries and to do all that is required of an initiate?'

'Well, of course. I think I'm trustworthy. It's just...'

'Right, you're one of us now. So go and bless the cave. I've got to get the prophecies out of Doreen.'

Lorraine stood with the bag in her hand and watched Alice turn to follow Doreen. She wailed at Alice's back, 'But what do I do?'

'For Goddess' sake woman! Improvise! Sprinkle the water, throw the grain about and bless the place in the name of the Mother.'

Alice lumbered along the path after Doreen, muttering to herself, 'Honestly, initiates these days! No gumption.'

Lorraine looked into the bag. There was a handful of porridge oats in the bottom, and a plastic bottle of water. She turned unhappily towards the cave.

Rev Dumfry parked the car and went straight into the church.

'Good morning, church,' he called loudly. The door banged behind him. He let his eyes take in the familiar shapes: the ranks of pews, the strip of carpet up the aisle, the arched timber roof, reminiscent of the timbers of an upturned boat. He looked at the tall windows. They let in plenty light, but the lower edge was six feet from the floor, so that the congregation would not be distracted by the world outside. His primary school had had similar windows. He shivered in the chill of the building. He walked over to the heating controls and snorted. Siller had turned it down a few degrees to save money. Honestly, the man was next thing to a miser. He turned the dial up then walked down the aisle and knelt at the front. He closed his eyes and began to pray.

After a few seconds, he opened his eyes and looked behind him. There was no-one there. He closed his eyes again, but couldn't settle. It felt almost as if someone was watching him. He opened his eyes and glanced around nervously.

He stood up and began to prowl the huge empty building, looking into the corners and hidden places. As he stalked around, he turned abruptly now and then, to catch the secret watcher, but saw no-one. His uneasiness increased. He found dust, he found chewing gum and he found a lone penny, but nothing that could explain his uneasiness.

At last he stood at bay, backed into a corner. He had searched every inch of the building and there was definitely no-one else here, but there was something very wrong in the church. He pressed back into the cold stone walls so that nothing could creep up on him.

'There's no-one here!' he called out. 'There's no-one here!'

The echoes rattled around the huge hall, and he felt the hairs rise on the back of his neck. That's what it was! No-one was watching him, because there was no-one there! The church was completely empty!

Doreen sat down on the soft couch, then fell over sideways and closed her eyes.

Alice looked down at her, calculating. Doreen was obviously tired, but that wasn't important. On the other hand, she was also feeling obstinate, and Goddess knew she was turning into a thrawn wee besom.

'I'll just get you a cup of tea,' she said.

Doreen didn't even open her eyes as she replied. 'And toast.'

Alice looked grimly down at the dozing figure. How had she turned into such an intractable defiant little... Perhaps she had been too slack with Doreen. But you had to let a Seer have her head or she'd never develop. Alice sighed. 'And toast,' she acknowledged.

Doreen did not fall asleep, though her body grew warm and comfortable and her eyes felt as if they were glued shut. She was gathering herself. She'd had enough, more than enough of this nonsense. It was time, and long past time, for a life of her own. She was strong enough now to hold out against Alice, but it was exhausting, having to be constantly ready to fend off Alice's bile and bad temper. She couldn't keep it up for a whole lifetime – there would be nothing left of Doreen. She saw herself fading away until there was just a hollow shell – a shell made up of nothing but spite and anger.

But where could she go? What could she do? There was nowhere on the Dark Isle that she'd be free from Alice. Perhaps nowhere in Scotland. There were relatives in Aberdeen, an aunt on her father's side. But she'd never met them.

You're being wishy-washy, she told herself. You can just get up and go. Everyone's got that option.

'Here's your tea.' There was a clonk as Alice put the mug down on the small table. Then another clonk as she put down a plate. 'And your toast.'

Doreen opened her eyes, sighed and sat up. The toast was half-burnt, the tea was weak. She picked up the mug and sipped. It was warm and sweet. She swallowed half the mugful.

'Now, dear. Let's hear what you Saw.'

Doreen looked at Alice's face, red and with an insincere smile on it. 'Nothing,' she said.

Alice chuckled. 'After a handful of Witches Eye I'm sure you didn't spend the night in a cave without Seeing something.'

Doreen gave in and let a rueful smile twist her mouth. Alice was right about that. She recalled the maelstrom of visions that had plagued her when she first arrived in the cave. Terrifying, bewildering. Then the effects of the herb fell into the familiar pattern – a series of long calm spells, each followed by a vortex of bright visions.

She opened her mouth, then stopped. She could recall the twisting whirlpool of visions, but not one image would come clear. It had all melted into a single bright and shapeless vision that would not release any meaning.

She shook her head. 'Nothing. I can't remember anything.' Alice's face grew hard and she stared into Doreen's eyes as if she might see the answers there.

The front door opened and Lorraine came through from the hall.

'I blessed the cave,' she said cheerfully. 'Goodness, Doreen, it must be awful, spending the night in such a place!'

'Be quiet!' said Alice, as Doreen was turning to acknowledge Lorraine's sympathy.

Lorraine's cheerful face fell.

Doreen turned back to Alice. 'I tell you, I saw nothing,' she said, and added spitefully, 'and I'm damned if I'm going in there again. That's the last time.'

'You've said that before.'

'But this time I mean it!'

'All right, all right. We'll talk about it later. But you must have Seen something!'

Doreen's jaw set. 'Listen, Alice, the fact of the matter is that I can't See. Never could. I've been making it up. Even the first time, I saw nothing.'

'Come on, just one little thing?'

Doreen almost laughed. Alice's wheedling skills were so primitive.

'All right,' she said. 'I saw George.'

'George?'

'George MacLear. As plain as the nose on your face.'

'Aha! I've wondered about that boy. There's something there – under the surface.'

Doreen smiled. 'But you see, Alice, he was really there. That's how I saw him.'

Alice nodded. 'I'm not surprised. I tell you, he's important in some way.'

'But I didn't really See him, not See. I just saw him! Like normal.'

'Yes, yes. What else?'

'You pig-headed idiot! Is it your ears or your brain that's going? Did you not hear what I said? He was really there! In the cave with me.'

'Doreen! There's no need to get upset. We both heard you. Now what else?'

Doreen felt like screaming and tearing her hair. 'Why don't you listen to me? I've told you, I can't See. It all just fades away. It means nothing.'

'Damn it, Doreen! Don't be so bloody self-indulgent! I know it's not easy being a Seer, but do you want to be a nobody?'

'All right! You want me to say something? I'll say something!' She threw back her hair and glared at Alice. Her eyes closed to a slit, she tightened her throat and let a creaky voice speak out her mouth, making up the details as the words appeared between her lips.

'I see Siller of the grey hand slipping through the mist in Cromness, taking the weak into his power, picking up that which has been forgotten.' Alice watched her, curious but unimpressed. 'The Vennels will fall into his hands, and unless he be thwarted, the life will depart from Cromness as from a rotting tree!' Alice looked worried. Doreen closed her eyes and continued, 'Christ's minister shall leave this world – yet will he return. Mor shall loose the lost beasts once more, the animals of the past, and the Gods will look on them with envy. He will become companion to the mare, that the Tuatha de Danaan may find a path to this world.

'For the Gods and Goddesses shall gather to break through into this world. Bringing with them death and pillage, their endless daft wars over Pigs and Cattle. And the beasts of the Gods shall trample the corn. There is one without a name, the grey woman and the grey man who are the same person, and It shall move among the people of the Dark Isle and none will be safe except they pay tribute.' She peeked under her eyelids. Alice was looking shocked. Doreen smiled to herself and continued.

'Where the sea now is, there shall be fields of grass! And the ships of the fishermen shall lie upon the dry land! Then there shall be wailing, tearing of hair and suchlike. The eyes of the world shall turn upon the Dark Isle and seek into its hidden places. Yea, the investigative journalists and the makers of documentaries shall infest the secret parts of the island and all mystery shall depart. Yea, all these things shall come to pass unless they are prevented. Surely, all must work together, for unless the pattern be broken, it may not be mended!'

She opened her eyes. Alice looked aghast and her face was even greyer than usual. She believed it! Hastily Doreen closed her eyes and intoned solemnly, 'And Doreen the Seer of Cromness shall depart where none may follow her. And there she shall find... shall find many interesting things and a reasonable amount of happiness.' She opened her eyes, sighed deeply and fell back on the couch with a theatrical moan.

'Bloody hell!' said Alice. 'This is serious.'

'Is she all right?' asked Lorraine.

'Hmm? Doreen? Of course she is. Just a bit tired. Get her a cup of tea.'

Lorraine put a cushion under Doreen's head while Alice sat, thoughtfully staring out of the window.

Extract from *The Book of the Celtic Gods: Being a Transliteration into English of the major texts concerning the Gods and Goddesses of the Celtic Race and an Explication of these same Matters* by Miles Gincourty d'Alis, published by the Mews Press, Abingdon (*c.* 1751)

...and being of one mind in this matter the Gods and Goddesses joined in Council to choose another to be Lord over them all. And when they had chosen their new Overlord, after due Sacrifice, by Debate and by their Arts which remain unknown up to the present time, then He that was their King aforetime, the Dagda, known also as Eochaid Ollathair, the Horse Father, departed from Ireland and took up His abode in a distant Island whose name is Dark to us. And there Manannan mac Lir went also, and many of their fellows went also, both Gods and Goddesses.

Should we now pay regard to the Geography of Ireland, we will speedily become aware that there may be found on the untilled land many Hillocks known among the unlettered cottars and peasants as 'shee' or 'sidhe', being by repute the Dwellings of such minor Gods and Goddesses as remained in their native Isle. None now but the most superstitious among the Natives pay them any notice, and by their abandoned and desolate state we may conclude that the most part of the Gaelic Pantheon did not long remain in Ireland thereafter, but followed their fellows to the Dark Isle whereof we have spoken.

'...cast into Hell not only the children of the unrighteous, but also those of the righteous, unless they believe and repent!'

Rev Dumfry closed the book on the lectern before he continued. 'Or so it is said. We are, of course, permitted to doubt.'

At these extraordinary words there was a stir among the congregation. Several men found it necessary to straighten the waistcoats of their dark suits, while the women clutched their hymn books nervously.

'We are permitted, if not by the Articles of our Faith, then at least by the constitution of our brain, which God has made marvellously to allow both belief and doubt.'

There was distinct stirring in the pews now, and a few words were muttered to neighbours from the side of the mouth.

'Brethren,' said Dumfry, smiling and raising his hands, 'and also Sistren, let me Bear Witness to you.' There was a sudden deadly hush of crushing embarrassment. 'When I came into the church this morning, I had a curious experience. Not a religious experience, I hasten to add. No, I did not feel the presence of God. Rather, I felt His absence. In the deepest sense, I felt that the church was empty. Completely empty.

'Yet is it not said that God is everywhere? Indeed, while avoiding the error of the Pantheists, who seem to believe that he is *only* everywhere, I think that we can assert that if God is anywhere, then He must be everywhere – and in all other places as well.' He chuckled, a sound that did not fit harmoniously in the church, where it broke into pieces and echoed back, so that people turned round to see who was behind them. 'Perhaps,' continued Dumfry, 'that is a little obscure, and it is doubtless more elegantly put somewhere in the Holy Book.' He gazed benignly at the ranks of worshippers – or potential worshippers – for they all looked suspicious and unsettled at the moment.

'Let me tell you a story, a parable, if you like. I had an egg for breakfast this morning and while I was eating it I was thinking deeply about the omnipresence of God. When I had finished, I was left with an empty eggcup. This very eggcup,' he said, holding up a china eggcup with a little yellow chicken painted on it.

'I thought about God as I gazed at this little vessel, this mundane Grail, as it might be. And I thought. In the dark, He is there. When the sun rises, He is there. When the rays of the sun warm my body, He is there. Where then shall I find Him – or rather, where shall I *not* find him? He is everywhere, He is even in this eggcup. Shall I catch Him in the eggcup?' He put his hand suddenly over the eggcup. 'Do I have Him now? Is He in the eggcup?'

He raised his hands slowly to his face and lifted his covering hand a fraction so that he could peep in with one eye.

'Yes!' he cried out. The congregation shrank back in their seats. 'Yes, He is in the eggcup! But no, I do not have Him now.'

He stood silently for a few seconds while everyone else watched him nervously. Then he spoke softly, but his voice carried to every ear.

'This church is like that eggcup.' He held up the white object with its painted chicken. Every eye followed it. 'If God is anywhere, then He is everywhere. Therefore He is here. Is He in the church when we gather together on the Sabbath? And when we shut the door, have we caught Him? Do you see Him now? Ladies and gentlemen, boys and girls, do you see Him?'

Dumfry shook his head sadly. 'Nor do I. The church is as empty as this little eggcup.' He dropped the eggcup. It smashed on the stone flagged floor.

'The eggcup is not meant to be a vessel for the Holy Spirit. We do not gather together to welcome the Holy Spirit into our crockery, we do not expect holiness in our bowls or sanctity in our saucepans.

'But we do expect this of our church! And if God is not in our church, where shall we find Him? This is not a theoretical question, this is an emergency! If God has left the church, then we must find Him! As your minister, this must be my task. To seek out the evidences of His existence. For if He has made this world for us and if He wishes us well, then surely there must be, somewhere in the world, clear evidence of His very Being! And I shall search out this evidence!'

He lifted his head high and nodded towards one or two shocked white faces in the ranks. 'I would like to ask the Elders of the church to remain behind after the service, as we have much to discuss.

'Now let us sing. This hymn is not in the standard book of Metric Psalms, so I have photocopied the words.' He divided a thick sheaf of paper amongst the people in the front row and they each took a sheet and passed the remainder back. 'Miss MacKay unfortunately does not have the music, so we shall have to sing unaccompanied. A capella. Perhaps she can join in as she picks up the tune. Now, follow me...'

Dumfry led the singing while the braver souls among the congregation tried to follow his tune.

'Jesus is on that Main Line
Tell him what you want
You just call him up and tell him what you want!'

George stayed in the house all that Sunday, waiting. There was an unsettling feeling of emptiness with his grandfather gone. It was almost as if no-one lived in the bleak cottage. George made himself cup after cup of coffee and tried to think calmly. Where could Grandad have got to? Sammy was competent and reasonably healthy, but he was also old. Perhaps he had broken a leg? Been caught poaching? Perhaps... A picture drifted into his mind: Sammy, more than half drunk, checking his nets. His foot getting caught in the net, Sammy falling, the waves covering his face. A pale old hand reaching out helplessly. Under the green water, white wisps of hair drifting one way then the other as the waves washed over him...

'Stop it!' he told himself. He stood up from the table and began to pace the room, sipping from his mug. The room was cold. Out of habit, he stood in front of the fireplace, even though there was no fire lit. He put his mug on the mantelpiece, pushing a clutter of envelopes to one side. One of them fluttered to the floor, the letter falling out of it. He bent to pick them up and idly scanned the letter. Then he looked more closely. It was from a company called Argent Enterprises, with a return address on the Isle of Jersey.

```
...note that your lease with D. MacLean and Sons expires
30th inst. D. MacLean and Sons is now a wholly-owned
subsidiary of Argent Enterprises.
We have to inform you that we do not intend to renew this
lease and we must ask you to vacate the premises by the
date given above.
    Yours Sincerely
    Peter Ullover, Land and Properties Dept.
```

George was reading the letter for the second time, although its meaning was perfectly plain, when he heard a vehicle stopping at the front door. He rushed down the hall to open it. Sammy was just stepping out of a Range Rover. His clothes looked even more rumpled than usual and there was a large bandage on his head.

Sammy waved to the driver and shut the car door. There was a design painted on it: a fish crossed with a rampant boar gules. George knew that design – it was from Redrock Estate.

'Grandad!'

Sammy turned towards George as the car drove off. 'Hello there, boy. I'd almost forgotten you were home.'

'Forgotten? Where have you been? Did you get caught?'

Sammy pushed past and down the dark hall to the kitchen. 'Caught?' He reached up and rubbed gently at the bandage. 'Yes, I suppose I did get caught. But that doesn't matter.'

'What? Are they not charging you?'

'Hmm?' Sammy had turned on the tap and was filling the kettle. 'No, no. We reached an understanding, Mr Mor and I.'

George sat down. 'You and Mr Mor... What about your job? Did you not lose your job?'

'Och, we never talked about that at all. We had other fish to fry. For an unscrupulous unprincipled capitalist bastard, he's quite a nice chap.'

George gave up. He watched Sammy prepare coffee. The old man was humming 'The Internationale' to himself, and his step was light. The room was dingy, but the dirt on the kitchen window was glowing in the sunlight.

Sammy plonked down two mugs on the table and poured in the boiling water.

'Grandad, you don't seem to be at all worried.'

'What's to worry about? Let me give you a quote that encapsulates the proper relationship of the state to the people: *The office of the sovereign consisteth in the end for which he was trusted with sovereign power, namely, the procuration of the safety of the people.* And am I not one of the people?'

George blinked and paused to think before he replied. 'But we haven't got a sovereign. Not in that sense. When Hobbes wrote that, the king had absolute power.'

'True, but the government occupies a similar position.'

'And are they going to protect you from Argent Enterprises?' George held up the letter which he had left on the table.

'Ah. No, somehow I don't think they will. Hobbes' analysis was idealistic but perhaps a little naive. In fact, as is plain from their heartless rapacity, the government is the tool of one privileged class, the capitalists, of which Argent is obviously a limb.'

'What will you do?'

Sammy shrugged. 'We shall fight! The eventual victory of the working classes is as inevitable as the flow of history!' His eyes grew bright as he stared at some vision that was not visible to George. 'They may break down the door, they may kill my body, but they can't kill me, for I am the spirit of the people, and the life of the land is my life...'

'Grandad, are you all right?'

Sammy looked at George and the light faded from his eyes. 'You can give up being a king,' he said, 'but you can't just give up the responsibility.'

George looked baffled. 'That's not Hobbes, is it?'

'No. That's just me being foolish. And now I'd better get some rest. I've been up all night.' He yawned and headed for the door. 'Damn!' he cried.

'What's the matter?'

'I forgot to put a stone through the Major's window.'

Rev Dumfry stood at the head of the table in the church hall. The Elders, in their daunting black suits, sat down on each side.

'Gentlemen,' cried Dumfry. 'Glad to see so many of you. This is a crucial moment for the church and for all of us. God has left the church, and we must find Him! At this time of need I am glad that so many of you have chosen to heed my call for action.'

Siller smiled thinly. There was no need to manoeuvre the fool out of his place. He was doing it all by himself.

Mr MacRae, with Siller's letter in front of him, raised his hand to attract Dumfry's attention.

'I think you misunderstand the reason for this meeting,' he began severely.

Siller put a thin hand on MacRae's arm. 'No, no. Do let him speak. It may well save us a lot of time.'

'Thank you, Mr Siller. As I was saying, it is plain that the Divine Being has left the church. I think we can all agree on that, though it may not yet be obvious to the less spiritually aware members of the congregation. The Church is hollow, a void. There is a lacuna where once there was a plenum. How can we continue? What course is open to us?' He looked into the faces of the Elders, who sat uncomfortably silent, waiting for someone else to speak.

Dumfry chuckled. 'You have my sympathy. Only a few days ago I too would have been confounded by such a situation, such an impasse. Can we coerce God? Can we bring him willy nilly back into the church? No. We cannot. Must we then sit idly waiting, with our spiritual gears in neutral, so to speak? Again I say no. There is a way forward – if not a solution, then at least a strategy.

'Where did I find this strategy? Not from God, but through one of His many mouths: through listening to the sound of many voices, through paying attention to the humblest among us. Do you remember the name of Harry Moncrieff, the man who brought back Noah's shirt?'

There was an angry stir among the Elders.

'The man was mad!' said MacRae.

Dumfry held up his hands placatingly. 'There is only a thin line between God's messengers and those we call insane. Indeed, they may sometimes be the same. However, I will agree with you that Mr Moncrieff was not a well-balanced individual. But I have heard tales of his exploits from Jimmy Bervie, and I believe that his method was sound.

'Somewhere in this world there must exist evidences of God. Not just clues hidden there by the Lord, as if this quotidian plane was a crossword puzzle – but the very traces of His Hand. Should we follow these traces, we must inevitably come before the Divine Seat!'

'This sounds like heresy to me,' said MacRae.

Siller spoke up. 'I hope you are not suggesting that we should all form a sort of search party? That I should close the bank and embark on a quest, or rather, a wild goose chase?'

There was a general mutter of agreement from the other men around the table.

Dumfry nodded. 'Of course not. It is plainly my duty, and mine alone. I shall search both highways and byways.'

'By all means,' said Siller heartily, or as heartily as he could manage, surreptitiously catching the eyes of the other Elders. He leant over to Mr

MacRae. 'We must humour him,' he hissed in his ear.

'Yes indeed,' said MacRae with a similar false enthusiasm. 'When do you intend to start this interesting project? We can't be left without a God, after all.'

'There are one or two small duties that need attended to first. We shall have to find a suitable replacement. A replacement for me, that is, not for God.'

He smiled and one or two of the Elders laughed politely.

'I think you can leave that to us,' said Siller.

'Yes, yes,' said MacRae. 'You be off post-haste. We'll soon find a replacement.' He turned from Dumfry to speak to the Elders. 'My nephew, by the way, has just left college. Good degree, too. Doctor of Divinity, honours, that sort of thing.'

A few heads nodded, and he turned back to Dumfry. 'There, that's settled. So where will you be looking?'

Dumfry looked thoughtful. 'I tend to think that I should just generally wander, leaving myself open to Inspiration. By looking for the Hand of God in all things, I will surely be led to the Lord.'

MacRae nodded. 'That certainly has a fine Biblical ring to it. Will you be gone long?'

'It may take some time. The ways of God are mysterious. But who knows? Perhaps I may find Him waiting outside the hall when I leave.'

'I don't think so,' said Siller. MacRae nodded his head in agreement. 'Perhaps you ought to look further afield.'

'Then I must leave you now and prepare for my journey. I will of course keep you all informed. Indeed, as it is a matter of concern for the whole congregation, I shall try to keep everyone up to date on my progress.'

Dumfry left the hall and they could hear him making his way along the gravel path to the manse.

Siller leant forwards. 'Mr Campbell. Among us, you are most conversant with Church Law. What course should be adopted if an incumbent is no longer fit for his post?'

Campbell inclined his head to acknowledge the compliment. 'We have various mechanisms for harmonising the wishes of the Elders, the congregation at large and the minister. The most severe of these is the Absolute Censure...'

'What about the Discommunication and Anathema?'

'I was coming to that...'

'I don't think we need go that far. Disvestment and Public Recantation should be quite sufficient...' There was a rumble of displeasure at this hint of leniency. '...and Apportionment of his Stipend, of course.'

'That's more like it.'

In the manse, Dumfry pulled on a pair of flared corduroy trousers and a polo-necked shirt. He gathered a few essentials for his quest and packed them in a small bag. He paused for a moment before the front door, then left the car keys hanging on the hook in the hall. As for transport, surely God would provide.

He whistled a jolly hymn tune as he walked down the road. Who would have thought the Elders would be so helpful?

From the *Rossland Advertiser*
(by special correspondent, Tom Moreton)

...in an unprecedented move, the Highland Constabulary have released without charge all those held at Inverness in connection with a recent alleged drugs smuggling operation. The operation, at Cromness Harbour and Redrock Estate, involved more than a dozen police, the Coastguard service, HM Customs and Excise and the captain and crew of the Castleton Ferry.

Inspector Morrison, in an exclusive interview, said that enquiries were continuing. Asked about local laird Mr Mor and his employees, Inspector Morrison said that they had been helping police with their enquiries and they had now been eliminated as suspects.

Further confusion surrounds claims that a white powder seized at Redrock turned out to be a marine fungicide for treating farmed salmon.

In a surprising development, an anonymous source has revealed that papers seized in the raid have been passed on to the Fraud Squad. Asked to verify these rumours, Inspector Morrison declined to comment. He also claimed that allegations of vindictiveness and spite were the fabrications of self-seeking underhanded back-stabbing persons of uncertain parentage.

As the summer advanced, the weather grew mild. But it was also damp, which was unfortunate for Rev Dumfry. He had committed himself fully to his quest, following every possible clue, likely or improbable, that might lead him to evidence of God. Sometimes he would climb off a bus at a random bus-stop or turn from the road on a whim and stride off along a faint path on the moor, as if to catch God unawares. This behaviour often led him far from human habitation by the end the day. At such times he had disciplined himself to accept the shelter of a bush or a haystack, and even to give thanks for this meagre shelter. Though he tried to be sincere in his thanksgiving, these privations only added to his deepening depression as his quest remained fruitless, day after day.

In Cromness, a replacement for Dumfry was soon found. The new minister moved into the manse, locked Dumfry's goods in a large cupboard, and soon made the house his own. The Elders were well pleased with his respectful demeanour and the sound doctrine in his sermons. The congregation also were satisfied. They collectively relaxed after his first Sunday service when he disdained to mention eggcups or to discourse on the whereabouts of God.

On the south side of the Island, Mr Mor's men continued their bizarre practice of catching salmon and then returning them to the sea. Mysterious vehicles were seen arriving at Redrock House during the night and there was a deal of speculation about this in the town. Bonnety Bill, who lived nearby, reported seeing men in white coats entering the farm steadings. This was tame stuff for Bill, who frequently claimed to see UFO's, giant figures walking the moors and even baying packs of red hunting dogs. None of this was generally accepted as reliable information, as most of these apparitions were seen during his long bicycle ride back from the Arms after closing time.

Doreen's visits to the boat on the Links became less regular. Sometimes she stayed at home of an evening, or if she did go out, came home early. More than once, she noticed that Lorraine and Alice fell silent as she entered the house. She did not even bother to question them, just went to her room to watch television, leaving them to their talk.

Elsewhere in the streets of Cromness, Sammy Poach walked with a step which was almost jaunty. He no longer spent every night in the bar, but sometimes stayed at home reading from his small collection of battered old books and writing notes in a cheap school jotter. This rediscovered industry extended even into his work. He arrived on the beach on time and even began to pull on the net along with Irwin. This was just as well.

Irwin, though his strength was undiminished, no longer put his heart into his work. Nor did his cheerful laugh ring out so often – and it had a hollow ring to it. Whatever was wrong with him, it was noticed that his new girlfriend was very understanding, sometimes even to the point of embarrassment. Despite her comforting presence, Irwin's face grew longer day by day. At last he gathered his courage, quelled his misgivings and visited the doctor.

Jimmy, meanwhile, raked the sand and grew ever more worried.

Le Placs walked slowly along the beach, breathing deeply of the bracing air. Near the harbour, where his garden petered out and became beach, Jimmy Bervie was standing and leaning on his rake, looking at the smoothly levelled patch of sand in front of him.

'Good day, Jimmy.'

Jimmy looked pleased to see him and waved him close. 'Good to see you. How is the surgeon's trade these days?'

'Fine. Always busy. And how is the sand-garden, my friend?'

Jimmy carefully scratched his bald pink scalp. 'Not so good,' he confessed. 'I thought that the worst of the anomaly had gone, but it came back with a vengeance a couple of weeks back. Then it disappeared again, for no reason that I can tell. Since then, well, everything looks fine, but now that I'm looking for it, I can see other disturbances in the pattern – small things that I might normally have missed. An odd configuration of sand grains – you see?' He pointed to a place where the raked sand looked exactly the same as everywhere else. 'Or an unusual angle of slippage.' He waved his hand vaguely over the sand then spread his arms wide. 'I might just be imagining it, but I think the sand is sort of getting ready for another major disturbance. As coming events cast their shadows before them.'

Le Placs looked at him sharply. 'These patterns in the sand, these marks of future events – it is not possible that you yourself are causing them?'

'Anything's possible,' said Jimmy, 'but not everything is likely. I've been watching the sand for long enough now, and interpreting it too, but this has me stumped. I haven't a clue what's causing it. I haven't been so baffled since... well, since 1425.'

Le Placs glanced at his watch. 'But it's only 8.35 now.'

Jimmy nodded. 'Just so,' he said vaguely. 'But I wonder,' he continued, 'I wonder if I might ask you...'

'Ah. I thought it possible you might ask.'

'Well, your run of good luck at the betting hasn't just been good luck, has it?'

'Not just good luck, no.'

'So perhaps you could take time off from predicting the winners at Epsom...'

'Very well. I will see what can be seen. But I cannot promise anything.'

'Anything you can do will help.' He shrugged. 'I can't see the situation clear, it's too vague. Too many strange shapes moving in the mist. If you could just have a wee look into the future and give me a hint, I'm sure it would help me to decipher the sand.'

Le Placs raised a forefinger. 'You understand, it is not like the old days. In ancient times, the haruspicier was a powerful man. If a chicken or a goat couldn't tell him what he needed to know, he could order a man killed and disembowelled. And not, perhaps, in that order.'

'Those days are gone and best forgotten.'

Le Placs nodded. 'Of course. I only mean to explain that I can't see everything. Don't expect too much. After all, I can just have a small look

– and I have to wait for the moment to be right.'

'When can you do the job?'

'Happily, I think I can do it this afternoon. There is a hip-joint to do later this morning, but in the afternoon there is a businessman with a gall-bladder operation. I think he will have the honour.'

'Good. Thank you. Now, since that has been dealt with, perhaps you might like to see something on a more positive note.' Jimmy took an envelope from his pocket and passed it over to Le Placs.

It was postmarked from the day before, Inverness area. Le Placs glanced up at Jimmy. 'May I?' Jimmy nodded and Le Placs removed the letter from the envelope, along with a bundle of folded pages. He unfolded the letter, evidently written on a sheet torn from a notebook. There was no return address on the page.

Dear James,

I hope that you will not mind my contacting you, but it seems to me that you are the person most likely to appreciate my position.

I have left Cromness temporarily to pursue a quest for the Divine Being, Who, I am sorry to say, has left the Church. The Elders, though men of probity and religious demeanour, are one and all too busy with other responsibilities. They do not have time to search for Him. In any case, as the Appointee for the Parish, I feel that it is incumbent on me to trace His whereabouts.

I have told the Elders that I will keep them informed about my progress, but I feel that the congregation also should be kept up to date. Considering the unexpected turns which my path is taking, I do not wish to burden the Elders with having to make a decision as to whether or not to inform the parishioners. Consequently I include here my Notes on progress so far. I hope I am not mistaken in believing that you will be in sympathy with my quest, and I would be obliged if you would see that one or two of the congregation are given copies of the Notes. Among others, Doreen, I think, would find them of interest. All being well, I will send you a new set of notes when available.

Thank you, in hope and expectation,
Rev John Dumfry

Le Placs looked up at Jimmy, his eyebrows raised.

Jimmy cocked his head and grinned. 'Dumfry has broken out, eh? I knew there was smeddum in that man! But read on, there's better yet!'

Le Placs began to read the notes on the folded pages. After a few seconds a smile appeared on his face and he leant closer to the pages, giving them his full attention. When he was finished, he folded the pages and handed them back to Jimmy.

'Strange things, indeed. Is the man sane?'

'He is no longer a victim of his sanity,' said Jimmy, judiciously.

'And about his request? What will you do?'

'Copies of the notes to one or two of the parishioners? I think we can do better than that. I think this lunchtime I shall visit the bar of the Harbour Hotel.'

'Cough, please.'

Big Irwin gave a small cough. Doctor MacEnery moved his stethoscope to another part of Irwin's massive chest.

'Again. And again.'

The doctor pulled the stethoscope from his ears and folded it into its case. He looked at Irwin quizzically. Irwin sat silently staring at the floor.

'Well, Irwin,' said the doctor, 'The good news is that you don't have athlete's foot, pneumonia or the Black Death. And you definitely aren't pregnant. Anything else you'd like me to check? Is there any body fluid we haven't looked at? Any internal organ we haven't prodded? Or would you like to just tell me what's wrong, hmm? My time is, unfortunately limited, and there is a queue of patients in the waiting room.'

Irwin gave a sigh and stood up. Looking straight at the wall across the room, he undid his trousers and let them drop. He pushed down his underpants.

'Ah,' said the doctor. 'I see.' He leant over. 'You must excuse me,' he said, as he prodded Irwin's penis with the tip of his pen. 'Your genitals – I take it they have not always been that size?'

'No!' The doctor looked up at him. 'Sorry. No,' Irwin continued. 'They've always been perfectly normal.'

'Do they work all right?'

Irwin blushed. 'Not always. Not recently.'

The doctor stood upright and tapped his forefinger against his pursed lips. 'And when did they begin to shrink?'

Irwin looked even more embarrassed. 'I don't really know. I noticed it a few months ago, I suppose.'

The doctor looked at Irwin's chest, his mighty biceps, his tremendous thighs. Then he shook his head and sighed. 'Well, we've taken a blood sample already and I know pretty well what the analysts should be looking for.' He walked round his desk and sat down. 'Get yourself dressed, man.'

Doctor MacEnery drummed his fingers impatiently on the desk as Irwin put his clothes back on. When he was fully clothed, the doctor looked at him severely.

'You've been doing well at the football recently?'

Irwin brightened up for a moment. 'Aye. We've had a good season. Never better. Until... until these last couple of weeks. I kind of lost heart. You know. With the... problem.'

'Have you had any injuries?'

'None at all. Well, one or two bumps and bruises, but they've all healed up double fast.'

'And what about last year? How was your form last year?'

Irwin grimaced. 'I was beginning to slow down a bitty. It's to be expected, I suppose. I'm twice the age of some of the younger players.'

'Now I'd like you to be honest with me, because it could be important. Why do you think you've improved so much?'

'I think it must have been that new coach that Mr Mor hired. He was only here for a few weeks, but what a difference!'

The doctor looked dubious. 'He didn't give you any medicines, did he?'

'Oh, aye. He brought a tub of embrocation for muscle strains. Grand stuff! We all use it. It stings a bit, though.'

'Yes... But anything else? Pills, capsules, powders?' Irwin shook his head. 'A special diet?'

'No. Just said I seemed to be healthy enough on tatties and herring.' Irwin leant forward confidentially. 'My granny said tatties and herring was good enough for generations of Highlanders and it would be good enough for me. That and porridge. And she was right.'

The doctor looked straight at Irwin. 'I expected a little more candour from you, Irwin. But I can see I must speak out. To be absolutely sure, I will have to wait for the results of the tests. I say nothing about the moral aspects, but for the sake of your continued health, I would strongly advise you, right now, to stop taking whatever drugs you are using.'

'Drugs?' Irwin looked astonished. 'I'm not using drugs!'

'I'm sorry, but the evidence says otherwise. Sudden surprising improvement in your athletic ability, rapid increase in musculature, quick healing of bruises and strains. And especially, shrunken genitals. Classical profile of the heavy user of steroids.'

'Steroids! I'd never use such things! My granny told me that tatties and herring built as good a man as any fancy diet and...'

Doctor MacEnery waved a hand to quiet Irwin. 'I may be wrong, but I doubt it. We should have the results of the blood test in a few days. For the moment... Well, please take my advice – and your granny's. Stick to tatties and herring.'

'But I do,' said Irwin as the doctor saw him out of the door. Another patient edged in past him. 'That's all I eat,' he said as the door closed. 'Tatties and herring. And porridge.'

The country singer was waiting outside, her long black hair stirring in the breeze. Irwin walked sadly out of the front door. She ran up to him and grasped his arm, looking up into his face. He shook his head glumly.

They walked off together along the seafront.

There was business to be attended to. Jimmy Bervie searched his wardrobe for suitable clothes. Over his dungarees, he pulled on a velvet smoking jacket, then hung a few sets of beads around his neck. He rummaged in a drawer. There he found a child's bath toy with a blue rubber sucker on the end. He licked the sucker to moisten it, then stuck it squarely on top of his head. Ready for his visit to the Harbour Hotel, he left his house, a yellow plastic tap rocking gently to and fro on his head as he walked across the road and into the hotel bar-room.

'Tom! The very man,' said Jimmy Bervie. 'What a surprise, to find a journalist in the bar at lunchtime!'

Tom Moreton looked at Jimmy. The velvet smoking jacket was elegant, the strings of beads were ornamental, the plastic tap stuck on his head was outrageous. 'Aha! Jimmy! Dressed to the nines, I see.' He frowned suspiciously. 'Visiting the bar at mid-day? Being sociable to a journalist? You are a man with a story if ever I saw one.'

'How do you do it, Sherlock? Let me buy you an Old Tobermory. Two Tobermories, Pauline.'

Pauline filled a couple of glasses and set them before the men.

'On the slate, Pauline,' said Tom, preventing Jimmy from paying. 'It's all paid for by the Arts Council. Research grant. I'm researching a book on malt whiskies and the distiller's art.'

'Now,' said Jimmy, when they had sampled the Old Tobermory and Tom had made a few notes. 'Have a wee look at this. It's from a local minister of my acquaintance.'

Tom Moreton looked over the pages of notes that Jimmy had given him. His eyebrows began to rise.

'Unusual... and entertaining.' He looked up from the pages. 'This reverend, would he be a minister of the First Ancient and Reformed Presbyterian church?'

'The very one.'

'That lot, eh? Sometimes I see them about their business. To a freethinker like myself, they seem a dark and sinister lot. A cabal. Even one of them by himself is a cabal.'

'But Dumfry has broken loose. A loose canon you might say.'

Tom swallowed his whisky as he looked dubiously at the pages. 'Pauline? Two glasses of – what haven't I had yet?'

'Glen Gobhan?'

'Fine. Two of them.' He turned back to Jimmy. 'What do you think is going through his head? What makes a man think like this?'

Jimmy shrugged. 'Metaphorically, God is like a windmill.' He pulled the Dalai Lama's windmill from inside his velvet jacket and waved it about. 'He is the whirly bit at the top, where all the activity is. But there must be a handle, otherwise it wouldn't work. Dumfry reasons that if there is something Divine in the world, working behind the scenes, then the evidence of It can't not be here.'

'I don't know if I understood any of that. For instance: *Can't not be here?*' Tom took a gulp of Glen Gobhan. 'What does that mean? A double negative, so that would mean...' He looked speculatively into the corner of the room.

Jimmy sipped at his glass then held up the windmill, waving it as he spoke, to keep the words in line. 'If it can't not be here, that means that it must be here.'

Tom looked dubious. 'Can I have that on paper? It doesn't seem like sound reasoning to me.'

'It's a perfectly respectable argument. René Daumal used it in one of his books.'

'Oh that proves it, I suppose.' Tom sat up haughtily and waved his drink. 'I refuse to accept the authority of authors I've never heard of. Anyway he sounds French.'

'Of course he's French. So was Nerval.'

'Nerval? The lobster man? I thought he was local.'

'Tom, I can see your education is a little patchy. Nerval was a poet and philosopher. Fascinated by the idea of an invisible world coexisting with this one.'

'He wasn't a lobsterman?'

'In a way. He wasn't completely sane – or so they say. But then, what do they know?' Jimmy shook his head sadly. The plastic tap on his head bobbed to and fro. 'He had a pet lobster and he used to take it for a walk in the Luxembourg gardens.'

'Ah! So that's the lobster connection.'

'That's why there's a Nerval Lobster prize in the Dark Isle Show. And René Daumal was a follower of this Nerval fellow. And Reverend

Dumfry is using the same sort of arguments as they did. It's a natural for the *Rossland Advertiser*. Confusing philosophical background and full of local connections. You could win the Pulitzer Prize!'

'It's an interesting document. Fascinating.' He put the pages on the bar in front of Jimmy. 'But I can't use it. Private correspondence and that. The boys in the *Sun* and the *Mirror* have no scruples about such things, but we live in a small community here.'

'But if Reverend Dumfry was in agreement?'

'Well, that would be a whole different pot of lobsters.'

Jimmy beamed as he handed over Dumfry's covering letter. 'Have a look at this, then.'

Tom finished his glass of Glen Gobhan then took the page. Jimmy bought a round of Glaickbea Glory while he read it.

Tom reached absently for the glass then looked up thoughtfully. 'Reading between the lines, it sounds to me like the Elders are trying to suppress it. I wouldn't mind thwarting that lot.'

'Good, that's settled then.'

'I'd have to select, mind. I couldn't publish the lot. Give it a snappy title. Sort of 'Diary of a Wandering Searcher for the Divine' sort of thing...'

'Pilgrim's Progress.'

'Hey, that's not bad. But I think it's been done. We need something punchy.'

'Hunting the Spirit...'

'Nah. That's the title of my book on Malt Whiskies. We'll work something out. Now how about another? Let's try the ten-year-old Clootie Special.'

The bank had closed for the day. In his flat above the bank, Siller sat at the table by the window. At the end of the street, the harbour was visible, with the blue-grey of the firth and the darker hills beyond. The sun was swinging towards the northwest, sending shafts of light down through the clouds. Siller did not see these. The street was nearly empty, but at Ali's shop, two women stood and talked. A truck drove out onto the pier. It was from Redrock Estate with a load of salmon tanks to be offloaded. Siller barely registered any of this.

There was a letter on the table. It had come from Reverend Dumfry. Siller was not pleased to hear from Dumfry. It had been agreed among the Elders that the man was dangerously unbalanced. Mr MacRae's nephew had proved to be a very suitable replacement and processes had been set under way that would permanently rid the parish of Dumfry. Even so, the man could still be a nuisance.

His mouth tightened as he looked again at the document which had arrived in the afternoon post. Dumfry evidently intended to keep the Elders exhaustively informed about his Quest. He had sent a set of notes and asked Siller to pass them on to the other Elders. He even suggested copying the pages and distributing them to the congregation! Siller glanced at the notes. They were all numbered under the heading 'The Footprints of God.' Number five mentioned a woman's undergarments! At that point, Siller had stopped reading and threw the pages down in disgust. Had the man any sense of propriety left, he would not even allude to such things.

He gathered the sheets of paper together and left the table to put them in the small safe in the corner of the room. If evidence were needed of the man's unfitness, then it was here. He would let the other Elders see it at the proper time. As for showing it to the congregation – thank God the letter had not been sent to some less responsible parishioner.

Before closing the safe, Siller took out a small package wrapped in oiled cloth. He carried this back to the table by the window and laid the package on it. He rubbed his fingertips gently together, then reached for the bundle. Slowly and with careful movements of his bony fingers, he unfolded and smoothed back the stiff cloth. The document inside was a will, hundreds of years old, but the parchment was still in good condition, and the ink had hardly faded.

He had read it before, but now he did so once more, his eyes moving slowly over the strange words. He reached up to the shelf beside him and picked out a book by Sir Thomas Farquhar. He laid the open book beside him, but he rarely had to consult it. After a few minutes he sat back, assured that there was no way round the terms of the will.

It had never been shown to its beneficiary, who did not even know of its existence. Consequently it could, if necessary, be destroyed with impunity. But there was no point in doing that if there was some way that it could be used.

He replaced the papers in the safe and brought out a further set of documents. These he slipped into the pocket of his long black coat. He put it on and left the house, locking it securely behind him.

Fergus wriggled on his seat and tried to devise some good reason to leave the house. But his mother would know. He only had to stand up and she would say, 'Where do you think you're going?'

'Out for a walk,' he would say, and she would look at him with that look that went right through you. His father only had to stand up and she knew he was going to the Harbour for a drink. Uncanny. In fact, his father was beginning to think about the pub right now, his glance straying towards the door.

The thing was, if Fergus had been really going out for a walk – as he sometimes did – she wouldn't even ask him, and if she did, he'd just tell her. So why couldn't he just get up from the couch with a casual air and say, 'It's a lovely evening. I'm going out for a walk.'

His father stood up, then stretched and yawned. He seemed to think that this somehow concealed his motives. 'Just going down to have a word with Tom,' he said.

'Hmph,' said his mother.

There was a knock at the door. His father looked annoyed. He went out into the hall and they could hear him open the door.

'Mr Siller! This is a surprise!'

'Indeed,' Mr Siller agreed. 'I wonder if I might have a few words with you, Mr MacFarquhar?'

'Ah. I was just going out.' There was the sound of the front door closing and Fergus's father backed into the room with Siller's black-clad figure almost treading on his toes. 'But you might as well come in,' he conceded.

'Good evening.' Siller looked at Fergus and his mother with a rictus of the muscles round his mouth. A symbolic smile with no good intent. He turned back to Mr MacFarquhar. 'Is there somewhere we could talk in private?' Mr MacFarquhar hesitated. 'It concerns your mortgage and other commitments at the bank.'

Mr MacFarquhar glanced quickly at his wife. 'Of course. Fergus, why don't you go out for a walk? It's no evening for a young lad to be stuck in front of the television.'

Fergus tried to conceal his elation. 'I suppose so,' he mumbled as he made for the door.

His mother eyed his father closely. 'What other commitments would these be?'

'Och, it's just a wee loan, dear.' Fergus shut the door and listened from the other side. His father was still talking. 'Could you give us a bit privacy for a few minutes, love? It's business.'

He heard his mother's angry grunt as she stood up and went through to the kitchen, shutting the door loudly behind her. Fergus shrugged and slipped out of the front door. The light was fading from the sky. Soon they would be meeting at the Foxes Dens. Fergus felt the tremble of excitement in his stomach.

This was the night of the Big Ceremony, the Great Invocation of Cromm Cruach. Donny MacLean had hinted that there would even be a sacrifice to the Old Gods, so Bad Bastard would have to do all those Persian ceremonial chants. That should be a laugh.

Clouds drifted across the dim evening sky. The air was clean and fresh. Suddenly his mother seemed less formidable. He could easily think up something to tell her if he got back late. He laughed for no particular reason. Freedom was a fine thing.

Back in the house, his father had slumped into a chair, trapped there by Mr Siller. 'Is there no way I can keep the house? Please, Mr Siller,' he begged.

'It's not my decision, Mr MacFarquhar,' lied Siller. 'It's the area manager in Inverness. He says we can't extend these finance terms any further. If you can't pay off some of your loans, we'll have to repossess the house.'

'Oh, my God! What'll the wife say?'

'You have my sympathy, but without some form of collateral, proceedings must be taken without delay.'

'Oh Christ!'

Siller's lips pursed in distaste. 'Please, Mr MacFarquhar. There is no need for such profanity.'

'No need? No bloody need? When will there be a need if not now? Christ's sake, man, you're going to make paupers of us, and you tell me there's no need for profanity!'

'Calm yourself. What must be will be.' He tried again to jog the man's memory. 'So there's nothing of value that you can use as further security, nothing you can sell?'

'Of course not! What would I have?'

'No shares, no securities...' asked Siller, slowly and emphatically.

'Just a minute, there's that batch of papers in the sideboard.' He opened the doors of the sideboard and rummaged. He handed them to Siller apologetically. 'I got them when my father died. They're just feudal rights, you know. For a couple of houses on Shore Road and School Brae. I get a few quid off them whenever the property changes hands – but that's all.'

'They're probably not worth much,' said Siller, 'but let us have a look at them.' He spread them out on the coffee table. 'Hmm. This is interesting,' he continued, as he perused the worthless documents. 'I think these may prove to be your salvation.'

'Really? Oh thank God!'

Siller looked closely at the papers and then shook his head. 'But no. I'm afraid it's no good. A very interesting batch, but it will take too long to waive the Fee Simple and assign the waivers. By then, the bank will have foreclosed on your mortgage.'

MacFarquhar put his head in his hands.

'Though there might be a way...'

MacFarquhar's face lifted. 'What? Tell me, for God's sake!'

Siller sucked at his teeth. 'But no. You wouldn't want to do that.'

'Of course I want to do it! What is it?'

'Well, it's not normal practice, Mr MacFarquhar, but I think we might be able to get the whole thing settled here and now if you could just sign these papers over to me as trustee.'

'To you?'

'Yes. Selling them would take too long. And if you assign them to the bank, they'll just hold the papers as security and you'll be no better off. In another few months they'll start demanding their money again. If you leave them in my hands, I think I can manage to pay off your outstanding debts, though not, of course, the mortgage, and leave you with perhaps a thousand pounds in hand.'

MacFarquhar was almost speechless. He swallowed a couple of times, then spoke. 'It's very good of you, Mr Siller, but... but...'

'Yes?'

'I don't know if I should be selling them. It's sort of my inheritance, you know. The boy should get them when, you know. When I die.'

'That's the beauty of it. You don't sell them. You just appoint me to administer these rights in your behalf. It's all perfectly normal practice. There's even a standard form for these circumstances. I might have one with me – yes, here it is.'

He took the document from his pocket and laid it on the table, with a pen beside it.

MacFarquhar began to read the document. At the other end of the table, Siller removed a cheque book from his briefcase. Beside it on the table he laid a large pile of notes.

'Cheque or cash?'

'Cash,' said MacFarquhar hastily. 'If it's all the same to you,' he added. Siller began counting out a pile of fifty-pound notes. MacFarquhar set to filling in the blanks on the form.

Siller finished counting and laid one gaunt hand on the pile of notes, watching MacFarquhar carefully. 'At that section there,' he pointed, 'Don't bother with the names of the properties. Just put in – All heritable properties held by me – Yes, excellent, that should do.' He clasped his hands and rubbed them slowly against each other.

Miss Semple's hands did not seem to be under her conscious control. They operated like a pair of bony animals in her lap, lifting and tweaking the woollen yarn and moving the knitting needles to and fro again and again. Meanwhile her pebble eyes were pointed forwards, apparently watching the woman on the stage of the Hugh Chandler Institute.

'Before looking at the Dark Isle, it might be as well to contrast it with the geology of neighbouring parts of Scotland.' Martha Nero clicked a button on the remote control and a slide appeared on the screen.

'This is a typical view of the East Coast. Bays, cliffs, rounded hills. A relatively harmonious assemblage of rocks with little real complexity. We can easily work out the order in which rocks were laid down.' There was a click and the slide changed.

Ellen leaned over to whisper to Miss Semple. 'You remember Mr Mor was arrested for drug running?'

'Mmhm.'

'Well, Bonnety Bill, from Nativvy, he says that there's chemists and pharmacists and people up there now. In white coats.'

Miss Semple raised her eyebrows politely, though this was old news. Martha Nero was pointing at the screen.

'If we look at the Northwest Highlands, however, we see that the terrain is quite different, an exceedingly complex set of rock layers that took us many decades to understand. The area around Assynt is still a veritable Mecca for the geologist, and it contains some truly ancient rocks, old even in geological terms. Look at it carefully: the rock faces, the shapes of the hills. Even the vegetation is determined by the underlying rock, so that it is possible to read the geology by studying the plants.'

'Irwin,' said Ellen, her eyes on the screen but her head beside Miss Semple's, 'he's still with that singer, Minnesota Mary. Or Kate Fromkansas. Something like that.' Miss Semple's eyebrows rose in surprise while her lips pursed in disapproval of Irwin's shenanigans. 'Or at least, she's with him. Hanging on to his arm, won't let him go. Poor man. He looks miserable. Someone should have a word with her.'

Miss Semple was not prepared to offer comment. Though Irwin was held in high esteem locally, she had her own opinion about his multitude of temporary liaisons. It was shocking enough that such things should go on, but everyone seemed to think that it was acceptable behaviour – for Irwin. All these young women, their reputations tarnished by his wanton ways. Her lips pursed further. It didn't bear thinking about.

'...from the chart to look at the slopes of this range here. You can see the typical shapes of a landscape formed by piggyback thrusting and imbrication, largely a horizontal activity.'

The slide changed again and Martha Nero pointed to the screen.

'Now we turn from the frenzied activity of the Northwest Highlands. This is our picture of the East Coast once again, and you can see the much more restful landscape resulting from a more recent deposition of rock, hiding the tortured evidence of ancient geological turmoil far below.'

'Sammy Poach,' whispered Ellen. 'He was in on it too. Inspector

Morrison it was that caught them. He's my uncle's brother-in-law.'

Miss Semple nodded vaguely. 'Yes, Victoria Glendinning has mentioned him.' She turned a little so that she could see Ellen's face. 'You know Victoria, don't you? Delightful woman. The Chief Constable's wife.'

'Yes, of course,' said Ellen. 'Vicky,' she added, daringly.

Miss Semple turned her eyes back to the stage as Martha Nero pointed to a new slide, showing a map of the Highlands.

'The Dark Isle, as you can see, is perched on the edge of the Great Caledonian Faultline, where there has been movement along a vertical plane, creating the vast hollow of Loch Ness and leaving a clear demarcation line between the north and the south of the Highlands. The mountains to the north have distinctly different features, even to the amateur eye, from those to the south.'

'I was speaking to the ploughman at Nativvy. He says there's wild beasts in Redrock Estate. He's heard them.'

'Indeed?' Miss Semple's lips barely moved. 'He didn't see them?'

'No. But it sounded like buffalo, he said. Like wild Cape Buffalo in the rutting season.'

Miss Semple's eyebrows lifted. 'He's been to South Africa, then?'

Ellen hesitated. 'No. But you know what he means. He probably saw a nature programme on TV.'

The screen now showed a field, with Castleton beyond. There were aluminium poles standing in the field, each hung with wires. The wires led to a caravan at the roadside with the letters TRE on the side in large capitals. Martha Nero stood by it, smiling at the camera.

'Here you can see our detection equipment. Our research team, from the Terrestrial Research Establishment, is in the north to investigate the deep structure of the rocks, and especially to record the intermittent grumblings proceeding from the depths of the fault.'

Ellen was almost out of gossip, but she had saved a good bit for last.

'And what about Reverend Dumfry?'

Miss Semple smiled a small contemptuous smile. This too was old news. 'Indeed. Doreen has much to answer for. I would have thought better of Reverend Dumfry.'

'No, no,' hissed Ellen. 'Not that. You know the Elders removed him from the church? Well, it was because he'd gone mad. He's been seen wandering the hills and even sleeping in a barn.'

Miss Semple's fingers twitched and she dropped a stitch. 'Oh, yes,' she lied. 'I believe I heard something about that.'

'You may have heard the news recently about earth tremors in and around Edinburgh? These were trivial events, no more than surface shiftings. The minor tremors which can be felt here in the Highlands are much more significant, resulting as they do from rock movements deep down, near the liquid rock inside the Earth.

'The Earth, you see, is solid only on the surface. Imagine a pot of lentil soup on the stove with pieces of toast floating in it. From beneath, the heat causes the liquid to circulate, so that pieces of toast shift and move. The toast is like the plates of rock that form the Earth's surface. They can move apart, slide past each other, or collide into each other. Pressure may build up, especially along the edges of the plates, and the sudden release of pressure between two plates can cause earthquakes as the Earth's crust fractures.'

She turned the main light on and switched off the slide projector.

'Any questions?'

A woman waved her arm in the air. 'Mrs Nero?'

'That's Ms Nero. You have a question?'

'This piggyback thrusting...'

'Yes?'

'Is it likely to happen around here?' There were giggles from one or two of the younger ladies. Martha Nero smiled tolerantly.

'Definitely not.'

'More's the pity,' Ellen whispered, but Miss Semple did not respond, except by pursing her lips once more.

'Piggyback thrusting,' continued Ms Nero, 'occurs when one piece of toast slides on top of another, and then that bottom piece slides over yet another. However, the current movements in the Caledonian Faultline are more like two pieces of toast sliding past each other. The Faultline formed millions of years ago, but it is still moving, causing minor earthquakes.'

'Earthquakes? Here?'

'Oh yes, too small to notice, most of the time. But we can detect them – and we can measure the extent of the movement. We can expect to see changes to the coastline quite soon.' She waited until the stir subsided before she smiled. 'Soon, that is, in geological terms. Over the next 100,000 years or so!'

Siller turned the key in the door, locking out the world. He climbed the stairs to the apartment above the bank. Once in his own room, he let himself relax and enjoy the glee within him. He took the papers from his briefcase and laid them on the table. He selected the document that MacFarquhar had signed and set it beside Farquhar's Will. Neither one was of any use without the other. But together, they gave him control of the Vennels.

Daniel MacFarquhar had been easy meat. No moral fibre. The effect of years of alcohol. Most of it bought with money which Siller had lent him, with his house as security. The poor fool thought that Siller had been doing him a favour.

Siller sat down to read the Will again.

> *...inasmuch as the parcell of land known as the Vennelles field is of an antiperistatick nature to the circumjacent area having the character of similar sacerdotal endroits pertaining to the purposes of worship or of precognitorie practices.*
>
> *This Vennelles field being in the sense herein explicated a fortallis of superquotidianarie nature this testimentarium doth fully entirely and omnitemporistically assign bequeath and dispone without fief or encumbrance or interest of utility or disposal save only that of the Gods said parcell of land bounded by the sea to the north by the Greatte Vennelle to the west by the Lessre Venelle to the east and by the Kirk Road to the south.*
>
> *Said land as thus described and as delineated in the diagrammaticall representation below being seven chains and fifteen yards by three chains and five yards or thereabouts to be disponed and bequeathed etcetera to the first born heirs on the male side or failing this by the female line so long as this Earth shall last or in perpetuity.*
>
> *By sundry calculations based on Arts Propheticall and Astrometricall and greatte study of the prophets of aforetime we have ascertained the date thereof to be coincident with the dawn of the second Millenium after Christ but should by mischance the Earth survive the Millenium this Will shall not lose its force.*
>
> *Let it be noted that we present for the consideration of our descendants the excellent saying of Titus Quintius testudo intertegumen tuta est.*
>
> *That is to say that the tortoise is safe within her shell though be it noted that we use it with an antitheticall intent.*

Siller gazed smugly at the document and its preposterous language. Sir Thomas Farquhar had a childish obsession with big words, but he knew how to frame a document that would stand up in court. Every one of the absurd terms used in the will was clearly explained in Farquhar's book *Ekskubalauron, or, The Gem in the Dunghill.*

What it meant, shorn of circumlocutions, was that Farquhar's descendants had absolute right to ownership but were not permitted to sell or dispose of the Vennels. An absurd constraint for him to lay on his children's children's children. None of his other properties were so constrained. But he'd had some ridiculous notions about the Vennels – proof that intelligence alone is no proof against superstition. Even in the will he'd let these primitive beliefs creep in. Indeed, he seemed to make a point of them. Saying, for instance, that none should put aside his descendants' claim except the Gods. And what was that nonsense about the tortoise being safe within its shell? But he meant it 'antithetically,' or so he said. What did that mean? That we were safe from the tortoise as long as it was within its shell?

Never mind. It was plain enough that the descendants of Farquhar were of course the MacFarquhars. Descendants of one Isabella Farquhar, who was, though married, loth to give up her name entirely and insisted that her children adopt her name in the old Celtic way.

And Dan MacFarquhar's document was now in his hand. The Vennels belonged to MacFarquhar, but as his trustee, Siller was in total control of it. Argent Enterprises would not long leave it undeveloped. The Thursday of the Dark Isle Show there would be a bulldozer coming over by low-loader. By Friday, there would be a field of rubble, ready for development, and big signs with 'Argent Enterprises' written in big bold letters.

Dusk was settling on the streets of Cromness, but light still gleamed in the window of the butcher's shop. Andy the butcher had decided that if the supermarkets had late night shopping, then he must do so too – once a week anyway – to compete. Business was not brisk. He was sitting in the back room having a cup of tea while Bad Bastard set up the gleaming sausage machine. Beside the machine was a large pile of pork offcuts, and leaning against the work table was a sack of soya rusk.

Andy nodded in approval. Trevor, locally known as 'Bad,' for some reason, was working with a semblance of efficiency. Usually, by this time of day, Andy had to constantly remind him that in a sense he was a labourer in the vineyard of the Lord.

The shop door went *Ting!* Andy put his mug down on the formica-topped table below the religious calendar. 'We need plenty of sausages, Trevor, so no slacking.' An unctuous smile settled on his face as he passed through the doorway to the front shop. 'Good evening, Ellen. And it's a fine evening too. What can I do for you this fine evening?'

Andy wiped his hands on a towel as he pointed his pink smile at Ellen across the counter. She did not smile back.

'It is not a fine evening Andy. It's been as dreich a day as I've seen at this time of year. Give me a piece of beef. And no fat, mind.'

'Yes, yes, a lovely day.'

'It is not!'

'Och, you know best, Ellen. And how's your husband getting on?' Andy lifted a slab of red meat from under the counter-glass and laid it on his chopping block.

'Well enough. Well enough. It's a pity he couldn't live a bit closer to home, but his post keeps him busy all hours. I'm sure you know how it is.'

'Yes, indeed,' said Andy, lifting his knife and running it a couple of times up and down the steel. 'So it'll just be yourself at home then.'

'Aye.' She glared at him. 'Though just what that has to do with you I cannot fathom.'

Andy lifted his mild eyes to her face. 'So you'll just be wanting a half pound or so of beef then?'

'Aye. That'll do. And a bit over, for a piece.'

Andy drew the blade back across the lump of red meat and the flesh fell into two pieces.

'I hope it's not tough, like that last lot you gave me.'

'No, no. Lovely tender meat, this. Hung to perfection.'

'Well, that's as may be.'

A thin layer of polythene was laid on the scales and the red meat spread itself upon it.

'That's just three pounds and seventy-five pence.'

'Have you a scrag end for the dog?'

'I think I've just the thing here.' Andy reached under the counter and brought out a lump of bone with bits of fat and meat still clinging to it.

'Losh, Andy, you cut it close.'

'That's a good bone, Ellen. Just the thing for the dog.'

'I suppose it'll do. Put it in the bag, then. Put it in the bag.'

She paid for the purchases and left. Andy went into the back shop. Bad Bastard had the machine humming and he was feeding it with meat and rusk, forcing the mixture down into the hopper with a plastic prod.

Seeing him busily at work, Andy nodded to him and went to stand by the table. The calendar on the wall had a picture of Jesus blessing the children. Andy looked at the picture for a few seconds, then straightened his shoulders. It was a hard task that was laid on him, but God never loaded you with more than you could bear.

Below the picture Andy had a small blackboard on which he kept score. Ellen had definitely held out against his good humour. She was tough. He sighed and marked a cross on the left side of the board. But he had managed to keep the smile on his face, despite her intransigence. He marked a cross on the right. At least he had come out even.

A regular thumping noise began as Trevor set to jointing a carcase. Andy turned and stared at him in surprise. Trevor was not usually one to look for work.

'Thought I'd joint this pig, then I can use the scraps for sausages,' said Bad Bastard. He smiled at Andy uneasily.

'By all means.' Andy looked up at the clock. It was not far from closing time but Trevor was still working! He watched his apprentice for a few minutes. The lad must have turned over a new leaf. Perhaps it was the leaflet on 'The Christian Life and how to Live it.' A powerful piece of literature, that was. He resolved to search out a new leaflet for the boy.

'Trevor,' he began, 'There's a visiting minister at the Church this Sunday, I wonder...' The bell jingled. 'Well, think about it,' he finished as he went through the doorway.

'Well then, Mr Inglis. Hasn't it been a lovely day?'

'Aye, aye. I daresay it has, if you can spend your day in a nice warm shop out of the elements. For the rest of us it's a bitter cold bastard of a day, if you'll excuse the Gaelic.'

'What can I do for you today, Mr Inglis?'

'A pound or two of sausage meat. Not the fatty stuff. That square piece, there.'

'And how's the family? Has Peter been home?' Andy picked up the pink lump with a piece of polythene and set it on the scales.

'Peter hasn't been home for ages, Andy.' He scowled at the butcher.

'Kept busy, I suppose. That's a pound and sixteen ounces. Will that do?'

'Busy with any damn thing but his mother and father. Doesn't give a damn about his family. Selfish, always was. Even when he was a young thing.'

'But he's a bright lad. He has a good job.' The pink lump was dropped in a white bag and tied off. Andy tapped keys on the face of the scales. It stuck out a tongue of paper. Andy peeled off a sticky label.

'Daresay. Daresay. Not many get to the top in electronics. Crowded field, you know. Not many can stand the pace.'

Andy put the package on the counter top. 'It'll be a well-paying job, then?'

'Suppose it is. But what's the use of that if you've no life of your own? He's got to work every hour God gives just to keep his place. Running to stand still, that's what he's doing.' He fumbled in his pocket, finding a handful of coins.

'Maybe time for a change. Two pounds seventy-eight.'

Mr Inglis nodded vaguely. 'Aye. He'll have a heart attack before he's forty.' He carefully counted out the exact money, then paused before handing it over. 'You mark my words. Then who'll pay the mortgage?' He plonked the coins on the glass beside the red RSPCA collecting box. Andy scooped the coins up.

'And how's the wee girl?'

'She's grand, Andy. A wee imp. As like her granny as they could be sisters. If you take a look at the old photographs of her, that is.'

'She'll be growing.'

'Aye. We had her third birthday last week. Peter brought them up to see us for the day. A long drive. He couldn't really afford the time off work, but he's thoughtful.'

'A good son.'

Mr Inglis stood for a moment looking suspiciously into Andy's mild Spam-coloured face, feeling that he had been somehow out-maneuvered. 'I'd better be off. Things to do.'

'Well, good day to you.'

As Mr Inglis opened the door, Andy turned from the counter and rang the money into the till. He walked soberly through to the back, then fairly skipped to the blackboard. He marked a white cross on the right side, then, savouring the moment, a second cross for a bonus. He'd turned Mr Inglis round like a teetotum.

He turned, whistling, to watch Trevor feeding scraps from the carcase into the machine. Large pink coils were piling up on the white enamel tray. The shop door opened again. He glanced through and flinched, then set a smile on his face.

'Good-day to you, Jenny,' he said. Jenny-Pet stood uneasily, halfway from the door to the counter. She was a tricky customer. Sociable to a fault in her own territory, she grew increasingly nervous the further she was from the Wee Vennel.

'A slice of square sausage and two bits of bacon, pet. And a bone for the dog?' Her gaze flickered around the shop restlessly.

'I think I have the very thing here.'

He reached under the counter and pulled out a thinnish haunch and held it up to show her.

Jenny's eyes rested on the meat for a moment and she nodded briefly.

'How is it along the shore this weather?' Andy cut a thin slice from the pink block of sausage meat and wrapped it. 'It's been gey breezy weather – and that's at this end of town.'

'Windy, pet,' she mumbled. 'Very windy.'

'The house will be draughty too, like as not.' He carefully peeled two rashers of bacon from the pile. 'You should get the council to draughtproof it for you.'

Her face worked for a few seconds. 'Council! Council!' For the first time she looked Andy in the face. 'If it's not landlords wanting to repossess it, it's that pack of lard-bottomed swindlers wanting to condemn the place. They'd tear it down around me if they had their way. Draughtproofing, indeed! It's all right for those as has money – oh yes, there's grants for them and to spare.'

Andy dropped his eyes, uneasily aware that she classed him among 'those as has money.' Thinking about rich men and eyes of needles put him off guard, and he almost let himself get into an argument. 'Well, there are lots of houses that need done up Jenny, and it's better to catch them before they get so bad they just have to be demolished.'

'Demolished! Let them try! I've lived in that place for forty years, pet, and it'll see me out. They won't get me out of there without bloodshed!'

Andy coughed. 'Well, good for you, Jenny. I daresay you're fond of the old place, eh?' He dropped the bits of meat into a plastic bag and jauntily twirled it shut.

Jenny smiled at him sadly. 'The old place is just a heap of junk waiting to fall down. Just the way I feel myself, pet.'

Andy's big fingers expertly twisted the little ears of the bag into a knot. Jolly her along a bit, he thought. 'Och it's surely just the weather. A bit of sunshine and you'll be as right as rain.'

'I'm just old, pet. Falling to bits. Probably won't see the year out, pet.'

Andy's repertoire of heart-warming comments ran dry at that. He gave the conversation up as a bad job and put the meat on the counter.

'Twenty pence, Jenny.'

Jenny-Pet looked shocked. 'That's four bob, pet.'

Andy nodded. 'I'm afraid so. Prices don't stand still.' Except for Jenny, he thought. She'd refused to pay more than twenty pence for anything since the advent of decimalisation, and he hadn't the heart to argue. She reached deep into her purse for the coin and clicked it onto the glass counter top.

Andy tried one more gambit. 'And how is the little fellow?'

She stopped with her hand on the meat and looked up at him, puzzled. 'The little fellow? What little fellow is that, pet?'

'The dog. How is he?'

She tucked the meat into a coat pocket and turned to the door. 'Oh, him. Dead, pet. Died two years past.' She pulled the door open, subsiding into her old coat in preparation for the wind outside.

Andy returned to the back room and picked up the chalk. She had not responded very well to his bonhomie. Definitely a failure. One cross on the left. He stood a long time looking sadly at Jesus. He could not deny it. His fund of good cheer had failed him. His heart heavy in him, he marked another cross on the left. He started totting up the columns, then heard Trevor pouring another scoop of rusk into the sausage machine. He turned.

'For goodness sake, Trevor! What do you think you're doing? It's time to close up.'

Bad Bastard looked up at the clock. His face expressed surprise.

'Sorry. I lost track of time.'

'Well, don't expect me to clean up after you! You'll just have to stay late.'

Bad Bastard shrugged. 'Oh well. I hadn't any plans for the evening anyway.' He smiled at Andy.

Andy removed the shop key from his pocket and laid it on the table. 'Lock up after you,' he said severely, 'and put the key through my letter box.'

Andy counted up the takings and left. Bad Bastard gave him a few minutes, then flicked the shop lights on and off twice.

Bad was working away in the back room when the car pulled up outside. The shop door opened.

'In here, Donny.'

Donny MacLean came through from the front shop.

'Okay, Bad?'

'Aye, Donny. Just let me clean this damned machine and we'll be on our way.'

'We should have a good turn-out tonight.'

Bad seemed to have adopted a personality to match his name as soon as Andy left the shop. He turned to Donny and scowled. 'They'd better all turn up or...' he reached for one of the sharp butcher's knives.

'Yes, yes,' said Donny. 'I know. Their privy members shall be cut off and shall be cast among the embers of the sacred fire and so forth.'

'Aye. But tonight,' he thrust the knife deep into a chopping block, where it stood, quivering. 'I mean it.'

As the streetlights began to flicker on outside, Lorraine brought in tea, along with a cake which she had baked herself. Doreen thanked her and looked at her with one eyebrow raised. Lorraine blushed. Alice grunted as she took a slice. She grunted again after she'd tasted it, so Lorraine knew that it was a good cake.

Doreen and Lorraine sat at the table by the window, continuing their discussion of Celtic religion, which had gone on all afternoon. The pattern of the conversation was that Lorraine asked, Doreen answered and Alice contradicted.

'What about priests,' asked Lorraine. 'Or priestesses. Can you have a religion without some kind of specialists, people with a vocation? Is there some sort of organised system of... well, clergy?'

'Oh, yes,' said Doreen, 'it's not that formal or even very well organised, but there are some of us around here I suppose you could call priestesses. But frankly, we're the underclass. There is what you might call a higher echelon.'

'Be quiet!' shouted Alice from her seat deep in the sofa. 'Haven't I told you often enough to keep your mouth shut in public!'

'In public?' asked Doreen. 'Who's here, Alice? Is the minister behind the sofa, is Ellen listening at the door? There's no-one here but you and me and Lorraine. Lorraine who seems to be living here now, Lorraine that you've been training up as a Seer...

Alice glared at Lorraine, who shrank before her gaze. 'No, I didn't tell her...'

'Of course she didn't say anything. She didn't have to. I'm not bloody stupid, though I think you might be, Alice.'

'You've been listening at doors, you wee bitch!'

Doreen laughed. 'Is that all you think I am, Alice? Don't you think I learnt anything from you? They say that envy can see a coin beneath a stone, and I think that's where you get your sharpness. Maybe I'll never be as sharp as you, but damn it, I'd have to be completely stupid not to see what's obvious.'

Alice looked unconvinced. Doreen sighed. 'Do I have to explain it to you, Alice? How could I not notice? Whenever we talk about the Seeing, Lorraine goes silent. But she's fascinated by anything else to do with the Celts. What do you two do when I'm out of the house? I don't know and you never talk about it. And she's started being extra nice to me recently, as if she was feeling guilty. She bakes cakes, for goodness sake, and I'm damn sure she doesn't do it for you. The trouble is, she's just too honest for your devious mind, Alice. She can't lie.'

Alice turned red and floundered her way out of the sofa. 'How dare you! When did I ever lie to you?'

'No, you don't lie, do you, but you haven't told Lorraine everything. I'm sure you haven't lied to her, but that doesn't make you honest.'

Alice's hand whipped out and struck Doreen on the cheek. 'Go to your room!'

Doreen, holding a hand to her face, laughed at her. 'Listen to yourself, Alice. Who do you think you're talking to? I'm not a terrified wee bairn, I'm not even a sullen teenager. How are you going to get me to my room? Of course, you're stronger than I am. Is it going to come down to that?'

Alice looked for a moment as if it might.

Doreen kept talking. 'You have to be top dog, don't you? But I'm not going to be your underdog. That time's long past. So what are you going to do?'

'I'm sorry,' said Lorraine. 'Perhaps I should leave.'

Doreen looked at her in surprise. 'Why?'

'It's obviously causing friction, me being in the house.'

Doreen smiled. 'Don't worry about that. It's only things that should have been sorted out long ago. Anyway, I don't think Alice will let you leave. I think you're part of her master plan. Whatever that might be.'

Alice struggled with herself for a moment, then accepted defeat as gracefully as she knew how. 'For any's sake, you horrible wee besom! If you spill all the bloody beans, all you end up with is an unholy mess!' But the venom was gone from her voice.

There were a dozen people on Kirk Road as Fergus made his way casually towards the old graveyard. It was always busy for dominoes night in The Fisherman's Arms. He walked up and down a couple of times, waiting for a quiet moment. Then he slipped surreptitiously into the unlit gloom of the Waye. Behind him he heard the sound of chatter and music as the pub door opened, then it was cut off as the door closed.

At the corner of the graveyard wall he paused and looked around in the gloom before ducking through the hedge into Ladies Walk. It was instantly pitch-black and he stumbled along with his hands held before him.

Someone grabbed his arm and thrust a piece of coarse cloth into his hand.

'Your robe.'

'Ta.' Fergus pulled the robe over his head and arranged it so that the hood was at the back. His eyes were beginning to adjust to the dark and he could just make out the path before him, and a flickering glow through the leaves.

The bushes thinned out just before the Foxes Dens. He pulled the hood up and stepped out into the circular grove of beech trees. In the centre of the clearing was a big bonfire, its smoke boiling up into the sky. Dark masses of cloud moved across the sky, obscuring groups of stars, revealing others. Figures in black robes were scattered about the clearing, bringing firewood, carrying stones, clearing twigs and litter from the ground. On a tree stump sat a stocky hooded figure who seemed to be directing everyone else without doing anything himself.

Bad Bastard, I bet, thought Fergus. He tried to keep moving, to look busy, so as not to be conspicuous. What were they all doing?

A figure approached the stump and spoke to Bad Bastard. Bad stood up and climbed on to the stump.

'Brothers of Cromm Cruach! We are all gathered!' His voice was deep and resonant, a ceremonial voice. Fergus giggled in the secrecy of his hood. It would be a laugh if he spoke like that in the butcher's shop. Madam, your Bacon is Prepared!

'Let the Wild Rumpus begin!' shouted someone.

There was a moment of pointed silence before Bad spoke again.

'This is the night of the Great Ritual. The Spirit of the Great One will walk among us and... and...' Bad held a slip of paper at an angle so that the fire would illuminate it. '...and his carnation will guide us.'

He stuffed the paper into a pocket. 'Have the sentinels been set?'

'At the east and the west, both below and above.'

'Right. Have the stones been placed by the sacred fire?'

'Yeah. Most of them.' A couple of figures lugged flat stones across the glade and set them near to the fire, flinching from the heat as they did so.

'Okay. Come and get it.' Black-hooded figures gathered round him. 'Don't push! There's plenty for everyone!' Bad reached into a plastic bag and pulled out a handful of sausages for each. 'Right. Put them on the stones. Not too close to the fire or they'll burn.'

Dark figures edged in towards the flames, laying the sausages out on the flat stones by the fire. As they finished, Bad lifted his arms and called out.

'Man yek pedar ra yek madar daram!'

At the sound of the ceremonial language, everyone fell into a circle round the fire. Bad stood straight on his podium, his arms raised, and as he chanted, the acolytes walked slowly counter clockwise round the fire.

'In asb-e-shoma nist, asb-e-man ast!'

Fergus felt a thrill of excitement. A wall of darkness surrounded the clearing, and within it the fire lit a stage whereon occult ceremonies would be performed. Great. Mysterious chanting figures circled the fire, their magnified shadows falling on the silver-grey trunks of the circle of beech trees at the clearing's edge. Above, the clouds had caught the silver light of the rising moon. They assumed strange shapes as they drifted over the glade. Fergus had the feeling that he belonged here. He had passed the initiation and was one of the group. Soon all their secrets would be laid bare before him.

The circling figures repeated Bad's chanted words as they paced. 'An mard ba asb miayad!' Fergus could only join in haltingly, but he thrilled to the sound of everyone chanting together. No longer just an onlooker, he was part of the secret circle of adepts. 'Adepts,' he mouthed to himself, 'Adepts.' It was strange and wonderful. He hardly knew anything yet, but he still felt a member of the group, an insider.

And yet it didn't feel quite right. No-one had ever said that it was wrong to chant in a foreign language while walking round a fire, but still, there was something about this whole ritual business that made him a little uneasy. Smoke blew in under his hood, bringing the smell of sausages with the woodsmoke. He smiled to himself, forgetting his uneasiness for a moment. That was one secret that he knew: where the sausages came from. What would Andy the butcher think if he knew that his sausages were being eaten by pagans?

Bad Bastard's voice rang out. 'Man khahar nadaram vali baradar daram!' Strangely, although he knew that the words came from Donny MacLean's Persian phrasebook, Fergus found himself stirred by the ritual. Stirred, and a little afraid.

The mysterious dark figures marched slowly round the fire.

The sausages sizzled and spat.

The Fisherman's Arms was full, and Jimmy Bervie leant back against the bar, demonstrating his latest novelty. He was wearing full Highland dress. The kilt, the sporran, the jacket, the shirt, the long woollen socks, the sgian dubh – and the wellington boots. On the toe of each boot was clipped a plunger and spring mechanism that whirled a small flywheel, producing a whizzing sound with each footfall. By varying the force and the speed of his tread he could produce a passable imitation of an ambulance siren, a car alarm, or, moving very slowly, the sound of a fat man snoring in a railway carriage. It took some imagination to hear this last, but Jimmy was prepared to rock slowly on his toes all evening rather than disappoint any of his less imaginative acquaintances.

'You'll get it in a minute, Irwin. Just you close your eyes now, and imagine you're in a railway carriage. Nailer, you can help. Rock your glass on the counter to give the *diddly dum, diddly dum* of the wheels. Good. Now Irwin, you just close your eyes... Well, keep them shut, if they're already shut, and...'

'Jimmy, my friend. May I have a word with you?'

'Aye, aye, just a minute till Irwin...'

'About our little project.'

'Oh, aye. Of course. Tell you what, Irwin.' Jimmy took off both wellington boots and handed them to Irwin. 'You have a shot by yourself while I have a word with Monsieur Le Placs here.'

Irwin looked dubiously at the boots which he had accepted from Jimmy without thinking.

'They'll not fit me, Jimmy.'

Jimmy looked down at Irwin's boots. 'No. I suppose not. But your lady friend could try them. They'll fit her.'

Irwin looked across to the table where Louisiana Lou sat. She wasn't working tonight, but she still looked like she'd stepped off the Deadwood stage. She had white gloves, a most becoming checked blouse, a suede waistcoat with dangly bits and a western dancing girl's dress with all the petticoatish things that made it sort of bounce when she walked. And dainty cowgirl boots.

Irwin sighed and walked over with a pint of lager, a tall glass of whisky and Coke and a pair of wellington boots that went 'WwweeeeEEEeeee.'

In the ancient beech grove on the outskirts of Cromness, mysterious dark figures still marched slowly round the fire. Moonlight, silvering the edges of the clouds, formed eldritch shapes against the starry sky. Fergus MacFarquhar walked with the others, in an elevated state of trance caused by the rhythmic chanting, the monotonous circular march round the fire and the smell of the sausages cooking on the stones near the flames.

Bad Bastard, leading the chants from his position on a convenient tree stump, raised his arms high and called out one last phrase.

'Inja sabr konid ta man biayam!'

Everyone stopped dead and stood still, each one looking at the back of the figure in front of him. Only the crackle of the fire and the sizzle of sausages broke the silence.

'Bring forth the sacrifice!' called Bad.

He beckoned to a group of five acolytes and they all disappeared together into the dark beyond the trees. A chilly breeze blew through the clearing. Fergus shivered as the sweat cooled on the back of his neck. As they all stood waiting, Fergus felt a growing apprehension. There was obviously an element of play-acting in these rituals, but who knew what Bad's idea of play might be? Would they really have to sacrifice something? A lamb? A hen? Maybe they would slit the throat of a black cockerel and the blood would splatter everywhere, like the Voodoo rites in Long *Night in Haiti*. That was a grisly film. They'd caught the blood, what they could, in a bowl and everyone had to sip some of it. Yuk. He looked shiftily from side to side to see if there was some way to slip off into the bushes.

From the trees came the sounds of six people lifting something heavy, and muffled swears as they manoeuvered it amongst the bushes. There was a loud hiss followed by a pop as one of the sausages split in the heat. There were a couple of nervous laughs from around him, and Fergus took comfort from the fact that the others were tense as well. Smoke drifted across his face, bringing the smell of sausage. He rubbed at his stinging eyes.

When he looked again, Bad and his assistants had entered the grove. They were carrying the trussed figure of a man, so tied about with ropes and fishing net that it was scarcely possible to make out his shape.

'Oh god!' groaned Fergus. 'Oh no.' He remembered what Donny MacLean had told him about the sacrifice of Cromm Cruach, about the entrails and the ashes and what was put in the jar. But that had died out hundreds of years ago. Human sacrifice didn't happen any more, except in weird cults in Switzerland or California. Somewhere far away. The chilling realisation came to him that Cromness was in fact a place far away from almost everywhere in the world.

He looked wildly from side to side. If he ran for it, they'd never catch him, once he reached the darkness of the path. Unless there really were sentinels.

Across the fire, one of the group stumbled. 'Damnation!' he said, as they almost dropped their load. 'Who left that rope there?'

'You did, you wally!'

'Get yourselves together at the front!'

It was so ridiculously commonplace that Fergus almost laughed at himself. It was obvious what was going on. It wasn't real, it was all a wind-up. It was an initiation. He'd been reading up on secret societies, especially about initiation rites. His own humiliation had been mild compared to some of them. In *really* secret secret societies, if you wanted to join, they put you through an ordeal and warned you that the penalty for failure was death. Then they made you think you were going to be killed and terrified the wits out of you. That's what was happening here, he was sure of it. Some poor bugger was all tied up and beginning to wonder if he was going to survive the initiation. It was a relief, but even so, it was pretty freaky. You'd think Donny would have mentioned it. God, what a fool he could have made of himself! Fergus blushed in the darkness as he thought about it. In fact, he was probably the only one here that didn't know what was really going on. The bastards! It was a test! Another test. Ha! They'd kept him in the dark to see how he'd react!

Someone had thrown a few branches on the fire. Through the flames and smoke, it was just possible to make out the assistants holding the victim upright while Bad leant over him, fastening a steel butcher's hook into the rope at the back of the man's neck. At least, Fergus assumed it was the back. There was so much net and rope that the man was practically featureless. Through the flames and the heat, the straining dark figures trembled and distorted. They looked like a fat black grub wriggling and twisting. Smoke drifted across his face again. The greasy smell made him feel ill.

They had finished the job on the other side of the fire. Two figures, one on each side, were supporting the victim in front of Bad, who was standing on his tree-stump again. The other three stood behind him, in one dark mass with many heads.

Bad's ceremonial voice rang out. 'Raise him! Raise the sacrificial victim!' The three attendants reached up, then pulled down. There was the creak of a pulley wheel in the dimness above the clearing, and the victim swung up off the ground until it hung in front of Bad, slowly twisting to and fro.

Bad leant down and spoke to one of the assistants.

'Get a stick and pull the sausages back from the fire! They're bloody burning!' He turned to the other, 'And you can bring the tin bath!'

One assistant got a long stick and worked his way round the fire, rolling the sausages away from the heat. The other hooded figure dashed out of the firelight and reappeared dragging an old tin bath by one of its handles. He pulled it across until it lay beneath the sacrificial victim's dangling feet. Bad jumped down from his podium and fussily arranged the tub just so, then took his place again. The flames of the fire were subsiding, leaving glowing wood that gave out waves of heat.

Everyone stood facing Bad, his assistants and the dangling victim. Fergus watched Bad reach out to the dangling figure and hold it for a moment, to stop it swinging. It was so casual, that action, as if a human being was no more than a piece of meat. For a moment he imagined what it would be like if this was all for real, if the sacrifice really did take place. Inside him, a vast abyss opened as he looked into the horror of it. The stink of the burnt sausages was thick in his throat. His stomach heaved.

A layer of cigarette smoke lay across the bar room of The Fisherman's Arms. Striding through the smoke, patrons brought drink from the bar to the tables. Below the smoke, competitors hid their dominoes in their hands and attempted to distract their opponents with items of gossip. Dominoes clacked and a folk singer tried to make himself and his guitar heard over the hum of chatter.

In one corner, feeling himself to be less conspicuous there, Irwin sat with Louisiana Lou. She had a pair of wellington boots in her hands and she was walking them to and fro on the table top, while Irwin vainly tried to imagine a fat man snoring. Lou had run out of other tactics in her attempt to enliven Irwin, who had succumbed to the melancholy common to those with shrinking genitals.

Nailer and Sammy Poach were playing dominoes, but they kept glancing over at Irwin. It was deeply unsettling that Irwin's rock-solid good humour should have failed.

In another corner sat Jimmy Bervie in full Highland dress, but with no footwear. He wriggled his toes as he and Monsieur Le Placs discussed the mysteries of foretelling, confident that they would not be overheard in the general hubbub.

'It doesn't look good,' said Le Placs.

Jimmy Bervie's face remained unruffled, like a man who has endured much tribulation and is not easily brought to a state of worry. He raised his glass in a questioning manner.

'But nothing urgent?' he asked. 'I mean, nothing is likely to happen in the next few minutes?'

'Perhaps not.' Le Placs looked uneasy. 'You have time to drink your whisky, my friend, but not to linger over it. No, no, take your time. It is probably too late already to intervene.'

'Then tell me about it as we drink.'

Le Placs sipped his brandy. 'The man that I was telling you about,' he said, 'had developed great pain, and we had to operate quickly.' His eyes half-closed as he remembered the details of the operation. 'The first incision was simple enough. We clamped back the muscle wall, and soon we were at the gall-bladder. I studied his intestines carefully while working and saw the evidence of some severe disturbances waiting to happen.' He leaned towards Jimmy and his eyes opened as he enthusiastically explained. 'It is all in how they glisten, and in their disposition. The intestines, you see, are soft and flexible – as also are all the internal organs – so in each person the intestines and organs take up their own particular configuration. By studying the patterns of the insides, we haruspiciers can foretell something of the future.'

Jimmy nodded. 'And what did you see?'

Le Placs shrugged. 'Well of course, from that first exploratory look I could see trouble ahead, but little more. The details escaped me.'

'Oh well, I suppose we'll have to make do...'

'But no. By a stroke of fortune, he had kidney stones too – hence the great pain. So I had the chance to delve deeper. And there, behind the main coil of the intestine, do you know what I found? An inflammation! Yes, just where the roll of the lower bowel meets the fatty tissue of the... Are you all right, my friend?'

Jimmy had removed a child's windmill from his sporran and was waving it to and fro. The Tibetan characters painted on the vanes seemed to dance in the air. He coughed. 'Just need to settle myself a bit. I get quite upset at news of trouble ahead. Perhaps you could summarise, without the details?'

'By all means. Perhaps, if we survive the disaster, we can discuss the details some other time?'

'Perhaps.'

'Then let me not beat about the bush. Some cataclysm is about to break on this quiet island. And not only on the physical plane. By no means. Even worse, there is, in the vicinity, some supernatural entity waiting to escape from the bounds imposed on it by nature. Sooner or later, others will follow. Mighty forces will be unleashed.'

'Crivvens! We must do something to prevent this.' Jimmy made to rise. 'I must get my rake.'

Le Placs put a hand on his arm. 'Alas, we have not the time. Even now, the thing is straining to be free. Before we could even muster our energies, it will have insinuated itself into the physical world. Once free, it will damage the delicate fabric of reality that we are pleased to enjoy in this corner of the world. Yes. Cromness may fade into the past, her people no more than peasant labourers on the thin soil of reality.'

'My goodness,' said Jimmy. 'You saw all this? Anything more?'

'Nothing. Although it seems that the Cromness football team may lose to Castleton. At least, it is a possibility. I just caught a glimpse – the anaesthetist was in a hurry to get to the golf course.'

The Nailer threaded his way amongst the tables to speak to the folk singer. Soon the strains of 'Tatties and Herring' filled the room. Cheery faces turned to the corner of the room where Irwin sat with Lou, expecting him to join in.

Irwin shrank into his seat. After a while, people turned back to their dominoes and a hush descended on the room. The folk singer, thinking it a tribute to his playing, beamed at the crowd, but his was the only smile in the room.

The long walls of the cellar were built of red sandstone. Shoulder-high partitions divided the room into working areas and the far end was closed off behind a transparent perspex wall. White plastic conduit was screwed to the ceiling and fluorescent tubes cast their cold light over everything. From the sandstone walls, the shapes of fossil fish stared out at the people working there.

Baldy swore as he tried to connect up the glass piping with the rubber tubes. 'Bastarn stupit stuff! Why the fuck's he pissing around wi this shit?'

The thin grey man working across the bench grunted. 'He's got his reasons. That's why he's the boss.'

Baldy shook his head. 'Nah. He's no the same man any more. Ah bin wi him fur ten years and Ah never seen him like this. Mebbe his brain's shot, wi the drugs.' He nodded thoughtfully to himself. 'You canny trust these South American geezers. They could be putting anythin in the coke.'

A white-coated figure took an armload of equipment from the bench. 'We need more reflux condenser assemblies and a semen implantation syringe.' He turned to carry the equipment down the long hall.

'Sure thing.' The thin man reached for the parts and began fitting them. Other people in overalls were at work on various items: some were testing electrical devices, others were drilling plastic tanks and fitting valves. One was tending a bank of incubators where small animals lay absorbing the warmth. Some of the animals were obviously piglets or lambs, but others, though they were obviously mammals, were less easily recognisable. Behind the perspex wall were other figures in white with masks over their faces, standing around a table. There was a live pig lying on the table and a man was washing its stomach. Beside him stood Mr Mor, watching.

The wee man handed Baldy a set of components. 'Make yourself useful.'

Baldy looked at the pieces in his hand and roughly twisted a piece of transparent silicon rubber onto a glass U-bend. 'Ah reckon he's losing his marbles,' he said. 'He's no whit he used tae be. No since we shifted up here an he got these pigs an the other animals.' He glanced towards Mor at the other end of the room and lowered his voice. 'Christ, you'd think he was a bloody farmer or something.'

The small man shrugged. 'He's got to keep up a front.'

'Ah know, Ah bloody know. But look at him up there, watching a pig drop its litter. No just pigs either, noo it's coos and... and other things. Meddling wi nature.' Baldy's big shoulders shuddered fastidiously. 'It's just no right. Know what Ah mean?'

'Dunno. He just told me they was needing help in the labs. "Do what the professor tells ya," he said. An the professor said, "Stick them pipes together like this," so that's what I'm doing.'

'But it's no what Ah call real work. Wid ye ca this real work? It's a job for poofs this. Nae bloody guns, he said, nae knives, nae violence. See whit it got him? I could of told him. No respect, that's whit. The coppers coming in and busting us!'

'He had it covered, Baldy. No-one's been put away and the head copper's been up to the house to apologise.'

'Whit? That Inspector Morrison? He apologised?'

'Sure. Had to. Arrived with a face like poison. Stayed a couple of hours. Him and the boss were thick as thieves by the time he left – handshakes all round, see you soon. Negotiating skills, that was. The boss has all his marbles all right.'

'Negotiating skills? Fuck that! Ah didny get in this line of work tae negotiate! You an me an Slippery Leon, lookin mean – that wis a' the negotiatin we needed.'

'Leon got cut in the belly, din't he?'

'Yeah! We took care o the guy that done it, but. He didny cut no other bastard after that, know what Ah mean?'

'How's Leon doin?'

'Nae sae bad. Don't have to use a tube now. They gave him a sort of permanent implant, so he can turn it on an off.'

A glass tube broke in his hand. Baldy swore as blood dripped from his hand. 'Bastard! Why din't he stick to running coke?' He wrapped a cloth round his hand and clumsily tied it. 'Gonny be heavy shit over that.'

'What you mean, heavy shit?'

'Physical complaints, know whit Ah mean? There's people wantin that coke and he just told them right out – no until he feels like doing it again.' One corner of his mouth lifted in a smile. 'Hey, they'll mebbe send a squad up to hit us! That would be a bit of action! Like old times! Whit d'ye say?'

The thin man looked across at him, his grey eyes weak and sad. 'You know this work?'

'Yeah.'

'How it isn't fit for a real man?'

'Yeah.'

'And how it's a job for poofs and girl's blouses and other things what you said?'

'Yeah?'

'Well, I like it, Baldy. It's a job with a future, a bit of job satisfaction. I don't know if the big man is off his head or what, but if he is, then long may he stay off it, I say.'

There was a moment of appalled silence from Baldy, then he snorted. 'Whit? You're joking! Or Ah bloody hope you are. You wis the handiest bugger ever tae slip a blade intae a set of kidneys!'

'Yes,' said the wee man. 'That's true. But somehow, being here on this island with lots of space and green things growing and things like that, and what with working with the fish and the boats and suchlike, well, I've got this hankering not to end up with a plastic faucet on my bladder. If I never handle a knife again, it'll be too soon.'

Baldy's lip curled. 'Christ, if Ah ever heard the like! Ah've had enough of this green-wellies country living shit, by the way. There's fuck all action. Ah tell you, wee man, Ah'm aboot ready tae chuck it in and clear oot.'

'Might be as well. But just you remember what you was saying about me being handy with a blade.' Suddenly there was a shining piece of steel in his hand. 'If I think you might talk, yours is the kidneys this'll be in. Okay?'

Baldy swallowed. 'Yeah.'

'Just joking, of course.' He made a small smile as he put the knife away.

'Of course.' Baldy's face replied with a stiff grin.

A door in the perspex wall opened and Mr Mor came through with one of the white-coated men. 'Good work professor,' he said. 'You'll let me know when the next one's due?'

The man smiled. 'That should be a mammoth task.'

Mor nodded. 'Right.' He turned and beckoned. 'Baldy. I need a driver. I have to go and talk to some people.'

Baldy grinned. 'Sure boss.' He stripped off his overalls and dropped them on the floor. 'Bit of action, this is more like it,' he whispered to the thin man as he left the bench. 'Where we going, boss?'

'Cromness. Ladies branch of the Rare Breeds Association,' he replied.

Baldy's shoulder's slumped.

'And for God's sake get a proper bandage on that hand! This place is supposed to be sterile and you're dripping blood like a slaughtered pig!'

'Sure boss.' Baldy glowered as he followed Mor out of the room.

Bad Bastard was standing with arms upstretched, chanting. He had one of his butcher's knives in his fist. Fergus shuddered. It was horribly impressive, the black figure with the shining blade, the firelight gleaming on the boles of the trees.

The circle of adepts stood still now, facing Bad.

'They are seven!' he called.

'Just seven!' everyone replied.

'In the abyss,' called Bad.

'They are seven.'

'Abase yourselves!' All the hooded figures round the fire fell to their knees. Fergus could feel the cold moist earth seep through his trousers. How could he explain muddy knees to his mother? It was so unimportant that he almost laughed. Bad was calling out the next line.

'For in the sky they are seven!'

Every hood turned up to the sky. The clouds were doing strange things.

Bad stood silent for a few seconds, his arms outspread, his head up to the sky. Then everyone rose from the ground as he continued the chant:

'In the empty houses, in the dark depths, in the hidden places

They swell up, they grow tall.

Not male, not female

They bear no children – for their number is seven.

Always seven.

In a silence heavy with tempests they live.

They are boars that have grown to great size, that devour mountains.

They tear up the roadways and the works of people are as nothing.

They lay waste the fields,
And they feed on the Gods!
They are the faces of evil, they are the faces of evil!
And they are seven as we are seven.'

A hideous feeling had come over the grove, as if something had begun to move that would not stop until it had reached its terrible outcome. There was no other choice, no way to change things, no escape. The clouds seemed to have lowered: in odd twisted shapes they lay just above the grove.

Fergus shook his head inside its cowl and leant over to his neighbour in the circle.

'God's sake,' he muttered. 'That's heavy stuff.'

The hooded figure turned towards him. It was not possible to see the face inside the cowl. 'The tool for the job,' replied the dark figure.

Alice was standing by the window, watching the moon over the housetops. Her voice was strained, as if she was being forced to speak, and sometimes her eyes grew glazed for a moment or two. She was speaking to Lorraine, but she did not look directly at Lorraine.

'Some there are who have special gifts.' she said. 'Some can call up the mist, or calm a disturbed herd of cattle – or see the future.' She nodded her head towards Doreen, but her eyes still looked out into the night. 'The Seers. And there are bards as well as prophets, and they are especially valued, by the people and by the Goddess.'

Lorraine opened her mouth to speak, but Doreen hushed her.

'On the other hand,' she continued, 'there are those who are not merely favoured. They take on the very qualities of the Gods.'

'Like Alice,' said Doreen.

Alice nodded curtly. 'Yes.' Her eyes moved slowly to and fro, the only part of her face that was moving. 'I am not just a priestess. I am more than a Seer.' Her voice had grown slow and thick, as if it was climbing out of her mouth. 'I am a Goddess.'

Lorraine looked at her with a mixture of curiosity and disbelief. Alice's face was flushed red and the roll of fat at her neck had left sweat-stains on the collar of her grey dress with the wee blue flowers.

'Indeed,' said Lorraine, without conviction. 'Which one?'

Alice's head jerked round, her mouth twisted as if she was about to spit. 'Not now, you stupid hussy! When the Need calls.'

'Oh,' said Lorraine, and nothing more.

'When people neglect the sacrifice,' Alice intoned, 'and the rumblings of discontent begin, then a bitter wind finds its way even into warm rooms, and the cries of the raven hang on the wind. Black feathers, black beak and red blood...'

'Oh come on, Alice. You don't have to make a meal of it.' Doreen turned to Lorraine. 'Look, I'll give you a couple of clues. She is a Goddess, that's true enough. Three syllables. Favourite bird the crow. Not completely unconnected with episodes of multiple violent death.'

'Morrigan!'

'Of course, bloody Morrigan. Now as we both know, Alice is bad enough – though we can learn to cope with her. But if Morrigan takes over...'

Lorraine had her hand to her mouth. 'Does it happen often?'

Alice had turned to face the blank TV, leaving Doreen to speak. 'No. Thanks be. And when the Need is gone they must go back to where they come from.'

'Are there others?'

Doreen looked uncomfortable. 'Perhaps it's best not to name Them,' she said. 'The more attention you give Them, the closer They come – and just at the moment, that might be a bad idea.'

Lorraine stood up straight. 'Come on, Doreen. I'm initiated now. Or are you keeping secrets too?'

Doreen sighed. 'All right. There's one or two that you might as well know. Epona the horse-goddess, that's the woman at Nativvy stables. There's not many horses around these days, but you should see her at the Dark Isle show, at the races. Sparks flying from her hair. You'd think the Goddess was damned near ready to break through. Then there's Nin, the Goddess of unregarded corners. She's around somewhere – probably Miss Semple or Jenny-Pet. It's hard to know what crisis of events would call her into possession in any case, so it's really a matter of conjecture.'

Lorraine glanced at Alice before speaking.

'What about, you know, male Gods?'

Doreen laughed. 'There's the question. We don't really know, except for the Dagda, and He's changing.'

'Changing?'

'Yes. Used to be easy to see. Big and brawny, a hero to one and all. Never beaten, rising anew to every fray.'

Alice snorted. 'It's a matter of what's rising.'

'Of course,' said Doreen, 'I'm told that he never favoured Alice with his attentions, not even when she was a young thing of forty and he was eighteen.'

'Shut your mouth, you wee hoyden!'

'But he's the man with vigour enough to serve a dozen maidens.'

'Irwin,' snapped Alice. 'She's talking about Irwin.'

'Irwin?'

'You've seen him, Lorraine. In the Arms. Big man. Reddish blond hair, big body. He likes to sing 'Tatties and Herring' when he's had a few drinks.'

Lorraine smiled. 'So that's Irwin. And he's the Dagda.'

'Was,' grunted Alice.

'Something's wrong,' said Doreen. 'He's lost form. Fighting was important to the old Gods, and that was where you would get the measure of the Gods, see who was boss. We don't have battles anymore, but the football pitch is a field of symbolic battle – and the football team is struggling. Irwin hasn't scored for the last couple of matches. The Dagda has deserted him for another, and we don't know who. Or why.'

'Does it matter?'

'Matter! Look around you. Just how likely is this place? Just how normal and natural is the Dark Isle? Do you find direct links to the Otherworld on every Scottish island? Does Morrigan fly with her crows down every country lane? It's a bloody strain on reality keeping it here. You have to hold the right rituals at the right times with the right people or phut! It's over. Or possibly boom! It's over. Who knows what will happen then.'

'It's not our job, but the men will have to find out who it is, and damn soon.'

'Why?'

'He has to perform the horse sacrifice at the Dark Isle Show.'

Lorraine's face paled. Her hand went to her mouth and her wide eyes looked at Alice. 'The horse sacrifice! Not really!'

'Not the whole bloody ritual! Of course not,' said Alice. Lorraine blushed and looked down. 'No, of course they don't really kill the horse nowadays. They just mimic it. But it has to be the leader of the tribe that does it. Not the political leader, of course, but the mythic leader. It should be Irwin – it was last year, and the year before – for the last decade in fact. But this year...'

'What'll happen if they can't do the ritual?'

'Don't even think of it! Goddess knows. Maybe the Dark Isle will sink beneath the waves, or be rent in sunder by earthquakes. The Gods might desert us.' Alice had a half-hopeful look on her face. 'Or worse.'

'Worse?'

Doreen nodded. 'They've got their people, like Alice – so they can manifest for a while and make mischief. Wreak a bit of vengeance or blight the crops...'

'It's not all bad,' muttered Alice.

'No, I suppose not. They bless the fishing, make the barley sprout, keep the sun rising and things like that. I suppose they do some good. And there are gates, thin places where their world and ours meet. The Drooping Cave, the Vennels, Glen Grian.'

'Doreen!'

'She might as well know. She is an initiate, after all.'

'I suppose,' Alice grunted.

Doreen turned back to Lorraine. 'There are tales of people disappearing into these places, never to be seen again. Humans can sometimes get in, but the Gods and Goddesses can also get out for a while, in their own person, and walk around among us. It's not easy for Them, but one or two of them can do it, if they are angry enough, or have some other reason. They might feel an urge to seduce some young woman or man – for purposes of their own, no doubt. It's an ancient tradition. Or perhaps we should call it a habit. As long as we do the rituals and show some respect, they mostly stay in their place. But if something goes wrong, and one or two of Them get loose, that would be bad. Very bad.'

'Would it?'

'That would be worse than you can imagine,' said Doreen. She nodded discreetly towards Alice as she kept her eyes on Lorraine. 'They're not human, you know.'

Miss Semple knitted awkwardly, pressed as she was between two other ladies.

There were ten rows of chairs in the Chandler Institute, eight chairs to each row, and every seat was filled by a bottom, though not all of them belonged to a member of the Ladies branch of the Rare Breeds Association. Many had slipped in by accompanying friends or, like Miss Semple, merely by smiling vaguely and looking harmless.

Mr Mor had recently become somewhat notorious while remaining, of course, eminently respectable as the Laird of Redrock Estate. So there was a big turnout, even though he was giving a talk on Palaeolithic Animals of the Golden Age.

Miss Semple had heard quite enough about her primitive forebears in recent lectures on the Picts and the Celts. She was on her guard now. Mr Mor hadn't mentioned any unspeakable practices yet, but he must be working his way towards it. These ancient peoples were pagans, every one of them. Running around dressed in nothing but blue paint. Her knitting needles clacked fiercely.

'Bottle gardens,' she hissed. 'Or herb gardens. Yes, herbs are a suitable topic for ladies.'

The woman next to her leant over and whispered, 'I beg your pardon?'

Miss Semple blushed. 'Just counting stitches,' she said.

Mr Mor looked at the ranks of women. He was not accustomed to public speaking, but he'd almost been eager when he'd been asked to give a talk. The Lady President had suggested suitable topics. 'Perhaps something on stock care, or old breeds?'

The truth was, she did not care what he talked about. It was just that he had such an aura of power – and there was mystery about him too. Even after he'd been in Cromness for four years, few people had even seen him. So, she'd thought, get him to give a talk. Everyone will turn up just for the chance to meet him.

For Mr Mor it was more than that. It was confirmation that he'd managed to find himself a respectable niche. And it was also a chance to talk about some things that had begun to fascinate him. The idea of the superman, the degenerative effects of climate change, the philosophy of stock breeding and the origins of the Atlantis myth.

He'd done his best, but he was not exactly sure that they were taking it all in. There was an old woman in the front row blindly knitting as her eyes drifted about the room, and most of the rest seemed to be assessing the cut of his clothes. He was beginning to feel somewhat irked, as he had taken some trouble finding facts to fit his ideas.

'...and during the last Ice Age, this whole region was deep in ice and so was North America. But not Siberia – it had no glaciers. In fact, Siberia was full of animals at the time. It was a warm place, fertile too. Lush grasslands. Hell, there were forty million mammoths alone, and they all needed to eat. And there was a whole range of other animals – hippo, rhinoceros, giant sloths, tigers – that kind of thing.

'So we were chilled to the marrow here, under hundreds of feet of ice, while the Siberians were basking in the sun. They had hardly any winter, just a long warm stable growing season.

'Why? I don't know, but that's what the geologists tell us. But, according to one scientist called Hapgood, it was all because the poles were in a different place, and they've moved since. The north pole was in Greenland, so that was the centre of the Arctic. And there was no tilt to the Earth, no axial tilt. So the weather was stable. It was always cold in the far North and the far South, and the icecaps grew there, sucking up the water from the sea so there was more land to live on. People could live on the continental shelves that are under the sea now. It was a Golden Age.'

Miss Semple picked out some words that she understood. 'Shelves?' she thought 'Golden age? He won't think old age is golden when he gets there. What does he know about it? He can't be over forty.'

'Nice-looking chap, though,' whispered her neighbour.

Miss Semple flushed red and dropped a stitch. 'Just counting,' she said.

At the entrance to the room, Baldy leaned against the niche where the bronze boar stood. He watched the street outside through a chink in the blinds. Nothing happening. He yawned. The boss was going on a bit. He shifted uneasily and looked at his watch. He hadn't even started talking about animal breeding yet.

'And in that Golden Age there lived certain special people.' Mr Mor stood silent for a moment, just looking at the women. There was a stir among the more alert members of his audience, who were still waiting for the relevance of all this to pedigree bulls and Arab stallions. 'They were not supernatural. They were much like you and me, but they were so much more powerful, bigger, stronger, tougher. They probably had skills and natural abilities that we can only dream of. So much more than us, that we can only call them gods or supermen.

'Then 12,000 years ago, the Earth shifted its axis, so that the weather suddenly became unpredictable. Siberia became an icy plain, the mammoths and the woolly rhinoceros and dozens of other species were wiped out. People survived, but they had to change.' He looked at the women. Most of them looked puzzled, but they were nearly all listening now.

'We are human beings,' he continued. There were a couple of nods of acknowledgement from the audience. 'And we are pretty well adapted to our environment. But it is not our natural environment. Do you know what happens if you take a pair of Percherons or a couple of Arab horses and let them breed in Mongolia? After a few generations, the descendants turn into stunted ponies like the native breeds. They adjust to the environment. These people I'm talking about, they were perfectly adapted to the environment of the late Palaeolithic. The climate changed suddenly, and they had to adapt. Take a few of these demi-gods and let them breed in a disturbed environment, one with violent seasonal changes, and what happens? They become dwarfed and impoverished shadows of their former selves.

'Where have these gods gone? We are them – or their descendants. We have shrunk, lost our strength, become Men. But our ancestors were remembered in stories, in myths, as gods. As we slipped into our degraded state, we remembered that time, and made tales of Eden or Atlantis or the continent of Mu. We liked to think that these great beings had somehow escaped the cataclysm caused when the Poles moved. So we said they had gone to the inaccessible places – to the mountains: to Mount Meru, Olympus, or Mount Zion.

'So, can we do anything about our miserable, poor impoverished state?' He looked around the audience. No-one had anything to suggest. 'We could move the Earth's axis of rotation,' he continued. 'That would help, but it's too big a job. What else can we do?

'Even now, after ten thousand years, we still have ancestral memories of mammoth, aurochs, boar, the giant sloth. Memories from the days when we were more than human. Some of these animals are gone for ever. But some are still here, changed by selective breeding and by the changing climate. If we can breed back to the original form, if we can have wolf and tiger, aurochs and boar once more at large, we will remember something of what we once were, we will get back something of our godhood.

'There are few untouched places left in the world. There is no room for such beasts to roam free. If you fence them in, they are stock, not free beasts.

'But here on the Dark Isle we have space and the natural boundaries of the sea. Here we could reintroduce some of these ancient animals, make a Golden Age in this small island state. People will flock here from all over the world to visit this new Eden.'

He opened his briefcase and took out a sheaf of leaflets which he placed on the table. DARK ISLE FREE STATE, they proclaimed. INDEPENDENCE NOW! 'Thank you. That is all.'

'May I ask a question?'

A woman in the audience had her hand up.

Mor frowned. 'I suppose so.'

'How can the Poles possibly have moved? The earth is pretty big. What could have caused such a change without destroying the Earth?'

'I don't know.' He pulled his briefcase towards him and opened it.

'But I can't believe...'

'Listen, I gave you the facts, all right? If you can't just accept the facts then that is really your problem, not mine. You ready, Baldy?'

Baldy had been dozing. He was alert in a moment. He leapt to the door, pulled it open and scanned the street.

'All clear, boss.'

'Yes, yes, I'm sure it is.'

The woman was still waving her arm. 'But you said this Hapgood had a theory.'

'Hapgood? Yes. A sad case. He became completely obsessed with explaining the facts scientifically. Made up some unlikely theory or other that didn't explain half of it. No-one believed him. Except Einstein, of course.'

Some members of the audience smiled and nodded. They had heard of Einstein.

A woman with a cream-coloured cardigan and a string of pearls stood up. 'Ladies, I'm sure we would all like to thank Mr Mor for his most illuminating talk.'

They all clapped politely, except the woman who had asked the questions. She sat steadfastly with folded arms.

'Right, Baldy, let's go.'

Baldy leapt out of the door and went down the path in a crouch, swivelling to cover each point of the compass.

Mr Mor came out of the door of the Institute. The lady with the cream cardigan was close behind him, trying to convince him to stay and mingle while they had tea. She stopped as she saw Baldy fling open the door of the Land Rover and check the interior, front and back.

'You must excuse him,' said Mor. 'He's very keen. But not very bright.'

Jimmy Bervie and Le Placs appeared out of Kirk Road. They were deep in discussion, but they paused to watch Baldy throw himself to the ground to check for booby traps under the car. Then he stood and held the car door open.

'Baldy,' said Mor, 'You don't have to make such a bloody performance of it.'

Baldy shut the car door and looked down the street. Nothing but a couple of harmless-looking teuchters. His hand slipped into his jacket and pulled out a clothes brush. he carefully brushed road-grit from his clothes, scowled menacingly then climbed into the car and drove off.

Inside the Institute, a hubbub of conversation arose from eighty ladies.

Smoke blew across the clearing. Moonlit clouds swirled across the dark sky. The crackling of the fire was backed by the moan of the wind through the branches.

'Now let everyone that is with us gather to beat the arse of this hero!'

The dark figures around the fire began to form into a line. Two hooded acolytes held steady the figure of the victim, suspended by a rope. The first in line raised a stick and whacked the suspended person. He handed the stick to the next in line and moved aside.

There was no chanting now, no sound but the hissing of wind in the bushes, the crackle of burning logs and the whack of stick on flesh, then a pause, then another whack. Fergus felt like a prisoner under surveillance, as if, from the darkness under each hood, everyone was watching to see how he behaved. His eyes slid from side to side, looking for escape, but there was none. The line moved forward, bringing him closer to the horrible figure hanging there. Through the bindings, he began to make out the person underneath. In the firelight, pink skin showed through trussings of rope and net. The poor bastard was naked.

Now there was only one person in front of Fergus. The stick whacked onto the pink rounded surface showing through a piece of brown fishing net. Fergus stepped forward and took the stick.

The strings of the net had made deep grooves in the pink flesh. A few coarse hairs poked out through the net. Along with his own fear, Fergus felt painful pity for the victim. Not only did he have to put up with the humiliation of the ritual, but he had a bristly bottom too.

He could hear the breathing of the next person in line. Bad Bastard and his assistants were all watching. Reluctantly, Fergus swung the stick at the sad pink behind, then handed it to the next in line.

Bad was on his makeshift podium again. Fergus tried to shrink away inside his robes. He had a sick feeling deep in his stomach. This was not going to end well. Don't be an idiot, he told himself. It's just an initiation. Soon the guy will be released and we'll all be sitting around eating sausages and laughing. But he was trembling uncontrollably and he could no longer follow the chant, but stood with his mouth half open. The smoke had left a greasy feel to his skin, his lips, his eyeballs. Evil was here, he could feel it, and it was watching him. Perhaps all these robes were empty, only disembodied eyes deep in the hoods. Watching.

The moment had come. All the hooded figures stood facing the hanging man. Bad Bastard had his shiny knife raised: Fergus saw moonlight slip down its edge. Two assistants held the victim firmly.

'So! Thus do we in Cromness, in the name of Cromm Cruach!'

Above the grove, grey clouds moved restlessly. They seemed to form into faces that looked down at the ritual in the clearing. The faces were not friendly ones.

The gathered figures chanted their response. 'Thus do we, in the name of Cromm Cruach!'

Bad Bastard leaned forward and placed the point of the knife at the groin of the sacrificial victim.

This is it. This is where he cuts the cords and the guy falls down. Then we all laugh and...

With a grunt of effort, Bad pulled the knife upwards. Entrails like strings of sausages spilled from the belly, falling towards the tin bath below.

'No!' Fergus screamed. 'No!'

The assistants gave the body a shake, the entrails flopped out and Bad reached with his free hand to guide the guts into the tub. Fergus stepped back, his hands to his face. There were no humans under those hoods, but only great evil.

The clouds above boiled into hideous organic shapes, then began to take form. Fergus watched as a face appeared, with strings of dirty hair. It grew downwards into a neck and shoulders, then a grey naked body with breasts hanging to the navel. Arms emerged from the clouds, reaching out towards Fergus, who was standing immobile with fear. The sagging belly appeared, and the crotch, with a dangling penis and scrotum. Still Fergus was unable to move, as knees grew out of the clouds, then shins, then the feet, planted among the trees.

The creature opened its mouth. Stars could be seen through its grey gullet. It groaned with a sound like a tempest. Clumsily, it stepped forwards, its grey foot mingling with the smoke from the fire.

With a wail, Fergus broke from his paralysis as the creature leant over the glade. Unable to find the path, he plunged into the bushes, smashing through them, falling, rolling, scrambling on hands and knees, anything to get away from the hideous creature and the terrible sacrifice.

Bad Bastard turned to Donny.

'Was that Fergus? What the fuck's wrong with him?'

Donny shrugged. 'Just highly strung, I guess.'

'Oh well. More for the rest of us. Okay everyone, let's have the sausages now.' Smoke swirled around the glade, clouds scudded overhead. 'Jesus, the wind's really got up.'

Bad picked up a sausage from near the fire. 'Hey, you two. Torquil and James. Get the victim down and untie him. And take care. All that meat has to be back in the shop before Andy notices it's missing.'

The hanging man was lowered and the bindings were cut. Joints of meat spilled into the tin bath on top of the strings of sausages.

'Christ's sake mind them bloody sausages! They're no good if you burst them!'

MacFearn plodded up the street, heading for The Fisherman's Arms. He was not in a good mood. Woe betide any publican tonight who thought he could flout the licensing laws in Cromness! Anger simmered in MacFearn's heart, anger and resentment at being excluded from the drugs raid. If he had been there, that drugs baron Mor would never have slipped out of the net. He'd have had him bang to rights.

He turned the corner, and there was the man himself. MacFearn slipped unobtrusively into a doorway and exercised his observational skills, mentally noting the details, to be transferred later to his notebook.

Mor was standing at the door to the Chandler Institute, in association with a woman wearing a cream cardigan and a grey woollen skirt. The woman looked perfectly respectable, but criminals could be cunning. She might be a pharmaceutical expert or a contact for organised crime. Perhaps the Institute was their meeting place. There were strange Masonic symbols above the door, too. If the Masons were involved, the scandal could run deep. His mouth set grimly. The Masons had never invited him to join, but he was sure that several police officers were members, including Inspector Morrison.

One of Mor's henchmen scuttled down the path from the Institute, looking around in a shifty fashion. MacFearn edged further into the doorway, peering round the doorframe. The henchman was an obvious criminal type with small eyes, a mean look on his face and a bald head. He reached the roadside, fell to the ground and rolled under the Land Rover. This was interesting. Perhaps he was sabotaging the vehicle. MacFearn thrilled to the thought. There was no honour among thieves, that was plain. Just across the street, Jimmy Bervie and that French fellow were standing, watching the performance. Excellent. A pair of witnesses. MacFearn whipped out his notebook as Mor walked down to the waiting vehicle. MacFearn's pencil scribbled on the small pages. *I was proceeding along Harbour Road when, turning into High Street, my attention was drawn to a suspicious character acting in a suspicious manner...*

The balding man was in the driver's seat now, and had the engine racing. Mor climbed in, and with a squeal of tyres, the Land Rover shot down the street and went round the corner on two wheels.

Driving at an excessive speed, the suspects left the scene, wrote MacFearn. *I observed that neither suspect had his seat belt properly fastened.*

He closed his notebook and thoughtfully proceeded along the street, which was now quiet and empty. Mr Mor needed watching, that was plain, and MacFearn knew that he himself was the man for the job. Perhaps some plain-clothes surveillance was called for.

There was a sound of running feet on the pavement and a dreadful moaning, which grew louder as the footsteps approached. Round the corner came a running figure, a tattered black cloak flapping around him. There was a hood to the cloak, but it had fallen back, revealing the face of a young man, his eyes wide open in terror, his hands held up to his white face, as if he was trying to stop it falling off.

'Hello, hello...' began MacFearn, but the fleeing youth was past him in an instant, turning down towards the harbour. MacFearn thoughtfully opened his notebook again. *Continuing to proceed along High Street*, he wrote, *a further suspicious circumstance occurred...*

Fergus ran down Harbour Road and turned into his own street. He ran up the garden path and threw open the front door. 'Oooaaagghhh!' he moaned.

From the kitchen he heard the chink of a cup going down onto a saucer.

'Fergus? Is that you?' It was his mother's voice. He felt no fear for her, did not care at all what she thought of his escapade, but in an instant, from the very familiarity of her voice, he knew that there was no help there. His very soul might be damned, but she could offer him no help. His home was a refuge no more. The very carpet and the wallpaper spoke to him of the everyday, the ordinary: they had nothing to do with hideous ceremonies and human sacrifice. He was surely lost.

In despair and terror, he moaned again as he turned and ran from the house. He ran blindly, his heart thundering, his mind whirling. Was there any place to go, anywhere he could find help? Should he throw himself in the harbour? But that would do no good. He would be dead, but he would still be damned. Should he go to the police? That would not bring back the dead man or wipe the horror from his soul. Still running and moaning, not knowing or caring where he was going, he came to the church. He clutched the iron railings and stared at the blind windows. Should he throw himself on the mercy of the minister? No, that was as futile as anything else. He turned again and ran, then slowed to a walk and finally stopped. The orange streetlights sapped all colour from the houses and the hedges. It looked unreal, it looked like a street in Hell. There was nowhere in the world he could go, nothing he could do to make things better. He fell to his knees in the middle of the road. He wrapped his arms around his head and howled.

Jimmy Bervie removed his jacket and laid it on an old fish-box. He removed his wig and laid it on the jacket. He rubbed his hands against each other, looking thoughtfully out over the sea towards the northern mountains. Then he took his rake from its place against the wall and strode down to the sand. Le Placs stood at a distance, respectfully watching.

'Well, then, *i graidh*, we shall see what story the sand has for us.' He seemed to be talking to the rake, or perhaps he was addressing the night itself.

He leant forward and reached out with the rake. The tines dropped into the sand and began to write their message as he pulled with a smooth powerful movement.

Le Placs watched Jimmy, not the writing in the sand. It seemed that he could see the influences at work on Jimmy's shoulders, on the muscles of his forearms, on his stance as he moved along sidestep after each pull. Now and then the moon shone through gaps in the clouds, and a glow hovered around Jimmy. Le Placs shivered as the wind blew cool on his neck. It seemed to him that he heard a desolate howl from far off. He listened, but the sound was not repeated.

When Jimmy had finished, he turned from the sand and walked up to the house. Le Placs watched him as he stood the rake in its accustomed place. He then put on his jacket and tucked the wig into his pocket.

'I suppose we'd better have a look, then.' But he did not move. 'Or perhaps you'd like a coffee first?'

'No, *mon brave*. I think it best not to delay.'

Jimmy sighed and walked down to the edge of the sand.

'Oh dear,' he said.

'*Merde*,' agreed le Placs.

Lorraine's mind was still in a state of turmoil. The various details of Alice's Godhood were lost on her. Or was it Goddesshood? Goddessness? Her face twitched into a nervous smile. It was too much. Really, she had to go back to basics and start all over again with a new notion of what was possible and what was not. It was either that, or disbelieve both Alice and Doreen. But those two usually disagreed so violently that it was difficult to dismiss something that they both agreed on.

Not long ago, Alice had subsided into a sort of weighty sulk. 'Something's happening,' she said, 'Something serious. I'd better see what it is.' Then she just went away, leaving her body slumped in a chair and a scowl on her face. Lorraine glanced at her now and then. Alice had immersed herself in her state of aggressive withdrawal and her forehead was wrinkled in a deep frown.

Pretty sure that nothing would disturb her in her present state, Lorraine turned to Doreen. 'These Gods and suchlike,' she began. 'I thought you were, well, sceptical about the whole business. You certainly don't hesitate to contradict Alice.'

Doreen shrugged. 'You know Alice. She's bigoted, bad-tempered, overbearing and her political stance is somewhere to the right of the Third Reich. On the other hand, she has a mind like a bucket of acid. If a fact goes in there and survives, you can be pretty sure of it. Oh yes, the facts of the matter you can rely on. Her opinions – well, you know what I think of them.'

'Where do they live, these Gods, when they're not out riding their human steeds?'

Doreen nodded. 'Yep. It's just like that.' She looked thoughtful. 'I suppose the best I can say is that they live beside us in another world. It's not really important where it is. It's just some other place.'

'But they can get out...'

'And sometimes people can get in. Some people. There was a preacher called Wandering John a long time ago. He disappeared, right in front of a crowd of fishermen. There are gates from here to there, but most people don't see them. They are disguised somehow, or guarded.'

'You mean there's someone watching over them?'

'Perhaps. Or a distraction of some sort, something like a magician's patter. You know, to keep your attention off the gate until you're past. It's not like there's a guardian with a bloody great sword. It's subtle. I'm sure there's a gate in the Wee Vennel, near Jenny-Pet's house, but I've looked hard and never found it. I bet Alice knows where it is, but she won't tell. There's a gateway in the Drooping Cave, and I never knew about that until George MacLear disappeared into it.'

Lorraine shivered. 'It's weird. I don't know if I can even believe it.'

Alice roused herself. 'Good,' she said. 'That's the right approach. Otherwise you end up woolly-minded and mystical like those Celtic New-Age people. Daft as brushes, the lot of them.'

Lorraine looked shocked. 'How can you say that? They believe just the same sort of thing that you do. They speak about respect for the Goddess and communing with the ancient Gods...'

Alice snorted. 'What did I tell you? They're away with the bloody fairies. The Gods and Goddesses live here, in the Dark Isle. Have done for centuries.'

Doreen looked at Lorraine and shrugged.

'It's so hard to believe in this when everything else is so – normal.'

From the street outside came a long drawn out howl of anguish and despair.

'Ah,' breathed Alice. 'That's it. Doreen, go and get him.'

Doreen went straight to the door. Lorraine pulled back the curtains to look. In the middle of the road a young man was curled up in a knot with his head in his arms.

Doreen entered the house with Fergus in tow. The tatters of his cloak hung around him and his face was a picture of misery and fear.

'So,' said Alice. 'It's the MacFarquhar boy. What have you been up to, eh?'

'Leave him be, Alice.' Doreen led him to a chair. 'Lorraine, get him a mug of coffee.' Fergus was shivering under her hand. She pushed him into a chair and went round the room turning up the radiators.

Lorraine returned and handed the boy a steaming mug.

'You're all right now,' said Doreen.

'He may be all right, but what about the rest of us? There's been something damned strange going on tonight, or my name's not Alice MacKerril.'

Doreen sat on the arm of Fergus's chair and put an arm round his shoulders. 'Don't bully him,' she said. 'He'll get round to it in his own time.'

Alice impatiently waited while Fergus calmed down under Doreen's soothing murmurs. He had stopped shivering, but his face was still pale.

'So, young man,' said Alice, with a ghastly attempt at a smile. 'Where have you been tonight, eh?'

Fergus stiffened, but Doreen patted him on the shoulder.

'Better tell us,' she said. 'You're going to have to tell someone.'

'The Foxes Dens,' he said reluctantly. 'It was a meeting.'

'Ah. The Sons of Cromm Cruach or whatever it is. Dabbling in things you know nothing about, I suppose.' Her fake smile disappeared. Her voice was sharp as a whip. 'What happened?'

'We did a ritual,' said Fergus, 'a horrible ritual. Then the clouds drew down and a thing came out of them, a huge being, a god or a demon or something, naked and grey and horrible.'

Alice's mouth pursed. 'I thought as much. Was it male or female?'

Fergus looked around at the women. 'I don't know. Both, I think.'

'What do you mean, both?'

'It was both.' Fergus blushed. 'It had, you know – it had a woman's chests and a man's... thing.'

Alice looked at him in outrage. 'It had dugs *and* a dongler?'

'Yes.'

Alice looked at the other two women. 'Who the hell was it?'

Doreen patted his shoulder. 'What ritual did you use?'

'Well, we marched round the fire and chanted...'

'Yes, of course,' Alice said. 'But what did you chant? Do you remember any of the words?'

'Man khahar nadaram vali baradar daram.' The three women looked at him in incomprehension. 'It's in Persian,' he explained. 'I think it means, That is not your horse, it is my horse.'

'What?'

'It was just made up. Just a joke, you know. Or at least I thought it was.'

Alice frowned at him. 'That's not going to raise up a supernatural, no matter how gullible you are. Was there nothing else?'

'There was one other bit I could understand. It was in English, just before the sacrifice...'

'What? A sacrifice! You idiots!'

'Stop it, Alice,' said Doreen. 'He's worried enough. Go on, then, Fergus. What was that bit?'

'I can't remember it all. It's something to do with Seven.'

'Come on, can you remember any of it?'

Fergus's face was dead white and frightened. 'I don't want to say it.'

Alice sneered at him. 'For goodness sake, it's already done its job. You can't make it worse now.'

Fergus shook his head. Alice glared at him. 'Doreen, give us a circle of protection.'

Doreen went to the kitchen and returned with a wooden spurtle and a jar of Allspice. Muttering to herself, she threw pinches of the aromatic spice to the corners of the room then, pointing with the spurtle, she turned around, marking out a circle that included everyone present.

'All right,' said Alice. 'You can tell us now. We're protected from evil influences.'

'Except from those already in this room of course,' Doreen whispered to Lorraine. Alice turned her eyes on her for an instant, then back to Fergus.

'Now let's hear it, or what you remember of it.'

Fergus swallowed and haltingly began.

'They are seven, only seven.'

Doreen nodded encouragement. His voice grew stronger.

'In the depths, seven
In the sky, seven
In the secret corners, in abandoned houses
They swell up, they grow tall.'

A cold draught blew through the room. Doreen leant over and turned the radiator up again.

'Neither man nor woman, without mother or father
They have no child,
For they are seven, always seven.
They are the faces of evil, the faces of evil.'

A gust of wind rattled the windows. Alice's head jerked round and she stared out of the window into the darkness of the street. Fergus's eyes closed, but his voice continued, full and strong.

'Their breath is pestilence.
They live in the silence of the tempest,
Their step lays waste the handiwork of man.'

Wind was moaning in the chimney. Smoke blew into the room. Doreen clutched the spurtle tightly. Lorraine sidled closer to her.

'Where they walk, the paths fall into ruin
They tear down the houses
They eat even the Gods
And they are the seven!'

The wind gave a final shriek and subsided.

'That's all I remember,' said Fergus. The coldness in the room began to dissipate.

'Just as bloody well,' said Alice. She looked at Fergus appraisingly. 'Has anyone ever told you that you have the power?'

Fergus coughed and blushed. 'Doreen once told me that I had a lot of vigour.'

Alice looked across at Doreen, who would not catch her eye. 'Hmph. It may be that she was referring to some other quality. Well, we'll let that go for the moment. It's just that someone let that thing loose, and the rest of those clowns haven't the imagination.'

'But I thought the ritual called it in.'

Doreen spoke. 'Sort of. But it's not just the ritual, there has to be belief too. You can murder a whole barnyard of cockerels and nothing will happen, unless you believe it will. If you have the power, and you imagine something strongly enough, it becomes real. It steps into this world.'

Fergus looked relieved. 'So it was just my imagination?'

'It was your imagination that brought it here,' said Alice.

'But how do you know it wasn't someone else? Donny or Bad Bast... I mean Trevor.'

'Because it was you that arrived here and not them.' Alice's voice was sure. It was plain that she thought that no further explanation was necessary.

'So if it's just my imagination, then that Grey Thing isn't really here?'

Alice chuckled nastily. 'Oh, it came here by way of your mind, but it's here now, make no mistake. And it doesn't need your mind any more.'

'Oh God.'

'But we're no closer to knowing who It is,' said Doreen, 'It was a damned strong invocation, but where did they get it from?'

Lorraine looked around at everyone. 'Sorry? I thought you'd have recognised it. It's very old, but it's quite well-known.'

'Well, I've never heard it before,' said Alice. 'Never heard of that Grey God either, and I know all the Celtic myths.'

Lorraine laughed. 'No, it's not Celtic. It's much older than that. It's Sumerian. Must be over four thousand years old.'

'Sumerian! What the hell's one of them doing here?'

Lorraine looked at her curiously. 'We don't know everything about the Celts – we don't even know where they came from before they arrived in central Europe. Who knows what mythological hangers-on they brought with them? This old grey being sounds a bit like Koschei the Deathless. Or the Enarees of the Scythians – they were half-male and half-female.'

'What have the Scythians got to do with it?'

'Maybe nothing – but the Scythians came from Iran into southern Russia and that's where they encountered the Celts. In fact, the Celts learnt their horsemanship from the Scythians. And lots of other things too.'

Alice frowned. 'It sounds like prehistoric miscegenation to me.'

Lorraine laughed. 'You can't get away from it. We've all influenced each other.'

'I'm not interested in bloody influences. Just in what's really here.'

'Like that Grey Thing,' said Doreen.

'Still can't see how it got here. Four thousand years – it must have been near moribund. It would take a hell of a ritual to call it up.'

'There was that invocation. It was pretty powerful.' Doreen looked at Fergus. 'And you said something about a sacrifice.'

Fergus's face grew paler, and he looked as though he was about to be sick.

Jimmy Bervie and Le Placs stood looking at the sand for a few minutes, saying nothing. There were no lights down here, but the moonlight was enough to reveal the patterns on the sand.

The first part of each stroke was straight and true, then there was an edge of turmoil, where the furrows twisted, as though the rake had deformed into another shape. Then there was nothing, a flat unmarked expanse of dry sand, though Jimmy had raked the whole area with a smooth and regular action.

Le Placs spoke at last. 'I think this does not need much interpretation, Jimmy my friend.'

'No, indeed. I think we have the situation in a nutshell.'

'It is bad, my friend, no?'

Jimmy nodded. 'Even in 1425 it wasn't this bad.'

Le Placs looked at him curiously. 'Before, you mentioned this date. Do you have some kind of record of this year?'

'None but my own memory.'

'Surely not!'

Jimmy waved a hand dismissively. 'It is not important.'

Le Placs shrugged. 'It seems important to me.'

Jimmy looked at him. His eyes were sharp as gems in his broad red face. 'Perhaps I should have said that it is not urgent.' He pointed at the sand. 'This is urgent.'

'*Mon Dieu*, it is certainly that. But what are we to do?'

'First, I think we must have some coffee, and I will tell you why I have such a long memory.'

Le Placs waved a hand towards the sand. 'But what about this urgency? Look at what the future has in store! Is this a time for coffee?'

Jimmy took his arm and led him towards the house. 'I said it is urgent, but that is no reason to be hasty. Let us have coffee and talk.'

Le Placs shrugged. '*Bon*. Let us drink coffee. Who am I to concern myself with disasters and calamities?'

'The first thing you must know,' said Jimmy as they entered the house, 'is that my name is not really Bervie. That is just a by-name. But I have been using it for so long that no-one here remembers my real name.'

From *Legends of the Celts* by C Stollerone
published by Gundestrup Press, 1894

...at that time, Saint Finnen lived in Donegal, and making occasion to pass by the stronghold of Tuan mac Cairell, he went to visit the ancient warrior and bard, asking for his hospitality. Finding the door shut against him, the saint sat upon the stone by the door and would not take food or drink. After three days, seeing that the saint knew the old customs, Tuan let him enter and the two sat down to meat.

Good relations having been established between them, the saint asked him his name and lineage – to which he received an astounding reply. 'My name is Tuan mac Cairell,' the man replied, 'but aforetime I was son of Starn, son of Sera. My father's brother was Partholan, the first of men to settle in Ireland. I myself sat in his council and gave judgements.'

The holy monk was astonished by this and asked Tuan to tell his story. The old warrior's life story contained within it the whole history of the country. As the histories of the divers races which have inhabited Eire are presented in Chapter Three, here I will give a paraphrase of Tuan's tale.

After the death of Partholan's people, I lived in waste places, avoiding all people, growing long-clawed, decrepit and wretched. At last I retired to a cave and died. Waking on the morrow, I found myself to have become a stag. I was young again, and gladness was in my heart. Through all the days of Nemed's people I remained a stag, king of the race of deer. When Nemed's race failed, I was old once more and I retired to that same cave to lie down and die. On the morrow I found that once again I was transformed. I stood at the cave mouth and cried out that I had put on a new form. I who had sung the judgements of Partholan was now a black boar, young again and glad.

As the cycles of invaders arrived in Ireland, Tuan took on the form of a sea-eagle and then a salmon, returning each time in old age to his cave to await his transformation.

As a salmon, however, he was captured in a net and taken to Cairell, the wife of a chieftain. She ate him whole and he passed into her womb to be born again as a man, known as Tuan son of Cairell.

Le Placs sat on a fish-box and sipped his coffee. In the dim light of an oil lantern Jimmy's face gleamed as he told his story.

'Saint Finnen was only the first of many and I could see the way it was going to go. The people of the church were growing plentiful and the Gods, who had once lived amongst us, had retired to live in hillocks, or gone far away. So then I left, too. Manannan and the Dagda went away to the Dark Island, and I followed. At first I stayed with them here on the Dark Isle. I took a wife and had children. But after many years, she died and I did not.

'Then I left the Dark Isle and wandered among the peoples of Scotland: in Arran, in Glasgow, in Argyll and in Berwick. In St Andrews I lived for many years, and also in the Long Island. But time and again I returned to this place, the Dark Isle. The Gods didn't live among men anymore. They had hidden themselves. But I knew that they were here, and although I had my differences with them, it was a comfort to me to know that someone else remembered the early days as I did. Each time I came back here, I took another wife and lived my life out, expecting to die. Each time, my wife died and I remained. People would have noticed after a while, so I would go wandering again until all who knew me had forgotten, or died.

'I left these shores and saw strange countries, strange people. When I came back here, I realised that most of the people I met were my children's children's children. That was when I decided to live by myself. No-one really notices an old man living alone. No-one finds his continuing existence remarkable. Since then, I have stayed here to watch over Cromness and my children.'

Jimmy picked up a windmill and waved it to and fro, the glow of the lamplight gleaming on its shiny vanes. He beamed at his guest.

Le Placs smiled back at him. 'Quite a story. But where did your name come from?'

'In Glasgow, if they don't know your name, they just call you Jimmy. So I took that name a good few years back. And my last name I took from the fish-box. Look.' He pointed to the box that le Placs was sitting on.

Le Placs read 'RETURN TO KINLOCHBERVIE.'

'Because I keep returning, you know.'

Le Placs laughed.

'Do you believe me?' asked Jimmy.

'I don't know. Must I believe you?'

'No. It's not important.'

'Not urgent, perhaps. I will think about it.'

Jimmy leant forwards. 'As to the more urgent matter...'

'Ah, yes. The imminent destruction of the world as we know it.'

Jimmy waved his hand. 'Or whatever it is.'

Le Placs shrugged. 'I have no idea of how to proceed. Did you see anything specific in the sand? Anything that might give us a clue?'

Jimmy frowned and sucked his teeth. 'It looks to me as if there will be serious damage to the local state of reality. But you will have noticed that yourself. It is possible that the Earth will split asunder, releasing monsters to go forth upon the world. Perhaps some disaster will occur that releases once more the caprices of the Gods upon us – for to tell the truth, they are an unruly and violent lot. Splendid, in their way, but their behaviour is not what we would today consider acceptable. As the herring are already in a beleaguered state, I expect little response from them, but it is likely that the mackerel will desert the sea. A couple of centuries ago, the Brown Seer told me that he was glad he would not be living when a man could walk dryshod across the sea at Castleton.' He looked seriously at Le Placs. 'For there will be the lowing of cattle and the squeals of distressed swine. More than one will die on that unfortunate day, so he said. And it's not long until the Dark Isle Show.'

'Pardon?'

'The local fishermen tie up their boats to make a bridge to the mainland. Then you can walk across dryshod.'

'This Brown Seer, did he say anything else?'

'Och, yes. Rakes of things. Some of them have almost come true.'

'But he has no concrete suggestions?'

'No, no. Nothing concrete...' He lifted his hand to his brow and fell silent. His eyes were dark shadows in his face.

'Is there anything wrong?' asked Le Placs, after a few seconds.

'I think I have it,' said Jimmy. 'It is uncertain and risky, but there is little else we can do.'

'What is it?'

'First thing in the morning, I'm going to buy a bag of cement.'

Constable MacFearn had decided to approach The Fisherman's Arms by a circuitous route. Walking along the seafront as if he was merely taking a stroll, he ascertained that the coast was clear before ducking smartly into the Muckle Vennel. He stealthily proceeded along the darkened lane, making no noise until he stumbled over a cat. It hissed at him from the deeper darkness of a doorway. MacFearn's involuntary swear must have alerted the late-night revellers, because there were no lights on in the Arms when he peered round into Kirk Street.

Thwarted, he plodded back through Cromness towards his own house down Harbour Road. In case of felons working under cover of darkness, he swung round by way of Wayland Crescent, then Inglis Road. Not far from the Harbour, he noticed a car drawing up beside the butcher's shop. To his delight, two figures furtively carried something from the car boot to the shop door. While they were trying to open the door he managed to creep up close to them. On the ground beside them was their burden, a metal tub with a sheet over it.

'Hello, hello! What's going on here then?'

Two shocked faces turned to him. Bad Bastard stepped forwards in an instinctive response – to strike out when in a tight spot – but Donny MacLean grabbed his arm.

MacFearn drew himself up to his full height. He was taller than Bad, but not so wide. 'Well, then, well, then. This looks very suspicious, indeed it does. And what do you two have in that big tub, eh?'

Donny stepped forwards. 'Ah, it's you, Sergeant MacFearn. What a relief.'

'It's Constable MacFearn, as yet,' he said gruffly, 'But promotion could be on the way if I can prevent a nasty bit of thievery taking place.' He raised his bushy eyebrows in enquiry.

'Yes indeed.' Donny spoke hastily. 'A well-deserved promotion, I'm sure. I suppose it does look a little suspicious, us being here at the dead of night, making a delivery to the local butcher.'

MacFearn stepped forward and whipped the sheet from the tub. It was full of joints of meat and skeins of sausage. 'I think there is a bit of explaining to be done.'

'Of course. I daresay it does seem a little odd.'

'That is why I would like an explanation.'

'The fact is, Sergeant MacFearn, that we are ourselves the victims in a sense. Yes. Victims of the new EC regulations.'

'I beg your pardon?'

'You'll know about the new regulations in the EC directive on Transportation of Meat and Meat Derivatives?'

MacFearn looked dubious.

'It says that meat and meat products have to be delivered in refrigerated transport only. That's the regulations now, and the fact of the matter is, we can't afford to have our vehicle upgraded.' He gestured to the car. His voice developed a pleading note. 'There's a maze of regulations covering small businesses now. All over the country, local traders are going down under the weight of red tape.'

'So.' MacFearn frowned as he looked from one to the other. 'You admit that you are breaking the law?'

'Not really,' said Donny. 'Well, a little bit, I suppose. It's purely a civil matter, you understand. If the EC Inspectors of Meat and Sundry Products should find us delivering meat in a non-refrigerated transport, they'll put us out of work. The Cromness farmers will be unable to sell their animals locally and may be forced to sell off their herds and lay off skilled workers.'

MacFearn frowned. He was naturally inclined to distrust regulations emanating from Europe, and he didn't like the sound of these jumped-up inspectors.

'So that's why we have to make our deliveries at night.'

MacFearn considered. It was true that he'd seen the car drawing up at the shop and the basin-load of meat had been brought to the shop, not taken from it. But there was one big hole in the story.

'So, how are you supposed to make deliveries when there's no-one in the shop?

'The butcher gave us the key.'

Bad Bastard held up the shop key and held it there while MacFearn looked at it and thought. The butcher obviously trusted them, if he let them have his key. And MacFearn was all in favour of the idea of community policing. The idea being, to keep folk from committing crime in the first place instead of catching them afterwards. It appealed to his avuncular nature. He looked at the two young men.

'Johnny MacDonald, isn't it? And Kevin Barkly?' Surprise appeared on Donny's face. MacFearn chuckled. 'I've got a trained memory, lad. Never forget a face. Now, Johnny and Kevin, I'm probably taking a risk here, but it seems to me that you're not hardened wrongdoers.'

'Oh no.'

'So just this once, I'm going to overlook this infringement of the regulations.'

'Thank you...'

He held up his hand. 'But if I catch you at this carry-on again, I'll throw the book at you. Understand?'

'Oh yes. Thank you.'

'So you open up that door and make your delivery and I'll just wait here until you're finished.' He folded his arms and stood over them while Bad fumbled the key into the lock and they carried the tub inside. Without another word, he watched them as they unloaded the joints of meat and then the strings of sausages into the cold store.

'Now lads,' he said after they had locked the door. 'Take my advice and speak to your bank manager. That Mr Dollar up at the bank, he's a reasonable man. Tell him you want to invest in a little refrigerated van.' He shook his head. 'This fly-by-night stuff, it's going to get you into trouble.'

'You're right, sergeant,' said Donny. 'We'll make an appointment tomorrow. Thank you for your advice.' They climbed into the car. 'Goodnight.'

MacFearn watched them drive off, feeling content. Stern but fair, that was the ticket.

'So what happened then?'

Fergus swallowed and clutched his mug. 'After we'd all spanked the hero...'

Alice snorted. Doreen managed to suppress a smile.

'Bad, I mean Trevor, he took one of his big butcher's knives. You know, those ones he uses in the shop. That's where he works. They've got a black handle and a big shiny blade.'

'Get to the point,' Alice growled.

'Two people held his legs, to keep him steady. Not Trevor's legs, the victim's.' A nervous smile flitted across his face and he glanced round at the women. Alice was glowering at him, Doreen was watching him with sympathy on her face. The other woman, Lorraine, had her eyes fixed on him and her expression was a strange combination of horror and wonder.

'Then he called out – Bad, that is, not the victim...' his face twitched again into a nervous smile.

'Get a grip, boy,' growled Alice, 'and tell us the bloody story!'

'In the name of Cromm Cruach, that's what he said, just before he did it.' Fergus was trembling. His knuckles were white as he clutched his mug hard, trying to keep his hands still. 'And then he did it,' he whispered. 'He killed him.'

'Yes, yes. But how did he do it? Tell us what he did for God's sake!'

Lorraine's mouth twisted in distaste as she looked at Alice. 'Surely we don't need the gory details.'

'Be quiet and let the boy answer.'

Fergus bowed his head. His spoke in a low flat voice. 'Bad Bastard put the knife in right at the base of his belly, then he ripped upwards so that the guts spilled out and fell into the tub on the ground beneath. That was when the Grey Thing stepped down out of the clouds. Bad Bastard was standing there and the guts were spilling into the tub and Bad reached right in and pulled out more and that's when I turned and ran.'

Alice sat in her chair, nodding her head. Doreen had drawn back from Fergus, so that he sat alone. Lorraine, very pale, left the room. There were retching sounds from the direction of the bathroom. After a few minutes, the toilet flushed and she returned.

'So,' said Alice, at last. 'What did they do with the blood?'

Fergus lifted his head to look at her. 'What do you mean?'

'Well, the guts spilled into the tub, yes? So what about the blood?'

Fergus did not move a muscle, but his face became blank as he looked inside himself at the dreadful moment when Bad ripped open the belly. 'There wasn't any blood.'

'No,' said Alice. 'Of course there wasn't. If you'd noticed that earlier we might all have been spared a lot of trouble.'

'But how... But why...'

'And now that Grey Thing is loose in the world, because you were too stupid to notice that there was no blood.'

Fergus's mouth was hanging open. 'If there was no blood,' he said, 'then he must have been already dead.'

'Have you got a grain of sense in that head? Why would they kill a man and then pretend to kill him later? No, the whole thing was a sham.'

'But we had to spank his bottom. I saw him tied up, I saw his skin.'

Alice snorted. 'It was dark, and I bet there was a lot of rope on him.'

'Well, yes. Ropes and net.'

'So you couldn't see much of him, eh? As for his backside, it could just have been a piece of meat. Pork, most likely.'

'That was why he had a bristly bottom!' Fergus suddenly looked much less pale. There was the hint of a smile across his face. 'Of course! Bad Bastard could get hold of any amount of meat that he wanted.' He laughed. 'So there wasn't any sacrifice at all. Thank God! It's all right.'

'It's far from all right, my lad. If you had half the gumption you were born with, that Grey Thing wouldn't be trollomping about the countryside right now.'

'Maybe I imagined it. It was dim, and I was frightened. If the sacrifice wasn't really real...'

Alice's face flushed and she practically bellowed at him. 'Did you not listen to a word Doreen said? Well listen to me, cloth-ears! The sacrifice isn't for the benefit of the gods or whatever you're calling up. It's to get you into the right frame of mind so that you can act as a bridge between the Otherworld and this one. Do you understand that, or do I have to say it again?'

Fergus nodded dumbly. Alice continued.

'You thought the sacrifice was real, didn't you? And because of that, the empty space which you call a mind was the right *shape* to let the Thing through. And now we're stuck with it.'

Fergus looked worried, but he still looked far more cheerful than before. 'What can we do?'

'We? You can't do bugger all. It's up to us to find some way to get rid of it.'

In his lap, Fergus's hands twisted together. 'It's just that, if it came here through me, perhaps it might go back the same way.'

Alice looked at him in surprise. 'Would you risk that? Or do you just think you ought to offer? No matter. The best you can do is go off home.'

Fergus suddenly looked terror-stricken. 'Oh no! What will Mum say?'

Alice peered at him, then laughed. 'It's like that is it? You'll tangle with the forces of darkness, but not with your own mother. Well, well.' She lifted herself out of the chair, went to the phone and dialled. She watched Fergus, with a grin on her face, as she waited for an answer.

'Alice here. Fergus is on his way home. He has been helping me. Do you understand? Good.' She put the phone down without another word. 'Don't tell her anything,' she said to Fergus.

He gaped at her. 'But I'll have to tell her something. She'll make me tell.'

'She will not, or she'll have me to deal with. If she tries to bully you, just say Alice told you to keep quiet.'

'Will it work?'

Alice glared at him. 'What do you mean, will it work? Of course it'll bloody work! Now off you go!'

Doreen took him by the shoulder and began to pull the tattered robe off him. 'Be as well to throw that thing out.' She shook her head. 'And the rest of your clothes are not much better. Come on through and get washed up.' She led him through to the kitchen and closed the door behind them.

'Come here.' She ran water into the sink and beckoned him close. 'Listen,' she said in a low tone,' 'You have to get out of this.'

'I'm just about to go home.'

'Not just this house, but right out of Cromness. Out of the Dark Isle.'

'Right now?'

'I'm serious. You're mixed up in some bad stuff and I don't like the way that Alice is taking an interest in you. You have to get out, soon.'

Fergus looked down. 'I can't.'

'Why not? There's a whole world out there.' She paused for a moment. 'So they tell me.'

'I want to! I want to get out of here. I'd like to go away to college – I'm doing well enough at school – but my mum says we need the money and I have to take a job in the bank.' He grimaced. 'With Mr Siller.'

'Can't you stand up to her?'

'Doreen, I can't. Do you know my mum? I mean, she is my mother, but she's...'

'Desperate to be respectable and hard as stone.'

'Well, I wouldn't say it like that, but...'

Doreen held up a hand, silencing him. A small frown appeared on her forehead and her eyes looked into the distance. 'So, we want her to change her mind. How can we make that happen?'

'You're not going to do magic on her are you, because...'

'No, no. But I think we can arrange something just as effective – but much more physical.' She looked him up and down. 'Get yourself washed. I'll be back in a minute. I've got some old clothes I can lend you.'

Mrs MacFarquhar, burning with curiosity, was waiting in the lounge when Fergus came home.

'I'm in here, dear,' she called. 'I was waiting up.'

'I'm a little tired,' Fergus called from the hall. 'I think I'll go straight up to bed.'

'Do come in and say goodnight,' she asked, her voice a little sharper.

'Of course.' Fergus walked into the lounge. His hair had been tied up in dozens of little bundles that stuck out from his head. His face had been painted dead white except for one red stripe across the bridge of his nose. He was wearing a torn black cloak over a pink ra-ra skirt and leopardskin tights. His chest was bare and he was wearing heavy black wellington boots. In one hand he held a trowel. Under the other arm he carried an old leather flying helmet.

'What on earth! My god, Fergus, what on earth have you been up to?'

Fergus held up his hand, the one holding the trowel. 'Sorry Mum, but Alice swore me to silence.'

'Yes, but... but...'

'Goodnight, Mum.'

Fergus slipped into the hall, closing the door behind him. Soon his mother heard the unusual sound of someone in welly boots skipping joyfully up the stairs.

The moon hung over Cromness, looking down through rifts in the clouds. The orange streetlights lit empty streets. MacFearn had done his bit to ensure that Cromness was a safer place, and was now sleeping deeply, his uniform neatly laid out by his bed.

In his house by the shore, Jimmy was pensively munching on some dried seaweed as he lay abed. He hung the strip of seaweed on a nail by the bed and turned off the light.

On the Links, Louisiana Lou was fast asleep in the too-narrow bed of her caravan home, with Irwin uncomfortably dozing beside her, as his mother would not allow him to bring his girlfriends to the house.

Fergus was racked by disturbed dreams of a grey pall that hung over his house. He looked up at the pall and said 'Alice told me to say nothing,' and the shroud faded away.

In her dirty old house, an empty sherry bottle on the floor beside her, Jenny-Pet twitched as she slept. In her own neat cottage, Miss Semple twitched also, though for other reasons.

George dreamt that he was walking with his father, a tall blond man who smelled of seaweed and moved like a fish through the liquid houses of the Vennels.

Even in his sleep, Siller's fingers moved slowly, counting pennies.

Cromness slumbered. But on the hill to the west, Mr Mor was still awake, not in his tower tonight, but in the steadings, watching a sow give birth.

PART 3

THE EASTERN HORIZON grew pale, the deep blue turned to the paler colour of washed-out denim. Birds began to sing among the dew-drenched bushes. Then the sun raised itself over the knife-edge of the North Sea – a wonder seen by few, but carefully noted by Dumfry in particular, up early this morning, and searching the clifftops for the Hand. As the air warmed, mist lying in hollows began to shrink away, though a strangely persistent grey haze remained hanging over some fields.

Sammy Poach lay snoring abed, an empty half-bottle on the table beside untidy sheets of paper and a pen. His scrawl covered a dozen sides of paper, with many crossings out and second thoughts. At the head of one page, the title could be seen: Socialism in a Small State – the Dark Isle as a Model for Development.

Elsewhere in the house, George skimmed close to the surface of sleep, trying to dive deeper into his dream. His feet were set deep in the mud, and he could feel nourishment pulsing up his legs as if he were a plant. The sun shone on his upturned face, and he felt the energy flowing in through his eyes and down through his body. Something strange was happening in the pit of his stomach, where the two flows met. His mother was standing in front of him, trying to feed him a spoonful of Milk of Magnesia.

'Come on, dear,' she said. 'This'll settle your tummy.'

At Redrock House, work was proceeding round the clock, but no-one saw the sun rise. They were working deep in the sandstone vaults that lay below the house and the steadings. Under bright fluorescent lights moved busy figures, clothed in white coats, insulated from their organic activities by masks and disposable plastic gloves.

Cromness began to stir. The milk-cart rattled up Harbour Road and turned down the High Street. A boy on a bicycle meandered along delivering newspapers.

In his flat above the bank, Siller woke. His letter box rattled as a newspaper was pushed through. He went downstairs in his drab dressing gown, picked it up and returned upstairs to breakfast on thin porridge and weak tea. He scanned the front page of the *Rossland Advertiser* then turned to the financial pages to study the exchange rates.

– Three stirks and a heifer for six gimmers; a cran of herring for four lambs; five fat hoggs for a bullock with calf at foot... No, that couldn't be right. He realised that he was not concentrating properly. There was something wrong. His lips pursed tighter as he considered what might have caused this distraction. It was something to do with the layout of the paper. Something new.

He turned back through the pages and found it. Ladies Guild News was not at its accustomed position on page three. It had been shunted to the bottom of the page, and above it was a new section. The heading was in a flashy type – something elaborate and not easy to read. It said – The Hunting of God. Siller sneered. What kind of nonsense was this?

He began to read, horror growing as he recognised the words on the page.

THE HUNTING OF GOD

The Newsletters of a Pilgrim – being extracts from the journals of
Rev John Dumfry of Cromness

(Disclaimer: Rossland has a long history of eccentricity of one sort or another, from the sublime intellectual fevers of Sir Thomas Farquhar to the more bucolic religious fervours of Wandering John. More recently, Angus of the Hills gave his croftlands to the poor of the parish, claiming that he had been transformed into a barley bannock and had no need of property. Homeless, he wandered the Dark Isle, asking strangers to dip him in their soup and eat. Though his behaviour often met with rough humour, there were always one or two good souls who saw more than madness in his ravings and gave him food and shelter. In this spirit of tolerance we are pleased to give space to Rev John Dumfry's meditations, without, however, endorsing any of his opinions. Ed.)

To the Elders and congregation of the First Ancient and Reformed
Presbyterian Church, Cromness.
As you will no doubt remember, it recently came to my notice that God had disappeared from the church, leaving our beloved building no more than an empty vessel. Consequent upon the discovery of His absence, I called an emergency session of the church Elders and it was decided that a suitable person must go forth and find God.

Being men of substance in the community, the Elders were of course unable to undertake the task, and it seemed meet and proper that I, as minister of the flock, should apply myself to the quest. After much deliberation it was decided that my quest must be to look for the Hand of God in all things.

For, somewhere in this world, there must exist evidences of God, the very traces of His Hand. I intended to follow these traces and so draw nearer to the Lord and present Him with my humble questions.

Ah, but how arrogant we are when we think ourselves humble, as you will shortly see. For I shall keep a journal of the quest. Yes, the departure of the Lord is plainly a matter of concern for the whole congregation, so I shall try to keep everyone informed of my progress.

This is the first newsletter, including extracts from my journal.

I left Cromness the same night, after that meeting, as the matter was clearly one of urgency. I trust that the Elders have found a replacement to minister to your needs satisfactorily until my return.

For the first few days of the august duty laid on me by the Elders of the First Reformed and Ancient Presbyterian Church of Cromness, I had no success. My appointed task, which I had undertaken with such optimism, seemed beyond my capacities. My spirits grew low, doubts assailed me, and I began to feel that I must return to Cromness and admit my failure.

I was residing in a respectable lodging house near Dingwall at the time, and I spent the evening composing a letter of resignation. I went to bed that night in a mood of great despondency, my dejection such that I spent many hours over my evening prayers, yet without much hope of aid.

Arising the next morning, I was taking breakfast in the dining room when I suddenly became assured that I had seen the Hand of God at work. This I will enter in my notebook as item No. 1.

I am happy to relate that having once seen His Hand, like a man picking berries I began to see It everywhere, and this greatly encouraged me in my task.

No. 1 The sun rose.

No. 2 After rain, the sun again.

No. 5 Mrs MacIntosh, my landlady in Dingwall, seemed to me a woman of unswerving rectitude and unmitigated, though just, severity. She was hanging out her washing. A small boy leapt over a hedge, landing feet first in her basket. Two boys and a girl, who had been chasing him, hung over the hedge, smiling slyly the one to the other, waiting for him to be chastised. Mrs MacIntosh took hold of the small boy and raised a hand to strike. As the hand descended, it was entangled in some undergarments hanging on the line. The hand, its force spent, descended gently, neatly depositing the undergarments on the boy's head.

Seeing what she had done, Mrs MacIntosh first stared in astonishment, then laughed. 'Get away with you,' she said, and let the boy escape.

No. 8 A strange tree on the moor touched by lightning.

No. 12 On the road, eating a crushed rabbit, there is a crow. The road here turns to descend into a gully, twisting back on itself to rise on the far side. The leaves and grass look unnaturally green in the evening sunshine. Moved by some emotion, I stand at the roadside and watch, noticing the way that darkness is mingled with light below the trees that overhang the road. This piece of road becomes a place, different from all others. The crow looks at me from the side of its head before flying away.

No. 17 The salmon leaps. Everything seems to be urging it onward, upward.

No. 27 Water pouring down a small cliff by the roadside. I touch the stone, it is wet.

No. 37 Academy Street, Inverness. I was standing in a shop doorway watching the passing throng for further signs of the Lord.

I had almost given up and was about to leave, when I perceived an intoxicated man making his way along the pavement. Should I step out, our paths would inevitably cross. To avoid this meeting I remained in the doorway.

A look of panic came over the man's face, and he turned towards the doorway in which I was standing. He bent over convulsively, and I realised with horror that he was about to vomit on my shoes. He glanced upwards, then turned away, and vomited in the other corner of the doorway. He wiped his eyes and looked up at me again. 'When I saw thon strange light about yer heid,' he said, 'I just couldnae throw up on yer feet.'

No. 39 This happened a long time ago. Something dark occurred under a tree, among the roots of a hawthorn. Whatever it may have been, I survived it.

No. 42 I can do it, muttered the old man. He glanced up and down the road: no-one was coming. He jumped the ditch, hooking his cane in the fence to keep his balance. The wild raspberries were ripe. The rusty fence began to give way, he leaned further and further back. There was nothing to hold onto except the prickly raspberry canes. The muddy ditch beckoned.

As the fence gives way, the old man picks another berry.

How delicious they are!

No. 47 The heron spreads its wings, picks up its legs and glides off downstream.

No. 58 My father's trousers were very patriarchal. A tweed that spoke of security and comfort, with a rich and pleasant tone of sternness.

He burnt them, one New Year's Eve.

He, a teetotaller, came home drunk and stood too close to the fire while jovially insisting that he'd had no more than a nip or two, and was by no means intoxicated.

No. 63 Strange things, strange things. Am I dreaming while awake? I am afraid for my reason.

No. 70 More strange things

No. 73 There are byways of the mind too bizarre to be wordable.

The moment before sleep, certain extremes of intoxication, the haze of those in utmost pain or otherwise stretched to a limit. Logic gives way to another imperative.

That moment when a bird elides properly and logically into a bicycle. The understanding of what has just occurred, as the bicycle becomes a crayfish which is suddenly aware. It describes the happening to itself, and it is, for the moment, more than a crayfish. A brush sweeps over a mirror, and it is gone.

Without reading further, Siller crumpled up the newspaper and threw it to one side. He sat staring out of the window, his lips twitching slightly. After a while he rose, crossed the room and picked up the paper. He carried it downstairs and dropped it into the rubbish bin, although normally he would have frowned on the extravagance of throwing away an almost unread paper. Then he closed the door and began to prepare the bank for opening.

Craig Dunain Hospital was an enormous place. It seemed almost impossible that the Highlands of Scotland suffered mental disorder on such a scale as to make so large an establishment necessary. Helplessly lost near the reception area, George was lucky enough to meet a nurse going the right way, and he tagged along with her. Once out of the reception area, they entered an extraordinarily long corridor. At the far end, two tiny figures could be seen coming towards them. George felt dwarfed by the scale of the place, unable to believe that such distances could exist inside a building. Then he laughed. Of course, the two tiny figures were reflections in a mirror at the far end of the corridor.

'I bet it gets every visitor,' he said. The nurse smiled vaguely, but did not reply. Her shoes clacked on the polished floor.

They walked on. George glanced through the doorways and windows to each side. Some rooms were wards with a dozen or more patients, others had only a single bed. Others were common rooms or occupational therapy rooms with patients weaving baskets or nets. There was a soft room with padded walls, ceiling, floor and chair, where a wild-eyed man threw himself around, thrashing against the walls, writhing on the floor. A woman stood nearby watching him, nodding encouragingly. No sound came through the glass panel in the door.

The mirror-images were getting closer. With a start, George realised that the other man was wearing pyjama trousers. In a moment of terror, he checked his own legs. He was wearing jeans. The two nurses nodded to each other as they passed. George had stopped dead. The other man had to detour round him and scamper after the nurse.

The corridor continued.

'Here we are.' The nurse opened a door to let George enter. 'George MacLear to see you,' she said, then closed the door. The clack of her shoes diminished as she continued down the corridor.

At the window, with her back to him, a woman stood. Her red hair was cut at the shoulders, and there were threads of silver in it. She stood still, as if she had not heard the nurse.

George felt as if he'd been summoned to an audience with the headmaster. He glanced around the room. The walls and ceiling were entirely covered in black plastic bin-liners, stapled in place. The thin plastic had pulled free in places and underneath, a layer of aluminium foil showed through.

The woman still had not moved.

'Mum?'

She turned to him, looking first at his feet, then slowly moving her gaze up to his face.

'I suppose so,' she said.

Her face was older than he remembered, thinner. Her eyes were deeper, if that was possible. Yet something about her face was so familiar that he almost tried to toddle towards her, as if he were still an infant. Instead, he laughed awkwardly.

'Thought I should come and see you.'

She nodded. 'Sit down, sit down.' She pointed to a bean-bag on the floor. 'The bean-bag is comfortable, the chair is not. I won't sit, myself,' she continued. 'Physical relaxation tempts the trained mind to lassitude. Have to stay on the ball here. Weird vibrations, you know. Even with the shielding.' She gestured to the walls.

'Ah. Vibrations. Perhaps I'd better not sit either.'

'Shouldn't matter. Not for you. But I've been sensitised, you see.'

'Sensitised?' George shifted from one foot to the other. His mother stood with her feet apart, knees slightly bent, as if ready to leap at an opponent.

'I suppose you think I'm talking about the Otherworld. I suppose someone told you about that episode.' She laughed. 'Lot of nonsense, I know that now. Just the dreams of a girl, you know. We carry a burden of dreams. Do you know how many adolescent girls think they've been impregnated by God? Walking among us radiantly expecting the Second Coming. There's hundreds of them. Thousands! If they all gave birth, Jesus could be his own apostles. He could feed himself with the loaves and fishes.'

'Oh,' said George. There seemed little else he could contribute.

'So don't expect me to tell you anything about Manannan mac Lir and how he comes from the dark Vennels, his skin rimed with salt, his muscles smooth and mighty as the wave. No, you won't hear me telling you about His country, where the Lady looks on you with green imperial eyes that make you feel as small as a beetle. No, no, though He stands between you and Her, you can never escape Her gaze.

'Not now, not ever. The mysteries of that land are not ours to divulge. The holy place of Manannan is hidden in the Vennels, behind protecting walls, where no-one may step in and desecrate, the worm may not corrupt and... and... Where was I?'

She looked baffled. Her hair hung over one eye as she cocked her head suspiciously.

'You were not going to tell me about Manannan's holy place.'

'Aye. Not for mortal to tell of how it may be entered by the Greater Gate and the Lesser Gate in the Vennels of Cromness, each with its guardian. One of them came here, by the way. Interesting woman. Wouldn't eat anything but black pudding, bacon and fried egg. Had to be sent home. She was mad as a hatter, but the cook refused to prepare food for her. Said it was unhealthy. Are you eating well?'

'Yes, yes I think so. I watch what I eat...'

'Yes, you have to, or someone might steal it off you. Oral cues.'

'What?'

'Good food, you see, is the basis of a sound mentality. I watch people at mealtimes, you can tell a lot about them. There was this man brought in, you'd swear he was one hundred percent sane – except that I could tell, you see. I know. Well, at meal time I strolled past his table and you know what? He hadn't eaten his pudding. Just pushed it to one side. Didn't even offer it to someone else. Ha! Thought he had everyone fooled, but not me. Oh, no. Where was I?'

George took a chance. 'You were telling me that you couldn't tell me how to escape from the attentions of the Gods and lead a normal life.'

'What? Utter nonsense. I was not saying no such thing. You can't escape. Not escape. Not until you've done whatever it was they wanted you for.' She looked at him craftily. 'At least, that's what I thought when I was a girl. Adolescent nonsense of course. Surrendering responsibility to a mythical concatenation of archetypal qualities in anthropomorphic form. Happens all the time.

'But Gods? Don't make me laugh. Ha. Ha. Remember whatsisname, the Celtic chief? Defeated by the Romans. Laughed himself to death when he heard that the Romans actually believed in Gods with human form!'

'So if they aren't Gods, what are they?'

'I didn't say they weren't Gods. Let's be clear on this. Because of course they don't exist, so they can't not be Gods. What they are really... Were such beings to exist, they would be no more than demi-gods. I think of the degrees of divinity like notes. Musical notes. Like quavers and crotchets on a musical staff. You'd get Gods, demi-gods, semi-demi-gods and hemi-semi-demi-gods. I'm sure you get the idea. Now, is there anything else you want to know?'

'My father?'

'Your father, of course, was a fisherman... or a merchant sailor. Connected with the sea, anyway. I took his name, although he abandoned me when I got pregnant. Foolish of me, perhaps, but I'm afraid I was rather a sentimental young woman. My father will have told you all about that.'

'Yes. I mean, that's more or less what Grandad told me. But...' His voice failed and he stood silently twisting his hands together.

'Go on, go on. I can't stand here all day answering your questions.'

George looked down at the floor. 'Why did you leave me for Gran and Grandad to bring up?' He stood and waited for her answer. He did not look up, though she spoke no word for a long time.

'I didn't want you to be drawn in,' she whispered, right next to his ear. George started away from her. She put a hand on his shoulder, to hold him near to her. 'I know now that it was all nonsense,' she continued, 'All illusion – or delusion – but then I thought differently. Half the time I thought it was real and I wanted to save you from it. The rest of the time I thought it was delusion, and I wanted to save you from me.'

There was a knock on the door behind George. His mother stepped smartly away from him. 'Come in.' A nurse entered.

'Sorry to disturb you, doctor. There is a new patient in ward 23, seems to be suffering from drug-induced psychosis. Would you mind having a look?'

'Bring him along. We're almost finished here.' The nurse left and his mother stepped forward and put her arms around George for a moment, then let go. It felt as if she was measuring him for a suit. It slowly dawned on him that it was meant to be an embrace.

'Goodbye,' she said.

George left and made his way alone back down the long, long corridor.

A foghorn cried its sad song, echoes returning from the cliffs that lay, invisibly, on either side. The channel was nearby but it was not possible to tell just where. The *Suitor's Lass* sat on the heaving grey water with its engines off. All afternoon the boat had motored along the coast, searching for the world's most northerly resident school of dolphins. None had appeared. All afternoon Barry Ellis and Maria had watched fog gathering over the Dark Isle. When it was time to return to harbour, the Dark Isle was invisible under a humped hill of cloud. They slowed as they headed into the fog. Within five minutes all navigation equipment had failed.

Barry glanced at his watch. As soon as the fog had closed around them it had become bitterly cold, but he was sweating. He should have made harbour two hours ago. The light was failing too. He could barely see the far end of the boat and the tourists seated near the cabin were looking distinctly uneasy. Several children were becoming quarrelsome. Their shrill complaints cut into his worsening headache.

'You'd better speak to them again,' said Maria.

'I suppose I'll have to. What'll I give them this time? The crusty old mariner or the sailor home from the sea or what?'

'No. Look at them. They're not in the mood.' She looked thoughtfully out at the passengers. 'You have to impress them with the deadly danger that they're in, and that you are saving them from. They have to know that you're in charge and they have to forget that they're tired and cold and uncomfortable.'

'I suppose I couldn't just tell them the truth, that we're lost?'

Maria looked at him scornfully. 'I hope that was meant to be a joke.'

'Well, why don't you go out there and speak to them? Damn it, you write the bloody routines anyway.'

'Come on, Barry. Show some backbone. This situation isn't in the script. Anyway, they'll know something's wrong if I go out there. I haven't got your style.'

'Haven't got the style! You bloody taught me!'

'Quiet! They'll hear you. Smile.' Maria pointed to a non-existent landmark in the thick fog. Barry nodded and managed a smile. 'It's up to you, Barry. The fact of the matter is, I haven't got a beard and I can't smoke a pipe with commitment. So they won't believe I know anything about boats or navigation.'

Barry grimaced sourly. 'Okay, okay. Take the wheel. But my leg's bloody killing me.'

She patted his arm as he slipped past her to the door. 'I'll see to it this evening, when we get ashore.'

'If.' Barry slid the door open and stepped out, turning with a reassuring smile to the passengers.

'Ladies and gennelmen, we have been at sea for two hours longer than normal. So I suppose there's one good thing to come out of this mist. You're all getting your money's worth.' No-one smiled. He stumped his way across to the box by the mast and sat down carefully, resting his wooden leg on a coiled rope. 'But I'm sure you'd all rather be ashore by now, and believe me, I wish we could be there too. But the fact of the matter is, conditions are not improving, though they're getting no worse.' Difficult to see how they could get worse, he thought, with visibility less than thirty feet and all our navigation equipment down.

'In conditions such as this, there is one golden rule. That is: safety above all. You can see for yourselves, or rather, you can't see, because of this dashed fog. We could make our way to shore,' if we knew where it was, 'but it would be a matter of feeling our way in blindly, risking the savage rocks of the Demon's Lair or the shoals of...' he cast about wildly for a suitable name, 'the Widow's Beds. We have Intelsatcom navigation equipment with pinpoint accuracy,' and the best thing to do with that is to throw it overboard and see if it hits rocks 'but still we can do nothing, because in this grey haar we could be within earshot of safe landing, without seeing the knife-sharp jaggy rocks of the Splintered Reef. Look at the swell, ladies and gentlemen. Not heavy enough to give a sound as it slips deceitfully past the coral reefs, yet powerful enough to break our back if we should stray a few feet out of the safe line through the Narrow Channel.'

Maria was right. The passengers seemed to have perked up at this litany of dreadful possibilities. A small boy put up a hand. 'Captain, sir. Mister Captain?'

'Aye, lad?'

'I thought coral reefs only grew to appreciable size in tropical or sub-tropical seas.'

Barry wondered for a moment whether to brazen it out, but decided to let it go. It showed that morale was improving.

'True enough.' He chuckled in a nautical fashion. 'For a moment there I was thinking about my time on the SS Dreadless. We were caught in a blanket of fog down in the Antipodes, with a broken rudder and no fuel. Three weeks we drifted, afraid to sleep except in exhausted snatches, dreading to hear the sound of waves on a reef. Sharks following us, waiting under our stern as thick as sardines in a tin. But that's another story. And at least we don't have to worry about sharks here.'

The passengers from the stern had moved closer so that they could see him more clearly. He took out his pipe and slowly began to pack it with dark black tobacco. His every move signalled ease and patience: a man in command of the situation.

'You seem incredibly relaxed about this,' called out a young man. 'What's that you're smoking?'

Barry grinned and winked. He held up the tin and read from the lid. 'A connoisseur's blend of Black Burley, Cavendish and Finest Burmese Plug – matured in old fish barrels.'

There was a general laugh. Barry glanced at the wheelhouse. Maria smiled and held up a thumb. He struck a match and held it to his pipe.

'So.' He sucked hard and let clouds of smoke drift around his face. 'If we're going to be drifting out here for weeks, perhaps we'd better draw lots, to see who gets eaten first when the rations run out.'

The young man waved a packet of crisps in the air. 'For sale by auction, one packet of smoky prawn crisps. Who'll start the bidding at five pounds?'

There was more laughter. Barry joined in with a chuckle. He reached for a rope loop and pulled himself upright. 'One moment. I may be able to save us from the necessity of cannibalism.' He raked about in a box by the cabin. 'Yes. There's some lines and hooks here. Anyone like to try their hand at fishing?' Two boys waved their hands excitedly in the air. Good. They can be fishing and their parents can be watching fondly. He set up the lines. Someone offered a cheese sandwich for bait.

'Now, I know it's unlikely we'll see the dolphins this evening, but would anyone like to try the hydrophones?'

He took out several sets of headphones and handed them round. In the wheelhouse, Maria surreptitiously slipped a cassette entitled 'Whalesongs of the North Atlantic' into the cassette deck.

'Wow!'

'Listen to that!'

'Jesus, they must be all around us.'

They looked intently out into the cold grey mist, hoping to see the smooth black shape of a dolphin.

'There's one!'

'Nah! Can't be. The fog's too thick.'

'It was! Well, it looked like it. There it is again!'

'Bloody hell, it is!'

Not twenty feet from the side of the boat, a dolphin's head rose from the waves. It exhaled loudly as it slipped forwards and away. Its dorsal fin had a white scar across the tip. Its tail smacked the water as it dived. Everyone looked out into the grey murk. A minute later the same dolphin reappeared, gliding past close to the bows.

Maria flipped a switch and a floodlight glared on the sea. The surrounding gloom was immediately more striking, but the dolphin gleamed like fire as it played beside the boat. Barry chewed hard on his pipestem, grateful for this stroke of good fortune. There was nothing worse than a boatload of disgruntled passengers, and this lot had not seemed likely to be gruntled in the slightest. Now the boredom of the long trip had been redeemed.

He coughed and spoke. 'Reminds me of Pelorus Jack.' Several people turned from the rail. 'Used to lead our ship through the narrows of Wellington Sound.'

'There it is again!'

They all crowded to that side, watching the dolphin rise into the light and slip away. Barry spoke louder. 'Yes, many's the time he saved us from sure and certain death.'

'Hey, maybe this one's trying to guide us in!' It was the boy who had turned out to be an authority on coral reefs. 'Look, see the way it keeps swimming past the front, as if it wants us to follow!'

There were a couple of excited comments. Barry thought he'd better nip this in the bud. 'It's generally believed,' he said, 'that instances of dolphins apparently acting as a guide are probably no more than the beast hitching a ride, so to speak, on the bow wave.'

'But what about Pelorus Jack?'

Someone else spoke up. 'Anyway, there is no bow wave. We're not moving.'

'Ah...' said Barry.

'Look at it!'

'See the way it flips its tail just before it goes under. It looks as if it's beckoning.'

'They're more intelligent than most people think. Everyone says so.'

'It is, you know, it's trying to guide us!'

Within a matter of seconds, Barry had lost control of the crowd. There was a mad gleam of mysticism in every eye. Every otherwise sane person in the boat seemed to believe that a dolphin they'd never seen before could know that they were in trouble and also know where they wanted to go.

'But...'

'Captain, we must follow it. It's our only chance.'

'He's right. We might drift on to the Widow's Rocks at any moment.'

'Or founder on the Narrow Reef!'

'And it's getting dark, too.'

Barry looked over at the wheelhouse and gave a despairing shrug. Maria beckoned to him. He plodded to the cabin and edged inside.

'What's going on?'

'They've all gone mad! Danny the Do-gooder Dolphin is going to bring us safe to harbour! It wags its tail and they think it's communicating messages of comfort and encouragement. It's this bloody mist. They're all out of their heads from sensory deprivation.'

'Maybe so,' said Maria. 'But...'

'But bloody what?'

'But we might as well humour them.'

'What!'

'There's bugger-all we can do until this fog lifts. Might as well keep them entertained.'

'But what if we go on the rocks?'

'Which rocks would that be? The Demon's Splintered Lair? Or the Widow's Weeds?'

'Of course not. But there's the Suitors.'

'We passed through the worst of the Suitors before the fog came down and we won't be going back that way.' She tapped on the glass of the binnacle. 'At least our compass hasn't broken down. So if we keep heading west, what's the worst that can happen?'

Barry glowered at her. 'We might run aground in Boblair Bay.'

'Then we'll all wade ashore and catch the bus back to Cromness. It'll be an adventure for them. Buy them all a meal in the Harbour Hotel and they'll be as happy as pigs in shit. And tomorrow we'll pick the boat up at high tide.'

Barry looked out at the impenetrable fog quickly becoming impenetrable dark. Within the circle of light, the dolphin rose once more. He sighed. 'All right, you're the boss. Let's start the engines. But keep it dead slow, okay?'

He left the cabin and made his way to the bows. The diesel engines began to throb. 'Okay, boy,' he called as the dolphin raised its gleaming head. 'Let's go home.'

The afternoon had taken a long time to pass, and now it looked as if the evening would be equally long. Alice had ceased trying to goad Doreen and was simply ignoring her. Lorraine had become her main assistant and general gopher.

Doreen tried to concentrate on whatever nonsense was on the television. Alice read the paper. Doreen had almost managed to stun herself into a state of somnolence when Alice began wheezing. This had happened before. It was Alice trying to laugh.

Doreen tried to ignore her, but Alice made no attempt to control her unpleasant laughter.

'Will you look at that! My goodness, the man's making a complete fool of himself!'

Lorraine frowned. 'Who is?'

'It's that minister fellow. Dumpy. Reverend Dumpy. Or is it Dumpty? Ha hah!'

'What's he done?'

'Och, you'll need to see it for yourself.'

Doreen reached out and grabbed the newspaper. 'Give it here.'

Alice laughed at her. 'Keen, aren't you? Of course, he was always a pal of yours, wasn't he?'

'Nothing of the sort, Alice, and you know it.' She scanned the page.

There it was. 'The Hunting of God.' She began to read.

Alice leant over towards Lorraine. 'Doreen's always been his favourite. Gave her special instruction, would you believe! At least, so the story goes. Myself, I think it was Reverend Humpty Dumpty that got the instruction.'

'Shut up,' said Doreen, but without much heat. She was absorbed in the newspaper article.

'So, this Humphrey Dumfry seems to have dropped his marbles all over the floor and been sent skedaddling by the Elders.'

'Shut your fat mouth.' Doreen spoke the words automatically. Alice's needling scarcely touched her. She was fascinated by Dumfry's mysterious notes.

'Doreen used to attend all his services. Said it was a duty to her poor dead mother, but I don't think so.' She winked lewdly at Lorraine, who turned away in embarrassment. Doreen kicked Alice's shin, but without looking up from the paper.

'Oho, that got home!' Alice leered, but Lorraine would not catch her eye.

Doreen folded the newspaper.

'Well?' asked Alice. 'Is he not out of his little head?'

Doreen stood up. 'I'm going out.' She closed the door firmly behind her.

'Goodness me, isn't she the sensitive wee thing tonight?'

Lorraine stood. 'I'm going out too.'

Alice watched her go, without finding a word to say.

Outside, Lorraine ran to catch up with Doreen. 'Wait!' Doreen let her catch up. 'I'm sorry.'

'What for? It was just Alice being Alice. Nothing to do with you.'

'I suppose I was apologising for being there.'

Doreen stopped and turned to look at her. She laughed softly and reached to touch her cheek. 'You shouldn't be here,' she said. 'You're just too nice to be up against Alice.'

'But I'm not up against her.'

'You will be.' She walked on, slowly enough for Lorraine to take it as an invitation. She joined Doreen at the corner of High Street.

'What did she mean? About your mother?'

'Mind your own business.' But she didn't sound serious.

'It's just that it seems strange, that you're involved in Seeing and the Old Religion and going to church too.'

Doreen laughed. 'Okay. I'll tell you. It doesn't matter any more, anyway.' She paused. 'I think it's the only time I got away with a direct lie to her. My father was drowned, swept overboard, before I was old enough to remember him. Then my mother went and died a few years later, leaving me at the mercy of Aunt Alice. I was terrified.'

'I can understand that.'

'Oh, she's not all bad. I knew she'd look after me well enough, but she's a powerful woman. I could feel it from the first time I saw her. I can remember her in the doorway, cutting off the light, dark like a thundercloud, full of lightning and heat. So here I was, under her protection, which meant that she would always be there to watch over me. To make sure I grew up exactly the way she wanted. I had to find some space of my own, some place to hide in, otherwise I'd just shrink away and become Alice's shadow. So I lied to her.'

'How did that help?'

'My mother was a member of the Reformed Church. Went to worship every Sunday. Used to drag me along with her. I hated it. But faced with the prospect of Alice, I lied and said that before she died, my mother made me promise to go to church every week. Alice wasn't happy, but she wouldn't say no to that.'

They had reached the end of High Street. The Links lay to the left, the grass glowing in the last of the sunlight. Doreen stopped.

'I'd like to be alone now.'

'Oh, sorry. I really didn't mean to impose myself.'

'It's all right, for god's sake. It's just private business, okay?'

Lorraine nodded. 'Of course. I think I'll go for a drink. I don't want to go straight back.' She turned down Kirk Road, towards the Arms.

Doreen walked down onto the grass of the Links, where a few people still walked in the last light, and where two upturned boats lay, side by side.

The nurse brought Wee Eck into the room and handed a folder to the doctor. She closed the door as she left and the black plastic bags fluttered on the walls.

Eck stared round the room. Every wall was covered with black plastic. He looked in amazement at the doctor. 'What the...'

'It's to keep out the vibrations,' said Dr MacLear, not looking at him but studying the notes in the open folder. She beckoned him to a chair. 'Possibly you understand?'

'Well, yeah. Of course. I just didn't expect that you would.'

'It may be that you were lucky that I was on duty this morning. Now, let us waste no more time. I have here the notes taken on your admission to Craig Dunain. Reading between the lines, you seem to be claiming that you have special powers, is that so?'

Eck nodded.

'May I know what these powers consist of?'

'Well, I can cure people. Fix headaches, bad trips, that sort of thing. I've got this energy going through me. Life energy. Direct connection. And I can suss out people and situations, you see what I mean?'

'Suss them out?' Doctor MacLear looked dubious. 'How do you do that?'

'It's just something I do.'

'Indeed. But how, precisely? Is it something in your mind that tells you? Do you hear voices speaking to you?'

'Nah, nah!' Eck laughed. 'That would be crazy.'

'So how do you know?'

'It's the colours.'

'Colours?'

'Yeah. Like, when I look around, it's what jumps out at me. Like for instance, when I walked into this room, I got this flash of blue. From that book cover there, on the desk. The colour of it just kind of jumped out at me. That's how I know you're all right.'

'And if I'd been not all right?'

'Well then, maybe I'd have caught sight of a bit of red or purple. It jumps out at me.'

'But there are many colours around us all the time. I wonder how you choose?'

Eck shrugged. 'I just know which one to choose. I'm guided.'

Dr MacLear tried another tack. 'So what guided you to the door of Cromness Kirk at four o'clock this morning, screaming for sanctuary?'

'Ah. Well.' Eck looked sheepish. 'That might have been an error of judgement on my part. You see, I'd had a few pints of beer, and perhaps that threw the guidance off a wee bit.'

'You'd also had, and I quote,' she looked at a form in her hand. 'Two disco biscuits, a couple of spliffs, a handful of mushies and three tabs of acid. I believe these are common names for ecstasy, hashish, psilocybin mushrooms and LSD respectively? I thought so. And these did not contribute to your error of judgement?'

'Nah. It's never happened before. The mist wouldn't have freaked me like that if it hadn't been for the beer, I'm sure of it.'

'What was wrong with the mist?'

'It was bad stuff.' Eck pursed his lips and shook his head slowly. 'I'd been at a party in Boblair and it was late at night. The party was slowing down. I went up on to the Ardmeanach ridge, to commune with the spirits of the hillside. I was walking out towards the east when I saw it coming up around me. There wasn't much light in the sky, but I could see it, creeping up from the sea. It looked like it was moving slow, but in a few minutes I was nearly surrounded by this grey rolling mist, rising up the hillside, left and right. There was no colour in it, no life, nothing. I kept looking for some colour, to give me guidance, you know, but there was nothing. Just mist on each side, and behind me too. All I could see was the ridge leading east towards Cromness.

'The mist was getting closer and I could feel the chill coming ahead of it. Somehow I knew that if that cold got inside me I was dead. I walked faster, trying to keep away from it, but it was getting closer and closer, and I kept falling over things in the dark. Heather and stones, other things too, that I couldn't make out – strange shapes. Then I saw street lights way ahead, and I knew it must be Cromness. There was just a strip of land now between the walls of fog. I climbed over a fence onto a road and began to run. I was still about half a mile from Cromness when the mist closed in front of me and I was trapped. Mist all around, slowly creeping closer. I could feel it watching me. I was shit scared. I knew I was lost. God, I was scared.' Eck breathed deeply, looking all around into the corners of the room.

'Don't worry. There's nothing here,' said Dr MacLear. 'Remember, the walls are protected. Go on.'

'Well, I knew that if I breathed the mist I would die, but I had to get to Cromness and the light. The only way was through the mist. I knew that I could hold my breath for over a minute – nearly a minute and a half. I timed myself once. And I reckoned that in an emergency like this I could run half a mile in under two minutes. Simple arithmetic. I might just make it. So I took a deep breath and ran for it, through the fog.' He shook his head sadly. 'But I didn't make it.'

'But the mist did not kill you?'

'No. But it was a close thing. When I couldn't hold my breath any longer, I had to let the mist come in. Pure evil. It was like breathing badness. I could feel its malevolence spreading through me and I knew I had to get help. See, I don't know Cromness well, but I do know the minister. Friend of mine. Met him at a rave. Course I didn't know he was a minister then. I don't have much truck with the Church, like. Basically I'm a pagan, but this gadgie was okay. So I ran to the church, as you mentioned, and asked for sanctuary.'

'You were screaming, they say.'

'Maybe. I was seriously in need of sanctuary, and the bloody gate was locked. I couldn't even get to the door. And then this guy that I'd never met came out of the manse and told me to go away or he was calling the police. Bloody unchristian thing to do. Anyway, I imagined if I stood near the church I might get some kind of holy overflow from it, something that would save me, so I wasn't going to let go of the railings. No chance. Then a cop turned up, with a doctor.'

'Constable MacFearn and Dr MacEnery.'

'Aye. The pig said – just like you'd imagine – What's going on here then? So I said I needed sanctuary. I explained that evil had found its way into me and I needed holy water to fight its influence. The doctor – he had slippers on – he looked in my eyes and said, I'll give you holy bloody water! That was a laugh. Well, you don't expect doctors to swear, you know. That was when I knew he was all right. It was his little psychological trick, to put me at ease. Subtle. Then he asked me what I'd taken. When I told him, the cop was all for arresting me, but the doctor wouldn't let him. He took a hypodermic syringe from his bag. What's in that, I asked, no drugs, I said. Holy water, he said, so I let him put it in my arm. I could feel it working right away. All the knots started coming undone and I kind of fell into a quiet place. The world was folding in around me, safe, you know. I was safe.' Eck sighed and smiled at Dr MacLear. 'Just as I floated away, the doctor's coat fell open and I saw that he was wearing blue pyjamas, so I knew everything was all right. I should never have doubted that it would come out right in the end.'

Dr MacLear grunted. 'You were lucky.'

'No. Not lucky. It was inevitable. I know, you see. I know I can't be harmed. When you hit the right level, everything works for you.'

'I see.' A bell rang and Dr Maclear picked up her papers. 'That's tea-time. I suggest you join the others. I'll speak to you first thing in the morning.' She stood up.

Eck frowned up at her. 'Why?'

She looked taken aback. 'To see how you're responding to treatment.'

'You mean I've got to stay here?'

'Of course.'

Eck stood up, looking outraged. 'But I'm all right now. It was just the beer. There's nothing wrong with me.'

'Nothing wrong? Perhaps I shouldn't say this, but my professional opinion is that you're mad as a hatter. This isn't just a temporary drug-induced psychosis but a severe and deep-rooted dislocation from reality. Possibly incurable.'

'What!'

'So I have two options. I can keep you here until you are cured. Which, in my professional opinion, will take forever. Or I can suggest that you might like to stay here for a day or two, until you at least learn to behave normally.'

'What if I want to leave?'

Dr MacLear shook her head sadly. 'In that case I shall have to call in another doctor to countersign the papers for your commitment.'

'You can't do that to me!'

'I'm afraid I can.'

'I want another doctor. A second opinion.'

'If you wish. But I should warn you that no other doctor in Craig Dunain would even consider the second option. You were lucky that I was on duty. Or perhaps it was inevitable?'

'Hah!'

Doctor MacLear pressed a bell push. A nurse entered. 'Take this young man to the dining room.' Eck went with the nurse. He turned at the door to glare at her. Dr MacLear nodded to him. 'Make sure you eat up your pudding,' she said.

The moorland around Redrock House was half-hidden in a grey mist. The sound of a vehicle drifted through the mirk. From the yard beside the house, Baldy peered at the gatehouse, just visible quarter of a mile down the drive. He had been instructed that Mr Mor was expecting a visitor, but it seemed unlikely that this guest would arrive in a battered pickup truck. To his surprise, the gatekeeper let them in, and the truck began to make its way along the drive.

Leaning against the corner of the steading a small grey man whittled a piece of stick into splinters with a wicked sharp knife.

Baldy gestured towards the vehicle. 'Who d'you think that is?' The small man just shrugged. 'Well, Ah wasn't telt about them.' Baldy moved to intercept the truck near the front door. As the occupants stepped out, he hulked at them menacingly and asked them the traditional question.

'Can Ah help youse?'

The Nailer straightened his overalls and stepped forward. 'We've come to see Mr Mor.'

'Well, Ah dinny think Mr Mor wants tae see you. Ah suggest you turn around an go back. Right now, know whit Ah mean?'

Aristide Coupar stepped up beside the Nailer. 'The gateman let us in,' he said. 'It's business.'

'Whose business?'

'The Ancient Order of Horsemen.'

'Ah.' Baldy was suddenly uneasy. This sounded like it might be one of them secret societies. Maybe the boss belonged to it – and maybe he didn't. He glanced at the small man with the knife, who shrugged. 'Did youse call him?'

'No. But I think he'll see us.'

Baldy frowned at them for a few seconds, then took a phone from his pocket. He looked from one to the other, then ignored the one with the overalls. 'An who are you?'

'I'm Aristide Coupar, from the football committee. And this is my friend, the Nailer.'

Baldy pressed buttons and waited. 'Boss? Ah've got a couple of visitors here. A guy called Aristide Coupar and his mate. Say they're from the Ancient Order of Horsemen. Okay.' He put the phone away and scowled at the two men. 'You're tae wait here.'

Aristide smiled at him. 'Thank you.' He and the Nailer gazed out at the mist as they waited, talking to each other.

'Damned unseasonable, this haar.'

'Aye. Not good for the crops at all,' replied Aristide.

'Not too good for the livestock either. I hear Henderson Glaickbea has lost two out of five calves. Lung problems. The vet can't do a thing.'

Baldy snorted in disdain. Aristide and the Nailer continued their conversation.

'Libby MacGurgle's in a bad way too.'

'Oh, aye?'

Baldy looked at the small man and raised his eyebrows, a sneer on his lips.

'Then there's the mullet problem,' said the Nailer, giving a half wink at Aristide. 'They can't grow properly when the air's moist.'

Aristide looked at the Nailer in surprise. 'You just have to turn the soil and mulch them with sawdust.'

The Nailer laughed. 'So that's why MacLing was in asking for sawdust. I had to tell him I'd given it off to Annie Dulse for her granny's poultice!'

Aristide sucked air through his teeth. 'She hasn't got scaly canker again?'

The Nailer nodded dolefully. 'The mist always brings it on bad. The itch is devilish bad. In them that's susceptible.'

Baldy watched the two men closely, scratching uneasily at the back of his neck.

'Starts on the back of the neck,' continued the Nailer. 'Then it creeps down onto the shoulders.'

The door opened and Mr Mor stepped out.

'I really am very busy,' said Mr Mor. 'How can I help you?'

Aristide Coupar looked at the Nailer, and they both looked at Baldy and the small man.

'It's a delicate matter,' said Aristide.

'Really?' Mor raised an eyebrow. 'All right. I'm expecting a visitor shortly, but I can give you ten minutes.'

In the library, he poured himself a drink and sipped it while waiting in silence for one of the two men to speak. He used this tactic to unsettle people, particularly unimportant people who might waste his time. It always worked. But Aristide and the Nailer did not seem to be at all uneasy.

'It's the horse sacrifice,' said Aristide. 'At the Dark Isle Show. We'd like you to do it this year.' Mor looked at him without speaking. He had never heard of the horse sacrifice. Both men were watching him calmly and expectantly, neither of them intimidated by the grandeur of the library nor by Mor. Mor himself grew uneasy. There was something odd about their behaviour. They looked as if they had just offered him a great favour. Under their calm expectant gaze he felt boorish and clumsy.

'I'm sorry,' he said. 'Let me get you a drink.'

He poured whisky into two chunky crystal glasses. 'Sit down. Please.'

They all sat in the deep leather armchairs. 'Now. Tell me about this horse sacrifice.'

'It's an old custom,' said Aristide. 'Very, very old.'

Baldy called through twenty minutes later.

'The Inspector has arrived.'

'Ask him to wait. In the main hall. Give him a drink.'

'But...'

'Do it!'

'Yes, boss.'

Down on the links, there were still a few people strolling in the evening twilight. A dolphin broke the surface of the sea, not far out, then dived. Doreen walked down to the beach, watching the waves, waiting for the dolphin to surface again. A cool breeze came in from the east. Near the horizon, a couple of dim lights winked, warning boats away from the rocks. The dolphin did not reappear. Doreen shrugged and returned to the Links. No-one was there. She made her way to the upturned boats and slipped under one of them. The dark space smelled of boat tar and old wood. It had been a long time since her last visit. From a nest on a rooftop, she could hear the wheezy call of a young seagull. There was a squawk, then silence. Either its mother had returned or some more dreadful fate had overtaken it.

She took a toffee from her pocket and popped it into her mouth. The strip of light at the lower edge of the boat was fading, and there was no sound now but the sucking of the toffee and the hush of waves on the shore. Surely someone would come soon. It was almost completely dark now. An oystercatcher flew along the shore piping its sad notes.

There was the sound of a foot on the grass, and a grunt as someone bent down and crawled halfway under the boat.

'Is that you, Doreen?'

'Who else would it be?'

The dark figure rolled in and lay beside her. He smelled of beer and aftershave. She couldn't remember his name, but he might be one of the ploughmen from the Mains.

A hand reached under her blouse and took hold of her breast. A forefinger pressed on her nipple as if it was a bell-push. His nose whuffled into her neck, just below the ear. He was still wearing his woolly hat. It must be Bill, from Nativvy.

He spoke to her collarbone, his voice muffled. 'Where you been?'

'I've been busy.' Bill's other hand had pulled up her skirt and he was stroking the tight fabric of her panties.

'I've been down here a few times, like, and you wernae here.' His fingers sneaked round the waistband and pulled downwards. Doreen arched her back to help him. His hand came back and settled on her crotch, scurrying and probing.

'So what did you do?' she asked. 'Did you just carry on without me?' All movement ceased as he realised that he was one hand short. Reluctantly, the hand between her thighs withdrew and there was the sound of a zip.

'What d'you mean?' He grunted as he undid a button. 'Aah!' Something large and meaty pressed against her thigh then prodded upwards a couple of times before finding the place sought for. He pushed harder. 'Oh, Jesus...' he moaned, his question forgotten. 'Oh Jesus!'

'Indeed,' said Doreen. She took the toffee from her mouth and prepared to give the exercise her full attention. She pulled his face to hers and kissed him.

His body tensed, he thrust hard, just once more, then he slumped on top of her. 'Oh, Jesus, that was great!'

Doreen lay silently for a few seconds as his panting slowed. 'Was it?' she asked.

From the *Rossland Advertiser*

Police in Inverness are investigating the most recent of a series of unusual incidents which have occurred in the Highland capital. A spokesman for the Highland Constabulary acknowledged that they had received reports from an Inverness woman complaining that her bicycle had turned into a crayfish. Our reporter interviewed Mrs Helen Gray (35) in her Lorne Street home shortly after the incident.

'It was ever so strange. I was riding along Feckle Road on my bike. There's a slope there, down towards the cemetery, and the bike was going like a bird. Then it happened. One moment I was sitting on my saddle, the next moment it was a thing like a lobster! I was thrown right over the handlebars. What used to be the handlebars.'

But the ordeal of this attractive blonde young mother of two was far from over. 'I didn't even have a bag to put it in! And when I explained the situation to passers-by, they just didn't want to know!' Brave Helen wrapped the crayfish up in her raincoat and carried it home!

According to Police reports, the crustacean later disappeared – presumably escaping via the cat flap in the front door.

Brion Sinclair, an accredited investigator for the *Fortean Times*, confirmed that a number of paranormal events had occurred in the area which is coming to be known as the 'Inverness Trapezoid.' He said that a rain of small stones had occurred within the boundaries of a sheep fank near the Struie, while the incidence of herons in the area significantly exceeded that to be expected by chance.

Donny MacLean was a considerate lover. He usually took the time to explore Doreen's body before he got down to business. She appreciated this. It was good to have a change of pace. Too many of her visitors were hasty, some to the point of rudeness.

But tonight, his wandering hands merely irritated her. She reached down and undid his trousers, pulling him to her impatiently. He seemed surprised at this treatment but was soon thrusting away vigorously. Doreen gave as good as she got, arching her back to meet his thrust. She knew Donny from way back, and over the months he had learnt both technique and staying power. By now, most of her paramours would have finished, zipped up and gone. But two minutes passed, then three, then five. God, would he be here all night? She reached underneath and squeezed his balls tightly as he rose.

He thrust again, groaned, and it was all over. Thank god, thought Doreen.

Donny leant down and kissed her, which irritated her beyond all reason.

'Oh, go away!'

'What?'

'Sorry, Donny. It's usually a pleasure to have you, but could you please just clear off.'

'What did I do?'

'Nothing, nothing. I just need to be alone.'

'But...'

She pushed him off and lay with her back to him. After a moment, he rolled out from under the boat. She heard him zip up and move away.

She sighed in relief and lay there quietly, thinking.

There was another footstep outside.

'No!' she said.

A voice spoke hesitantly. 'Doreen?'

It was Fergus.

'Oh, it's you. Come in.'

Fergus scrambled in beside her. 'Guess what! I'm going! Mum's letting me go away – to university, if I want!' He put his hand on her body and moved it around until he found her bosom. 'In fact, she insisted. Said that I had to get away from certain influences.' He laughed. 'I think she meant Alice.' He squeezed her breast gently through her blouse. She put her hand on his, held it there.

'Sensible woman,' said Doreen.

'I'm leaving quite soon,' Fergus said, trying to impress her with the urgency of the situation. 'So I won't be in Cromness for much longer.' He tried to explore her breast, but Doreen's hand remained firmly on top of his.

'Fergus,' she said, 'I wonder if you could do something special for me.'

Fergus shivered in excitement. This was it. She must want him to do something really, well, really exciting, more than normally lascivious, something truly libertine. He'd heard about such things, though he was unsure of the details. 'Anything.'

'You're a dear.'

That didn't sound right at all. Surely a woman did not say that to a man who was about to fulfil her sexual dreams?

'You see, I can't get a moment's peace at home. It's impossible to think clearly with Alice in the house. She fills the entire mental space. Do you know what I mean?'

Fergus's heart sank. This did not sound hopeful at all.

'I mean, this was the only place I could find some quiet, some privacy. Live my own life, you know. Or, if not my own, at least not Alice's.'

Fergus nodded sadly.

'But people keep coming in. You know I don't mind that. Usually. It's just that... Well, you remember the minister caught you here one night?'

Fergus shuddered.

'Well, he was quite sweet. No, really. He tried to save my soul. Night after night, he lay under the next boat, singing hymns. No-one came to visit me. Except Bonnety Bill. And even he said the singing put him off.

'But I liked it. For the first time ever, I had space to myself, space to think. I used to lie here all evening, just thinking to myself, while the minister sang.'

Fergus sighed deeply. 'So you want me to go.'

'No, no. If you go, someone else will turn up. Someone who isn't so understanding as you.'

Fergus dubiously wondered if this was a compliment. 'So what do you want me to do?'

'I wonder if you could go under the next boat and sing.'

'What!'

'It'll keep people away.'

'I can't do that!'

'Of course you can.' She patted his hand, which still lay on her breast. 'I wouldn't have asked just anyone, you know.'

Jimmy Bervie walked along the Links. In defiance of the chilly fog, he wore only a string vest and a woollen blanket tied round his waist. The natural fibres somehow seemed to keep him tuned in to the wordless information that flowed from the grass blades, the small pebbles, the insects that crept along near the ground. He needed information about the world, he needed guidance, and the very humility of these indicators of the Balance of the World was reassuring to him. At a time like this, with the very weave of the world tearing on the loom, he did not feel inclined to rely on the showiness of ritual disembowelling or even the stylish elegance of sand-raking. Listen, he told himself. Listen to the very worm that creeps.

Sometimes, he was deaf to the nuances of the inaudible. At such times it was not possible to make anything of the silent song that was the music of the world happening. Even its rhythm escaped him.

But then again, some nights it almost seemed he could hear the melody played on the tuning forks of God. Tonight was such a night. Emerging from the background sound of waves on the beach was the faint sound of music. The melody was an old one, familiar. He listened intently. Even the words were almost audible. His breathing stilled as he listened. Yes, there it was...

'Oh-oh, linger a while ere you leave us, do not hasten to bid us adieu, but remember the Red River Valley...'

Another voice broke in. A woman's voice. It was Doreen.

'No, not that one. Try a hymn.'

There was silence for a few seconds, then the first voice hesitantly began to sing.

'Onward Christian Soldiers...'

'That's better,' Doreen called. 'Louder!'

Jimmy wandered closer to the sound. It was coming from under one of the derelict boats. It sounded like young Fergus. 'Onward Christian

Soldiers' reached its close and after a short silence, Doreen's voice came from the other boat.

'Try one of the psalms now.'

There was a silence as Fergus searched his memory. Falteringly he began:

'I to the hills will lift mine eyes, from whence doth come my aid...'

'Yes. That's a good one. Keep going.'

Jimmy waited through the tune, which did not take long, as Fergus frequently had to resort to la-la-ing.

'What about 'Rock of Ages'?' Fergus sounded rather dejected.

'Just keep singing.'

'Rock of Ages, cleft for me...'

Jimmy nodded to himself and walked past the boats. Sometimes the song of the universe could be a little obscure

Under her boat, Doreen settled down to think. Though there didn't seem to be much to think about now. She felt sad, but in a pleasant sort of way. As if she wanted something, but didn't know what it was. Fergus, unable to remember the words, sang nonsense sounds to any ecclesiastical tune he could recall.

Along the track that crossed the Links, several young men wandered, but none came close.

In the deep ditch across the road from Redrock gatehouse, Constable MacFearn lay and shivered as he tried to write in his notebook. He had not intended to hide in a damp ditch. His chosen spot was farther away, in one of the fields of Nativvy Farm, but the damned mist had settled in to stay. And it wasn't just that it was thick: there seemed to be things in the mist. Living things – or at least things that moved. He'd tried calling out, 'Hello, hello. Is there anyone there?' But there was only a series of hissing sounds and then a dead silence. It would have made him very uneasy if he had not been a police officer. He did not call out again.

While remaining huddled down out of sight, he documented his observations.

'Having taken up my post across from the gatehouse of Redrock Estate, I remained concealed in order to observe traffic. At seven thirty-two p.m. two male persons of local habitation, being known to me as one Aristotle Jack, a lobster fisherman, and his accomplice, commonly known as the Nail, arrived at the Estate. After a few minutes' delay they were admitted and proceeded along the drive in the direction of Redrock House.'

From the west he could hear another vehicle approaching, though its headlights were not yet visible. He quickly finished up his notes and lay low, with just his eyes above the roadside grasses.

The vehicle appeared out of the murk, a dark shape with an enormous halo of diffused light around each headlamp. It stopped at the gate and the driver wound his window down. As he leaned out to speak to the gate-man, MacFearn sucked in a breath and ducked down. He knew the driver. Knew him well. So this was how Mr Mor had escaped prosecution! Collusion! His heart pounded. This could be dangerous. The conspiracy ran deep.

The gate opened and closed again. The red tail lights disappeared along the drive. MacFearn opened his notebook.

'At eight twenty-one a person arrived at the gate, whom I was able to identify positively. As he is a person in a position of some considerable influence within the Highland Constabulary, I will refer to him only as N. It seemed that N was expected, as he was immediately admitted.'

MacFearn chewed on the end of his pencil. There was little more intelligence to be obtained at this location. Yet there were obviously nefarious dealings afoot up at Redrock House. He had his own suspicions about what might bring a boat owner and a Police Inspector together with a drug dealer. There was the reek of corruption in the air.

He considered his options. If he went ahead with his plan, he might not survive the night. Mr Mor was not a man who would stick at murder, that was plain. If MacFearn was caught spying, he could end up as lobster bait. He would also have to commit criminal trespass in order to get to the bottom of the whole sordid business. MacFearn was deeply opposed to law-breaking in any form. Yet, if he succeeded, he would rid the Dark Isle of a nest of vipers. And might well be promoted to Sergeant.

Or, he could pass on his suspicions and his notes to a superior. Who would laugh at him and ask for hard evidence.

MacFearn gritted his teeth and made his decision. But before he made his break, he had one last thing to do. He took out his notebook and wrote.

'Eight thirty-two. I am about to proceed to Redrock House, where I expect to find further evidence of the collusion of Mr Mor and N.'

He chewed the shattered end of his pencil for a few seconds, then added:

'Should I not survive this mission, N is Inspector Morrison.'

Out in the sea-roads, the foghorn uttered its mournful cry. Jimmy Bervie glanced towards the sound as he walked along Shore Road. Even the sound of the waves was hushed by the fog. It would not be a good night to be out on the sea.

He stopped and looked along the gloomy length of the Muckle

Vennel. At least, as far as he could make it out. The streetlights lit only the first few yards and the fog made the gloomy unlit alley even darker than normal. The narrow street seemed to wind on forever into the dimness, the tiny cottage windows blindly peering at each other across the alley. He shivered involuntarily. It looked eldritch enough to justify its reputation.

Many villagers would not use the Vennel after dark. Some would not use it at all. It was said that now and then the odd tourist mysteriously failed to return from a visit to the Dark Isle, last seen in Cromness. Wandering John had disappeared in there, not a hundred and fifty years ago, in plain sight of dozens of fishermen and other townsfolk.

Sir Thomas Farquhar had trouble there too, in the seventeenth century. Why, after all, did Farquhar give up on his plan to clear the Vennels? Supposedly there was popular resistance to his plans, but a man who could trace his ancestry back beyond Adam and Eve was scarcely likely to take much account of the rabble of a fishing village. So there was some other reason. He must have discovered something about the nature of the Vennels, something important enough to make him change his plans.

That was when he'd taken up pig-breeding. Plainly the man was an eccentric beyond even the normal eccentricities of his class. The Hog Graveyard, for instance, was a gem of its type. Then of course there was his book, *Ekskubalauron, or, The Gem in the Dunghill*, littered with Farquhar's ideas for the perfect language. But not content with one layer of meaning, he had hidden subtexts within it. Even in the title. The Gem in the Dunghill! What could it refer to except the crystals of saltpetre found in the heart of manure heaps, the essential ingredient of gunpowder. Referring back in turn to the explosive power of the perfect language. A language whose every word perfectly and inevitably represented the thing it referred to. So that it would be possible, by the power of speech alone, to affect the world directly.

Jimmy found himself strolling along Shore Road, looking up into the grey night and musing. Damn! This had happened to him before. Every time he got close to the Vennels, something distracted him.

He turned and marched back to the Muckle Vennel. He adjusted his string vest, hitched up the blanket around his waist and began to creep slowly along the Vennel. Whatever was hidden here, someone did not want him to find it. He peered into every indistinct nook and cranny. At the far end of the Vennel was a dim orange glow from a streetlight, but it gave almost no illumination to the depths of the alley. On the other hand, he'd walked this mean street hundreds of times in broad daylight without seeing anything. Perhaps some other sense was required.

Suddenly a cat dashed out of a doorway, across his path and into the shadows at the other side. There was a small, shrill cry, then a crunch as the cat began to eat whatever it had caught. Jimmy looked in the direction of the crunch, but could see nothing. It was a subtle cat, that one, despite its ferocity. Practically invisible except for the moment it took to get across the street and catch its prey. He shook his head as he stepped past the shadows, which had developed a purring sound. It was amazing how often that cat caught something just as you approached that part of the Vennel.

'Ah!'

Jimmy had a fair idea of what he was looking for. A doorway of some sort. He also knew who had inhabited the Vennels area in the olden days, and he knew something of their customs. If there was a gate, there was a gate-keeper. And there was no reason that the gate-keeper should be human. He turned and walked back down the lane, waiting for the cat to show itself. It launched itself across the alley again. This time he did not let himself be distracted. The gate was nearby, he was sure of it.

Jimmy closed his eyes and began to feel his way along the cottage walls. Behind him, the cat mewled savagely. He ignored it.

Beneath his fingers, he felt a gap at the edge of a house. A gap that should not be there. 'I have you now!' He stepped forwards, but could not go past the corner. He tried to shoulder his way in sideways, but for all his effort, could go no further as if the air had grown too thick to pass through.

'Let me in!'

There was no reply.

Jimmy reached into a fold of his blanket and pulled out his child's windmill. Waving it to and fro before him, he stepped forwards once more. From the pitch black depths in front of him there was a sound of laughter. Not friendly laughter. Jimmy could move no further.

Then there was a voice, speaking in an old tongue that no-one else alive could understand.

'Go away,' it said.

'Damn it,' said Jimmy. 'What the hell do you lot think you're doing?' There was no answer. 'There's nothing here for you. Why can't you just stay out there and leave us alone?' The darkness was thick and silent. 'Listen, I'm looking after this place. This island is my home too, and these are my people. You put your pestilential feet out of your own dimension and I'll... I'll not be answerable for my actions! I'm warning you! Remember, you're not invulnerable.'

An icy blast of air threw him backwards against the other side of the alley. In the hiss of the wind he heard the words once more.

'Go away.'

He straightened up and glared at the blank wall, where he could see no sign of the gateway. He tucked the windmill back into his blanket and headed for the lights of Kirk Road. The Fisherman's Arms was brightly lit. Before he went in, he stood and thought about his encounter.

'I suppose that went as well as could be expected,' he muttered to himself, then pushed through into the light and the warmth.

MacFearn crept along the ditch until he was out of sight of the gatehouse, then ran across the road in a crouch, diving down into the long grass at the foot of the fence. The fence was made of heavy-grade wire mesh. He set his feet on the wire and tried to climb, but his boots could not find enough purchase. After a few attempts, he slipped back across the road to the ditch and returned with his bicycle. He leant it against the fence and climbed on to it. Above the top of the mesh was a triple line of barbed wire. He smiled grimly and reached into his back pocket, pulling out a pair of pliers. He opened the jaws and offered them up to the barbed wire.

Even in the mist, the blue flash was visible from the gatehouse. A bell began ringing and the gateman swore as he pulled on his jacket and picked up his torch. The phone bleeped at him.

'Yes? Oh, it's you, Baldy. Yes, of course I noticed. Of course I'm bloody going! I'd be there and back by now if you hadn't called! Of course I don't need help, it's not a gang of do-or-die ninjas. You can come down if you want, but it'll be one of these stupid geese flying into the wire again.'

He slammed the phone down, opened the gate and stamped along the road, with his torch spraying a cone of light into the mist.

A dazed MacFearn, who had managed to scramble back into the ditch with his bike, took the opportunity to stagger along the road and through the open gates.

A hint of gloom had settled on The Fisherman's Arms. It was doubtless related to the pall of mist that had lain over the Dark Isle recently. The barman had engaged a local ensemble to brighten up the evening. The main attraction of the group was the virtuoso accordionist known as John Thatch. Although his other faculties were not sharp, he had a natural flair for the accordion, and could produce an unbroken flow of reels, jigs and folk tunes all evening without repetition, if he was not stopped.

Jimmy Bervie jigged at the bar, his elbows well flung out and his blanket flying. A few feet away, a ring of people watched and clapped their hands. Among them, Le Placs whistled and clapped along with the rest. At the other end of the bar a couple of farmers discussed the weather, shouting to each other over the din.

'It'll be mildew yet, you mark my words! Nothing good ever came of mist, certainly not at this time of year.' He pursed his mouth and sucked in breath with a thin whistle. 'Mildew on the barley. I'm telling you.'

His companion was even more pessimistic. 'Mildew? That'll be the least of it. I wouldn't be surprised if we don't have another attack of the green gyadders this year.'

'Christ, I haven't seen that since, oh, the year that Bill MacKerril was swept away in the flood.'

The music changed from a jig to a Highland Scottische. Jimmy stopped dancing and leaned on the bar, reaching for his glass. 'Well,' he said. 'What do you make of that?'

'The dancing?' Le Placs considered. Then he smiled, having found a suitable idiom. 'This is to raise the level of the vibrations, no?'

'Not entirely,' said Jimmy. 'I was testing the universe. If the gloom can be relieved by such methods, then we have a temporary trough in an otherwise healthy community. But in this case I think that other measures are called for. Raising the vibrations will not work.'

'Why so?'

'Vibrations are fundamentally vector phenomena.' The barman, hearing Jimmy even through 'The Braes o' Enzie,' looked suspiciously at him.

Le Placs raised his eyebrows. 'Is that so? How does this cause a problem?'

'I suspect that the world is more closely represented by a mosaic of scalar fields.' He picked up a cardboard beer mat and flexed it in his hand.

'Jimmy, my friend, does this mean anything?'

'Indeed. At least, I think so.' He gratefully accepted another whisky and sipped it thoughtfully. Then he took the beer mat and carefully tore two small slots in each side as he spoke. 'The fact that there are four fundamental forces in nature, for instance, is probably a matter of chance.' He flexed the beer mat and held it against his string vest, then let go. The beer mat sprang flat again, the slots catching in the mesh. Jimmy patted it, then looked up again at Le Placs. 'In other parts of this same universe there may be five forces, or none. And there are similarities with...'

Le Placs held up his hands. 'Jimmy, Jimmy. I do not understand this at all. *Mon Dieu*, where do you get these ideas?'

Jimmy absently reached for another beer mat and began to prepare it. 'I was reading one of these scientific journals in the library. Probably just speculation, but I liked the sound of it.' He clapped his hand to his chest and another colourful disk of pasteboard hung there.

In the corner sat Big Irwin. His muscles seemed as glorious as ever, but his posture was poor. He was slumped over the table in utmost dejection. There were many empty glasses on the table. Louisiana Lou had her hand on his shoulder. He was talking, not to Lou in particular, just talking.

'I've done it every year since, since the first year I did it, and no-one has ever done it but me since then. Not since that first year when I did it. When I was sixteen.'

Lou patted his shoulder soothingly. 'I know,' she said. 'It's dreadful.'

'Every bloody year. And now they want that, that, that eejit Mr Mor to do it. What does he know about tradition and Horse rituals and, and... you know what I mean. Serve them all right if he turned out to be a zoophilist. Ha! Then we'd see what was what and what wasn't!'

'What are you talking about, Irwin?'

He lifted his face towards her. The glower slowly slipped from his face to be replaced by a look of cunning. 'Men's stuff,' he said. He tried to tap the side of his nose, but missed. 'Damn!' He rubbed at his smarting eye.

'You know what would make me feel better?' he continued. 'You know. It would make me feel better if. If.' He lifted a clenched fist and waved it in front of his own face. 'One good whack in the face of that bloated capitalist bastard!' He looked around the room and saw Sammy Poach nearby. He cried out, 'Come on the revolution!' Sammy smiled at him, then turned to play a domino.

The door opened and Aristide and the Nailer came in. Irwin slowly focused on them. 'There's the Nailer! Look, bold as brass! He works for that bastard! He works for that bastard Mor. I'll knock his bloody head off!' He rose to his feet, but Lou held his arm.

'Irwin,' she said, 'you work for Mr Mor too.'

'Ah. You are right.' He sat down again, looking defeated. He swallowed the rest of his beer and looked into the empty glass. 'Things can not get worse,' he said. 'Not worse.' He suddenly looked up at Lou. 'Do you know how many goals I've scored for Cromness? Do you?'

'No, I don't.'

'I've scored, I've scored, I've scored so many goals I don't know how many goals. I've scored. Lots. More than enough. So what if I haven't scored for the last three games? What about the times when I scored more than we needed, eh? Why don't they count them?'

Lou made a sympathetic sound.

'And who's the chairman of the bloody football club, eh? Mor again. I've had more than enough of Mor. And it's not enough that they're wanting to put someone else in my position, oh no. That's not enough.' He lowered his head until his nose rested on the rim of his glass. 'Balls like marbles,' he muttered. A tear fell into his glass. 'Smaller than marbles.'

He looked up angrily. 'And the doctor says it's drugs. What the hell does he know? I bet he doesn't have balls the size of peanuts!'

Lou stood up. 'Another drink?'

'And then they come and tell me they want Mr Mor to do the Horse Ritual at the Dark Isle Show.' His face crumpled. 'And I always done it, ever since that first time when I was just sixteen...'

'Another beer?'

'No.' Irwin looked up at her. 'No. I want you to sing that song. The sad one.'

Lou looked puzzled. 'Which sad one? There's lots of sad ones.'

'The saddest one.'

'Oh, that one.'

Jimmy Bervie and Le Placs watched Louisiana Lou walk over to the band.

'Now,' said Jimmy. 'Now you'll see what I'm talking about.'

Lou approached the band. Thatch was playing at the front, merrily giving it laldy on the squeezebox. As Lou approached, other members of the band waved to her frantically. She ignored them. She stopped in front of Thatch and spoke to him.

'An interesting example,' said Jimmy to Le Placs, as the accordion stopped in the middle of a phrase. The backing musicians kept playing, watching Thatch closely in case he suddenly began again. 'He can play tunes all night, but he can't think and play at the same time. If you speak to him, he has to stop playing.'

Lou turned away from Thatch. He instantly began playing again, from the very note at which he'd stopped. The others tried to find their place, stumbling for a few bars before joining him.

'You see, with Thatch you can have music or talking but not both.'

Le Placs' usual placidity had become a bit ruffled. 'But what has this to do with what we were talking about? The man with the accordion is not too bright, is that not all?'

Jimmy shrugged. 'It's just an example. There are two properties that exclude one another. On the Dark Isle at the moment, I think there is something in the air which excludes, for instance, happiness. Oh, people may think they are happy, but it is only a memory of what it is like to be happy. Gloom is the quality of the moment.'

'Pish, my friend. You are unnaturally pessimistic tonight. Let us try and see if some brandy will change that. Barman!'

The music reached a conclusion and Thatch stepped to the microphone.

'Ladies and Gentlemen, by request we now have, eh, Louisiana Lou to sing for you one of her own songs that she wrote herself to an old tune.'

Lou stepped up and took the mike. There was a smattering of applause.

'Thank you. This is just a little thing I wrote recently, with a little help from a good friend.' She sent a smile in the direction of Irwin, but he was getting ready to be really sad and could only return a nod. 'I hope you like it,' she continued. 'It's kinda sad, but pretty-sad, if you know what I mean.'

The band played a few slow introductory bars, while Lou swayed in rhythm. Then to the tune of 'The Beaches of Port Elphinstone', she began to sing:

I'm deeply and sadly unhappy
Don't know what's the matter with me
When I go for a walk
I don't go very far
So I'll be back in time for my tea.

But oh, the life that was in it
The silvery thrash of the sea
The heart of my life was within it
But that was
before I knew you
And before you knew me.

The distant horizon is empty
The fish have deserted the sea
The depths of the ocean
Hold nothing but sand
And it means very little to me.

Almost all other activity had ceased in the Arms. The Nailer swayed slowly in time to the mournful music, his dominoes forgotten in his hand. Sammy Poach coughed and rubbed at his eyes while surreptitiously glancing at the dominoes which the Nailer had left showing. Lou sang the chorus again, while Irwin mournfully joined in.

Then she repeated the last verse, and every fisherman in the place was lost in a wave of melancholy. Even the farmers were affected.

The fish have deserted the sea
The depths of the ocean hold nothing but sand
And it means very little to me.

A miasma of sadness washed through the room. Jimmy Bervie turned to Le Placs. Tears were running down his cheeks. 'You see what I mean?' he asked. 'This is not normal drunken anguish. This is teleological distress, and we must find the first cause.'

In the courtyard at Redrock House the floodlights created a series of bright cones in the mist. Baldy went from one island of light to the next, carrying two sacks, one in each hand. He put one down to open the steading door, then carried them both across to the bench. The wee grey man was opening a large cylindrical tin. Baldy dropped his burden.

'Heavy bastards,' he said.

One sack had blue lettering on it, announcing: GREAT ORM MILL, DRUMNADROCHIT. PINHEAD OATMEAL. CONSERVATION GRADE. 25KG. The other announced, in black writing: REALITY FOODS. FINEST ORGANIC POTATO POWDER. 25KG.

'Pit them up there.'

With no sign of effort, Baldy lifted them both on to the bench. A sharp knife appeared in the wee man's hand. 'Now we open them along the bottom.' He tucked the point of the knife into the thread that bound the edge of the paper sack and began to unpick it.

Baldy watched him unenthusiastically. 'Why the bottom?'

'So it doesn't look as if it's been tampered with. People look at the top of a sack, they don't look at the bottom.' He tugged at the thread-end and the stitching pulled out neatly. 'Bring that tub over.'

Baldy pulled a half-barrel into position and poured the oats out into it. 'Why bother? D'you think that bone-head wid notice?'

The wee man looked at him. 'Maybe not, but that's the right way to do it, okay?'

'Awright, awright. Just asking.'

'Right, now we put the stuff in.' He reached for a mug and dipped it into the cylindrical tin, lifting it out brimful of white powder.

'Sure that's the right dose?'

'Course I am. Two mugfuls.'

'How d'you know? Ah didny know you was a chemist.'

'Course I'm not. But the Professor is, and the Professor tole me. Wrote down the instructions. Here it is.' He held up a grubby bit of paper. 'Look for yourself.'

Baldy looked at the piece of paper. It said: 2MG PER 25KG.

'Guess it must be right, then.'

Two mugfuls were poured in and they mixed it thoroughly with trowels. Then they shovelled the oats back into the sack. The wee grey man shook it to get the oats to settle.

'You going to sew it up, or will I?'

'Ah'm not going tae bloody sew! That's a woman's bloody job!'

The wee man picked up a reel of thread and a needle. The knife appeared in his hand once more. 'Whatever you say.' He cut off a length of thread and the gleaming blade vanished again. 'Now why don't you open the other sack. At the bottom. Carefully.'

Baldy began to unpick the next sack inexpertly, swearing to himself.

Outside one of the small dark windows of the steading, MacFearn watched closely as they followed the same procedure with the second sack. He scribbled in his notebook: 'Between nine eleven and nine forty-three p.m. two suspects were observed concealing a white powder in sacks of foodstuffs. This may be the key to their distribution network.'

Baldy took both sacks and put them in the back of the Land Rover.

The moment they were gone, MacFearn removed a small penknife from his pocket. He slipped across to the vehicle, opened the rear door and cut a small hole in each of the paper sacks, just big enough to prise out a sample of the contents. He sealed the samples in small plastic bags, writing details on the outside of each, then put them in his breast pocket, the one with the zip. He patted the pocket. That lot would be on its way to an analyst first thing in the morning.

He turned and headed into the murky night, satisfied with a job well done. Now he only had to work out how to return to his bicycle in the ditch, preferably without being electrocuted again.

Every farm in the North had been busy for days. As the day of the Show approached, the best animals were selected, the finest sheaves of corn were picked out and carefully arranged and wrapped. In one or two of the smaller farms, even the hanging ears of the oats were burnished before the sheaf was wrapped in tissue paper and laid carefully in a padded basket.

The fishermen too were busy, hauling in their last few catches before the boats were sailed in convoy down to Castleton, to take their places in the causeway.

The day before the Show, the roads from Perth to Wick began to rumble with the wheels of lorries hauling livestock to the Dark Isle. In every house, best clothes were chosen and ironed, last minute chores were finished so as to be out of the way for the morning.

Everywhere, people were responding to the mysterious force of gravity that on this one day of the year, would draw everyone for twenty miles down from the hills and along the glens, into the maw of the Show.

Veronica was alone in the kitchen at Rossfarm, eating breakfast and reading yesterday's paper with some interest. The Aga purred in the corner, keeping the room warm. It was only ten o'clock in the morning, but the lights were on, countering the gloom cast by the fog that pressed against the windows like a cat. She reached the end of the article, put down the newspaper and shook her head.

As a local paper, it was no worse than most of them. Usually it carried stories about a drunken labourer in court, a report on the church whist drive or local notes from the Ladies Guilds. Amongst this dull quasi-news, Reverend Dumfry's article shone out like a bauble in a dung heap.

The door opened, letting a gust of chilly air enter along with Mr Ross. He pulled off his flat cap and beat it against his leg. Droplets spattered the floor. 'Bloody turnips!'

Veronica picked up the *Rossland Advertiser* again. 'Hmm?'

'Can't find them. Would you believe it? I can't find the turnips on my own bloody farm.' He stuffed his cap in beside the Aga to dry it out.

'Indeed?' Veronica turned a page. 'Tricky wee fellows, turnips.'

Mr Ross's complaint died in his mouth. He looked at his daughter. That had almost sounded like humour. He began again, uncertainly. 'It's not just the turnips. It's the whole bloody field.'

'A whole field of turnips?'

'That's what I'm saying. It's the turnips and the field, the whole lot missing.'

Veronica finally lifted her face. 'You can't be serious. Fields don't go missing. It must be the mist.'

'Of course it's the bloody mist!' He glared at her. 'I didn't mean the field had been stolen. Though dammit, it might as well have been.'

'Aren't you being a bit melodramatic, father? Anyway, why do you want the turnip field so badly? Is there a turnip famine in Central Scotland? Is some entrepreneur cornering the turnip futures of Europe?'

Mr Ross sat down and looked at her suspiciously. She was every bit as acid as normal, but this was almost certainly her attempt at light banter.

'No. I do not expect to make a killing in the turnip field. I merely want a turnip for the Dark Isle Show – it's on tomorrow and I haven't got a damn thing to show! My best calves have got some kind of respiratory infection, the bull's got the skitters and the sheep have hoof-rot! It's this blasted mist. In the whole farm there's not one animal worth taking to the Show.' He sighed. 'But I had great hopes for the turnips. They like that field above the glen. There were some big buggers in that field.'

Veronica's eyes had dropped back to a bizarre account of the ecclesiastical wanderings of a local minister. She replied absently. 'That's the field beside the barley?'

Mr Ross let his mouth drop open. 'Ronny! This is amazing! You've finally worked out what barley is?'

She looked up at him severely. 'Of course. It is an awned cereal. Grows well in poor soil that will not support other cereal crops.'

'And you've seen the turnips?'

'Dad! I'm not completely blind and I do have a couple of brain cells in my head.'

'Well, where are they?'

'The brain cells?'

'No, blast it! The turnips!'

She threw down the paper and stood up. 'Dad, this is a stupid joke. Just let it go, okay?' She turned to leave.

'No, wait a minute, Ronny, please. I honestly can't find the turnips. Honestly.'

Veronica looked back at him, puzzled. 'Why not?'

'I don't know! I was beginning to wonder if, you know, if I might be getting that Alzheimer's or something, you know, losing my memory. Because I'd swear the turnips were growing right where you said. But I can't find them.'

'Can't find them,' Veronica said flatly.

'No.'

'Past the barn, down the track, just before the barley field.'

'No. They're not there. I can't even find the field.' He put both hands on the edge of the table and looked at them. They were brown and weather-beaten, a working man's hands. But they were not old. Not very old. 'So would you go and have a look?'

Veronica felt her eyes smart as tears sprang. He looked really shaken, sitting at the table, looking down at his hands. 'Of course.' He'd never asked her to do anything important for him. Never had to. Until now. Go and find the turnip field for him. 'Sure. Do you want me to bring back a turnip?'

He nodded. 'If you can find a good one.' Veronica pulled on a coat and left the kitchen. She was visible for a moment in the farmyard, then was lost in the fog.

Mr Ross sighed. Perhaps it was time to sell out and retire? He grimaced at the thought. He'd never considered that option before, and a chill went through him. He reached across the table and picked up the paper. It was folded to the section that Ronny had been reading. He let his eyes lead him down the page.

THE HUNTING OF GOD

The Newsletters of a Pilgrim – being extracts from the journals of John Dumfry of Cromness.

No. 77 The heron, once more, miraculously floating on the air.

No. 85 The grain in a walnut burr.

No. 89 The furrow that the fishing boat ploughs across the perfect planar sea. Exactly the effect that is created by the cause. Not an iota more, not an iota less.

No. 93 Last night I sang as we sat around a fire. It was not completely tuneless.

No. 107 The baby falls from the breast, almost instantly into a doze, warm milk on the pink mouth.

Before sleep comes, however, there is a moment of almost supernatural contentment which is neither self-absorbed, as in sleep, nor outwardly absorbed, as when suckling.

No. 121 The sun came up again.

No. 145 The Goddess Demeter is unrelievedly sombre in the search for Her lost child. The woman of the household in which She takes shelter rebukes Her by exposing her private parts to the Goddess, at which She is so delighted that She blesses the house and family.

No. 180 A slug creeps down a damp plank, racing the rising sun to the cool damp grass and the dark places.

No. 226 The sudden intrusion of God into otherwise pleasant circumstances.

No. 243 In the family rooms above a small draper's shop in Inverness, a young Gujarati girl goes through the chore of buttering the family lingam. Suddenly she understands and blushes. She glances around self-consciously to see if anyone is watching her perform this normally mundane act.

No. 298 By the harbour, a Greek man, off a ship. Old, but with the wrinkled face of a boy, cruel and thoughtless, and scarcely human.

No. 302 The salmon leaps, again. This time...

No. 334 Suddenly, God.

No. 371...

No. 393

Veronica walked past the barn and trudged down the track. Something was wrong. Dad didn't forget things like that. He knew to an ounce the yield from every one of his fields. He knew which fences needed attention, which cow gave the best milk. He knew his farm better than the back of his hand. He would only notice the back of his hand if it changed in some way, but he had to know the farm better than that.

The fields to the side of the track were barely visible. She tried to keep clear of the tall grass that grew down the centre of the track, which was drenched with mist. She stumbled on a tussock and swore. Past the barley field, the track turned into a path which led under the trees of Glen Grian. As she passed beneath them, droplets fell from the leaves and twigs. When she brushed against a bush, her whole leg became soaked. It was a silly time to be out here, really. The dark shapes of trees loomed, strangers to her in the mist. The path was nearly invisible.

She stopped and laughed. She'd done exactly what her father had done, walked right past the turnip field! She turned and climbed back up the path, still smiling to herself. She was still smiling faintly when she reached the barn.

Next time, she walked purposefully, keeping a close watch on the fields. Somehow she found herself past the barley field again, without seeing the turnips. A cold shiver ran up the back of her neck. She stood with her spine perfectly straight and breathed deeply. She closed her eyes, silently repeating to herself certain mantras that she'd found in books.

When she'd become calm, she opened her eyes again. In front of her, the heads of barley drooped under the weight of the droplets from the air. 'A wet blanket of awns,' she said to herself. That phrase came from the night she was here with George and Eck. The memory came clear to her. Eck had called up the spirit of the Barley, then the spirit of the Turnip. She smiled at the memory of Eck's discomfiture.

A cool damp air washed over her. Cooler and damper than the mist. She looked around, suddenly alert.

'Is that you?' she called. 'Spirit of the Turnip?' Mist rolled slowly down the track. It seemed to form into a round, sad face. Veronica watched it slow and stop before her. 'Where have you gone? What's going on?' The sad face did not seem able to communicate anything but sadness. Veronica stamped her foot.

'Oh, for goodness sake, show a little backbone!' The Spirit of the Turnip looked more melancholy than ever. 'How dare you go away! Do you know what you've done to my father?' The shape began to retreat into the mist. 'No, wait. I'm not pleased with you, not at all. But we do need a turnip. Can you do that for us? A good turnip for the Show?'

The shape gave a slow nod and faded away. There was a dull thump from further along the track. 'Thank you,' said Veronica and walked into the mist towards the barn.

Back in the kitchen, Mr Ross was beginning to worry about Veronica. Should she be out there alone, where fields vanished inexplicably? Don't be daft, he told himself. She was old enough to look after herself. Wasn't she?

The door opened and a huge clump of greenery entered. Red-faced, Veronica dropped a monstrous turnip to the floor.
'I could only get the one. Will it do?'
He gaped at it. He'd never seen the like for size: huge and purple and perfectly formed. 'My God! Where did you get that?'
'From the Spirit of the turnip field, where else?' She smiled, and he laughed uneasily. 'But I did the exact same thing that you did. I walked right past the field twice. Missed it in the fog.'
'Ah.' He shook his head ruefully. 'Damned if I know how I did that.'
'But I found it eventually and here's your turnip.'
'So I see.'
Veronica twisted her hands together awkwardly, not looking at him. 'But I wouldn't bother going down there again. Not just now.'
Mr Ross, to his own surprise, nodded. It sounded like good advice, though he didn't know why.

From the *Rossland Advertiser*
Boblair 2, Cromness 1

This, the last match of the season, should have been a gala occasion for Cromness, league champions for the third year in a row. A remarkable achievement, due in part to injections of cash from local businessman Mr Mor. But most of the credit for the spectacular success of the Cromness club must be given to Big Irwin, player of the year. What a phenomenon this man has become! Surely an encouragement to all the rest of us who reckon sporting achievements out of our grasp after the age of thirty-something.

So where was Irwin today? It almost seemed possible that his weel-kent muscular torso was hidden in the mist which descended on the Boblair pitch. Certainly there were times when both goals were practically invisible from the centre spot. Had the result been in any way crucial to the outcome of the season, the referee would have been justified in abandoning the match. As it was, this disappointing game was played out by two teams of grey ghosts among whom Irwin was conspicuous by his absence.

Sadly, it is not difficult to understand why he was dropped from the team. Newcomer 'Bad' Trevor was awkward and unsettled, but he was no worse than Irwin has been on his last two outings. Perhaps, after all, this is the end of the phenomenon that was Irwin...

The Planning Committee was going through its usual monthly grind, trying to rush through the agenda so they could all go home and prepare for the Show next day. Apart from the speed with which decisions were being made, the meeting was distinguished only by the surprising fact that several members of the public sat along the benches at the far end of the hall. Among them was Alice.

'Next item, ladies and gentlemen.' Alma Keivor breathed deeply, her proud bosom straining at her cardigan. Several people seated at the long Council table flinched. 'The vexed question of the Vennels.' She put her hand on top of a pile of papers. 'Again.'

Halfway along the table, Siller lifted one hand from his lap and straightened a notepad in front of him. Then he folded his hands in his lap once more. Alma noticed this uncharacteristic agitation and wondered at it.

'We have received a reminder from Building Control in Inverness. More than a reminder. A warning. They have pointed out that there is a demolition order on most of the buildings in the Vennels, due to their condition of decrepitude. Some of these orders date back over ten years.' She looked around. 'Nothing new in that. But the buggers have also pointed out that until we serve orders on the owners, we are liable for any damage or injury caused by these buildings.' She paused. 'Liable both as the Town Council and as individuals.'

There was muttering along the table.

'What?'

'Personally responsible? That's ridiculous!'

'But if we can't find out who owns the houses...'

Alma broke in. 'Apparently, it is our responsibility either to serve the orders or demolish the houses ourselves and send the bill to the owners. If we don't do so, fines may be levied on the Council for non-compliance.'

'Fines? How much?'

'At the discretion of these Jacks-in-office in Inverness, but not to exceed one hundred thousand pounds.'

'That would bankrupt us!'

Alma nodded. 'Further non-compliance after three months will be met with another fine.'

Siller spoke. 'Then they must be demolished.'

There were affirmative noises along the table, though one or two people shot glances at Alice, sitting in the public benches. She did not look back at them.

'However,' put in Alma, 'there is also a Conservation Order on the entire area. No changes or alterations are permissible without the express permission of the Secretary of State for Scotland. Again, we are bound to inform the owners, and until we find them, we as a council are responsible for the protection of these buildings.'

Siller leaned forward slightly as he spoke. 'Is there certainty about the legality of this order? After all, no-one has any idea of who the owners might be.'

Alma looked at him suspiciously. 'It's a bit late in the day to question its legality, Mr Siller.' She gestured to the papers before her. 'As you must know, I have copies here of all the Orders, served to Cromness Council.'

'One Order is as legal as the other then?'

'Yes. And we have to decide which has priority.' Siller opened his mouth to speak, but Alma forestalled him. 'With no record of the owners, we appear to be the executors by default. This is a hot potato which I for one would be pleased to pass on to anyone with the faintest claim to a legal interest in the matter.'

Siller smiled thinly and sat back in his chair. At the far end of the room, Alice prodded Lorraine, who stood up and waved her hand in the air.

Alma looked across at her. This woman was obviously an acquaintance of that awful Alice. She cast a severe gaze at Lorraine. 'Yes? You have something to say?'

'I believe I can shed some light on the matter of ownership.'

Siller was on his feet in a moment. 'I must object, madam chair. This is not a public debate but a meeting of the Planning Committee.'

'I'm afraid,' said Alma, looking as if she'd tasted something unpleasant, 'that I must agree with Mr Siller. Only submissions by interested parties are allowed. Or experts called to give testimony.'

'I am an expert. My name is Doctor Lorraine MacDonald.'

There was general puzzlement around the table.

'You have some sort of medical evidence?'

'No, my Degree is as a Doctor of Philosophy.'

'Really?' Alma looked interested. There were nods from around the table.

Siller rose from his seat. 'Madam chairman, if we allow unscheduled interruptions, the business of this committee will grind to a halt. Adequate procedures exist to allow interested members of the public to comment on cases before the committee. Should this woman have something to say, then she should have submitted a Form of Intent a minimum of three working weeks before the meeting. Such forms are freely available to...'

Alma broke in impatiently. 'Under the circumstances, Mr Siller, I think we may waive procedures. She claims to be an expert in something. Perhaps she can clear up this mess of paperwork.' She gestured at the mound of papers on the table.

'Furthermore,' Siller continued, as if she had not spoken, 'experts must be called by a member of the committee or their agents...'

Alma looked annoyed. 'All right, I'll call her then!'

'...and be lodged as such in the agenda,' continued Siller, 'not less than three working days before the meeting.'

Alma glared at him. 'Then I called her three days ago! Surely in a case like this we can dispense with formalities. Let's hear what she has to say.' She looked around at the other officials at the table. 'Agreed? Good. In that case...'

'I object,' put in Siller.

'Carried with one abstention,' said Alma to the secretary.

'I did not abstain! I objected!'

'I beg your pardon. One objection.' She smiled sweetly at Siller before turning to Lorraine. 'Now, my dear, what is your area of expertise?'

'My doctorate is in Highland Studies, and my Doctoral dissertation was on Celtic traditions in the Highlands of Scotland.'

Alma frowned. 'How is this cogent to the ownership of the Vennels?'

Siller tried again. 'Really, madam chairman, I must object in the strongest possible...'

'Overruled.' Alma tried to read Siller's face. His lip twitched, almost imperceptibly. What was his interest in this? 'Well, Doctor MacDonald?'

'I don't know how much you know about the Vennels. Not just the streets, but the area that lies between them.' Lorraine looked around the Council Chamber.

'Assume we are all ignorant,' said Alma, looking around also at her fellow members of the Planning Committee. 'You will not be far wrong.'

'Then the first thing that I would like to make plain is that the Vennels are by far the most ancient part of Cromness. In fact, the Vennels are nearly two thousand years old. When the Celtic heroes left Ireland, this is where they came. To a Dark Island, so the tales tell. This very Dark Isle, in fact.'

Siller was watching her with a mixture of bafflement and relief. This did not sound like any kind of challenge to MacFarquhar's documents.

At the end of the long table, Alma watched with curiosity tinged with impatience. 'This is ancient history. How can it possibly be verified?' she asked.

'It can't. But this is merely background to later developments.'

'Get on with it then, girl, get on with it.'

'The Vennels was the homestead of one of the greatest of these heroes. Indeed, it has to be said that he was regarded as a God, as were many of his companions. Their names are familiar to many of you. Epona. The

Dagda. Scathach. Manannan mac Lir. Even today, many regard them as gods. Manannan mac Lir had his abode in the Vennels area. It was, and I believe it still is, a sacred precinct. A religious sanctuary.'

'Lady chairman!' Siller was on his feet again. 'This is not only irrelevant, it borders on the blasphemous! As a God-fearing community, should we have to listen to this superstitious prattle about pagan gods?'

Alma looked at him. Siller needed squashed regularly, and she was the woman to do it. 'I'm sure we are all God-fearing, Mr Siller, and you more than most.' She paused. 'Perhaps with good reason. But I believe we are all, or most of us, robust enough in our faith to listen to Doctor MacDonald's intriguing presentation without fear of being corrupted by false doctrine. Any who feel compromised by the subject matter are free to leave the chamber. Please continue.'

'Manannan mac Lir, in time, along with the rest of them, faded away. Some say he died, others say he slipped into another world that is separate from this one, though linked to it. In any case, a temple was built on his old domain. Late records remain. Inverness Library holds the Register of Sasines and Parcelline Trow, where there are details of the building and the extent of the surrounding land that was considered sacred. I have a copy here.' She laid it on the table and it was passed from hand to hand up to Alma. 'As you will see, it is closely equivalent to the Vennels.'

Alma shook her head. 'What of it? This was all hundreds of years ago. Even if the place had some semi-legal status back then...'

Lorraine smiled. 'Yes, but there are serious implications. Many believe that Manannan mac Lir still inhabits the place. As a sacred precinct, it has been, in a sense, his home for at least eighteen hundred years. Under the Homestead and Enclosures Act, (1734), if a man occupies a building where he is not charged rent, after seventeen years it becomes his property.'

There were smiles along the table. Alma snorted loudly. 'Do you expect us to take this seriously?'

'Why not?'

Siller spoke up. 'Whoever this person was, he is plainly long dead. It is not admissible for a dead person to possess any material thing.'

Lorraine bowed her head slightly, acknowledging the point. 'No, of course not. We can't know if Manannan mac Lir is dead or alive. But I am not trying to establish his claim to the place.'

'Then whose?'

'His son.'

'His son!'

'George MacLear. Resident of this town. Here is a copy of his birth certificate.'

This time, Lorraine handed the certificate directly to Alma. She snatched it and read every detail carefully. She looked along the table. Siller's notebook was awry and his cheeks showed a hint of purple. She'd rarely seen him so upset.

'Well, bugger me with a fishfork!' A wide smile split her face. 'Well, who is this boy George? George MacLear is it? Well, who is the lad, eh?'

Dumfry tramped along the narrow back road to Inverness, where he intended to offer his services to some deserving charity. Really, the Hand of God was appearing everywhere, and he might as well be doing some good works while he was searching for It.

Recently, life had been interesting but not comfortable. In the broad thoroughfares of commerce and down in the dark alleys of Inverness he had looked for the Hand of God. In the hills and glens, yea in the thorny gullies on the hillside, there also he searched.

And found evidence that He had been there. In the eyes of strangers he saw evidence, in the small rain that fell and in the gleam of moonlight on a wet stone. Last night he had seen the Hand of God in a dream, had seen His touch on a meadow of flowers, a blessed place where Dumfry had lain and found his heart's ease. Was that any different from seeing it in the wide world? Had not God made his mind also?

He took out a notebook and stopped for a few minutes to write.

No. 453 From out of the 5th dimension emerged a certain something that had the nature of a breast. A perfect breast: rounded, beautiful, its skin as smooth as eucalyptus bark.

Inverness lay along the river, its streets reaching up out of the valley and along the hillsides, its outlying tentacles grasping at the green land beyond, inexorably turning farmland and forest into desirable bungalows and stylish detached houses with Fyfestone cladding and double garages. The breast moved on in its mysterious way, the warmth of its all-pervasive ambience soothing the senses of any who might have been watchful for this moment.

The breast from the 5th dimension languidly rested itself on several acres of new development to the south of Inverness, and there it stayed, while the houses and streets folded away beneath it, shrinking away as if they had never been.

At that moment God, green-skinned and awesome, appeared before the breast. He raised one Hand on high and poised Himself, ready to utter a banishment. Then, with His many eyes, He simultaneously looked at the breast, at the forests and farms in front of Him and at the sprawled houses behind Him.

He patted the breast lightly, and vanished.

He tucked the notebook away and walked on, ever watchful. And yes, there he saw the Hand of God in the gorse bush on the hillside – he saw it in the shape of each of its tiny flowers. The glow of divinity seemed to emanate from within, as if God looked out through the blazing gold of the bush.

He looked around. A hawk floated high over the green hill slope. Sheep grazed on the short grass or lay against an outcrop of rock. Slender rowans grew against the small cliff nearby, leaves waving in the breeze. There were other bushes, but this one, the gorse bush, seemed to speak to him. Odd, he thought, that this particular block of colour and shape should speak to me. Why not a patch of grass or a lump of rock? Was there something special about the bush?

A disturbing thought struck him. He tried to ignore it. He drew a deep breath and contemplated the flowers, a solid block of gold, with the green thorns showing through here and there, sticking out dagger-sharp. Almost involuntarily, he found himself walking round the gorse bush. Every inch of it was gold flowers with thin sharp thorns protruding.

That's ridiculous, he thought. Absurd. Yet he knew that he would have to investigate. If God was displaying Himself in the blossom of the bush, then perhaps He Himself was there, inside the bush. That's ridiculous, he thought, even as he wrapped his arms around his head to protect his eyes, bent down and began to force his way into the bush.

The interior was dim and filled with gnarly branches and twigs and a carpet of old dry thorns. He twisted around, and lay uncomfortably among the thorny twigs, contemplating the branchings and contortions of the bush. It seemed that a great deal of hidden structure was needed to hold together a gorse bush, and most of this structure was prickly. The thorns had torn both his clothes and his skin. Pulling a few thorns from his hand, he reflected that if He chose to inhabit the interior of a thorny bush, then perhaps He did so in a form visible only to some suitable life-form, such as a beetle.

After all, although He was everywhere, He was not necessarily visible everywhere. The prickles of the gorse bush, its branches, twigs and roots are the means by which He manifests in the bloom, in a form that humans, who are not designed to live inside such a bush, can understand and appreciate from the outside.

His mind drifted into deep thoughts about the branching nature of the world around him. He wondered whether it was possible to see the entire cosmos from outside and see, not the complicated structure, but the whole effect – just as he had recently been viewing, from the outside, the golden log of the gorse bush.

Feeling that he had done his duty by the gorse bush, he began to wonder how he was to get out of it. Crawling backwards would force thorns and twigs into parts of him that had hitherto escaped laceration. It might be better to crawl right through the bush. He looked dubiously at the wall of thorns in front of him.

There was a growling sound somewhere in the world outside the bush and a pain in one foot.

'Stop that, Shep! Drop it! Drop it!'

The pain ceased, though the growling continued. Then the voice spoke again, nearer at hand.

'Hello.'

'Good morning.'

'Are you all right? In there? That's my bush, by the way. At least, it's growing in my field.'

'I'm fine, thank you. I didn't really think about whose bush it might be. Sorry.'

'That's all right, I wasn't using it. Truth to tell, I suppose it's a weed.'

'It's a beautiful bush.'

'Aye. Gives shelter to the sheep in bad weather, too.'

'The sheep don't eat it do they?'

'Well, they get a nibble out of it, when there's nothing else to eat.'

'So it's not an entirely useless plant.'

'No, I suppose not.' There was a silence of a few seconds. The dog was still growling, but it sounded less ferocious. The farmer spoke again. 'Are you sure I can't help you in some way?'

'Please. Perhaps you could you pull me out?'

Two strong hands took hold of his ankles and Dumfry once more wrapped his arms around his head and was dragged from the thorny dimness of the bush.

Once clear of the gorse, he stood up and tried to brush thorns and other detritus from his clothes.

The farmer watched, shaking his head. 'For god's sake, man, what were you doing in there?' Then he noticed the clerical collar. 'Begging your pardon, Reverend.'

'I was, eh, looking for something.'

'Ah. You had lost something. I see.' He paused and looked at the bush and the hole where there had recently been a minister. 'In the gorse bush.' Dumfry smiled vaguely at him. 'Something valuable, most likely.'

'Hmm.' Dumfry tried to winkle some thorns out from behind his collar, but they merely slipped down inside his clothes.

'I see, Reverend. Something valuable and no doubt irreplaceable.' He pointed at the sheep on the hillside. 'I just came out here to fetch a ram. For the Show tomorrow. But perhaps I'd better take you down to the house,' he said, 'and get you cleaned up.'

'Thank you. I would be most grateful.'

Dumfry brushed ineffectually at his ruined clothes. The farmer shook his head, looking at the minister's trousers with the arse torn out.

'And we'd better see if we can find something to replace those trousers.'

After the Planning Meeting had broken up, Alice had remained in silence for a long while. First it was a satisfied silence, then it gradually changed into a thoughtful silence, and by the time they got home, it was grim and concentrated. Deep in her chair she slumped, and picked up a bundle of wool and knitting needles. She seemed to be knitting a scarf, which was made of several different unmatched colours. The abstracted look on her face was almost genial, until she dropped a stitch.

'Damn and blast!' She unpicked a few stitches and began again, needles rattling angrily for a few seconds, then settling into a merely forceful clack clack.

Doreen had fallen silent too, and she now sat at the table by the window, working away with a crochet hook. The doily she was working on was oversize and misshapen. Or perhaps it was a small rug. The streetlights were on outside, the orange glow choked by fog.

Lorraine brought in a tray and set it sharply on the table. Three cups rattled as they were set on saucers, teaspoons clattered.

Alice glared at her. 'It's time you were helping. There's plenty of wool.'

'Help with what? For goodness sake, you told me we had to do something, but you won't tell me what.'

'Just get started on some knitting or crochet – even darning. Surely you can do that? It's simple enough.'

Doreen looked up from her doily. 'Something repetitive to keep the mind busy,' she said. 'We've got plans to make, things to discuss, but we don't want any of the Other People – if you know what I mean – to hear us.'

Lorraine poured the tea slowly and carefully. 'Why knitting, then? What about making a jigsaw?'

'Hmm. Might work. But knitting's better. There's something far wrong with the world – with the Dark Isle anyway. So we're joining strands together. Weaving, crochet, anything like that will do. It's the physical action that represents what we want the world to do. Hold together.'

'I've not seen you do it before.'

Alice glowered. 'Most of the time there's plenty of women out there knitting. That's part of the compact. That's what women have to do, knit together the strands of the world. And most of them haven't a clue what they're doing.'

'So why now?'

'Because there's no-one else knitting. Everyone's getting ready for the Show, tomorrow. But we can't wait. We've got to do something soon, something really serious, to stop what's happening. Whatever it is. Maybe they're going to steal something.'

Lorraine laughed. 'Steal what?'

'A herd of cows would do for starters. But I don't really think that's what They want. This time I think it's more serious.'

'Like coming through here to stay,' said Doreen. 'Having Them living in the world next door is fine, even though They come through from time to time. But if They stayed here, they'd be deadly.'

Lorraine glanced uncertainly between the women. 'So why do you... I don't know... worship these deities?'

Alice shrugged. 'I'm a priestess, and so's she, of a sort. And it's our job to worship...' her mouth pinched sourly, as though the word did not taste good, '...and we do so, up to a point. But it's a damn sight more than just that.'

Lorraine looked from one to the other helplessly. 'Well tell me, then. What more is there?'

Alice grunted and jerked a shoulder at Doreen, but Doreen shrugged and turned away.

'All right,' said Alice with bad grace. 'We have to keep the balance. Too much worship and they'll get too big for their boots. They'll be in here, in our world, like wasps in a jam jar. But if people don't pay them enough attention, they'll withdraw, go somewhere else. The Island would become just like any other place.'

'What would happen then?'

'Use your imagination, girl! There's a big difference between a wind from the north because of an anticyclone over Norway and the same wind when you know it's the breath of Nanag, goddess of unborn children. You can't do anything about an anticyclone, but you can bring Nanag round if you tell her how terrible she is and how awesome. She likes to hear that. But you've got to be careful. They get kind of drunk on too much worship. It's like drinking mead, for them.' She looked almost frightened, though her face wasn't well shaped for that emotion, and her voice fell.

'And that's when they can come right through, without even borrowing a body. Now and then, one does get through: usually Manannan or Lugh, out on the randan. Sometimes Scathach.' She shuddered. 'Or Morrigan, out for something much worse than a quick fuck.'

Lorraine opened her mouth to speak, but Doreen butted in. 'I don't like to speak well of Alice, but in this she's right. I can feel it – and I'm sure you do too. The walls of the world are bulging with the pressure from the other side. Something is impending, something really heavy. So we're going to have to devise a ritual of some sort. But we have to wait for the right moment. And until then, we're keeping ourselves busy, keeping ourselves hidden from Them.' Lorraine opened her mouth to speak. 'That's enough, Lorraine. If you want to talk, you have to do some knitting, to keep the walls up between you and Them.'

Lorraine looked dubiously at the darting crochet hook and Alice's clacking needles. 'Well, I did French knitting in primary school...'

'Damn and blast, girl, it doesn't matter what language it's in! Here, take a pair of needles.'

'I don't need needles. Have you got a hammer and some wee nails?'

They both watched Lorraine in bafflement as she tapped a few tacks into a cotton reel and wrapped wool around the nails. Then she slowly began to turn scraps of wool into a multi-coloured rat's tail.

'I suppose it'll do,' said Alice at last, continuing with her knitting. The scarf was coiled at her feet. By the window, Doreen settled the doily over her knees and worked around the edges with her crochet hook. 'I think we all know how serious the situation is,' Alice continued, 'and how little time we have.'

'Do we?' Lorraine flinched as the other two looked at her. 'You're talking as if doom is waiting in the wings, but maybe you're over-reacting.'

'Is that so?' Alice said. 'Pray tell us how you see the situation.'

Lorraine blushed, but spoke up. 'Well, there's the mist,' she hazarded. 'And as far as I can see, that might be all there is. It's a bit gloomy, and people are maybe getting a bit unsettled by it. Perhaps that's why the boy Fergus was so hysterical. Isn't that all it is? I mean, you're both obviously feeling uneasy, but I honestly can't see why.'

Alice snorted. 'That's it, eh? Well, I suppose if you don't know the place, that's all it seems like. But for someone born here, raised here...'

'And stuck here like a limpet,' put in Doreen.

'Indeed. Someone who is firmly committed to this place, someone whose roots are here, can see the signs. The fog, for instance: listen to the weather reports – nowhere else is affected by it. Mist on the Dark Isle has never lasted this long, nor been so dense. This mist is not natural, take my word for it. Or ask the farmers. Their beasts are afflicted by everything from the green gyadders to Chinese foot rot, and the barley is rotting on the stalk. Turnips seem to be surviving, but everything else is blighted. You might blame it all on the unseasonal dampness, but it's more than that.

'Calves and lambs are being born with two heads – or none at all. It might have a perfectly natural cause – it could just be leakage from the nuclear power station in Caithness. But I think not.

'As for Fergus, think about that invocation he recited. A person that didn't feel the power in that would have to be made of putty. Don't tell me that was just hysteria – I saw your face. And then there's that Grey Being that appeared. A nasty piece of work that one. The whole business started off as just a few boys larking about, and normally nothing would have come of it, but damn it, there's something in the air, I can feel it. Things of the Otherworld are perilously close to this world at the moment.

'Everyone is behaving oddly, too. You'll have noticed that Doreen has not been frequenting the Links recently? And what about the minister, that Dumpty fellow...'

'Dumfry. You know he's called Dumfry,' said Doreen.

'Whatever. Have you read his newsletters in the paper? Pure daftness from end to end. Except that I happen to know Helen Gray, and she tells me that her bicycle really did turn into a crayfish.'

'So she says.'

'Aye. So she says. But I've known her and her family since before you were born, and there's not one of them more imaginative than a boulder. I don't know which is more unlikely, a transforming bicycle or Helen inventing that story. But hell, it doesn't matter which it is, how did Humfry Dumfry know about it? And what about Jimmy Bervie – have you seen him recently? Cavorting like a heathen – though that's scarcely to be held against him – and dressed up like a clown. Perhaps he's finally gone crazy. Maybe that's all it is. But I don't think so. When so many things are out of kilter, do we try to find a cause for each one, or do we look for a single cause for everything?'

'Occam's Razor,' said Lorraine, nodding.

Alice looked at her sharply. 'What's wrong with his razor?'

'Nothing. It's a principle. William of Occam said that we shouldn't multiply entities unnecessarily.'

'Entities? Like this Grey Thing that Fergus called out of Scythia or whatever? This Occam fellow's on the ball there, all right. One bloody entity like that is one too many.'

'No, not that kind of entity. I think he meant... Oh, never mind. I see what you're saying. That there's one cause that's creating all these situations.'

Alice grunted, and stared into nowhere, thinking.

Lorraine spoke again. 'So what is it?'

'What?'

'This one cause.'

'Oh, that. I don't know for sure. But you can bet your boots it's Them that's behind it. I can feel Them looming, peering into the world as if we were nothing but goldfish in a bowl. They're watching us. We have muddied the waters a bit, at the planning committee, in plain view of everyone. With any luck They'll think we're concentrating on the gateways in the Vennels.' She looked at Doreen. 'But now we need to find out what They're up to.'

'No,' said Doreen.

Alice shook her head. 'Not in the Cave. We don't have time for that. We'll do it tomorrow morning, in the back garden.'

'No.'

'We have to. Fortunately we don't have to do the purification. I imagine you're pretty pure at the moment, now that Humfry Dumfry has gone.'

Doreen was on her feet in a moment, spitting.

'My life is my own business, you nasty lump of lard!'

'Stop it, stop it, stop it!'

Doreen stopped with her mouth open. Alice looked at Lorraine in surprise.

'Why do we always have to go through this? Alice spits bile around the room and Doreen tries to throw it back. Why can't we discuss, for God's sake?'

'There's nothing to discuss. She has to do the Seeing. There's too much at stake.'

'You're right about one thing! There is nothing to discuss. I'm not doing it!'

'Stop right there!' Lorraine jumped in again, just in time. 'Before you start mauling each other, why don't we consider what other options there might be?'

'Options? What bloody options?' said Alice. 'We've got to do the Seeing. There's no other way. Unless...' She paused to think, then smiled at Lorraine. 'I don't suppose it has to be Doreen.'

'There you are! I knew there was bound to be a solution if we just talked about it.'

Doreen frowned at Alice. 'Who?'

Alice kept looking at Lorraine. Doreen looked at her too. She looked back, first at one, then the other.

'Me? Oh no. Definitely not.'

'Why not?'

'Because... because I'm not ready.'

'Yes, you are. You've studied it and read about it and I've told you just about everything I can. Now you have to do it.'

'But...'

'Good. That's settled then. Doreen, first light tomorrow, you go off to the beach and get some Witches Eye. Lorraine, lie down on the couch and relax. Let Doreen get you a nice cup of tea. No, stay there, she'll get it. You must relax or you'll be fit for nothing.'

From the *Inverness Crier*

...Police were today investigating allegations that a part of South Inverness, around Heatherdale, disappeared during the night. From reports, it appears that the police have as yet been unable to gain any coherent information, even from the few eye-witnesses, one of whom claims that the housing estate 'just went round a corner and didn't come back.' Several residents who were outside the Heatherdale area at the time of the disappearance were still too shocked to speak about the events. They appear, according to a Northern Infirmary spokesperson, to be suffering from a great trauma.

Our reporter spoke to Dr MacLeod at the Infirmary. 'Never seen anything like it,' said Dr MacLeod. 'Half of them unconscious and the other half in a trance. There's a man in there, wearing brown corduroy trousers and a blue anorak. Despite this, he has a smile on his face and he keeps saying – Take me, please take me – But of course this is confidential, so don't quote me...'

At a press conference in Highlands Constabulary HQ Inspector Morrison read from a prepared statement, admitting that he had received unverified reports that an unspecified part of Inverness could not be located and had possibly been removed. Investigations were continuing, he said, and criminal activity had not been ruled out.

Asked if anyone had claimed responsibility, Inspector Morrison said, 'No comment.'

Asked if the disappearance had a political motive, Inspector Morrison said, 'No comment.'

At the west end of the Dark Isle, just above the ramp where the ferry docked, lay the Mannies Field. For most of the year it was a pasture, growing poor grass, barely enough to support a flock of sheep. Now, the open pasture was criss-crossed with temporary fencing, pegged-out roadways and a horse-racing track overlooked by a stadium. Next to these, brightly painted trucks and trailers stood. They had been gathering for a couple of days, to give time to erect the stalls and sideshows and fairground rides that would blaze into a city of coloured lights on the day of the Dark Isle Show. A few of the vans had already begun trading, selling hamburgers and hot drinks to the other traders who were setting up their stalls. The mist had spread even to the west end of the Island and the lights from the stalls shone like stars in the gloom.

A few farmers had begun to arrive too, bringing their vehicles and livestock over early to take advantage of the ferry. Traditionally the ferry would stop running in the early hours of the morning before the Show – as soon as the causeway of boats had been completed. When the first drover crossed the wooden causeway with his animals, the ferry tied up and would not move again until the day after the Show.

Boats were moving in Castleton Sound even now, heading for the slipways at Castleton and on the beach below the showground. Stacks of timber and bales of rope lay on each slipway, and a small army of fishermen and riggers hauled and tied, building a wooden roadway that stretched across the decks of the first few fishing boats that had moored to each other, broadside on, stretching out into Castleton Sound. As each boat tied up, the road was extended across its decks. More boats waited to the north, ready to tie up as needed. South of them, two ferries steamed to and fro across the Sound: the big new boat, with a ramp at each end, capacity thirty-six cars and up to one hundred and twenty passengers, and the old ferry, *Eilean Dubh*, with only one ramp and a revolving deck. She could carry nine cars and up to fifty passengers. She had been retired from daily service five years past, but was always brought back for this busiest time of the year.

At the forefront of the growing causeway was the Nailer. On the shore, Aristide Coupar shouted at the squad.

'Come on, lads, let's get to the other side before they get to us!'

Some laughed at the old joke, others passed a sustaining bottle of whisky from hand to hand. The causeway slowly grew as the day lengthened. Floodlights came on as night fell, and the work continued.

All across the Highlands, the rumble of heavy traffic that had congested the roads throughout the day continued long into the night. At Castleton, the ferries clanked and roared, animals bellowing from the slatted sides of the tall trucks and from trailers and pick-up trucks and even, muted, from the back of estate cars. The ferry crew were on double time, and handled the work with dour good humour.

Waiting for their chance to cross, a long queue of vehicles snaked across the car park and slowly moved towards the ferry. Among the agricultural traffic, an incongruously shiny and new limousine edged forward and waited, then edged forwards again. In the passenger seat, David MacLing MP laid aside his papers and looked around at the bustling scene, smiling from time to time.

'It's years since I've seen all this,' he said. 'I remember coming here when I was small enough to walk under a pony. I remember the first time I walked across the causeway. It moved and shifted and creaked. It sounded like a live thing.'

The driver showed little interest in either the reminiscence or the busy scene around him. 'It'll be hours before we even get across,' he complained. 'Bloody poor way to organise an event.'

'It's traditional.'

'That excuses it, I suppose.'

MacLing smiled at him. 'You're just going to have to put up with it, Torquil. This meeting is important.'

'Important it may be, but it's too damned clandestine for my liking. One slip and the party will have you out on your ear – and I'll be persona non grata too.'

'If it works, I won't care, and neither should you. But the party don't even have to know about it, if the whole thing falls through. I don't like the secrecy either, but that's why we're doing it this way.'

The queue moved forwards again, a few feet, then stopped.

'There's some pretty dubious customers among them too. This man Mor – what about him? There's rumours of drugs, and other things. And I've heard that man will be there too. You know the one.'

'Sammy Poach?'

'Yes. He must be a bit past it by now. What's he doing there?'

MacLing's lips tightened. 'That's what decided me, Torquil. Sammy's all right. Everyone else has an axe to grind, but if he's in on it, there's at least one honest man among them.'

'But.' Torquil hesitated. He coughed. 'What about the rumours – about him and... well, you?'

'They were rumours. It was nothing but hearsay. Anyway, it was years and years ago.'

'Damn it, David, it was in the newspapers! It doesn't matter if the stories were true, people will think they were.'

'Yes, of course I know. As an election agent, Torquil, you are good. Very good. There's a place for you,' he paused, 'or someone like you, in this enterprise. But underneath it all, you're an old woman. There are always rumours, or if there aren't, someone will make them up. Ignore them. Face them down and smile.'

WRITING IN THE SAND

The truck in front tipped forwards then rolled down the ramp onto the *Eilean Dubh*. Torquil pulled forward and the car also rumbled down onto the ferry. A man in an orange see-me coat waved him forwards into the last space, which was clearly too short for the car.

'I can't get in there! For God's sake, does he think this is a bloody Mini?'

The crewman's hand beckoned as he watched the space between the car bumper and the licence plate of the truck in front. Torquil stopped. The man looked up and frowned, then beckoned him on. Torquil let the car edge forward a few inches, then stopped the engine and pulled on the handbrake. 'That's it. He'll have me right into the back of that truck.'

'Come on,' the crewman mouthed, with an expression of barely curbed impatience. Torquil folded his arms stubbornly. The crewman shrugged and waved to the man at the ramp controls. The ramp came up behind them, thumping the back of the car, pushing it forward.

Torquil flushed. 'Bastards! What have they done to my car!'

'Relax. It was just a wee knock. Your rubber bumpers will take more than that.' The car began to vibrate as the ferry engine revved up, then the whole deck began to rotate.

'Jesus!' said Torquil, gazing contemptuously at the wooden rails, the old and many-times-painted cabin, where the captain looked down on them. 'What is this Dinky toy?' He lit a cigarette and stuffed the match into the ashtray.

MacLing laughed. 'Don't say that too loud. It's easy seen you're not a seaman. The *Eilean Dubh* worked this route for over thirty years.' He looked up at the red-faced, grey-haired mariner in the bridge. 'One of the best New Year's parties ever was held on this deck, when that captain ran aground on a sand-bank on a falling tide. They were stuck out here for eight hours, until the tide came back in. People first-footing in Castleton came down to the shore to join them in the songs, bellowing a chorus out into the Sound. Seals lay on the sand-bank, turned their bellies to the east wind and gave tongue with the rest.' He smiled wistfully. 'This boat's like an old girlfriend to the crew. The first and best.'

The ferry began to move. To one side of the car, a crewman leant on the wooden rail, watching over the side to make sure that they were clearing the jetty. The rail gleamed under the lights. As the ferry began to respond to the swell of the sea, he turned and waved to the captain, then bent to a heap of rope that had been disturbed by passing feet. Taking the free end, he began to lay it carefully in a new pile, the disordered heap slowly turning into a shipshape coil again.

Torquil laughed. 'Look, the munchkin's tidying his sad little boat!'

MacLing's voice had an edge. 'That's not funny, Torquil. You talk about people like that and it gets to be a habit. Then one day you'll say it to the wrong person, someone who matters.'

'Sorry. I'm nervous. You'll appreciate that I've never been involved in a revolution before.'

'It's not, and you won't be. It's merely a declaration of independence. And you will stay safely out of the way until afterwards.'

Torquil sighed and stubbed his cigarette out in the ashtray. 'Why couldn't you have chosen a place with decent roads and a bridge instead of this ridiculous ferry.'

MacLing looked across to where the Dark Isle was beginning to appear out of the fog. 'I didn't choose it, Torquil. It chose me. This is where I'm from, and there's people here that I owe some loyalty to. And the only way this can work is because it's an island. Isolated. Can you imagine trying to close off all lines of communication to Moray or Aberdeen? Couldn't be done.'

Torquil lit another cigarette and tried to stuff the match into the full ashtray. 'I'm smoking too much,' he said. He unclipped the ashtray, wound down the window and dumped out the ashes onto the steel deck. Mist drifted in. He shivered and closed it again.

The crewman had been watching from his post at the rail. He reached for a broom and a shovel that stood in a rack nearby.

'Hey, look,' said Torquil. 'The munchkin's coming to tidy up!'

With a broad grin on his face, he watched the man hurry between the cars, then bend and brush the cigarette ends and ashes into the shovel.

'Good boy,' said Torquil, beaming and giving him the thumbs up. The man nodded back, opened the car door and carefully tipped the shovelful of dirt back into the car.

'Shit!' said Torquil.

MacLing laughed.

The crewman neatly replaced shovel and broom in the rack.

Lorraine leant forward and threw up into the bowl. Doreen handed her a damp face cloth, to wipe her face.

'It can take you like that, the first time,' she said.

'So, what did you See?' Alice sat on the sofa, hands gripping the arms, eyes small and bright and intense.

'I saw all sorts of weird stuff. I can hardly remember it. It's all slipping away.'

'That's why we're asking you now. Get on with it.'

'I saw a country, a wild country. There were sheep on the hillside and in the valleys. The valley sheep were fatter, but...'

'Bugger the sheep! Get on, girl!'

'There were oxen too, wild oxen – and I thought I saw a rhinoceros.' Her pale face managed a small smile. 'Imagine that! A sort of hairy rhinoceros!'

'And...'

'And a forest filled with life. Boar rooting in the leaf mould, deer browsing in the clearings. Giant bulls on the uplands were bellowing at each other across the valley. Cows, half the size of the bulls, but fiercer, watched over the calves, eyeing the wolf and lynx at the forest edge. Kites hung in the sky, watching for smaller prey.'

Alice yawned. 'Mph. What else?'

'Hounds, red and white, with jaws like bear traps, fawning on men with wild red hair. And a woman with a long red braid lying over her bare shoulders. Gold ornaments on her clothing, a bronze moon at her throat. Green eyes, hard and sharp. And there were smaller men and women too, with dark hair. They were carrying baskets of earth up a hillside. Children were working with them, and there were younger children fierce as dogs one minute, cowering by their family the next.'

'Yes, yes. Is that all?'

Lorraine's eyes lost their faraway look and she looked angrily at Alice. 'Yes! That's all! And it wasn't easy, either.' She began to cry. Doreen put an arm round her shoulders.

'Sshh. It's all right. It gets me like that too.' Doreen glared at the impervious Alice, then turned back to Lorraine. 'Afterwards you feel like a piece of thin cloth, yes? As if light could shine right through you.'

Lorraine nodded and reached an arm round Doreen's waist. Alice's face twisted.

'Come, come. You're a grown woman. Pull yourself together for God's sake. Tell me what else you saw.'

'Nothing! I told you!'

'Of course you did! I don't want to hear your daft romantic notions! So you saw forests and animals in some imaginary other place. What the hell is the use of that?'

'It was real! Realer than this!'

Alice threw up her hands. 'Maybe it does really exist, somewhere, but we don't need to know. We need to know about what's happening here, right now!'

'But I told you what I saw!'

'All right, you saw it! But that's no bloody use to us! You must have seen something else.'

'There was lots more, but it's all gone, like a dream. There was nothing else.'

'YES! THERE! WAS!'

Lorraine collapsed, weeping. 'I didn't see anything else. Nothing. Except the apple.'

'Aha. The apple?'

'Yes. It was after I stopped Seeing. I saw an apple. There were wasps on it, scraping at the skin, trying to get through to the sweet stuff, the fruit.'

'Go on.'

'Why? This was real. It really happened. In the garden.'

'Of course. Now go on.'

'They were just wasps, Alice. On an apple. On that tree, out there.'

'And?'

'They were scraping at it, with their jaws, not really getting anywhere. The skin was too tough. Then two of them put their heads together so they were working on the same bit. Then another came, and another until there were four or five of them scraping away together.' She shuddered. 'I don't like wasps.'

'You've done well,' said Alice. Lorraine stared at her in astonishment. 'Were they all gathered there? At the same spot?'

'No. Just a few of them. Some of the others tried to join in, but they were chased away.'

'Ah. Good, good. Then we have a chance. Anything else?'

'Then I felt sick and Doreen and I left you and went inside.'

'Hmm.'

'I stopped in the kitchen for a drink, and when I looked out of the window I could see you, in the garden.'

'Yes, yes. That's enough.'

'You were on the bench, by yourself, frowning.'

'All right! That's enough. You can stop talking now.'

'All by yourself.'

Alice sat, grim and silent, with her eyes half closed. After a minute, Lorraine looked at Doreen, who shrugged and cast her eyes upward.

'I'll clean up the bowl. Do you feel fit for a cup of tea?'

Lorraine gave her a squeeze and let go of her waist. 'Yes, thanks. I'll help.'

Doreen nodded towards Alice. 'She could be like this for a long time.'

Half an hour later, Alice's eyes flicked open. 'Right! Where They're going to get the energy from, I don't know, but I think I can see what They're up to. They're going to try to come in here – not just one at a time, but a bunch of Them all at once. And we've got to stop Them, because if they once take over, we're never going to be rid of them. Doreen, give me a bit of that cake and get knitting.'

Alice pushed a slice of cake into her mouth and lifted her knitting needles from the basket. Doreen rummaged in a chest and pulled out the clumsy-looking doily. Lorraine picked up her gaudy rat's tail.

'You can make some fresh tea,' said Alice. 'And then I'll tell you what we've got to do. And we've got to do it soon.'

In his croft house on the hillside, Ruaridh Beag woke before the dawn. The clock ticked loudly by his bed. He lay beneath the blankets wondering why he was awake so early. Then he heard a lamb bleating from the steading and he felt the flame of anticipation lick at him.

He threw back the blankets and clambered out of bed, shivering as he fumbled his way to the light switch. He pulled on the old tweed trousers that lay on the floor, without removing the long-johns he'd slept in. Even in summer, nights were chilly this high on the Ardmeanach Ridge, and this night seemed full of more than the normal chill.

He threw sticks into the Rayburn stove and set it alight, yawning as he did so, but he was beginning to feel the excitement growing big within him. 'Ach, you're just a big child,' he chided himself.

The Dark Isle Show. He attended each year, but always as an onlooker, a spectator. Oh, he showed an animal sometimes, for the sake of the thing, but there was never a chance of winning a prize. The bigger farms on the good land lower down could always produce fatter heifers, sleeker stirks. And as for crops... well, the soil up here was too thin to grow anything but tough grass, scarcely enough to feed the sheep.

But this year he was in with a chance. He smiled to himself as he buttered a slice of porridge. This year he had a lamb that would surely take the champion's rosette. The fattest lamb he'd ever seen. And why should it not be? All day long it ate twice as fast as the other lambs – and during the night it could sleep while it ate and eat while it slept.

The fire in the stove was crackling now and the kettle was hissing on the hot plate. There was just time for a wee bit grooming before the water boiled. He pulled on his wellies and went out into the dark, rubbing his hands together and chuckling as he made his way across to the steading. There was a steady munching sound from the first stall. He turned on the overhead light and leant over the wall. There was the lamb, almost the size of a yearling, though it still had the soft curling lambswool. It turned its head briefly from its feed and bleated. He scratched it roughly on the top of its head and it pushed against his hand, bleating. The commotion woke its other head, and Ruaridh reached over to scratch that one too.

Then he climbed in and began to brush the wool, sprinkling on a few drops of 'Silverlite – the hair-tint for the mature woman, gives body and lustre.' He'd learnt that trick from Granny Island. While he brushed at its fleece, both heads munched at the enriched lamb feed. It cost a pretty penny, but it was worth it, for a beast like this one. When he'd finished the brushing, the lamb's wool gleamed like silver. Then he lifted each hoof in turn and carefully fitted a tiny leather collar round the top of each, to protect the wool. Then he polished the hooves with 'Cherry Blossom' dark tan shoe polish.

'There's my bonny,' he said as he undid the little gaiters. 'You'll bring home a ribbon for your uncle Ruaridh, won't you, my wee lambie.'

The lamb turned to watch as he climbed out of the stall. The other head kept eating.

Inverness Evening News
EDITORIAL

...tragedy, on the very eve of the Dark Isle Show. Yet our stalwart Police Force remain baffled. Or perhaps blinkered would be a better word. We would like to invite them to read the comments of our own eminent political analyst, Dr Gyre, on page three. With his usual trenchant insight, he has pointed out that Heatherdale is, or rather, was an area of residual Conservatism, and was also a stronghold of the Greater Britain movement. He described this section of Inverness, locally known as 'Little England,' as a beleaguered island within the housing schemes, which have a long history of left-wing activism and Scots Nationalist sentiments.

Need we look further?

However effective the Highlands Constabulary might be in 'moving on' buskers and catching drunk drivers, it is plain that they are out of their depth in confronting political terrorism. What are we to make of the response of the local police? First they say that they cannot verify the disappearance of Heatherdale. (Presumably this is because they cannot find it!) Then they advise us to remain calm and they claim that the situation is under control. Sheep-dip, as our grandmother used to say.

The Police also say that several people are helping them with their enquiries. We expect that these people will turn out to be no more than 'the usual suspects'.

To add insult, they are trying to fob us off with broad hints of criminal activity by an organised gang.

They might as well claim that it was caused by a breast from the fifth dimension!

International terrorism has entered the twenty-first century, while our Law Enforcement lags in the eighteenth!

Eck knew it was inevitable, but he didn't really want the Millennial catastrophe to happen. At least, he didn't want to want it. It wouldn't be humane to want all those people to die, as they must. After all, it was prophesied. Yet deep below the rather thick veneer of Eck the Wildman of Blairfiddich, there was a sense of unease, because part of him longed for it, wanted the dross of the world cleared away. So he just tried to think of it as something inevitable. And his job was to survive it. In the chaos as the ages turned, he would come into his own. He would help bring in the new world.

Yes, he looked forward to that time. There was something in him that longed to burst out of his earthly guise and display himself in his butterfly glory. Then they'd see. But at the moment, he was a guest in Craig Gobhan Mental Hospital. Voluntarily, of course. But if he walked out, they'd make it compulsory. And all because he'd had a few pints of beer, just to relax himself.

Keenly, but inconspicuously, he assessed the other people in the common room. He could, of course, see instantly who was who. There were some poor sad souls who had looked into the magnificence at the heart of the human soul and had shrivelled at the sight. And there were the over-defended, the snails, locked into their protective shells, not risking anything, not gaining anything. And a good proportion of trembling alcoholics, desperate to escape from the everyday world, but stretched beyond their metabolic capacity. And there were some few who were still in shock from circumstance or deliberate abuse, in here for their own protection as much as anything.

And there was Eck.

Was there no-one else of any stature?

None. There was just one fallen angel here.

He swore to himself. It was that beer. Everything would have been fine but for the beer. And yet it was a good beer, Orkney Dark Island, one of the best. What else, though, could have caused his downfall and left him here?

He thought about that night when he had wandered the long ridge of the Dark Isle, while the mist rose around him, and he'd thought it was going to get him.

Damn it! That was the way the doctor wanted him to think. But the mist wasn't just a meteorological phenomenon, it had been coming for him. And because he'd been afraid, he'd lost the chance to confront it, to discover what it meant.

Perhaps the mist was the enemy – or perhaps not. It might be an ally. Whichever it was, he had to deal with it, had to meet it on its own ground.

So maybe he hadn't blown his chances after all. As he chewed it over, things began to fall into a new perspective. He wasn't a prisoner in a mental hospital, but an honoured guest in a sanctuary. He was meant to be here at this time. His train to Eden had not been derailed.

So that meant that everything he needed was here.

'Think of it as an opportunity,' the doctor had said. The crazy doctor. Perhaps she'd been right. He looked down at the book she had given him.

From *Psychic Attack: A Manual of Self-defence*

'...that all around us, separated from us by the flimsiest of veils, lie other forms of consciousness, ready at a touch to emerge in their full-blown splendour.'

So said William James. What he did not know – or maybe he deliberately kept it quiet – was that those other states of consciousness may equally well be seen as different worlds, parallel to this one. There are many such worlds, and they time-share with this one. The human mind is like a radio receiver: adjust the vibrations of your mind and body and you can tune yourself into the universe next door.

Eck put down the book and looked around the common room. It wasn't hard to believe. Several of the people wandering around in hospital dressing gowns looked blank. Perhaps they were brain dead or stupid or drugged, but it was just as easy to imagine that those eyes were looking into another world, beside this one.

A young man, a doctor, was going round, talking to the patients, speaking a few words, listening, nodding, then moving on. The doctors wore no uniforms, but it was easy to tell who they were. They were neatly dressed. It wasn't just that, though. There was the air of certainty. No-one was going to refuse to let them out of here. They didn't have to be careful what they were saying and thinking.

'You're right.'

Eck looked suspiciously at the wee grey-haired woman on the chair beside him. 'About what? I didn't say anything.'

'No, but you were thinking quite loudly.'

'Thinking loudly?'

'Aye, pet. That's what I said. And what was going through your head was – we have to watch what we're saying all the time. One wrong idea and you're in a secure ward with no privileges.'

'Aye, I was thinking along those lines.'

'No, it's not easy, watching yourself all the time. It drives you crazy. Really it does. That's why half the people are in here. They were fine when they came in, but now they're all crazy.'

'You don't seem crazy. Well, not very crazy.'

'No. But that's because I'm a doctor.'

Eck jumped involuntarily in his seat.

'You are?'

'Naw. Just joking. But you see what a shock it gave you. You were talking to me like a human being, more or less, then you thought I was a doctor. What was the first thing that went through your head?'

'I, eh, I kind of thought...'

'You thought, omigod, what have I said that I shouldn't have, eh?'

'Something like that.'

'Well, that's good. Eventually that'll get you out of here. When you get the hang of it, asking yourself before you open your mouth, what can I say to this person, what will seem normal?' She leant closer to Eck and her hair hung around her face. Her eyes were bright and fierce. 'Oh yes, you'll get out of here all right, when you've learnt that. That's the instructions they want to install in you. But once it's there, you'll never be free again! Never!'

'Easy, easy. People are looking.'

She nodded thoughtfully. 'They do though. They put a filter in your brain.' She grabbed Eck's hand and leant forward, hissing fiercely. 'It lets through the water, you see, but it strains out every living thing, leaving the pollywogs and larvae stranded and wriggling in your head. You can see them. Look, look into my eyes!'

Eck looked. Her eyes were jerking around, flickering here and there, never settling. 'Look,' she said. The flickering movement lessened, then stopped. She had grey eyes, with a lighter rim next to the pupil. The eyelids trembled, but did not blink, and he found himself gazing into the clear black depths of her pupils. It was true. He could see something moving in there, he could almost see what it was.

'Yes, you can look, look deep into my eyes...'

There was something there, something disturbing but fascinating...

'Mrs Dixon! Stop that this moment!'

Suddenly Eck found himself looking into the face of an old woman, her eyes turned downwards to her hands, clasped in her lap.

'Wasn't doing nothing,' she whispered.

'Are you all right?'

Eck shook his head to clear it and looked up. It was Dr MacLear.

'Yeah. I think so.'

'She's very naughty. I said, you're very naughty, Mrs Dixon.'

'Yes, doctor,' she muttered, still looking down.

'If I catch you doing that again, you'll have to stay in your ward.'

Eck felt confused. 'What was she doing?'

Dr MacLear turned to face him. 'She was hypnotising you.'

Eck laughed. 'She was not. We were just having a chat about... about something.'

The doctor gave him a small smile. 'But you can't remember the details now, eh?'

'Well, no.'

'And it didn't seem as if you were looking into her eyes for rather a long time?'

'No, no. I just glanced at her eyes, like you do when you're talking, and I noticed how deep they were. Deep and dark, and bright at the same time, as if there was a light in there... Ah. I see.'

'Hmm. Well, no harm done, this time.'

Eck looked around for the old woman, but she had slipped away. 'How did she learn to do that? Is she a psychologist or something?'

'No. She's been here for years. One time she got hold of a white coat from the laundry room and wandered around wherever she pleased. Everyone thought she was a doctor. She's a very plausible liar. She wandered around picking up books from the library, reading about things that shouldn't concern her, such as rapid trance induction.'

'Is that so?' Eck tried not to look as if he was interested.

'I would warn you to watch out for her, but I have been told that you ate your pudding last night. And your toast this morning. So you are free to go.'

'Go? You mean I'm out of here?'

She frowned. 'Not yet, obviously. Only when you go out that door will you be out of here.'

'I mean, I can leave, right now?'

'Yes.'

'Yay!' He stood up and handed her the book.

'No, keep that for now. You can bring it with you next week. Here's your appointment card.'

Eck was too jubilant to object. 'I'll be there.'

'Good. And you'll remember to eat your pudding, right?'

From *Drugs Say No!*
published by the Rossland Athletics Association

... a generally soporific effect, hence Quaaludes are used only in slow-moving games such as darts and bowls.

RITALIN: *See Amphetamines and Related Substances*

STEROIDS: This is a general term applied to anabolic steroids, which are derived from the male sex hormone testosterone. They are used to build up muscle tissue and provide extra strength. Steroids are banned from almost all competitive sports. Taking anabolic steroids can reduce the sex drive of men, in some cases causing impotence. With extreme use, the genitals may shrink. Steroids cause aggressive tendencies, which help the user to train harder, but can also make them violent. This is known as 'roid rage.' Anabolic steroids are a Class C substance, available only under prescription. It is illegal to supply the drug (although possession is not by itself illegal.) Other names for steroids: Dianobol, Stanozolol, Durabolin, Horse Gonads, Donkey Juice.

VENUS NIGHTWORT
This plant, reputed to give endurance and stamina, is also occasionally used for its supposed aphrodisiac powers. There are two identified active ingredients: Nightwortol is known to stimulate the adrenal and pituitary glands, while Octomorphase is an enzyme which breaks down the messenger chemicals which signal fatigue. Occasionally, this drug has caused withdrawal by athletes, particularly swimmers, embarrassed by its very visible effect upon the manly member. Female athletes, while not so conspicuously affected, should also steer clear of this substance.

WITCHES EYE: A drug that is said to stimulate precognitive perception, it is sometimes used by goalkeepers hoping to anticipate the next shot at goal. However, Witches Eye interferes with logical thought processes and can cause spontaneous mystical episodes. Suffering from an unstable sense of reality, the keeper may attempt to block a ball which has not yet been kicked, or one which will not arrive until the next match.

Witches Eye is only used extensively within remote areas of the Highlands and has not yet been banned. Its use is not recommended.

Sammy Poach put on his best jacket, which was, in fact, his only one. 'I'll see you at the Show, eh? I'm off.'

'Already? If you wait an hour, I can give you a lift.'

'How are you going to do that? Carry me to Castleton?'

George smiled. 'I've got a car. Donny lent me his old car for the day. If it runs all right, I might buy it.'

'But who's going to drive it? You? No thanks, boy. I'll take the bus.'

'Come on. I've had a couple of lessons. It'll be safe enough.'

'No chance. I've got a meeting, an important meeting, and I want to get there on time.'

'Aye? What's that about?'

Sammy tapped the side of his nose and winked. 'Never you mind, my lad. You'll find out about it soon enough. Tomorrow morning, if all goes well, the world will know.'

George laughed. 'Oho, a secret conspiracy. Ten to one Ellen already knows about it, and if she knows, everyone else will within the hour.'

Sammy scowled. 'Damn all she knows about it. I'm more worried about that sneaking boyfriend of hers.' He stood silent for a minute, thinking.

'What's up, Granda?'

'Ach, it's just that Major, Ellen's boyfriend. A prying weaselly sort of fellow. He's been asking some gey queer questions around town.'

'What about?'

'Oh, nothing. Nothing important, I suppose. Anyway, I haven't seen him since the night I gave him a flea in the ear. Maybe he's slipped back under his stone. Let's hope so.'

'You'd better be off then. I hope you find who you're looking for.'

Sammy grinned. 'They'll be there,' he said. 'And I'm damned sure that I'll be there too, to speak for the poor and the oppressed, the day-labourer and the serf. Today we may strike a blow for freedom that will not soon be forgotten!' He gave a jaunty wave. 'The Revolution is nigh!' he called as he walked out of the door.

George shook his head as the door closed. He cleared his dishes off the table and filled the ancient electric kettle before fetching fresh clothes. It was good that his grandfather was feeling optimistic, but ever since George could remember he'd been devising plans for a Socialist revolution. He had finally realised that World Revolution was out of reach, and over the years had narrowed his scope to Britain, then Scotland, then the Highlands. Nothing ever came of it, and nothing would this time. He was probably just going to meet a few cronies in the beer tent to talk about infiltrating the Community Council.

The kettle still had not boiled, so he filled the kitchen sink with cold water and located a sliver of green soap. The Dark Isle Show came but once a year, and he intended to make the most of it. He turned on the radio and stripped his clothes off.

'...extra police have been drafted in to control traffic. Visitors are advised to park outwith the Castleton area and use public transport.'

George turned the dial to another station. A strange mixture of guitar and trumpet rang out. He checked the dial. Rossland FM. He shrugged and began to lather up the soap.

two Flamingos in a fruit fight!
coming out into striped light!
everything's wrong –
but at the same time it's right...

The guitars and the drums did strange rhythmical things as the voice declaimed its peculiar lyric. George jigged around the kitchen. This was the stuff! Tonight was his! Veronica would be at the Show and they'd arranged to meet there. He rubbed lather deep into his armpits, then scooped water from the sink in his hands and splashed himself with it. Cold water dribbled down his sides. He shuddered and let it become part of his dance as a crazed voice sang out:

the tunes have no patterns
for me tonight
I'm playing this music
so all the young girls
will come out
to meet the monster tonight!

'Ha!' he yelled at the end of the verse. 'Let's see who gets to be the monster tonight!'

He turned the volume up. It didn't sound like the sort of music that Rossland usually played. It was good. Weird, but good. He shoogled himself as he rubbed up the soap again and slapped it onto his groin.

Meet that monster tonight!

More cold water from the sink, and his genitals shrivelled from the shock. George didn't mind. He swung his way around the grimy kitchen, avoiding the chairs and the table, drying himself now with his grandfather's thin towel. That was one thing about his grandfather's house: it was grimy and poverty-stricken, but it was definitely real. Yes, there was no nonsense about Celtic gods and inter-dimensional gateways here. And maybe that was why he'd risked coming back to stay here for the summer. His grandfather had a no-nonsense pragmatic approach to reality. He had his little foibles, like his adherence to the Communist Party, but at heart he was a down-to-earth son of the soil. He threw the towel onto a chair-back and reached for his clean T-shirt.

On the radio, the drums rolled down as the crazed voice invited:

how would you like to be the girl,
to be the one
to feed the monster tonight?

George began to put on his fresh clothes. The music finished and the fast patter of Totie MacCuish rattled from the radio.

'Well that was interesting, ladies and gentlemen. Interesting and surprising. That was supposed to be "The Captain of Her Heart", but the search facility in our music archives gave us Captain Beefheart instead, with "Tropical Hot-dog Night". Apologies to all you easy-listening fans out there. Now it's the top of the hour and time for our weekly programme, *Local Investigation*, with our roving reporter Les Black. Are you there, Les?'

'Yes, Totie, Les Black here. Though 'Man in Black' might be more to the point this week, with the strange goings-on over here in Inverness.'

'I understand that a part of the town has disappeared?'

'Indeed, Totie. It seems that part of a new housing scheme has been lost. Most careless of the City Fathers, eh? Let me first describe the scene. I am standing at the edge of the Heatherdale area of Inverness, beside the barrier that the police have thrown around a section of what appears to be a virgin green field site. Until yesterday there was a thriving housing scheme somewhere in that field, with 2- and 3-bedroom detached houses each with twin garages and vernacular Fyfestone bow-window features. Where are they now? No-one can tell.

'But fortunately we have with us in the field – literally as it happens – Martha Nero, a distinguished geophysicist from the Terrestrial Research Establishment...'

'Hello, Les.'

'...who will enlighten us as to the forces at work in this tragic event. Hello Martha. Now there have been suggestions of terrorist activity and...'

George listened with half an ear as he finished dressing. The kettle finally boiled and he began shaving himself in the fly-specked mirror. The distinguished geophysicist was talking.

'It is almost certainly a manifestation of the underlying tensions in the Great Caledonian Fault. Unfortunately our seismographic equipment was out of order at the time so we have no data which we can consult. Damp has been getting into the recording equipment. But I have no doubt that what we see here is the result of Lateral Plane Thrust. It will help if you think of the earth's crust as a laminar arrangement of more or less horizontal planes consisting of different rocks. The rocks are, of course, of different consistencies, with differing characteristics.'

'Like the layers of a lasagne?'

Martha Nero's reply was frosty. 'If it helps you to visualise the situation. There is a bed of sulphurous coal for instance, that extends below the town of Strathpeffer. One of the lesser-known characteristics of sulphur is, under conditions of great pressure and heat, to polymerise with itself to form molecules not unlike those of graphite or its more complex molecular relative, known as Buckminsterfullerene – or Buckyballs for short.'

'Well thank you, Martha...'

'I hadn't finished.'

'I beg your pardon.'

'Under extreme conditions, such as pertain in the environs of the Caledonian Faultline, this polymer can act as a lubricant, allowing one sheet of rock to slide under another.'

'Thank you, Martha, but I'm afraid that's all we have time for...'

George turned the radio off. He looked in the mirror. He was neatly turned out and almost, he admitted to himself, handsome. In the heady festival atmosphere of the Show, Veronica would undoubtedly melt into his arms. 'Take me,' she would beg, and he would carry her off into the dark, where they would spend the night enfolded in the shelter of a rhododendron bush. George blushed and stuck his tongue out at the mirror. 'Don't be stupid,' he said. 'She might let you have a kiss.' He laughed at himself. 'If you're lucky.'

From the *Rossland Advertiser* letters page

Dear Editor,

No-one is more concerned about the state of the local economy than I, and it goes without saying that the tourist trade is an invaluable boost to an economy that relies on dwindling stocks of fish and increasingly centralised farming commodities to survive. Yet sometimes the sheer thoughtlessness of some of these tourists beggars belief. For several days now, it has been well-nigh impossible for anyone to find parking space near Cromness Harbour. Why? Because the public thoroughfare is practically blocked by tourists' cars. Complaints to the local police have been less than useless, as the local constable, who shall remain nameless, promptly wheel-clamped the offending cars, making them impossible to move.

Why oh why do we have to put up with this thoughtless anti-social behaviour from visitors to the town? Who, after all, benefits? The local Hoteliers perhaps, but none of the rest of us. Perhaps it is time to send them all back home where they belong! Take your thirty pieces of silver, we on the Dark Isle can do without your type!

Yours sincerely,
A concerned resident of Cromness (name and address withheld)

Aristide Coupar was sleeping in his cabin, groggy from the work and the whisky of the night before. Animals were arriving all through the night, but the clatter of hooves and the complaints of sheep and cattle failed to awaken him, and he slept on until he heard the cheery chatter and the tramp of many feet as half the population of Rossland walked across the Sound of Castleton, and across his deck.

Eventually he climbed the companionway and stuck his head out into the bright sunlight. Across his deck and that of the next boat and the next ran the wooden walkway, wide enough for ten people abreast, that ran from the shoreline at Castleton to the Dark Isle.

Constructing the floating road was no easy task, and it required every boat from the Dark Isle and the Inner Firth, and the assistance of every member of their crews.

A farmer stopped to speak. 'How's it going, Ari?' His family carried on without him, joking and laughing.

Aristide waved. 'Is that yourself, Sandy? Try to stay out of the beer tent will you, at least until you've seen something of the Show.'

'I was expecting to find you in there already.'

'No, no. Maybe later. We had a hard night of it.'

'Never done complaining are you? I was up late myself, grooming the beasts.'

'Aye, I'm sure. But we were a boat or two short. Barry was missing, and all.'

'Barry? What's up with him?'

Aristide shrugged. 'Hasn't been seen this last few days. And he was the man with the schedule for the bridge. I had to do the planning off the cuff, more or less.'

'That's hard on you, surely.'

'I've done it often enough in the past, but it was Barry's turn this year. And he's due at a meeting later on. Hope he turns up.'

Sandy's family called to him. 'See you.'

Aristide watched him go. Here at the west side of the Sound, the sun danced bright on the waves, but as Sandy walked away, he and the rest of his family slowly faded from sight. The melancholy groaning of the causeway ropes provided a suitable accompaniment to the wall of mist that hung across the causeway. From the mainland, it was not possible to see the Dark Isle at all, though bright lights from the fairground hung in the grey firmament.

Aristide pulled himself together. He was going to have to face up to it. If Barry and Maria didn't turn up, then he himself was going to have to represent the fishermen of the Dark Isle at the unholy conclave later on. And co-ordinate the boats later, after the announcement at midnight. One wrong move then and the whole damn plan would fail. That was where Barry was essential. Or more likely, Maria. He was pretty sure that she was the power behind that particular throne.

He considered who would be at the meeting. Mr Mor was going to be there, of course. Nothing would have happened but for him. A high-powered man and no mistake. Most likely one of his hard men would be with him too. And Sammy Poach – though what he was doing there was anyone's guess. There would be a politician or two as well, no doubt. And there would be Alma Keivor. His heart quailed within him.

At a roadside encampment by the old A9 road, a man swore as a screw gave way and the petrol tank of his pickup truck fell on top of him. It was so rust-ridden that it had bent in the fall. He pushed it aside and crawled out from underneath.

A woman in a grimy dress looked down at him. 'Likely we'll not make it to the Show this year,' she said in as resigned a voice as possible.

'Damned if I'll stay here, with everyone else at the Show. I'll get the bastard thing working.'

She sighed. If they'd gone with the rest of the clan, they'd be there by now, enjoying the Show. But himself wouldn't hear of it. 'That pickup's just about ready to go,' he'd said. He'd been saying it for the last four hours as the vehicle fell apart beneath his hands.

'Even if you get it going,' she said, 'You can't drive it with no licence. If you get caught again...'

He grinned at her. 'But I've got a licence.'

'Whose? Not yours, for sure.'

'Ah, never you mind. We'll get it all worked out.'

'But what about the petrol tank?'

He kicked at it, and stove it in.

'Jottered,' he said. 'Emergency measures are called for.' He wandered around the encampment looking into the caravans and the various makeshift tents. Then his eyes lit on a bucket beside the muddy stream. 'There it is,' he said. 'There's our petrol tank.'

The fax machine extruded its strip of paper. MacFearn tugged at the paper to make it come out faster. He'd been on edge for days, ever since he'd sent the samples off for analysis, waiting for the results. This was the big one. On the results of this chemical test, his future lay. He might receive a commendation. He could be made sergeant. As soon as the machine stopped, he tore the paper off and took it to the desk. He smoothed it out and began to read the blurred letters.

Analysis of samples from Redrock Estate, by way of Constable Alick MacFearn.

Sample (a) was mainly (98%) dried potato powder. The potato contained starch and protein in a proportion characteristic of the 'Laird's Delight' potato, grown only in Strathnaver. The Kinlochbervie Potato Works still use this particular potato despite an EC ruling that this potato is not considered suitable for processing.

The remaining 2% of the sample consisted of the anabolic steroid known as Durabolin.

Sample (b) was mainly (98%) commercial grade pinhead oatmeal. The proportion of different glutens strongly suggests that this oatmeal was grown south of Aberfeldy. Striations on the grains suggests that the oatmeal was stoneground. Careful study of the microscopic details revealed marks consistent with the use of stones with 'feather-pitched' dressing. The water-powered mill at Darnaway uses such stones, as does the Great Orm Mill at Drumnadrochit.

The anabolic steroid known as Durabolin constituted the remaining 2% of sample (b).

Underneath, in the space headed 'Notes', someone had written:

MacFearn: well done, indeed. We'll have a squad of police down on Mr Mor's neck for this! Having located the source of these foodstuffs, we can now cut off the supply and smash the gang known as the Porridge Smugglers. The Potato Pirates will likewise get their desserts.

By the way, it may have escaped your attention that possession of steroids is not a criminal offence.

Excellent work, MacFearn, you blithering idiot!

MacFearn's face fell. His visions of a glittering rise through the ranks fell as dust around him. Scarcely knowing what he was doing, he stumbled out of the Police Station, the sheet of paper still clutched in his hand. In the street, he turned and followed his normal route up Harbour Road, but his steps were guided by habit alone. He saw nothing of the street around him.

How could he have made a mistake? How had Mr Mor escaped? It must be the influence of that Inspector Morrison. The whole thing was probably set up purely to discredit MacFearn within the Police Force. His hands clenched in anger and the chemical analysis crumpled in his fist. He stared at it, then threw it to the ground and stamped on it viciously.

'It's a fine day for it.'

MacFearn lifted his head. It was Jimmy Bervie.

'Ah, yes,' said MacFearn, aware that he had not been behaving in a manner consonant with the dignity of the law.

'Yes, a grand day for the Show,' continued Jimmy, watching him curiously.

MacFearn coughed. 'Indeed. Yes. I shall be there later. Perhaps I shall see you there also?'

'No, I have other things in hand tonight. By the way, I couldn't help noticing that you...'

MacFearn broke in. 'Yes, I'll be there as usual. Extra duty, you know. Drafted in, as usual. Extra police, you see.' He coughed again and drew himself up straight. 'Good day.' He strode stiffly to the corner and turned down High Street, his face red. He stepped into the Chandler's doorway and let himself slump against the door. After a long while he sighed. Best look on the bright side. At least it was only Jimmy that saw him. And disappointment or not, there was still the Show to look forward to. Best job of the year. He stood up straight and began to walk again. A small smile appeared on his face. Yes, the Show.

After all, basically he was a country Constable, and the glitter of high position was not for him. Walking the beat, giving out stern avuncular warnings, that was the ticket. There was lots of that at the Show. The hustle, the bustle. Sometimes there were fights to break up, with a severe but fair, 'Well then, well, then! What's going on here?' Sometimes there were lost children and distraught parents coming to MacFearn, the reassuring constable. Better to be an honest constable than a corrupt Inspector. His stride became proud and even jaunty as he went down the hill towards Shore Road.

Back on Harbour Road, Jimmy stood for a while thinking about MacFearn. But Jimmy was himself preoccupied by other matters and he could make nothing of the constable's behaviour. Idly he picked up the crumpled piece of paper and smoothed it out. It was a good bit of paper. There must be something he could make out of it.

As he strolled towards the door of the Harbour Hotel, he folded the sheet. A paper horse began to take shape in his hands. He stepped through the door of the public bar. 'Pauline,' he called, 'A Glen Grian, please. As fast as you like.'

At a table in the corner sat Irwin, nursing a pint of beer. Louisiana

Lou sat beside him, trying vainly to cheer him up. She looked almost as miserable as Irwin.

Jimmy strode up to the table. 'Irwin,' he said, 'You've not been looking yourself. You need something to do. Melancholy cannot remain in the concentrated mind, as my old friend Ch'utz-pa On-yig Tze Fong used to say. Look at this now – here's something to keep your hands busy. A fine wee horse made out of nothing more than a sheet of paper. Let me show you how it's done.' He sat down and unfolded the paper in front of Irwin. Now, you just make the first fold here, like this.' He pushed the paper across the table. 'Now you try.'

Irwin's big hand fell listlessly on the paper. He picked it up. He looked at it. The word 'steroid' leapt out and caught his eye.

'You have to fold it diagonally first.'

Irwin ignored him. His lips moved as he slowly read the crumpled fax.

The stance for the bus to Castleton was crowded. Dumfry stood in the queue beside a young woman who was carrying a radio. It was tuned to Rossland FM, and as the music faded out, Dumfry could hear the News.

Unusually, the first item of the news was a local story, a story that jolted Dumfry to the soles of his shoes. The name Heatherdale was not known to him, but all the other details were disturbingly familiar.

A couple of days before, in the local paper, he had read the story about the woman whose bicycle had turned into a crayfish. Of course, he had dismissed that as a bizarre coincidence. No reason to assume that there was meaning behind it. After all, the newspapers did not carry stories about the millions of bicycles that behaved normally. In any case, there was a good chance that the woman was unbalanced. Even within his own congregation, there were several people who might have invented just such a story.

But now, on the radio, he heard that a housing estate on the outskirts of Inverness had disappeared. This time he felt less inclined to dismiss the outrageous connections that his mind was making, thoughts that he would normally have dismissed out of hand.

But Dumfry was not himself at the moment. Or, more accurately, part of him was himself, but the rest was not. Not what he usually thought of as himself, at any rate.

The part which he had been accustomed to call himself was still there, talking away to itself: concerned with his pastoral duties, concerned about the moral laxity evident in the big city, worried about the impression he must be giving as he wandered around Inverness in such strange clothing, peering intensely at people and plants, stopping now and then to write in his notebook.

The rest of him, the new Dumfry, was calm and confident, aware of the old Dumfry chittering away at the back of his mind and watching him with tolerant amusement.

So the present John Dumfry was not the same as the old John Dumfry. Nor, as he glanced around, did Inverness High Street look the same as usual. Partly it was the effect of the wall of mist over the Dark Isle, reflecting sunlight back at strange angles. But mostly it was the curious persistence of vision that afflicted Dumfry now and then. For minutes at a time, sometimes hours, everything would be normal. And then, like just now, he would begin to see trails around everything: people, cars, dogs, insects. Trails like the wake of ships, but floating in the air, trails that led backwards into the past, or sometimes forwards, into the future. He could even see, with an inner sense, the long extended being that was called John Dumfry, with its echoes of the past and its echoes of the future.

He couldn't see very far into the future but what he could see worried him. There he was, or at least, his shadow-self was, entering the headquarters of Highlands Police. And of course there was at least one thing that he thought he should mention to the police, though he was not at all sure that he *could* explain it.

He sighed. Right in front of his mind's eye, looking a little dejected but resolute, he could see himself catching a No. 68 bus to Old Perth Road.

Very well, then, best to come clean. And afterwards, if he wasn't locked up, he could go to the Show. Something had been worrying him about the Show. Something rather serious. He turned to look at the ominous wall of mist that somehow managed to look grey even with the sun on it. Something over there was not right. He could feel it in his bones as he travelled in those strange places that he often found himself visiting on his Quest. Whatever the matter was, he could sense that it concerned Doreen, and after all she was his spiritual responsibility. A responsibility that he had sadly missed since his quest had begun.

But first, he had to speak to the police. He sighed once more, and moved to another, shorter queue, for the 68 bus.

The incoming plane from London was visible through the office window. The tortured roar reached in through the double-glazing, almost swamping the conversation. The helicopter pilot sat at the coffee table in one corner of the office. Behind the desk a man in a suit looked straight at him.

'Sorry, Bud' he said, though his voice did not sound sorry. 'If you reckon the fog's too thick over the Dark Isle...'

Bud stood up and turned to the map. 'It's as thick as lentil soup from there to there. All round the Dark Isle. We can't take a copter to the Dark Isle Show. It would be suicide to fly in that. You can't even see the island from Castleton.'

'Then we'll just have to cancel the flights. And there's nothing else. You might as well go home.'

The pilot swore. 'But I'll get paid for the day?'

'You'll get paid,' he looked at his watch, 'three hours.'

'Three hours! You can't do that! It's not my bloody fault if there's no work. That's your job.'

'Take it or leave it.' The man in the suit leaned forward and spoke again. 'In fact, you can take it – or leave.'

Bud hesitated. 'What do you mean? I've got a contract...'

'Yes, you do. I think you'll find that the admirably flexible terms of that contract set an upper limit to the hours you spend working here, but no lower limit.' He smirked. 'A contract cuts both ways.'

'Shit!'

There was a knock on the door. 'Yes?'

A woman came in, holding a long thin package with a lump at one end.

'A priority package, sir. It came in on the flight from London.' She turned to hand the package to Bud. 'It's to go to...'

The manager spoke. 'Hold it.'

'But it's priority.'

'Tough. Bud's just going home for the day. Aren't you?' He looked at Bud, who glared back at him. 'It's not worth warming up the engines just for one package. He can take it out tomorrow, after he's picked up the lobsters from Tain.'

'But sir, it's an Emperor-class package...'

He looked suddenly thoughtful. He tapped on the desk with his fingers.

'...and if we don't deliver it right away, someone's sure to complain.'

'Yes, Miss MacLean, I think that I can deal with that.'

'And head office has already made it clear that...'

'I said I can deal with that!'

'Yes sir.' There was a long pause before she ventured to speak again. 'It's just that, well you know what they said last time.'

He swore. 'Of course I bloody know!' He stubbed out his cigar fiercely. 'Where's it for?'

'Cromness. On the Dark Isle.'

The man sat up straight. 'Emperor-class, you say?'

'Yes sir.'

'Right.' He reached for the package. 'Leave it here. Bud will take it.'

Miss MacLean left the room. He looked at Bud. 'Okay?'

'No. Not if it's for the Dark Isle.' Bud pointed out of the window. The day was bright and clear, and beyond the airfield, flat land stretched to the sea. Where the island should have been visible in the Moray Firth, a long grey shape lay, with mountains peering over it from beyond. 'Look at it. Visibility is about twenty yards. I'd have to stop and ask the way.'

'Then that's what you'll bloody do, okay?' He held out the package. Bud did not take it.

'I'll take it out as soon as the mist clears.'

'Oh no you won't. You'll take it now. Or if you won't, there's a queue of helicopter pilots down at the Job Centre. One of them will take it.'

Doctor Hislop and the rest of his group of academics made their way across the wooden causeway that led from the beach at Castleton across to the Dark Isle. Among them, tethered by a silken leash, they had the latest arrival in their famous flock of sheep, each one genetically identical to all the others. This one was called Barbie, and she was a fine plump lamb with curling wool. The group were gathered tightly, protectively around their charge. Dignitaries from the Highlands University fluttered around the outside of this famous research team, trying to pick up a few hints as to the next development in the field of genetic engineering.

About twenty yards in front of them, a cameraman walked backwards, his camera flashing every so often as he spotted a good picture of the group. Certainly it was an impressive progress, the besuited flock picked out now and then by the swaying lights overhead. They wended their way through lively knots of farm-hands and townsfolk making their way to the Show, progressing along a street of trawler cabins, under a canopy of aerials, loops of electric cable and stubby masts hung with flags.

They passed a pair of American tourists dressed in tartan. They were trying to explain the significance of the Highlands Agricultural Fair to some Danish back-packers who could not well understand them and thought that they had luckily made the acquaintance of some genuine locals. Ahead of them, a boisterous group of farm-hands in their best clothes had stopped to take a drop of whisky, to celebrate the fact that they were standing in the middle of Castleton Sound.

'Excuse me, Dr Hislop,' called the Principal of the Highlands University, as he moved forward a few steps to deflect the group around the young men. Dr Hislop's tread did not waver.

'Want a drink? Hey man, want a drink?'

'Nah! Stuck-up bastards!'

The voices fell away behind them and the Principal took the opportunity to fall in alongside the Doctor. 'I hope you will enjoy the show,' he said. 'It has some very interesting features, though perhaps it is not the equal of the Smithfield Show or... or some other shows. Though I have to say that we have a much more interesting show than Nairn.'

'Is that so?'

'Oh, yes. And the Dark Isle Show is also older. Its antiquity is much more... extensive. More prestigious. Though of course, your presence lends prestige to the event, rather than the other way round. And of course, the presence of your protégé. Your, eh, your companion.'

Hislop nodded. 'Indeed. Come, Barbie.' He tugged on the leash and the yearling sheep trotted to catch up with him.

'A fine sheep,' said the Principal.

'Do you think so? She wasn't selected for her positive agricultural traits, but rather for a history of good health.'

'And of course you had to consider also a range of biochemical factors in the uterine environment of the host mother,' put in the Principal, rather heavily.

'Yes,' Hislop replied vaguely. 'Of course, those.'

'Such as,' the Principal's voice slowed, and he enunciated clearly, 'the harmonious functioning of endocrine glands coupled with optimum proportions of oestrogen and progesterone.'

Hislop laughed. 'You are well-informed.'

'Thank you.' The Principal leaned over confidentially. 'Dr MacReady took it on himself to inform me about the process of cloning. He runs a fine lab there, up at the Agricultural College. We may not be cloning sheep yet,' he bent to pat Barbie on her woolly nose, 'but we are ambitious. In fact, we have initiated a feasibility study to see if we can adapt our Domestic Science wing into genetics labs – we might even be able to utilise the same equipment. While you're in the area, I wonder if you might...'

'No,' said Hislop.

'I beg your pardon?'

'I want nothing to do with your rinkydink Agricultural College. I am not a farmer, I am a scientist, and I am here for one reason only. We must, unfortunately, court publicity in order to attract funding.' At the shoreline ahead of them, a camera flashed, then another. Hislop smiled and raised a hand. 'That's why I have to travel with this band of semi-professional sycophants to visit a series of second-rate agricultural shows and congratulate second-rate farmers on their second-rate beasts.' As they approached the shore, Hislop paused and knelt down with one hand on Barbie's head. A dazzling barrage of flashes lit the scene. Hislop soothed Barbie, the crowd stood as close as they could to the great

Doctor, and only the Principal's face was not smiling.

From *Psychic Attack: A Manual of Self-Defence*

There are many ways of changing the vibrational state of the human mind, and in this chapter we will be looking at some of these.

To look at a familiar example first, music can be used as one such method. Mystical musicians are part of the traditions of the East and Middle-East. More recently, certain types of popular music have developed in the West, with the purpose of changing the vibrational rates of many people simultaneously and thus breaking down the barriers between minds. Such reckless experiments are not to be recommended – we have already seen, in Chapter One, how mental states can directly affect reality. In the overexcited state that such popular concerts can encourage, there is the danger that an intense positive feedback loop may be established between the musicians and the audience. The immense amount of power harnessed may create the conditions necessary for mass hallucinations or even local distortions in time and space. There is a risk of serious damage to the mental functioning of people exposed to such experiences unprepared.

Eck looked through the book as he waited by the roadside, hitching. Among the stream of cars, a bright blue one passed as he read the paragraph about the effects of a positive feedback loop. He read it again, feeling the excitement of discovery. The warnings did not worry him at all. It sounded like an ace way to raise the energy and make weird things happen.

The cars rushed by, ignoring his out-held thumb. Eck didn't mind. He was waiting for the right one, the vehicle sent to take him where he was going. He flexed his muscles, stretched his back, rolled his head and closed his eyes, sounding a secret syllable inside his head.

Certainty settled on him: he knew where his future lay. 2nd Tribal Railroad were doing the sound for the bands at the Dark Isle Show, and he, Eck, would be there, playing a part, raising the energy.

First the idea, then the action. He imagined himself in an enclosed space. Then he visualised the space opening and saw himself flying, his wings spread, like an eagle. He had to get from here, the roadside by Craig Gobhan, to there, the show at Castleton. That wouldn't be too hard: he could feel things falling into place.

A battered blue truck pulled to a halt at the grass verge. The man on the passenger seat moved over against the woman at the wheel. Eck stuffed the book into a pocket and reached up to open the door.

'Ta, man. Going to the show?'

'Aye. Climb in.'

He climbed up and squeezed in beside the man. There was a smell of sweat and burnt rubber in the cab, possibly coming from the man, and a powerful smell of petrol. Eck leaned against the door to give himself as much space as possible. The man leant the other way, muttering to the woman.

There was a jerk as the truck started.

'Easy!' said the man. 'Less throttle.'

The truck eased out into the road, then there was another jerk as the man changed gear.

Eck looked at the couple in amazement. The woman had her hands folded in her lap. The man's right hand rested lightly on the steering wheel. As the truck neared a corner, his hand flicked the wheel, flicked and grabbed, then rested lightly on the rim, letting it glide back into the straight. The truck picked up speed and the man's left hand snapped out like a snake, changed gear without benefit of the clutch, then came back to steady the bucket he was holding between his thighs.

'Jesus Christ!'

Eck stared in horror at the bucket. It was three quarters full of petrol and there was a plastic tube over the rim and down, to pass through a hole in the metal floor.

The man turned to Eck. His face was blue-black where he had shaved recently, dark with oil and smoke everywhere else.

'Bastards took ma licence,' he said. The petrol slopped in the bucket as the woman reached into her pocket for a packet of cigarettes. 'Easy, fafucksake, Mary.' He gestured at her. 'But she's got a clean licence.'

'So why doesn't she drive, then?'

'Ah, well, it's like this. Mary can't drive. Never learned.'

'Aye, aye.' Eck nodded as if he understood. The truck swung into a bend and the petrol climbed up to the rim of the bucket, then subsided. As soon as the road was straight again, he risked a question. 'So how did she pass her test then, if she can't drive?'

The man laughed. 'Mary? Dinna be daft, man. She hasny passed her test. She'd be driving this van if she had.'

'But you said...'

The man turned an enquiring eye on Eck. The truck hurtled on. Somehow the man managed to steer round a bend while watching Eck.

'...you said she had a clean licence.'

'Oh, that. Aye, she's got a clean licence all right. But it's not hers. It's her sister's. See?'

Eck nodded and closed his eyes. Every being is a star, he thought.

A star. Not this body, but a star. Which was just as well, because this body might not last too much longer.

Several large, high-sided trucks pulled away from the gates of Redrock Estate, leaving a thick animal stench hanging in the moist air. The bellowing that came from the trucks faded as they slid into the fog. As the last one drove off towards Castleton, the gatekeeper swung the gates closed and locked them. He was walking back towards the gate lodge when Lou's motor caravan emerged from the mist and stopped at the gates. The horn sounded as Irwin jumped out. The gatekeeper glanced round, dismissed Irwin with a glance and kept going.

The gates rattled as Irwin shook them. 'Wait a moment, wait a bloody moment!'

The gatekeeper walked slowly back from the gatelodge, appraising the situation. There was a massively-built man standing at the gate, his great fists clenched round two of the steel bars. Behind him in the mist stood a motor-caravan, its lights on, its engine still running. A woman with long dark hair sat at the steering wheel. She smiled nervously as he glanced at her.

He stopped a few feet back from the gates. 'Well?'

'Where's that bastard Mor?' Irwin's face was red. He thrust it forward, almost pushing it through between the steel bars.

'Got an appointment, have you?'

'No, I haven't got a bloody appointment!' He rattled the heavy gates again. 'Open up!'

The gateman put his hands in his pockets and sucked at his teeth 'That's unfortunate, that is. I'd like to let you in. I'm an obliging sort of chap, everyone says so.' He looked Irwin up and down. 'But it's more than my job's worth to let in an enraged yokel with hay in his ears. Especially if he hasn't got no appointment.'

'I want to see the bastard now!'

'Oh do you? Well, the best I can do is to suggest that you go back down the road and phone the Big House. Perhaps your girlfriend can dial, if you don't know your numbers yet. Then you can come back in a day or two – if the Big Man wants to see you, which I doubt.'

'Open these bloody gates!' Irwin shook the gates violently.

'Now, now. Bad language never got no-one nowhere. And I'd advise you to let go of them gates, because I'm just going inside to turn on the electrics. You'll get 24,000 volts right though you if you don't let go.'

He looked over to the motor caravan, smiled and winked at the woman, then turned round and walked towards the lodge. Behind him there was a prolonged grunting sound and a creak of metal, followed by a loud 'Ping!'

Before he could turn, a huge fist caught him by the shoulder, lifted him and pushed him up against the wall.

'Right. I asked you a polite question, and I'm waiting for a polite answer. Where's that bastard Mor?'

'Gnnh gnoak ak ih ghuuse!'

Irwin released the pressure and the man's face separated itself from the wall. A fist was poised nearby.

'Well?'

'He's not here! Honest. He's gone to the show!'

The big fist hovered for a moment longer, then the man slumped to the ground as Irwin let go of his shoulder.

'Right.' Irwin turned and walked through the gateway. 'We're going to the Dark Isle Show,' he said.

Louisiana Lou nodded and shifted into gear as Irwin climbed in the passenger door.

'Thanks,' he called to the gateman as the van began to move.

'What about the gates? Jesus Christ! Look what you've done to the gates!'

The red tail-lights of the van disappeared into the mist.

Le Placs and Jimmy Bervie sat on a fish-box at Jimmy's front door, sipping coffee. Although the sun had not set, the street lights were on, an orange necklace of lights past the harbour and along Seaview, fading into the mist. Jimmy was wearing a length of tartan cloth wrapped round his waist to make a kilt, with the loose end thrown over his shoulder. On another box, perched on bricks to make a table, were dozens of strings of beads.

'The mala of neem seeds, certainly,' Jimmy said, separating them from the others. 'And the cowrie shells.' He lifted the plaid from his shoulder and tucked it in at his waist. Slowly he raised the strings of beads and settled them round his neck. 'What else, do you think?'

Le Placs was stirring at black paint in a jam jar. Two other jars on the table held red and yellow. He waved a hand at the pile. 'Why don't you put them all on?'

'Perhaps I will, but this is ceremonial: I have to choose them one at a time.' He opened a small wooden box and lifted out a string of roughly spherical beads, a dull yellow colour. 'These ones, for certain. I've had these since I was a lad.' He mumbled a few words to himself and put them to one side. 'But I'll save them until last.'

Then he continued separating strings one by one until the table was empty and his naked chest was swathed in strings of beads.

'Now, my friend, perhaps you could put the last string on for me?'

He held out his hand.

Le Placs put down the paint pot and took the last string of beads from him. It was surprisingly heavy. Jimmy spoke a few incomprehensible words in a slow ceremonial voice as Le Placs settled the beads on top of the others.

'Thank you.' Jimmy lifted an old copy of the *Fishing Times* from the ground, pulled out a few pages and tucked them around his neck, to protect the beads. 'Right. Fire away.'

'You are sure about this?' asked Le Placs.

'Yes. Go ahead.'

Le Placs gave the black paint a final stir and lifted a paint brush. Jimmy sat straight and steady, studying the harbour. It was just possible to see to the far side, where the harbour lights gleamed hazily. There were hardly any boats left – all the trawlers and lobster boats were round at Castleton for the show. Only a few dinghies and cobles bobbed on the oily water. But Jimmy paid them no heed. He was looking at the berth of the *Suitor's Lass*. It was still empty. Under the streetlights at the harbour's edge, several tourists' cars were beginning to develop a dull white coating of salt.

'I see Barry's still out,' said Jimmy, 'seeking the wild dolphin. They must be gey elusive. That's two days he's been gone.'

'You are concerned?'

'Not for their safety, no. But it might be linked to the imminent disaster which we are trying to avert.' Small waves plashed on the shore. Almost everyone was at the Show and all was silent but for the far-off sound of a heavy vehicle crawling down the Dinny Hill. The rumble faded as it headed towards the east end of Cromness.

'Right. That's the paint mixed.'

Jimmy leant down and picked up his mop-head wig and gave his shiny bald head a wipe with it. 'Carry on.'

'I don't know how well I can do this.'

Jimmy shrugged. 'Do your best.'

Le Placs dipped a brush in the paint and with intense concentration, began to paint a black circle around Jimmy's skull. When he had finished, he stood back to look. 'Not too bad. It just takes a steady hand and some concentration. Perhaps you would like me to do a symbol of some sort?'

'Wheesht man, the circles will do fine. It's just for the sense of occasion. To get me in the mood.'

Le Placs picked up another jar and began to paint a second, concentric circle, in red. 'In the mood for what, Jimmy? I still do not know what you have planned.'

Jimmy stared into the mist beyond the harbour. The light was failing badly now. 'Well, I'm not completely sure myself. The situation is dire, there can be no doubt of that. Someone must do something, and we seem to be the people on the spot. But I have a natural disinclination to go messing with the forces of nature.'

His cheerful face slumped, and for a moment he looked ancient, instead of just very old. Le Placs put a hand on his shoulder. 'You look weary, *mon brave*. Perhaps we can leave this until tomorrow...'

'No, no. You have seen it in the entrails, and you know the matter is urgent. I can feel it myself, in the cold wind that moves over the earth without disturbing the mist, and I have seen the writing in the sand. It must be tonight, if it is to be done at all. But I am still waiting for a sign, a message.'

'Ah, yes. You have talked of this before. The small signs that speak to you from the lie of the grass, from the songs of the birds, even the tiny movements of insects.'

'Aye, something of that sort. It is no small thing to disturb the balance of the universe, and I would not like to proceed without a sign of some sort. I have asked for advice: let's hope an answer comes.' He shivered, then held his head up straight. 'Paint on, maestro.'

Le Placs dabbed again at Jimmy's skull. The silence in Cromness was profound. The streets were empty now, and even the bar of the Harbour Hotel was closed for the Show. The soft plashing of waves that reached them from the shore seemed to accentuate the deep quiet. Jimmy suddenly lifted his head. Le Placs' brush slipped.

'*Merde*!' A drop of red ochre trickled down over Jimmy's forehead.

'What's that?'

'I hear nothing.' Le Placs stood still, paint brush in hand. In the air there was a faint fluttering, as if someone was blowing into the end of a rolled-up newspaper while moving it rapidly to and fro in front of the lips. 'A helicopter?'

'Ah, yes. This is it.'

'What, your sign?'

'I think so.'

Le Placs shrugged. 'But it is just a helicopter.'

'We will see.'

The sound grew, and soon they could hear the thudding of the engine. Lights appeared through the mist as the pilot slowly made his way into the wall of fog that surrounded the Dark Isle.

Trucks with the arms of Redrock Estate ground their way along the muddy tracks among the pens and stalls. Baldy walked in front, clearing the way. 'Make room! Oot the way!'

The wee grey man worked the other side of the thoroughfare, clearing a path quietly but just as effectively. Mr Mor arrived as one truck stopped at the cattle pens and reversed into place. The back of the truck folded down into a ramp and an enormous bull was guided out, led by ropes around its wide spreading horns. It was of no traditional breed. As much as anything, it resembled the beasts in the ancient cave-paintings of Lascaux. Other bulls nearby bellowed, catching its smell. There were groups of people at each pen, discussing the merits of the various bulls, the sweep of the back, the spread of the horns, the hang of the balls. They all converged around the newcomer.

'Jesus, what's that?'

'It's the bloody Minotaur!'

One of them leant to read the card on the gate. 'Owner, Redrock Estate. Age, 18 months. Breed, Aurochs. Aurochs? What the hell kind of breed is that?'

Baldy stood near to Mr Mor, watching the crowd, one hand close to the bulge under his jacket.

Mor took the cigar from his mouth. 'Take it easy, Baldy. No-one is going to steal it. This is an agricultural show, they want to see the animals. The worst that's likely to happen is some drunk might pick a fight.'

A bunch of young men swaggered past, drinking from cans. Baldy stepped forwards to fend them off.

'Bloody teuchters,' he said, as they disappeared into the crowd.

The other trucks had moved on, one of them stopping in the pig section. There was a specially reinforced pen there, marked with the Redrock shield. Nervous-looking men opened the back of the truck and a boar hurtled out and into the pen. It turned in an instant, but the gate had been closed. It rammed the steel gate with its flat slimy nose, but the gate too was reinforced. It reared up with its front trotters on the top of the gate and screamed in rage. Froth dripped from its muzzle, and the white tusks gleamed. A man edged forward and hung a red sign on the steel bars: WILD BOAR. THIS BEAST IS DANGEROUS. KEEP CLEAR.

The trucks moved through the fair, unloading animals in their particular sections. Several of them were in the exotic breeds section, where they quickly drew crowds.

The last truck stopped among the sheep pens, and several rams the size of cattle trotted into the enclosure. The registration card on the pen declared that they were Mouflon.

'That's the lot, Baldy.' Mor was looking smug. 'That lot should win a few prizes.'

'Dunno why you bother. Bloody animals.'

Mor chewed on his cigar as he looked Baldy up and down. 'It's politics,' he said, 'So maybe it's beyond you. You see, no-one here gives a damn about your reputation in Glasgow or your influence in the corridors of power in Edinburgh. And they don't much care if you've lived here for twenty years. You're still an outsider. But if you can raise a good beast, if you can show a champion bull or a sheep, then you belong. You've got something they can appreciate.'

Baldy looked at the sheep pens around him and sniffed at the air. Men, women and children in their best clothes hung over wooden fences and steel poles comparing the lambs and ewes.

Baldy shook his head. 'Right,' he said, grimacing.

A man turned from admiring the mouflon and walked over. 'Mr Mor?'

'Ah. Aristide Coupar, isn't it?'

'I wonder if I could have a word.'

'The ritual?'

'No, it's about the meeting. Barry is still missing and I'll have to organise the boats.' He looked around and lowered his voice. 'For later, you know.'

Mr Mor looked around. 'Let's you and me find a place to talk. Baldy, walk around, enjoy yourself. If you can. Be at the tent at seven – and make sure it's secure.'

'Okay.'

Baldy looked around.

The sheep bleated in their pens, young men strutted down the muddy thoroughfares shouting and joking, some of them with young women on their arms. A woman, smart in black jacket and jodhpurs, led an immaculately groomed pony through the crowds: a man, in tweeds and a flat cap, looking the worse for drink, led a Clydesdale horse the other way. They called to each other as they passed.

'Good afternoon, Mr MacLeod.'

'Aye, aye. It's yourself, Clementina.'

Red faced farmers strode through the mud, ignoring the splatters on their shoes and trousers. Children ate candyfloss and demanded fairground rides or food. Music from the fairground and the food tent and the stalls drifted over the noisy throng, and the hearty farmyard smells permeated everything.

Baldy, with a scowl on his face, pushed his way to the blue striped marquee, where he could see a huge crowd at the bar. Old packing crates had been scattered around for use as tables and seats. Most of the tables were covered with used plastic tumblers. All the seats were taken. Several people had brought dogs in with them, and there were even a couple of goats and a sheep.

Baldy, by force of muscle, just managed to get to the front without causing a fight. He bought a pint, pushed his way out and leaned against the tent pole to drink it. There was barbed wire wrapped round the pole, presumably to stop people climbing it. One or two ebullient youths eyed it anyway. Baldy glared at them. There was a 'Baa!' from nearby. The men with the sheep were at the nearest crate. Baldy looked down at them with a sneer. Just see that happening in Glasgow. You'd maybe get away with a dog, if you were a regular customer. But a sheep!

He could hear the two farmers talking.

'Dash me, that's a fine sheep you have there, Tommy.'

'She's bonny, right enough.'

'Neat wethers on her.'

'Aye.'

Baldy resigned himself to a miserable afternoon and swallowed another mouthful of warm beer.

In the big marquee, a man sat before a sound desk studded with dials and knobs and sliders. 'That one's fine,' he called. 'Next.'

On stage a denimed roadie stepped up to another mike.

'One two, one two.'

'That's great. And the last one.'

'One two, one two.'

'Hey man, I could do that! Can I do that, Zak?'

'Eck?' The man at the mixer turned, beaming. 'They let you out, then.'

'Couldn't keep me in, man!' Eck shrugged. 'I needed to be here, so I called in the energy – and here I am.' He thought about his journey. 'By the skin of my teeth, risking death by live cremation.'

'Ha, ha! I'm sure. So what are you up to?'

'Well, Zak, I had this vision. An amazing vision. So real you could touch it.'

'So they couldn't cure you, hey?'

'I saw the energy rising over the Dark Isle, gathering over the showground. It was ablaze with light, like fireworks and lasers.'

'That would be the firework display, later tonight. Twenty thousand pounds worth of fireworks. Should be something to see.'

'No, no. This wasn't physical. This was something special. Energy pouring from one dimension to another.'

Zak looked at him, frowning. 'Did you see this while you were in the Craig?'

'Right.'

'And what drugs were they giving you?'

Eck winked. 'Nothing. I palmed them.' He reached into his pocket. 'Here they are. You can have one if you want.'

'No thanks. Don't trust medical pills.'

'Anyway, man, when I saw it, it was like I saw my future laid out before me. I knew that I had to be here, doing it!'

'Right! Do that thing.'

'So that's why I was looking for you.'

'Eh?'

'This is the centre of the energy, the main marquee in the centre of the show. This is where the big bands are going to be playing, raising the energy, breaking down the barriers between minds – and I've got to be doing something, contributing. Working that energy.'

'Yeah?'

'So can I work the sound desk? I mean, later on, when the big bands are on, around midnight?'

Zak held up his hands, shaking his head. 'No, I don't think so.'

'You can show me how to do it. Look, you can watch and make sure. It's just, I have this vision – and I need this, man, I really, really need it.'

Eck leant forward, trying to convince him. Zak was pinned in his chair by the intensity in his eyes.

'But I can't let you...' Zak paused, thinking furiously. 'Well, maybe if...'

'Right!'

'Look, you just can't do it all by yourself. There isn't time to show you how. It takes months to learn your way round the desk.'

'But...'

'Wait. You can't work the whole desk, but you could operate the master slider.'

'The Master Slider? Hey!'

'Yeah. It, eh, it controls the energy level. It's that one on the far left.'

Eck took the handle and slid it up and down. 'Like this?'

'That's it. Pull it down to the bottom for low and subtle. Up to the top for high and hard.'

Eck slid it to the top and held it there, grinning.

'But not all the time, right?'

'Okay.' Eck slid it down and up again, making police siren noises. 'You're a pal, Zak. Wooooeeeoo! Eeeoo! So what does it actually do?'

'It's the Master Slider.'

Eck laughed. 'Hey, it's the one I'm working – of course it's the Master Slider. But what does it control?'

Zak laughed too. 'You know. You can use it to raise the energy level.'

'Yes, but how does it do it?'

'What d'you mean? Like, on the physical plane?'

'Yes.'

'Well, what it does actually is, it controls the level of the bass. The deep bass. The low notes, you know.'

'Sure, I know what bass means. That sounds great to me. So why is it slider number forty-eight, right at the end here?'

'That's just the way it happened,' said Zak, shrugging and flashing a bright smile.

Eck looked at him, and kept looking at him, with eyebrows slightly raised. Zak gave up.

'It's not really an important control, Eck. Sorry. This bank is really just a graphic equaliser and that slider controls the very lowest notes. Hardly any of the bands have got anything that goes that low. Hell, people could hardly hear it even if they did. Most of the time it's just an open channel with nothing going through it.'

'That's great!'

'What?'

'That's just what I need. Better than doing the whole desk. I've got one clear channel, all to myself.'

'But Eck, unless someone turns up with a pipe organ or a six-foot war-horn, there won't be anything in that channel!'

'Oh yes there will. I'll send my energy right through that open channel and it'll pour out of the speakers, amplified to glory!'

'Oh yeah, right. Sorry, I thought we were talking on the physical plane.'

'But we are! We certainly are. It's becoming clearer to me all the time.' He sat down on a chair next to Zak. 'See, it's like this. The mind can affect the physical plane directly, at the quantum level.'

'Is that so? The quantum level, huh?'

'Oh, yes. I was reading about it. It's amazing. Personally, I don't think the scientists even know what they've discovered. Sometimes, right, if you set it up in the right way, if you look at an electron, it behaves like a particle, and if you don't watch it, it behaves like a wave.'

'So how do you know it's behaving like a wave, if you're not watching it?'

'I guess you have to look at it afterwards.'

'When it's stopped behaving?'

'Yup. And sometimes you find it in places where it shouldn't be. Spooky, huh?'

'Dead weird.'

'Anyway, that's just one example. There's lots more, but you get the idea, yes?'

'Right. But that's on a kind of small scale, isn't it?'

'Aye. Tiny. Down at the atoms. Smaller.'

'So it can't affect very much. I mean, I'd not even notice if you did this quantum thing right beside me.'

'True enough. Usually. But what if you're in a state of sensitive dependence on initial conditions? What then, eh?'

'What's that mean?'

'Remember the story of the butterfly in China, the one that flapped its wings?'

'Right, a Zen story, isn't it? You were telling us about it at that party over at Boblair. The Buddha fell asleep with a butterfly on his chest...'

'No, no. This is a different butterfly. Listen to this, right. The weather is incredibly complex, I mean, you just have to look at the clouds – it's dead complex, yeah? And so there's always places that are in a super-sensitive state, all poised and ready to go one way or the other. Then the butterfly flutters its wings and that affects the local system, and that affects the next one and that starts a storm right round the other side of the world, in Kansas.'

'I don't suppose we could catch the butterfly and...'

'No, man. You can't tell which one it is, because of Heisenberg's uncertainty.'

'Right.'

'It was just an example, okay?'

'Anyway, we don't have that kind of weather here do we?'

Eck held up his hand. 'It doesn't have to be weather. Anything that's complex enough, it'll get into that state sooner or later. And look around you, man. Look at the Show! Thousands of people moving around in groups, groups that break up and form again, crowds that dissolve. And they're doing all sorts of different things. People talk to each other, fall out, make up. They buy candyfloss, they drink and fight and swear, they make deals and they lie and they go on the rides. There's layers and layers of them – the horse people and the dairy farmers and the market gardeners and the fishermen and people from every damned walk of life. Usually they have bugger all to do with one another, but there's just this one day of the year when they all come together and the place hums. You can feel the buzz, can't you? Well, that's a complex system, all right. Just as complex as the weather patterns over China.

'All I have to do is be here ready to take advantage of it. At the right moment, a tiny subatomic mental push will set off quantum cascades, growing like a whirlpool. Resulting in events in the realtime world of you and me, energy flowing out to those who can hear. An invisible link from mind to mind.'

'And this is what you're going to do?'

'Yeah. But you got to do it at the crucial moment, when the state is right. So you've got to be really sensitive to what's happening around you. Not everyone can do it.'

'And you're going to amplify this through my sound desk?'

'I am!'

'Wow. But if you break it, you pay for it, okay?'

Inspector Morrison was at his desk, clearing away unfinished business before the meeting. There were papers to secrete and files to encrypt, just in case. He was uneasily aware of the quasi-legal nature of the whole enterprise and the shadowy past of at least some of his co-conspirators.

The phone rang.

'Yes, what is it?' he barked.

The desk sergeant spoke in an even tone, not wishing to invite the sarcasm of his superior. 'There's someone here to see you sir. Yes, I know you're busy sir, but he insisted on seeing you. A Reverend Dumfry, he says, from Cromness.'

'Cromness?' Morrison thought quickly. This could be a message from Mor. Unlikely, but possible. 'What does he want?'

'It's about the Heatherdale business, sir. He says he has important information. Knows what happened, apparently.'

'Really?' This could be the breakthrough. It would be worthwhile cracking this case before moving on. 'Send him up. No, bring him up yourself.'

'If you say so, sir.' There was a long pause.

'What is it, man?'

'He's dressed rather strangely, sir.'

'What the hell does that have to do with anything? I don't care if he's dressed up in a kangaroo suit, if he has the information we need.'

The sergeant spoke stiffly. 'Very well, sir.'

A few minutes later, the door opened.

'Reverend Dumfry, sir,' said the sergeant, smugly.

Morrison stood, ready to step forward to shake hands, when the sergeant ushered in a man wearing a dog-collar, a very old and threadbare kilt and a shirt that looked as if it had been through a thorn bush.

Wanting something to do with his outstretched hand, Morrison waved at a chair in front of the desk. 'Ah, take a seat, please.'

Dumfry sat, and rearranged the folds of the kilt as well as he could. He adjusted the dog collar at his neck and nervously patted at his ragged shirt.

Morrison realised he was still standing. He sat. 'I am led to believe that you can throw some light on the alleged disappearance of Heatherdale.'

'I'm afraid so.' Dumfry blushed. 'It seems that I may have been instrumental in its disappearance. Inadvertently, I assure you.'

'Indeed?' He looked at Dumfry, sizing him up. Odd he certainly was, but he had none of the look of the hardened criminal. In fact he had the naive, slightly surprised look of a child. 'That is a most unlikely statement. But if this is so, I am not prepared to bargain with you. I must ask you to give us the names of your accomplices.'

'Oh, it was just one... well, one person, if you can call it that.'

'One person? Don't be ridiculous. No-one can even find Heatherdale, or what remains of it. Over one hundred houses have been moved or destroyed, not to mention the cars, the roads, the streetlights and most of the people who lived there! They have disappeared off the face of the earth!'

Dumfry sat forward in his seat and raised one finger. 'Not exactly. They have indeed disappeared, but I think they are still on the earth. Or very close to it.'

'What the hell does that mean? Listen, I have looked, my constables have looked, Aviemore Mountain Rescue team has looked. That housing estate is not there.'

'It is hidden from sight. But it is there, I assure you.'

Morrison laughed: not a happy sound. 'Where and how could you possibly hide an entire housing estate?'

'It's difficult to explain.' Dumfry frowned. 'It may be what is called a different dimension. Things work differently there, my goodness they do! There seem to be several of these dimensions, and I was in one of those places, the night before last. Just before I fell asleep.'

'You are claiming that you were in bed at the time of the disappearance?'

'Yes. But wait. I suppose I was dreaming in a way, although I was still awake. I remember, I was dreaming about...' He thought about that evening, two days ago. He'd been in a profound reverie. Thinking, as far as he could recall, about a warm, pillowy, comforting bosom in a meadow filled with wild flowers. It had been quite overwhelming, and he now had the uneasy feeling that he had not dismissed the thought quite as authoritatively as he should have. It had been so pleasant and so deeply comforting...

'Reverend Dumfry?' Morrison's voice was sarcastic. 'Are you with us?'

'I beg your pardon.' Dumfry coughed. 'Lost in thought for a moment. Anyway, I believe that I unintentionally allowed an entity to enter this world, and it pushed the estate out of its proper place. And I assure you that I will put it right, if I can. Up until now, I've mostly been an observer in these other dimensions – apart from small incidents, such as the bicycle and the crayfish. So I'm afraid I'm not quite sure how to do things. Nevertheless, I accept responsibility for this accident and I feel I must try to put it right.' He looked hopefully at Morrison's stony face. 'I'm sorry I can't be more precise. It's hard to find the right words.'

'I find it difficult to find words also. Do you realise that you could be prosecuted for wasting police time? Do you expect me to take this nonsense seriously?'

Dumfry held up a hand, looking distressed. 'No, no. I assure you. Heatherdale is still there, and safe. I simply can't explain where it is. It's probably best to say that it has been hidden behind itself, and just leave it at that.'

'I think you should be on your way, Reverend. Sergeant, could you please show...'

'No, please. If you can just give me a couple of minutes, I'll see what I can do. I have to ask this entity,' he paused and blushed, 'to restore Heatherdale to its accustomed position.'

He closed his eyes and began muttering to himself.

Morrison glared at the sergeant. 'Why did you let this nutter in?'

The sergeant spoke with studied forebearance. 'Sorry, sir. But you can never be sure with clergy. He might have been on the square.'

'On the square? This idiot's round the twist.'

Dumfry had fallen silent. Morrison glanced at his watch. 'This has gone on quite long enough, Dumfry. Do you hear me?' Dumfry did not stir. 'Right, that's it. Sergeant, remove that man.'

As the sergeant stepped forwards, Dumfry's eyes snapped open. 'I think that's done it,' he said. 'Remarkable. She, or possibly it, was most co-operative.'

'Thank you for your assistance, Reverend. I'm sure the people of Heatherdale will also be grateful.'

Dumfry did not notice the sarcasm. 'No thanks needed,' he smiled. 'I'm happy to have been able to put things right.'

'Indeed. Well I'm sure you're busy, and I certainly am. Sergeant, could you please show Reverend Dumfry to the door – unless you have any other crimes you would like to put right, hmm?'

'Not at the moment,' said Dumfry, as he was hustled to the door. 'In any case, I have important business at the Dark Isle Show.'

'Coincidentally, Reverend Dumfry, so do I. Goodbye. And Sergeant?'

'Yes sir.'

'I'd like a word with you once you have seen this man off the premises.'

As the door closed behind them, the phone rang.

'Yes? Morrison here.'

'Thank God I've got through at last! Something terrible has happened. We're trapped here, can't get out.'

'Calm down. Explain yourself.'

'I can't explain. I don't know what's happened – except that Inverness has completely disappeared!'

Morrison glanced out of the window. 'Might I suggest that you look again? Inverness looks perfectly solid to me.'

'No, I assure you, it's not there.' There was the sound of a door opening. 'Oh my God! It's come back! Thank God, the world's come back! I thought we were done for, trapped here in Heatherdale forever, unable to go anywhere...'

Inspector Morrison broke in abruptly. '*Where* did you say you were calling from?'

Rossland FM News Roundup

In an astonishing development, Heatherdale returned to Inverness this afternoon. Its apparent disappearance has been a nine-days wonder for the last two days. There has been wild speculation about the cause of its disappearance, but with its return, all bets are off. We spoke to a member of the local residents' group, who disappeared along with the housing estate:

'This is a quiet, respectable place. Things like this don't happen here. Heatherdale has the cleanest streets in the Highlands and a responsible attitude to dog control. Now we just want to put this behind us and get on with our lives.'

A heartfelt plea from the residents of Heatherdale. Despite the brave faces of local residents, some remain uneasy about the event. I asked a police spokesman whether the problem might recur.

'This case has been thoroughly investigated, and it is plain that this is a one-off event. Similar cases in the past have been carefully studied and the causes are well understood. In every case, the cause has turned out to be just one thing: mass hypnosis, mass hysteria and over-reaction by the Press. As far as Highlands Police are concerned, the matter is closed.'

Meanwhile, on the Dark Isle, the festival atmosphere is growing as the Show moves into full swing. This year's show was formally opened by David MacLing MP, local boy made good. David, originally from Cromness Mains Farm, is now Minister for Shellfish Harvesting & Pelagic Farms. Some political analysts consider this to be a dead-end job but David has recently given hints that he has his eye on another, more important post.

Events still to look forward to are the finals of the Tractor Pulling competition, the greasy pig competition and a visit by the world-famous sheep, Barbie, cloned by Dr Hislop of Aberdeen College of Agriculture. Later this afternoon, he will give his keenly anticipated keynote speech: Clones and Chimeras – the Physiological Constraints on Development.

Ruaridh Beag had kept his lamb carefully concealed all the way to the show. He hid its extraordinary features under a shapeless hood as he led it to its allotted pen. Once there, he arranged a tarpaulin in one corner and coaxed the sheep beneath it before slipping off to visit the beer tent and the fairground. The sheep was happy enough nibbling two turnips and bleating at itself from time to time.

Hislop strode about the show with his entourage scuttling behind him. The care of Barbie the sheep had been delegated to an underling. 'A splendid animal,' Hislop said for the umpteenth time, posing for a photo with his hand on the neck of a bull. He managed to turn a yawn into a wide smile and glanced at his watch. Forty minutes until his talk in the main tent. But he doubted if any of these people would understand a word of it. They just wanted to know if cloning could produce a sheep that would grow fast and healthy – an understanding of the processes involved was far beyond them.

He smiled at the crowd as he walked through. His smile muscles were beginning to cramp. Approaching the area set aside for sheep, he glanced back to see that Barbie was close by. He looked critically over the animals. Despite his comments to the Principal of Highlands University, he was quite well aware of the good qualities of sheep and did not expect to see anything better than Barbie. They were reasonably good specimens, healthy enough, but nothing outstanding. He shed empty pleasantries to left and right indiscriminately. Up ahead he could see a farmer, obviously inflamed by drink, arguing with an official.

'Perhaps we might go this way,' said one of the toadies, trying to lead him away from the altercation. Hislop ignored him. The voices grew louder as he approached.

'Dash it, I don't see why I have to uncover the sheep! I'll bring it out when the judges come round – not a minute before.'

'You're just making it hard on yourself, Ruaridh. Let me have a look at it, that's all I'm asking.'

'For why? We never had an inspection last year, nor any other year that I recall.'

'No, that's true. But there's special circumstances.'

Ruaridh Beag folded his arms stubbornly. Hislop paused to watch the stand-off. The official sighed and lifted a pen to his clipboard.

'Either you let me see the beast or you're disqualified.' He held his pen against the paper and looked at Ruaridh. 'I'm sorry, but that's the way it is.'

'All right, all right. But I'll be making a complaint about this, you mark my words.' Hislop had lost interest and began to walk by. Ruaridh climbed over the fence and pulled the tarpaulin to one side. The lamb lifted its two heads and bleated.

'Aha!' The official pointed at the sheep. 'Another one!' He began to make a note.

'What?' Hislop had stopped in his tracks. 'What on earth is that?' The entourage bustled up, chattering and pointing.

Ruaridh looked at him sulkily. 'It's my lamb. Bloody good lamb too.'

The official waved his clipboard at Ruaridh. 'It may well be a good lamb, Ruaridh, but she's got two heads, plain as the nose on your face.'

'But that's impossible,' said Hislop.

Ruaridh ignored him and continued his argument with the official. 'And what's wrong with that? Is there a rule that says a sheep can't have two heads?'

'Not as such, no. Not normally. But there's special rules this year...'

'Special rules! What bloody special rules are these?'

'That's not a real lamb!' Hislop's entourage had gathered around him and he turned to lecture them loudly. 'Look at this travesty, gentlemen. What an obvious fake!' He laughed, and several other academics laughed also, to keep him company. 'The genetic material simply doesn't have coding for this sort of thing! I mean, what about the two oesophaguses? Eh? How could they possibly join up? And if they did, what about the stomachs?'

The Principal of Highlands University spoke up. 'But we've all heard of two-headed calves, now and then.'

Hislop looked at him with contempt. 'Yes, of course! But how long do they live? This sort of thing,' he waved at the pen, 'I tell you, it's just impossible.'

The Principal stepped up to the fence and inspected the sheep. 'It certainly doesn't look impossible,' he said. 'In fact, it looks quite healthy.'

'It's a fabrication!'

'It certainly is not!' Ruaridh Beag had become aware of the discussion about his lamb. 'It's a merino cross blackface and I raised it myself.'

The official broke in. 'Whatever its breed, Ruaridh, it has to go into a special class. New rule. Sheep with two heads have a special category.'

'What? There's more of them?' Ruaridh's hopes of a medal faded. 'Dash me, how many are there?'

The clipboard was consulted. 'Fifteen, including yours.' He looked at the sheep again. 'But you've got a good chance, Ruaridh. That's a lovely fleece, and she has the prettiest hooves I've ever seen.'

Ruaridh beamed. 'Do you say so? Well come along with me and have a dram and I'll tell you how I got her to look so good. First of all, don't stint on the food. None of the cheap stuff, now...' They walked off.

The Principal leaned into the pen and scratched the sheep on its necks. His eyebrows lifted. 'Can't feel the join,' he said. 'Want to try?' A couple of people reached in to touch the sheep. Hislop snorted and turned away. The Principal left the pen and caught up with him. 'Well, it certainly feels like a real live sheep to me. And there are fifteen of these impossible sheep, I believe.'

'It's a clever deception, I'm sure,' said Hislop, 'but I'm not here to gawk at fairground attractions.'

'Indeed? So you won't be mentioning these sheep in your talk, then? It's all about Physiological Constraints, is it not...'

Hislop walked faster, heading for the cattle pens. The Principal followed, looking a good deal happier than he had all afternoon. They had not gone a hundred yards when Hislop stopped again, shocked out of his dignified silence.

'What in God's name is that?'

The Principal stared at the animal for a second, then gleefully hurried up and read the card on the fence. He glanced again at the huge ox-like beast and then at Hislop. 'The host-mother was an Aberdeen Angus cow, it says here. The natural parent, so to speak, was an extinct aurochs found in a glacier in the Caucasus. Quite a nice beast, don't you think? Raised by one of our local farmers, a Mr Mor.'

Hislop didn't stop to answer, but turned towards the main tent, taking a short cut through the exotic breeds section. He did not go far.

'What the hell...'

The Principal dashed in and read the card with delight. He had to shout over the chattering and astonished laughter. 'It's a woolly rhinoceros, Dr Hislop. The host mother was a pig, apparently.' He made a surprised face at the crowd. 'How unusual!' They laughed, and his smile widened. 'Oh, look,' he invented. 'It's won a rosette for the best-groomed extinct ungulate!' There was a roar of laughter. 'It's one of Mr Mor's entries again, and the DNA for this beast came from the Republic of Georgia.' He stood up and turned to face Hislop. 'We must suggest that Mr Mor gets the next one from elsewhere, don't you think? Give the woolly rhinoceros a better gene pool.'

Hislop stalked away, not even turning to look at a sheep the size of a cow.

'Mr Mor's stock, again,' shouted the Principal. 'An extinct breed called a mouflon. It's only been extinct for four thousand years, though, so it's scarcely in the same league as the eohippus over there...'

George had spent a long afternoon drifting through the Show, looking for Veronica. It was a very pleasant quest at first, his anticipation giving an edge to his enjoyment. He knew she was here, but he didn't know where. Along the way, he'd stopped at various stalls that were offering free drink – the *Inverness Crier*, for instance, was giving a complimentary whisky with every copy of their paper. The rubbish bin outside stood deep in a drift of unread newspapers. He had also drunk, at his own expense, several different beers, including one from Orkney called 'Dark Island,' and he was beginning to feel that he should slow down if he intended to last through the day.

Veronica, however, had not appeared. He wandered through the produce tent, looking at the various agricultural offerings, interspersed with choice selections of the marine harvest – line-caught sea trout at one display, a basket of lobsters at another. There was an enormous turnip on one table, with her father's name beside it, but the turnip gave no clue to Veronica's whereabouts.

Evening came on, and he began to feel a resigned disappointment. Perhaps she had gone home. Perhaps she was with someone else. He drifted despondently among the farm animals, barely looking at them. Then he stopped. In a massively built pen was a wild boar, attributed to Mr Mor of Redrock Estate. The boar's back was high and sharp, like the keel of an upturned boat, its chest was wide as a barrel and on its side was a curved white mark, like a crescent moon. It turned and looked at George. He leant on the reinforced fence and looked back. They watched each other for several long minutes.

There was something special about this beast, apart from its enormous size. Oddly enough, it looked familiar. Certainly George had seen pigs before, and he'd even seen pictures of wild boar in books, but this was different. What illustration could give the overwhelming sense of its strength, its majesty, its bristliness? And what book could even hint at its deep rich smell? There was something about its smell that George found deeply comforting, as farmyard smells can be, to those who know them well.

And then there were its eyes. They were small and bright, but did not give the impression of meanness and stupidity that went with the description 'piggy eyes'. More than anything, the shiny blackness suggested intelligence and curiosity. It stood at the back of its stall and looked at George, and George looked back at it. It was almost as if he knew this pig, knew it personally. Half an hour went by in contemplation. Now and then, the beast moved forward a step, until it was right next to the fence. George reached up his hand and laid it on the animal's head. The boar closed its eyes. George closed his.

'Careful, George. It says that the boar's dangerous.'

George shook his head clear and turned to see Veronica beside him.

'I was just looking at the boar,' he said. 'What an animal.'

Veronica looked doubtfully at the beast. It snorted and turned away. She watched its huge hairy backside shaking from side to side as it burrowed into a pile of straw at the far edge of the pen. Its powerful snout turned out soil and a couple of boulders, leaving a hollow to lie down in.

'It's an animal, all right,' she said.

George tried to find something to say.

'Eh,' he said.

Veronica smiled at him, a small smile, but encouraging.

'Eh, have you seen the aurochs?'

'No, I've been helping Clementina with her pony. A beautiful mare. It's about half the size of that boar.'

'Oh.' He couldn't think of anything to say about horses. 'Would you like to see the mouflon? It's not far.'

She laughed. 'By all means. I've got half an hour before they judge the turnips. Dad would like me to be there.' She took his arm and leant close. 'By the way,' she whispered, 'I don't even know what a mouflon is.'

He winked at her. 'It's a kind of etching.'

She laughed more than the joke was worth, and so did George, hugging her arm in his as they walked. They looked at the mouflon, and then they went on to laugh at the exotic breeds and the hand-reared lobsters. The next half hour went as smoothly and pleasantly as a burbling stream, until George saw her glance at her watch.

'Time for the turnips?' he asked.

'I'm afraid so.'

'Will I see you later?'

She turned towards him, then frowned. 'How barbaric,' she replied. She pointed at a poster hanging on fence, with the heading GREASY PIG COMPETITION.

BE IT KNOWN BY ALLE THE KING'S SERVAUNTS THT THERE SHALLE BE THYS DAY AT YE DARK ISLE SHOW, A PURSUIT FOR ALL ABLE-BODIED MEN. AFTER YE SUNSETTE, A PIGLET SHALL BE THOROUGHLIE

GREASED IN LARDDE AND SET FREE AMONG THE REVELLERS OF THE
SHOW. HE THAT CATCHETH SAID PIGGE SHALL THIS SAME DAY, AT
THE GRAND MARQUEE DANCE, RECEIVE THE TITLE OF PIG KING, AND
ALLE MUST BOWE TO HIM. FURTHER, HE SHALL RECEIVE THE SAID
PIGGES WEIGHT IN PRIME PORK, BACON AND SAUSAGES (KINDLY
DONATED BY ANDY CUMBERLAND, FAMILY BUTCHER, HARBOUR
CLOSE, CROMNESS). THYS TITLE SHALLE HE BEAR FOR THE SPACE
OF ONE YEAR, UNTIL WE, HIS FAITHFUL SUBJECTS, SHALLE GATHER
ON THYSSE SAME DAYE ONE YEAR HENCE FOR YE DARK ISLE SHOW.

'I mean, what century are we living in? It's savagery, pure and
simple.'

'I suppose it is,' said George. Pity, really. It sounded quite fun, and
he felt just about ready for some kind of physical activity, something to
prove himself. He watched Veronica's animated face as she talked about
the greasy pig.

'...when the Anti-Blood Sports League hears about this!'

Her cheeks were flushed and her black hair caught tiny electric
glimmers from the coloured lights. Green light shone in her eyes.

'Listen,' George butted in, then stopped, since he wasn't sure what he
was going to say next. 'Do you want to come over to the big marquee? I
mean, later. To the dance?'

'I'd love to, but...'

'There's some great bands playing. There's Dead Leopard and
Shooglenifty...'

'Really? They're pretty good, but...'

'I'll be going... I suppose.'

'But I've got to help Clementina with her horses...'

'Oh, well, that's all right then, it's just that...

'But after that,'

'If you'd like...'

'Damn. I forgot. I have to leave at ten. My dad's giving me a lift home.'

'Well, I could, you know. Give you a lift, if you like.'

'You've got a car?'

'It's not much of a car, but it goes.'

Veronica tried to look George up and down without him noticing. He
noticed. They both smiled. 'Yeah,' she said. 'Okay. I'd better find Dad
and let him know. I'll see you there,' she glanced at her watch, 'in an
hour, maybe two.'

'Two hours?'

'Sorry. It's just that Clementina wants me to help her groom Dander
– that's her horse.' George looked disappointed. 'Listen – if I didn't want

to come, I'd just say no, okay? But I promised Clementina I'd help. She wants to give Dander a special grooming – ribbons and pleats in the tail and everything. She says she wants her to look like a bride going to her wedding. I'll see you later, but now I've got to go.' She took his arm, stood high and kissed him quickly.

And then she was going, leaving a hint of perfume behind her.

George stood with his hand to his face, watching her. When she was out of sight he did a little dance. After a while he realised that people were looking at him. He stopped and turned to see what he could do for the next couple of hours. His stomach rumbled, and he realised how long it had been since breakfast. He thought of the food tent, where the jazz band played while farmers and their families exchanged banter and gossip: and where happy smiling waitresses brought venison, salmon and fine scotch beef to the white-clad tables.

But Veronica was a vegetarian, so George thought he had best avoid meat too, which meant there was practically nothing at all to eat in the showground. Even the standard fare of sausages, hamburgers, and bacon rolls was out of bounds.

Diagonally across the thoroughfare was the beer tent. The roar from that marquee was audible even in the constant noise of the showground. Another pint of beer would go down well, or a nip...

He heard a blurred voice blaring through the PA in the main showground. A loud roar went up from the crowd. The Greasy Pig competition was about to start! But Veronica was probably right. It was the shameful remnant of ancient rituals based on ignorance and superstition. Man debased to savagery by primitive urges. The mindless excitement. The thrill of the chase.

George pulled himself together. There seemed to be three immediate options, none of them ideal. It was meat, alcohol or the pig.

'What a dilemma,' he muttered. 'Or is it a trilemma when you've got three choices?'

A tall man with a pony-tail called from the crowd. 'Hey man! What's doing?'

'Oh, hi, Eck. Just filling in time until the bands start.'

'Hey! I'll be there too – working the sounds, you know, for the big stage. I'm on the mixing table. High energy stuff!'

'Right, Eck.' He paused, thinking that it would be only friendly to offer Eck a drink. 'Fancy a beer? They've got Dark Island on draught in there. It's really good.'

Eck shrank back from him. 'No, man,' he said, in a low voice. 'Not beer, man. Bad vibes, beer.'

George shrugged. 'A whisky, then?'

'No, man. Tell you what...' He looked around and pointed to a dark alley. 'C'mon in here and I'll give you a blast of some righteous stuff.'

George hesitated. 'You're going to preach a sermon?'

Eck grabbed his arm. 'Nah! Got some smoke off a friend. Great stuff. It's called skank, man, and it's real clean weed. Blows the top off your head without otherwise affecting you.'

Dry sand and scraps of seaweed whipped up from the beach and into Jimmy's garden. Jimmy and Le Placs made their way through the wind to the edge of the beach. Beams of light shone onto the moving surface of the sand as the helicopter swept down out of the mist and landed. The door opened and a man came running under the blades. He was carrying a package, a long thin package, with a cross-bar at one end, like a crucifix with the top part removed, or like a garden rake wrapped in brown paper. He waved to the two men, then he saw Jimmy and he halted at a respectful distance.

'Special delivery,' he shouted. 'I'm looking for ...' he checked the label on the parcel. 'Bervie-san, Harbour Cottage, Cromness.'

'That'll be for me.'

The pilot looked at the strange apparition in front of him. The tartan plaid hung in loose folds from Jimmy's waist. Below, he wore a pair of battered black wellington boots. Above the waist, he was bare, except for many strings of beads: amber beads, shells, gaudy plastic, wood. A sheet of newspaper flapped loosely at his throat. Concentric circles of paint ringed his bald head, and there was a wide red smear across his forehead.

'Are you sure?' The pilot glanced at the other man, who was much more conventionally dressed.

'Yes,' said Le Placs, 'It is he.'

The pilot did not move. 'It has to be paid for on delivery. Emperor-class high-priority air freight from Japan.'

'That's fine,' said Jimmy.

'Two thousand six hundred and seventy-three pounds and sixty-nine pence. Plus VAT.'

Jimmy stripped off the top string of beads, the dull yellow ones. 'Here. This should cover it.'

'What?'

'Take it. It's gold.'

The pilot fell back a step. 'I can't take that! I need a certified cheque, or a credit card. Or cash, even. But not a bloody string of beads.'

'This will cover the amount.'

'How the hell do I know that? I've only got your word that it's gold.'

Le Placs took the string of beads from Jimmy, stepped forwards and held them out to the pilot. 'If Jimmy says it is gold, then it is so. Here, take it.'

The pilot let Le Placs drop the rough beads into his hand. He looked at the pile of beads in surprise.

Le Placs nodded. 'Yes, it is heavy, is it not. Perhaps as much as half of a kilo.'

The man weighed the beads in his hand, brow furrowed, thinking. 'Half a kilo of gold?' He looked at Le Placs. 'Why do people bite gold coins? In films, you know?'

'Because pure gold is soft.'

The man lifted his hand and bit hard on one of the rough beads. 'Wow! It really is gold!' He stood uncertainly, not quite ready to hand over the package. 'But even if it does cover the cost...'

'Twice over, I'm sure.'

'But even so...'

'And the change is for you. A tip.'

The pilot stood perfectly still for a moment, then grinned and handed over the package. 'Okay. Sign this.' Still nervous of Jimmy, he gave the book and pen to Le Placs, who carried it to Jimmy, and brought it back.

The pilot waved and ran to the helicopter. In a minute, it had disappeared from view, its lights fading more slowly until they too were swallowed by the mist.

Where was he? And where was the toilet?

George looked around. The lights all had haloes round them. The tents had haloes round them. The people had haloes round them, and there was no sign of a toilet anywhere. His eyes sought out a dark gap between two marquees: the food tent and the craft fair, where he could hear the stalls being dismantled.

Waiting for his moment, George slipped into the dark gap, hoping that no-one had seen him, and pulled down the zip of his trousers. He leaned his head against the canvas wall of the food tent as the pressure in his bladder eased. 'Aah! Thank God!' The sound of the jazz band playing inside drowned out his voice. He tucked himself back in and stood upright. 'Veronica!' he said. He spoke louder. 'Veronica!' He reached one clenched fist up to the sky. 'Tonight you shall be mine!'

There was a lull in the music. His voice sounded embarrassingly loud. He glanced around. There was nothing but a couple of generators and some cables and empty beer cans. With the band silent, he could hear music from the side-shows, a few salesmen still trying to sell a dozen bath towels and the roar of the heavy tractors, each still trying to pull a heavier weight than the last.

He turned and lay back against the canvas of the tent. 'At least I hope she will.' He stood there in a dwam for several minutes, letting Veronica hold his attention. She had some strange ideas, it was true, but balanced against that – well, she certainly was lovely, with her long black hair, the swell of her breasts, the way she moved. But mostly it was her eyes and the way she looked at him.

What kind of look was it? As if she was curious about what he was. As if he was a cake and she was wondering whether he'd taste good. As if she was a little girl and wanted to be asked to play.

Really? Was that it? A smile spread over his face. He raised his hands in the air, and a surge of energy rose through him.

'I am the night-runner, the beast of the crescent moon! I am the mighty one, strong without equal, and I rend the flesh of the Earth that She shall be fruitful! She is my lover and to Her I go when She calls!'

He dropped his arms. What? What the hell was that about? A couple of people glanced down the dark alley as they passed. George shrank back against the tent canvas, frightened and exhilarated at the same time. He was shivering, his body shaking in deep shudders that slowly subsided. He hugged himself until his body was still. Too much to drink, he thought, as well as Eck's skank. That might also account for the lightness of spirit which he was feeling, though that was more likely due to the fact that he had at last managed to come to an arrangement of sorts with Veronica – including giving her a lift home.

Technically, the arrangement would end there, on her doorstep. But the night was young and full of song. He shivered again. There was something in the air. Something in him felt glorious tonight, majestic even. He strode back into the lights and surveyed the scene. The salesmen had nearly all gone from their stalls but the crowd was as thick as ever. The jazz band played on in the food tent and a rock band was tuning up in the stage marquee.

There was a roar of laughter near the car park and a small pig, shiny with grease, raced into sight, pursued by a crowd of yelling men.

'Go, pig! Go!' George shouted. The pig and the mob disappeared among the tents. He shook his head. 'Poor pig. No-one to save it. I bet Veronica would really go for that – if someone rescued the greasy pig. A hero.'

He listened to the sounds of pursuit. They seemed to be on the far side of the food tent. There was a confusion of shouts.

'The bugger's gone in between the tents! After him!'

'Aargh!'

'Watch out for the guy ropes!'

'Quick, he's getting away!'

'Shit! And the fucking cables!'

Right in front of George, the pig appeared in the alley between the two tents, and he knew instantly what to do. With a joyful cry, 'For you Veronica!' he leapt on the pig and rolled over with it, up against the food tent. Holding the slippery squealing beast as tightly as possible, he wriggled his way under the canvas of the tent, and into the darkness behind the podium where the jazz band were playing.

He managed to clamp one hand over the pig's muzzle, trying to keep it quiet. Outside, the bewildered pursuers shouted instructions to each other as they tried to work out where the pig had gone.

Meanwhile, George was busy. Waiting for a loud part of the music to conceal the squeals, he wrestled the pig in under his sweatshirt. The piglet was only a few weeks old, but it was stronger than George had bargained for. He struggled to hold on to it, alternating soothing phrases with profanity.

At last he managed to get it to lie quiet against his stomach, though he had to clench his elbows in against his sides to restrain its legs. He clasped his hands underneath, so that it did not sag out of the bottom of the strained sweatshirt.

Bent forward over his paunch, he stepped out from behind the stage into the crowded tent. The pig wriggled and squealed once or twice, but no-one noticed except the bandleader, who gave the trumpet player a hard look.

George headed for the far end of the tent, shuffling confidently among the tables. Then he stopped.

Very sensibly, the management had put in two doorways, one for coming in, and one for going out. George hoped to slip out without attracting attention. But there was a problem.

Police Constable MacFearn was full of community spirit. The Agricultural Show always brought out the best in him, he thought. No points duty, no officious superiors constantly checking on him – no real need to apprehend wrongdoers. Rules were relaxed for the day. If he found a couple of young men fighting, as it might be, he just loomed over them and said, 'Now, now, then. What's all this? On your way now, and don't let me catch you again.'

And the show was a friendly affair. People talked to you. 'Can you tell me how to get to the show-ring, please?' 'Got a light, mate?' 'Do you know what time the heavy horses are on?'

Better than that, was when you got the chance to become really involved. 'I wonder if you could help me, officer. I seem to have locked my car with the keys inside.' That was a good one. The wink of camaraderie as you say seriously, 'Now you're not to watch how I do this...' The bent wire, the pull, the door pops open. The amazement when they see how easy it is. A perfect chance to tell them about the benefits of steering locks and window etching.

But best of all was lost children. 'Officer, my little girl's missing. Please, please help. I don't know where she's gone!'

Then it was the country bobby approach. 'Now, now then.' That was always a good beginning. 'Calm down. Take it easy. We'll find her for you. I've been coming here for fifteen years, and we haven't lost one yet.'

Then out with the notebook. 'Now, let's have the details...'

Missing pets were almost as good. In fact, better sometimes. It was amazing how attached people were to their animals. 'Officer, my dog has run off...' 'A big dog ran away with Robbie, my rabbit...' 'My lamb's gone missing..' '...three of them, a billy and two nannies. Tormod, Eliza and Jane.' Oh yes, there was variety in animals.

And when you brought that kind of investigation to a successful conclusion, that was when you really got a bit of respect, a bit of gratitude.

Job satisfaction.

And there was always something to do. Like acting as doorman at the food tent. Just for the last couple of hours before it closed, to keep out those who had spent too much time in the beer tent.

He passed an approving eye around the busy marquee. The favoured seats, near the band, were full. Several people had dogs with them, and one family even had a pet lamb, still with its red ribbon round its neck, barely leaving room for the waitresses to pass between the tables. Despite the crush, there was no sign of trouble – the diners were either sober or still capable of behaving as if they were.

A flicker of annoyance disturbed his bonhomie. He had missed one.

In the corner of the tent, beside the band, there was a young man shuffling along. He was bent over, and obviously so drunk that he could hardly walk. It looked as if he was incapable of causing any sort of disturbance, but...

Perhaps it would be best to escort him from the premises.

'Excuse me officer, I wonder if you could help us? Do you know anywhere we could get food at this time of night?'

An elderly couple looked up at him expectantly. He glanced over at the young man. He was on his way out in any case. He turned back to the couple.

'Now, now, then. Let's see what we can do about this little problem, shall we?'

Indigent Workers' Association

The charity known as the Indigent Workingman's Association was set up by Rev Walachi Merton in the years before the First World War as a temporary measure to address the problems caused by large scale unemployment and general indigence. The IWA served two generations of workingmen through two World Wars, offering comfort and a modicum of hope to many decent men 'down on their luck.' In the general prosperity of the late fifties and sixties, the Association found its services less in demand and assumed an advisory role, which itself grew less with the widespread development of the Citizen's Advice Bureau. The IWA seemed to have outlived its usefulness.

However, the Association was saved from a premature demise by the Conservative Government and its policies. As unemployment grew to unheard-of levels in the seventies and eighties, the IWA experienced a resurgence, and now maintains a presence in every city throughout Britain.

In tune with the time, the name was changed to the Indigent Worker's Association, and the IWA policies were reviewed. Since 1976 it has no longer been necessary for clients to declare their belief in Christ as their saviour, though workers in the shelters and drop-in centres are still mainly recruited from among the clergy or the ranks of theology students.

The Inverness branch of the IWA, at No 10, Barren Sailors Alley, is currently addressing a shortfall of £50,000 and has raised an appeal for refurbishment of the premises. Donations are welcome. All proceeds from this stall go directly to the funds of the Inverness branch, and will help to keep the high standards that IWA has always maintained.

Bless you.

The crèche had been busy all day, as people took the opportunity to enjoy themselves for an hour or two without their children. It closed for business at evening, as small children reached the limit of their endurance and were taken home to recover from toxic quantities of candy floss and hot dogs. It was widely known that the tent was empty after seven o'clock, and it was used thereafter as an informal place of assignation, where amours were pursued, scores were settled in private or other less legal pursuits were followed. Next to the crèche was a food stall. Indigent Workingman's Association, said the sign above it. A small poster on the counter begged money for the association.

A few people leaned on the counter and behind it, a man dispensed coffee and burgers.

A large man wearing a battered overcoat picked up a plastic mug from the counter. 'Not goin to see the rest of the show, John?' he asked. 'There's some cracking beasts.'

Reverend John Dumfry shook his head. 'I believe I should remain here, Trevor. The IWA needs my assistance more than the show does. Should circumstances change, no doubt God will give me a sign.'

The big man guffawed. 'Jesus, you're a card, John. You shoulda been a minister.'

'Perhaps. Though I have developed some misgivings about that particular way of serving God.'

The next man in the queue elbowed his way to the counter. 'Izzat so? Well, how's about serving me? Large black coffee, two sugars.'

Dumfry smiled at him and passed him a mug.

'Fifty pence, please.'

'Fifty pence! That's robbery! That's...'

'That's how much it costs,' said Trevor. 'If you want to argue about it, how's about you and me go next door and argue in private?'

The man put down a coin and slouched away, grumbling and spilling his coffee as he went.

'Awright John?'

'Thank you for your intervention,' said Dumfry. 'It was most timely.'

'Heh, heh. You're a card, so you are.'

Over the last few weeks, Dumfry had learnt to speak in a more demotic register, so as to be more easily understood and accepted. However, when he was concentrating on other things, he naturally fell into the religious rhythms that he had been practising for years. This more sonorous, almost courtly speech, burbled out without thought, leaving his mind free to wander.

When the queue had subsided, he turned from the counter to prepare more food for later, buttering rolls, slicing tomatoes, arranging sausages and burgers on the hotplate. The work was mindless and his mind drifted.

Suddenly, with a small shock, he realised that he could see himself doing these small tasks, almost as if he was outside himself, watching. He moved upwards, and further up, surprised and delighted by this new freedom, until he was floating high above the stall.

From his empyrean, he looked down on the firefly flutter of the show, and beside it, the roadway that meandered from the Ferry Pier at Castleton. He hung in the air, watching the Dark Isle. Despite the dark, he could see the island perfectly. Indeed, by adjusting the focus of his... well, his eyes, he could see not only the surface of the ground below, but he could see behind it as well. How it used to look many years before.

Just there, the tarmac road faded back into a stone-laid track, then a rutted cart track, perhaps a century or two ago. Even then it was an old, old road. A thousand years back, if he looked carefully, it was a seasonal drovers' track, pitted by the feet of cows and sheep, muddy where it was not stony, puddled with mire in damp weather, lost in the snow of winter. And long before that, it was a path for wild animals and tough, barefooted men and women.

None of this was particularly odd – although, of course, the fact that he could see it was a little strange – but Dumfry was intrigued by one strange fact. If he looked closely enough, it seemed that the track had been there even before the land. It was there, as a tiny thread-like form in the ur-stuff of creation, before the island ever appeared, and the world had coalesced around it, shaping itself to the form of the track.

In order for the track to become manifest, it was necessary that these rocks be there, and this shallow strait be there, that the hillside should shape itself just so – and only later had the landscape been marked by the passage of feet and by the thirling of wheels.

Nor was this the only place like this. The Dark Isle had a web of tracks and roads growing out from each other, tracks which made a network that in some peculiar way seemed actually to hold together the rock and soil – and seemed also to constrain or empower the living things of the island. Not just the animals and plants, but the people too. The wind blew, the rain fell, the animals moved and the Dark Isle flexed and breathed like some enormous animal.

And there were certain places that were like anchors in the net, places more ancient still, seed-crystals from which the features of the island had grown. There was one at the Clooted Well, several along the Ardmeanach Ridge, one on top of the Suitor... With a sudden wrenching in his heart, he saw that something was happening there, on the Suitor. Something involving Doreen...

Doreen! His quest had occupied him so much that she'd slipped into the back of his mind, in the way that you forget the sun until darkness falls. Now she returned to him suddenly, with resounding force. She was there, on the Suitor. No... She would be there, sometime soon. She was doing something dangerous, something dangerous but fascinating that he couldn't quite make out. Something involving other people – Alice and another woman. He looked around, but the fog over the Dark Isle clouded his inner eye just as it clouded his physical eyes. Frantically he searched in the grey mist, calling for Doreen, desperate for any clue to her whereabouts. But the mist defeated him, coiling across his eyes. All he could see was the inexorable path that led her to the Suitor. He could not find her, he could not go to her. He wanted to weep.

Those women were going to be doing something noxious, he could tell that, but he could not see exactly what, nor what he could do to prevent it. His own quest seemed a paltry thing now, if Doreen was still in thrall to the dark arts of that heathen woman. His heart fell and he found himself once more in the stall, in front of the hotplate. He was surrounded by the smell of hot grease and onions and he had a spatula in his hand. He poked miserably at the sausages and burgers.

At the entrance to the food tent was a large policeman, full of the spirit of community policing, advising an elderly couple. George didn't want to go near that policeman. He wasn't sure if the pig was now stolen property, but he knew he didn't want to reveal its existence to the authorities. The exit was the only way out. Past the cash desk.

George edged his way towards the exit, sure that he was going to be challenged by the cashiers. What could he say? 'No I didn't have anything, thank you. I was just passing through.' Would they believe him? Would they call the waitress over to check? The pig was momentarily less restless, but delay could be fatal.

'Excuse me please.' A waitress pushed by him in the narrow aisle. The pig wriggled. George scanned the tent, desperately looking for an escape route. There was none.

Just as he gloomily accepted this fact, an idea leapt into his mind.

Amazing, he thought, how the mind works under pressure. No messing about. He staggered towards a nearby table. The perfect solution to each problem as it occurs. Thinking on your feet, that's what it is.

Miss Semple had had a good day at the show. She had managed to beat down that trader from twenty-seven pounds to eighteen for a dozen bath towels. She had also steadfastly outfaced that Glendinning woman, who after all had only married into the name, over the matter of whose household had a cook to help whom to win first prize in the cake competition, when it, the prize, that is, was properly hers.

'Mine that is,' she muttered, and glanced anxiously at the next table in case anyone had heard.

She had met all her friends, her many friends, and had told them what she thought, and about whom she thought it. And she had just finished a meal which, if it was not quite what she could have made herself, at home, without all that haute cuisine equipment, was at least augmented by a free dessert slipped onto her table by Maureen, a girl known to her, Miss Semple.

'Me, that is, myself.'

She looked up anxiously, in case of eavesdroppers, and looked right into George's flushed, sweaty face, at a distance of about ten inches.

George had seen the waitress place the bill on a saucer at the edge of the table. Clutching the pig with both elbows and one hand, he leant over and stared straight into the face of the woman at the table. The pig grunted. George had the woman's undivided attention for one second, while his free hand lifted the bill off the saucer.

'Sorry. I thought you were someone else.'

George turned and headed for the exit. At least the queue was short. He tried to hold the pig steady while groping in his pocket for money.

Miss Semple sat aghast and watched George cross to the queue. Her thought processes took some time to recover, then tumbled out from where they had been hiding.

That man was drunk! He certainly was! Disgraceful! Why do they let people in here in such a state? I shall not sit idly by and... and... I shall make a very strong complaint about this to my friend Tilda, who is one of my very closest friends and the wife of the chairman of the licensing board.

'I certainly shall!'

She glanced around anxiously, and found the waitress by her side, looking at her.

'Are you alright, madam?'

'No, Maureen, I am not. I have been... uh, just been... insulted by that horrible man in the queue there.'

'Oh Miss Semple! What did he do?'

She remembered the encounter, and shuddered. 'He looked at me.'

'Oh.'

Miss Semple glared at her. 'He looked at me from very close. And he... grunted.'

Holding the pig with one and half arms, George approached the table that served as a cash desk and leaned over to lay down the crumpled bill and a five pound note.

'Have a good meal?'

'Yes, thank you.'

The man stared at George curiously. 'You alright?'

Having regained use of his other hand, George clutched tighter at his paunch. The pig grunted.

'Uunk.'

'Beg your pardon. Stomach.'

The man looked at him sympathetically. 'I'd take it easy if I were you. Been in the beer tent?'

'Uunk.'

'God, that sounds bad! Look, do you want to sit down?'

'I'm okay.'

'Or there's the first aid tent...'

'No! I mean, I just need to get some fresh air.'

'Right, I understand. Just let me get your change.' He turned to the cash register.

'Well perhaps it doesn't sound so very bad to you, Maureen Lifferty, but I can assure you that it was not a pleasant experience. I shall make a very strong complaint to the management. Now where is my bill? I am leaving.'

'I put it in the saucer.' She pointed to the empty saucer.

'Well it's not there now. Do look, Maureen. Where can it have gone?'

Maureen looked under the table, checked the ground nearby.

'I can't see it, madam.'

'Oh this is really just too bad! Are you sure you put it there?'

'Yes. Look, I've got the duplicate here in my book.'

Already upset, Miss Semple was thoroughly vexed by this silly incident.

'For goodness sake, Maureen, if you can't find it, write me out another one.'

'Oh, I can't do that. It would put the books all wrong.' She started to check under the chairs once more. Her head came up and she laughed. 'Well, at least no-one would have stolen it.'

'That's four twenty-five, four thirty, four fifty, five pounds.'

George leant forward, trying to grab the coins without letting go of the pig.

As for the pig, it had had just about enough. Tied up, painted with lard, then chased through a mad world of lights and noise. After that, grabbed and pulled about and muzzled and stuffed into a small dark place. That small place had been warm and quite comfortable, for a while, but now all this squeezing and bending – it was more than could be asked of a pig.

As George's fingers scrabbled with the coins, the pig got its head free and tried to push it up and out of the top of the sweatshirt. Its mouth snapped open and shut.

George clamped a hand on top of the wriggling head, bending nearly double, trying desperately to control the pig. He managed to push the head down. He could hear shouting from behind him. He hoped it had nothing to do with him.

'...and then there's the Honey Bucket Chinese restaurant at the end of Market Street.' Constable MacFearn looked at his watch. 'If you hurry you should just make it.'

He waved goodbye to the couple then turned to cast a benevolent gaze over the tables in the food tent. He was feeling mellow. A good day's work, and home soon. His only minor disappointment was the shortage of lost children. Only one there had been, all day. Another couple of lost kids and it would have been a perfect day. Or an animal, of course. Lost animals were good too.

He heard someone calling. It was a middle-aged woman of less than average height and light build. She was several tables away, but coming closer.

'Constable! Constable! That man...' She pointed at the cash desk. He looked around.

There, at the head of the queue was the drunk young man. He was bent over – perhaps he was being sick. The rest of the queue were keeping back from him.

'He's taken my bill!'

He turned back to the woman. She was close enough to speak to now. He readied his reassuring tones.

'Now, now then. What's all this fuss? Bill, eh? Probably mistook it for his own pet.'

For the first time in memory his reassuring approach failed.

'How dare you speak to me like that! If you had been doing your job properly that man would not have been in here in the first place!' She pointed at the queue. 'There he is, now. I insist that you arrest him!'

George bent over once more to reach for the coins, and the pig took its chance. It lunged upwards and its small but powerful jaws fastened on the soft flesh around his nipple.

'Aaaah!'

He abandoned the money. 'Give it to the hospice!'

He staggered out the door. The pig began to squeal.

'Eee! Eeee! Eeeee!'

'Aah! Aaah! Aaaah!'

The cashier watched, mouth open, as George lurched towards the car park. He turned to his assistant and the small crowd gathered beyond. He shook his head dolefully.

As the crowd began to clear, the assistant cashier leant close.

'Did you see his stomach?' he asked in a low voice.

The cashier let out a long breath. 'I hope I may never see anything like it again.'

'It was heaving like a thing alive.'
'And those screams.' He shook his head. 'Poor man.'
There was a long silence at the cash desk.
'What did he have?'
The bill was smoothed out.
'Venison.'
'Better tell the cook venison's off.'

'He has stolen my bill, and I insist that you do something about it! Now!'
PC MacFearn tried to regain his stride.
'Very well, madam. If I could just have a description...'
'Bother it, you fool! He's getting away!' She pointed out of the doorway, where George was dodging among the crowd. 'Look, he's gone round the corner! He's heading for the car park!'
'Ah!'
Suddenly MacFearn grasped the possibilities of the situation. The young man had stolen something. He was a Wrongdoer. And he was trying to escape. A beam of sunshine seemed to light up MacFearn's features. His very favourite! Pursuit!
MacFearn threw his fifteen stones down the thoroughfare, the blood singing in his head.
A perfect day!

Jimmy and Le Placs walked back up the path to the house. They sat at the door and Jimmy began to unravel the wrapping paper from the rake-shaped parcel. 'Let's see what this is.' It did indeed contain a rake, with blued-steel tines and a bamboo handle. Jimmy nodded, not looking particularly happy. 'Ah well. I thought that's what it was. Still, it's as well to have confirmation. Now let's have a look at the letter.' From beneath the folds of his plaid, he took out a Swiss army knife and unfolded the scissors, carefully cutting a flap in the clear plastic envelope that was fixed to the wrapping. He took out a folded sheet of paper. Inside it was another sheet, smaller. He unfolded one, then the other. Le Placs glanced over at them and pointed at the larger one.
'What language is that?'
'Japanese, I think,' said Jimmy. For some time he looked at the smaller note. It said:
We regret to inform you that Suzuki-Roshi left this mortal plane several decades ago. However, since your query concerned sand-gardens, we have sent your letter to the gardening monk at Ryoanji, where he labours in the world-famous stone garden.

He put the note aside and looked at the other piece of paper. It said:

```
Haikei BERVIE-san.
    Kyôten iwaku.
    Ningen no Tamashii wa Rôsoku no honoo no yôda. Ittpon-
no-rôsoku no hi kara Tsugi no-rôsoku e to Rôsoku wa
utsuri-kawatte uku-keredo, Honoo wa itsumo onajida.
    Rôsoku wa hitotsu no yso ni suginai ga, Honoo wa
chigau.
    Tamashii wa hitotsu no yôtso dewanai to iu-koto o
shimeshite iru.
    Mata, Kyôten ni kakarete-iru-yôni, Yoi shigoto o
shitari, Kôhei de attari-suru Hito no jinsei wa, Ttsugi-
no-yo demo yahari Yoi-mirai ga hirakareru to iwarete
iru.
    Nazenara, Tamashii wa nikutai-teki-na rôdô ni eikyô
sareru to iu-koto ga dekiru kara.
    Kyôten no kotoba no haigo niwa watashi-tachi wa Shisaku
suru-koto o sokushin shinai. Kangae-sugiru-niwa oyoba-
nai to ieru.
    Watashi no tsumara-nai comments ga anata no mondai ya
Nayami kaishô no oyaku-ni tateruto iinodakeredo.
    Kono tegami o sokutatsu no air mail de okurimasu. Datte,
anataga totemo oisogi no yô-dakara. Demo, mazushii kurashi
o shiteiru watashi-tachi niwa Kono yûbin o shiharau koto
ga deki-masen, shitagatte, kore ga Uketori-nin-barai de
aru koto o kini-shinakereba iinodakeredo.
    Minasan ga Oshiawase de arimasu-yôni.
    Shigoto-jô no kyodai yori
    Tsuishin:
    Saiko no Kumade o present to-shite dôfû itashi-masu.
Anata no oshigoto no te-dasuke ni nareba to omoi-masu.
```

'I see,' said Jimmy.
'What is it?'
'I sent a letter to DT Suzuki, in Japan, asking for advice.'
'DT Suzuki?'
'Yes, you must have heard of him. Wrote a couple of books. *Manual of Zen Buddhism*, that was one. He had a lot of insight, that fellow. So I wrote and asked for advice about what we're going to do tonight. Whether we should go ahead, you know.'
Le Placs frowned. 'And what does the letter say?'

'The letter? It tells me that causes have effects, you know, but who can tell which is which. That sort of thing. Deep, I don't doubt.'

Le Placs looked down at the ground awkwardly. 'Jimmy,' he said, 'Suzuki has been dead for many years.'

'Och, I know that fine,' said Jimmy. 'I wasn't sending it to him direct. I put his name on the envelope and sent it to Japan – to the space he used to occupy. To see what answer I got.'

Le Placs smiled and shook his head. 'Well, someone has replied – but what if it had just been thrown away, and there was no answer?'

'That has meaning too. No answer is also an answer.'

'But... how did you learn Japanese?'

'I don't know a word of Japanese.'

'But, *mon Dieu*, that means that you cannot possibly understand the message.'

Jimmy laughed. 'No, no.' He waved the sheets of paper. 'This is not the answer.' He pointed to the rake. 'That is the answer.' He sighed deeply. 'It says most clearly that we must continue with the plan. I'm sorry to say that there seems to be nothing else for it. We must rake the sand.'

Cromness was quiet. Lights gleamed in a few windows, and now and then a car would drive along the streets – a young family returning from the show, children tired and whining in the back seats, or a farmer returning disappointed with livestock in his trailer. But most people would be staying until late, enjoying the cosmopolitan atmosphere, rubbing shoulders with farmers from Perth or getting the news from Portree.

A large lorry rumbled down the Dinny Hill, its headlights emerging out of the mist. It was a low loader, creeping along with a massive yellow bulldozer on the trailer. It passed the road junction where Lorraine's car was waiting to turn right.

'Who's needing a bulldozer?' asked Doreen.

'No matter. We have other things on hand.' Alice sat in the back seats, being too large for the front. 'Drive on Lorraine.'

'I don't know the road very well, and in this mist...'

'I'll direct you.'

Lorraine turned up the Dinny. Past the street lights, visibility shrank to fifty feet, then forty.

'Are you sure we should go? It's getting worse.'

'We have to go to the show.'

'But can't we do the ritual here, in Cromness?' said Lorraine. 'I understood...' Alice made an insulting grunt, but Lorraine continued. 'I understood that ritual space was outside of space and time.'

'Normally, yes. But right now, the show is the centre of all human energies – in this area anyway. And we need all the energy we can get. We don't know where the Gods are working, nor exactly what they're doing, but you can be sure there's at least Manannan and Lugh and Scathach there, and we've got to distract them. So we're going to do a ritual.'

'But surely that's just what we don't need just now, if they're getting too strong. A ritual will just give them more power.'

'It's too late for normal measures. The wasps are in the jam pot.'

'What?'

'If the wasps are in the jam pot, you put out a drop of honey. Jam is sweet, but honey is nectar. They'll leave the jam and head straight for the honey.'

'But what good will that do? It'll just make them even stronger.'

'Then we take the honey away.'

'And then they'll just go back to the jam pot.'

'Possibly. In that case, all we've gained is a bit of time. But if I set it up the right way, and if we're lucky, and if I read them right, they'll fall out among themselves, and fight.'

'Jesus!' Doreen sat up in the front seat and turned round to look at Alice. 'What do we do then?'

'Ah. Then we have to be very careful not to get stung.'

Doreen looked at Alice with awe. 'For God's sake, Alice! What kind of a plan is that?'

'It's the best I can come up with.'

Doreen began to laugh. 'Well, I bet Lorraine can run faster than you, and when the time comes, I'm damn sure I'll be well ahead of her.'

The car groaned up a hill. The damp branches of birch trees hung at the edges of the road. The car reached a junction. 'Which way?'

Doreen looked uncertain. 'Left I think. That was the Dinny, wasn't it?'

Alice snorted. 'We went up the Dinny ages ago. That was the Petty Hill. We need to go right.'

Doreen shrugged. 'If you say so.'

The car turned right, descending into a valley by way of a single-track road with hairpin bends.

Doreen laughed. 'Petty Hill is it? This is the Corkscrew Road. We're on the wrong side of the Island!'

Alice grunted from the back. 'Well, just keep on. We can turn up onto the Ardmeanach road when we get to Boblair.'

The car whined down the hill in low gear. Lorraine's hands were tense on the steering wheel. Her dipped headlights showed only a few feet of the road ahead. Beyond that, the mist made a brilliant white barrier, throwing the light back at them. The wall of mist twisted and swirled sluggishly as if it was about to turn into something hideous. Tendrils of thicker mist rose over the parapet of the bridge and lay across the road. They seemed to caress the car as it passed through, oozing through the windows and into the car.

Doreen shivered. 'It's cold.'

'There's a blanket in the back.'

'So there is,' said Alice. She spread the blanket over her legs and tucked the edges in around her thighs. 'That's better.'

'Thanks,' said Doreen, looking at Lorraine. 'That was thoughtful of you.'

'Don't mention it.'

Alice glowered. 'Can't you go a bit faster?'

'It's the mist,' said Lorraine. 'And the roads are so twisty. I hope it's not like this all the way to Castleton.'

The car crested the hill and drove onto a straight road with moorland on each side.

'What the hell are you doing, girl? Where are we?'

'I don't know! I've just been following your directions.'

'No you haven't! You've got it wrong.'

'No, Alice. She did exactly what you said.' Doreen looked around her, though little was visible beyond the road verges. 'But I haven't a clue where we are now.'

A crossroads appeared out of the mist. There was no signpost. Lorraine stopped and waited silently for instructions.

'Well, I think we should go left here.'

'Or right? Or possibly straight on.'

A long mournful wailing sounded over the moorland.

'My god! What's that?' Lorraine's hands gripped the steering wheel hard. Her knuckles were white. The sound came again, and was answered by another long moan.

Doreen laughed. 'Got it! I know where we are. We must be on the moor beside Redrock estate. That'll be one of Mr Mor's animals. He's got bison and all sorts roaming the estate.'

'Maybe. In that case, try the right. It should take us to Nativvy. If not, it'll be...'

'Glen Grian?'

'Yes. Probably.'

'I'm just the driver.' Lorraine turned right. There was a tense silence in the car for a few minutes, then the car drove past a pine tree, then another, then they were deep in a pine forest. On the left, a metal pipe spouted a stream of water into a carved stone bowl. The trees round about were festooned with ancient scraps of cloth and newer bits of clothing: neckties, bras, socks, scraps of cloth.

'It's the Clooted Well! How did we get here?'

Lorraine was leaning forward, her face close to the windscreen, trying to peer into the mist. She ignored the heated discussion between the others. As she drove, the trees disappeared, and they were once more at a crossroads. 'Is this the same place? It looks the same. Shall I try the left this time?'

'Stop! Stop right now! Something's far wrong.'

'I know that! But it's not my fault, right? I'm just the driver.' Lorraine pulled to a halt, the headlights shining back from the mist.

'We're being bamboozled,' said Alice. 'But how? Something is directing us, stopping us from getting to the show.'

'I can feel it,' said Doreen. 'Something is turning us the wrong way. It must be Them.'

Lorraine spoke with a tremble in her voice. 'Them? Are you sure?'

Doreen looked worried. 'But how could They know? We did everything we had to, didn't we?'

'But, wait a minute...' Alice sat and thought. 'Turn off the engine.'

Lorraine reached out for the ignition key, then stopped. The engine sound was a comfortable purr in the grey evening, the warmth from the car heater kept more than the physical chill at bay. 'Why?'

'Please. I need to think.'

In a state of shock, Lorraine turned off the engine. Silence poured into the car like a physical thing. 'Well, what now?'

Alice held both fat hands in the air. 'Quiet for a moment. Please.'

The mist swirled glacially at the windows. Chill crept into the car. Alice stared unseeing into the distance. 'Can't you feel it?'

'Yes,' Doreen whispered. 'Something's here. It's close. Very close.'

'We have to know what it is,' said Alice. 'Look carefully.'

Lorraine reached up with both hands to rub the crawling skin on the back of her neck. 'Stop it,' she said quietly, her voice shaking.

Doreen turned round to face Alice. When she spoke, her voice was charged and vibrant. 'Alice? It's us, isn't it.' The sound cut through the silence in the heart of the fog. Lorraine looked up in shock and saw Doreen as if for the first time, the fierce intensity in the way she held her head, as if waiting for something to pounce on, to hold. She looked like a predator. Her eyes gleamed in the dim light.

'Oh Christ,' Lorraine breathed. Alice and Doreen had locked their eyes. Lorraine could feel something in the air between them, invisible but almost palpable in the cramped car. Something that was not physical, but sent fear through every part of her body. She fumbled behind her, reaching for the door handle. 'Get out of this, get out,' she whispered.

Her hand grasped the handle, but she was too weak to pull it.

'No.' Doreen reached out and touched Lorraine's arm.

Lorraine flinched and pressed back against the car door. 'Leave me alone!'

Doreen turned to face her. 'It's all right. It's all right, Lorraine. It's just us. You and me and Alice. We're doing it.' She reached out with both hands and held Lorraine's face gently. 'It's us. You can relax.'

Lorraine's muscles unclenched and a deep breath flowed into her body.

'That's right. It's just us.'

'Us.' Lorraine breathed out, and a great sense of relief filled her. 'But how can we be doing it?'

'There's you and me and Alice here, and individually we don't know bugger all. Then there's the three of us together, and all together we make a different person, one that knows things that you and I don't, and can do things that none of us can do by ourselves. There's all three of us together. And perhaps not just us.'

'Not just us,' said Alice, firmly. 'Others are here with us, helping.'

'We're linked together, and because of that, we know more than we know,' said Doreen. 'We're in charge. All together, we've got the power.'

Lorraine looked up eagerly. 'A gestalt consciousness?'

Alice snorted, but without the normal amount of vituperation. 'Call it whatever you like.'

'We has taken over and it's steering us somewhere. We don't want us to go to the show, that much is obvious.' Doreen gestured at the featureless murk outside the car. 'We just have to assume that we know where we are going. So let's go.'

Lorraine nodded, and started the car. The headlights lit the three roads ahead. 'Which road?'

'I don't know,' said Doreen. 'But we do.'

'Yes, we do, don't we.' Lorraine laughed, chose a road and drove into the mist.

Alice said nothing.

After a while, Doreen said, quietly, 'Alice?'

'What?'

'You said please.'

Lorraine laughed. 'She's right. In fact, you said it twice!' Doreen and Lorraine giggled together as the car drove on.

Alice said nothing.

The low-loader rumbled along the narrow streets of Cromness, and stopped at the bank. Leaving the engine running, the driver climbed down and knocked on the heavy oak door. A thin man in a dark suit opened it. There was a very sour look on his face.

'I'm looking for a Mr Siller.'

'I am he. And you must be Mr Grigor. I perceive that you have brought your bulldozer with you.'

'Aye. That's it on the trailer.'

'So I see. It was supposed to be here this morning.'

The driver shrugged. 'Nothing to be done. The traffic's been snarled since this morning. You know what it's like when the Show's on.'

Mr Siller's mouth pursed. 'I specified the time in our original contract.'

'Eh? What contract?'

'A verbal contract...'

'Oh. One of them.'

'And a verbal contract is, as I'm sure you know, considered binding. And when I make a contract, I expect all parties to keep to the terms of that contract.'

'Bloody hell! It wasn't my fault!'

'In consequence of which I feel well within my rights in requiring you to work late.'

The driver pulled himself upright. 'Not tonight, I don't. Any other night I might have said yes, but I've got business at the show.'

'Then it will have to wait.' Although Siller was half the bulk of the driver, he stood like a rod of iron before him. The driver hesitated before Siller's unbending determination.

'Come on. This is the Show. Be reasonable.'

'I assure you, I have the law on my side in this.'

The driver hesitated, looked around, then bent forward conspiratorially. 'But do you have the League of Ancient Horsemen on your side? That's what I'd ask myself.'

Siller looked taken aback. 'What do you know of them?'

The driver smiled a broad smile. 'I have two words for you, Mr Siller. Horse. Ritual. And I'm the First Stableboy.' He put his hands in his pockets and sucked air in past his teeth. 'I'd like to oblige you, but you know what the Horsemen are like. When they call out "First Stableboy, advance and loosen the harness," and I'm not there – well, my life's not going to be worth tuppence. You see how it is.' Seeing that Mr Siller had no answer to this, he continued. 'So I'll have to be off. I'll be back first thing in the morning.'

'But that will be too late. I will have no use for it then.'

'You mean I've just got to take it away again?'

'Indeed. And I don't expect to be charged for this.'

'Damn. Well, I'd better uncouple it anyway.' He glared balefully at Siller as he leant over to let down the jacks on the trailer.

'You can't leave it here! It will block the street.'

'So where do you suggest? I'm not taking it back along the Dark Isle tonight – it was difficult enough getting here.'

'One moment.' Siller looked thoughtful. 'Perhaps after all it may be of some use.' He lifted an overcoat from a hook and came out, locking the door behind him. 'You can leave it on Kirk Road tonight. I'll guide you.'

The truck crawled along the narrow streets. There was no other traffic.

'There. Beside the Vennels, just before The Fisherman's Arms.'

Siller stood on the pavement and watched silently as the driver jacked up the trailer and uncoupled the cab.

'I'll be back first thing in the morning,' he said.

'Good. But there is no hurry. I daresay you might want to have a drink with some of your friends, the Horsemen. So just turn up whenever you can.'

Grigor looked at him suspiciously, unable to fathom Siller's sudden bonhomie. Then he shrugged, climbed into the truck and drove off with a parting wave.

As the rumble of the engine faded into the night, Siller approached the trailer and studied the battered yellow bulldozer. It couldn't be too difficult to drive. A check of the street assured him that there were no observers. He stepped up onto the trailer, climbed up on the caterpillar treads and opened the door.

He smiled to himself. In a few minutes, the first of these pestilential hovels would fall, and by morning, there would be nothing left of the Vennels but rubble on a development site by the waterside. Let the Council make of that what they could.

He sat down in the seat and closed the door. He grimaced. The cab smelt of sweat and tobacco and diesel. But there was plenty of room. The controls were laughably simple, no more than a few levers. There remained faint traces of a white arrow on the knob of one lever. That one was probably for lifting the bulldozer blade. Up and down, that's all that was needed. Perhaps up and down and tilt? That would be two of the levers. So what were these other ones for?

As he looked from one to the other, he realised why there was so much space in the cab.

Where on earth was the steering wheel?

Beginning to panic, he looked more closely at the dashboard, then around him, to left and right, on the floor, even behind him on the rear wall. There was no ignition key either. There wasn't even a keyhole.

Desperately he began to search the cab for an instruction manual.

Somehow, George staggered through the show to the car park. He leant over the car boot so that his weight would restrain the pig, and turned the handle.

'Grab the little swine by the hind trotters just so, milad. Lift boot lid, swing piggy forward and drop him in. Close the lid, and one more victim of agrarian exploitation is saved! Wahey!!'

He jumped into the air with his fist jabbing at the sky. And that was when PC MacFearn's fifteen stones took him in a flying tackle, threw him a long way to the ground, and landed on him.

MacFearn lay across his captive and smiled. The perfect capture. Of course, it was no contest really. These young lads didn't know what they were letting themselves in for.

A groan came from beneath him. He rolled off and stood up.

'Now, now then,' he said severely, and readied himself for a formal address. 'I have information that leads me to believe that you are in possession of stolen property. May I ask you to unlock the boot of your car?'

'Argh.'

'I beg your pardon?'

'It's not locked.'

MacFearn turned the handle, lifted the lid.

'My God, it's a pig!'

George was trying to get up, favouring the side with the broken rib.

'Well of course it is. What else would it be?'

'I didn't know, really. But I didn't expect a pig.'

MacFearn tried to imagine a middle-aged woman of less than average height and light build keeping a pig as a pet. Just an ordinary pig. He shook his head. He'd heard of it happening in London, but they were foreign swine.

Still, an animal was an animal. He hadn't had an animal today, so this rounded the day off nicely. And it was a rescue too, not just a finding. He felt warm and benevolent.

He picked up the pig, which had been thoroughly cleaned of lard by the fluffy interior of George's sweatshirt, and stuck it under one arm. It squealed once. He patted its nose and told it that it was a good boy.

'All right, lad.' He looked closely at George. 'Don't I know you? It's Stevan, isn't it?'

'George,' George mumbled. 'George MacLear.'

'Oho! Think you can get one by me, eh? It's Stevan MacCormack, right? Never forget a face! Now, then, come along with me.'

MacFearn shortened his stride to match George's shamble.

'Now it's up to the lady whether we press charges or not, so you be nice to her. Understood?'

'I didn't know it was hers.'

'Oh don't you try that on with me! You're in trouble, milad, and no mistake.'

George groaned. A rib on the other side seemed to be broken too.

MacFearn relented a little. 'We should be able to keep it out of the courts. You had been drinking, I suppose?'

George nodded.

'A bit of youthful folly, eh? Won't do it again, I shouldn't think?'

'No chance.'

The pig snuggled its way into MacFearn's armpit. He chuckled. 'I can see why she keeps it. It's an affectionate wee soul.'

George kept silent. It seemed best.

'Do you think he'll catch him, madam?'

'He most certainly will, Maureen.'

Miss Semple was having a good day. From the depths of adversity she had wrenched something... something better than adversity. She would tell Victoria Glendinning about this. She remembered their earlier disagreement. Never mind. She would forgive Victoria and then tell her the story. 'Stole my bill and expected to get away with it, would you believe it. Didn't know who he was dealing with, you see.'

Miss Semple, feeling magnanimous, smiled graciously at Maureen. 'Thank you so much for your help, Maureen.'

She turned and smiled vaguely in the direction of the car park. The policeman was on his way back now with the prisoner. She was glad to see that the young man was coming peacefully. Though it was scarcely surprising. The constable was a powerfully built man. So reassuring, so dependable. We are safe while we have such guardians of the law.

But why was he carrying a pig?

Baldy's attention was drawn by the sound of Mr Mor's voice. He'd never heard him talk like this, well, only once, at the Ladies Guild in Cromness. But now he was in full flight. The words were muffled, outside the tent, but Baldy had heard mention of the shipyard at Boblair, the Holiday Village around Rossmarty, and now he'd started on the Primaeval Park.

At that point, the excited chatter from inside the tent grew into a torrent and Baldy could restrain himself no longer. He looked around quickly. He was supposed to be guarding the tent, keeping the meeting secure. But everything was fairly peaceful here on the outskirts of the tented town. Small groups of people plodded through the mud, laughing and talking. The occasional couple drifted along arm in arm, intent on one another and watching out for the possibility of a hidden place where their romance might express itself in a more intimate and physical fashion. The main crowds, and most of the drunken marauding hordes of farmboys, had moved over to the fairground and the big Marquee, where loud music was playing accompanied by flashing lights that shone through the canvas, visible even in the mist.

Baldy parted the tent flaps and risked a look inside. Mr Mor was standing at one side of the long table which had been made by pushing a few trestles and planks together. The MP, David MacLing, was at the head of the table, watching Mr Mor with something close to awe. The dozen or so people around the makeshift table were interrupting with comments and occasional cheers. Alma Keivor was standing, which meant that she was about the same height as those sitting, and she was leaning over the table towards Mr Mor, demanding figures and explanations and assurances. Her bosom was more than normally protuberant, due to her posture, and although Mor was oblivious to this, the councillor for Rossmarty was not. He excitedly encouraged Alma, and even patted her on the back once, this being the most physical contact he could risk in the crowded tent.

Mr Mor was gesticulating over a map of the Dark Isle as he spoke.

'...at the edges and the boar will clear the ground. Up here, on the Ardmeanach Ridge, we can release the mouflon. They are tough enough to stand the conditions.'

A big red-faced farmer spoke up. 'They're bloody great big sheep, aren't they? They'll eat all the growing trees. I mean, look at bloody Sutherland – half of the bloody Highlands, come to that. Sheep deserts. So you'll need fences, won't you, or there goes your natural regeneration.'

'I don't think so. They won't stray far.'

'What's to stop them then, eh?'

'The wolves and lynx, lurking in the woods.' The farmer subsided as Mr Mor continued. 'At Boblair Loch I think we've room for a few woolly rhinoceros. We can't allow too much breeding, though. My man tells me that the gene pool is too small at the moment.'

As people crowded round to study the map, he drew an antique snuff box from his pocket and took a pinch of white powder from it. Down the length of the table, he caught Sammy Poach's eye and winked, then snuffed deeply at his fingertips. He closed the lid with a snap and tucked the box back into a waistcoat pocket.

'Anything else? Oh yes. Eohippus on the Blackadder Bog. We'll have to divert the road, but it's worth it.'

'Eohippus?'

'Yes. Small primitive horses. Extinct, except for the one in the stall here. They're not as spectacular as the aurochs, but we'll get plenty of kudos from the academics for breeding them.'

'Kudus? Aren't they a small gazelle? African, surely. How will they fit in?'

Mr Mor glanced at the Principal of Highlands University, dismissed both the man and the question as unimportant, and continued with barely a pause. 'This wildlife park will have real wild life. As little intervention as possible.'

'And what do you expect to get out of it?'

Sammy Poach spoke quietly, but everyone heard. Most of them did not know who he was or why he merited a seat at the table, but Mr Mor and MacLing seemed to know him, and that was enough. Alma Keivor, who knew him as a rather disreputable body around the streets of Cromness, was baffled by his presence and a little nervous, though she did not show it.

Mr Mor smiled. 'The Dark Isle Republic and all its citizens will benefit from Independence – and I intend to benefit also. Once we are free of the strangling bureaucracy of the Scottish Parliament, I expect to become rich, as will all the farmers and landowners whose land will become part of the Primaeval Park or the Rossmarty Holiday Village or any of the other developments which are planned. I intend to exploit all the relaxed rules of the new Republic to the utmost. For instance, when we legalise recreational drugs...' There were a few murmurs of dissent. '...as I believe we should, then I will no doubt develop connections in that area. These opportunities will of course be available to everyone. Relaxed banking rules will attract money and investment...'

'And these relaxed laws will also attract sharks of all sorts, the vermin that prey on honest folk!'

'He's right. What's to stop the Dark Isle becoming a haven for criminals and other riff-raff? I think you know the kind of people I mean.'

Mr Mor nodded towards Inspector Morrison, who had put aside his uniform and was dressed in an inconspicuous tweed suit. 'Our new head of police will be up to dealing with any problems, though I doubt we'll have many. Unjust and inappropriate laws create criminals.'

'I see,' said Alma Keivor, rather acidly. She leant forward so that she overhung the table. The Rossmarty councillor watched her in awe. 'Perhaps we should abolish the laws against stealing, so that we have no thieves?'

Mr Mor nodded. 'A radical suggestion, Mrs Keivor, but I think that's a matter for the new government, after the elections.'

'I wasn't being serious!'

'In that case, perhaps I might continue?' Mor took another pinch from his snuffbox. 'Prosperity will attract investment, and if we can restore half of the Dark Isle to a state of primaeval forest, a nursery and a sanctuary for extinct animals – most of you have seen at least one of the animals that we have cloned or grown from frozen ova? Yes? How did you feel? As if you were remembering something from the distant past, from a time when men were giants and walked the earth as demigods! And those times will come again! Neitzche was not daring enough! We are as gods, and...' He paused and looked around at the faces, some bemused, some enthralled. He shrugged. 'Purely in commercial terms, people will come from the other side of the world to see a park with wild animals from thousands of years ago. We already have lynx, aurochs, mouflon, giant beaver – and that's just the small fry.'

Mr Mor reached into his wallet and pulled out a sheaf of photos. 'I've been keeping this one back.' He handed the photos around, then pulled a cigar from his pocket and lit it as people ogled the photos in amazement.

'Good god!'

'It's a...'

'A bloody mammoth!'

'Yes. A mammoth. Well, mostly a mammoth. Her genes weren't complete, so we had to splice her DNA in with an Indian elephant. But she's the best mammoth in the world and she's called Buttercup.' Mr Mor beamed around the table. 'She was over fifty pounds at birth. She's still a baby, but she's doubled her weight in the last few weeks.'

'But where did you get her? And the others?'

'We cloned them from the remains of tissue from dead animals. Some of our first successes came from the Hog Graveyard in Cromness, where we obtained DNA from Lord Farquhar's champion pigs – he embalmed them before burial, so they were still in remarkably good condition. But more recently, we have used frozen ova and tissue samples from the remains of animals dead for thousands of years. When the last Ice Age descended on us, it came so fast that many animals were frozen solid before they had time to decay. They've been in cold storage for thousands of years, some of them locked in chunks of ice. Most of the cells are damaged, but if you search long enough you can find good ones, where the DNA is usable. We brought some samples here – from the republics that used to be part of the USSR, for the most part. Georgia, Kazakhstan, Siberia – and then we cloned them, with cows or pigs for host mothers.'

'Mr Mor, this is amazing! I had no idea that it was so easy!'

'Easy?' Mor laughed. 'It's not easy. There are only a handful of people in the world that could perform such a miracle. Fortunately we have one of them – a very distinguished scientist – working for us.'

'Hislop?'

'Oh no, not that clown. One of his rivals. His biggest rival. You can probably guess who I mean.'

'Not Wilmot!'

'I'm saying no more.'

The red-faced farmer spoke up. 'But how did you get the samples into this country? The regulations I have to face, just to export meat these days...'

Mr Mor drew on his cigar and blew out a plume of smoke. 'I have my own lines of communication.' He looked over at Sammy, who looked back without saying anything.

'Can you clone other animals, Mr Mor? Dinosaurs?'

'Not dinosaurs, no. Can't get the cell samples. They've been dead too long.'

'How about a sabre-toothed tiger? Why don't you get one of them?'

'We don't plan on it.'

'Too dangerous, are they?'

'No, not exactly.'

'Then why not? Hell, everyone loves an enormous predator. At a distance, of course. And look at those huge teeth! Terrifying!'

Mor nodded. 'Like walrus tusks, aren't they?'

'That's right. Great big buggers.'

'Well, think for a moment about those huge teeth. What could the tiger have done with them? It could possibly leap at a deer and stab it to death with them, but what then? Those teeth are like the bars of a cage, and its mouth is behind those bars. How's it going to bite off bits of deer? In fact, I don't think it did. It didn't have to. The walrus uses its tusks to dig out oysters and clams from the sea bed, and I suspect the sabre-toothed tiger did much the same, ambling along the beach digging cockles and razorfish from the mudflats. Perhaps we can get one for the kiddie's cuddle corner later on, but first we want to establish a functioning ecosystem.'

There was a general disappointment at this revelation about the diet of an extinct big cat. In the silence, David MacLing spoke. 'Any other business? The balloon goes up in less than two hours, and everything has to be ready. How about you, Aristide?'

Aristide Coupar sucked air in over his teeth and shook his head dubiously. 'I'm sure I can manage, but I wish Barry and Maria were here.'

MacLing looked up the table. 'Barry Ellis is in charge of the fleet, or was supposed to be, but he went missing a couple of days ago.'

Aristide smiled grimly. 'Barry, in charge? In a way. But it's Maria, really. She's the power behind the throne.'

MacLing frowned. 'But Barry is the union representative, isn't he? And he runs his own business?'

'Aye, I suppose that's true, but it's Maria that planned it all – and she invented Barry too. So they say.' Everyone leant forward to catch this piece of gossip. Aristide lowered his voice so they all had to lean further. 'When she met him, he was selling insurance. He wasn't very good at it, either. She said to him, "If you grew a beard you'd look like a sea captain. Do you fancy a job?" Groomed him and taught him how to run a forty-foot launch. And how to talk like a sea-captain. That's the story I heard, any rate.'

'But we can manage without them, can't we?' asked MacLing. 'Are the fishermen ready?'

'They'd better be.' Aristide looked around the table. 'Now let's be clear about this. The entire strategy depends on the fishermen. It will only work because this is an island and we can control the seaways.'

The farmer waved a hand. 'Yes, yes. Of course. That's understood.'

'I hope it is,' said Aristide, 'because farmers couldn't do it. And neither could politicians.' He didn't have the nerve to face Alma, so he looked at the Rossmarty councillor, who nodded appeasingly.

'Of course.'

'So I want to feel that we're being appreciated. Do you understand?'

'Of course,' said David MacLing. 'Appreciation for the fishermen is the first thing on the list of priorities. We'll claim a fifty-mile exclusion zone around the Dark Isle. Island fishermen only. There will be farmers in Moray that can't even fish in their own streams.'

'Well, I'm sure we'll come to some arrangement with them,' said Aristide. 'But fishing's not an easy life you know, and it's getting harder all the time. Every bastard with a boat big enough to carry a net is in our waters, taking our fish, while the Ministry of Agriculture and Fisheries leave us sitting on the shore twiddling our thumbs. We're only allowed to fish for half the year! How's a man meant to make a living at that, I ask you!'

'But they are ready and waiting?'

'Yes. We've got at least one sober man on each boat.'

'And they're all set for midnight?'

'Yes, right after the Horse Ritual.'

'Of course. At midnight you and your hand-picked crew will slip the ropes on the causeway and then...'

'Correct.' Aristide looked down the table. 'I rigged the boats up specially so that we can dismantle the causeway in about fifteen minutes.'

One or two people nodded approvingly. 'It's all down to the ropework, you see. Not many people know their knots these days, even fishermen. Sad days, sad days. Anyway,' he continued, 'I had to use the Turkoman's Bladder at the bow, secured with a Slipping Dreadknot. But, here's the secret, I tied a double Snakeline at the stern, so when you take the tension off the standing end it will come undone as sweetly as you please. My dad showed me that trick, for getting to sea fast when you're in a stack of boats at the quay.'

MacLing butted in. 'And then? After you have loosened the ropes...'

'Oh, right. Then the ferry captain will tow a section of ten boats to blockade Castleton harbour. I'll lead half the boats myself and we'll deal with Rossmarty, Redrock Bay and the other wee ports on the south side, then on to Cromness. Barry should have been setting up the blockade along the North coast, but the skippers will just have to work on their own initiative.'

'Let's hope it works. And Mr Mor's men...'

'They're ready,' said Mor. 'Every radio and TV mast on the island will be in our hands within a few minutes of midnight. I also have a man dealing with Rossland FM, and that's where we'll broadcast our announcement, right after midnight.'

The Rossmarty councillor spoke up. 'How will he get in? I hope there won't be any violence.'

'Of course not.' Mr Mor waved his cigar and grinned. 'He's just going to pick up a T-shirt that he won in a competition last week.'

'Oh, was that the competition where you had to identify strange noises?'

'I heard that one! They were dead easy – except for the last one. It was a bit tricky. I think it was a farmer sitting down in a padded tractor seat.'

'Nonsense! It was a cork extractor thingy. One of those where you pump air in.'

Mr Mor broke in. 'And I also have it on good authority – perhaps I should have mentioned this earlier, Inspector Morrison – that some unidentified vandal has been tampering with the power supply to the Highlands Police Communications Centre.'

Inspector Morrison frowned. 'It might fail at an awkward moment, is that what you're saying? Such as during the coup? Not to worry. It will seem a relatively trivial matter by this time tomorrow, and in any case I'll be far too busy elsewhere. And that brings me to another matter. I understand that all police officers are to be retained?'

David MacLing frowned. 'Yes. Otherwise we wouldn't have the support of the Public Service Unions. Haven't we dealt with this already?'

'It wouldn't be possible to make an exception for one Constable MacFearn?'

'Afraid not.'

'Damn. Well, I suppose I'll just have to post him somewhere harmless.'

Alma Keivor coughed. MacLing turned to her. 'Mrs Keivor?'

'I have ensured that local retailers have been discreetly apprised of the situation. I told them that central government were bringing the New Year forward by four months. They have all stocked up on essentials to get us through the period of disruption. Black bun, shortbread and whisky. And in case of hardship, our ladies at the guild have volunteered to run a soup kitchen. For which I think they deserve a vote of thanks, by the way.'

'I'll note that, Mrs Keivor.'

The Principal of Highlands University held up his hand. 'I've got a team of postgraduate computing students working on electronic voting forms and a tamper-proof system. Full encryption and... and things like that.'

The Rossmarty councillor spoke again. 'Students, eh? Are they up to the job?'

'Of course! They are graduates, you know.'

'From Highlands University?'

'Yes.'

'Are you sure they're up to the job?'

'I resent your implication! Anyway, we've got Andy MacInnes supervising. He's back from Oxford to visit his mum and he said he'd help out. Is that good enough for you? He knows computers from the bottom up.'

'So he should. He started off designing mouse mats, didn't he?'

MacLing stepped in once more. 'Please, I'm sure the principal has it in hand. Now, if we have no more business? Then good luck everyone, and a toast.' From a side table he brought over a tray of glasses and a forty-ounce bottle of Glen Grian. He poured a glass for everyone and they raised them together. 'We wake tomorrow to a new Republic!' They all cheered and drank it down.

'I don't think we are dealing with a hardened criminal here, Miss Semple. I think it was just youthful high spirits. And he said it was all due to an extra drink he had that he shouldn't have had.'

Constable MacFearn was having a wonderful time. A pursuit and apprehension and a rescued pet. And now the icing on the cake: a bit of negotiation, bit of street justice. He looked around. Well, showground justice. Anyway, keeping the young lads out of trouble until they're old enough to know better.

'Oh, and he said he was sorry and he won't ever do it again. Isn't that right?'

George nodded his head. 'Oh yes. That's what I said, all right.'

'So it's up to you, madam. Do you wish to press charges?'

Miss Semple savoured the moment. She was in charge. She could send this young man to prison if she desired, with just one word. Or she could give him one last chance to mend his ways.

'Young man.'

George lifted his head, tried to look alert.

'I think that your behaviour was thoroughly reprehensible... but if you promise never to do it again...'

'Absolutely. Never again.'

'Then I shall not press charges.'

George felt a surge of relief.

'Okay, lad. You got off with it this time. Be on your way now.'

George turned and tried to jog away into the crowd. 'Argh!' He tried to walk. 'Argh!' He stumbled as fast as he could, looking for a bolt-hole to hide in until the misunderstanding cleared itself up.

MacFearn and Miss Semple watched until he was out of sight.

'I hope he's learnt his lesson.'

'I hope so too, constable. Now, could I have my bill please?'

'Of course, Miss Semple. I almost forgot I had him.' He lifted the pig up to his face and rubbed its little wet nose with his own. 'Who's a good boy, then? Time to go back to mama, Bill.'

He held out the pig to Miss Semple. She stepped back.

'What on earth do you think you're doing?'

Something was wrong. This was the bit where the owner should fall on the pet with cries of joy, and wonder how she could ever thank MacFearn enough. MacFearn offered the pig again. 'It's yours, isn't it?'

'What?!' Dreadfully wrong.

'This is your Bill.'

'It most certainly is not!'

All the pleasure ebbed away. He felt tired.

'Please, madam, just take the pig and go home. We've all had a long day.'

'But it's not mine!'

MacFearn's patience came to an end. He roared in rage.

'It must be, you silly woman! It was the only pig he had!'

Aristide and Mor went out together, discussing details of the Horse Ceremony. 'After you're welcomed into the sacred enclosure, you'll be given a potion to drink,' said Aristide. 'It's just part of the tradition. A few harmless local herbs like Venus Nightwort.'

'Not psychedelic, is it?'

'No, no. A sustaining and fortifying drink.'

Alma left alone, but closely trailed by the Rossmarty councillor who was as smitten as a puppy. Others left in singles or pairs, not to make a conspicuous crowd in this quiet part of the showground. At last only Sammy and MacLing were left.

'Well?' asked Sammy.

'Well, what?'

'Well, why did you get me involved?'

'Me? What's it got to do with me?'

'Come on. Mr Mor catches me poaching and the next thing he's asking me to be part of the interim government of the Dark Isle. he wouldn't have let me in without pressure from someone.'

MacLing smiled, and something of his success as a politician was revealed. It was a genuine smile, and his face shone for a moment as though there was a light beneath his skin. 'All right, I admit it. I asked him to watch out for you. In fact, I told him that I'd have nothing to do with the scheme unless you were on the committee.'

'Why?'

'Because I owed it to you and the island. I know we don't see eye to eye...'

Sammy snorted.

'...but I wanted someone honest among us.' He shrugged ruefully. 'I have become a little too much of a politician, I'm afraid. I have to listen to Torquil more than I like. He keeps his eye on the political weather and advises me which way to trim my sails. And Alma Keivor and the other councillors are in similar case. More interested in looking good than doing good, more interested in power than responsibility. Mor is a business man with flexible ethics, if indeed he has any at all. Aristide is representing the Seamen's Union, and puts their concerns above all else. As he should, of course. But there's too much politics, too little principle. And this is a once-in-a-lifetime chance. It's too important to be left to vested interests and politicians.'

'Damn it, I have my own political convictions, you know!'

'Don't I remember? Sammy, I wouldn't ever have left the farm if it wasn't for you. I'd have been nothing more than a farmer's son and then a farmer...'

'And happy with it.'

'Probably. But there are more important things.'

'So you think you're doing more important things?'

'Sammy, please. I know you weren't pleased with the way things worked out, and I'm sorry. It just became obvious that World Revolution was not going to happen, not in my lifetime anyway. But you inspired me, really you did. I wasn't happy any more with the way things were. So I looked for what could be done. Some way that I could change things. And I found it.'

'Well let me tell you, David, I don't trust you any more than that unprincipled capitalist bastard Mor. I'm here to watch you as well as the rest of them. There's no-one but me to speak for the poor and the downtrodden, the common man – and the common woman. This could be the brave beginning of a new order, or it might be the start of just another damned useless, careless, thoughtless mess. A free election within three months, that's what we've agreed to and that's what we'll do, or you'll have me to deal with! And then we'll see what's what!'

'Come on, Sammy. I'm not that despicable am I?' He held out one hand, pleadingly. 'If I've made anything of myself, it's because of you.'

They were both standing at one end of the table by the whisky tray, only a foot or two separating them. When MacLing reached out, his hand touched Sammy's shoulder.

Sammy tensed, then relaxed. He shook his head and laughed, sadly. 'Ach, Davie, Davie. You were the fine one, when you were young and I was... Well, I was young too, not even so old as you are now.'

'Those days, Sammy. The excitement, the new ideas. They changed my life.'

'Just the ideas?'

'No, of course not. You too.'

'It was hard when you went. Twenty years, no, thirty. Who would have thought it would last that long? But I remember it like it was yesterday.'

He reached for the younger man and in a moment his arms were around him.

'Sam,' said MacLing.

'Davie.'

They held each other tightly, neither one remembering where they were or when. There was a brilliant flash from the doorway.

'David! David!'

They stepped apart. Torquil was standing wild-eyed at the doorway. 'A man has been listening, he's got a camera too. He's running off down that way!'

'Shit!'

Sammy got to the door first and looked out. He saw the figure running off, dodging his way through the thinning crowd.

'It's the Major! That's it! I'll get the bastard this time!'

'No, Sammy!'

But Sammy was already out of the tent, heading for the Major, who was slipping into the darkness among the parked trucks.

'Hey! You! Come back here you blaggard!'

Sammy broke into the best run he could manage, but even as he did so, the air grew thick with the smell of pigs, and an immense boar shot past him, each coarse bristle standing out on its ridged back. It dashed down the muddy track and without pausing, leapt in among the trucks. There was a hideous snort, then a scream of terror, abruptly broken off.

Sammy reached the trucks. He heard a few muffled snorts and a crunch, then the sound of something heavy being dragged along. After some hesitation, he walked carefully into the darkness. There was the rank smell of wild boar, but there was nothing to be seen, nothing to hear. Beyond the trucks was a rough pasture and as his eyes grew accustomed to the dark, he saw a crushed trail of grass, as if something had been dragged across the field. Beyond that, the hillside, vaguely lit by stray light from the show, was dotted with the darker shapes of gorse bushes and patches of bracken. There might have been a movement in the bracken – or maybe not.

'Are you there? Sammy?'

MacLing and Torquil had arrived.

'I'm here.' Sammy turned and made his way back to them.

'Are you all right? Did you catch him?'

'I'm fine. I didn't catch him, but I think we need not worry about that particular problem any more.'

'What do you mean?'

'Don't worry. I think the Major has been dealt with, finally.'

Sammy stepped out into the light and MacLing put a hand on his shoulder. 'Are you sure you're all right? You're white as a sheet.'

'I'm okay. But I have to go.'

'Where? What for?' Torquil turned to MacLing. 'Look, I think we'd better cut our losses and get out of this while we can.'

Sammy grimaced at MacLing. 'I see your right-hand man is feeling a bit shaky. But it's all right, the Major is gone. I can't stay to explain. There may be other things afoot on the Dark Isle tonight. More important matters.'

'More important?' Torquil's voice was high and nervous. He looked at the old shrunken man in his none-too-clean suit. 'Damn it, man, we've got a coup happening in a couple of hours! What on earth could be more important just now?'

Sammy looked at him. 'It's not your concern.' Torquil sputtered and tried to speak. Sammy turned to MacLing. 'Stick with it, David. This is the best chance we've ever had.' He turned and walked away.

'Come back here! You can't just...'

MacLing put a hand firmly on Torquil's shoulder. 'Let him go.' When Sammy had gone there was only the empty track and a cold wind blowing.

From the heap of tools in the shed, Le Placs and Jimmy took a few and carried them down to the shore. A scythe, a sledgehammer, a turnip slicer, the rake and a garden sprayer filled with a yellow liquid.

'For what do we need these?'

'Wait.'

They dropped the tools at the edge of the sand.

'Now,' said Jimmy, 'we mark out the space.' He paced out a rectangle on the sand.

'You are marking out a sacred space?'

'Aye, if you want to put it like that. What we're going to do is dangerous – it might disturb the planets in their orbits, or alter the weather patterns throughout the northern hemisphere. Or affect the interest rate in Guam. We don't want that sort of thing to happen. The problem is centred on the Dark Isle, so we have to set limits on it – and that's what the rectangle is for. Now, the turnip slicer, if you will.'

Together they carried the rusty old mechanism and set it on its legs at the north-west corner.

Le Placs stood back and examined it. 'This is symbolic, non?'

'Yes, I daresay it is.'

'Symbolic of the food cycle and our source of physical energy?'

'Yes, that's quite good.' Jimmy nodded. 'We use the turnip cutter to slice the whole turnip into parts so that we may feed it to the pigs and sheep and... and then they amalgamate it into the mystic whole once more. Yes, that will do nicely. Now...'

He took the garden sprayer and placed it to the south-west. Le Placs looked baffled. 'The power of water?'

'Aye, good. Represented by the hydraulic action of the pump sprayer.' He scratched thoughtfully at his forehead, smearing the red ochre. 'The fact that it changes the liquid into a semi-gaseous form is also symbolic, I don't doubt. You can work that out later, if you can be bothered.'

In the south-east he placed the sledgehammer. He looked over at Le Placs, raising his eyebrows.

'The laws of the physical universe? Cause and effect?'

'Aye. That seems to fit.' Jimmy nodded slowly. 'You can't stop a sledgehammer once its swing is started. Not without some violent result.' He sighed. 'I should have thought of that before. If I'd dealt with this business earlier... There were clues enough, even back in 1425.'

Le Placs picked up the scythe. 'And this goes in the last corner, yes?'

Jimmy nodded. 'The scythe. Symbolic of the sharp edge of the mind. The power of the intellect.' He held Le Placs with a long look. 'And of course, a symbol of death.'

Le Placs carefully positioned the scythe and returned to stand by Jimmy. To the north was pitch blackness. The sacred space was illuminated only by a faint glow from the quarter-moon behind the mist. A long cry came from the Whistler buoy out in the Firth. It sounded as if it was at the world's end.

'The turnip cutter,' said Le Placs.

'Yes?'

'It is a most unusual ritual item.'

'It is that.'

'Also, the garden sprayer.'

'You are right. You have to work with the materials to hand.'

'And the cement? What is its role?'

'Ah, yes. The cement. Let us fetch it.'

By the garden gate was a sack of Blue Circle cement. They took an end each and heaved.

'The crucial element,' Jimmy grunted as they lifted the sack. 'The bonding material that links all the powers, that binds together the thousand things of the material world.'

Together they staggered down the garden towards the sand.

'*Mon Dieu*, could you not get a smaller bag?'

'This'll do. Drop it now.' The sack thumped onto the sand and Jimmy straightened his back. 'Yes, everyone sells it in small bags now. Half this size.' He nodded his head approvingly. 'Health and Safety regulations, you see. Too easy to strain your back on the big bags.'

Le Placs stayed bent over for a few seconds, breathing heavily. 'So why have you this big sack?'

Jimmy looked at him solemnly. 'It's old stock.' Le Placs looked puzzled. 'So I got it half-price.'

The MC came onstage as the band left. He wore tartan trousers and a jacket checked in black and yellow. He stepped up to the microphone and his voice brayed out into the crowd. 'Thank you to Breeks off the Donkey!'

His voice was so loud that the rasp of his breath buzzed in every ear, an intimacy that few of the audience desired.

'I think you'll agree that last song was something of a knee-trembler, yes, a real tear-jerker and no mistake. Let's have another big hand for the band!' He stepped back from the microphone, clapping and whistling along with the crowd.

As the applause subsided he stepped up to the mike again. 'Now if you can be patient, we'll have a wee diversion while the next band set up.' Busy figures moved about the stage, plugging in and setting out a boraan, a drum set, a rack of bagpipes and a glass fiddle. 'Well worth waiting for, oh yes! Because next we have the amazing, the indescribable, the unique Shooglenifty! If anyone typifies the new Celtic revival with their dazzling mix of grainy kailyard and brazen in-your-face virtuoso don't-give-a-damn flamboyant good-time acid-croft mania, it is them! An overnight success wherever they play, this is the band described by one reviewer five years ago as too much too soon – but not for us! We can take what they give us, and then some! Because this is Castleton and this is the Dark Isle Show!

'Now, while they are setting up we have a special presentation, the last of this year's show. The winner of this year's Greasy Pig competition! Yes, some lucky lad – or lassie, we are not prejudiced here – yes, some lucky lad or lass that has captured the elusive pig will be receiving his accolade, his prize and the homage of us all, at the end of this perfect day, for I'm to be Queen of the May, Mother, I'm to be Queen of the May!

'Sorry, folks! I got carried away for a moment – it's that Peruvian marching powder, it always takes me that way! No, seriously, what we are looking at here, lads and lassies, is the crowning of the Pig King! Lord of the Dark Isle for a year and a day!'

George was in the crowd, pressed close to Veronica, with one arm round her waist. He was very aware of Veronica leaning companionably against him and very little else in the noisy throng took his attention. At the mention of the greasy pig, he felt her stiffen slightly and he was suddenly fully alert. He felt a certain uneasiness about his role in the capture of the pig. It would take some explaining, especially as the pig had not in fact been set free, but had instead fallen into the hands of the law. In an attempt to distract Veronica from the proceedings, he leant over and nuzzled her ear. She giggled, sounding surprised as well as amused, but did not move her ear very far away. He breathed gently right beside her ear. She turned in towards him and hugged him briefly.

'Just a minute George. This is all about that barbaric competition. I think we should hear what's going on.'

She looked earnestly up into his face, but George had become more interested in her closeness than his attempt to distract her. He pulled her closer, looking into her eyes. She kissed him, quickly, on the lips. Then again, for a little longer. George lost all sense of time and space and sank into the vortex of sensation made up of the feel of Veronica's cool lips, her warm tongue, her scent and the hiss of her breath as they held each other close.

'Wow.'

Veronica's face had no expression as she looked at George, but it was full of possibility, as if it might change in a moment. As if it was poised ready to avalanche into any imaginable emotion.

'Yes,' said George. 'You're right.'

'What did I say?' A slight puzzlement showed itself on her face, disturbing the smooth skin.

'Wow.'

Now her face tumbled from its equilibrium, falling into a wide smile.

'Yes. That wasn't quite what I expected.'

'Oh?'

'Better.'

George laughed and let his face do what it wanted, which was to grin like a pumpkin.

'...so we'll have to wait until later, ladies and gentlemen. In the meantime, it seems the office of Pig King is still open, and the little swine itself is still loose. If you should happen to see a greasy pig, grab it and bring it backstage! You could be the lucky one!'

A small bit of George's attention noticed this development and relaxed. With luck, Veronica would never know about his ignominious involvement with the pig.

'Well I hope the poor beast escapes,' said Veronica. 'In fact, I think the organisers should be reported to the RSPCA.'

'Now, it's the band you've been waiting for! Shooglenifty!'

All lights went out. Then the weird strains of a fiddle cut the silence, followed by a pipe drone. There was a rattle of drums and the lights came up onstage. In a moment, the crowd transformed itself into a wild many-headed dancing animal. Uncaring of how he looked, George leapt and whirled with the best of them while Veronica's long hair whipped and floated around her. Bodies barged against each other without complaint. The temporary wooden floor shuddered with the impact of thousands of feet.

At the sound desk against the back wall of the marquee, Wee Eck worked his slider, keeping an eye on the crowd as well as the band, moving the energy up the scale, up and down, nowhere near the top yet, but moving ever higher. He sucked fiercely on a large roll-up and blew out a long plume of smoke. 'Easy skankin,' he said as he passed it over to Zak.

At the entrance to the marquee, Constable MacFearn stood, with the pig tucked under his arm, and argued with the ticket man.

'I am in charge of this pig and I wish to return it to the rightful owner.

My enquiries lead me to believe that those responsible for the beast may be found inside this premises.'

The ticket man had been drinking, and besides, he had been lifted for speeding on the Culblair straight just the day before.

'Well, you're not getting in here without a ticket. Not to exceed twelve hundred persons – that's what it says on our licence. We've sold all our tickets, and if you haven't got one, you can't go in.'

'But this is a police matter!'

'Then why don't you take it up with your boss? Inspector Morrison signed the licence, and it doesn't say twelve hundred persons plus any police constable with a pig who wants to get in for free.'

'Right. I'm going round the back, where I may find someone with a bit more common sense!' MacFearn settled the pig under his arm and strode away with dignity.

An old man stepped up to the desk.

'I'm needing to get into the tent. I'm looking for my grandson.'

'Sorry. All the tickets are sold. More than my job's worth to let you in.'

Sammy's hand slid across the table. The corner of a five pound note was showing. The ticket man slipped his hand over Sammy's then pulled back again. The note had disappeared.

'Thank you sir. Have a good time now.'

Sammy Poach walked into the turmoil of the tent.

The car drove up yet another unremarkable hill, passing more wind-blasted larches and juniper that appeared out of the mirk and disappeared again.

'It's hard to believe we're still on the Dark Isle,' said Doreen. 'We must have been driving for hours. I'm beginning to wonder if we're ever going to get anywhere.' She half turned towards Alice, in the back seat, but Alice remained heavily silent.

'Well, I've been wondering exactly what we're going to do when we get there.' Lorraine waved vaguely at the featureless grey ahead. 'Wherever we're going.'

Doreen turned to face front again. 'I think Alice is right, They're trying to get in here. They are intent on some sort of gourmet meal, possibly with us as the main course. It'll be Manannan and the Dagda – and Morrigan of course. She won't keep Her head down if there's anything violent going on. Probably Lugh too – but not all of Them, which is lucky for us.'

'If They're going to try to get in here, to our world, why won't They all work together?'

'Because each and every one of Them is as petty and greedy as a spoilt child. The ringleaders will want to lord it over the others and keep the spoils for Themselves too – bigger shares. I imagine there's a bit of resentment boiling away in the ranks. That's why Alice wants to distract the ringleaders – to give the underdogs a chance to rebel. If They start fighting among Themselves, which is the normal state of affairs, then we've got some sort of chance.'

'A chance to do what?'

'I don't know.' She turned round. 'What are we going to do then, Alice?'

Alice gave no sign of hearing. Doreen turned front again and shrugged.

'Personally I think it's like getting between a pack of starving Dobermans and their food, only more dangerous. But I can't think of anything better.'

'It won't be easy to distract Them, will it?'

'Well, if Alice is interpreting your Seeing right, then they're not through the apple skin yet – not through into our world. Before they manage that, we need to give Them something really enticing, something that will really grab Their attention.'

'What would that be? A human sacrifice?' Lorraine changed down a gear as they reached a contorted stretch of hill road.

Doreen's face twisted into a grimace. 'Don't even mention it,' she whispered loudly. 'I wouldn't put anything past Alice. It's just as well she needs both of us for the ritual, or I wouldn't fancy your chances of surviving the night.'

Alice came out of her silence. 'I heard that, you little besom.'

'I meant you to.'

A beech trunk gleamed in the headlights. Broom bushes overhung the road from the high bank, scraping at the car with their long green fingers.

'What we do,' said Alice, 'is we wait and see. There's the three of us and that's all we've got. We have to work with the materials at hand.' She gestured, indicating the grey world outside. 'There are patterns forming.'

Doreen nodded. 'So we have to watch out for something special. Something to guide us.'

Lorraine giggled. 'Like talking toadstools? Friendly rabbits?'

Alice forebore to comment.

'Seriously, what are we looking for?'

'Anything. Anything that'll help.'

'Help how?' As far as the headlights reached, which was about forty feet, the road was straight. She moved up into third gear. 'I mean, I don't know if I should be looking out for a farm implement or a mystic herb or a grocer's shop.'

'It'll be obvious. You won't miss it.'

Lorraine snorted. 'That's what people say when they're giving directions. It usually means that you'll need a native guide to find it.'

Out of the grey mist a black shape flew straight towards the windscreen. Lorraine screamed and braked hard as the bird smacked into the glass with a heavy thump. The car slewed and stopped, and Lorraine sat still, breathing hard. She relaxed and lifted her foot off the clutch. The car jerked and then stalled. The headlights flickered and dimmed, and a thick silence descended.

'What was that?' breathed Lorraine.

'A crow,' said Alice, with satisfaction in her voice. 'Go and pick it up, will you?'

Lorraine shuddered. 'It's injured. Maybe dead.'

'Break its neck,' said Alice.

'I can't.'

Alice opened her mouth to shout, then changed her mind. 'No, you can't, can you. In fact, it would be much better if you did it, Doreen.'

'You're right,' said Doreen. She climbed out and walked round the back of the car.

Lorraine's hands gripped the steering wheel, clenching and unclenching. 'Sorry,' she said. 'I know it's better to kill the poor thing, but I just can't do it.'

Alice grunted.

'I can't stand thinking of it, in pain there on the road. I mean, it's not that I'm inhumane, I just can't do it.'

'Inhumane? What's that got to do with it? It's just a matter of balance.'

The back door opened and Doreen handed a limp black object in to Alice.

'Have you got a plastic bag?'

Lorraine looked back at her in surprise. 'There's one I keep here to put rubbish in.'

'That'll do. Hand it over.'

Alice took the bag, tipped the sweet wrappers and empty diet cola tins out of the open door, then put the crow into the bag. 'You broke its neck?' she asked.

'Yes,' said Doreen.

'Good.' There was the rustling of plastic in the back as Alice wrapped the crow in the bag and then tucked it under the blanket.

'Alice,' said Lorraine. 'You have a dead crow in the back of my car.'

'Yes.'

'Why?'

'For goodness sake girl, why do you think?'

'I don't know, and it's worrying me.'

'You tell her, Doreen. And see you don't use any big words. She's not too swift on the uptake tonight.'

'It has been provided,' said Doreen. 'It's for the sacrifice.'

'Oh my god!'

'The triple death, you see.'

'What?'

'You hit it with the car, I broke its neck and Alice – well I'm sure she'll devise a suitable way to bring it to its final end. When the time comes.'

'Indeed,' said Alice. 'Now drive on.'

Lorraine tried to start the car. The engine barely turned over. 'Oh shit.' She tried again. The engine turned slower and slower. The headlights were giving out a dim yellow glow. 'We're stuck,' she said.

'Ah!' said Alice. 'We're here.'

'We're not anywhere! The car won't go!'

'I can see that. And if we can't go anywhere else, then we must be here. This is it. This is where we're going. Now you two go and look around and see if you can find out where here is, and I shall remain here in the car and look after the crow.'

'But it's pitch black out there!'

'No, no. Once your eyes adjust, I think you'll find that you can see well enough not to fall over cliffs and suchlike. If you're afraid, you can hold each other's hand. Won't that be nice?'

Doreen sighed. 'We'd better go, Lorraine. She's in her element now, and that's worse than her normal obnoxiousness.'

They climbed out and slammed the doors.

Alice opened a window and shouted after them.

'And see if you can find some dry wood while you're at it!'

Eck had really got the hang of the slider now. He was treating it with respect. Just a nudge now and then, at the beginning of the song, then a long slow push as the music mounted towards the climax. Yeah, it didn't take much to work the machine, not if you had the knack.

He looked across to Zak, who had his eyes on the band, adjusting a knob or a slider now and then. He had the skill all right, but he didn't have the concentration, the absorption that you could give the job when you only had one control.

The pace of the music mounted. Eck watched the crowd and

played them like an instrument. The music was about to change, one, two, now – and Eck twitched the slider. On the dance floor everyone jerked at exactly the same time. Great. This was being in tune with it all!

He spotted George and Veronica in the crowd and felt a pang of regret. She was some dame, that Veronica, but it looked as if George was on her mind. More music, more slider and Kapow! a long final moment of high power, then close it down. There goes George towards Veronica and she's stepping towards him and Now! Although the music had stopped, he gave the slider a push. George and Veronica put their arms round each other. Hey! This was great! He slid it slowly down again and the couple became still. They looked at each other, she turned her face upwards, his face began to fall towards hers... He gently moved the slider and their lips grew closer...

Zak reached across and flipped the power switch.

'Damned loose connection somewhere,' he said as he pulled out one jackplug after another. 'Ah, it's this one I think.' He tightened the cover on a plug and pushed it back in. He flicked the power switch and held a set of headphones to his ear. 'Yup. That's it.'

Eck looked past him. George and Veronica weren't holding each other now. There was an old man talking to George, who was not looking happy.

'You want to tell me about what?'

'The Fir Bolg!'

'What? Right now?'

'Yes!' Sammy shouted, but his voice was barely audible above the music. 'It's important that you know who they were!'

'But this is important too!' George looked over at Veronica. She lifted her eyebrows a little. 'Just a minute,' he called to her.

'I have to tell you this. Because one person has died already, and although he has been greatly improved by the fact, killing people can get you in bad trouble. You have to restrain yourself, or who knows what else may happen?'

George looked frantically from Sammy to Veronica and back. 'Tomorrow, Grandad, please. I'll listen to you then. Any time you like but not now!'

'George, it has to be now. I'm sorry about your lass, but you must be told who you are.'

'Eh?' Sammy took his arm and led the baffled George to the entrance, where the music was not so loud. Veronica followed.

''Scuse me,' she said. 'But you have taken my boyfriend. Can't you find another?'

Sammy looked at her open-mouthed for a second, then laughed. 'Sorry,' he said. 'It was rude of me taking him away, but it's too noisy in here. I'm his grandfather, and I have to speak to him for a moment. Outside.'

George stepped up to Veronica and spoke in her ear. 'I'd better hear him out. Give me a few minutes?'

'OK. But don't you go off with him!'

He leant to kiss her, but she was gone. Sammy pulled him through the open tent flaps and into the middle of the muddy thoroughfare. The music of Shooglenifty was still audible, but muted, and it was mixed with John Thatch playing the accordion in the next tent. Somewhere nearby, a woman was crooning a sad sweet song in Gaelic.

George turned towards Sammy, and scowled at him. 'I hope this is worth it.'

'Now listen,' said Sammy, who did not appear to be intimidated by either George's attitude or his scowl. 'You know the Scots came from Ireland originally? Good. Because this story starts off in Ireland, where we came from. Now listen, because we can't waste time.

'The original settlers of Ireland were the people we know as the Fir Bolg. Then the Celts arrived from Europe and defeated them. From then on, the Fir Bolg were the underclass, slaves to the Celts. They did the work and the Celts got the benefit. Sound familiar? Of course it does. Isn't it the tale of the class struggle everywhere?

'Then things got too hot for the Celts, and their leaders left Ireland. They went away to a dark island, and many others went with them. And if I know them at all, I'm sure they took a bunch of their slaves with them. Only the names of the biggest and baddest of the oppressors come down to us. Lugh. Morrigan. The Dagda. But of course no-one remembers the names of the Fir Bolg.'

'But those names, they were the gods of the Celts – weren't they?'

'Gods or warlords, what does it matter? They oppressed us.'

'Us? Come on, they didn't oppress me. Or you either.'

'No, but your great to the nth degree grandfather and grandmother knew the lash of their whip, and a divine whip is just as bad as any other kind.'

'Listen Grandad, are you all right? This just isn't like you. I never even knew that you knew all this stuff.'

'No, you wouldn't. It's a difficult matter to discuss, and until now I've had no reason to do so. I've been a communist all my life, ever since I first understood what the word meant.' He looked around, in case anyone else was listening. He spoke as quietly as possible. 'But before I was a communist, I was a king. King of the Fir Bolg.'

'What?' George grinned, despite his annoyance. 'How did that happen, did you pull a sword out of a stone? And what was the coronation like? And how come you live in that wee house in the Vennels?'

'No, no, it's not like that. There's no coronation. No ceremony, no recognition, even. It is a duty that descends upon you, and nobody knows but you. Unless you tell someone.'

'Grandad, this is all very interesting, but I've got other things to think about. Veronica...' He looked around. She was standing just inside the main marquee, arms folded. He waved to her. She didn't wave back.

'Listen. I know what you're thinking. I know I drink more than is good for me, but this is not a delusion. There are signs that mark out the king among all others.'

'Like what? A mole on your arse?'

'Blank spots in your life, times when you haven't a clue where you've been, and no-one else does either. A feeling that you belong to the world, as if it owns you, not the other way round. And a tendency to turn into a monstrous boar with sickle moons on its flanks.'

'Oh. That would be quite convincing, I suppose.'

'And my grandad told me. When he was dying, he asked to speak to me before he went. He'd been king for decades, but he never told anyone. By then my father was dead and he had no other male relatives...'

'So it fell on you.'

'Yes, I was born to be the bloody king, and my grandfather before him and some relative of his before that, all the way back to the Fir Bolg in the bogs of pre-history! But I would have nothing to do with it! The proletariat are better served by an activist than another bloody king.'

'That's it all over, then. Probably just as well.' He looked over at Veronica again. She was fending off a farm labourer. 'Look, it's interesting, Grandad. At the right time, it might be fascinating, but it's not really urgent, is it? And Veronica's waiting for me.'

'No, no. It's not over. They must have a king. There must always be a king, and I don't have any other male relatives.'

'Hmm?'

'So you're the king of the Fir Bolg.'

'Me?'

'Yes.'

'But...'

'Strange absences when you couldn't be found anywhere. Sounds familiar? And you told me you had a vision of a boar.'

'A dream, Grandad. It was a dream.'

'You think so? Listen, I was in trouble, earlier on. Tonight. Someone was spying on a secret meeting. It would have been disastrous for me, and even worse for my friend. Then what should happen but a great boar appeared out of nowhere and dealt with the problem, in a very precise and final way. It wasn't just any marauding wild boar out on the rampage. It killed a man, and it killed the right man. No accident. It was very convenient for me, but it wasn't very responsible of you.'

'Of me?'

'Yes, you. It couldn't be anyone else. Who else would care for an old man and his friend and their predicament? Who else could deal with it in just that way? You are him. The Boar and the King.'

'But I didn't.'

'Sorry, George, but I think you did. You just don't remember everything that you do while you're a boar.'

'Who have you told about this?'

'You.'

'So I'm the only one that knows?'

'Yes. Just you and me.'

George laughed hysterically. 'You're not having me on?'

'No.'

'So what do I get from this? There aren't any ancestral robes, are there? Or jewels?'

'No. Nothing like that. What you get – and it's about all you get – is responsibility. You have to look after your people.'

'Me? Responsible for who?'

'Well, the Fir Bolg, of course.'

'Oh aye? Where are they? Is that a tent-full of them over there? Or do they have a secret handshake?'

'No, no. Now you're just being daft. No-one knows any longer just who the Fir Bolg are. We are not a race. We are anyone and everyone. Everyone that can't look after himself because the rules are crooked. Everyone who suffers because of despotism and slavery, all the victims of inhumane ideas. The poor and downtrodden. When it falls on you, it becomes your life.'

George stepped back. 'No thank you. I don't want to do that. I've got a life to live. My own life.'

Sammy slumped. 'You're probably right. After all, I gave it up. I couldn't believe that a king could have anything to give, not at this time in history, if ever.'

'Right, you gave it up. So if I'm the king now, then I'll just abdicate too. Problem dealt with. No more boar, no more weirdness, no more absences.'

'I hope you can, George, but it may not be that easy.'

'Of course I can. Watch me.' He drew breath and shouted. 'I abdicate!'

Hardly anyone looked at him. 'That should do it, eh?'

'I hope so. But there's one other thing I ought to mention. Until you know this you can't make a reasonable choice.'

'What's reason got to do with any of this? It sounds about as sane and reasonable as my mum having sex with Manannan, the God of the Sea!'

'Aye, well, that was the other thing I was thinking I ought to talk to you about.'

'But Grandad, it's nonsense! She's doolappy! If she wasn't a doctor she'd be locked away.'

Sammy rubbed at the back of his neck and looked at the ground. 'Well, now, perhaps she's not completely out of her mind.'

'What?'

'And think what it would mean, if she was right. If your dad really was Manannan. I'm only asking you to think about it now, theoretically. Just in case.'

'Theoretically? Well I suppose... Look, don't be daft.' He laughed. 'That would make me, at one and the same time, king of my people and the son of one of the overlords, the oppressors of my people! How schizophrenic would I have to be?' He laughed again. 'Not just that, I would be a demi-god!'

'Aye. I'm afraid so.'

'A demi-god...' George's eyes glazed over. He stared up into the vast darkness of the night and beneath his feet, the earth fell away. His scalp tingled with the flames of the sun, of a million suns. Clouds of interstellar hydrogen rasped at his skin. The darkness between the stars split like a melon, the light of a billion stars streaming out and into him.

At the same time, he could feel his toes searching in the cool damp ground and he could feel nourishment rising like sap within him. The deep rich smells of the earth sang to his body and the wind whispered at his ears, whispered words that fell into his heart. A woman laughed and somewhere a bell rang, then again. The sweet voice of a singer chimed through the air and pleasure flowed through every sense.

'Holy shit,' he whispered, just before he fell flat on his face in the mud.

Lights gleamed away into the mist and the causeway shifted and moaned as the waves slapped against the boats that supported the wooden road. A sign at the shore said, 'Causeway closed for routine safety check.' Several unhappy people waited by the barrier, where a couple of men kept guard.

Aristide and Mr Mor approached, with Baldy nearby, keeping a close watch, doing his bodyguard routine. The men slid a section of barrier aside then set it in place again once they'd passed.

'How come they got to go through?'

'Engineers. Checking the causeway.'

Halfway across the causeway, there was a rope across the wooden road, a silken rope. Ten yards beyond it was a tent, but not like the tents of the Showground. This tent was strung from the rigging of the boats, and it was made of silk, each panel a piece of sumptuous brocade showing scenes of horses. Horses running, walking, rolling in the grass, mating; stallions fighting, mares with their foals; drawing carts and ploughs; in races and in battle.

Aristide and Mor stopped at the rope and stood there waiting. Baldy grimly looked around for hidden danger while two men dressed as ostlers approached from the tent. One of these men addressed the other in an awkward, formal tone.

'Two men are without. Know you these people?'

'Nay, surely they are strangers.'

The first ostler turned to the newcomers. 'Why do ye strangers approach this sacred place? Have ye business with our brethren?'

Aristide spoke up. 'I am no stranger, but a brother come from afar, bringing the one who is expected.'

'Has he thin shanks, and a hairy fetlock? Doth he have a dam who stood over him when he was young? And are his teeth yet good?'

'Yes, he hath all of these and more besides! For he is the horse-husband and his thews are mighty. As for his teeth, he is here as a gift and a benison to the horse-mother, and ye may in no wise inspect them.'

'If he be the horse-mother's own, then let him enter.' They lowered the silken rope and Aristide and Mor stepped over it. Baldy made to enter too, but they raised the rope again to prevent him.

'Oy!'

One of the men coughed and looked at the other, who shrugged. 'Eh, but, who is this stranger,' he improvised. 'This... other stranger?'

'He is, hmm. What is he?' Aristide looked from Baldy to Mr Mor uncertainly, then continued. 'He is attendant unto the Horse Lord. Let him enter the enclosure. But let him not enter the Temple, but prevent him.'

'What's that?' Baldy stepped over the rope. He appealed to Mor. 'Ah gotta come in, boss. This is no like a ordinary meeting. We dinny know these gadgies fae Adam.'

'Sorry Baldy. You stay out here and keep watch.'

'But boss...'

'What is it with you, Baldy?' Mor frowned at him. 'Look around you.

There's just one way in and one way out, this causeway, and you can keep a watch both ways. Besides, there's guards at each end.'

'They're no oor guards,' said Baldy, sullenly.

Mor pointed to the wooden boards. 'You stay here. I'm going in there. Understood?'

'If you say so. But Ah dinny like it.'

'If that's all settled,' said Aristide, 'can we continue?'

Baldy glowered at the two attendants.

'Youse two staying out here an all?'

They nodded. Baldy settled himself against the railing and ostentatiously checked both ways.

Aristide continued. 'Brother, welcome to the holy precincts. Your protector is nigh and your sponsor speaks for you. Within this temple you will encounter the secret beyond the secret. At this gate,' he gestured to the silk walls of the tent, 'you leave your name and your self. You will take on your inner name. And that name is,' he leaned over and whispered into Mor's ear. 'Now let us enter.'

The two attendants stepped forward and held the tent flaps.

'Two beg entrance, the initiate and his guide, both bridled to the Horseman's Way.'

From inside the tent, a voice responded. 'No-one may enter save he be naked as a foal.'

Aristide called out, 'Then let us enter, for beneath our clothes we be one skin!'

'Truly we are of one skin. Let the initiate drink from the chalice and then may ye both enter.'

The curtains drew aside. Several robed figures stood there, their faces unseen beneath their hoods. One stepped forwards, holding out a leather cup. Aristide took it and held it out to Mor. 'Take this and drink, for surely this is the blood of the mare and the flesh of the stallion.'

Mor looked dubiously at the green scummy liquid, then lifted it and drank it off in one long swallow.

'Now may ye enter, but speak not of the mysteries within, or thy tongue shall be cut out and cast upon the temple midden!'

The curtain was drawn open and Mor and Aristide disappeared inside. Baldy scowled at the other two, then turned to lean over the railing. Lights glistened on the dark waves. To left and right it was possible to see the long string of lights suspended from the mast-heads, but despite the illumination, the causeway itself faded into the fog after twenty yards. He arranged himself against the railing for the best view each way and kept his hand near his pocket, where a heavy object made the cloth bulge.

From inside the tent came a series of chants and responses, muffled by the swathed silk. This went on for a long time. Eventually, a drum began to beat and the light of flames danced on the silk. Smoke dribbled up through a hole at the peak of the tent. There were the sounds of rhythmically tramping feet, the vibrations travelling through the wooden causeway, growing faster and more frantic. Occasional loud cries came through the cloth, and sometimes a whinny, followed by a soothing voice. Smoke fell down and spread through the mist, carrying smells both sweet and acrid.

Baldy looked at the other two guards. Their eyes were bright and they spoke in low voices to one another. Another, deeper drum joined the first and a reedy flute sang out thin notes that clawed at Baldy's spine. The chanting continued, without response now, on and on, a ceremonial liturgy that was backed by the primitive music but did not conform to it. Baldy huddled into his jacket. The warm smoke hung in the air, making his eyes sting. He blinked, then closed his eyes, just for a moment.

Dumfry put more food on the hotplate to cook and returned to buttering rolls. His mind was no longer on his work – in fact, he was looking forward to finishing for the night. He wondered dolefully if he should continue with his quest. Doreen's backsliding was a sore blow. He had hoped that she would foreswear her dubious activities and come fully into the fold of the church. Other hopes had been less well-formed, but perhaps even more powerful.

He sighed deeply and lifted the knife to chop a tomato, then laid the knife down and listlessly studied the unsliced tomato. Once more, he drifted up into the night, leaving himself behind, a tiny figure in the glow of the IWA stall, almost lost among the lights of the show, hunched over the chopping board, sadly buttering rolls. He left the sadness behind him and went higher. He could see Castleton spread out below, and then, almost before he knew it, he was so high that he could see the curve of the earth and the moon beyond it. He watched in wonder as the earth and moon diminished and then disappeared into the background and he saw the sun shrink away also until it was only one tiny star among thousands more. And still he travelled, rushing further and further, as if he would never stop. The feeling of wonder subsided and despair crept in to take its place. The heavens were oppressively enormous. Was there no end to it? Nothing solid, nowhere to stand?

A thought dropped into his mind: if you travel that way, there is no end.

He slowed in his flight, then slipped sideways – but not in any physical direction. Rather, he edged through the physical dimensions until he was outside them. The stars disappeared, the darkness disappeared...

'Ah, this is it!'

Unbelievably complex, a new world lay around him, a world made up of layer upon layer of light, entwined threads and sheets of light. His stunned mind began to sift the impressions, trying to make sense of them. The light-forms were bewildering in their variety, but there did seem to be patterns, simpler patterns, in the way that they were arranged. A sense of perspective emerged, the shapes fell into place in his mind and he recognised them.

'Sausages?'

He shook his head in some non-material way and looked again. There was indeed something very sausage-like about what he was seeing. The lights seemed to congregate in separate forms, each surrounded by a membrane. Each form was connected to others by a narrow throat, a constriction in the membrane. These connections, like the twists in a string of sausages, were the only links between them.

'But what is it?'

He stretched and turned, beginning to move among the bewildering shapes which lay across and even through each other without losing their identity. Slowly, chaos began to fall into order and he saw what it all meant.

That flow of gold, shading into green at the edges – that was the sun, its endless path laid for a moment in front of him. And that swirl was the energy of its light, condensing into forms. Into shapes. Into life. Light growing thick as cream, with lumps of light coalescing like butter.

He reached, in some very real though non-material way, to touch the shapes and forms, to feel them.

'Ah.' And this lump was the world, this right-now world. It lay within a membrane and all round about it other worlds had their own membraneous borders. They occupied more dimensions than normal sausages and so they had many more links. These links tied them together, but they were also a barrier, for scarcely anything could pass through such contorted, twisted space.

He was full of admiration for the harmony of it all, while remaining rather surprised at the homely resemblance to such a down-to-earth foodstuff.

His attention was drawn to his own world. Home. He looked more closely. There was something happening there. He closed in on the odd activity that he could see there at the joining of the worlds. Oh dear. There was something going on, and it didn't look harmonious at all. It looked for all the world as if one of the neighbouring sausages was trying to untwist itself at one end.

He shivered. Surely not. That couldn't be right. It didn't match the general feeling of harmony. He squinted at the activity, straining to see details. Someone was in there – in fact there were a few of them, digging into the twisted knot, manipulating the membrane of the universe. How could anyone use such forces? The strain must be enormous! He moved closer, trying to understand what he was seeing. Whoever they were, it looked as if they were trying to open up a passage from one sausage to the next. Dumfry frowned. Surely that would be dangerous. It could distort the sausages badly. And what would that mean to the world inside the sausage?

He moved in and studied them intently. He couldn't make out what they were, but they behaved like a team of insects, burrowing their way through the twisted membrane. But why? It looked like a hopeless task. Unless there was someone else working from the other side, they couldn't possibly succeed. He glanced across to the next sausage, his own world.

He saw the Dark Isle, and the place was a seething mass of energy pulling this way and that, an incomprehensible turmoil. But as he studied it, he saw that the energy was not all undirected. In fact, below the surface there were powerful undercurrents that dragged people along whether they wished to or not. And beneath even them, a great tide was gathering itself, with forces that could tear open the gate to the next world.

Dumfry looked desperately at the world, his world. Had no-one noticed what was going on?

Yes, in among the thoughtless mass, there were also people trying to stem the tide that looked fit to sweep away the Dark Isle. But they were ignorant of the real scale of the tragedy. Not that they could do anything anyway. They were trying, but they were so pitifully few, and too small. He shuddered. They would be swept aside like chaff in a storm.

From his place to one side of the world, he looked down at Eck working his slider and at Mor in the horse tent. He saw George climbing onto a stage and he saw Barry and Maria in their dolphin boat, lost and drifting in the Firth. He watched Jimmy and Le Placs at their desperate endeavour, on the beach, and he saw Sammy and MacLing and Aristide Coupar plotting to cut the Dark Isle free of the mainland. All of these he saw, and they seemed like threads, pulling events into an unholy whole that was straining the fabric of reality to breaking point. And then he realised what was going to happen if They broke through.

'Oh, my God!' he said, and he was not praying.

Then he heard a loud voice calling to him from a far place, saying, '... and nae onions!'

In the last moment before he fell back into the IWA stall, he saw Doreen and he saw Alice, and then he knew who was coming through the walls of the world. He could also see what would happen to Doreen and Alice.

'No... No!'

Dumfry found himself back at the counter. A farmer in best tweeds, smelling of strong drink, was staring at him belligerently.

'And why no? Are ye no open for business?'

'Yes, yes of course.'

Guessing at the missed part of the sentence, Dumfry slipped a hamburger into a sesame roll, added a couple of slices of tomato, wrapped it in a paper napkin and handed it over.

'One pound fifty,' he said.

The man handed over the coins and walked off, eating his way through both hamburger and napkin.

Dumfry strode to and fro in the cramped stall, trying to settle his thoughts. How can it be, he thought, that such a terrible thing should be happening within the harmonious structure of God's universe? He began slicing onions, a simple and soothing activity. The onions fell into silvery rings. I can do nothing about it, he said. I was allowed to see the structure of the world, he told himself. It was a grace and a gift. I have no cause to go meddling with the inner workings of the universe. Even if I could. Without a doubt, from a different viewpoint, this impending disaster is part of a greater harmony, which I do not yet understand.

Probably.

But what about Doreen? Did he not have a duty to protect her? He laid his arms down on the counter and hid his face in his hands.

From the hotplate came the smell of burning sausages.

'Damn!' he said.

Once everything was prepared, they sat in the house, drinking coffee, not talking much. Jimmy seemed unusually reserved, even melancholy. 'The garden,' he said. 'I like it to remain just as it is. It was never meant to be cultivated. Cultivated flowers creep in, of course, and even the occasional vegetable. They are welcome, but they must not take over from the plants whose home it is. You understand?'

'I think so. You are keeping a refuge for wild plants. This is a little den of wildness.'

'Just so. It is important that you understand that. The sand-garden has one purpose, and this garden has another. It tells me of the health of the world.'

Le Placs shifted uneasily on his seat. 'Has this to do with the task of tonight?'

'No. Not directly. But there are not many people that I can speak to as I do to you. Not many can understand. And so I tell you those things that someone must know.'

Le Placs reached out and put a hand on Jimmy's shoulder for a moment. 'You also, *mon brave*. I value your conversation. You have a clear mind.'

Jimmy smiled broadly. 'There are not many who would say that.'

'Then they do not listen, my friend.'

'Thank you,' said Jimmy. 'A friend is a fine gift from the world.' He stood up and stretched. 'But now, the time is near. We must grab the opportunity upon the cusp. Taken at its flood, the tide leads on to success, as it says in the *I Ching*.'

Le Placs looked dubious. 'You are certain of this?'

'No. Perhaps it was the Bible? A source that had authority, at any rate. Now give me a hand with these.'

By the door, a box held many jam jars and candles. They carried it between them out into the clammy night. On the shore they laid out the jars around the rectangle that they had marked out earlier, then lit candles and placed each in a jar for protection against the breeze. Dampness fell from the air onto every exposed surface. Jimmy's bare skin glistened and the ochre on his head ran down his forehead in little driblets.

'Now the cement.' Jimmy bent and slit the side of the bag with a small knife. They picked it up together and walked to and fro across the space, letting the cement powder spill out onto the sand. When they'd finished, the area was trampled and streaked with the fine cement. There were grey smears over Le Placs' trousers and Jimmy's bare legs. Le Placs folded the empty bag and put it to one side.

Jimmy adjusted a few of the jars and picked up the Japanese rake. He held it upright, tines at the top, facing forward into the mist. Candlelight flickered on his damp skin. He stood absolutely still for a long while. Out in the roads, the Whistler Buoy moaned, then, after a long silence, moaned again. Le Placs shivered in the cold clammy air, but did not speak.

At last Jimmy stirred. He shrugged his shoulders. 'Well,' he said, 'Better get on. Now feels like the right time.' He cleared his throat, then spoke in a ceremonial voice. 'East is the rising sun,' he said, gesturing to his right with the rake. 'It is associated with rebirth and new beginnings in many religions and myths.

'West has its own connotations,' he said, 'not least of which is the idea of the Western Paradise, the land of the eternally young. We may expect to see Angus Og there, when we die.' He turned his head to look at Le Placs. 'Perhaps you have heard of him? God of love in one mythology, friend of Lachie Mor in another.' He gestured behind him. 'South is the land of the Sun, of course, and we need say little more about it than that.

'North, however, is a direction which escapes most of the baggage of religious associations – except that I believe some of the native American peoples believe it to be the source of strength and the power of introspection. They represent it with the black bear, as I recall. I shan't quarrel with them on that score.' He tapped his temple with an index finger, looking upwards thoughtfully. 'And of course, there is also a particular Buddha associated with that direction, though his attributes escape me for the moment.' He threw his arms wide and laughed. 'Well, I suppose if you look deep enough, you'll find that someone has claimed everything on this earth as some sort of symbol. But north seems to be less lumbered than the other directions, so that's the direction that I face.'

Le Placs stepped back to give him room.

'Watch closely,' Jimmy continued. 'It is best if someone knows how to do this.'

'But what is it that we are doing? You are raking the sand, no?'

'Not quite. Tonight we are trying something quite different, though it begins the same.' Jimmy turned to look directly at Le Placs. His eyes were bright and clear. 'Do not try this by yourself. The outcome is not certain. What we are about to do is dangerous. Mortally dangerous.'

Jimmy breathed deeply and closed his eyes. Le Placs saw that his muscles were trembling, and he felt dread descend on him. For an instant, he saw the sacred rectangle and the implements which bounded it, as if from another's eyes, through the eyes of a foreigner, an alien. Meaningless but threatening pieces of equipment gloomed in the dimness, flames encased in glass flickered wildly. A half-naked man stood in the half-light contemplating some dreadful purpose which he could tell to no-one else.

Jimmy breathed out, then raised the rake, holding it level across his chest. Le Placs felt the pressure of the unknown making the walls of the world bulge. Jimmy had ceased to be a friend: he had become anonymous, a stranger, an archetypal figure with no name. Unseen membranes of reality trembled as Jimmy reached out with his rake and Le Placs felt the Unseen reaching dark claws towards him.

Then the tines dropped into the sand and it was only Jimmy after all, raking the beach. The sand spread itself before the rake with a soft hiss as the cement folded into it, until the grey powder had disappeared into the matrix of the beach.

Somewhere at the show, Mor was hiding. But there was an astonishingly large number of heavily built men with black hair and wearing suits. Big Irwin had already confronted most of them, and apologised loudly afterwards. He was beginning to lose his impetus.

He stopped to rest and take stock. He was in the central area of the show, between the fairground, the big marquee and the various smaller performance tents. Here was as good a place to stand as anywhere. Everyone must pass by here some time in the night. Irwin's burning anger was no longer so close to the surface, but it was still there, smouldering. He lifted a bottle to his lips and swallowed a large quantity of whisky. The anger flared and glowed deep in his belly. Good. It was still there. He shivered and pulled his jacket shut against the penetrating chill from the clammy air. He wished Lou was here. Right now, he needed to talk to someone, explain his grievances – and she would understand. But he'd lost her in the first mad rush through the show, searching among the stock pens for the hated figure of Mr Mor.

He took another gulp of whisky and glared aggressively into the shifting faces of the crowd. The sound of acid-croft music thundered from the main tent. Bubblegum pop blared from the fairground rides. A few bars of a Gaelic song fell on his ears, mixed with the fast incomprehensible patter of a comic filling in between acts on another stage. Happy voices drifted from the promenading people, lovers walked hand in hand. Everyone was enjoying this opportunity for excess and revelry. Everyone but Irwin.

The Gaelic song ended and then, slipping through the fairground cacophony, came sweet sad chords that plucked at his heart-strings. It was 'The Dark Island'. The song of his own birthplace, the song of the land that he loved. He sobbed involuntarily, rubbed at his eyes and swallowed another large dram. Unbearably lovely, the tune found its way into his breast, where it took control and tugged him, gently towards its source. 'I'm coming,' he called. 'I'm coming.'

The crowds opened before him, as if there was some magical quality to this simple man, two metres tall and built to match, who carried a bottle of whisky in his upraised hand and blundered aimlessly through the fair.

'It's yourself, Irwin,' said the man at the entrance, to ensure that Irwin recognised the fact that he was there and did not fall over him.

'S Th' Dark Island,' Irwin howled. 'Haunt me till I die... Thass what'll it do.' Irwin tried to fumble money out of his pocket, using the hand with the bottle in it. The cork came out and whisky poured down his leg. 'Oops.' Since the bottle was open in any case, he finished it off in a couple of long gulps. He waved the empty bottle to emphasize the importance of what he had to say. Everyone gave him a wide berth. 'Le' me in. I have. To go in.'

'Why don't you just go in then, hey? No, no, don't you worry about a ticket. Complimentary.'

'Thanggs. Best damn ticket man in a Dark Isle, you. Have a dram. No it's gone. Have a bottle. Good bottle. How's your famly keepin, eh?'

The music called to him once more and he struggled briefly with the conflicting claims of courtesy and the sad song.

'Gotta go.'

He stumbled into the tent, his feet barely keeping up with his body. Several people made room for him at the central tent-pole and he hung on to it, his cheek nestling against the barbed wire wrapped around it. He sang along to the song, mostly la-la-ing, except when it got to the bit about 'haunt me till I die', which he joined in loudly. Tears dribbled down his cheeks. 'Bess damn song,' he called, as everyone applauded the band. 'Bess one ever.'

The band struck up again. A familiar tune. So familiar that he didn't even recognise it at first, it was just there in his ears, as close as his heartbeat. His head moved in time with it, and a smile appeared on his face. Irwin's body was there, responding to the rhythm, the melody, but the rest of him was absent. Until they got to the chorus, and the crowd joined in.

'...them that was raised

'Upon tatties and herring!'

A raging fury took hold of Irwin and he swung a huge fist against the tent pole. 'Tatties and herring is it!' The marquee trembled, and everyone turned to look. The music stopped. Irwin roared again, shaking his bruised fist in the air. 'That basstard Mor! I know where he is! I know!'

He turned and ran from the tent, knocking people to left and right.

The singer looked nervously around the silent tent. 'Well, I've never had that reaction before.' A buzz of talk arose as fallen people were helped to their feet. 'Perhaps we'd better sing something else, hey? No-one's gonna object to, eh, 'Flower of Scotland', is that okay? Come on, lads, play up.'

Something wet was rubbing his face. Something that smelled of beer. George pushed it away and opened his eyes. Veronica was looking at him, with concern on her face and a bar towel in her hand.

'Are you all right?'

'Yes. I think so.' There was a long wailing sound in his ears. He held a hand to his head, then realised that the sound was outside him, a fiddle playing up to a crescendo. He looked around and saw that he was back in the main marquee. Drums pounded, the fiddle shrieked and the wooden floor shook as people danced wildly. He raised his voice. 'What happened?'

'I don't know!' Veronica shouted. 'You were talking to your grandfather and then you fell down. Fainted, I think.'

'Aye. You fainted,' put in Sammy. 'Then we dragged you back in here.

You all right now?'

'I'm fine. Let me up.' George struggled to his feet, Veronica holding his arm.

'Right,' yelled Sammy. 'I'll leave you two alone now, but you remember what I was saying. Power and responsibility go hand in hand. And I think you've still got the power, eh?'

'Sure, Grandad. I'll think about it.'

'Could you take the bar-cloth back?' Veronica handed it over to Sammy, who disappeared out of the tent, leaving George and Veronica looking at each other. 'What was that about?'

'I'm not completely sure,' George shouted over the music. 'It's too complicated to explain.'

Veronica looked him straight in the eyes. 'What?'

'It's too complicated to explain! Too complicated to shout about, anyway,' he bellowed. The music stopped. 'Look,' he said, 'it's sort of a family responsibility, but I'm having nothing to do with it.'

Veronica nodded dubiously. 'You don't have to tell me if you really don't want to. But you just fainted because your grandfather revealed some dreadful secret about your great-aunt Minnie or some other aberrant family member and I'm curious to know what could have that effect on you. On anyone. Your family must be much more exciting than mine.'

George shrugged hopelessly. 'It's not the right time,' he said. 'I'll tell you later. If you want. The band will be playing again in a minute.'

As the singer came up to the mike to announce the next song, the MC came onstage and stopped her. 'One moment! Hold everything, we have a winner! Listen everybody, we have a Pig King! Quiet everyone, someone has caught the pig!'

'Oh my God,' said George.

'Shocking,' said Veronica. She took George's hand.

'Yes, this year's heir to the throne is none other than...' He beckoned towards the wings and Constable MacFearn was pushed out onto the stage, still clutching the pig. He stood where he was, staring out into the lights. The MC brought the mike over and whispered, 'What's your name?' then bellowed, 'Our very own Constable MacFearn! The greasy pig was caught by a... No, better not.' The crowd laughed and MacFearn turned red.

'A policeman!' said Veronica.

'Tut, tut,' said George, in relief.

The MC was pressing the microphone on MacFearn again. 'So, Constable MacFearn, how does it feel to be King Constable?'

'I don't know what you're talking about. I am weary and I want to go home. Does anyone here own this pig?'

'But Constable, you caught it, so you are the new Pig King of the Dark Isle!'

'Caught it? I certainly did not! I confiscated it.'

'You what?'

'In the course of my duty, I apprehended a young man that I had reason to believe had come by this animal dishonestly.'

The MC laughed. 'Well, who was it? Ladies and gentlemen, the excitement mounts! The Pig King may be among us at this very moment, incognito! Lights, please!'

The main lights came on. Someone called out, 'Who caught the pig!' In a moment, everyone took it up as a chant, farm labourers and fishermen alike calling out, 'Who caught the pig! Who caught the pig!' The chanting grew louder and louder. 'Who caught the pig! Who caught the pig!' MacFearn opened his notebook and searched through the pages. George tried to move back towards the doorway, but Veronica tugged him close to her again.

'This year's Pig King is,' said the MC.

MacFearn found the relevant entry. 'Stevan MacCormack.'

'Stevan MacCormack? Step forward, Stevan.'

MacFearn had a smug look on his face. 'He said his name was George MacLear, but I knew who he was. Never forget a face.' He glared out into the crowd. 'You can't pull the wool over my eyes!'

'Dammit, man, which one was it? Stevan MacCormack or George MacLear?' The MC turned to the crowd. 'George MacLear! Is he here?'

Veronica stepped away from George. 'George! You... you caught that poor pig?'

'Listen, I can explain! I was trying to...'

'George!'

The crowd around them roared, and George was bundled helplessly from hand to hand through to the front. He clambered up onto the stage and blundered forward, blinded by the stage lights. The MC took his arm and led him to centre stage.

MacFearn glared at George as he handed the pig over. 'It's not my fault,' hissed George.

'King George MacLear, ladies and laddies! Let's have three cheers for the new King! Hip, hip, hooray!' Two roadies brought out a dining chair covered in aluminium foil. The MC led him to it and forced George to sit, with the pig on his lap. A young woman stepped forward. She had a tiara on her head and a blue sash over her shoulder that announced 'Dark Isle Herring Princess.' She placed a tinsel and cardboard crown on his head and handed him a glittery plastic sceptre. She leant forward and kissed him on the cheek. Then she stepped to one side of the throne and stood there smiling and waving.

The MC faced the crowd and bellowed. 'May our Royal Incumbent exercise his *droit de seigneur* with valour and discretion throughout the coming year!

'And now a word or two and a presentation from the sponsor of this year's investiture, the Cromness butcher... Yes, here he comes. Let's hear it for our patron!' He read from a scrap of paper. 'Andy Cumberland, Family Butcher, Harbour Close, Cromness, who will present King George with his tribute – the pig's weight in prime lean pork, sausages and bacon.'

Andy the butcher blushed in the glare of the lights. 'I am honoured, to present, this tribute of the best, produce of this land, to our new, King George. And wish him, all the best, and offer him, our allegiance, over, the coming year.'

He dropped the plastic-wrapped meat into George's lap and took the pig, while the crowd cheered and whistled. Andy stood to the left of the throne, smiling stiffly at the audience and cradling the little pig. George sat dumbly under the weight of all the attention and the butcher's goods.

'And what do you have to say to us, your loyal subjects?' The MC thrust the mike in his face.

'I abdicate!'

'Ha, ha! You can't do that! You're not even properly invested yet! Wait till you hear what's next!' He turned to the audience. 'Because, guys and gals, we have a rather special surprise tonight. At no expense, I mean, of course, with no expense spared, we have Kenny John with us tonight and he has brought with him the carnyx! The ancient Celtic battle horn, reconstructed from remains found in the depths of the Blackadder Bog!'

A smallish man with a goatee beard entered stage right holding a brazen horn, six feet long. He beamed as he held it up for everyone to see. At the bell end, the horn was moulded into the shape of a boar's head, open-mouthed and grinning. Its sycamore-wood tongue flapped as he shook the horn at the roaring crowd.

'But I abdicate,' said George.

'Quiet,' hissed the MC. 'Just sit there quietly for the next few minutes and then you can abdicate all you bloody well like.' He lifted the mike to his mouth. 'And tonight we have a rare treat. Especially for this evening, we have a new composition, especially written for this special occasion. Written by Kenny John and Shooglenifty, it's a tribute to the Pig King and this is its first ever performance! It'll be a stoatir, I don't doubt! And it's called 'Hog in the Bed'! Take it away!' He lowered the mike. 'And you sit there until it's finished. Please.'

The house lights went down and George sat in his shiny chair that crackled when he moved. Veronica is out there, somewhere, he thought. I can't see her, but she can see me.

There was dead silence in the tent for a few seconds, then the first note of the carnyx sounded. It started off almost too low to hear, all by itself, very quiet and very deep and it slowly rose up to a wild earsplitting roar, the tongue of the bronze boar flapping and clattering, the smooth bellow of the horn broken into fragments as if the carnyx was a live beast, enraged and not caring who knew it. George was in the midst of it, his very thoughts driven from his head by the sound. Then the sound began to subside and he realised that all the rest of the band, pipes, drum-kit, fiddles, mandolin and other assorted noisemakers were giving it laldy behind the roaring horn, and showed no signs of stopping for some time.

Oh hell, he thought. I caught the bloody pig, didn't I, and that makes me the Pig King.

Behind him, the band played his tune, and in front of him they were dancing and cheering for him. He waved his sceptre high towards his appreciative subjects, who were, presumably, somewhere on the other side of the lights. They cheered and whooped while George rose from his chair and stepped, exultant, to the edge of the stage, arms spread, holding the sceptre high. The MC had left his microphone upon its stand. George stood in front of it, opened his mouth and roared triumphally, his mouth grinning like the bell of the carnyx.

Siller pressed the big button and held it down. He had already tried half a dozen times, and the machine had failed to start. His thumb felt as if it was ready to break. 'Fifteen, sixteen, seventeen,' he counted, then turned the starter.

The thick foggy Cromness silence was once again split by the broken, straining roar of the bulldozer trying to start. Clouds of stinking black smoke vented into the night, but then the roar became smoother and the smoke cleared until it was merely a regular blast of diesel smoke and fumes.

Someone else might have punched the air and cried out in triumph, but Siller merely nodded to himself and said, 'Good.'

He sat still for a moment, going over the next step. He turned a switch and headlights came on, pitifully weak against the thick fog. Nervously he reached for two of the big levers. His slender hands seemed barely big enough to grasp the handles at the top of each lever. The levers were shaking with the rumble of the engine and he could scarcely force his hands to close on the shiny worn metal. He pulled the handles in and tugged. He pulled again. The levers wouldn't move. He took one lever in both hands and heaved. It gave way and out of the dusty cracked window he saw the right hand track begin to roll.

The huge mass of the bulldozer swung to the left, slewing off the low loader and down onto the road. Siller pulled himself back into the seat and desperately reached for the other lever. It clanked into place and the other tread turned, swinging the bulldozer to the right. Its big blade gently touched a garden wall, which crumbled into a heap of rubble.

Siller let go and grabbed at the first lever again, correcting just in time to clip the last lamp post before the darkness of the Muckle Vennel swallowed up the headlights.

No-one was there to see the bulldozer jerking and lurching into the Vennel, but had anyone been there, they would have seen Siller frantic and animated as never before, trying to keep the yellow monster on course. It lumbered first one way, then the other. Even the vibrations of the great beast were enough to tumble thatch and slates from the older hovels. What with the clouds of dust and the fog, the darkness was almost complete in the Vennel, but Siller kept on, the blade striking the houses, ripping the fronts off them. Chunks of masonry fell onto the cab and bounced off. The machine rocked and tilted as the caterpillar treads mounted fallen stone and crushed old bricks to dust. Behind, shaken walls fell, their desolate interiors open to the night air for a moment before roofs collapsed and ancient dust gusted up in clouds, making a thick gaseous porridge along with the clinging mist.

From the bulldozer came the frenzied cry of Siller, caught up in the wildness of destruction and noise and power. His wandering path brought him out into the alley again. A tom cat ran across the Vennel in front of him and disappeared into a doorway that fell in on it an instant later.

The street lights of Shore Road were beginning to show ahead of him and Siller in mad excitement grabbed both levers, one in each hand, and threw himself this way and that. The carterpillar tracks turned together and the bulldozer zigzagged its way into the lurking collection of hovels.

The seafront was close ahead of him now. He looked back over his shoulder for a moment, to get his bearings. The upper lights of The Fisherman's Arms could just be seen. A rictus twitched his face, a smile trying to appear. A line heading for the Arms would take the bulldozer right through the labyrinthine mess of the Vennels, wiping out shacks and sheds that no-one had seen for decades or even centuries. Perhaps, and Siller's almost-smile grew broader, perhaps the machine would not stop when it reached the Arms. Wine was a mocker always, and it would be a worthy thing to remove a cause of unrighteousness.

He turned to face front again. The bulldozer was pushing flat the last row of tumble-down cottages before Beach Road. Just watch them tumble down, thought Siller, with what was very nearly humour.

Dumfry's mind was disturbed. He could not think straight, and there was one place he knew that would afford him the necessary quiet to contemplate the situation and his best course of action.

He tipped the burnt sausages along with the hamburgers and the rolls into the bin. He threw the sliced vegetables in after them and then he drew down the shutter at the front of the stall. There was a world to be saved, and his responsibility to the IWA hamburger stall could not be allowed to stand in his way.

He walked out of the showground towards the north-west. Beyond the lights, the dark was nearly impenetrable. The road was narrow but well surfaced and until his eyes adjusted, he proceeded mainly by touch, turning back onto the road when wet broom bushes stroked his face or when his feet fell on the grass verge. Someone coughed nearby. He jumped, looking around, trying to pick out a human shape in the darkness. There was another cough and a munching sound and he relaxed. It was a sheep in the nearby fields. He heard footsteps and he managed to make out the shapes of a young man and woman going the other way.

'Good evening,' he said.

'Aye, aye,' said the man. The woman giggled as they hurried past towards the showground.

Ahead of him, he could see the dark silhouettes of several sombre trees against the general darkness of the night, which was lightened somewhat by the moon behind the mist. The road widened, then entered a large parking area. The dark shapes of several parked cars were just discernible. Music could be heard from more than one of them.

Another car approached and he stood out of the way. It pulled up beside the others, and the lights went off. Strangely, no-one got out. Curious, he ambled towards the cars, wondering what they were doing here. With a rush of embarrassment, he realised that more than one of the cars was moving in a rocking motion. There were couples in those cars, and they were coupling. He blushed deeply. Perhaps they thought he was here to spy on them.

He turned to one side and there was a pair of gates in front of him, wrought iron, between two large pillars. He sighed with relief. It was the cemetery. He pushed through the gates and a soothing quietness fell on him. He adopted his meditative walking position and began to meander among the half-seen gravestones, pondering. Now, what is to be done? There is a most unseemly distortion in the fabric of the universe. I have been graced with a vision of its inner workings, but that region does not belong to Man. It is the realm of God. So, no matter what appears to be going on, it would be arrogance for me to try to interfere.

There was a cough from nearby. He stopped dead and looked around. Were there sheep in the graveyard? He saw a bulky shape beside a gravestone. It reared up and gave a moan, then subsided again. There was a silence and then the bulky shape said. 'Oh Gary, Gary. I love you. Do you love me?'

'Course I do,' it replied. 'Want a fag?'

Dumfry felt a surge of most unecclesiastical anger. 'Will you all just stop it,' he roared. 'I came here for some peace and quiet!'

There were urgent whisperings from around him and the sounds of several people grumbling as they sneaked away among the stones.

Dumfry stood silent, trembling. He was aware that his anger was not completely righteous. There was a dreadful longing in him, which he recognised as an old wound. He had not felt it this strong since he had been at college, when it had seemed that everyone except him was finding comfort in the company of a member of the other sex.

As he walked on among the stones, he began to calm down. His mind turned to the cosmic situation and what he could do about it, if anything. With so many people and other beings involved, there didn't seem to be anything much that he could do, beyond praying. That was certainly worth doing, but somehow it was not enough – as if he were to call on God for help while someone was drowning. I am God's servant, His representative, he thought. There are people here who are my responsibility. Like Doreen, who is deeply embroiled in this, and may not survive the night.

He felt a sudden surge of more than ordinary energy as he thought of Doreen's dear sweet face, and could not help thinking also of her warm welcoming bosom and her long legs. And indeed, every part of her was important. He felt a stirring within himself, felt strength come to him. Surely, after all, it was his duty to help his fellow man and woman.

'Yes,' he cried. 'I am coming, Doreen.'

Someone sniggered in the dark of the graveyard, but Dumfry did not notice. He had already slipped into the space between the worlds, but not merely as an observer this time. He was driving inwards with intent, like a salmon heading upriver.

He found himself a suitable vantage point and looked at the complexity of the worlds. The chaos began to fall into order as he recognised the forms and shapes. He saw the world of men and women and he saw the world next door – and there he saw the beings at their infernal work. Now that he knew of Alice's involvement, he recognised them as the

Gods to which she owed service. They were hard at work, struggling to open the gate between the worlds, intent on opening a permanent doorway. He shuddered at their ghastly shapes. They may take on human form as it suits them, but in their own realm, their shapes were hideous. He glanced at the world that he knew, the Dark Isle. Human were pretty ghastly too, he admitted. They looked all right if you could only see them one moment at a time, but when you could see them in four dimensions, they were disturbingly like a barrel of worms tipped out on the ground.

Putting aside the chauvinism of body shapes, it was still important to stop them. Perhaps they knew what they were doing, or perhaps they were simply driven by their own natures, but the consequences for the people of the Dark Isle would be too dire to let anything like compassion intrude. When they succeeded in their task, as it seemed they would, the disturbance of equilibrium could not last long. For a short while they could hold a connection open between their world and ours, then the membranes of the world would twist back into a new configuration, leaving the Dark Isle isolated in a bubble universe. The island would disappear from the world, leaving nothing but a blank bit of sea off the coast of Rossland. Soon, everyone would forget it had ever been there, but in the unseen bubble world, these Gods would rule over the Dark Isle, and every human on the island would feel the lash of their otherworldly whip.

Dumfry metaphorically stood up straight. He was going to have to do something. He bowed his head momentarily. If it was allowed. He gathered himself, then tentatively stretched his notional muscles. The earth shuddered.

Far off in the showground, animals lowed in their pens and the lights of the fairground flickered all together. A wave larger than any others smacked against the causeway. Eck neglected his slider for an instant and as the band faltered, George and Veronica paused and turned to each other, then took the next step in the dance. Far off, Jimmy Bervie stopped in his tracks and stared into the darkness of the night. And in her mobile lab in a field near to Castleton, Martha Nero stared amazed at her dials.

Le Placs stayed off to one side in the flickering light, watching Jimmy rake the sand, listening to the regular chink of the beads as Jimmy leaned forwards then pulled back, with a half-step sideways every so often to reach a new bit of sand. Jimmy was wholly absorbed in handling the rake, barely glancing at the patterns appearing on the raked beach. But Le Placs saw them, and shivered. It was difficult to look at the distorted patterns of ridged lines. They were like a hologram, projecting another dimension into this one, and though Le Placs had only the most rudimentary ability to interpret the signs, it was plain that the other dimension was not a pleasant one. When the Whistler Buoy moaned, it sounded almost cheerful by comparison.

'Well, that's it,' said Jimmy at last. He turned from the space and walked up to lay the rake carefully against the garden wall.

'So what now? What does it say?'

'Och, I'm sure you can see as well as I that there's nothing good in the sand tonight. And I'd rather not know the details. Not tonight, of all nights.'

'So that's it?'

'No.' Jimmy bent and picked up the garden sprayer. Now it's time for this.' He gave a dozen strokes of the piston, then stepped to the edge of the raked area. 'Best stand upwind, I think. There's no telling what this stuff will do to your lungs.'

Le Placs stood back and Jimmy pressed the trigger. A fine yellow spray emerged from the nozzle. Jimmy carefully covered every inch of the raked area, pumping the sprayer again when it began to lose power. Finally it began to sputter, and Jimmy laid it aside.

'Well, that's it.'

'Good. Can you now tell me what it is?'

'It's accelerator. For the cement.'

'It makes the cement go fast?'

'In a way. It makes it set fast. You usually mix the accelerator with water and the cement sets in a couple of hours. If you use it neat, the cement sets in a few minutes.' Jimmy sat down on the sand. Le Placs took a seat beside him.

'You are not being very forthcoming this evening.'

'No, I know. Intentionally so, I'm afraid. But it should all become clear quite soon.' Jimmy reached into his sporran and pulled out a half-bottle of whisky. He poured a nip into the lid and handed it to Le Placs, then took a swig from the bottle. 'Let me explain. You recall we talked once about the effect that a Seer has on the world?'

'About whether the Seer affected the future that he was predicting?'

'Yes. The way I see it, there's a link between the Seer and the event. And if what you're doing is Seeing the state of the world, you become very close to it. Intimately bound to it.'

'Go on.'

'So that if you make an artifact like this sand-garden, the world and it are linked together.'

Le Placs laughed. 'Well, of course. But the world affects the sand a lot.

The sand affects the world only a little.'

'But they are linked. And when the world is in a very delicate state of balance – as it is right now – a tiny cause can have big effects.'

'So, have you done it? You have changed things?'

'No.' He shrugged. 'If your mind is trying to change the world, it no longer mirrors the world. So then the writing is not a true picture.'

Le Placs pointed at the sand. 'So, this is false?'

'By no means. That is a good and true picture, probably the best I have ever done. I was not trying to change anything at all.'

'*Mon Dieu*!' Le Placs looked exasperated. 'I thought you were going to do something about this business! To fix it!'

'Patience. It is happening. I'm sure you can feel it.'

'No!' Le Placs looked around into the dark. He shivered and buttoned his jacket up to the collar.

'More whisky?' Jimmy poured Le Placs another dram. 'Keeps the cold out.' He set the bottle upright in the sand.

Le Placs swallowed the whisky and rubbed at the back of his neck, where small hairs were lifting of their own accord.

Jimmy nodded. 'Oh yes. You can feel it all right. I was afraid that it wouldn't work – and I hoped that it wouldn't, but here we are, and I can feel it and so can you.'

'What is happening?' Le Placs jumped up and looked desperately into the dark around him. He could feel things moving out there, he could feel vast powers writhing and struggling behind the face of reality.

Jimmy spoke quietly. 'The cement is setting and as it sets, They are becoming locked in. For just a few minutes, the nature of local reality cannot change from what it was when I raked the sand. And They are trapped in that reality.'

He walked over to the south-east corner of the rectangle and stared down at the sledge-hammer on the ground. 'And that, I hope, will give us time to do something.'

The fire crackled and blazed on its fuel of straw and old fence-posts, flames trying to leap high, but somehow quelled by the dampness in the air. In the heart of it, bigger lengths of dead branches were beginning to catch, and the women stood back from the fierce heat.

'All this stuff came from Dan Finlayson's old farm,' said Doreen. 'It's been abandoned since Mor bought him out. There's all sorts of stuff lying around.'

Lorraine bent down and grabbed a double-handful of old straw and threw it on. Alice ducked her head and turned away from the eruption of blazing flecks.

'That's enough! Let it go down a bit. This is a ceremonial fire, not a bloody funeral pyre.'

'Might as well be warm,' said Doreen, but she dropped her own armful back onto the pile of mouldering straw.

'You'll be wanting to roast tatties in the embers next!'

'No, no.' Lorraine glanced at Doreen and took a half-step sideways to hide a small pile of potatoes.

But for the crackle and hiss of the fire, the Dark Isle was silent in the impenetrable dark around them. Steam rose from the moist ground near the fire. An icy draught hit each woman on the back. Alice pulled her blanket tighter. Lorraine turned round slowly, trying to warm herself evenly, shutting her eyes as the smoke stung them.

The women moved silently and uneasily around the fire, dodging the smoke, waiting for the flames to subside. Gradually and unconsciously they fell into a three-cornered dance as the smoke drifted this way then that. The fire slowly collapsed in on itself, becoming a red-hot pile of embers. The Whistler Buoy complained from out in the water. Doreen glanced towards the sound. The cliffs lay over that way, not far beyond the circle of firelight.

A large branch burned through and fell into the red-hot coals, throwing up a cloud of sparks. Alice put her foot against one end of the branch and pushed it into the fire. She threw on a couple of logs. More sparks flew.

'It is time,' she said. Her face was grim. 'We are in deep trouble, and we must take serious measures.'

Doreen was watching the sparks fade and vanish into the darkness. 'Man is born to trouble, as the sparks fly upwards,' she muttered.

'Pish and nonsense,' said Alice. 'We are here between the night and the dawn, between the land and the sea. Between this world, and a calamity. And as long as we can lift a hand for ourselves, we are born to make what we bloody well can of this momentary flicker of light that we call life.'

Lorraine huddled over her folded arms. 'Well that's a comfort,' she said, but not very loudly.

'Now, take your posts around the fire,' said Alice.

Lorraine bent and lifted a rotted fence post from the pile. 'Will this one do?' She laughed shrilly then dropped it again when she saw Alice's scowl. 'I'm sorry. I don't know what got into me.'

Doreen grinned at her across the fire. 'The night and the mist and the dark. And three women on a deserted clifftop trying to save the world from ravening hordes of otherworldly beings.'

Lorraine smiled back. 'I guess so. That's just the sort of thing to bring on hysteria.'

'If you're quite finished? Right then.' The fiery glow picked out the three faces, all pale and tense, all intent. 'Now, can you feel it? Let it come close so that we can feel it, and know what it is we are fighting.'

The cold of the night bit into faces and necks. The air itself grew thick.

Eck was well into it. This was the big one, and he knew it. The band were playing their hearts out and Kenny John's carnyx filled the tent with its deep bass note until it felt as if the ground trembled. This underlying note was the ground on which everything else rode, and Eck was in control of it, working his slider with intensity, barely aware of the people around him. The note of the carnyx had its own pace, its own pattern within the music. The bray of the horn spoke to Eck, telling him about the power that would be unleashed when it reached its peak. The energy was mounting, the melody swirling around the brazen pillar of sound, unbearably near to breaking through the unseen barrier. The walls bulged, the crowd were howling as they danced, adding their energy to the band's, feeding it back to them. Eck had nothing in his mind now but the shape of the music, the urgency of the force behind it. More and more music, the melody as sweet as nectar, as strong as steel, ropes of light hauling the world up onto another level, shaping itself into the gates of a new world.

The slider moved up and up as the carnyx howled louder and louder, its red sycamore tongue flapping. Eck had given almost all that he could, and still the music wanted more. But he was waiting for the right moment. It was coming, it was coming! Another roar almost swamped everything else for a moment, a sound that was almost human. Eck threw everything into one last surge of energy. He poured it into the channel, riding on the sound of the carnyx and urging it on towards its goal.

And the music broke through, as if it were emerging from a chrysalis. People danced for its heartbeat and the band played like its thoughts and there was Eck, for one instant still as a stone, mind sharp as a diamond, holding the slider at the top of its range.

And Eck looked out into a new world, where the music had gone silent, but every note was a light trembling on a leaf, the thrum of the carnyx was the skeletal rock that lay under the hills, giving them shape. And the melody spread itself wide before him, a river running through a world so beautiful that he could not breathe. But that was no problem, because time had stopped also. For a few seconds, he lived there forever. That's what he said afterwards – and there was an afterwards, though he did not wish there to be.

I did it, he thought, just before the world came back with the force of several trillion tons of universe returning to its place.

George had run out of yell for the moment. He raised his sceptre above his head and waved it. Behind him, he heard a new sound in the music. He turned from the microphone. Kenny John had laid the carnyx against the throne and was now playing the saxophone. On the other side of the throne, Andy the butcher was struggling with the pig. The pig was no longer greasy, but it was strong, and it was upset.

George drew breath to yell into the mike once more – and the music stopped. Yet it was still there, it had stopped where it was. Fiddle notes hung like a shoal of minnows in the air, drumbeats fenced space into wire frames, the saxophone shot hot metal plates through everything. George stood in a still and silent centre where nothing was happening, only the next note waiting to happen.

A shudder ran through him and his mind opened up, releasing memories of another place and people of a different race, unlike those playing music or dancing wildly in the tent. He remembered another life, a larger life, full of space and light.

He turned, and there They were, the people he remembered – immense and ghostly for a moment, then immense and solid, while everything else around him faded; the stage, the tent, the showground, the Dark Isle, all becoming small and meaningless.

There in front of him was Manannan, taller than a circus tent, gazing into his face. And beside him, the woman with emerald eyes, her long red braid hanging between her breasts, her full mouth inviting and cruel at the same time.

Behind them stood others, Lugh and Morrigan and Nanag – he knew all their names, and more, he knew who they were. He knew that Nanag liked to eat the black bee and wore a caul for a choker. Knew that Lugh could not be trusted to count the dogs in his own pack, but had the strength of a mountain and could eat a pair of oxen at one meal. Knew that Manannan had fits and rages where he would attack anything that moved and only one person could calm him – and that was the woman without a name. Though she had no name, he knew her too, knew her fascinating beauty and the use she made of it. He knew that the green of her eyes was a lake and she cared not at all how many drowned there.

But he had never seen them like this, standing unconcealed in this world.

'Dad,' he said. 'What are you doing here?'

And as he spoke, he realised that he was looking Manannan straight in the eye, that he was as tall as they.

'We have come to take this.' Manannan swept his arm around. 'It was ours once, ours alone, and it will be ours again.'

'You are coming here to stay, to live here?'

'This will all be our domain, and you will be with us. You are my son, so this will be your place also, to hunt the deer by day and to feast by night, to take whom you will from those people to be your servant – or what you will.' He winked at George and his great eyebrows waggled suggestively.

George felt himself blushing. 'I will be one of you?'

Morrigan pushed her way in beside Manannan, her mouth twisted up on one side. 'You'll have to fight for it,' she hissed. 'No matter who your father is.'

Manannan flushed red and faced her down. 'This is my son. It is not your concern!'

The woman with green eyes leaned towards George and smiled. 'Yes, you will be one of us,' she said, and George saw what she promised, and he felt himself falling into the depths of her eyes.

'Yes,' said Manannan. 'One of us forever. You must help us, then you will belong with us and rule over this place.'

'Help you? How?'

Manannan gestured at the crowd behind George. 'These people are yours to command. They are small creatures, but even they may be of use, especially when they are many. Call on them to follow us – they will listen to you. Then the way will be made clear and we shall enter the world.'

'Why should they listen to me?

'You are their king. Has this not been told to you?

'Yes. I suppose it has.'

'Then call on them! The time is close. Even now, the horse sacrifice is being performed, as it has not been for many centuries past.' His red tongue slipped over his lips, disturbing the golden hairs of his moustache. 'And you are destined to help us. You are my son and I have watched over you, so that when this time came you could join us.'

Thoughts slipped into George's head, memories of growing up without a father, mostly without a mother. Of time spent in another world, a glorious place but rough and violent, where he was mostly disregarded or ridiculed. 'You have watched over me,' he said flatly.

Manannan frowned. 'If you won't help,' he said sharply, 'we shall break in anyway, and then we will lay waste the Dark Isle. Ninety and nine of a hundred shall die. But there is no need for that. You can save these people. You are my son, and to these people you are more than a king, you are a god. Look at them.'

George turned to look at the crowd, a many-limbed animal far below, stopped in the moment of waving and cheering – for him. Manannan laid his hand on George's shoulder. 'It is good to be one of us,' he said.

Then George looked out into the sky. He could see the paths that the planets moved on, he could see the lives of stars. Light poured into him and exaltation gripped his innards. Breath filled his lungs, flooded his body like a river of fire.

I remember this, he thought. He reached out with his mind and felt the curve of the earth, held in his grasp.

When Baldy opened his eyes, he felt as if he was waking from a dream – or into a dream. He looked around, baffled, slowly piecing together the elements of his surroundings. There was a silken tent perched on a causeway built on a long string of boats, there was the smell and the sound of the sea and there were two men nearby in strange clothes. They were silent, but watching the tent closely. That was where Mr Mor was. There was no music now, but a high concerted moaning noise was coming from many throats inside the tent.

Baldy shook himself and rubbed his hands together.

'What's going on now, then?'

One of the men glared at him and raised a hand, enjoining silence.

'Just asked a bloody question.'

'Sshh!'

The moaning grew louder. Baldy shivered and pulled his collar up. His hand crept nervously into his pocket. He licked his lips, trying to clear the taste of smoke from them.

'Fuck this,' he muttered. He checked the causeway, both ways. It was still empty as far as he could see. Shivers ran up his neck as the sounds from the tent mounted towards a crescendo, then stopped dead. In the sudden silence, Baldy could hear the sounds of the night, the creak of wood and ropes, the slap of the waves against the boats, a brief whinny from the tent, then another long one, then a cry of triumph and a chant in many voices.

'It is done, it is done! Manannan smile upon us, Manannan bring us plenty! Let the silver fish swim to our nets, let the waves run in the barley that our crop may be good and may our seed increase a hundredfold!'

There was a muffled crash from the end of the causeway and cries came faintly through the mist. Baldy and the two men turned to look at the blank wall of mist. There was a regular thumping through the wood of the causeway, then the sound of feet pounding and out of the mist, looming large, came an enormous man, running at an incredible speed.

'Jesus Christ!'

Baldy's hand darted into his pocket and came out again with his pistol clenched in it.

'It's Irwin! Hey, Irwin, what's up?'

'Stop right there!' Baldy had his gun up and pointing at Irwin.

One of the men stepped across to him. 'What the hell do you think you're doing? It's just Irwin!' He pushed Baldy's arm to one side. There was a stunning explosion as the gun went off and the bullet kicked up a burst of splinters from the causeway.

Before Baldy could recover, Irwin was on them. Baldy took an arm in the chest, the other man was shouldered aside. With barely a pause, Irwin grabbed the tent cloth and heaved. The silk ripped from the rigging. Irwin threw it to one side and leapt forward.

Inside the remains of the tent, exposed now to the night air, two dozen men in improbable costumes were kneeling in a half-circle before Mr Mor, who was standing beside a glossy chestnut pony, its mane and tail pleated and beribboned. He was smoking a cigar and had one arm over the horse's neck. He was wearing a cloak which was open at the front, under which he was naked but for a leather apron which hung slightly askew.

An elderly man struggled to his feet.

'Who dares disturb this sanctuary?'

With a wordless cry, Irwin sprang at Mr Mor. He grabbed him by the shoulder and raised a mighty fist.

'Tatties and herring, you bastard!' he yelled as he put all his strength into a fearsome blow aimed at Mor's astonished face.

There was another explosion, and Baldy's shot hit Irwin in the shoulder like a hammer-blow. Irwin's hurtling fist grazed Mor's face and struck the mare on its forehead with a solid thump. The horse staggered and stumbled backwards, its weight crushing the railing.

'No!' Irwin cried out as the mare toppled sideways towards the water.

A horrified cry arose from the surrounding crowd. 'You've killed her!'

Irwin gaped at this sudden disaster, then pushed Mor aside and reached for the mare, but though his hand grasped her braided mane, he could not hold her. The mane slipped through his fingers, coloured ribbons tearing loose. She hit the oily black waves, sending water over the side, drenching Irwin. Blood and water ran on the rough planks as he threw himself down onto the causeway, reaching for her – but his arm would not do what he told it. The mare's head sank below the water without a struggle, then rose again on a wave, her eyes closed, unconscious, bubbles streaming from her nostrils as sea water poured into her lungs.

A heavy throbbing in his ears, Irwin tried to reach for the horse with his uninjured arm. 'Dander!' he yelled. 'She's drowning! Help me!' A few yards away, the glossy back of a dolphin rose briefly from the night-black water, then went under again with a hiss of breath.

Out of the mist, its diesel motors throbbing, the *Suitor's Lass* appeared, bearing down on them. Irwin looked up. The bow loomed high into the night as she headed straight for him. Standing at the bow, his legs spread wide and peering ahead with his hand shading his eyes, Barry Ellis stood.

'No!' Irwin cried, reaching up as if to keep the sharp prow from the drowning horse. But nothing could stop the boat. Its bow ploughed into the horse. Irwin was thrown to one side as the boat hit the causeway and smashed it to splinters. His head struck the railing, and the last thing he saw was the beakish laughing face of the dolphin as it rose from the waters, stained red with the mare's blood.

Alice reached under her blanket and pulled out the dead crow. It hung from her hand, little more than a bunch of black feathers. The three women walked around the fire, and as they went, Alice swung the crow out over the fire, so that feathers singed and the acrid smell stung the nostrils. 'Taste that, oh Great One, see what a feast we have for you here. Twice-killed and still warm. Come then for your offering! It is for you, Morrigan, this third death of three!

'Once, struck by the chariot!

'Twice, its neck was thrawn!

'Three times, I give the bird to the flames!

'To thee Morrigan I give your own, your sacred bird!'

She hurled the bird into the ashes and they all flung themselves aside as a tower of ash and sparks leapt upwards, a fountain of fire that dropped hot coals and foul smoke over them.

The wind moaned in the night, a long cry that sounded like pleasure and anger together, that sounded like some awful thing savouring the stink and the fire and the death.

George was in ecstasy, barely aware of his body, but acutely aware of everything else. Great Beings stood before him – Beings made of light, as he was. They were waiting for something. They were waiting for him to join them. Why were they waiting? Already he was one of Them. There was nothing to decide.

Then he looked down, and on the stage below, far away and very small, he saw a tableau. The tiny figure that was Andy the butcher was reaching out, trying to catch the pig. It had escaped from his arms and was running for the edge of the stage. Veronica was standing there and she had her arms stretched out to catch it.

'I remember,' said George. He looked up and into the face in front of him. 'I remember that there is another choice.'

Manannan flushed. 'There is only one choice!'

The woman stepped forward and took George by the shoulders. Her green eyes held his for a moment, but he turned away.

'No,' he said. 'You say these people are mine to command. Well, if they are mine, then I am theirs.'

The woman pushed him away. 'You fool!'

George shook his head. 'The bones of drowned men are in your eyes, and you can promise me nothing that I want.'

Manannan laughed, harshly. 'She is right, you are a fool. If you are my son, you are not the only one!' Morrigan smiled grimly and stepped forward once more.

The woman put her hand on Manannan's shoulder, her emerald eyes looking coldly into George's. 'He is lost. Leave him and let us finish our work. Afterwards, you can father many sons.'

'If you will be mortal then you will die as they do!' Manannan pointed at him angrily and George saw him and the others grow colossal as he shrank back to the stage below. The music was still paused, still poised, waiting for time to start again.

Morrigan spoke from high above. 'Now you have not your father's protection, I will kill you, as I should have done long since.' Her face, hideous with hate, loomed over him.

Beside her shoulder, George saw a flash of emerald green as the woman turned away. Manannan and Lugh and Nanag looked down at him contemptuously and he saw that they cared less for him than they did for their dogs and he felt what he had lost, his exaltation draining out of him, leaving him shrunken. He had made his choice and there was nothing he could do.

Above him, an immense figure leant down. Morrigan reached out her taloned hands for him, not even using a weapon.

Why, he thought. If I am no more than anyone else, why does she bother to kill me? There is nothing I can do to stop them.

Around him the slow air sucked at him like treacle, so that he could not run, could barely move. He half-turned, hoping even now for some escape, and a gleaming shape caught his eye. A step away, the carnyx lay against the throne, light glinting on the flared horn. The eye of the boar's head gleamed, so that it seemed to look at him, and something stirred inside him, more defiance than hope. He strained towards it, struggling against stopped time, stepping slowly, slowly across the stage. Morrigan's hand began to close around him, her breath a thick stink of ordure.

Then her face changed. Her squint mouth opened wide, her eyes flickered and then went blank, her hand trembled and withdrew. 'Oh, yes,' she hissed. Her head turned and she looked towards the east. Her nostrils flared, sucking in the stink of burnt flesh and feathers from far away. Her purple tongue licked at her thin lips. For a moment, her attention was gone, and George finished his step. As he touched the carnyx, the music came through again and the roar of the excited crowd lifted him through the treacly air. His hand grasped the cool metal and dauntless he lifted the horn to his lips and blew a blast, the boar's tongue flapping wildly in the ancient battle call. The crowd roared as if from one great throat.

Even the gods turned, to hear that call.

Dumfry felt his way in, seeking for the right moment. He would not get more than one chance, he knew. Yet They were so powerful and ancient, would there even be one chance? His smallness was an advantage – they had not noticed him. But if they did... He shuddered. He stretched himself again, taking comfort in the way that the world trembled when he did so. He was not completely powerless. He edged in closer. What could he possibly do?

The savage Beings were now deeply embroiled in the twists of the world and from the other side there came a sudden flood of energy as events on the Dark Isle conjoined. To his dismay, he saw the Beings wriggle one last time and they were suddenly there. They had opened a doorway to the Dark Isle, they were crossing through. Nothing stood before them, and already Dumfry could see the world-membrane twitching, a peristalsis that was going to fold the Dark Isle away, leaving it forever closed off from the rest of the world, part of the realm of these ancient beings.

Despair filled him. It was already too late! The edge of the world was closing in on the Dark Isle as the Gods reached into their new realm to claim it.

Then They paused. Something was holding Them, and Dumfry looked around. He could see Alice, demonic with flames leaping before her. He saw Jimmy reaching for a sledgehammer. He saw George lifting the carnyx to his lips, and he saw Them lose the focus of Their intent, distracted and baffled for a moment.

He let time slow down while he slid into the centre of events, into the focus. How to fix this? How to heal this rift in space and time?

His mind opened wide enough to contain the entire continuum. His mind draped itself around the form of it, stretching through the various relevant dimensions, computing and calculating, working backwards through time and space until he found, far off and very distant in time, a delicately balanced configuration of events that was crucial. He gave a quick look around, in case God was watching, sent out a mental apology, then reached in and with the touch of a finger, changed the flow.

There was a moment of complete stillness. In the showground, music stopped and hung in the air, generators fell silent. Animals ceased bellowing, drink paused on its way down a thousand gullets. Then the ground heaved, pushed up hard. Ten thousand knees buckled, five thousand people fell to the ground, beer spilt and the causeway lurched from end to end. Then the ground dropped.

Le Placs waved his hands in exasperation. 'But what can you do?'

Jimmy shook his head. 'Sadly, there are times when it is not possible to do anything constructive. Sometimes, the only positive action is a destructive one.' He grunted as he bent over to lift the sledgehammer. 'I've never wanted to change things,' he said. 'The way things are is marvellous enough for me. The most wonderful thing in the world is the music of the way things are. So they say. A lovely phrase. But I must put a stop to this bit of music.' He lifted the big sledgehammer in both hands and swung it up onto his shoulder. He stepped into the rectangle. The raked sand was solid.

'I don't know what will happen,' he said, 'But things will change.'

As Le Placs stepped forwards, Jimmy raised the hammer high and brought it down on the rock-hard pattern. A star of cracks appeared. He raised the hammer again and brought it down. The pattern split. Once more he lifted it. 'This time,' he grunted, and swung a mighty blow down at the sand.

The cement shattered into a thousand pieces. Jimmy staggered and dropped the hammer.

The ground dropped below him, fell eighteen inches then returned and smacked into his falling body. Jimmy collapsed like an empty puppet onto the broken patterns, the hammer beneath him.

Dumfry saw the constriction ease and unfold and saw the world settle into stability once more. His heart sang. Everything was well.

Then he looked again.

From the skin of the world, the Gods rose up and flocked at him, outraged. He waved them away like a cloud of gnats.

'Go away. Your time is done.'

But they kept coming, looming like stormclouds over him, more and more of them, until he was bewildered in their midst, striking out to left and right, barely keeping them at bay.

Then, in the middle of his fear and confusion, he found a deep well of silence. He looked into that well and knew what to do. With one hand he kept Them at bay while he leant out of the empyrean to gaze on the earth. And there was what he needed. Exactly what he needed. He smiled to himself. Mr Mor's fences were torn and broken and dozens of panicking pigs had galloped out onto the moorland.

He slipped sideways again into another dimension. In the world next door, he could be any size he wanted. He made himself large, then reached through to where the Gods were. He took the whole cloud of Them in one hand and thrust Them, buzzing and howling, through the walls of the world and into the pigs.

And then there were none, and Dumfry felt himself returning to the world that he knew. But before he did so, he took the opportunity to change one small thing. While the universal book-keeping was still trying to readjust itself to multiple disruptions of reality, he took advantage of the confusion and moved his body twenty miles east before he fell back into it.

Light gleamed along the blade of the knife. Totie MacCuish wiped sweat from his eyes, then leant over to the microphone. 'That was Breeks off the Donkey with their new single, "Eat the Sheets". He glanced nervously at the wee grey man with the sharp knife, who indicated graphically what would happen to him should he try to give the alarm. 'And to take us up to the news at midnight, we have Shooglenifty and "The Duck's Walk Through the Kailyard".'

He turned off the microphone and reached for a cassette tape.

The knife jerked towards him. 'What do you think you're doing?'

'It's the station jingle. I've got to play it right after the news. Honest, it's more than my job is worth to miss it out.'

'Hand it here.'

The wee man investigated the cassette tape, shrugged and handed it back. 'But no funny business, see? After that, you play this.' He took a cassette out of his pocket and laid it on the table, 'Then I go away and you never see me again. And most important of all, no-one gets hurt. Right?'

Totie nodded. 'Right.' 'The Duck's Walk Through the Kailyard' ended and Totie cued in the pre-recorded news. As the first news story was read out, the floor trembled and the lights flickered. The wee man looked suspiciously through the glass to the dim, deserted office next door. Totie took the opportunity to tug out a short section of the tape. He ignored the news and its litany of dire events and celebrity gossip and tried to manipulate the flimsy tape without attracting notice. Totie had grown up reading books where intrepid boys hoisted flags upside down, as a distress signal. He'd never had the chance to try it, but in the books it always worked.

Rossland FM had no flag, but the listeners knew its jingle by heart. Nervously twiddling the tape case, he tugged at the tape, twisted it and pushed it back in again. The man with the knife didn't notice a thing.

The news finished, and Totie slipped in the cassette.

Odd musical sounds came out as the jingle played backwards. The wee man frowned. Come on, thought Totie, someone out there must realise it's a distress signal.

'!Meffednalssor stissey... ! Meffednalssor vodnoous eth sissith...' The jingle finished with the sounds of guitar notes being sucked into guitars.

The man and his knife walked to the desk and leant over Totie. He pointed at the cassette player. 'See that music?' he said. 'It sucks. Now put this tape in and play it.'

Mor's voice came from the speakers, broadcasting across the Highlands: 'This is the voice of the Independent Dark Isle. Ladies and Gentlemen, from midnight tonight all routes into and out of the Dark Isle have been closed. All ports are blockaded and the ferry has been impounded...'

Totie's jaw dropped as Mor continued with his speech about the Unilateral Declaration of Independence. 'This can't be serious...' He turned to the wee man, who flipped his knife and caught it without taking his eyes off Totie. Totie swallowed hard.

'Totie, are you there? Totie?' A small voice was coming from his headphones. He lifted them to his ears.

'Hello? Is that you Les?'

The wee man was instantly suspicious. 'What's this? Let me hear!'

Totie pressed a button and Les Black's voice came out of a speaker. 'It's terrible, Totie! There's been an earthquake! Right here at the show! It's a shambles, the fairground has collapsed and now there's animals and people stampeding in the dark. For God's sake, Totie, get help. The sea's come right in. I'm on the top of the radio car, Totie, but it's havoc here, I don't know how much longer I can...'

The voice cut off and in the studio there was only Mor's voice explaining the benefits of an independent Dark Isle.

Totie reached for the phone.

'What do you think you're doing?'

'Phoning the emergency services, what do you think?'

'Did I tell you could do that?'

'No, you didn't. But I'm doing it anyway.' Totie deliberately dialled 999. 'Hello? Police, ambulance and fire brigade. And the coastguard.

There's big trouble at the Dark Isle Show.'

The wee man stood with his knife poised, listened to Totie talking to the operator.

'No, there's no lights…' Totie looked at the wee man. 'No, the ferry's not available. Yes, I'll stay by the phone.' He put down the phone and said in a conversational tone, 'There will be helicopters and coastguards and police and god knows who else on the Dark Isle in a few minutes. I just thought you'd like to know.'

Mr Mor was coming to the end of his speech. '…has been decided that until free elections can be held, we will form an interim government, and the following have consented to be office bearers.'

The wee man's face twisted as he thought hard. 'Maybe you'd better turn that off.'

Totie smiled and folded his arms. 'No.'

'Bastard!' The wee man leapt over the desk, pushed him out of the way and stared frantically at the complex deck in front of him.

'First Minister,' said Mr Mor, as the man poked wildly at buttons with no effect. 'This post will be filled by…'

He gave up on the buttons and swung his leg back. The front of the deck shattered as his boot smashed into it.

'David Mac…' The tape stopped.

The wee man poked at the ruined plastic with his knife, prising the damaged tape from the wreckage. He turned threateningly towards Totie. 'I was never here,' he said.

'Of course not,' said Totie. The phone rang. Totie put his hand on it. 'This is probably the police,' he said.

The man swore and ran from the room, doors banging as he hurried through the office to the front door.

'Hello, this is Totie MacCuish at Rossland FM.'

'Hello, Totie, this is Hamish here, from Lairg. Listen, man, are you on the wacky baccy or what? First there's that god-forsaken modern music, so-called, and then after the news there's some lunatic talking about politics. What I want to know is, what happened to the Late-night Sermon?'

Doreen lifted herself to her hands and knees and looked around.

'What the hell was that?'

Alice floundered onto her front and tried to rise. Her expression was a mixture of fear and delight. 'I don't know what it was,' she said, 'but damn, there was power in it!'

The ground trembled again and the women braced themselves, but it subsided into a shudder and disappeared.

'Oh, my god,' said Lorraine, looking from Doreen to Alice in awe.

'Do you do that often?'

'Never felt anything like it,' said Doreen.

'Was that Morrigan coming?' Lorraine looked around, trying to see any hint of an otherworldly presence.

Alice was on her feet now. 'No,' she said. 'That was more than Morrigan can do. She would sell all her kin for that kind of power. The whole damned earth moved.'

'What's that noise?'

Carried on the wind was a far-off piping sound, high-pitched and irregular.

'Animals?' They all stood still to listen. The squealing grew louder and harsher, sounding angry, angry and afraid. 'I hope so.' Doreen looked across at Alice. 'Unless it's something else that we've let loose.'

Lorraine moved closer to her. 'It's coming this way.'

There was a cacophony of squeals now, closer and louder, sounding like a farmyard in pain. Lorraine and Doreen quickly moved to the other side of the fire, keeping it between them and the tortured cries. Alice lumbered over to join them and they stood staring out into the dark.

Among the cries they could now hear the thudding of many feet and deep grunting sounds among the squeals. The women huddled close together, focused on the impenetrable dark, where the sounds must be coming from. The noise grew to a cacophony and out of the dark burst a mob of pigs, their muzzles high and wide open, slime trailing from their jaws. Their tiny piggy eyes glinted in the firelight as they rushed down on the women. One or two of the pigs managed, even in their terror, to look imploringly towards the women for a moment. Then they had gone into the dark again, leaving behind the thick stench of terrified swine.

The women turned, eyes straining into the darkness towards the cliffs, though there was nothing to be seen. The cries diminished, then there was a new outbreak of terrified squeals, followed by a few meaty thuds, then a series of splashes, then silence.

'My, God,' whispered Lorraine, 'What was that?' She shuddered and turned away from the cliffs, reaching for the warmth of the fire. 'And what the hell is that?'

Floating in the air on the other side of the fire was a streak of light. It grew bigger and brighter, as if the darkness were folding back to reveal sunshine behind it. Inside the light was a tiny figure, far far away. It grew closer and closer, rushing towards the hilltop and the fire. Then it stopped, and it was a man, sitting in the air in a ragged patch of light.

'Good evening, ladies,' he said.

'Oh my god, it's John,' said Doreen.

Alice, astonished as she was, still managed a contemptuous snort. 'Well, well,' she said. 'It's Humfry Dumfry the flying nun. What do you think you're doing here? This is a private ceremonial.'

'The Dark Isle has been saved,' he said. 'But there is a rather severe problem remaining.' He blushed. 'I may need a little assistance.'

Once the earth had settled, Le Placs went out to the harbour. One of the harbour lights had survived the shock and shone wanly on the oily waters. Several sunken boats showed their broadsides to the sky, one or two masts stuck out of the water. In the village, torches showed as people ran from house to house, trying to find out what had happened.

Le Placs searched around until he found a half-sunken rowing boat that could be retrieved. He climbed into it and used a rusty can to bail out the water until the boat began to bob rather than wallow. Then he untied the mooring rope and clumsily manoeuvred it out of the harbour, using an oar to pole it past the wrecks and the wallowing cobles.

At the beach below Jimmy's house, he nosed the boat into the sand and clambered out, wading through the waves to the shore. Jimmy's body lay, a darker shape on the dark beach. He put his hands under Jimmy's arms, dragged him down the beach to the water's edge and by dint of much effort, managed to lift him into the boat. He settled Jimmy's body in the bows, then pushed off into the dark sea, pulling on the oars, chanting a long sad song in French. The scant lights of Cromness disappeared as he rowed, and the thick black air closed around him. There was nothing visible in the world, there was only the sound of the oars in the water and the touch of the mist on his face, like the palpable fingers of darkness. Le Placs rowed on, unseeing. The boat rocked with the waves, and he began to get the feel of the oars.

What possessed him he could not have told, and he wondered at himself. Despite the chill of the night air and the dense darkness, he felt no concern about what he was doing. The chance of sinking or simply losing himself in the night did not worry him. There was only a distant curiosity, as if he was watching himself and the boat from nearby, an uninvolved watcher. Perhaps, he thought, I shall lower his body into the deeps. When the time is right. Or perhaps I shall row to Norway. Not understanding what he was doing or why, he simply kept pulling on the oars until blisters rose on his delicate surgeon's hands. The pain did not concern him. He kept pulling. The cold night slipped away behind him as he rowed.

After many hours, he noticed a change. The air was no longer so clammy and stars had appeared in the sky. He could make out the shape of his hands and the oars, could almost see the stern of the boat. He looked around. The dark shape of the island cut a sharp edge across the drifts of stars. The mist had gone. Nearby, the Whistler Buoy groaned. He shivered at the sound. After a few minutes it sounded again, and he turned the boat inexpertly to head away from it.

As he rowed on, light spread up from the eastern horizon. He had fallen into an exhausted reverie, nothing in his mind but this boat on the glimmering sea, his hands pulling the oars, and Jimmy's empty body in the bows behind him.

There was a scrape from the keel, then a thump that threw him backwards from his seat, striking his head on the gunwale. Raising himself groggily, he found that the boat had grounded in a small bay below the Suitor. Jimmy's body had been thrown to one side by the impact and one of his arms lay stiffly on the gunwale, as if pointing up the beach. Le Placs looked at the cliff face that bounded the bay and saw there an oval opening, rimmed with white limestone. A cave.

'Why not?' He looked at Jimmy. 'Why not, *mon brave?* Who knows what will come, and this is a better end than lying in the cold deep.'

He climbed out of the boat and pulled it a couple of feet forward onto the shingle. He hooked his hands under Jimmy's armpits and heaved.

'You are heavy, my friend,' he grunted as Jimmy's body thumped onto the stones. He took a new grip. 'But I cannot leave you here. Help me, if you can. This will not be easy.' Grunting as he heaved, he dragged Jimmy's body across the beach to the foot of the cliff. From the boat he took a length of rope. He tied it round Jimmy's chest then climbed up the slippery rock and into the cave entrance.

Several hours later, Le Placs walked into Cromness. His normally neat clothes were ruined – soaked with sea water, torn and streaked with white. He held his hands close to his chest, the fingers curled protectively. He staggered with weariness. He had to detour by way of Church Road, as the sea had claimed several streets, including the Vennels. The barman was sitting at the upstairs window of the Arms, looking down at the water just a few feet below. Other people were in the street, carrying household goods or moving them in barrows. Children wailed and trailed along behind their parents or played wild games in the waves, splashing and shouting. A few tractors were braving the sea, towing trailers axle-deep to ferry people and goods from half-sunken houses along Shore Road. Out in the sea, barely visible, the cab of a bulldozer showed.

Among this, Le Placs shambled like a derelict, but attracted little notice and no comment. He was merely another in the crowd of unfortunates.

Lorraine blinked and shook her head. The sun was looking over the horizon, right into her eyes. 'Doreen? Alice?' She turned to look around her, stiffly, as if she had been standing here for too long. And indeed, the whole night had somehow passed away.

'I'm here,' grumbled a voice.

'What happened?'

'Why don't you tell me,' said Alice. There was no sign of Doreen.

'I don't know. It all happened like it was a dream. Is this? A dream? Are we real?'

'Oh, be quiet and tell me what happened.'

'Sorry, Alice. It's just too...'

'Stop it!'

'Right.' Lorraine took a deep breath and clenched her fists. 'This happened: after the pigs went squealing over the cliff, Reverend Dumfry arrived in the air, wearing only a kilt. He sat in the air, and I could see him although it was dark. He told us that the gods had gone, that he'd turned them away.'

'Humph,' said Alice. 'He would. Trying to impress Doreen, most likely.'

'But he was sitting in the air, Alice.'

'What did I say? Showing off.'

'But how could he do that?'

'So he's a magician! So what? Carry on.'

'He said there was something he couldn't do. He couldn't banish the Old Grey One, that thing that Fergus called up, because it was neither male nor female and he could do nothing with it.'

'And then?'

'And then he asked for help, and he reached out, and you said...'

'Never mind what I said.'

'And I didn't know what to do, but Doreen stepped forward. Forward and up, as if there was an invisible step, and she climbed up into the air in front of him.'

'Well? Come on, girl, what then?'

'They had a private conversation and then she, Doreen I mean. She, eh,' Lorraine blushed and avoided Alice's eye. 'She kissed him for a long time, and then she moved his kilt aside and sat in his lap. I think they were, you know. Conjugating.'

'Humph. I think so too.'

'And then a light began to come from them, and it grew brighter and brighter until I couldn't see them anymore, but I still had to look, and there was nothing there, nothing but light... more and more light...' She fell silent, gazing into the rising sun. Alice stepped forwards and shook her. 'And then I woke,' Lorraine continued, 'and found myself staring into the sun, the night all gone and the mist gone with it.'

Alice's face was twisted into a scowl, as if she was thinking.

'Is that what you saw too?' asked Lorraine.

'Yes! Yes, it was. Unfortunately, that was exactly what I saw.' She looked Lorraine up and down. 'Well, then, how does it feel to be the Seer of Cromness?'

'What?'

'Well, I'm pretty sure Doreen's not coming back. You're not fully trained yet, but you're the best we've got.'

Lorraine looked at Alice then looked around at the bright fresh morning. A lark was rising over the moorland, singing as it went. Where the hillside fell away to the cliffs, the sun lay on bushes and trees. Light glinted on the wide sea, far below.

'No,' she said. 'I don't think so.'

'No? You mean you're not going to... You're turning your back on...'

'That's right. I'm sorry to disappoint you, but I've had enough of shadows.'

'God damn it girl! What else are you going to do with yourself? Back to bloody academia, is it?'

'I have more choices than that: you or academia. I don't quite know what I will do, but I'm sure I can find a better life than that.'

Alice glared at her, but Lorraine was paying her little attention. She was breathing in the fresh air, turning her head to let the wind whip her hair.

'You'll rue this day, my girl! You'll never find an opportunity like this, nor a place like this.'

'Perhaps. I'll make do with something less, then. Something not so intense, that suits me better.' She turned to look at the car. It was parked on a slope and should be easy enough to start. 'Do you want a lift? We'll have to bump-start the car.'

'So, after all I taught you...'

But Lorraine had turned towards the car and Alice had to grumble her way after her.

'...have to find someone else, God only knows where, now Doreen's gone. Have to start over again – and who's likely to take the training? It takes years, bloody years.' She clambered into the back seats of Lorraine's car, still muttering. 'Ye gods! I'll have to do the Seeing myself until I can get some girl trained up.' She did not look happy at the thought.

Rossland FM special news report

Despite these clues, you couldn't predict the event?
No, earthquakes are notoriously difficult to predict. But I did have my equipment located within half a mile of the epicentre – a unique

occurrence. Our analysis of the readings may take months, but you can be sure that the information will be jolly significant.

So, can you tell us exactly what happened?

Not in detail, not yet, but the main outline is clear. There must have been tension building up for a long time and finally the geological plates moved. There was a minuscule shift along the length of the Caledonian Faultline.

Minuscule? But look what happened to the Dark Isle!

That is a most interesting point, Les. You see, the Dark Isle is part of a distinct geological plate which is separate from those to the north and south. It is balanced between them and so it responds sensitively to the tiniest movements of the Caledonian Faultline.

That sounds bad. Are we going to have more quakes?

I don't think so. The earthquake was a relatively localised geophysical event, and the imbalances in crustal stresses were resolved locally. To the west, this plate slid up and over the main plate and this was compensated by the corresponding subsidence of the eastern edge of the Dark Isle.

Causing half of Cromness to sink beneath the sea...

Indeed. It was very fortuitous. Not only did it balance out the stresses in an almost miraculous manner, but it gives us clues to the behaviour of small crustal plates, which I have called Microplates. Indeed the Dark Isle Microplate is the first of its kind known.

And you happened to be on the spot?

Yes indeed, for the first ever Microplatonic event, as I have chosen to call it.

A feather in your cap. But are you quite sure we won't have a repeat performance?

No, no. The Microplate has settled in its new position now and I do not think we need fear another movement for quite some time. Tens of thousands of years, I expect.

Thank you, Martha Nero.

Thank you, Les.

Now back to the studio, where Totie is waiting to present our weekly Agricultural Phone-in.

Mr Ross returned to the farm at about five in the morning. The showground, or what remained of it, was chaos. No-one was seriously injured, but he couldn't help worrying, against all good sense, that Veronica might be the exception. There was no sign of her.

Eventually he'd managed to get his pickup out through the stranded vehicles and broken fences and made his way home.

'Veronica!' he called as he came in the door. No answer. 'Ronnie?' He quickly checked the downstairs rooms then ran upstairs to her room. Without even knocking, he threw the door open and put the light on.

'Dad!' There was Veronica, in her bed, sheet drawn up high to her neck.

'Thank God you're safe, I didn't know where you were. The phone lines are down and half the roads on the Island are blocked.'

'Well I'm perfectly safe, Dad.'

'What happened to you? Did you get hurt?' He spotted a pile of clothes on the floor, muddy and torn. 'Look at your clothes! Did you have a fall?' He bent down to pick them up from the white carpet.

'It's okay, Dad! Just leave them.'

Mr Ross stood up with a puzzled look on his face. 'These aren't the clothes you were wearing. And what's this?' He rubbed his fingers together cautiously and grimaced.

He looked at Veronica again. Her face was bright red and she was holding the sheet very high. Mr Ross' mind was working very slowly. His arm lifted of its own volition and he pointed at a bump under the sheet.

'What,' he said, then stopped. He backed slowly towards the door. 'Sorry,' he said. 'I was worried, you know.'

'It's okay.'

'I'll just go now.' He glanced again at the strange clothes on the floor. 'See you later, then.'

'Right, Dad.'

He stepped back into the corridor and took hold of the door handle to pull the door shut. His fingers slipped on the knob. He grasped tighter and pulled the door firmly shut. From inside the room he could hear stifled giggles. He stood there for a few seconds, blankly staring at his greasy fingers while trying to work out how he felt about this development. It was true that he'd hoped that Ronnie would loosen up a bit, but this was so sudden. Surely he should at least know something about the young man. Surely there were some questions to be asked...

He knocked softly on the door. 'Ronnie?'

The giggles stopped. 'What is it, Dad?'

'Why has he got lard on his sweatshirt?'

From the *Inverness Crier*

An event like this occurs only once in a blue moon, but when it does, it separates the sheep from the goats. The cost in human misery is incalculable. The people of Cromness are only now beginning to realise the extent of the devastation. Yet the story has its humorous side. A local worthy, who shall remain nameless, was swept out to sea by the tidal wave, and saved himself only by clutching the cab of a bulldozer that was also swept away by the wave. This extraordinary freak of nature has officials scratching their heads in amazement.

Now that the Dark Isle is connected to the mainland at Castleton, the Council plan to put in a road as soon as possible. Surveyors are already out mapping the route and bulldozers have begun work on the approach roads. However, the new road is not good news for everyone.

'It's a hard day for the ferry crew,' said Donald Jack, 55, captain of the ferry. 'It's all very well for the motorists and pedestrians and people like that, but where will we find another job? There's been a ferry here since the middle ages, but people just don't care about tradition nowadays.'

Irwin and Lou waded down the street and carefully climbed up the makeshift stairs. There was no handrail, just a length of nautical-looking rope along one side. At the top, Lou opened a shutter of rough timber. Dominoes clacked cheerily amid the music and general din that drifted out as Lou stepped through the upstairs window of The Fisherman's Arms.

The regulars had responded with enthusiasm to the new layout, and the place was busier than ever, even though it was necessary to wear wellies to wade along Kirk Road to the Arms, unless the tide was out.

Once inside, she helped Irwin to clamber through. His right hand was in plaster and much of the rest of him, including his head, was bandaged.

Then she helped Le Placs climb out. He was not so much injured as drunk, and rather melancholy with it. He carried a glass in his hand and was giving it more attention than it needed, trying not to spill it. Descending the rickety stairs, he stumbled and grabbed at the rope, wincing with pain. Rowing the boat had blistered his hands badly and they were still healing.

Le Placs sat with his feet on the bottom step, just above the water, and sipped at his whisky. One or two streetlights were working, but most of the street was in darkness. As he sat and thought and sighed and thought some more, he became aware of a regular splashing sound, and out of the darkness came Alice, lumbering wild-eyed along Church Road.

He stood up and stared aghast at her appearance. '*Mon Dieu*! Are you all right?'

'All right? Of course I'm not bloody all right! I see rivers of blood, I see a spectre stalking the streets of Cromness!'

Le Placs looked at the blood trickling down from her torn knees, the hideous white smears on her clothes and across her face. 'Have you looked in a mirror?'

'A mirror? Of course not! I looked into the depths of the Drooping Cave, but I'm damned if I'll try that again. Filthy place.'

Le Placs regarded her with alarm. 'This cave is in the cliff, yes? And it is surrounded by this white stuff?' He gestured at the daubs on Alice's clothing.

'Of course. And it's not only wet and filthy, it's too small.'

'Ah. Too small for you to get in, yes?'

'Of course it is!'

'But you climbed up, yes?' He looked at her ruined clothes and torn knees. 'Did you see anything?'

'I told you, I saw rivers of blood, I saw...'

'No, I mean in the cave.'

Alice scowled. 'What's to see? It's pitch black in there. I heard some strange noises, though, animal noises. But that darkness is thick as treacle, thick as blood. I could see nothing at all. Nothing but a forest, a great forest where boar and deer ran and no-one set foot. Ancient gnarled trees there were, and giant pines and saplings reaching high. Green glades among the trees, where streams ran through shade and light. Bright they were, and lively, and the living water clear as wine, but no-one was there to drink. No, not human nor spirit, but only the animals of the forest.'

Alice's eyes flickered here and there as she spoke. Her feet performed an incongruously delicate skipping dance, her feet splashing in the shallow water. 'All my days might I spend in that place, the moss for a bed, the high branches a roof to my dwelling place. The leaves on the trees spread themselves to the light, sucking sunlight from the warm breast of the sun, and I would live on sunlight too, suckling at the same tit. Bright is the sky in that place and light are the feet of the deer. Time does not touch that place, though a thousand years may go by in a breath.'

Le Placs looked closely at her eyes, seeing the widely distended pupils and the brightness of tears waiting to fall. 'I see,' he said gently. 'And now you go home to think about this some more, hein?'

Alice did not acknowledge him, but looked up past the housetops to the stars.

'So you saw nothing on the physical plane, as one might say?'

'Darkness,' she said. 'That's all there was, darkness and strange noises. And some beast that leapt at me from out of the cave. It knocked me to the ground and ran away. I did not see it, but it smelt like a pig.'

She turned to lumber off, splashing carelessly through the shallow waves.

To the east, the moon was beginning to show itself. Le Placs thought of Jimmy's body in that cold wet cave, where he had thought it safely hidden, and he thought of the pig that had knocked down Alice. 'Perhaps I had better go to the cave, just to check,' he said to himself. Then he sighed and sat down on the bottom step. 'No. There has been enough foolishness.'

He sipped at the whisky and watched the wavelets splashing at his feet.

From Rossland – the East Coast Route
published by the Highlands Tourist Association

...in addition to deer, red kites and the occasional eagle, the Dark Isle also has a population of wild sheep – a primitive form of the domesticated sheep. There are also rumoured to be wild horses in the depths of the Ardmeanach forest. Indeed, if the rumours are to be believed, the Dark Isle is home to everything from woolly rhinoceros to the giant sloth! No doubt the proximity to Loch Ness encourages such tales, as the Dark Isle vies with her more famous neighbour for a share of the tourist trade!

Unverified rumours aside, it is certain that there is a small herd of wild pig roaming the Island, keeping mainly to the moorland and forest margins along the Ardmeanach ridge. They are secretive creatures and best avoided, as they can be dangerous. Those who wish to view such exotic breeds in safety may visit the Dark Isle Safari Park, at Redrock, where various unusual animals are on display.

Siller huddled at one end of the long polished mahogany table, his grey face lined and old.

'A sad day, a sad day,' said Mr MacRae. 'All those poor people losing their homes, all along Shore Road – even as far back as Kirk Road.'

Siller grunted, though whether in the positive or negative sense was not discernible. The rest of the Elders adopted serious expressions and nodded their heads wisely.

'It was a mercy that they were all insured, eh, Mr Siller? And mostly due to you,' MacRae said. 'It has not gone unnoticed that you have worked tirelessly over the years to encourage them to insure their houses, without which they would now be destitute and a burden on the community.'

Another man leaned forward. 'It is certain, now, that the insurers will pay? Most of the householders were with the Argent Insurance Company, I believe. I myself know little of them.'

Siller raised his head. 'I believe we are here to discuss church matters,' he said sharply.

'That is so, Mr Siller. Let us then call this meeting to order.'

A beam of sunlight filled the room, dazzling the assembled crowd. When they could see again, they found that there was another person in the room, standing in the light.

'Dumfry! Is that you?'

'Dumfry?'

Siller half rose from his chair, his face twisted in a compound of anger and revulsion. He spluttered a few times before he managed to speak. 'How did you get in? What do you think you are doing here? This is a conclave of Elders, a private meeting and as you no longer hold any position within this church, you are neither invited nor welcome!'

Dumfry smiled. 'I am aware that I have been relieved of my post as minister of this church. Nevertheless, in view of my other responsibility, I am duty-bound to attend regularly, whether or not by your invitation.'

'If you once had any responsibilities, then you are relieved of them!'

'I'm afraid not, Mr Siller. Only the Highest Authority can relieve me of this duty. Indeed, it is in that respect that I am here today, to report to you on my progress.'

'What are you talking about?'

'Come Mr Siller. Surely you remember the august duty laid on me in this very room and by this very conclave. To seek for the Hand of God.'

There was a low mutter around the table. Mr MacRae tried to speak, but Siller stood up and waved him quiet. His dull skin burned red on his cheeks. He leant towards Dumfry and spoke clearly and forcefully. Occasional specks of spittle flew from his mouth, small comets in the bright sunbeam. 'I think I can speak for all here when I say that this so-called quest of yours has no authority from this church. It is a personal and baseless fantasy probably related to deeper problems that doctors nowadays would call a mental illness. Our forefathers, more bluntly, called it demonic possession.'

Dumfry did not look at all abashed. He nodded. 'Possibly they would have called it that. But our forefathers were not always right.'

There were several shocked gasps from around the table. Mr MacRae stood up. 'We don't have to sit here and listen to this! Reverend Dumfry, we have been indulgent with you on account of your unfortunate mental condition, but even compassion has its limits. I demand that you leave!'

'Certainly. But before I do, I must leave you my most recent notes.' He laid a sheaf of papers on the table. 'You need not distribute them to the congregation – the local newspaper has been obliging enough to publish them in full. I shall return in six months to let you know how I am progressing in my search for the Divine Being.' He smiled and the sunlight seemed to grow stronger around him. 'I haven't found the bugger yet, but I'm on His trail!' Then the light grew too bright, and when they could see again, Dumfry had left the room, though no-one heard the door open.

In the weeks following the earthquake, there was a large quantity of livestock running loose on the Dark Isle. Most of the animals had escaped from the showground, where the pens had been breached by the violent tremors. Le Placs, in what he admitted to be a sentimental gesture, adopted a piglet which he had found wandering aimlessly on the beach. The beast responded well to training, and had become his constant companion.

Le Placs had studied the transcript of the Japanese letter more than once, but could find no comfort in it. He read it now, out loud, though there was no-one to listen except the pig.

Greetings, Bervie-san, from your brother in labour.

The scriptures liken the human spirit to a flame that is passed from one candle to the next, always changing, yet still the same. This suggests that the spirit is not itself material in the sense that the candle is.

Yet it is written that, by good works and detachment we may improve our lot in the lives to come. Hence it is implied that it is possible to affect the non-material realms by physical means. Beyond that, we are not encouraged to speculate.

I hope my humble comments will help to resolve your problems.

I will send this letter by express air-mail, as you have indicated that the matter is urgent. As we live in poverty, I cannot pay for the postage. I hope you will not mind paying for it when it arrives.

May all beings be happy.

PS I enclose my best rake as a present to you, and to help you with your endeavour.

He sighed and tucked the piece of paper away. 'Does it truly mean anything? Hmm?' He leant down and scratched the little pig behind the ears. 'I think not. It is only a courteous letter from a pious Buddhist monk.'

He sighed again and rubbed at the stubble on his face. 'I must shave. And I must change my clothes.' He looked at his hands, where new pink skin had grown over the blistered palms. 'And I must go back to work.

But I am sad, little pig, sad. Jimmy has gone – and for what? Perhaps he was a foolish old man, but he was not *only* a foolish old man. He was a friend. Perhaps I am to blame, that I humoured him in his fancies? I fear it is so.'

There was a knock at the door. 'And what now, hein?'

At the door stood a policeman, a man in a business suit and a security guard carrying a briefcase. Le Placs looked at them in surprise. The policeman stepped forward and spoke.

'Mister Le Plank?'

'Possibly.'

'Constable MacFearn gave us your name.'

'Of course.'

'I am Inspector Morrison, and this is Mr Brown, from the National Museum of Antiquities in Edinburgh.' He did not introduce the security guard. 'Apparently you were a friend of one James Bervie, of Harbour Cottage.'

Le Placs nodded. 'I had that honour.' He braced himself.

'Mr Bervie of course is no longer with us.'

'Swept out to sea,' put in Le Placs, quickly. 'By the tidal wave. After the earthquake.'

The inspector waved a hand vaguely. 'Yes, yes. You have my sympathy, but we are here on other matters. May we come in?'

'Why not? Enter. Don't mind the pig, he's a house guest, until I have a pen built for him.'

In the lounge, the security guard stepped up to the table and laid down the briefcase. It was chained to his left wrist.

'We would like you to inspect an item we have here,' said the Inspector.

The guard slipped a key into a lock on the left side of the case. Mr Brown inserted a similar key on the right side. They turned their keys simultaneously and the lid flipped open. Lying on a padded bed of velvet was a small plastic bag, and inside the bag was a dull yellow bead.

'Now, Mr Plank, do you recognise this?'

Le Placs glanced at it briefly. 'Of course. It is one of Jimmy's beads.'

'Good. Can you tell us where and when you last saw it?'

'Why?'

'Just answer the question, please. This is important.'

All the men were standing tensely, eyes set on Le Placs. He shrugged. 'It was the night of the earthquake. Jimmy gave them to a helicopter pilot. Did he get into trouble trying to sell them?'

'You might say that. Why did Mr Bervie give him the beads?'

'It was payment for a special-delivery parcel.'

'And that was all?'

'Yes. Of course. And anything left over was a tip for the pilot.'

'Aah...' All three men breathed out at the same time. Le Placs looked from face to blank face.

'Well, bugger me,' said the security guard, at last.

'Lucky bastard,' whispered the inspector.

'The pilot? I suppose so,' said Le Placs. 'A thousand pounds or so for an hour's work.'

A strange smile appeared on Mr Brown's face. 'Look at that bead,' he said.

Le Placs, puzzled, leant over and looked again, more closely. The bead was a miniature boar's head. 'I see. It is pretty, no? Quite valuable, I imagine.'

'Pretty? Pretty?! It is beautiful, it is...' Nothing more came out. Brown waved his hands wildly. 'It is priceless! It is...'

'It is nearly two thousand years old,' put in the inspector.

Mr Brown recovered his speech. 'Only one bead like this has ever been found, badly crushed. Even that one could have bought him his own helicopter. And he has a whole string of them, in perfect condition...'

'Except for...' the inspector began.

'Except for one which has the pilot's teeth marks on it.'

Le Placs smiled. He felt as if he hadn't smiled for years, but now there was something worth smiling about. 'Two thousand years, you say?'

'Yes,' said the inspector. 'Two thousand years, give or take a century or so. So how and where did this James Bervie get them?'

Still beaming, Le Placs shrugged. 'They belonged to him, I am sure. I think he always had them.'

Mr Brown spoke sharply. 'Yes, yes. But who had it before him?'

'Jimmy was very old,' said Le Placs.

Mr Brown snorted. 'Don't be ridiculous. That necklace is immeasurably older than any human being.'

Le Placs smiled even more broadly. 'You remember, you were trying to tell me how much the beads are worth? And you could not find the words?'

Mr Brown nodded.

'Well,' said Le Placs, 'That is how old he was.'

Seaweed and sponges grew on the ancient chain of the Whistler Buoy. Mussels hung from it, next to sea anemones. Crabs and small fish grazed up and down its length. At its lower end, where the seaweed grew thick, it merged into the sea bed without a visible join.

Tethered by the chain, the dark bulk of the buoy leaned over as the tide ripped past. Its winking light warned vessels away from this part of the sea, where the buoy sat like a tiny dark island to the east of Cromness. On dark nights, when the fog was down, its siren moaned and complained. Fishermen, hearing it, shivered, though they relied on its sound to lead them safely home.

After the earthquake, the buoy began to misbehave. Its light worked perfectly and the siren blasted out its warning when fog was around, but even on the sunniest day there was a low moaning sound from the buoy which reached as far as Cromness. The sound was just at the edge of hearing and not everyone noticed it, but those who did complained bitterly. Jenny-Pet had been relocated in sheltered housing on Kirk Road, and although her new house had no stand-pipe outside, Jenny would stand by her door with bucket in hand listening intently to the sound from the buoy. There at the roadside she would trap passers-by and make them listen too.

'Hear that, pet? No? It sounds like lost souls lamenting at the bottom of a barrel. Now do you hear it?'

Eventually the Northern Lighthouse Board sent an engineer out to look at it, but he could find nothing wrong with the mechanism. Yet there did seem to be a low moaning sound coming from the buoy, almost too low to hear. The engineer replaced the diaphragm of the siren and checked the coils on the electromagnet. He investigated the wiring with the probes of his oscilloscope, then he tested the siren. Once the echoes of its mighty bellow had died away, he tested everything again. Nothing was obviously wrong, but the low sound persisted, like many small voices whining and bickering.

The engineer sat back and scratched his head. He could think of nothing else to test. He leant on the gunwale of his boat and pondered, and while pondering, he let his gaze drift across the water. Although the day was mild and sunny, he had trouble making out the cliffs of the Dark Isle. His own boat was strangely indistinct too, as if the buoy had its own private darkness hanging round it. He shivered and climbed into his boat. Halfway back to shore, he found that he had left his tools on the buoy, but he did not go back.

The engineer's report said that the buoy was in excellent operating condition and strongly advised that it be replaced as soon as possible. The Northern Lighthouse Board could make nothing of these contradictory statements and so they merely recommended that the engineer take a few days' leave and left the buoy alone.

There was thick cloud over the Firth and heavy rain squalls swept across the steep waves. Rain and spray blew into the face of the man who stood by the sea wall. Icy water splashed now and then into his wellington boots, but he did not move. Staring into the deepening darkness, he seemed to be listening to something, though the tumult of the wind covered all but the loudest sounds.

Out in the Firth, the tide gripped the Whistler Buoy and pulled, the waves crashed against it and the buoy moaned like a live thing and pulled at its chain. Many years of corrosion had weakened the chain and the waves that accompanied the earthquake had strained it badly. Now the storm completed the task: rust flakes fell from the shackle and the pitted metal bent and twisted. At last, the fatigued steel broke and the vertical forest of seaweeds and marine animals fell silently to the sea bed.

Le Placs stood on the shore, hearing the buoy's siren calling. He frowned and cocked his head. The sound had grown fainter. He wiped rain from his face and waited. In a few minutes, the siren sounded again, distinctly more distant now. Le Placs waited for a long time, listening to the sound slowly fading away as the buoy rounded the headland and drifted into the wide sea, out of the kenning of man.

Le Placs pulled up the collar of his raincoat and turned to wade up the Muckle Vennel towards The Fisherman's Arms. The waves were low here, damped by the rough piles of rubble to each side, all that remained of the ancient cottages that used to crowd the lane. The visibility was poor so he felt his way carefully, heading for the orange streetlight at the far end. Below the streetlight, something moved. It was the pig, waiting for him. As Le Placs grew close, it stepped into the waves and nuzzled his leg.

The upstairs windows of The Fisherman's Arms were brightly lit. At the top of the stairs, someone opened the makeshift door. Le Placs heard the sound of many voices, a background of music and the hint of dominoes chattering on tables.

Le Placs set his foot on the bottom step. 'Come along, James,' he said to the pig, and they climbed up to the warmth and the light.